DISCOVERY AND RESPONSE

DISCOVERY AND RESPONSE

The Strategies of Fiction

James Hart
Stanley Johnson
Judah Bierman
Portland State University

Winthrop Publishers, Inc.
Cambridge, Massachusetts

Cover by: Robert and Marilyn Dustin

Printed in the United States of America 87626-184-5. Current printing (last number): 10 9 8 7 6 5 4 3 2 1.

Library of Congress Catalog Card Number: 75-163998.

ACKNOWLEDGEMENTS

"Appointment in Samarra", reprinted by permission of the Literary Executor of W. Somerset Maugham and William Heinemann, Ltd. "The Owl Who Was God", Copyright © 1940 by James Thurber. Copyright © 1968 by Helen Thurber. Reprinted from *Fables For Our Time*, published by Harper & Row. Originally printed in *The New Yorker*. "The Snapping Turtle and the Wisteria Vine", and "Aesop's Last Fable", reprinted by permission from *99 Fables by William March*, edited by William T. Going. Copyright © 1960 by The University of Alabama Press. "The Bound Man", from *The Bound Man and Other Stories* by Ilse Aichinger, reprinted by permission of Farrar, Straus & Giroux, Inc. Copyright © 1956 by Ilse Aichinger. "In the Basement", by Isaac Babel from *Modern Soviet Short Stories*, Selected, Edited and Translated by George Reavey. Copyright © 1961 by George Reavey. Reprinted by permission. "Sonny's Blues", copyright © 1957 by James Baldwin. Reprinted from *Going to Meet the Man* by James Baldwin by permission of the publisher, The Dial Press. "My Sad Face", from *Children are Civilians Too* by Heinrich Böll, translated by Leila Vennewitz. Copyright © 1970 by Heinrich Böll. Used with permission of McGraw-Hill Book Company. "Funes the Memorious", from *Labyrinths* by Jorge Luis Borges. Copyright © 1962 by New Directions Publishing Corporation. Reprinted by permission. "The Scythe", from *Dark Carnival*, copyright © 1943, 1970 by Ray Bradbury, reprinted by permission of the Harold Matson Company, Inc. "Hollywood Heart", from *The Murder of the Frogs and Other Stories*, copyright © 1944, 1969, by Don Carpenter. Reprinted by permission of Harcourt Brace Jovanovich, Inc. "Anna on the Neck", from *The Portable Chekhov* edited by Avrahm Yarmolinsky. Copyright © 1947 by The Viking Press, Inc. Reprinted by permission. "Blow-Up", from *End of the Game and Other Stories* by Julio Cortazar. Copyright © 1967 bvRandom House, printed by permission of Random House, Inc. "Pig", from *Kiss, Kiss* by Roald Dahl. Copyright © 1959 by Roald Dahl. Reprinted by permission of Alfred A. Knopf, Inc. "The Poet", by Hermann Hesse. Reprinted by permission of Farrar, Straus & Giroux, Inc. from *Great Stories by Nobel Prize Winners*, Edited by Leo Hamalian and Edmund L. Volpe. Copyright © 1959 by the Noonday Press. "The Stroller in the Air", from *The Colonel's Photograph and Other Stories* by Eugene Ionesco, translated by John Russell. Reprinted by permission of Grove Press, Inc. Copyright © 1967 by Faber and Faber Limited. "The Jolly Corner", by Henry James, reprinted by permission of Charles Scribner's Sons. "In the Penal Colony", reprinted by permission of Schoken Books, Inc. from *The Penal Colony* by Franz Kafka. Copyright © 1948 by Schocken Books, Inc. "The Pond:", from *Tomato Cain and Other Stories* by Nigel Kneale. Reprinted by permission of Nigel Kneale and A. M. Heath & Company, Ltd. "The Horse-Dealer's Daughter", from *The Complete Short Stories of D. H. Lawrence*, Volume II. Copyright © 1922 by Thomas B. Seltzer, Inc., renewed 1960 by Frieda Lawrence. Reprinted by permission of The Viking Press, Inc. "Mario and the Magician", from *Stories of Three Decades* by Thomas Mann translated by H. T. Lowe-Porter. Copyright © 1931, renewed 1959 by Alfred A. Knopf, Inc. Reprinted by permission of Alfred A. Knopf, Inc. "The Vane Sisters", from *Nabokov's Quartet* by permission of Phaedra Inc., Publishers, New York. Copyright © 1966 by Vladimir Nabokov. "Upon the Sweeping Flood", from *Upon the Sweeping Flood and Other Stories* by Joyce Carol Oates. Copyright © 1963, 1966 by Joyce Carol Oates. Reprinted by permission of The Vanguard Press, Inc. "Greenleaf", from *Everything that Rises Must Converge* by Flannery O'Connor. Copyright © 1956, 1965 by the estate of Mary Flannery O'Connor. Reprinted by permission of Farrar, Straus & Giroux, Inc. "Ouagadougou", from *New African Literature and the Arts*, vol. I, edited by Joseph Okpaku. Copyright © by Gregorie Ouedrago. Reprinted by permission of The Third Press. "The Jar", by Luigi Pirandello. Reprinted by permission of Toby Cole. "The Grave", from *The Leaning Tower and Other Stories*, copyright 1944, by Katherine Anne Porter. Reprinted by permission of Harcourt Brace Jovanovich, Inc. "When the Priest Is Not at Home", from *The Night Visitors and Other Stories*, by B. Traven. Copyright © 1966 by B. Traven. Reprinted by permission of Hill and Wang, Inc. "The Christian Roommates", from *The Music School*, by John Updike. Copyright © 1964 by John Updike. Originally appeared in *The New Yorker*. Reprinted by permission of Alfred A. Knopf, Inc. "Death of a Travelling Salesman", from *A Curtain of Green and Other Stories*. Copyright © 1941, 1969 by Eudora Welty. Reprinted by permission of Harcourt Brace Jovanovich, Inc. "The Hour of Letdown", from *The Second Tree From the Corner* by E. B. White. Copyright © 1951 by E. B. White. Originally appeared in *The New Yorker*. Reprinted by permission of Harper & Row, Publishers, Inc. "The Lost Boy", from *The Hills Beyond* by Thomas Wolfe. Copyright © 1937 by Maxwell Perkins (as Executor); renewed 1965 by Paul Gitlin as Administrator, C.T.A. Reprinted by permission of Harper & Row, Publishers, Inc. "The Mark on the Wall", from *The Haunted House and Other Stories* by Virginia Woolf, copyright © 1944 by Harcourt Brace Jovanovich, Inc., reprinted by permission.

CONTENTS

INTRODUCTION

Where the modern short story is successful, its success calls to mind the poet Rilke's

> *image of the "Torso of an Archaic Apollo." A full and comprehensive view of the statue is unnecessary because the radiance of the torso suggests an intense unity. The torso, though only a part of the whole, radiates the power of the greater entity which is not described but suggested. The short story aspires to the intensity Rilke ascribed to the torso.*[1]

Some of the stories in the present collection achieve the radiance and intensity of the archaic torso. All of them—such is the nature of the genre—aspire to it, in that they necessarily suggest far more than they describe. For, generally speaking, the short story limits itself to a single situation within which the important actions (or abstentions from action) occur. Antecedent events are omitted altogether, or are introduced by implication, by brief narrative statement, or, occasionally, by flashback. If by the latter, the flashback must be held to such brevity as to prevent diffusion of the single situation.

These conditions of the genre indicate that the characters too will be presented as "torsos," for here again there must be more suggestion than full-length portraiture (or ample development of psychological complexity). Yet we learn enough about the characters to recognize, at the end of the tale, whether they have changed their ways of viewing the world and their criteria for making value-judgments,[2] or, by contrast, have been unmoved by experience or so little moved as to leave their prior values intact. Where the story succeeds, it sets in motion reverberations that reach beyond its spatial limitations, its limited word-count. Such extension of meaning is a further implication of Rilke's torso-image.

The successful tale achieves its aim because it creates a self-sufficient world of its own: not necessarily a "real" world, but a self-sufficient one, from which irrelevancies are excluded. The storyteller *shapes* that world, even if he seems merely to be imitating the confusions of life. His people suffer unexpected calamities just as we do from day to day. The author, however, has known the calamities were coming; he has made them happen. He has a grasp of the way cause and effect operate in the lives of his characters. To be sure, he is not necessarily aware,

[1]Edward Mitchell & Rainer Schulte, eds., *Continental Short Stories: The Modern Tradition*, 1968, "Afterword," pp. 162–163.
[2]Ibid., p. 163.

at the moment he sets about creating his world, of all there is to know concerning the people he has imagined. Such knowledge is progressive and it is cumulative. Nevertheless, as he explores the nature of his persons and the relationships of their actions, he is clarifying his own response and determining how best to evoke in us a parallel response. By such means he establishes and sustains the relevance of his created world (however evidently circumscribed—however like Rilke's torso) to the world we inhabit.

The stories in the anthology are listed in alphabetical order. The editors have chosen this order to impose minimal restrictions on the reader. We do, however, presume to offer suggestions as to variant approaches.

I. A Chronological Reading

The history of the short tale, especially if it includes the verse-tale as well as the prose, is a long one; for our purposes it opens in the 6th century BC with Aesop. But in fact the story emerges as a sub-genre of narrative fiction only in the 19th century. The literary genre that has commanded widest popularity since the middle of the 18th century—prose fiction—began with the novel and with minor exceptions the novel preoccupied the storyteller until well into the following century. The short story begins in America with Irving, Poe and Hawthorne, in Britain with Dickens, in France with Balzac (though the stature of both of the latter writers rests on their achievements as novelists).

Even granted a limited history of 150 years, no single anthology can hope adequately to serve the needs of a chronological approach unless it serves in fact no other. Yet the reader of the present selection can usefully introduce himself to the short story by starting with Aesop and the ensuing fables. The fable as a type of story has altered little over the centuries: Maugham's is a retelling of ancient materials, and though March and Thurber are very much of our own age in spirit, they follow the ancient form closely. Hawthorne's "Ethan Brand" (1845) serves to introduce *story* much as the modern world has come to conceive it, a narrative generously expanded beyond the anecdotal fable, and complex in its mixture of elements; "Ethan Brand" is rooted in the material world, yet it contains a touch of the fantastic, and its close is allegory. That is, Hawthorne's tale offers in the end the kind of direct judgment previously associated with the brief fable. Chekhov's "Anna on the Neck" (1895) is realistic comedy centered on a marriage of mismatched persons; though Chekhov doubtless also throws into comic relief the rigidities and confinements of provincial bureaucracy, his own voice is not in evidence, so that judgments rise from our grasp of character and incident. In "The Jolly Corner" (1908, a late story), Henry James offers what one risks calling a realistic ghost-tale, in the sense that the ghost encountered and confronted is the protagonist's own, the ghost of what Spencer Brydon might have become; a mark of this story, common to most of James's mature work, is the internalization of its significant conflicts, including, indeed, the conflict with the appalling apparition itself. Lawrence's "The Horse-Dealer's Daughter" (1916) might well come next, since it is a story in which, within a wholly realistic setting, a symbolic baptism brings awakened life to the central characters. And Lawrence's use of symbolic action to produce the climax of his tale may serve here as reminder of a needed readiness on the part of the reader of 20th century stories to examine such stories simultaneously on more than one level, to read, if one may borrow a musical analogy, contrapuntally. Such readiness is indispensible, for example, in approaching Thomas Mann's "Mario and the Magician" (1929), whose meticulously realistic surface offers the performance, in a provincial Italian seaside resort before an international audience, of a corrupt, drunken and cynical stage-magician. Taking, however, Mann's clues (the name he gives his magician is one of them: Cipolla = *onion*, and, by extension, "onion-head", the reader recognizes in the story a powerful political parable of the rise of modern tyrannies. Here it is the action in its entirety, including general audience-response, that is symbolic, not merely, as in Lawrence's story, a single action production of climax.

It may be ventured that writers of the short story here presented from Hawthorne to Mann have tested the limits of the genre without fundamentally questioning the "objective reality" of the external world in which their tales take root. Our century, however, which has had to digest as best it can two world wars, and, more fundamentally, the implications of quantum theory and atomic physics, has been host to other writers less certain about the stability of the objective external world and less ready, as a consequence, to base stories on the assumption of that stability. Hence a chronological use of the present collection must at this point return in its tracks to, say, 1914, and confront in Kafka's "In the Penal Colony" more radical experimentalism, for his is one of those contemporary stories that suggest the nightmare actualities of our world by scrupulously observing the canons of realism while at the same time suspending the laws of nature. Virginia Woolf, writing in 1917 her "The Mark on the Wall," distrusted the well-ordered narratives of her predecessors because they violated the nature of human life as experienced from moment to moment, arbitrarily centering on *external* events instead of on states of consciousness. "The Mark on the Wall" is therefore hardly a story at all by traditional measurement, but rather a sustained interior monologue. Here is a story without plot, almost without character except for the disembodied voice of the narrator. And yet, as we reach the end, we recognize that the reflections evoked by "the mark on the wall" have, as a recent critic has pointed out, "arranged themselves not by accident into a meditation on life, time, and history culminating in an apocalyptic vision." As a story, then, Mrs. Woolf's moves by a series of free associations toward an unsettling climax, in the process putting the reader into immediate contact with the texture of a human consciousness.

Such a chronological approach: the fables, Hawthorne, Chekhov, James, Lawrence, Mann, followed by Kafka and Woolf, should introduce the reader to the range of the short story. It may enable him as well to reach certain tentative conclusions concerning the modern development of the genre. Thereafter, it is hoped, he should be ready to explore the limits of the collection, from Baldwin's "Sonny's Blues," say, to Roald Dahl's "Pig" or Ionesco's "The Stroller in the Air."

II. A Thematic-Substantive Reading

"Appointment in Samarra," a fable, begins with the futility of fleeing death, then develops an anecdote appropriate to the "fleshing out" of the initiating moral. Hawthorne's tale, also cautionary, is yet more story than fable and makes its human characters subject to the largest of human ambitions; in the end pointing the way to damnation or (by negative example) to salvation. James's ghost story raises the issue of identity, and also, by the reader's inference, draws contrasts between value-options in the Europe and America of the turn of our century. And Mann's story is centered less on magic than on the corruptions of power-politics and the vulnerability of constituencies. Perhaps a majority of recent fiction anthologies have ordered their stories under thematic categories such as the foregoing sentences will have suggested. A similar approach is applicable to the present collection.

Most stories focus on the significant and the unusual rather than the commonplace, and on conflicts from which the participants emerge measurably altered. The brevity and the potential intensity of the story make it an effective vehicle for what James Joyce calls "epiphany," the revelation that overtakes a character in the wake of a single, sharply registered experience. Such tales are often called tales of *initiation*, particularly when they open the eyes of a young protagonist to the nature of his world. Thomas Wolfe's "The Lost Boy," Isaac Babel's "In the Basement," and Katherine Anne Porter's "The Grave," develop this theme.

Death is a central concern of Maugham's fable and of Miss Porter's "The Grave," mentioned above, but death is also central to Eudora Welty's "Death of a Travelling Salesman." If salvation (or damnation) within orthodox systems is Hawthorne's theme in "Ethan Brand," so is it also, though far more obliquely, Kafka's in the story of the penal colony. And death as imminent reality permeates those tales by European contemporaries whose knowledge of the modern police-state shapes their stories: Heinrich Böll's "My Sad Face," Ilse Aichinger's "The Bound Man," and, once again, Mann's "Mario and the Magician." The capacity of the irrational to destroy those who fail to understand or refuse to acknowledge its power is at the core of Bradbury's "The Scythe" and Cortazar's "Blow-Up." It plays a significant role, especially as regards Mario and the various members of the magician's audience, in Mann's parable.

But there is a further thematic category, made up of stories which directly question the ethical and/or spiritual premises on which, confronted by dilemma, we finally act as individuals and as citizens. Once again, Mann's tale demands inclusion, as do Kafka's "In the Penal Colony," Ionesco's "The Stroller in the Air," Carpenter's "Hollywood Heart," and, perhaps most transparently, Hawthorne's "Ethan Brand."

The reader will have noticed substantial overlapping in the categories suggested above, the re-entrance of the same story from one pigeonhole to another; and this fact points to the danger of the thematic approach. Categories risk a pre-determining of the reader's response, at the same time permitting and implying a simplistic interpretation. A warning is therefore appropriate, a warning against approaching any story as if the mere identification of its theme were equivalent to grasping its complexities through comprehensive reading. The fact that "Mario and the Magician," as an example, appears under four headings in the brief list of suggestions above should militate against confusion of thematic identification with meaning.

III. An Analytical Reading

Among the technical considerations important in analyzing a story we single out four: point of view, structure (the ordering of the story's events), language, tone and feeling. To consider point of view is to ask, "To whose voice am I listening?" Or, taking the story as a whole, "Whose voices?" Further, the voice we listen to at a given moment is connected to a pair of eyes, so that a second question must be asked, "through whose angle of vision are the events and persons of the story being refracted toward me?" For one's response to a tale is largely controlled, even manipulated, by the author's selected angle of vision. Does the angle of vision belong to the protagonist, speaking in the first person, as it does in Babel's "In the Basement?" or to an interested observer, also speaking in the first person, as in Borges' "Funes the Memorious"? Point of view raises more complex problems as well; the author may elect to shift from one voice to another, to place responsibility for a share of the narrative in the hands of that character whose "authority" is clearest; or to withdraw from his characters altogether and address the reader from behind the mask of an anonymous persona (narrator) endowed with omniscience, free to enter the consciousness of each of his characters in turn, as his plot prescribes. The omniscient storyteller can be heard in D. H. Lawrence's "The Horse-Dealer's Daughter," and the nameless persona is here to be trusted wholly. By contrast (and in illustration of the complexities just mentioned), Kafka's "In the Penal Colony" also uses a third-person narrator, a nameless persona, who shifts (in the earlier sections of the tale) from Officer to Explorer, and even to condemned soldier; but his omniscience is less real than apparent, for increasingly Kafka reveals his subject to us through a single center of consciousness, that of the Explorer, and the Explorer's ultimate responses to his bizarre situation are not at all to be trusted as indicators of value. His liberal, enlightened view of the Penal Colony would be anathema to the author. Hence the reader of a story must raise and probe such questions as the trustworthiness of the narrator, both with respect to his knowledge and his candor, and the degree to which his stance is ironical or may be accepted at face value. One may add by way of pointing to additional complexities that in Cortazar's "Blow-Up" and Thomas Wolfe's "The Lost Boy" point of view shifts (though in clearly different ways) between omniscient third-person and first-person narrative.

The distinction between story and plot is not easily grasped by most readers; definitions are slippery. When Alice asks the King of Hearts where she should begin her story she's told to begin at the beginning, go on until she reaches the end, and then stop. And this instruction is consonant with novelist E. M. Forster's definition of *story* as "a narrative of events in their time sequence." Such a narrative may suffice, says Forster, for an account of "life in time," life measured by hours; but it will hardly suffice for an account of "life by values," life measured by intensity. Hence the writer concerned with more than "story" examines his imagined events, seeking, among them, causal relationships, relationships that transcend simple chronology; he presses his subject to disclose to him intimations of value inherent in it. On the basis of his discovery, he includes this minor incident, rejects that major one, juxtaposes events at the cost of defying chronology, thrusts one aspect of character into prominence while abandoning a second to shadow. The writer shapes his materials, and his criterion for selection is relevance. But relevance to what?

Not the story as such, for loosely speaking, *everything* is relevant to the *story*—the number of heart-beats per second no less than a struggle for the presidency. What determines relevance is in fact the shape the author has discerned within his subject, a shape that can emerge into visibility for the reader only through suppression of everything that might blur its profile. The achieved shape of the finished story will, like Rilke's "torso," accommodate the author's "intimation of value," and it is the product of composition, of the act of composing or plotting.

"Let us define a plot," Forster writes:

> *We have defined a story as a narrative of events in their time-sequence. A plot is also a narrative of events, the emphasis falling on causality. "The king died and then the queen died" is a story. "The king died, and then the queen died of grief" is a plot. The time-sequence is preserved, but the sense of causality overshadows it. Or again: "The queen died, no one knew why, until it was discovered that it was through grief at the death of the king." This is a plot with a mystery in it, a form capable of high development. It suspends the time sequence, it moves as far away from the* story *as its limitations allow.*[3]

Story then remains content to establish chronology; plot aims higher, at providing reasons, that is, revelations of cause. And to achieve its aim with clarity, plot can suspend chronology for the sake of bringing together events whose relationship, chronologically, might well be disguised from us.

Further, to establish cause is to reveal pattern, to create order, and, ultimately, to point the way to meaning and value. But (allegory and fable aside) stories *only* point the way to meaning and value. *Their* discovery—"epiphany" for the reader—demands collaboration. Forster continues:

> *Consider the death of the queen. If it is in a story, we say, "and then?" If it is in a plot we ask "why?" That is the fundamental difference between these two aspects . . . A plot cannot be told to a gaping audience of cave-men . . .* They *can only be kept awake by "and then—and then—"* They *can only supply curiosity. But a plot demands intelligence and memory also.*[4]

It appears therefore that the storytellers in this collection are unlikely to have followed the instructions given to Alice; that, on the contrary, they have ordered their events toward erecting a final structure of relationships, which is not, yet, an end in itself, but which, discerned by the collaborating reader, will reveal something approximate to the

[3]E. M. Forster, *Aspects of the Novel*, London, 1963, pp. 82–83, Editor's emphasis.
[4]*Ibid.* Editor's emphasis.

author's initiating vision. Collaboration often takes the form of questions. Why, for example, does Mann's narrator not remove the children during the intermission of the Magician's performance? Is "inertia" (the reason offered) adequate to the circumstances? Why does he reserve Mario himself and the obscene caress to the end of the tale? Why does Kafka devote so much space to the Officer's reminiscence of the "bliss" attaching to the "sixth hour"?

"In the Penal Colony" raises, as a corollary, a subsidiary issue. Bradbury's "The Scythe" evokes at first encounter a world remote from that of Kafka's colony, but they are alike in their suspension of the laws of nature. They are alike in a second way: no two stories in the collection are more determinedly held at the lower end of the ladder of abstraction, more determined in their appeal to the reader's immediate sense perceptions of concrete reality.

Tone and feeling constitute a troublesome pair of tools for analysis because their identification and definition arise and are resolved in subjective responses to the literary work. Conventionally *tone* is defined as the tone-of-voice in which the author addresses his reader; it measures the writer's relation with his reader. Feeling, by contrast, points to the writer's attitude toward the subject, the materials-of-the-subject about which he is writing. Tone and feeling within a given story are often consonant, and when they are, we tend to ignore them; such is the case, for example, in a majority of newspaper cartoon-narratives, like "Mary Worth's Family" or "Rex Morgan, MD" or "Judge Parker." We accept the gravity the cartoonist assigns to particular situations, and if we smile, it is because the cartoonist sees occasion to smile. By contrast one turns to the example of satire, in which the writer's tone of voice may be sweet reasonableness, even one placatory toward the reader, while his attitude to his material may range from laughter to savage denunciation. Jonathan Swift's "A Modest Proposal" is the *locus classicus* of such discrepancy between tone and feeling; but within the tales here included one might instance Roald Dahl's "Pig," with its near-fairytale opening, or the fable by Thurber, "The Owl Who Was God;" and special attention might be directed to the "innocence" of Ouedrago's piece, and to the problematic view which Nabokov takes of his reader in "The Vane Sisters."

Stories selected for inclusion in any anthology appear for varied reasons: the author's ambition and his relative achievement, but often his failure of vision or fulfillment as well for his willingness to expand the genre, irrespective of his success. Above all, some few appear for the reason that, from a varied experience of the short story, the reader may come to an awareness of that radiance and intensity by means of which, at its finest, the genre can approximate the achievement of Rilke's "Torso of the Archaic Apollo."

DISCOVERY AND RESPONSE

A Group of Fables

Aesop

THE FOX AND THE GRAPES

What little is known about the Greek fabulist Aesop is based on inference rather than on direct information. He was a Phrygian slave who lived from about 620 to 560 B.C.; thus he is one of the earliest writers known by name in the western world. He was probably freed from slavery, perhaps for some service to the state. Aristotle mentions him as a public defender. The fables attributed to him were not all original, for some older versions have been found in Egyptian, Oriental, and other sources. But Aesop put his own stamp on them, revealing human vices and follies succinctly and humorously through the personae of his talking birds and animals.

One hot summer day, a Fox was strolling through an orchard when he noticed a bunch of Grapes that had just turned ripe on a vine that was growing overhead. "Just what I need to quench my thirst," he thought. Stepping back a few paces, he took a run and a jump, and just barely missed the bunch of Grapes. Turning around, he tried again, but with no better success. Again and again he jumped after the Grapes, but could never quite reach them. Finally he gave up the attempt, and walked away with his head in the air, saying to himself,

"Well, I'm sure they are sour, anyway."

W. Somerset Maugham

APPOINTMENT IN SAMARRA

Once highly popular, the prolific Somerset Maugham suffered a decline in reputation during the latter part of his life. The autobiographical novels of his early years and the sophisticated stage comedies of the 1920s no longer seemed as fresh as they once had, and his cynical, mocking tone was taken as a literary pose rather than as honest expression. However his plots are skillfully if somewhat artificially constructed, and he is particularly good at showing how the stresses of setting and environment break down the composure and the mannered behavior of worldly, civilized characters. Born in England in 1874, he studied medicine, and used his experiences as an intern in London slums for his first novel, Liza of Lambeth *(1897). Other major novels include* Of Human Bondage *(1915), a long, autobiographical novel, and his best-known work;* The Moon and Sixpence *(1919), a novel based on the life of the painter Gauguin; and* Cakes and Ale *(1930), a satire of British literary life. He also wrote a series of bright, witty stage comedies, including* The Circle *(1921),* Our Betters *(1923), and* The Constant Wife *(1926). Maugham died in 1965, rich and famous, in his villa on the Riviera. The fable used here is his adaptation of an ancient Persian fable; it appears as a preface to the published version of his play* Sheppey *(1933).*

DEATH SPEAKS: "There was a merchant in Bagdad who sent his servant to market to buy provisions and in a little while the servant came back, white and trembling, and said 'Master, just now when I was in the market-place I was jostled by a woman in the crowd and when I turned I saw it was Death that jostled me. She looked at me and made a threatening gesture; now, lend me your horse, and I will ride away from the city and avoid my fate. I will go to Samarra and there Death will not find me.' The merchant lent him his horse, and the servant mounted it, and he dug his spurs in its flanks and as fast as his horse could gallop he went. Then the merchant went down in the market-place and he saw me standing in the crowd and he came to me and said, 'Why did you make a threatening gesture to my servant when you saw him this morning?' 'That was not a threatening gesture,' I said, 'it was only a start of surprise. I was astonished to see him in Bagdad, for I had an appointment with him tonight in Samarra.' "

James Thurber

THE OWL WHO WAS GOD

Probably the best-known comic writer in America in the twentieth century, James Thurber shows, better than anyone since Mark Twain, the uses of comedy for serious purposes. Born in Columbus, Ohio, in 1894, Thurber attended Ohio State University, was turned down by the army during World War I for poor eyesight, and then went into newspaper work. Eventually he joined Harold Ross and E. B. White as one of the guiding spirits of the New Yorker *magazine, helping to establish its tone which combined serious intent and satire. Despite his impaired vision that eventually ended in blindness, he continued to draw cartoons and write stories in which he exposed human pretensions with great relish. He also treated fondly the desperate small attempts of beleagured man to maintain sanity in an absurdist world. He died in 1961. His works include* Is Sex Necessary? *(written with E. B. White, 1929),* The Owl in the Attic and Other Perplexities *(1931),* My Life and Hard Times *(1933), and a play,* The Male Animal *(written with Elliot Nugent, 1940), as well as the collection of* Fables for Our Times *(1940), from which this fable comes.*

Once upon a starless midnight there was an owl who sat on the branch of an oak tree. Two ground moles tried to slip quietly by, unnoticed. "You!" said the owl. "Who?" they quavered, in fear and astonishment, for they could not believe it was possible for anyone to see them in that thick darkness. "You two!" said the owl. The moles hurried away and told the other creatures of the field and forest that the owl was the greatest and wisest of all animals because he could see in the dark and because he could answer any question. "I'll see about that," said a secretary bird, and he called on the owl one night when it was again very dark. "How many claws am I holding up?" said the secretary bird. "Two," said the owl, and that was right. "Can you give me another expression for 'that is to say' or 'namely'?" asked the secretary bird. "To wit," said the owl. "Why does a lover call on his love?" asked the secretary bird. "To woo," said the owl.

The secretary bird hastened back to the other creatures and reported that the owl was indeed the greatest and wisest animal in the world because he could see in the dark and because he could answer any question. "Can he see in the daytime, too?" asked a red fox. "Yes," echoed a dormouse and a French poodle. "Can he see in the daytime, too?" All the other creatures laughed loudly at this silly question, and they set upon the red fox and his friends and drove them out of the region. Then they sent a messenger to the owl and asked him to be their leader.

When the owl appeared among the animals it was high noon and the sun was shining brightly. He walked very slowly, which gave him an appearance of great dignity, and he peered about him with large, staring eyes, which gave him an air of tremendous importance. "He's God!" screamed a Plymouth Rock hen. And the others took up the cry "He's God!" So they followed him wherever he went and when he began to bump into things they began to bump into things, too. Finally he came to a concrete highway and he started up the middle of it and all the other creatures followed him. Presently a hawk, who was acting as outrider, observed a truck coming toward them at fifty miles an hour, and he reported to the secretary bird and the secretary bird reported to the owl. "There's danger ahead," said the secretary bird. "To wit?" said the owl. The secretary bird told him. "Aren't you afraid?" he asked. "Who?" said the owl calmly, for he could not see the truck. "He's God!" cried all the creatures again, and they were still crying "He's God!" when the truck hit them and ran them down. Some of the animals were merely injured, but most of them, including the owl, were killed.

Moral: You can fool too many of the people too much of the time.

William March

THE SNAPPING TURTLE AND THE WISTERIA VINE

It is one of the ironies of recent literary history that William March's only real success was his last novel, The Bad Seed, *published posthumously in 1954, a few months after his death. The book was also dramatized successfully that same year by Maxwell Anderson, and later was made into a film version. Never widely known or read during his lifetime, March came to be praised after his death, especially by British reviewers, as a major though neglected novelist of his time. This attention created a revival of interest in him, and brought about the republication and rediscovery of some of his earlier work. Born in Mobile, Alabama, in 1893 (as William Edward March Campbell), he grew up in Southern towns with little formal schooling. He then served in the marines in Europe during World War I. Out of his war experiences came one of his best novels,* Company K *(1933). His other works are set chiefly in the South—*Come In at the Door *(1934),* The Tallons *(1936), and* The Looking Glass *(1943); but one brilliant satirical novel,* October Island *(1952), is set on a South Sea island, where a staid missionary couple try to reform the natives, but are themselves changed instead. The fables that March had written throughout his lifetime were collected and published as* 99 Fables *in 1960.*

Of all the creatures of the forest, the snapping turtle was the most tenacious: once he seized an enemy in his jaws, he wouldn't turn loose until his adversary admitted he was beaten or until it thundered. One day he was crawling through the underbrush when a big snake, hanging down from a tree, swung forward and struck him between his near-sighted eyes. The turtle stopped in his tracks, wondering if the affront were intentional or not; then deciding it was not, he continued on his way, saying over his shoulder, "Do that again and I'll bite you; and if I bite you, I'll hold on until you admit you've had enough or until it thunders. I have great strength of character, as anybody will tell you, and I mean what I say."

He'd hardly finished before the snake swung back, this time catching the turtle in the rear. The turtle, furious at the insult, seized the tail of the snake in his jaws—and instantly he knew his poor eyesight had betrayed him again. It wasn't a snake at all; it was only the dangling end of an old wisteria vine.

For a time the turtle hung on, knowing he had made a mistake but unwilling to act contrary to the traditions of his kind, and after a while the other animals gathered to watch the spectacle of a live turtle fighting a dead wisteria vine. "It's nothing but a vine," they said. "The vine can't admit it's beaten, so why don't you turn loose and go home to supper?"

"I'll turn loose when it thunders, and not before," said the turtle. He glanced upwards, but there was not a cloud in the sky, and it looked as though it would stay fair for a long time. And so things went, with the friends of the turtle urging him to turn loose and with him shaking his head stubbornly. "When it thunders," he said. "Not until it thunders."

Nobody was surprised when, toward the end of the week, the turtle died and fell to the ground. His friends gathered about him and said, "Sometimes it's hard to tell the difference between strength of character and plain stupidity."

William March

AESOP'S LAST FABLE

Aesop, the messenger of King Croesus, finished his business with the Delphians and went back to the tavern where he had taken lodgings. Later, he came into the taproom where a group of Delphians were drinking. When they realized who he was, they crowded about him. "Tell us," they began, "is Croesus as rich as people say?"

Aesop, since the habit of speaking in fables was so strongly fixed in him, said, "I can best answer your question with a parable, and it is this: The animals gathered together to crown their richest member king. Each animal in turn stated what he possessed, and it was soon apparent that the lion had the largest hunting preserves, the bee the most honey, the squirrel the largest supply of acorns, and so on; but when the voting began, the difficulty of arriving at a decision was plain to all, for to the bee, the nuts that represented the wealth of the squirrel were of no consequence; to the lion, the hay that the zebra and the buffalo owned was worthless; and the panther and the tiger set no value at all on the river that the crane and crocodile prized so highly."

Then Aesop called for his drink, looking into the faces of the Delphians with good-natured amusement. He said, "The moral of the fable in this: Wealth is an intangible thing, and its meaning is not the same to all alike."

The stolid Delphians looked at one another, and when the silence was becoming noticeable, one of them tried again: "How was the weather in Lydia when you left home?"

"I can best answer that question with another fable," said Aesop, "and it is this: During a rain storm, when the ditches were flooded and the ponds had overflowed their banks, a cat and a duck met on the road, and, wanting to make conversation, they spoke at the same instant. 'What a beautiful day this is,' said the delighted duck. 'What terrible weather we're having,' said the disgusted cat."

Again the Delphians looked at one another, and again there was silence. "The moral of that tale," said Aesop, "is this: What pleases a duck, distresses a cat." He poured wine into his glass and leaned against the wall, well satisfied with the start he had made in instructing the barbarous Delphians.

The Delphians moved uneasily in their seats, and after a long time, one of them said, "How long are you going to be here?"

"That," said Aesop, "can best be answered in the Fable of the Tortoise, the Pelican, and the Wolf. You see, the pelican went to visit his friend the tortoise and promised to remain as long as the latter was building his new house. Then one day as they were working together, with the tortoise burrowing and the pelican carrying away the dirt in his pouch, the wolf came on them unexpectedly, and—"

But Aesop got no farther, for the Delphians had surrounded him and were, an instant later, carrying him toward the edge of the cliff on which the tavern was built. When they reached it, they swung him outward and turned him loose, and Aesop was hurled to the rocks below, where he died. "The moral of what we have done," they explained later, "is so obvious that it needs no elaboration."

Questions

1. The fable is both one of the oldest and one of the most contemporary fictional forms. Account for its survival. Enumerate and discuss some of the characteristics—brevity, pithiness, etc.—that have made it both an enduring and a useful form.

2. The fable's characters are usually birds, animals, trees, even inanimate objects or abstractions, all of which usually possess human characteristics and speak with human voices. Cite examples from the fables used here.

3. By what other means (use of human emotions, human reasoning, etc.) does the fabulist make it clear that he is really writing about human beings?

4. Why is one of these tales necessarily Aesop's "last" fable? What is William March implying here about the role of the moralist, and the public's reaction to him? Is he right?

Ilse Aichinger

THE BOUND MAN

Not widely known in English-speaking countries, Ilse Aichinger has a a high reputation and has won literary prizes in her native Austria for both fiction and poetry. She was born in Vienna in 1921. She has studied medicine and is concerned with the tensions and the psychological anxieties in Europe during the aftermath of World War II. Her works available in translation include The Bound Man and Other Stories *(1956) and* Selected Short Stories and Dialogues *(1966).*

"The Bound Man" reveals Miss Aichinger's affiliation with the Kafka-like use of nightmarish fantasy as a means of communicating some of the stresses and dilemmas of the modern world. Although the surface of the story seems straightforward enough, and its details are realistic and literal, the allegorical portrayal of the "bound" man who finds a certain safety in his bondage raises disturbing questions about the nature of freedom, political or otherwise.

Sunlight on his face woke him, but made him shut his eyes again; it streamed unhindered down the slope, collected itself into rivulets, attracted swarms of flies, which flew low over his forehead, circled, sought to land, and were overtaken by fresh swarms. When he tried to whisk them away, he discovered that he was bound. A thick rope cut into his arms. He dropped them, opened his eyes again, and looked down at himself. His legs were tied all the way up to his thighs; a single length of rope was tied round his ankles, criss-crossed up his legs and encircled his hips, his chest and his arms. He could not see where it was knotted. He showed no sign of fear or hurry, though he thought he was unable to move, until he discovered that the rope allowed his legs some free play and that round his body it was almost loose. His arms were tied to each other but not to his body, and had some free play too. This made him smile, and it occurred to him that perhaps children had been playing a practical joke on him.

He tried to feel for his knife, but again the rope cut softly into his flesh. He tried again, more cautiously this time, but his pocket was empty. Not only his knife, but the little money that he had on him, as well as his coat, were missing. His shoes had been pulled from his feet and taken too. When he moistened his lips he tasted blood, which had flowed from his temples down his cheeks, his chin, his neck, and under his shirt. His eyes were painful; if he kept them open for long he saw reddish stripes in the sky.

He decided to stand up. He drew his knees up as far as he could, rested his hands on the fresh grass and jerked himself to his feet. An elder branch stroked his cheek, the pain dazzled him, and the rope cut into his flesh. He collapsed to the ground again, half out of his mind with pain, and then tried again. He went on trying until the blood started flowing from his hidden weals. Then he lay still again for a long while and let the sun and the flies do what they liked.

When he awoke for the second time the elder bush had cast its shadow over him, and the coolness stored in it was pouring from between its branches. He must have been hit on the head. Then they must have laid him down carefully, just as a mother lays her baby behind a bush when she goes to work in the fields.

His chances all lay in the amount of free play allowed him by the rope. He dug his elbows into the ground and tested it. As soon as the rope tautened he stopped, and tried again more cautiously. If he had been able to reach the branch over his head he could have used it to drag himself to his feet, but he could not reach it. He laid his head back on the grass, rolled over, and struggled to his knees. He tested the ground with his toes, and then managed to stand up almost without effort.

A few paces away lay the path across the plateau, and in the grass were wild pinks and thistles in bloom. He tried to lift his foot to avoid trampling on them, but the rope round his ankles prevented him. He looked down at himself.

The rope was knotted at his ankles, and ran round his legs in a kind of playful pattern. He carefully bent and tried to loosen it, but, loose though it seemed to be, he could not make it any looser. To avoid treading on the thistles with his bare feet he hopped over them like a bird.

The cracking of a twig made him stop. People in this district were very prone to laughter. He was alarmed by the thought that he was in no position to defend himself. He hopped on until he reached the path. Bright fields stretched far below. He could see no sign of the nearest village, and if he could move no faster than this, night would fall before he reached it.

He tried walking and discovered that he could put one foot before another if he lifted each foot a definite distance from the ground and then put it down again before the rope tautened. In the same way he could actually swing his arms a little.

After the first step he fell. He fell right across the path, and made the dust fly. He expected this to be a sign for the long-suppressed laughter to break out, but all remained quiet. He was alone. As soon as the dust had settled he got up and went on. He looked down and watched the rope slacken, grow taut, and then slacken again.

When the first glow-worms appeared he managed to look up. He felt in control of himself again, and his impatience to reach the nearest village faded.

Hunger made him light-headed, and he seemed to be going so fast that not even a motorcycle could have overtaken him; alternatively he felt as if he were standing still and that the earth was rushing past him, like a river flowing past a man swimming against the stream. The stream carried branches which had been bent southward by the north wind, stunted young trees, and patches of grass with bright, long-stalked flowers. It ended by submerging the bushes and the young trees, leaving only the sky and the man above water level. The moon had risen, and illuminated the bare, curved summit of the plateau, the path, which was overgrown with young grass, the bound man making his way along it with quick, measured steps, and two hares, which ran across the hill just in front of him and vanished down the slope. Though the nights were still cool at this time of the year, before midnight the bound man lay down at the edge of the escarpment and went to sleep.

In the light of morning the animal-tamer who was camping with his circus in the field outside the village saw the bound man coming down the path, gazing thoughtfully at the ground. The bound man stopped and bent down. He held out one arm to keep his balance and with the other picked up an empty wine-bottle. Then he straightened himself and stood erect again. He moved slowly, to avoid being cut by the rope, but to the circus proprietor what he did suggested the voluntary limitation of an enormous swiftness of movement. He was enchanted by its extraordinary gracefulness, and while the bound man looked about for a stone on which to break the bottle, so that he could use the splintered neck to cut the rope, the animal-tamer walked across the field and approached him. The first leaps of a young panther had never filled him with such delight.

"Ladies and gentlemen, the bound man!" His very first movements let loose a storm of applause, which out of sheer excitement caused the blood to rush to the cheeks of the animal-tamer standing at the edge of the arena. The bound man rose to his feet. His surprise whenever he did this was like that of a four-footed animal which has managed to stand on its hind legs. He knelt, stood up, jumped, and turned cartwheels. The spectators found it as astonishing as if they had seen a bird which voluntarily remained earthbound, and confined itself to hopping.

The bound man became an enormous draw. His absurd steps and little jumps, his elementary exercises in movement, made the rope dancer superfluous. His fame grew from village to village, but the motions he went through were few and always the same; they were really quite ordinary motions, which he had continually to practice in the daytime in the half-dark tent in order to retain his shackled freedom. In that he remained entirely within the limits set by his rope; he was free of it, it did not confine him, but gave him wings and endowed his leaps and jumps with purpose; just as the flights of birds of passage have purpose when they take wing in the warmth of summer and hesitantly make small circles in the sky.

All the children of the neighborhood started playing the game of "bound man." They formed rival gangs, and one day the circus people found a little girl lying bound in a ditch, with a cord tied round her neck so that she could hardly breathe. They released her, and at the end of the performance that night the bound man made a speech. He announced briefly that there was no sense in being tied up in such a way that you could not jump. After that he was regarded as a comedian.

Grass and sunlight, tent pegs driven into the ground and then pulled up again, and on to the next village. "Ladies and gentlemen, the bound man!" The summer mounted toward its climax. It bent its face deeper over the fish ponds in the hollows, taking delight in its dark reflection, skimmed the surface of the rivers, and made the plain into what it was. Everyone who could walk went to see the bound man.

Many wanted a close-up view of how he was bound. So the circus proprietor announced after each performance that anyone who wanted to satisfy himself that the knots were real and the rope not made of rubber was at liberty to do so. The bound man generally waited for the crowd in the area outside the tent. He laughed or remained serious, and held out his arms for inspection. Many took the opportunity to look him in the face, others gravely tested the rope, tried the knots on his ankles, and wanted to know exactly how the lengths compared with the length of his limbs. They asked him how he had come to be tied up like that, and he answered patiently, always saying the same thing. Yes, he had been tied up, he said, and when he awoke he found that he had been robbed as well. Those who had done it must have been pressed for time, because they had tied him up somewhat too loosely for someone who was not supposed to be able to move and somewhat too tightly for someone who was expected to be able to move. But he did move, people pointed out. Yes, he replied, what else could he do?

Before he went to bed he always sat for a time in front of the fire.

When the circus proprietor asked him why he didn't make up a better story he always answered that he hadn't made up that one, and blushed. He preferred staying in the shade.

The difference between him and the other performers was that when the show was over he did not take off his rope. The result was that every movement that he made was worth seeing, and the villagers used to hang about the camp for hours, just for the sake of seeing him get up from in front of the fire and roll himself in his blanket. Sometimes the sky was beginning to lighten when he saw their shadows disappear.

The circus proprietor often remarked that there was no reason why he should not be untied after the evening performance and tied up again next day. He pointed out that the rope dancers, for instance, did not stay on their rope overnight. But no one took the idea of untying him seriously.

For the bound man's fame rested on the fact that he was always bound, that whenever he washed himself he had to wash his clothes too and vice versa, and that his only way of doing so was to jump in the river just as he was every morning when the sun came out, and that he had to be careful not to go too far out for fear of being carried away by the stream.

The proprietor was well aware that what in the last resort protected the bound man from the jealousy of the other performers was his helplessness; he deliberately left them the pleasure of watching him groping painfully from stone to stone on the river bank every morning with his wet clothes clinging to him. When the proprietor's wife pointed out that even the best clothes would not stand up indefinitely to such treatment (and the bound man's clothes were by no means of the best), he replied curtly that it was not going to last forever. That was his answer to all objections—it was for the summer season only. But when he said this he was not being serious; he was talking like a gambler who has no intention of giving up his vice. In reality he would have been prepared cheerfully to sacrifice his lions and his rope dancers for the bound man.

He proved this on the night when the rope dancers jumped over the fire. Afterward he was convinced that they did it, not because it was midsummer's day, but because of the bound man, who as usual was lying and watching them with that peculiar smile that might have been real or might have been only the effect of the glow on his face. In any case no one knew anything about him because he never talked about anything that had happened to him before he emerged from the wood that day.

But that evening two of the performers suddenly picked him up by the arms and legs, carried him to the edge of the fire and started playfully swinging him to and fro, while two others held out their arms to catch him on the other side. In the end they threw him, but too short. The two men on the other side drew back—they explained afterward that they did so the better to take the shock. The result was that the bound man landed at the very edge of the flames and would have been burned if the circus proprietor had not seized his arms and quickly dragged him away to save the rope which was starting to get singed. He was certain that the object had been to burn the rope. He sacked the four men on the spot.

A few nights later the proprietor's wife was awakened by the sound of footsteps on the grass, and went outside just in time to prevent the clown from playing his last practical joke. He was carrying a pair of scissors. When he was asked for an explanation he insisted that he had had no intention of taking the bound man's life, but only wanted to cut his rope because he felt sorry for him. He was sacked too.

These antics amused the bound man because he could have freed himself if he had wanted to whenever he liked, but perhaps he wanted to learn a few new jumps first. The children's rhyme: "We travel with the circus, we travel with the circus" sometimes occurred to him while he lay awake at night. He could hear the voices of spectators on the opposite bank who had been driven too far downstream on the way home. He could see the river gleaming in the moonlight, and the young shoots growing out of the thick tops of the willow trees, and did not think about autumn yet.

The circus proprietor dreaded the danger that sleep involved for the bound man. Attempts were continually made to release him while he slept. The chief culprits were sacked rope dancers, or children who were bribed for the purpose. But measures could be taken to safeguard against these. A much bigger danger was that which he represented to himself. In his dreams he forgot his rope, and was surprised by it when he woke in the darkness of morning. He would angrily try to get up, but lose his balance and fall back again. The previous evening's applause was forgotten, sleep was still too near, his head and neck too free. He was just the opposite of a hanged man—his neck was the only part of him that was free. You had to make sure that at such moments no knife was within his reach. In the early hours of the morning the circus proprietor sometimes sent his wife to see whether the bound man was all right. If he was asleep she would bend over him and feel the rope. It had grown hard from dirt and damp. She would test the amount of free play it allowed him, and touch his tender wrists and ankles.

The most varied rumors circulated about the bound man. Some said he had tied himself up and invented the story of having been robbed, and toward the end of the summer that was the general opinion. Others maintained that he had been tied up at his own request, perhaps in league with the circus proprietor. The hesitant way in which he told his story, his habit of breaking off when the talk got round to the attack on him, contributed greatly to these rumors. Those who still believed in the robbery-with-violence story were laughed at. Nobody knew what difficulties the circus proprietor had in keeping the bound man, and how often he said he had had enough and wanted to clear off, for too much of the summer had passed.

Later, however, he stopped talking about clearing off. When the proprietor's wife brought him his food by the river and asked him how long he proposed to remain with them, he did not answer. She thought he had got used, not to being tied up, but to remembering every moment that he was tied up—the only thing that anyone in his position could get used to. She asked him whether he did not think it ridiculous to be tied up all the time, but he answered that he did not. Such a variety of people—clowns, freaks, and comics, to say nothing of elephants and tigers—traveled with circuses that he did not see why a bound man should not travel with a circus too. He told her about the movements he was practicing, the new ones he had discovered, and about a new trick that had occurred to him while he was whisking flies from the animals' eyes. He described to her how he always anticipated the effect of the rope and always restrained his movements in such a way as to prevent it from ever tautening; and she knew that there were days when he was hardly aware of the rope, when he jumped down from the wagon and slapped the flanks of the horses in the morning as if he were moving in a dream. She watched him vault over the bars almost without touching them, and saw the sun on his face, and he told her that sometimes he felt as if he were not tied up at all. She answered that if he were prepared to be untied, there would never be any need for him to feel tied up. He agreed that he could be untied whenever he felt like it.

The woman ended by not knowing whether she was more concerned with the man or with the rope that tied him. She told him that he could go on traveling with the circus without his rope, but she did not believe it. For what would be the point of his antics without his rope, and what would he amount to without it? Without his rope he would leave them, and the happy days would be over. She would no longer be able to sit beside him on the stones by the river without arousing suspicion, and she knew that his continued presence, and her conversations with him, of which the rope was the only subject, depended on it. Whenever she agreed that the rope had its advantages, he would start talking about how troublesome it was, and whenever he started talking about its advantages, she would urge him to get rid of it. All this seemed as endless as the summer itself.

At other times she was worried at the thought that she was herself hastening the end by her talk. Sometimes she would get up in the middle of the night and run across the grass to where he slept. She wanted to shake him, wake him up and ask him to keep the rope. But then she would see him lying there; he had thrown off his blanket, and there he lay like a corpse, with his legs outstretched and his arms close together, with the rope tied round them. His clothes had suffered from the heat and the water, but the rope had grown no thinner. She felt that he would go on traveling with the circus until the flesh fell from him and exposed the joints. Next morning she would plead with him more ardently than ever to get rid of his rope.

The increasing coolness of the weather gave her hope. Autumn was coming, and he would not be able to go on jumping into the river with his clothes on much longer. But the thought of losing his rope, about which he had felt indifferent earlier in the season, now depressed him.

The songs of the harvesters filled him with foreboding. "Summer has gone, summer has gone." But he realized that soon he would have to change his clothes, and he was certain that when he had been untied it would be impossible to tie him up again in exactly the same way. About this time the proprietor started talking about traveling south that year.

The heat changed without transition into quiet, dry cold, and the fire was kept going all day long. When the bound man jumped down from the wagon he felt the coldness of the grass under his feet. The stalks were bent with ripeness. The horses dreamed on their feet and the wild animals, crouching to leap even in their sleep, seemed to be collecting gloom under their skins which would break out later.

On one of these days a young wolf escaped. The circus proprietor kept quiet about it, to avoid spreading alarm, but the wolf soon started raiding cattle in the neighborhood. People at first believed that the wolf had been driven to these parts by the prospect of a severe winter, but the circus soon became suspect. The proprietor could not conceal the loss of the animal from his own employees, so the truth was bound to come out before long. The circus people offered the burgomasters of the neighboring villages their aid in tracking down the beast, but all their efforts were in vain. Eventually the circus was openly blamed for the damage and the danger, and spectators stayed away.

The bound man went on performing before half-empty seats without losing anything of his amazing freedom of movement. During the day he wandered among the surrounding hills under the thin-beaten silver of the autumn sky, and, whenever he could, lay down where the sun shone longest. Soon he found a place which the twilight reached last of all, and when at last it reached him he got up most unwillingly from the withered grass. In coming down the hill he had to pass through a little wood on its southern slope, and one evening he saw the gleam of two little green lights. He knew that they came from no church window, and was not for a moment under any illusion about what they were.

He stopped. The animal came toward him through the thinning foliage. He could make out its shape, the slant of its neck, its tail which swept the ground, and its receding head. If he had not been bound, perhaps he would have tried to run away, but as it was he did not even feel fear. He stood calmly with dangling arms and looked down at the wolf's bristling coat under which the muscles played like his own underneath the rope. He thought the evening wind was still between him and the wolf when the beast sprang. The man took care to obey his rope.

Moving with the deliberate care that he had so often put to the test, he seized the wolf by the throat. Tenderness for a fellow creature arose in him, tenderness for the upright being concealed in the four-footed. In a movement that resembled the drive of a great bird (he felt a sudden awareness that flying would be possible only if one were tied up in a special way) he flung himself at the animal and brought it to the ground. He felt a slight elation at having lost the fatal advantage of free limbs which causes men to be worsted.

The freedom he enjoyed in this struggle was having to adapt every movement of his limbs to the rope that tied him—the freedom of panthers, wolves, and the wild flowers that sway in the evening breeze. He ended up lying obliquely down the slope, clasping the animal's hind legs between his own bare feet and its head between his hands. He felt the gentleness of the faded foliage stroking the backs of his hands, and he felt his own grip almost effortlessly reaching its maximum, and he felt too how he was in no way hampered by the rope.

As he left the wood light rain began to fall and obscured the setting sun. He stopped for a while under the trees at the edge of the wood. Beyond the camp and the river he saw the fields where the cattle grazed, and the places where they crossed. Perhaps he would travel south with the circus after all. He laughed softly. It was against all reason. Even if he continued to put up with the sores that covered his joints and opened and bled when he made certain movements, his clothes would not stand up much longer to the friction of the rope.

The circus proprietor's wife tried to persuade her husband to announce the death of the wolf without mentioning that it had been killed by the bound man. She said that even at the time of his greatest popularity people would have refused to believe him capable of it, and in their present angry mood, with the nights getting cooler, they would be more incredulous than ever. The wolf had attacked a group of children at play that day, and nobody would believe that it had really been killed; for the circus proprietor had many wolves, and it was easy enough for him to hang a skin on the rail and allow free entry. But he was not to be dissuaded. He thought that the announcement of the bound man's act would revive the triumphs of the summer.

That evening the bound man's movements were uncertain. He stumbled in one of his jumps, and fell. Before he managed to get up he heard some low whistles and catcalls, rather like birds calling at dawn. He tried to get up too quickly, as he had done once or twice during the summer, with the result that he tautened the rope and fell back again. He lay still to regain his calm, and listened to the boos and catcalls growing into an uproar. "Well, bound man, and how did you kill the wolf?" they shouted, and: "Are you the man who killed the wolf?" If he had been one of them, he would not have believed it himself. He thought they had a perfect right to be angry: a circus at this time of year, a bound man, an escaped wolf, and all ending up with this. Some groups of spectators started arguing with others, but the greater part of the audience thought the whole thing a bad joke. By the time he had got to his feet there was such a hubbub that he was barely able to make out individual words.

He saw people surging up all round him, like faded leaves raised by a whirlwind in a circular valley at the center of which all was yet still. He thought of the golden sunsets of the last few days; and the sepulchral light which lay over the blight of all that he had built up during so many nights, the gold frame which the pious hang round dark, old pictures, this sudden collapse of everything, filled him with anger.

They wanted him to repeat his battle with the wolf. He said that such a thing had no place in a circus performance, and the proprietor declared that he did not keep animals to have them slaughtered in front of an audience. But the mob stormed the ring and forced them toward the cages. The proprietor's wife made her way between the seats to the exit and managed to get round to the cages from the other side. She pushed aside the attendant whom the crowd had forced to open a cage door, but the spectators dragged her back and prevented the door from being shut.

"Aren't you the woman who used to lie with him by the river in the summer?" they called out. "How does he hold you in his arms?" She shouted back at them that they needn't believe in the bound man if they didn't want to, they had never deserved him. Painted clowns were good enough for them.

The bound man felt as if the bursts of laughter were what he had been expecting ever since early May. What had smelt so sweet all through the summer now stank. But, if they insisted, he was ready to take on all the animals in the circus. He had never felt so much at one with his rope.

Gently he pushed the woman aside. Perhaps he would travel south with them after all. He stood in the open doorway of the cage, and he saw the wolf, a strong young animal, rise to its feet, and he heard the proprietor grumbling again about the loss of his exhibits. He clapped his hands to attract the animal's attention, and when it was near enough he turned to slam the cage door. He looked the woman in the face. Suddenly he remembered the proprietor's warning to suspect of murderous intentions anyone near him who had a sharp instrument in his hand. At the same moment he felt the blade on his wrists, as cool as the water of the river in autumn, which during the last few weeks he had been barely able to stand. The rope curled up in a tangle beside him while he struggled free. He pushed the woman back, but there was no point in anything he did now. Had he been insufficiently on his guard against those who wanted to release him, against the sympathy in which they wanted to lull him? Had he lain too long on the river bank? If she had cut the cord at any other moment it would have been better than this.

He stood in the middle of the cage, and rid himself of the rope like a snake discarding its skin. It amused him to see the spectators shrinking back. Did they realize that he had no choice now? Or that fighting the wolf now would prove nothing whatever? At the same time he felt all his blood rush to his feet. He felt suddenly weak.

The rope, which fell at its feet like a snare, angered the wolf more than the entry of a stranger into its cage. It crouched to spring. The man reeled, and grabbed the pistol that hung ready at the side of the cage. Then, before anyone could stop him, he shot the wolf between the eyes. The animal reared, and touched him in falling.

On the way to the river he heard the footsteps of his pursuers—spectators, the rope dancers, the circus proprietor, and the proprietor's wife, who persisted in the chase longer than anyone else. He hid in a clump of bushes and listened to them hurrying past, and later on streaming in the opposite direction back to the camp. The moon shone on the meadow; in that light its color was both of growth and of death.

When he came to the river his anger died away. At dawn it seemed to him as if lumps of ice were floating in the water, and as if snow had fallen, obliterating memory.

Questions

1. In what way does the opening situation—the bound man's acceptance of his absurd position—prepare the reader for a story which is something other than a realistic narrative?

2. Account for the bound man's appearance with the circus. Why is he greeted with "a storm of applause"? Why does he become "an enormous draw"? What do the spectators see in him? Why are they interested in inspecting his knots and in learning how he came to be bound?

3. Why does the man voluntarily remain bound, even at night when he is off duty and could be untied? Why does he even feel elated at being bound, as if this is somehow a special distinction?

4. Explain and account for the bound man's relationship with the wolf that escapes. Why does he refuse to repeat his battle with the wolf?

5. Why is the bound man never given a name? What does this lack of a name suggest about his function in the story? What do he and the other characters "represent"?

Isaac Babel

IN THE BASEMENT

Babel was born in an Odessa ghetto in 1894 to a middle-class Jewish family. Through his university studies he became interested in the French realistic writers, especially Flaubert and de Maupassant, whom he imitated, especially by learning to write in French. His varied military experiences probably helped contribute to the spirit of ironic detachment with which Babel came to view human affairs in his writing. He first served in the Tsar's army, on the Rumanian front, and then, after the Russian Revolution, was a member of a Cossack cavalry detachment in Poland. However, his lack of orthodox writing about the changing political regimes in Russia of the early 1900's made him something of an outcast. He disappeared after 1938, and is believed to have died or to have been executed in a concentration camp about 1939. The work he left includes Red Cavalry *(1926),* Lyubka the Cossack and Other Stories *(1963), and* The Lonely Years *(1964), a collection of previously unpublished stories, letters and personal documents. His story "In the Basement" is a notable demonstration of the irony made possible by skillful use of point of view.*

As a small boy I had the vaguest idea of truth. This was the result of too much reading and an over-excitable imagination. I was always poring over books: stealthily in class, during the breaks between lessons, on the way home, and in the evenings, squatting surreptitiously in the shadow of our dining-room table. For books I sacrificed all the most popular amusements, such as the secret excursions to the port during school-time, the billiard-parties in the Greek Street coffee-houses, and the swimming on the Langeron. I had no friends: for who would care to consort with such a bookworm?

One day at school I caught sight of a book about Spinoza in the hands of Marc Borgman, our head boy. He had just finished reading it and was unable to resist the temptation to tell the other boys about the Spanish Inquisition. What he said had an erudite flavour, but sounded very dull. There was no poetry in his words. And I simply had to break in. I edified my audience with tales of old Amsterdam, of its gloomy ghetto, of the philosophers and the diamond-cutters. My account, based on a knowledge gleaned from books, was greatly embroidered by my own invention. But that was only to be expected. My imagination intensified the dramatic scenes, found mysterious and complicated motives and surprising conclusions. Spinoza's death, that free and lonely death, loomed in my imagination like a battle. The Sanhedrin urged him to repentance, but the dying man was adamant. And then I introduced Rubens, whom I saw standing by Spinoza's bed taking a mask of the dead man's face.

My audience listened open-mouthed to this fantastic and animated recital. And, in the next break, Borgman came up to me and, taking my arm familiarly, led me off for a stroll. Before long we had become the best of friends. Borgman was not a bad type of head-boy. His powerful brain had already out-distanced our school-boyish wisdom, and he seemed bent upon the discovery of greater truths. Even we, thoughtless twelve-year-old boys, could realise that a career of unusual distinction lay in store for him. And now this brilliant and reserved youth grew attached to me because of my peculiar knack of spinning the most fantastic tales on the least provocation.

That year we had moved up into the third form. One day towards the beginning of summer Borgman invited me to spend a day at their country house. Borgman's father was manager of the Russian Foreign Trade Bank, and was one of that generation of men who were transforming provincial Odessa into a Marseilles or Naples, but he still had in him the leaven of the old Odessa merchants. Fond of the society of sceptical and affable men of the world, he avoided when possible talking in Russian, preferring to express himself in an English that smacked of the rough and abrupt jargon of Liverpool sea-captains. When the Italian Opera had come to town in April, the Borgmans gave a dinner in honour of the company. And the self-indulgent banker, the last of the old Odessa merchants, had then proceeded to carry on a vigorous intrigue with the generously-bosomed prima donna, who departed after two months, taking away with her only some memories which did not weigh too heavily on her conscience, and a necklace chosen with taste, but of negligible value.

Borgman's father was also Consul for the Argentine and Chairman of the Stock Exchange Committee; his business abilities were generally recognised. I had been invited to his house, and my Aunt Bobka was not slow to make the most of this, and soon the news spread far and wide. On the great day, my aunt dressed me up with the greatest possible style, and I caught the local train for Bolshaya Fontanka.

The Borgman house stood on a low red cliff overlooking the sea. In its grounds, sloping gently to the edge of the cliff, a garden had been laid out, planted with fuchsias and mulberry trees trimmed into sphere-like shapes. Coming as I did from an indigent and disorderly household, this tastefully appointed residence sent me into raptures. Wicker-work chairs gleamed whitely in the foliage-shaded alleys; the lunch-table was elegantly laid and adorned with flowers; the window-frames were picked out in green; and a low and spacious wooden colonnade stretched in front of the house.

The bank-manager himself arrived in the evening. After dinner, setting a wicker armchair near the edge of the cliff overlooking the restless plain of the sea, he lit a cigar and engrossed himself in the *Manchester Guardian*. The guests, Odessa ladies for the most part, sat on the verandah, playing poker. A slender samovar with narrow ivory handles stood steaming on a table. Gamblers, profligates in secret, these dainty Odessa women in their negligently fashionable dresses fanned themselves languidly as they staked gold pieces. The sun reached them filtered through a hedge of wild vine. Its fiery disc appeared enormous and its reflection glowed like bronze on the women's dark hair. Sparks of sunset glittered in their diamonds—jewels that sparkled everywhere, in the hollow of their breasts, on their delicately tinted ears, and on their plump white fingers.

It grew dusk. A bat flittered by. The darkening sea rolled down upon the red cliff. My twelve-year-old heart was bursting with the joy and happiness of other people's good fortune. Borgman and I strolled down the furthest alley hand in hand. He told me of his intention to become an aviation engineer. There was a rumour too that his father would soon be appointed representative of the Russian Foreign Trade Bank in London and that Marc would thus be able to finish his education in England.

At home, at Aunt Bobka's, nobody ever talked of such things. I had nothing with which to repay these moments of endless delight. But I told Borgman that, though my home life was very different, yet my grandfather Levvi-Isthok and my uncle Simon Woolf had travelled all round the world and had gone through thousands of adventures. These I recounted in order; and my sense of the probable forsaking me, I conducted Simon Woolf through the Russo-Turkish campaign and then to Alexandria and Egypt. . . .

Night settled itself darkly on the rigid poplars; stars began to stud their heavy branches. I talked on and on, gesticulating. The hand of the future aviation engineer quivered in mine. With difficulty breaking the spell, he promised to return the visit on the following Sunday. And cherishing this promise, I caught the local train back home, to Bobka's.

Throughout the week I imagined myself a banker. I made million-rouble deals with Singapore and Port Said, and had a private yacht in which I sailed on business. But on Saturday it was time to awake, for Borgman's visit was due the very next day.

There was, of course, not an ounce of truth in the tales I had told him. The facts were in a way far stranger, but then I had not yet learned to respect the truth of this world. My grandfather Levvi-Isthok, the rabbi, who had been dismissed from his post for forgery, was looked upon as a madman by our neighbours and the boys of the district. My uncle Simon Woolf was unbearable because of his rowdy eccentricity, his bullying manner and his fiery, meaningless abuse.

Aunt Bobka alone was presentable. And she was proud too that I should have made friends with a bank manager's son. She looked upon this friendship as the first step in my career, and she baked a jam strudel and a poppy-seed cake in honour of the occasion.

But our great problem was how to get grandfather, with his battered top-hat and ragged bandages swathing his swollen feet, out of the way; we finally entrusted him to the care of our neighbours, the Apelhots, and I implored him not to show himself until the guest had departed. We disposed of Simon Woolf as well. All my efforts went to packing him off for the rest of the day, and I even gave him three roubles I had painfully saved up. He went off at last with his fellow-jobbers to drink tea at the Bear Tavern. Three roubles were not so easy to spend, and vodka being obtainable on the premises, we felt sure that Simon Woolf would not put in an appearance till late in the evening. Borgman would thus never suspect that the stories of my uncle's prowess were false.

That morning Bobka had donned a brown cloth dress, tightly clasping her kindly voluminous bosom. She also put on a neckerchief with black printed flowers, the one she usually wore to the Synagogue at Atonement Day and Rosh Hashanah. Then she set out the cakes, the jam and pretzels on the table, and settled down to wait.

We lived in a basement. Borgman raised his eyebrows as he walked over the uneven floor of the passage and saw the butt of drinking water standing in the hall. As soon as he entered our living room I did my best to distract him with all sorts of curiosities. I showed him the alarm clock which my grandfather had made with his own hands down to the very last screw. A lamp was attached to it, which lit up whenever the hour or half-hour struck. I also showed him a little barrel of boot polish, an original recipe of grandfather's who jealously guarded the secret. We then read through a few pages of Levvi-Isthok's manuscript, written in Hebrew on square sheets of yellow paper as large as wallmaps and entitled "The Headless Man." In it were described all of Levvi-Isthok's neighbours during the past seventy years of his life. Undertakers, cantors, Jewish drunkards, cooks come specially for the circumcision festivals and rabbis come to perform the ritual operation, such were Levvi-Isthok's heroes. They were all fantastic, stuttering fellows with bulbous noses, pimply pates, and crooked rumps.

We drank two glasses of tea each and helped ourselves to the *strudel,* and then Bobka left the room, bowing and walking backwards. With joyful abandon I struck an attitude and began to declaim the lines I valued above everything else in the world.

"Friends, Romans, countrymen, lend me your ears:
I come to bury Caesar, not to praise him . . ."

Thus Antony, bending over Caesar's corpse, begins his harangue to the Roman mob. Panting, I clutched my breast:

"He was my friend, faithful and just to me:
But Brutus says he was ambitious;
And Brutus is an honourable man.
He hath brought many captives back to Rome,
Whose ransoms did the general coffers fill:
Did this in Caesar seem ambitious?
When that the poor have cried, Caesar hath wept:
Ambition should be made of sterner stuff:
Yet Brutus says he was ambitious—
And Brutus is an honourable man.
You all did see that on the Lupercal
I thrice presented him a kingly crown,
Which he did thrice refuse: was this ambition?
Yet Brutus says he was ambitious,
And sure he is an honourable man. . . ."

Brutus' face loomed through the smoke of eternity before my eyes. It had grown whiter than chalk. The Roman populace bore down upon me with a thunderous roar. I raised my arm—Borgman followed it obediently with his eyes; I shook my clenched fist, my outstretched arm pointed through the window, and I saw—my uncle Simon Woolf coming across the courtyard accompanied by the jobber Leykhach. They were carrying between them a clothes-hanger shaped like a pair of antlers and a red trunk with lion-headed spring locks. Bobka had evidently seen them too, for, oblivious of the guest, she came rushing into the room and clutched me with trembling hands.

"My pet, they've been buying furniture again!"

Borgman stood up in his prim little uniform and bowed in perplexity to Bobka. The outer door was flung open with a crash. There was a thundering of boots in the corridor and the noise of the trunk being dragged in. The voices of Simon Woolf and the ginger-headed Leykhach were raised in a deafening roar. They were in high spirits.

"Bobka!" bellowed Simon Woolf, "guess how much I paid for these antlers. . . ."

Though he blared like a trumpet, a note of uncertainty could be detected in his voice. Although drunk, Simon Woolf no doubt remembered how much we detested Leykhach, who encouraged our uncle in his senseless extravagances, which only lumbered the house with useless and inconvenient pieces of furniture.

Bobka did not say a word. Leykhach squealed out something to Simon Woolf. Then, to drown his snake-like hissing, to drown the alarmed beating of my heart, I cried out in the words of Antony:

> "But yesterday the word of Caesar might
> Have stood against the world: now lies he there.
> And none so poor to do him reverence.
> O masters, if I were disposed to stir
> Your hearts and minds to mutiny and rage,
> I should do Brutus wrong and Cassius wrong,
> Who you all know are honourable men. . . ."

At this point there was a thud. It was Bobka falling, knocked down by a blow from her husband. She must have made some bitter comment about the antlers. And now the familiar, almost everyday scene repeated itself. Simon Woolf's voice stopped up all the crannies of eternity. He shouted as always on such occasions:

"You're tearing the heart out of me," he complained thunderously. "You're tearing the heart out of me to stuff your own rapacious mouths with it. . . . Work's been my perdition . . . And who has hung this millstone round my neck? It's you . . . you accursed harpies, who have fastened it there. . . ."

Heaping Bobka and myself with Yiddish curses, he gave us an assurance that our eyes would ooze out, that we should not have time to bury each other and that finally we should all be dragged together by the roots of our hair to a common grave.

Borgman had risen. He was pale, and kept looking uneasily round. Though uninitiated into the subtleties of Yiddish blasphemy, he was familiar enough with the Russian variety of curses. Nor were these disdained by Simon Woolf. The bank manager's son stood twisting his cap. His figure grew blurred in my eyes as I attempted to shout down the immense evil of the world. My own mortal despair, and Caesar's already accomplished death, were blended into one. I was already dead but I went on ranting. Hoarse moans welled up from the very depths of my being:

"If you have tears, prepare to shed them now.
You all do know this mantle; I remember
The first time ever Caesar put it on;
'Twas on a summer's evening in his tent,
That day he overcame the Nervii:
Look, in this place ran Cassius' dagger through:
See what a rent the envious Casca made:
Through this the well beloved Brutus stabbed;
And, as he plucked the cursed steel away,
Mark how the blood of Caesar followed it. . . ."

But nothing could drown Simon Woolf. Bobka was still lying on the floor, blubbering and sniffling. The imperturbable Leykhach was moving the trunk behind the partition. Then my crazy grandfather decided it was the moment to create a diversion. Having eluded the vigilance of the Apelhots, he crept up to our window and began sawing on his fiddle, in the hope very probably of preventing the passers-by from overhearing Simon Woolf. Borgman glanced out of the basement window and stepped back aghast at the sight of my grandfather grimacing there with his blue twisted lips. He had on his battered top hat, a black wadded mantel with bone buttons, and ragged bandages on his elephantine feet. His straggling tobacco-stained beard tossed to and fro. Borgman took to his heels.

"Excuse me," he muttered, breaking away, "I hope you don't mind . . . I must go. . . ."

His little uniform and cap flitted across the courtyard.

With his departure my agitation subsided. In its place came decision and peace of mind.

I waited for evening. As soon as my grandfather had finished scrawling his hooked Hebrew characters upon the square sheets of paper—that evening he was portraying the Apelhots, with whom he had spent the day on my account—and had stretched himself out in his bunk to sleep, I stole into the corridor. Barefoot, in a long patched nightshirt, I groped my way in the dark along the cold earthen floor. From the streets, through chinks in the wooden walls, came a sharp steely flicker of moonlit cobbles. The water-butt stood in its usual place in the corner. I lowered myself down into it. The icy water cut me in two, and I bobbed up, spluttering. A cat on a shelf above was looking down at me drowsily. The second time I held out longer: the water gurgled as my gasping breath bored through it like a screw.

Opening my eyes I saw the fold of a shirt and a pair of small feet hugging each other at the bottom of the butt. My resolution deserted me once more and I got out. Grandfather was standing by the butt in a jersey. His single tooth was chattering to itself.

"My grandson,"—he uttered the words clearly and contemptuously—"I am going to take a dose of castor-oil to have something to lay on your grave. . . ."

Beside myself I screamed and plunged headlong into the water. Grandfather's feeble arm dragged me out. Then, for the first time that day, I burst out weeping; and the world of tears was so vast and beautiful that all else vanished from my eyes.

I came to myself in bed, wrapped warmly in a quilt. Grandfather was striding up and down the room, whistling. Aunt Bobka was warming my hands at her breast. I let her keep them there.

"How he trembles, our little fool, our child," Bobka said. "Where does he find the strength to tremble so?"

Grandfather tugged at his beard, whistled, and took up his pacing again. Simon Woolf was snoring painfully in the next room. He always had his fill of battles by day, and never woke in the night.

Questions

1. How "old" is the narrator, i.e., how far removed from the events is he? What is his attitude toward the events at the Borgman villa and in the basement? Show how the tone that serves as a filter for those experiences reveals Babel's attitude and helps create the reader's attitude.

2. "In the Basement" portrays part of the initiation of a young boy into the world beyond his family. Describe the speaker's sense of himself at the beginning of the story and at the end, especially as it is revealed in the phrase about "the world of tears."

3. Discuss the quality of the life Babel creates in the wonderful world of the household in the basement. What has each of the strange characters who live in there contributed to the boy? Why is he so ashamed of them? How is it different from life at the Borgman villa?

4. What function does Antony's "Funeral Oration" play in the story? Does it seem out of place coming from this boy at this time?

James Baldwin

SONNY'S BLUES

Both an articulate and an angry spokesman for his race and his generation, James Baldwin is probably one of the major contemporary black writers. Born in New York City in 1924, he grew up experiencing the poverty of all ghetto people. He matured in a revivalist atmosphere as the oldest of the nine children of a Harlem preacher. Rebelling against the treatment of his race in America, he went to Paris in 1948 and lived there and in Switzerland for nine years. There he began writing in a variety of forms. His first published work was Go Tell It on the Mountain *(1953), a somewhat autobiographical novel. He later wrote* Notes of a Native Son *(1955), a collection of essays the title of which paid tribute to his sponsor, Richard Wright; another novel,* Giovanni's Room *(1956); and another collection of essays,* Nobody Knows My Name *(1961). By this time he had returned to America, where he was able to combine the expatriate experience with a fresh view of black life. In quick succession two major works, a novel,* Another Country *(1962), and an apocalyptic vision of the racial crisis,* The Fire Next Time *(1963), became best sellers. He has also written two plays,* Blues for Mister Charlie *(1964) and* The Amen Corner *(1968), a collection of short stories,* Going to Meet the Man *(1965), and another novel,* Tell Me How Long the Train's Been Gone *(1968).*

"Sonny's Blues," from Going to Meet the Man, *is one of Baldwin's best short stories and one of the most sensitive treatments of the black world from the inside.*

I read about it in the paper, in the subway, on my way to work. I read it, and I couldn't believe it, and I read it again. Then perhaps I just stared at it, at the newsprint spelling out his name, spelling out the story. I stared at it in the swinging lights of the subway car, and in the faces and bodies of the people, and in my own face, trapped in the darkness which roared outside.

It was not to be believed, and I kept telling myself that as I walked from the subway station to the high school. And at the same time I couldn't doubt it. I was scared, scared for Sonny. He became real to me again. A great block of ice got settled in my belly and kept melting there slowly all day long, while I taught my classes algebra. It was a special kind of ice. It kept melting, sending trickles of ice water all up and down my veins, but it never got less. Sometimes it hardened and seemed to expand until I felt my guts were going to come spilling out or that I was going to choke or scream. This would always be at a moment when I was remembering some specific thing Sonny had once said or done.

When he was about as old as the boys in my classes, his face had been bright and open, there was a lot of copper in it; and he'd had wonderfully direct brown eyes, and great gentleness and privacy. I wondered what he looked like now. He had been picked up, the evening before, in a raid on an apartment downtown, for peddling and using heroin.

I couldn't believe it: but what I mean by that is that I couldn't find any room for it anywhere inside me. I had kept it outside me for a long time. I hadn't wanted to know. I had had suspicions, but I didn't name them, I kept putting them away. I told myself that Sonny was wild, but he wasn't crazy. And he'd always been a good boy, he hadn't ever turned hard or evil or disrespectful, the way kids can, so quick, so quick, especially in Harlem. I didn't want to believe that I'd ever see my brother going down, coming to nothing, all that light in his face gone out, in the condition I'd already seen so many others. Yet it had happened and here I was, talking about algebra to a lot of boys who might, every one of them for all I knew, be popping off needles every time they went to the head. Maybe it did more for them than algebra could.

I was sure that the first time Sonny had ever had horse, he couldn't have been much older than these boys were now. These boys, now, were living as we'd been living then, they were growing up with a rush and their heads bumped abruptly against the low ceiling of their actual possibilities. They were filled with rage. All they really knew were two darknesses, the darkness of their lives, which was now closing in on them, and the darkness of the movies, which had blinded them to that other darkness, and in which they now, vindictively, dreamed, at once more together than they were at any other time, and more alone.

When the last bell rang, the last class ended, I let out my breath. It seemed I'd been holding it for all that time. My clothes were wet–I may have looked as though I'd been sitting in a steam bath, all dressed up, all afternoon. I sat alone in the classroom a long time. I listened to the boys outside, downstairs, shouting and cursing and laughing. Their laughter struck me for perhaps the first time. It was not the joyous laughter which—God knows why—one associates with children. It was mocking and insular, its intent was to denigrate. It was disenchanted, and in this, also, lay the authority of their curses. Perhaps I was listening to them because I was thinking about my brother and in them I heard my brother. And myself.

One boy was whistling a tune, at once very complicated and very simple. It seemed to be pouring out of him as though he were a bird, and it sounded very cool and moving through all that harsh, bright air, only just holding its own through all those other sounds.

I stood and walked over to the window and looked down into the courtyard. It was the beginning of the spring, and the sap was rising in the boys. A teacher passed through them every now and again, quickly, as though he or she couldn't wait to get out of that courtyard, to get those boys out of their sight and off their minds. I started collecting my stuff. I thought I'd better get home and talk to Isabel.

The courtyard was almost deserted by the time I got downstairs. I saw this boy standing in the shadow of a doorway, looking just like Sonny. I almost called his name. Then I saw that it wasn't Sonny, but somebody we used to know, a boy from around our block. He'd been Sonny's friend. He'd never been mine, having been too young for me, and, anyway, I'd never liked him. And now, even though he was a grown-up man, he still hung around that block, still spent hours on the street corner, was always high and raggy. I used to run into him from time to time, and he'd often work around to asking me for a quarter or fifty cents. He always had some real good excuse, too, and I always gave it to him, I don't know why.

But now, abruptly, I hated him. I couldn't stand the way he looked at me, partly like a dog, partly like a cunning child. I wanted to ask him what the hell he was doing in the school courtyard.

He sort of shuffled over to me, and he said, "I see you got the papers. So you already know about it."

"You mean about Sonny? Yes, I already know about it. How come they didn't get you?"

He grinned. It made him repulsive and it also brought to mind what he'd looked like as a kid. "I wasn't there. I stay away from them people."

"Good for you." I offered him a cigarette and I watched him through the smoke. "You come all the way down here just to tell me about Sonny?"

"That's right." He was sort of shaking his head and his eyes looked strange, as though they were about to cross. The bright sun deadened his damp dark brown skin and it made his eyes look yellow and showed up the dirt in his conked hair. He smelled funky. I moved a little away from him and I said, "Well, thanks. But I already know about it and I got to get home."

"I'll walk you a little ways," he said. We started walking. There were a couple of kids still loitering in the courtyard and one of them said good night to me and looked strangely at the boy beside me.

"What're you going to do?" he asked me. "I mean, about Sonny?"

"Look. I haven't seen Sonny for over a year, I'm not sure I'm going to do anything. Anyway, what the hell *can* I do?"

"That's right," he said quickly, "ain't nothing you can do. Can't much help old Sonny no more, I guess."

It was what I was thinking and so it seemed to me he had no right to say it.

"I'm surprised at Sonny, though," he went on—he had a funny way of talking, he looked straight ahead as though he were talking to himself—"I thought Sonny was a smart boy, I thought he was too smart to get hung."

"I guess he thought so, too," I said sharply, "and that's how he got hung. And how about you? You're pretty goddamn smart, I bet."

Then he looked directly at me, just for a minute. "I ain't smart," he said. "If I was smart, I'd have reached for a pistol a long time ago."

"Look. Don't tell *me* your sad story, if it was up to me, I'd give you one." Then I felt guilty—guilty probably, for never having supposed that the poor bastard *had* a story of his own, much less a sad one, and I asked, quickly, "What's going to happen to him now?"

He didn't answer this. He was off by himself someplace. "Funny thing," he said, and from his tone we might have been discussing the quickest way to get to Brooklyn, "when I saw the papers this morning, the first thing I asked myself was if I had anything to do with it. I felt sort of responsible."

I began to listen more carefully. The subway station was on the corner, just before us, and I stopped. He stopped, too. We were in front of a bar and he ducked slightly, peering in, but whoever he was looking for didn't seem to be there. The juke box was blasting away with something black and bouncy, and I half watched the barmaid as she danced her way from the juke box to her place behind the bar. And I watched her face as she laughingly responded to something someone said to her, still keeping time to the music. When she smiled one saw the little girl, one sensed the doomed, still-struggling woman beneath the battered face of the semi-whore.

"I never *give* Sonny nothing," the boy said finally, "but a long time ago I come to school high and Sonny asked me how it felt." He paused,

I couldn't bear to watch him, I watched the barmaid, and I listened to the music which seemed to be causing the pavement to shake. "I told him it felt great." The music stopped, the barmaid paused and watched the juke box until the music began again. "It did."

All this was carrying me someplace I didn't want to go. I certainly didn't want to know how it felt. It filled everything, the people, the houses, the music, the dark, quicksilver barmaid, with menace: and this menace was their reality.

"What's going to happen to him now?" I asked again.

"They'll send him away someplace and they'll try to cure him." He shook his head. "Maybe he'll even think he's kicked the habit. Then they'll turn him loose"—He gestured, throwing his cigarette into the gutter. "That's all."

"What do you mean, that's *all*?"

But I knew what he meant.

"I *mean*, that's *all*." He turned his head and looked at me, pulling down the corners of his mouth. "Don't you know what I mean?" he asked softly.

"How the hell *would* I know what you mean?" I almost whispered it, I don't know why.

"That's right," he said to the air, "how would *he* know what I mean?" He turned toward me again, patient and calm, and yet I somehow felt him shaking, shaking as though he were going to fall apart. I felt that ice in my guts again, the dread I'd felt all afternoon; and again I watched the barmaid, moving about the bar, washing glasses, and singing. "Listen. They'll let him out and then it'll just start over again. That's what I mean."

"You mean—they'll let him out. And then he'll just start working his way back in again. You mean he'll never kick the habit. Is that what you mean?"

"That's right," he said, cheerfully. "*You* see what I mean."

"Tell me," I said at last, "why does he want to die? He must want to die, he's killing himself, why does he want to die?"

He looked at me in surprise. He licked his lips. "He don't want to die. He wants to live. Don't nobody want to die, ever."

Then I wanted to ask him—too many things. He could not have answered, or if he had, I could not have borne the answers. I started walking. "Well, I guess it's none of my business."

"It's going to be rough on old Sonny," he said. We reached the subway station. "This is your station?" he asked. I nodded. I took one step down. "Damn!" he said, suddenly. I looked up at him. He grinned again. "Damn if I didn't leave all my money home. You ain't got a dollar on you, have you? Just for a couple of days, is all."

All at once something inside gave and threatened to come pouring out of me. I didn't hate him any more. I felt that in another moment I'd start crying like a child.

"Sure," I said. "Don't sweat." I looked in my wallet and didn't have a dollar, I only had a five. "Here," I said. "That hold you?"

He didn't look at it—he didn't want to look at it. A terrible, closed look came over his face, as though he were keeping the number on the bill a secret from him and me. "Thanks," he said, and now he was dying to see me go. "Don't worry about Sonny. Maybe I'll write him or something."

"Sure," I said. "You do that. So long."

"Be seeing you," he said. I went on down the steps.

And I didn't write Sonny or send him anything for a long time. When I finally did, it was just after my little girl died, he wrote me back a letter which made me feel like a bastard.

Here's what he said:

> Dear brother,
>
> You don't know how much I needed to hear from you. I wanted to write you many a time but I dug how much I must have hurt you and so I didn't write. But now I feel like a man who's been trying to climb up out of some deep, real deep and funky hole and just saw the sun up there, outside. I got to get outside.
>
> I can't tell you much about how I got here. I mean I don't know how to tell you. I guess I was afraid of something or I was trying to escape from something and you know I have never been very strong in the head (smile). I'm glad Mama and Daddy are dead and can't see what's happened to their son and I swear if I'd known what I was doing I would never have hurt you so, you and a lot of other fine people who were nice to me and who believed in me.
>
> I don't want you to think it had anything to do with me being a musician. It's more than that. Or maybe less than that. I can't get anything straight in my head down here and I try not to think about what's going to happen to me when I get outside again. Sometime I think I'm going to flip and *never* get outside and sometime I think I'll come straight back. I tell you one thing, though, I'd rather blow my brains out than go through this again. But that's what they all say, so they tell me. If I tell you when I'm coming to New York and if you could meet me, I sure would appreciate it. Give my love to Isabel and the kids and I was sure sorry to hear about little Gracie. I wish I could

be like Mama and say the Lord's will be done, but I don't know it seems to me that trouble is the one thing that never does get stopped and I don't know what good it does to blame it on the Lord. But maybe it does some good if you believe it.

Your brother,
SONNY

Then I kept in constant touch with him and sent him whatever I could and I went to meet him when he came back to New York. When I saw him, many things I thought I had forgotten came flooding back to me. This was because I had begun, finally, to wonder about Sonny, about the life that Sonny lived inside. This life, whatever it was, had made him older and thinner and it had deepened the distant stillness in which he had always moved. He looked very unlike my baby brother. Yet, when he smiled, when we shook hands, the baby brother I'd never known looked out from the depths of his private life, like an animal waiting to be coaxed into the light.

"How you been keeping?" he asked me.

"All right. And you?"

"Just fine." He was smiling all over his face. "It's good to see you again."

"It's good to see you."

The seven years' difference in our ages lay between us like a chasm: I wondered if these years would ever operate between us as a bridge. I was remembering, and it made it hard to catch my breath, that I had been there when he was born; and I had heard the first words he had ever spoken. When he started to walk, he walked from our mother straight to me. I caught him just before he fell when he took the first steps he ever took in this world.

"How's Isabel?"

"Just fine. She's dying to see you."

"And the boys?"

"They're fine, too. They're anxious to see their uncle."

"Oh, come on. You know they don't remember me."

"Are you kidding? Of course they remember you."

He grinned again. We got into a taxi. We had a lot to say to each other, far too much to know how to begin.

As the taxi began to move, I asked, "You still want to go to India?"

He laughed. "You still remember that. Hell, no. This place is Indian enough for me."

"It used to belong to them," I said.

And he laughed again. "They damn sure knew what they were doing when they got rid of it."

Years ago, when he was around fourteen, he'd been all hipped on the idea of going to India. He read books about people sitting on rocks, naked, in all kinds of weather, but mostly bad, naturally, and walking barefoot through hot coals and arriving at wisdom. I used to say that it sounded to me as though they were getting away from wisdom as fast as they could. I think he sort of looked down on me for that.

"Do you mind," he asked, "if we have the driver drive alongside the park? On the west side–I haven't seen the city in so long."

"Of course not," I said. I was afraid that I might sound as though I were humoring him, but I hoped he wouldn't take it that way.

So we drove along, between the green of the park and the stony, lifeless elegance of hotels and apartment buildings, toward the vivid, killing streets of our childhood. These streets hadn't changed, though housing projects jutted up out of them now like rocks in the middle of a boiling sea. Most of the houses in which we had grown up had vanished, as had the stores from which we had stolen, the basements in which we had first tried sex, the rooftops from which we had hurled tin cans and bricks. But houses exactly like the houses of our past yet dominated the landscape, boys exactly like the boys we once had been found themselves smothering in these houses, came down into the streets for light and air and found themselves encircled by disaster. Some escaped the trap, most didn't. Those who got out always left something of themselves behind, as some animals amputate a leg and leave it in the trap. It might be said, perhaps, that I had escaped, after all, I was a schoolteacher; or that Sonny had, he hadn't lived in Harlem for years. Yet, as the cab moved uptown through streets which seemed, with a rush, to darken with dark people, and as I covertly studied Sonny's face, it came to me that what we both were seeking through our separate cab windows was that part of ourselves which had been left behind. It's always at the hour of trouble and confrontation that the missing member aches.

We hit 110th Street and started rolling up Lenox Avenue. And I'd known this avenue all my life, but it seemed to me again, as it had seemed on the day I'd first heard about Sonny's trouble, filled with a hidden menace which was its very breath of life.

"We almost there," said Sonny.

"Almost." We were both too nervous to say anything more.

We live in a housing project. It hasn't been up long. A few days after it was up it seemed uninhabitably new, now, of course, it's already rundown. It looked like a parody of the good, clean, faceless life—God knows the people who live in it do their best to make it a parody. The beat-looking grass lying around isn't enough to make their lives green, the hedges will never hold out the streets, and they know it. The big windows fool no one, they aren't big enough to make space out of no space. They don't bother with the windows, they watch the TV screen instead. The playground is most popular with the children who don't play at jacks, or skip rope, or roller skate, or swing, and they can be found in it after dark. We moved in partly because it's not too far from where I teach, and partly for the kids; but it's really just like the houses in which Sonny and I grew up. The same things happen, they'll have the same things to remember. The moment Sonny and I started into the house I had the feeling that I was simply bringing him back into the danger he had almost died trying to escape.

Sonny has never been talkative. So I don't know why I was sure he'd be dying to talk to me when supper was over the first night. Everything went fine, the oldest boy remembered him, and the youngest boy liked him, and Sonny had remembered to bring something for each of them; and Isabel, who is really much nicer than I am, more open and giving, had gone to a lot of trouble about dinner and was genuinely glad to see him. And she'd always been able to tease Sonny in a way that I haven't. It was nice to see her face so vivid again and to hear her laugh and watch her make Sonny laugh. She wasn't, or, anyway, she didn't seem to be, at all uneasy or embarrassed. She chatted as though there were no subject which had to be avoided and she got Sonny past his first, faint stiffness. And thank God she was there, for I was filled with that icy dread again. Everything I did seemed awkward to me, and everything I said sounded freighted with hidden meaning. I was trying to remember everything I'd heard about dope addiction and I couldn't help watching Sonny for signs. I wasn't doing it out of malice. I was trying to find out something about my brother. I was dying to hear him tell me he was safe.

"Safe!" my father grunted, whenever Mama suggested trying to move to a neighborhood which might be safer for children. "Safe, hell! Ain't no place safe for kids, nor nobody."

He always went on like this, but he wasn't, ever, really as bad as he sounded, not even on weekends, when he got drunk. As a matter of fact, he was always on the lookout for "something a little better," but he died before he found it. He died suddenly, during a drunken weekend in the middle of the war, when Sonny was fifteen. He and Sonny hadn't ever got on too well. And this was partly because Sonny was the apple of his father's eye. It was because he loved Sonny so much and was frightened for him, that he was always fighting with him. It doesn't do any good to fight with Sonny. Sonny just moves back, inside himself, where he can't be reached. But the principal reason that they never hit it off is that they were so much alike. Daddy was big and rough and loud-talking, just the opposite of Sonny, but they both had—that same privacy.

Mama tried to tell me something about this, just after Daddy died. I was home on leave from the army.

This was the last time I ever saw my mother alive. Just the same, this picture gets all mixed up in my mind with pictures I had of her when she was younger. The way I always see her is the way she used to be on a Sunday afternoon, say, when the old folks were talking after the big Sunday dinner. I always see her wearing pale blue. She'd be sitting on the sofa. And my father would be sitting in the easy chair, not far from her. And the living room would be full of church folks and relatives. There they sit, in chairs all around the living room, and the night is creeping up outside, but nobody knows it yet. You can see the darkness growing against the windowpanes and you hear the street noises every now and again, or maybe the jangling beat of a tambourine from one of the churches close by, but it's real quiet in the room. For a moment nobody's talking, but every face looks darkening, like the sky outside. And my mother rocks a little from the waist, and my father's eyes are closed. Everyone is looking at something a child can't see. For a minute they've forgotten the children. Maybe a kid is lying on the rug, half asleep. Maybe somebody's got a kid in his lap and is absent-mindedly stroking the kid's head. Maybe there's a kid, quiet and big-eyed, curled up in a big chair in the corner. The silence, the darkness coming, and the darkness in the faces frighten the child obscurely. He hopes that the hand which strokes his forehead will never stop—will never die. He hopes that there will never come a time when the old folks won't be sitting around the living room, talking about where they've come from, and what they've seen, and what's happened to them and their kinfolk.

But something deep and watchful in the child knows that this is bound to end, is already ending. In a moment someone will get up and turn on the light. Then the old folks will remember the children and they won't talk any more that day. And when light fills the room, the child is filled with darkness. He knows that every time this happens he's moved just a little closer to that darkness outside. The darkness outside is what the old folks have been talking about. It's what they've come from. It's what they endure. The child knows that they won't talk any more because if he knows too much about what's happened to *them*, he'll know too much too soon, about what's going to happen to *him*.

The last time I talked to my mother, I remember I was restless. I wanted to get out and see Isabel. We weren't married then and we had a lot to straighten out between us.

There Mama sat, in black, by the window. She was humming an old church song, *Lord, you brought me from a long ways off*. Sonny was out somewhere. Mama kept watching the streets.

"I don't know," she said, "if I'll ever see you again, after you go off from here. But I hope you'll remember the things I tried to teach you."

"Don't talk like that," I said, and smiled. "You'll be here a long time yet."

She smiled, too, but she said nothing. She was quiet for a long time. And I said, "Mama, don't you worry about nothing. I'll be writing all the time, and you be getting the checks. . . ."

"I want to talk to you about your brother," she said, suddenly. "If anything happens to me, he ain't going to have nobody to look out for him."

"Mama," I said, "ain't nothing going to happen to you *or* Sonny. Sonny's all right. He's a good boy and he's got good sense."

"It ain't a question of his being a good boy," Mama said, "nor of his having good sense. It ain't only the bad ones, nor yet the dumb ones that gets sucked under." She stopped, looking at me. "Your Daddy once had a brother," she said, and smiled in a way that made me feel she was in pain. "You didn't never know that, did you?"

"No," I said. "I never knew that," and I watched her face.

"Oh, yes," she said, "your Daddy had a brother." She looked out of the window again. "I know you never saw your Daddy cry. But *I* did—many a time, through all these years."

I asked her, "What happened to his brother? How come nobody's ever talked about him?"

This was the first time I ever saw my mother look old.

"His brother got killed," she said, "when he was just a little younger than you are now. I knew him. He was a fine boy. He was maybe a little full of the devil, but he didn't mean nobody no harm."

Then she stopped, and the room was silent, exactly as it had sometimes been on those Sunday afternoons. Mama kept looking out into the streets.

"He used to have a job in the mill," she said, "and, like all young folks, he just liked to perform on Saturday nights. Saturday nights, him and your father would drift around to different places, go to dances and things like that, or just sit around with people they knew, and your father's brother would sing, he had a fine voice, and play along with himself on his guitar. Well, this particular Saturday night, him and your father was coming home from some place, and they were both a little drunk and there was a moon that night, it was bright like day. Your father's brother was feeling kind of good, and he was whistling to himself, and he had his guitar slung over his shoulder. They was coming down a hill, and beneath them was a road that turned off from the highway. Well, your father's brother, being always kind of frisky, decided to run down this hill, and he did, with that guitar banging and clanging behind him, and he ran across the road, and he was making water behind a tree. And your father was sort of amused at him and he was still coming down the hill, kind of slow. Then he heard a car motor and that same minute his brother stepped from behind the tree, into the road, in the moonlight. And he started to cross the road. And your father started to run down the hill, he says he don't know why. This car was full of white men. They was all drunk, and when they seen your father's brother they let out a great whoop and holler and they aimed the car straight at him. They was having fun, they just wanted to scare him, the way they do sometimes, you know. But they was drunk. And I guess the boy, being drunk, too, and scared, kind of lost his head. By the time he jumped it was too late. Your father says he heard his brother scream when the car rolled over him, and he heard the wood of that guitar when it give, and he heard them strings go flying, and he heard them white men shouting, and the car kept on a-going and it ain't stopped till this day. And, time your father got down the hill, his brother weren't nothing but blood and pulp."

Tears were gleaming on my mother's face. There wasn't anything I could say.

"He never mentioned it," she said, "because I never let him mention it before you children. Your Daddy was like a crazy man that night and for many a night thereafter. He says he never in his life seen anything as dark as that road after the lights of that car had gone away. Weren't nothing, weren't nobody on that road, just your Daddy and his brother and that busted guitar. Oh, yes. Your Daddy never did really get right again. Till the day he died he weren't sure but that every white man he saw was the man that killed his brother."

She stopped and took out her handkerchief and dried her eyes and looked at me.

"I ain't telling you this," she said, "to make you scared or bitter or to make you hate nobody. I'm telling you this because you got a brother. And the world ain't changed."

I guess I didn't want to believe this. I guess she saw this in my face. She turned away from me, toward the window again, searching those streets.

"But I praise my Redeemer," she said at last, "that he called your Daddy home before me. I ain't saying it to throw no flowers at myself, but, I declare, it keeps me from feeling too cast down to know I helped your father get safely through this world. Your father always acted like he was the toughest, strongest man on earth. And everybody took him to be like that. But if he hadn't had *me* there—to see his tears!"

She was crying again. Still, I couldn't move. I said, "Lord, Lord, Mama, I didn't know it was like that."

"Oh, honey," she said, "there's a lot that you don't know. But you are going to find it out." She stood up from the window and came over to me. "You got to hold on to your brother," she said, "and don't let him fall, no matter what it looks like is happening to him and no matter how evil you gets with him. You going to be evil with him many a time. But don't you forget what I told you, you hear?"

"I won't forget," I said. "Don't you worry, I won't forget. I won't let nothing happen to Sonny.

My mother smiled as though she were amused at something she saw in my face. Then, "You may not be able to stop nothing from happening. But you got to let him know you's *there*."

Two days later I was married, and then I was gone. And I had a lot of things on my mind and I pretty well forgot my promise to Mama until I got shipped home on a special furlough for her funeral.

And, after the funeral, with just Sonny and me alone in the empty kitchen, I tried to find out something about him.

"What do you want to do?" I asked him.

"I'm going to be a musician," he said.

For he had graduated, in the time I had been away, from dancing to the juke box to finding out who was playing what, and what they were doing with it, and he had bought himself a set of drums.

"You mean, you want to be a drummer?" I somehow had the feeling that being a drummer might be all right for other people but not for my brother Sonny.

"I don't think," he said, looking at me very gravely, "that I'll ever be a good drummer. But I think I can play a piano."

I frowned. I'd never played the role of the older brother quite so seriously before, had scarcely ever, in fact, *asked* Sonny a damn thing. I sensed myself in the presence of something I didn't really know how to handle, didn't understand. So I made my frown a little deeper as I asked: "What kind of musician do you want to be?"

He grinned. "How many kinds do you think there are?"

"Be *serious*," I said.

He laughed, throwing his head back, and then looked at me. "I *am* serious."

"Well, then, for Christ's sake, stop kidding around and answer a serious question. I mean, do you want to be a concert pianist, you want to play classical music and all that, or—or, what?" Long before I finished he was laughing again. "For Christ's *sake*, Sonny!"

He sobered, but with difficulty. "I'm sorry. But you sound so—*scared!*" And he was off again.

"Well, you may think it's funny now, baby, but it's not going to be so funny when you have to make your living at it, let me tell you *that*." I was furious because I knew he was laughing at me and I didn't know why.

"No," he said, very sober now, and afraid, perhaps, that he'd hurt me, "I don't want to be a classical pianist. That isn't what interests me. I mean"—he paused, looking hard at me, as though his eyes would help me to understand, and then gestured helplessly, as though perhaps his hand would help—"I mean, I'll have a lot of studying to do, and I'll have to study *everything*, but, I mean, I want to play *with*—jazz musicians." He stopped. "I want to play jazz," he said.

Well, the word had never before sounded as heavy, as real, as it sounded that afternoon in Sonny's mouth. I just looked at him and I was probably frowning a real frown by this time. I simply couldn't see why on earth he'd want to spend his time hanging around night clubs, clowning around on bandstands, while people pushed each other around a dance floor. It seemed—beneath him, somehow. I had never thought about it before, had never been forced to, but I suppose I had always put jazz musicians in a class with what Daddy called "good-time people."

"Are you *serious*?"

"Hell, *yes*, I'm serious."

He looked more helpless than ever, and annoyed, and deeply hurt.

I suggested, helpfully: "You mean—like Louis Armstrong?"

His faced closed as though I'd struck him. "No. I'm not talking about none of that old-time, down home crap."

"Well, look, Sonny, I'm sorry, don't get mad. I just don't altogether get it, that's all. Name somebody—you know, a jazz musician you admire."

"Bird."

"Who?"

"Bird! Charlie Parker! Don't they teach you nothing in the goddamn army?"

I lit a cigarette. I was surprised and then a little amused to discover that I was trembling. "I've been out of touch," I said, "You'll have to be patient with me. Now. Who's this Parker character?"

"He's just one of the greatest jazz musicians alive," said Sonny, sullenly, his hands in his pockets, his back to me. "Maybe *the* greatest," he added bitterly, "that's probably why *you* never heard of him."

"All right," I said, "I'm ignorant. I'm sorry. I'll go out and buy all the cat's records right away, all right?"

"It don't," said Sonny, with dignity, "make any difference to me. I don't care what you listen to. Don't do me no favors."

I was beginning to realize that I'd never seen him so upset before.

With another part of my mind I was thinking that this would probably turn out to be one of those things kids go through and that I shouldn't make it seem important by pushing it too hard. Still, I didn't think it would do any harm to ask: "Doesn't all this take a lot of time? Can you make a living at it?"

He turned back to me and half leaned, half sat, on the kitchen table. "Everything takes time," he said, "and—well, yes, sure, I can make a living at it. But what I don't seem to be able to make you understand is that it's the only thing I want to do."

"Well, Sonny," I said gently, "you know people can't always do exactly what they want to do—"

"*No*, I don't know that," said Sonny, surprising me. "I think people *ought* to do what they want to do, what else are they alive for?"

"You getting to be a big boy," I said desperately, "it's time you started thinking about your future."

"I'm thinking about my future," said Sonny, grimly. "I think about it all the time."

I gave up. I decided, if he didn't change his mind, that we could always talk about it later. "In the meantime," I said, "you got to finish school." We had already decided that he'd have to move in with Isabel and her folks. I knew this wasn't the ideal arrangement because Isabel's folks are inclined to be dicty and they hadn't especially wanted Isabel to marry me. But I didn't know what else to do. "And we have to get you fixed up at Isabel's."

There was a long silence. He moved from the kitchen table to the window. "That's a terrible idea. You know it yourself."

"Do you have a *better* idea?"

He just walked up and down the kitchen for a minute. He was as tall as I was. He had started to shave. I suddenly had the feeling that I didn't know him at all.

He stopped at the kitchen table and picked up my cigarettes. Looking at me with a kind of mocking, amused defiance, he put one between his lips. "You mind?"

"You smoking already?"

He lit the cigarette and nodded, watching me through the smoke. "I just wanted to see if I'd have the courage to smoke in front of you." He grinned and blew a great cloud of smoke to the ceiling. "It was easy." He looked at my face. "Come on, now, I bet you was smoking at my age, tell the truth."

I didn't say anything but the truth was on my face, and he laughed. But now there was something very strained in his laugh. "Sure. And I bet that ain't all you was doing."

He was frightening me a little. "Cut the crap," I said. "We already decided that you was going to go live at Isabel's. Now what's got into you all of a sudden?"

"*You* decided it," he pointed out. "*I* didn't decide nothing." He stopped in front of me, leaning against the stove, arms loosely folded. "Look, brother, I don't want to stay in Harlem no more, I really don't." He was very earnest. He looked at me, then over toward the kitchen window. There was something in his eyes I'd never seen before, some thoughtfulness, some worry all his own. He rubbed the muscle of one arm. "It's time I was getting out of here."

"Where do you want to *go*, Sonny?"

"I want to join the army. Or the navy, I don't care. If I say I'm old enough, they'll believe me."

Then I got mad. It was because I was so scared. "You must be crazy. You goddamn fool, what the hell do you want to go and join the *army* for?"

"I just told you. To get out of Harlem."

"Sonny, you haven't even finished *school*. And if you really want to be a musician, how do you expect to study if you're in the *army*?"

He looked at me, trapped, and in anguish. "There's ways. I might be able to work out some kind of deal. Anyway, I'll have the G.I. Bill when I come out."

"*If* you come out." We stared at each other. "Sonny, please. Be reasonable. I know the setup is far from perfect. But we got to do the best we can."

"I ain't learning nothing in school," he said. "Even when I go." He turned away from me and opened the window and threw his cigarette out into the narrow alley. I watched his back. "At least, I ain't learning nothing you'd want me to learn." He slammed the window so hard I thought the glass would fly out, and turned back to me. "And I'm sick of the stink of these garbage cans!"

"Sonny," I said, "I know how you feel. But if you don't finish school now, you're going to be sorry later that you didn't." I grabbed him by the shoulders. "And you only got another year. It ain't so bad. And I'll come back and I swear I'll help you do *whatever* you want to do. Just try to put up with it till I come back. Will you please do that? For me?"

He didn't answer and he wouldn't look at me.

"Sonny. You hear me?"

He pulled away. "I hear you. But you never hear anything I say."

I didn't know what to say to that. He looked out of the window and then back at me. "OK," he said, and sighed. "I'll try."

Then I said, trying to cheer him up a little, "They got a piano at Isabel's. You can practice on it."

And as a matter of fact, it did cheer him up for a minute. "That's right," he said to himself. "I forgot that." His face relaxed a little. But the worry, the thoughtfulness, played on it still, the way shadows play on a face which is staring into the fire.

But I thought I'd never hear the end of that piano. At first, Isabel would write me, saying how nice it was that Sonny was so serious about his music and how, as soon as he came in from school, or wherever he had been when he was supposed to be at school, he went straight to that piano and stayed there until suppertime. And, after supper, he went back to that piano and stayed there until everybody went to bed. He was at that piano all day Saturday and all day Sunday. Then he bought a record player and started playing records. He'd play one record over and over again, all day long sometimes, and he'd improvise along with it on the piano. Or he'd play one section of the record, one chord, one change, one progression, then he'd do it on the piano. Then back to the record. Then back to the piano.

Well, I really don't know how they stood it. Isabel finally confessed that it wasn't like living with a person at all, it was like living with sound. And the sound didn't make any sense to her, didn't make any sense to any of them—naturally. They began, in a way, to be afflicted by this presence that was living in their home. It was as though Sonny were some sort of god, or monster. He moved in an atmosphere which wasn't like theirs at all. They fed him and he ate, he washed himself, he walked in and out of their door; he certainly wasn't nasty or unpleasant or rude, Sonny isn't any of those things; but it was as though he were all wrapped up in some cloud, some fire, some vision all his own; and there wasn't any way to reach him.

At the same time, he wasn't really a man yet, he was still a child, and they had to watch out for him in all kinds of ways. They certainly couldn't throw him out. Neither did they dare to make a great scene about that piano because even they dimly sensed, as I sensed, from so many thousands of miles away, that Sonny was at that piano playing for his life.

But he hadn't been going to school. One day a letter came from the school board, and Isabel's mother got it—there had, apparently, been other letters but Sonny had torn them up. This day, when Sonny came in, Isabel's mother showed him the letter and asked where he'd been spending his time. And she finally got it out of him that he'd been down in Greenwich Village, with musicians and other characters, in a white girl's apartment. And this scared her and she started to scream at him, and what came up, once she began—though she denies it to this day—was what sacrifices they were making to give Sonny a decent home and how little he appreciated it.

Sonny didn't play the piano that day. By evening, Isabel's mother had calmed down but then there was the old man to deal with, and Isabel herself. Isabel says she did her best to be calm but she broke down and started crying. She says she just watched Sonny's face. She could tell, by watching him, what was happening with him. And what was happening was that they penetrated his cloud, they had reached him. Even if their fingers had been a thousand times more gentle than human fingers ever are, he could hardly help feeling that they had stripped him naked and were spitting on that nakedness. For he also had to see that his presence, that music, which was life or death to him, had been torture for them and that they had endured it, not at all for his sake, but only for mine. And Sonny couldn't take that. He can take it a little better today than he could then but he's still not very good at it and, frankly, I don't know anybody who is.

The silence of the next few days must have been louder than the sound of all the music ever played since time began. One morning, before she went to work, Isabel was in his room for something and she suddenly realized that all of his records were gone. And she knew for certain that he was gone. And he was. He went as far as the navy would carry him. He finally sent me a postcard from somewhere in Greece, and that was the first I knew that Sonny was still alive. I didn't see him any more until we were both back in New York and the war had long been over.

He was a man by then, of course, but I wasn't willing to see it. He came by the house from time to time, but we fought almost every time we met. I didn't like the way he carried himself, loose and dreamlike all the time, and I didn't like his friends, and his music seemed to be merely an excuse for the life he led. It sounded just that weird and disordered.

Then we had a fight, a pretty awful fight, and I didn't see him for months. By and by I looked him up, where he was living, in a furnished room in the Village, and I tried to make it up. But there were lots of other people in the room, and Sonny just lay on his bed, and he wouldn't come downstairs with me, and he treated these other people as though they were his family and I weren't. So I got mad and then he got mad, and then I told him that he might just as well be dead as live the way he was living. Then he stood up and he told me not to worry about him any more in life, that he *was* dead as far as I was concerned. Then he pushed me to the door, and the other people looked on as though nothing were happening, and he slammed the door behind me. I stood in the hallway, staring at the door. I heard somebody laugh in the room and then tears came to my eyes. I started down the steps, whistling to keep from crying, I kept whistling to myself. *You going to need me, baby, one of these cold, rainy days.*

I read about Sonny's trouble in the spring, Little Grace died in the fall. She was a beautiful little girl. But she only lived a little over two years. She died of polio and she suffered. She had a slight fever for a couple of days, but it didn't seem like anything and we just kept her in bed. And we would certainly have called the doctor, but the fever dropped, she seemed to be all right. So we thought it had just been a cold. Then, one day, she was up, playing. Isabel was in the kitchen fixing lunch for the two boys when they'd come in from school, and she heard Grace fall down in the living room. When you have a lot of children you don't always start running when one of them falls, unless they start screaming or something. And, this time, Grace was quiet. Yet, Isabel says that when she heard that *thump* and then that silence, something happened in her to make her afraid. And she ran to the living room and there was little Grace on the floor, all twisted up, and the reason she hadn't screamed was that she couldn't get her breath. And when she did scream, it was the worst sound, Isabel says, that she'd ever heard in all her life, and she still hears it sometimes in her dreams. Isabel will sometimes wake me up with a low, moaning, strangled sound, and I have to be quick to awaken her and hold her to me and where Isabel is weeping against me seems a mortal wound.

I think I may have written Sonny the very day that little Grace was buried. I was sitting in the living room in the dark, by myself, and I suddenly thought of Sonny. My trouble made his real.

One Saturday afternoon, when Sonny had been living with us, or, anyway, been in our house, for nearly two weeks, I found myself wandering aimlessly about the living room, drinking from a can of beer, and trying to work up the courage to search Sonny's room. He was out, he was usually out whenever I was home, and Isabel had taken the children to see their grandparents. Suddenly I was standing still in front of the living-room window, watching Seventh Avenue. The idea of searching Sonny's room made me still. I scarcely dared to admit to myself what I'd be searching for. I didn't know what I'd do if I found it. Or if I didn't.

On the sidewalk across from me, near the entrance to a barbecue joint, some people were holding an old-fashioned revival meeting. The barbecue cook, wearing a dirty white apron, his conked hair reddish and metallic in the pale sun, and a cigarette between his lips, stood in the doorway, watching them. Kids and older people paused in their errands and stood there, along with some older men and a couple of very tough-looking women who watched everything that happened on the avenue, as though they owned it, or were maybe owned by it. Well, they were watching this, too. The revival was being carried on by three sisters in black, and a brother. All they had were their voices and their Bibles and a tambourine. The brother was testifying and while he testified two of the sisters stood together, seeming to say, Amen, and the third sister walked around with the tambourine outstretched and a couple of people dropped coins into it. Then the brother's testimony ended, and the sister who had been taking up the collection dumped the coins into her palm and transferred them to the pocket of her long black robe. Then she raised both hands, striking the tambourine against the air, and then against one hand, and she started to sing. And the two other sisters and the brother joined in.

It was strange, suddenly, to watch, though I had been seeing these street meetings all my life. So, of course, had everybody else down there. Yet, they paused and watched and listened and I stood still at the window. "*'Tis the old ship of Zion,*" they sang, and the sister with the tambourine kept a steady, jangling beat, "*it has rescued many a thousand!*" Not a soul under the sound of their voices was hearing this song for the first time, not one of them had been rescued. Nor had they seen much in the way of rescue work being done around them. Neither did they especially believe in the holiness of the three sisters and the brother, they knew too much about them, knew where they lived, and how. The woman with the tambourine, whose voice dominated the air, whose face was bright with joy, was divided by very little from the woman who stood watching her, a cigarette between her heavy, chapped lips, her hair a cuckoo's nest, her face scarred and swollen from many beatings, and her black eyes glittering like coal. Perhaps they both knew this, which was why, when, as rarely, they addressed each other, they addressed each other as Sister. As the singing filled the air, the watching, listening faces underwent a change, the eyes focusing on something within; the music seemed to soothe a poison out of them; and time seemed, nearly, to fall away from the sullen, belligerent, battered faces, as though they were fleeing back to their first condition, while dreaming of their last. The barbecue cook half shook his head and smiled, and dropped his cigarette and disappeared into his joint. A man fumbled in his pockets for change and stood holding it in his hand impatiently, as though he had just remembered a pressing appointment further up the avenue. He looked furious. Then I saw Sonny, standing on the edge of the crowd. He was carrying a wide, flat notebook with a green cover, and it made him look, from where I was standing, almost like a schoolboy. The coppery sun brought out the copper in his skin, he was very faintly smiling, standing very still. Then the singing stopped, the tambourine turned into a collection plate again. The furious man dropped in his coins and vanished, so did a couple of the women, and Sonny dropped some change in the plate, looking directly at the woman with a little smile. He started across the avenue, toward the house. He has a slow, loping walk, something like the way Harlem hipsters walk, only he's imposed on this his own half-beat. I had never really noticed it before.

I stayed at the window, both relieved and apprehensive. As Sonny disappeared from my sight, they began singing again. And they were still singing when his key turned in the lock.

"Hey," he said.

"Hey, yourself. You want some beer?"

"No. Well, maybe." But he came up to the window and stood beside me, looking out. "What a warm voice," he said.

They were singing *If I could only hear my mother pray again!*

"Yes," I said, "and she can sure beat that tambourine."

"But what a terrible song," he said, and laughed. He dropped his notebook on the sofa and disappeared into the kitchen. "Where's Isabel and the kids?"

"I think they went to see their grandparents. You hungry?"

"No." He came back into the living room with his can of beer. "You want to come someplace with me tonight?"

I sensed, I don't know how, that I couldn't possibly say no. "Sure. Where?"

He sat down on the sofa and picked up his notebook and started leafing through it. "I'm going to sit in with some fellows in a joint in the Village."

"You mean, you're going to play tonight?"

"That's right." He took a swallow of his beer and moved back to the window. He gave me a sidelong look. "If you can stand it."

"I'll try," I said.

He smiled to himself, and we both watched as the meeting across the way broke up. The three sisters and the brother, heads bowed, were singing *God be with you till we meet again.* The faces around them were very quiet. Then the song ended. The small crowd dispersed. We watched the three women and the lone man walk slowly up the avenue.

"When she was singing before," said Sonny, abruptly, "her voice reminded me for a minute of what heroin feels like sometimes—when it's in your veins. It makes you feel sort of warm and cool at the same time. And distant. And—sure." He sipped his beer, very deliberately not looking at me. I watched his face. "It makes you feel—in control. Sometimes you've got to have that feeling."

"Do you?" I sat down slowly in the easy chair.

"Sometimes." He went to the sofa and picked up his notebook again. "Some people do."

"In order," I asked, "to play?" And my voice was very ugly, full of contempt and anger.

"Well"—he looked at me with great, troubled eyes, as though, in fact, he hoped his eyes would tell me things he could never otherwise say—"they *think* so. And *if* they think so—!"

"And what do *you* think?" I asked.

He sat on the sofa and put his can of beer on the floor. "I don't know," he said, and I couldn't be sure if he were answering my question or pursuing his thoughts. His face didn't tell me. "It's not so much to *play*. It's to *stand* it, to be able to make it all. On any level." He frowned and smiled: "In order to keep from shaking to pieces."

"But these friends of yours," I said, "they seem to shake themselves to pieces pretty goddamn fast."

"Maybe." He played with the notebook. And something told me that I should curb my tongue, that Sonny was doing his best to talk, that I should listen. "But of course you only know the ones that've gone to pieces. Some don't—or at least they haven't *yet* and that's just about all *any* of us can say." He paused. "And then there are some who just live, really, in hell, and they know it and they see what's happening and they go right on. I don't know." He sighed, dropped the notebook, folded his arms. "Some guys, you can tell from the way they play, they on something *all* the time. And you can see that, well, it makes something real for them. But of course," he picked up his beer from the floor and sipped it and put the can down again, "they *want* to, too, you've got to see that. Even some of them that say they don't—*some*, not all."

"And what about you?" I asked—I couldn't help it. "What about you? Do *you* want to?"

He stood up and walked to the window and remained silent for a long time. Then he sighed. "Me," he said. Then: "While I was downstairs before, on my way here, listening to that woman sing, it struck me all of a sudden how much suffering she must have had to go through—to sing like that. It's *repulsive* to think you have to suffer that much."

I said: "But there's no way not to suffer—is there, Sonny?"

"I believe not," he said, and smiled, "but that's never stopped anyone from trying." He looked at me. "Has it?" I realized, with this mocking look, that there stood between us, forever, beyond the power of time or forgiveness, the fact that I had held silence—so long!—when he had needed human speech to help him. He turned back to the window. "No, there's no way not to suffer. But you try all kinds of ways to keep from drowning in it, to keep on top of it, and to make it seem—well, like *you*. Like you did something, all right, and now you're suffering for it. You know?" I said nothing. "Well, you know," he said, impatiently, "why *do* people suffer? Maybe it's better to do something to give it a reason, *any* reason."

"But we just agreed," I said, "that there's no way not to suffer. Isn't it better, then, just to—take it?"

"But nobody just takes it," Sonny cried, "that's what I'm telling you! *Everybody* tries not to. You're just hung up on the *way* some people try —it's not *your* way!"

The hair on my face began to itch, my face felt wet. "That's not true," I said, "that's not true. I don't give a damn what other people do, I don't even care how they suffer. I just care how *you* suffer." And he looked at me. "Please believe me," I said, "I don't want to see you—die—trying not to suffer."

"I won't," he said, flatly, "die trying not to suffer. At least, not any faster than anybody else."

"But there's no need," I said, trying to laugh, "is there, in killing yourself?"

I wanted to say more, but I couldn't. I wanted to talk about will power and how life could be—well, beautiful. I wanted to say that it was all within; but was it? Or, rather, wasn't that exactly the trouble? And I wanted to promise that I would never fail him again. But it would all have sounded—empty words and lies.

So I made the promise to myself and prayed that I would keep it.

"It's terrible sometimes, inside," he said, "that's what's the trouble. You walk these streets, black and funky and cold, and there's not really a living ass to talk to, and there's nothing shaking, and there's no way of getting it out—that storm inside. You can't talk it and you can't make love with it, and when you finally try to get with it and play it, you realize *nobody's* listening. So *you've* got to listen. You got to find a way to listen."

And then he walked away from the window and sat on the sofa again, as though all the wind had suddenly been knocked out of him. "Sometimes you'll do *anything* to play, even cut your mother's throat." He laughed and looked at me. "Or your brother's." Then he sobered. "Or your own." Then: "Don't worry. I'm all right now and I think I'll *be* all right. But I can't forget—where I've been. I don't mean just the physical place I've been, I mean where I've *been*. And *what* I've been."

"What have you been, Sonny?" I asked.

He smiled—but sat sideways on the sofa, his elbow resting on the back, his fingers playing with his mouth and chin, not looking at me. "I've been something I didn't recognize, didn't know I could be. Didn't know anybody could be." He stopped, looking inward, looking helplessly young, looking old. "I'm not talking about it now because I feel *guilty* or anything like that—maybe it would be better if I did, I don't know. Anyway, I can't really talk about it. Not to you, not to anybody." And now he turned and faced me. "Sometimes, you know, and it was actually when I was most out of the world, I felt that I was in it, that I was *with* it, really, and I could play or I didn't really have to *play*, it just came out of me, it was there. And I don't know how I played, thinking about it now, but I know I did awful things, those times, sometimes to people. Or it wasn't that I *did* anything to them—it was that they weren't real." He picked up the beer can; it was empty; he rolled it between his palms: "And other times—well, I needed a fix, I needed to find a place to lean, I needed to clear a space to *listen*—and I couldn't find it, and I—went crazy, I did terrible things to *me*, I was terrible *for* me." He began pressing the beer can between his hands, I watched the metal begin to give. It glittered, as he played with it, like a knife, and I was afraid he would cut himself, but I said nothing. "Oh well. I can never tell you. I was all by myself at the bottom of something, stinking and sweating and crying and shaking, and I smelled it, you know? *My* stink, and I thought I'd die if I couldn't get away from it and yet, all the same, I knew that everything I was doing was just locking me in with it. And I didn't know," he paused, still flattening the beer can, "I didn't know, I still *don't* know, something kept telling me that maybe it was good to smell your own stink, but I didn't think that *that* was what I'd been trying to do—and —who can stand it?" And he abruptly dropped the ruined beer can, looking at me with a small, still smile, and then rose, walking to the window as though it were the lodestone rock. I watched his face, he watched the avenue. "I couldn't tell you when Mama died—but the reason I wanted to leave Harlem so bad was to get away from drugs. And then, when I ran away, that's what I was running from—really. When I came back, nothing had changed, *I* hadn't changed, I was just—older." And he stopped, drumming with his fingers on the windowpane. The sun had vanished, soon darkness would fall. I watched his face. "It can come again," he said, almost as though speaking to himself. Then he turned to me. "It can come again," he repeated. "I just want you to know that."

"All right," I said at last. "So it can come again. All right."

He smiled, but the smile was sorrowful. "I had to try to tell you," he said.

"Yes," I said. "I understand that."

"You're my brother," he said, looking straight at me, and not smiling at all.

"Yes," I repeated, "Yes. I understand that."

He turned back to the window, looking out. "All that hatred down there," he said, "all that hatred and misery and love. It's a wonder it doesn't blow the avenue apart."

We went to the only night club on a short, dark street, downtown. We squeezed through the narrow, chattering, jam-packed bar to the entrance of the big room, where the bandstand was. And we stood there for a moment, for the lights were very dim in this room and we couldn't see. Then, "Hello, boy," said a voice, and an enormous black man, much older than Sonny or myself, erupted out of all that atmospheric lighting and put an arm around Sonny's shoulder. "I been sitting right here," he said, "waiting for you."

He had a big voice, too, and heads in the darkness turned toward us.

Sonny grinned and pulled a little away, and said, "Creole, this is my brother. I told you about him."

Creole shook my hand. "I'm glad to meet you, son," he said, and it was clear that he was glad to meet me *there*, for Sonny's sake. And he smiled. "You got a real musician in *your* family," and he took his arm from Sonny's shoulder and slapped him, lightly, affectionately, with the back of his hand.

"Well. Now I've heard it all," said a voice behind us. This was another musician, and a friend of Sonny's, a coal-black, cheerful looking man, built close to the ground. He immediately began confiding to me, at the top of his lungs, the most terrible things about Sonny, his teeth gleaming like a lighthouse and his laugh coming up out of him like the beginning of an earthquake. And it turned out that everyone at the bar knew Sonny, or almost everyone; some were musicians, working there, or nearby, or not working, some were simply hangers-on, and some were there to hear Sonny play. I was introduced to all of them and they were all very polite to me. Yet, it was clear that, for them, I was only Sonny's brother. Here, I was in Sonny's world. Or, rather: his kingdom. Here, it was not even a question that his veins bore royal blood.

They were going to play soon, and Creole installed me, by myself, at a table in a dark corner. Then I watched them, Creole, and the little black man, and Sonny, and the others, while they horsed around, standing just below the bandstand. The light from the bandstand spilled just a little short of them and, watching them laughing and gesturing and moving about, I had the feeling that they, nevertheless, were being most careful not to step into that circle of light too suddenly: that if they moved into the light too suddenly, without thinking, they would perish in flame. Then, while I watched, one of them, the small, black man, moved into the light and crossed the bandstand and started fooling around with his drums. Then—being funny and being, also, extremely ceremonious—Creole took Sonny by the arm and led him to the piano. A woman's voice called Sonny's name, and a few hands started clapping. And Sonny, also being funny and being ceremonious, and so touched, I think, that he could have cried, but neither hiding it nor showing it, riding it like a man, grinned, and put both hands to his heart and bowed from the waist.

Creole then went to the bass fiddle and a lean, very bright-skinned brown man jumped up on the bandstand and picked up his horn. So there they were, and the atmosphere on the bandstand and in the room began to change and tighten. Someone stepped up to the microphone and announced them. Then there were all kinds of murmurs. Some people at the bar shushed others. The waitress ran around, frantically getting in the last orders, guys and chicks got closer to each other, and the lights on the bandstand, on the quartet, turned to a kind of indigo. Then they all looked different there. Creole looked about him for the last time, as though he were making certain that all his chickens were in the coop, and then he—jumped and struck the fiddle. And there they were.

All I know about music is that not many people ever really hear it. And even then, on the rare occasions when something opens within, and the music enters, what we mainly hear, or hear corroborated, are personal, private, vanishing evocations. But the man who creates the music is hearing something else, is dealing with the roar rising from the void and imposing order on it as it hits the air. What is evoked in him, then, is of another order, more terrible because it has no words, and triumphant, too, for that same reason. And his triumph, when he triumphs, is ours. I just watched Sonny's face. His face was troubled, he was working hard, but he wasn't with it. And I had the feeling that, in a way, everyone on the bandstand was waiting for him, both waiting for him and pushing him along. But as I began to watch Creole, I realized that it was Creole who held them all back. He had them on a short rein. Up there, keeping the beat with his whole body, wailing on the fiddle, with his eyes half closed, he was listening to everything, but he was listening to Sonny. He was having a dialogue with Sonny. He wanted Sonny to leave the shore line and strike out for the deep water. He was Sonny's witness that deep water and drowning were not the same thing—he had been there, and he knew. And he wanted Sonny to know. He was waiting for Sonny to do the things on the keys which would let Creole know that Sonny was in the water.

And, while Creole listened, Sonny moved, deep within, exactly like someone in torment. I had never before thought of how awful the relationship must be between the musician and his instrument. He has to fill it, this instrument, with the breath of life, his own. He has to make it do what he wants it to do. And a piano is just a piano. It's made out of so much wood and wires and little hammers and big ones, and ivory. While there's only so much you can do with it, the only way to find this out is to try and make it do everything.

And Sonny hadn't been near a piano for over a year. And he wasn't on much better terms with his life, not the life that stretched before him now. He and the piano stammered, started one way, got scared, stopped;

started another way, panicked, marked time, started again; then seemed to have found a direction, panicked again, got stuck. And the face I saw on Sonny I'd never seen before. Everything had been burned out of it, and at the same time, things usually hidden were being burned in, by the fire and fury of the battle which was occurring in him up there.

Yet, watching Creole's face as they neared the end of the first set, I had the feeling that something had happened, something I hadn't heard. Then they finished, there was scattered applause, and then, without an instant's warning, Creole started into something else, it was almost sardonic, it was *Am I Blue*. And, as though he commanded, Sonny began to play. Something began to happen. And Creole let out the reins. The dry, low, black man said something awful on the drums. Creole answered, and the drums talked back. Then the horn insisted, sweet and high, slightly detached perhaps, and Creole listened, communicating now and then, dry, and driving, beautiful and calm and old. Then they all came together again, and Sonny was part of the family again. I could tell this from his face. He seemed to have found, right there beneath his fingers, a damn brand-new piano. It seemed that he couldn't get over it. Then, for a while, just being happy with Sonny, they seemed to be agreeing with him that brand-new pianos certainly were a gas.

Then Creole stepped forward to remind them that what they were playing was the blues. He hit something in all of them, he hit something in me, myself, and the music tightened and deepened, apprehension began to beat the air. Creole began to tell us what the blues were all about. They were not about anything very new. He and his boys up there were keeping it new, at the risk of ruin, destruction, madness, and death, in order to find new ways to make us listen. For, while the tale of how we suffer, and how we are delighted, and how we may triumph is never new, it always must be heard. There isn't any other tale to tell, it's the only light we've got in all this darkness.

And this tale, according to that face, that body, those strong hands on those strings, has another aspect in every country, and a new depth in every generation. Listen, Creole seemed to be saying, listen. Now these are Sonny's blues. He made the little black man on the drums know it, and the bright, brown man on the horn. Creole wasn't trying any longer to get Sonny in the water. He was wishing him Godspeed. Then he stepped back, very slowly, filling the air with the immense suggestion that Sonny speak for himself.

Then they all gathered around Sonny, and Sonny played. Every now and again one of them seemed to say, Amen. Sonny's fingers filled the air with life, his life. But that life contained so many others. And Sonny went all the way back, he really began with the spare, flat statement of the opening phrase of the song. Then he began to make it his. It was very beautiful because it wasn't hurried and it was no longer a lament. I seemed to hear with what burning he had made it his, with what burning we had yet to make it ours, how we could cease lamenting. Freedom lurked around us and I understood, at last, that he could help us to be free if we would listen, that he would never be free until we did. Yet, there was no battle in his face now. I heard what he had gone through, and would continue to go through until he came to rest in earth. He had made it his: that long line, of which we knew only Mama and Daddy. And he was giving it back, as everything must be given back, so that, passing through death, it can live forever. I saw my mother's face again, and felt, for the first time, how the stones of the road she had walked on must have bruised her feet. I saw the moonlit road where my father's brother died. And it brought something else back to me, and carried me past it. I saw my little girl again and felt Isabel's tears again, and I felt my own tears begin to rise. And I was yet aware that this was only a moment, that the world waited outside, as hungry as a tiger, and that trouble stretched above us, longer than the sky.

Then it was over. Creole and Sonny let out their breath, both soaking wet, and grinning. There was a lot of applause and some of it was real. In the dark, the girl came by and I asked her to take drinks to the bandstand. There was a long pause, while they talked up there in the indigo light and after a while I saw the girl put a Scotch and milk on top of the piano for Sonny. He didn't seem to notice it, but just before they started playing again, he sipped from it and looked toward me, and nodded. Then he put it back on top of the piano. For me, then, as they began to play again, it glowed and shook above my brother's head like the very cup of trembling.

Questions

1. The narrator both admires and resents Sonny's approach to life. Why? To what degree does either character envy the other? Describe the way of life, the goals, the things that are important to each.

2. James Baldwin is noted for his intense concern with racial issues. Is "Sonny's Blues" a racial story, or something else? To what extent does its tension depend on racial issues, and to what extent does it transcend them?

3. Does the reader identify with one brother more than another? If so, why? Is this identification intended? Consider the use of point of view in this respect. Are the reader's responses the same as the narrator's? What does the reader think of the narrator?

4. This is a "memory" story—it consists of the narrator's recollections of various events from the past in connection with his brother. Why does he remember the particular events he does—the death of his daughter, the death of an unknown uncle, the revival meeting, the trip to a night club to hear Sonny play? What do they tell us of his past life and his relationship with Sonny?

Heinrich Böll

MY SAD FACE

One of the significant writers to emerge in Germany after World War II, Heinrich Böll has taken a critical attitude toward modern society, certainly not sparing his own country. Born in Cologne, Germany, in 1917, he came to prominence in 1951 when he won a German literary prize. He was associated with a group of young writers who attacked war, raised questions about the direction of post-war society, and exposed the spiritual emptiness of modern life. His works available in translation include the novels Billiards at Half-Past Nine *(1962),* The Clown *(1965), and* End of a Mission *(1968), and a collection of short stories,* Children Are Civilians Too *(1970), from which "My Sad Face" is taken. The story itself, like much of Böll's other work, describes an absurdist situation in a realistic way. Its distortions emphasize one kind of political madness of the writer's time.*

As I stood by the harbor to watch the gulls, my melancholy face attracted a policeman who walked the beat in this quarter. I was completely absorbed in the sight of the floating birds, who shot up and plunged down, looking in vain for something edible: the harbor was desolate, the water greenish, thick with dirty oil, and in its crusted skin floated all kinds of discarded rubbish. Not a ship was to be seen, the cranes were rusty, the warehouses decayed: it seemed that not even rats populated the black debris on the quai; it was quiet. For many years all connections with the outside had been cut off.

I had fixed my eyes on one particular gull whose flight I was watching. It hovered near the surface of the water, nervous as a swallow that senses the approach of a thunderstorm; only once in a while did it dare the screeching leap upward to unite its course with that of its companions. If I could have made one wish, I would have chosen bread to feed it to the gulls, to break crumbs and fix a white point for the purposeless wings, to set a goal toward which they would fly; to tighten this shrieking web of chaotic trails by a toss of a bread crumb, grasping into them as into a pile of strings that one gathers up. But like them, I was too hungry; tired too, yet happy in spite of my melancholy because it was good to stand there, hands in my pockets, and watch the gulls and drink sadness.

But suddenly an official hand was laid on my shoulder, and a voice said: "Come along!" With this, the hand tried to jerk me around by the shoulder. I stood where I was, shook it off, and said calmly: "You're crazy."

"Comrade," the still invisible person said to me, "I'm warning you."

"My dear sir," I replied.

"There are no 'sirs'," he cried angrily. "We're all comrades!" And now he stepped up beside me, looked at me from the side, and I was forced to pull back my happily roaming gaze and sink it into his good eyes: he was serious as a buffalo who has eaten nothing but duty for decades.

"What grounds . . .," I tried to begin . . .

"Grounds enough," he said, "your melancholy face."

I laughed.

"Don't laugh!" His anger was genuine. At first I had thought he was bored, because there were no unregistered whores, no staggering sailors, no thieves or absconders to arrest, but now I saw that it was serious: he wanted to arrest me.

"Come along . . .!"

"And why?" I asked calmly.

Before I became aware of it, my left wrist was enclosed in a thin chain, and at this moment I realized that I was lost again. One last time I turned to the roving gulls, glanced into the beautiful gray sky, and tried, with a sudden twist, to throw myself into the water, for it seemed better to me, after all, to drown alone in this filthy water than to be strangled in some backyard by the myrmidons or be locked up again. But the policeman, with a jerk, drew me so close that escape was no longer possible.

"And why?" I asked again.

"There's a law that you have to be happy."

"I am happy," I cried.

"Your melancholy face . . .," he shook his head.

"But this law is new," I said.

"It's thirty-six hours old, and you know very well that every new law goes into effect twenty-four hours after its proclamation."

"But I don't know it."

"That's no excuse. It was announced day before yesterday, over all the loudspeakers, in all the papers, and it was published in handbills to those," here he looked at me scornfully, "those who have no access to the blessings of the press or the radio; they were scattered over every street in the area. So we'll see where you've spent the last thirty-six hours, comrade."

He dragged me on. Only now did I feel that it was cold and I had no coat, only now did my hunger assert itself and growl before the gates of my stomach, only now did I realize that I was also dirty, unshaven, ragged, and that there were laws that said every comrade was obliged to be clean, shaved, happy and well-fed. He shoved me in front of him like a scarecrow who, convicted of stealing, had to leave the home of its dreams on the edge of the field. The streets were empty, the way to the precinct not long, and although I had known they would find some reason to arrest me again, still my heart grew heavy, because he led me through the places of my youth, which I had wanted to visit after viewing the harbor: gardens that had been full of shrubs, lovely in their disorder, overgrown paths—all this was now planned, ordered, neat, laid out in squares for the patriotic leagues which had to carry out their exercises here Mondays, Wednesdays, and Saturdays. Only the sky had its former shape and the air was like in those days when my heart had been full of dreams.

Here and there in passing I saw that already in many of the love barracks the state sign had been hung out for those whose turn to participate in the hygienic pleasure was on Wednesday; also many bars seemed authorized to display the sign of drinking, a beer glass stamped out of lead with stripes of the patriotic colors of the area: light-brown, dark-brown, light-brown. No doubt joy reigned already in the hearts of those who had been entered in the state lists of Wednesday drinkers, and could partake of a Wednesday beer.

The unmistakable sign of zeal adhered to everyone who met us, the thin aura of industry surrounded them, probably all the more when they caught sight of the policeman; they all walked faster, showed a perfectly dutiful face, and the women who came out of the stores tried to give their faces an expression of that joy which was expected from them, for they were commanded to show joy, vigorous cheerfulness about the duties of the housewife, who was encouraged to refresh the public worker with a good meal in the evening.

But all these people avoided us skillfully, so that no one had to cross our path directly; wherever signs of life were evident on the street, they disappeared twenty steps ahead of us. Everyone tried to step quickly into a store or turn a corner, and many may have entered an unfamiliar house and waited uneasily behind the door until our steps had faded away.

Only once, just as we were passing a crossing, an older man met us; briefly, I recognized the badge of the schoolteacher on him; it was too late for him to dodge us, and he now tried, after he had first greeted the policeman according to the prescribed regulations (that is, he hit himself three times on the head with a flat hand as a sign of absolute humility), then he tried to fulfill his duty, which demanded that he spit in my face three times and call me the obligatory name: "Traitorous swine." He aimed well, but the day had been hot, his throat must have been dry, because only a few meager, rather unsubstantial drops hit me— which I—against regulations—automatically tried to wipe off with my sleeve; whereupon the policeman kicked me in the behind and hit me with his fist in the middle of my backbone, adding in a calm voice: "Stage 1," which meant the first, mildest form of punishment every policeman could use.

The schoolteacher hurried away quickly. Otherwise everyone succeeded in avoiding us; only one woman, a pale, puffy blonde, taking her prescribed airing beside a love barrack before the evening pleasure, quickly threw me a kiss and I smiled gratefully, while the policeman tried to act as though he hadn't noticed anything. They are urged to allow these women freedoms that would immediately bring any other comrade a heavy punishment. Since they contribute substantially to the improvement of general working morale, they are thought of as standing outside the law, a concession whose significance the state philosopher Dr. Dr. Dr. Bleigoeth branded in the obligatory Journal of (State) Philosophy as a sign of beginning liberalization. I had read it the day before on my way to the capital, when I found a few pages of the magazine in the outhouse of a farm. A student—probably the farmer's son—had glossed it with astute comments.

Luckily we were about to reach the police station, when the sirens started to sound, which meant that the streets would overflow with thousands of people whose faces bore an expression of mild joy (for it was "recommended" not to show too great a joy after work since it would indicate that work was a burden; jubilation, however, was to reign at the beginning of work, jubilation and song)–all these thousands of people would have had to spit at me. Actually the sirens indicated that it was ten minutes before closing, for everyone was expected to indulge in a thorough washing for ten minutes, in accordance with the slogan of the present Chief of State: Happiness and Soap.

At the door to the precinct of this quarter, a plain concrete structure, two guards were posted who bestowed upon me in passing the usual "physical measures": they hit me violently on the temples with their bayonets and cracked the barrels of their pistols against my collarbone, following the preamble to State Law No. 1: "Every policeman except the arresting officer is to prove himself before every apprehended (they mean arrested) as an individual power; to the arresting officer falls the good fortune of executing all necessary bodily measures during the interrogation." The State Law No. 1 itself has the following wording: "Every policeman *may* punish anyone; he *must* punish everyone who has been found guilty of a transgression. There is, for all comrades, no exemption from punishment, but a possibility of exemption from punishment."

We now walked through a long, bare corridor, with many large windows; then a door opened automatically, because in the meantime the guards had announced our arrival, since in those days when everyone was happy, good, orderly, and everyone exerted himself to consume the prescribed pound of soap a day, in those days the arrival of an apprehended (an arrested) was indeed an event.

We entered an almost empty room, which contained only a desk with a telephone and two chairs; I was to place myself in the middle of the room; the policeman took off his helmet and sat down.

At first it was silent and nothing happened; they always do it that way; that's the worst part; I felt how my face sagged more and more, I was hungry and tired, and even the last trace of that joy of melancholy had vanished, for I knew that I was lost.

After a few seconds a tall, pale man entered in the brownish uniform of the pre-examiner; he sat down without saying a word and looked at me.

"Occupation?"

"Simple Comrade."

"Born?"

"1.1 one," I said.

"Last employment?"

"Prisoner."

The two looked at each other.

"When and where released?"

"Yesterday, house 12, cell 13."

"Released to where?"

"To the capital."

"Papers."

I took my release paper out of my pocket and handed it over. He fastened it to the green card on which he had started to write my statements.

"Former offense?"

"Happy face."

The two looked at each other.

"Explain," said the pre-examiner.

"At that time," I said, "my happy face attracted a policeman on a day when general mourning was ordered. It was the anniversary of the death of the chief."

"Length of punishment?"
"Five."
"Conduct?"
"Bad."
"Reason?"
"Lack of initiative."
"That's all."

Then the pre-examiner stood up, walked up to me and knocked out exactly three front middle teeth: a sign that I should be branded as a backslider, a measure I had not reckoned with. Then the pre-examiner left the room and a heavy fellow in a dark brown uniform stepped in: the Interrogator.

They all beat me: the Interrogator, the Senior Interrogator, the Head Interrogator, the Preliminary and Final Judge, and also the policeman carried out all the physical measures, as the law commanded; and they sentenced me to ten years because of my melancholy face, just as five years ago they had sentenced me to five years because of my happy face.

But I must try to have no face at all any more, if I succeed in enduring the next ten years with happiness and soap.

Questions

1. Show how the narrator's attitude toward his society is revealed by the way he reacts to officials, and what he expects from them—the policeman who arrests him, the schoolteacher, the guards, etc.

2. How does the apparently realistic beginning prepare the reader for what is to come? Is there any relation between the narrator's observation of one particular seagull and his own plight?

3. How much self-knowledge does the narrator have of his own situation? Does he understand why he is being arrested?

4. What is the point of the revelation at the end of the story that the narrator has previously been arrested for having a "happy" face?

5. The narrator says that, when he ends his new prison sentence, he "must try to have no face at all any more." What does he mean? What does his remark imply about the requirements for survival in his society?

6. Does the story have any allegorical elements? Note particularly any political implications.

Jorge Luis Borges

FUNES THE MEMORIOUS

A distinguished, versatile man of letters, Jorges Luis Borges is probably South America's best-known writer, and has often been mentioned for the Nobel Prize. He has become a kind of cultural bridge, making Latin American literature known to the rest of the world and also translating into Spanish such modern writers as Gide, Faulkner, Virginia Woolf, and Kafka. Born in Buenos Aires in 1899, Borges traveled and was educated in Europe, then returned to Argentina and began writing poetry. Criticial essays on metaphysics, mythology, and literature followed. As poor health overtook him and his eyesight failed, he turned to the writing of short tales of the grotesque and esoteric, much influenced by Poe and Kafka. Some of his works in translation are Ficciones *(1962),* Labyrinths *(1962),* Dream-tigers *(1964), and a collection of essays,* Other Inquisitions *(1962).*

"Funes the Memorious," from Labyrinths, *illustrates several of Borges' tantalizing qualities. Like many of his stories, it has elements of the fable and the parable; it seems to exist in a dream world, yet its details are disturbingly real, and it appears to offer a "meaning" that is just beyond reach. The reader will want to consider why the story is told by a narrator rather than by Funes himself.*

I remember him (I have no right to utter this sacred verb, only one man on earth had that right and he is dead) with a dark passion flower in his hand, seeing it as no one has ever seen it, thought he might look at it from the twilight of dawn till that of evening, a whole lifetime. I remember him, with his face taciturn and Indian-like and singularly *remote,* behind the cigarette. I remember (I think) his angular, leather-braiding hands. I remember near those hands a maté gourd bearing the Uruguayan coat of arms; I remember a yellow screen with a vague lake landscape in the window of his house. I clearly remember his voice: the slow, resentful, nasal voice of the old-time dweller of the suburbs, without the Italian sibilants we have today. I never saw him more than three times; the last was in 1887 . . . I find it very satisfactory that all those who knew him should write about him; my testimony will perhaps be the shortest and no doubt the poorest, but not the most impartial in the volume you will edit. My deplorable status as an Argentine will prevent me from indulging in a dithyramb, an obligatory genre in Uruguay whenever the subject is an Uruguayan. *Highbrow, city slicker, dude:* Funes never spoke these injurious words, but I am sufficiently certain I represented for him those misfortunes. Pedro Leandro Ipuche has written that Funes was a precursor of the supermen, "a vernacular and rustic Zarathustra"; I shall not debate the point, but one should not forget that he was also a kid from Fray Bentos, with certain incurable limitations.

My first memory of Funes is very perspicuous. I can see him on an afternoon in March or February of the year 1884. My father, that year, had taken me to spend the summer in Fray Bentos. I was returning from the San Francisco ranch with my cousin Bernardo Haedo. We were singing as we rode along and being on horseback was not the only circumstance determining my happiness. After a sultry day, an enormous slate-colored storm had hidden the sky. It was urged on by a southern wind, the trees were already going wild; I was afraid (I was hopeful) that the elemental rain would take us by surprise in the open. We were running a kind of race with the storm. We entered an alleyway that sank down between two very high brick sidewalks. It had suddenly got dark; I heard some rapid and almost secret footsteps up above; I raised my eyes and saw a boy running along the narrow and broken path as if it were a narrow and broken wall. I remember his baggy gaucho trousers, his rope-soled shoes. I remember the cigarette in his hard face, against the now limitless storm cloud. Bernardo cried to him unexpectedly: "What time is it, Ireneo?" Without consulting the sky, without stopping, he replied: "It's four minutes to eight, young Bernardo Juan Francisco." His voice was shrill, mocking.

I am so unperceptive that the dialogue I have just related would not have attracted my attention had it not been stressed by my cousin, who (I believe) was prompted by a certain local pride and the desire to show that he was indifferent to the other's tripartite reply.

He told me the fellow in the alleyway was one Ireneo Funes, known for certain peculiarities such as avoiding contact with people and always knowing what time it was, like a clock. He added that he was the son of the ironing woman in town, María Clementina Funes, and that some people said his father was a doctor at the meat packers, an Englishman by the name of O'Connor, and others that he was a horse tamer or scout from the Salto district. He lived with his mother, around the corner from the Laureles house.

During the years eighty-five and eighty-six we spent the summer in

Montevideo. In eighty-seven I returned to Fray Bentos. I asked, as was natural, about all my acquaintances and, finally, about the "chronometrical" Funes. I was told he had been thrown by a half-tamed horse on the San Francisco ranch and was left hopelessly paralyzed. I remember the sensation of uneasy magic the news produced in me: the only time I had seen him, we were returning from San Francisco on horseback and he was running along a high place; this fact, told me by my cousin Bernardo, had much of the quality of a dream made up of previous elements. I was told he never moved from his cot, with his eyes fixed on the fig tree in the back or on a spider web. In the afternoons, he would let himself be brought out to the window. He carried his pride to the point of acting as if the blow that had felled him were beneficial . . . Twice I saw him behind the iron grating of the window, which harshly emphasized his condition as a perpetual prisoner: once, motionless, with his eyes closed; another time, again motionless, absorbed in the contemplation of a fragrant sprig of santonica.

Not without a certain vaingloriousness, I had begun at that time my methodical study of Latin. My valise contained the *De viris illustribus* of Lhomond, Quicherat's *Thesaurus*, the commentaries of Julius Caesar and an odd volume of Pliny's *Naturalis historia*, which then exceeded (and still exceeds) my moderate virtues as a Latinist. Everything becomes public in a small town; Ireneo, in his house on the outskirts, did not take long to learn of the arrival of these anomalous books. He sent me a flowery and ceremonious letter in which he recalled our encounter, unfortunately brief, "on the seventh day of February of the year 1884," praised the glorious services my uncle Gregorio Haedo, deceased that same year, "had rendered to our two nations in the valiant battle of Ituzaingó" and requested the loan of any one of my volumes, accompanied by a dictionary "for the proper intelligence of the original text, for I am as yet ignorant of Latin." He promised to return them to me in good condition, almost immediately. His handwriting was perfect, very sharply outlined; his orthography, of the type favored by Andrés Bello: *i* for *y*, *j* for *g*. At first I naturally feared a joke. My cousins assured me that was not the case, that these were peculiarities of Ireneo. I did not know whether to attribute to insolence, ignorance or stupidity the idea that the arduous Latin tongue should require no other instrument than a dictionary; to disillusion him fully, I sent him the *Gradus ad Parnassum* of Quicherat and the work by Pliny.

On the fourteenth of February, I received a telegram from Buenos Aires saying I should return immediately, because my father was "not at all well." May God forgive me; the prestige of being the recipient of an urgent telegram, the desire to communicate to all Fray Bentos the contradiction between the negative form of the message and the peremptory adverb, the temptation to dramatize my suffering, affecting a virile stoicism, perhaps distracted me from all possibility of real sorrow. When I packed my valise, I noticed the *Gradus* and the first volume of the *Naturalis historia* were missing. The *Saturn* was sailing the next day, in the morning; that night, after supper, I headed toward Funes' house. I was astonished to find the evening no less oppressive than the day had been.

At the respectable little house, Funes' mother opened the door for me. She told me Ireneo was in the back room and I should not be surprised to find him in the dark, because he knew how to pass the idle hours without lighting the candle. I crossed the tile patio, the little passageway; I reached the second patio. There was a grape arbor; the darkness seemed complete to me. I suddenly heard Ireneo's high-pitched, mocking voice. His voice was speaking in Latin; his voice (which came from the darkness) was articulating with morose delight a speech or prayer or incantation. The Roman syllables resounded in the earthen patio; my fear took them to be indecipherable, interminable; afterward, in the enormous dialogue of that night, I learned they formed the first paragraph of the twenty-fourth chapter of the seventh book of the *Naturalis historia*. The subject of that chapter is memory; the last words were *ut nihil non iisdem verbis redderetur auditum*.

Without the slightest change of voice, Ireneo told me to come in. He was on his cot, smoking. It seems to me I did not see his face until dawn; I believe I recall the intermittent glow of his cigarette. The room smelled vaguely of dampness. I sat down; I repeated the story about the telegram and my father's illness.

I now arrive at the most difficult point in my story. This story (it is well the reader know it by now) has no other plot than that dialogue which took place half a century ago. I shall not try to reproduce the words, which are now irrecoverable. I prefer to summarize with veracity the many things Ireneo told me. The indirect style is remote and weak; I know I am sacrificing the efficacy of my narrative; my readers should imagine for themselves the hesitant periods which overwhelmed me that night.

Ireneo began by enumerating, in Latin and in Spanish, the cases of prodigious memory recorded in the *Naturalis historia:* Cyrus, king of the Persians, who could call every soldier in his armies by name, Mithridates Eupator, who administered the law in the twenty-two languages of his empire; Simonides, inventor of the science of mnemonics; Metrodorus, who practiced the art of faithfully repeating what he had heard only once. In obvious good faith, Ireneo was amazed that such cases be considered amazing. He told me that before that rainy afternoon when the blue-gray horse threw him, he had been what all humans are: blind, deaf, addlebrained, absent-minded. (I tried to remind him of his exact perception of time, his memory for proper names; he paid no attention to me.) For nineteen years he had lived as one in a dream: he looked without seeing, listened without hearing, forgetting everything, almost everything. When he fell, he became unconscious; when he came to, the present was almost intolerable in its richness and sharpness, as were his most distant and trivial memories. Somewhat later he learned that he was paralyzed. The fact scarcely interested him. He reasoned (he felt) that his immobility was a minimum price to pay. Now his perception and his memory were infallible.

We, at one glance, can perceive three glasses on a table; Funes, all the leaves and tendrils and fruit that make up a grape vine. He knew by heart the forms of the southern clouds at dawn on the 30th of April, 1882, and could compare them in his memory with the mottled streaks on a book in Spanish binding he had only seen once and with the outlines of the foam raised by an oar in the Rio Negro the night before the Quebracho uprising. These memories were not simple ones; each visual image was linked to muscular sensations, thermal sensations, etc. He could reconstruct all his dreams, all his half-dreams. Two or three times he had reconstructed a whole day; he never hesitated, but each reconstruction had required a whole day. He told me: "I alone have more memories than all mankind has probably had since the world has been the world." And again: "My dreams are like you people's waking hours." And again, toward dawn: "My memory, sir, is like a garbage heap." A circle drawn on a blackboard, a right triangle, a lozenge—all these are forms we can fully and intuitively grasp; Ireneo could do the same with the stormy mane of a pony, with a herd of cattle on a hill, with the changing fire and its innumerable ashes, with the many faces of a dead man throughout a long wake. I don't know how many stars he could see in the sky.

These things he told me; neither then nor later have I ever placed them in doubt. In those days there were no cinemas or phonographs; nevertheless, it is odd and even incredible that no one ever performed an experiment with Funes. The truth is that we live out our lives putting off all that can be put off; perhaps we all know deep down that we are immortal and that sooner or later all men will do and know all things.

Out of the darkness, Funes' voice went on talking to me.

He told me that in 1886 he had invented an original system of numbering and that in a very few days he had gone beyond the twenty-four-thousand mark. He had not written it down, since anything he thought of once would never be lost to him. His first stimulus was, I think, his discomfort at the fact that the famous thirty-three gauchos of Uruguayan history should require two signs and two words, in place of a single word and a single sign. He then applied this absurd principle to the other numbers. In place of seven thousand thirteen, he would say (for example) *Máximo Pérez;* in place of seven thousand fourteen, *The Railroad;* other numbers were *Luis Melián Lafinur, Olimar, sulphur, the reins, the whale, the gas, the caldron, Napoleon, Augustín de Vedia.* In place of five hundred, he would say *nine.* Each word had a particular sign, a kind of mark; the last in the series were very complicated . . . I tried to explain to him that this rhapsody of incoherent terms was precisely the opposite of a system of numbers. I told him that saying 365 meant saying three hundreds, six tens, five ones, an analysis which is not found in the "numbers" *The Negro Timoteo* or *meat blanket.* Funes did not understand me or refused to understand me.

Locke, in the seventeenth century, postulated (and rejected) an impossible language in which each individual thing, each stone, each bird and each branch, would have its own name; Funes once projected an analogous language, but discarded it because it seemed too general to him, too ambiguous. In fact, Funes remembered not only every leaf of every tree of every wood, but also every one of the times he had perceived or imagined it. He decided to reduce each of his past days to some seventy thousand memories, which would then be defined by means of ciphers. He was dissuaded from this by two considerations: his awareness that the task was interminable, his awareness that it was useless. He thought that by the hour of his death he would not even have finished classifying all the memories of his childhood.

The two projects I have indicated (an infinite vocabulary for the natural series of numbers, a useless mental catalogue of all the images of his memory) are senseless, but they betray a certain stammering grandeur. They permit us to glimpse or infer the nature of Funes' vertiginous world. He was, let us not forget, almost incapable of ideas of a general, Platonic sort. Not only was it difficult for him to comprehend that the generic symbol *dog* embraces so many unlike individuals of diverse size and form; it bothered him that the dog at three fourteen (seen from the side) should have the same name as the dog at three fifteen (seen from the front). His own face in the mirror, his own hands, surprised him every time he saw them. Swift relates that the emperor of Lilliput could discern the movement of the minute hand; Funes could continuously discern the tranquil advances of corruption, of decay, of fatigue. He could note the progress of death, of dampness. He was the solitary and lucid spectator of a multiform, instantaneous and almost intolerably precise world. Babylon, London and New York have overwhelmed with their ferocious splendor the imaginations of men; no one, in their populous towers or their urgent avenues, has felt the heat and pressure of a reality as indefatigable as that which day and night converged upon the hapless Ireneo, in his poor South American suburb. It was very difficult for him to sleep. To sleep is to turn one's mind from the world; Funes, lying on his back on his cot in the shadows, could imagine every crevice and every molding in the sharply defined houses surrounding him. (I repeat that the least important of his memories was more minute and more vivid than our perception of physical pleasure or physical torment.) Towards the east, along a stretch not yet divided into blocks, there were new houses, unknown to Funes. He imagined them to be black, compact, made of homogeneous darkness; in that direction he would turn his face in order to sleep. He would also imagine himself at the bottom of the river, rocked and annihilated by the current.

With no effort, he had learned English, French, Portuguese and Latin. I suspect, however, that he was not very capable of thought. To think is to forget differences, generalize, make abstractions. In the teeming world of Funes, there were only details, almost immediate in their presence.

The wary light of dawn entered the earthen patio.

Then I saw the face belonging to the voice that had spoken all night long. Ireneo was nineteen years old; he had been born in 1868; he seemed to me as monumental as bronze, more ancient than Egypt, older than the prophecies and the pyramids. I thought that each of my words (that each of my movements) would persist in his implacable memory; I was benumbed by the fear of multiplying useless gestures.

Ireneo Funes died in 1889, of congestion of the lungs.

Questions

1. In a first-person narrative, the question of the reliability and credibility of the narrator always arises. In this story the narrator is seemingly an observer rather than a participant in the action. Does the question of his reliability occur? What are some of his characteristics? His limitations? At one point he calls himself "unperceptive." Is this true? Do he and the reader mean the same thing by it?

2. What is accomplished by having this story told by an outside narrator rather than by Funes, himself? In what ways are the narrator's observations and judgments different from those that would come from Funes himself?

3. Why does the narrator bother to tell the story of Funes at all? What makes him think that it is worth telling?

4. The narrator says he finds a certain "stammering grandeur" in Funes' accomplishments. What does he mean? Why is he impressed? What kind of tribute is he paying to Funes?

5. Explain: "In the teeming world of Funes, there were only details." What judgment does the word "only" imply? What is absent from Funes' world?

6. Is there any significance in the manner of Funes' death? What is it?

Ray Bradbury

THE SCYTHE

The name of Ray Bradbury is so closely associated with popular science fiction that some readers may have difficulty accepting his work at more serious levels. Yet the serious core is there. Born in Waukegan, Illinois, in 1920, he began writing early, and during the 1940s he had stories accepted by such magazines as Weird Tales, Amazing Stories, Astounding Science Fiction, *and* Captain Future, *whose titles tell their own story. The serious uses of the impossible and the futuristic began to show themselves in the stories Bradbury published in book form in the 1950s:* The Martian Chronicles *(1950),* The Illustrated Man *(1952),* The Golden Apples of the Sun *(1953), and* A Medicine for Melancholy *(1959); and in a novel,* Fahrenheit 451 *(1953). In a variation from the pattern, he produced the short novel,* Dandelion Wine, *in 1957, a sensitive and beautifully written story about a boy growing up in the midwest and his last golden summer before his initiation into the terrors of the adult world.*

Bradbury has always seemed aware that he was writing about the present as well as the future, and that the seemingly fantastic elements in his stories were only imaginative extensions of contemporary actualities. In one well-known remark about his work, he said, "I have always told myself there is a bit of the known in the unknown, there is a bit of the unknown in the known; look *for it,* find *it." The reader of "The Scythe" may shrink from what he finds in that story, but he can hardly deny that its "unknown" terrors bear a disturbing resemblance to his own perceived world. The story is from Bradbury's first published collection,* Dark Carnival *(1942).*

I

Quite suddenly there was no more road. It ran down the valley like any other road, between slopes of barren, stony ground and live oak trees, and then past a broad field of wheat standing alone in the wilderness. It came up beside the small white house that belonged to the wheat field and then just faded out, as though there was no more use for it.

It didn't matter much, because just there the last of the gas was gone. Drew Erickson braked the ancient car to a stop and sat there, not speaking, staring at his big, rough farmer's hands.

Molly spoke, without moving where she lay in the corner beside him. "We must of took the wrong fork back yonder."

Drew nodded.

Molly's lips were almost as white as her face. Only they were dry, where her skin was damp with sweat. Her voice was flat, with no expression in it.

"Drew," she said. "Drew, what are we a-goin' to do now?"

Drew stared at his hands. A farmer's hands, with the farm blown out from under them by the dry, hungry wind that never got enough good loam to eat.

The kids in the back seat woke up and pried themselves out of the dusty litter of bundles and bedding. They poked their heads over the back of the seat and said:

"What are we stoppin' for, Pa? Are we gonna eat now, Pa? Pa, we're awful hungry. Can we eat now, Pa?"

Drew closed his eyes. He hated the sight of his hands.

Molly's fingers touched his wrist. Very light, very soft. "Drew, maybe in the house there they'd spare us something to eat?"

A white line showed around his mouth. "Beggin'," he said harshly. "Ain't none of us ever begged before. Ain't none of us ever goin' to."

Molly's hand tightened on his wrist. He turned and saw her eyes. He saw the eyes of Susie and little Drew, looking at him. Slowly all the stiffness went out of his neck and his back. His face got loose and blank, shapeless like a thing that has been beaten too hard and too long. He got out of the car and went up the path to the house. He walked uncertainly, like a man who is sick, or nearly blind.

II

The door of the house was open. Drew knocked three times. There was nothing inside but silence, and a white window curtain moving in the slow, hot air.

He knew it before he went in. He knew there was death in the house. It was that kind of silence.

He went through a small, clean living room and down a little hall. He wasn't thinking anything. He was past thinking. He was going toward the kitchen, unquestioning, like an animal.

Then he looked through an open door and saw the dead man.

He was an old man, lying on a clean white bed. He hadn't been dead long; not long enough to lose the last quiet look of peace. He must have known he was going to die, because he wore his grave clothes—an old black suit, brushed and neat, and a clean white shirt and a black tie.

A scythe leaned against the wall beside the bed. Between the old man's hands there was a blade of wheat, still fresh. A ripe blade, golden and heavy in the tassel.

Drew went into the bedroom, walking soft. There was a coldness on him. He took off his broken, dusty hat and stood by the bed, looking down.

The paper lay open on the pillow beside the old man's head. It was meant to be read. Maybe a request for burial, or to call a relative. Drew scowled over the words, moving his pale, dry lips.

> To him who stands beside me at my death bed: Being of sound mind, and alone in the world as it has been decreed, I, John Buhr, do give and bequeath this farm, with all pertaining to it, to the man who is to come. Whatever his name or origin shall be, it will not matter. The farm is his, and the wheat; the scythe, and the task ordained thereto. Let him take them freely, and without question—and remember that I, John Buhr, am only the giver, not the ordainer. To which I set my hand and seal this third day of April, 1938. (Signed) John Buhr. *Kyrie eléison!*

III

Drew walked back through the house and opened the screen door. He said, "Molly, you come in. Kids, you stay in the car."

Molly came inside. He took her to the bedroom. She looked at the will, the scythe, the wheat field moving in a hot wind outside the window. Her white face tightened up and she bit her lips and held onto him. "It's too good to be true. There must be some trick to it."

Drew said, "Our luck's changin', that's all. We'll have work to do, stuff to eat, somethin' over our heads to keep rain off." He touched the scythe. It gleamed like a half-moon. Words were scratched on its blade: WHO WIELDS ME—WIELDS THE WORLD! It didn't mean much to him, right at that moment.

"Drew," Molly asked, staring at the old man's clasped hands, "why—why's he holdin' that wheat-stalk so hard in his fingers?"

Just then the heavy silence was broken by the sound of the kids scrambling up the front porch. Molly gasped.

IV

They lived in the house. They buried the old man on a hill and said some words over him, and came back down and swept the house and unloaded the car and had something to eat, because there was food, lots of it, in the kitchen; and they did nothing for three days but fix the house and look at the land and lie in the good beds, and then look at one another in surprise that all this was happening this way, and their stomachs were full and there was even a cigar for him to smoke in the evenings.

There was a small barn behind the house and in the barn a bull and three cows, and there was a well-house, a spring-house, under some big trees that kept it cool. And inside the well-house were big sides of beef and bacon and pork and mutton, enough to feed a family five times their size for a year, two years, maybe three. There was a churn and a box of cheese there, and big metal cans for the milk.

V

On the fourth morning Drew Erickson lay in bed looking at the scythe, and he knew it was time for him to work because there was ripe grain in the long field; he had seen it with his eyes, and he did not want to get soft. Three days sitting were enough for any man. He roused himself in the first fresh smell of dawn and took the scythe and held it before him as he walked out into the field. He held it up in his hands and swung it down.

It was a big field of grain. Too big for one man to tend, and yet one man had tended it.

At the end of the first day of work, he walked in with the scythe riding his shoulder quietly, and there was a look on his face of a puzzled man. It was a wheat field the like of which he had never seen. It ripened only in separate clusters, each set off from the others. Wheat shouldn't do that. He didn't tell Molly. Nor did he tell her the other things about the field. About how, for instance, the wheat rotted within a few hours after he cut it down. Wheat shouldn't do that, either. He was not greatly worried. After all, there was food at hand.

VI

The next morning the wheat he had left rotting, cut down, had taken hold and come up again in little green sprouts, with tiny roots, all born again.

Drew Erickson rubbed his chin, wondered what and why and how it acted that way, and what good it would be to him—he couldn't sell it. A couple of times during the day he walked far up in the hills to where the old man's grave was, just to be sure the old man was there, maybe with some notion he might get an idea there about the field. He looked down and saw how much land he owned. The wheat stretched three miles in one direction toward the mountains, and was about two acres wide, patches of it in seedlings, patches of it golden, patches of it green, patches of it fresh cut by his hand. But the old man said nothing concerning this; there were a lot of stones and dirt in his face now. The grave was in the sun and the wind and silence. So Drew Erickson walked back down to use the scythe, curious, enjoying it because it seemed important. He didn't know just why, but it was. Very, very important.

He couldn't just let the wheat stand. There were always new patches of it ripened, and in his figuring out loud to no one in particular he said, "If I cut the wheat for the next ten years, just as it ripens up, I don't think I'll pass the same spot twice. Such a damn big field." He shook his head. "That wheat ripens just so. Never too much of it so I can't cut all the ripe stuff each day. That leaves nothin' but green grain. And the next mornin', sure enough, another patch of ripe stuff. . . ."

VII

It was damned foolish to cut the grain when it rotted as quick as it fell. At the end of the week he decided to let it go a few days.

He lay in bed late, just listening to the silence in the house that wasn't anything like death silence, but a silence of things living well and happily.

He got up, dressed, and ate his breakfast slowly. He wasn't going to work. He went out to milk the cows, stood on the porch smoking a cigarette, walked about the backyard a little and then came back in and asked Molly what he had gone out to do.

"Milk the cows," she said.

"Oh, yes," he said, and went out again. He found the cows waiting and full, and milked them and put the milk cans in the spring-house, but thought of other things. The wheat. The scythe.

All through the morning he sat on the back porch rolling cigarettes. He made a toy boat for little Drew and one for Susie, and then churned some of the milk into butter and drew off the buttermilk, but the sun was in his head, aching. It burned there. He wasn't hungry for lunch. He kept looking at the wheat and the wind bending and tipping and ruffling it. His arms flexed, his fingers, resting on his knee as he sat again on the porch, made a kind of grip in the empty air, itching. The pads of his palms itched and burned. He stood up and wiped his hands on his pants and sat down and tried to roll another cigarette and got mad at the mixings and threw it all away with a muttering. He had a feeling as if a third arm had been cut off him, or he had lost something of himself. It had to do with his hands and his arms.

He heard the wind whisper in the field.

By one o'clock he was going in and out of the house, getting underfoot, thinking about digging an irrigation ditch, but all the time really thinking about the wheat and how ripe and beautiful it was, aching to be cut.

"Damn it to hell!"

He strode into the bedroom, took the scythe down off its wall-pegs. He stood holding it. He felt cool. His hands stopped itching. His head didn't ache. The third arm was returned to him. He was intact again.

It was instinct. Illogical as lightning striking and not hurting. Each day the grain must be cut. It had to be cut. Why? Well, it just did, that was all. He laughed at the scythe in his big hands. Then, whistling, he took it out to the ripe and waiting field and did the work. He thought himself a little mad. Hell, it was an ordinary-enough wheat field, really, wasn't it? Almost.

VIII

The days loped away like gentle horses.

Drew Erickson began to understand his work as a sort of dry ache and hunger and need. Things built in his head.

One noon, Susie and little Drew giggled and played with the scythe while their father lunched in the kitchen. He heard them. He came out and took it away from them. He didn't yell at them. He just looked very concerned and locked the scythe up after that, when it wasn't being used.

He never missed a day, scything.

Up. Down. Up, down, and across. Back and up and down and across. Cutting. Up. Down.

Up.

Think about the old man and the wheat in his hands when he died.

Down.

Think about this dead land, with wheat living on it.

Up.

Think about the crazy patterns of ripe and green wheat, the way it grows!

Down.

Think about . . .

The wheat whirled in a full yellow tide at his ankles. The sky blackened. Drew Erickson dropped the scythe and bent over to hold his stomach, his eyes running blindly. The world reeled.

"I've killed somebody!" he gasped, choking, holding to his chest, falling to his knees beside the blade. "I've killed a lot—"

The sky revolved like a blue merry-go-round at the county fair in Kansas. But no music. Only a ringing in his ears.

IX

Molly was sitting at the blue kitchen table peeling potatoes when he blundered into the kitchen, dragging the scythe behind him.

"Molly!"

She swam around in the wet of his eyes.

She sat there, her hands fallen open, waiting for him to finally get it out.

"Get the things packed," he said, looking at the floor.

"Why?"

"We're leaving," he said, dully.

"We're leaving?" she said.

"That old man. You know what he did here? It's the wheat, Molly, and this scythe. Every time you use the scythe on the wheat a thousand people die. You cut across them and—"

Molly got up and put the knife down and the potatoes to one side and said, understandingly, "We traveled a lot and haven't eaten good until last month here, and you been workin' every day and you're tired—"

"I hear voices, sad voices, out there. In the wheat," he said. "Tellin' me to stop. Tellin' me not to kill them!"

"Drew!"

He didn't hear her. "The field grows crooked, wild, like a crazy thing. I didn't tell you. But it's wrong."

She stared at him. His eyes were blue glass, nothing else.

"You think I'm crazy," he said, "but wait 'til I tell you. Oh, God, Molly, help me; I just killed my mother!"

"Stop it!" she said firmly.

"I cut down one stalk of wheat and I killed her. I felt her dyin', that's how I found out just now—"

"Drew!" Her voice was like a crack across the face, angry and afraid now. "Shut up!"

He mumbled. "Oh—Molly—"

The scythe dropped from his hands, clamored on the floor. She picked it up with a snap of anger and set it in one corner. "Ten years I been with you," she said. "Sometimes we had nothin' but dust and prayers in our mouths. Now, all this good luck sudden, and you can't bear up under it!"

She brought the Bible from the living room.

She rustled its pages over. They sounded like the wheat rustling in a small, slow wind. "You sit down and listen," she said.

A sound came in from the sunshine. The kids, laughing in the shade of the large live oak beside the house.

She read from the Bible, looking up now and again to see what was happening to Drew's face.

X

She read from the Bible each day after that. The following Wednesday, a week later, when Drew walked down to the distant town to see if there was any General Delivery mail, there was a letter.

He came home looking two hundred years old.

He held the letter out to Molly and told her what it said in a cold, uneven voice.

"Mother passed away—one o'clock Tuesday afternoon—her heart—"

All that Drew Erickson had to say was, "Get the kids in the car, load it up with food. We're goin' on to California.

"Drew—" said his wife, holding the letter.

"You know yourself," he said, "this is poor grain land. Yet look how ripe it grows. I ain't told you all the things. It ripens in patches, a little each day. It ain't right. And when I cut it, it rots! And next mornin' it comes up without any help, growin' again! Last Tuesday, a week ago, when I cut the grain it was like rippin' my own flesh. I heard somebody scream. It sounded just like—And now, today, this letter."

She said, "We're stayin' here."

"Molly."

"We're stayin' here, where we're sure of eatin' and sleepin' and livin' decent and livin' long. I'm not starvin' my children down again, ever!"

The sky was blue through the windows. The sun slanted in, touching half of Molly's calm face, shining one eye bright blue. Four or five water drops hung and fell from the kitchen faucet slowly, shining, before Drew sighed. The sigh was husky and resigned and tired. He nodded, looking away. "All right," he said. "We'll stay."

He picked up the scythe weakly. The words on the metal leaped up with a sharp glitter.

WHO WIELDS ME— WIELDS THE WORLD!

"We'll stay. . . ."

XI

Next morning he walked to the old man's grave. There was a single fresh sprout of wheat growing in the center of it. The same sprout, reborn, that the old man had held in his hands weeks before.

He talked to the old man, getting no answers.

"You worked the field all your life because you *had* to, and one day you came across your own life growin' there. You knew it was yours. You cut it. And you went home, put on your grave clothes, and your heart gave out and you died. That's how it was, wasn't it? And you passed the land on to me, and when I die, I'm supposed to hand it over to someone else."

Drew's voice had awe in it. "How long a time has this been goin' on? With nobody knowin' about this field and its use except the man with the scythe . . .?"

Quite suddenly he felt very old. The valley seemed ancient, mummified, secretive, dried and bent and powerful. When the Indians danced on the prairie it had been here, this field. The same sky, the same wind, the same wheat. And, before the Indians? Some Cro-Magnon, gnarled and shag-haired, wielding a crude wooden scythe, perhaps, prowling down through the living wheat. . . .

Drew returned to work. Up, down. Up, down. Obsessed with the idea of being the wielder of the scythe. He, himself! It burst upon him in a mad, wild surge of strength and horror.

Up! Who wields me! Down! Wields the world!

He had to accept the job with some sort of philosophy. It was simply his way of getting food and housing for his family. They deserved eating and living decent, he thought, after all these years.

Up and down. Each grain a life he neatly cut into two pieces. If he planned it carefully—he looked at the wheat—why, he and Molly and the kids could live forever!

Once he found the place where the grain grew that was Molly and Susie and little Drew he would never cut it.

And then, like a signal, it came, quietly.

Right there, before him.

Another sweep of the scythe and he'd cut them away.

Molly, Drew, Susie. It was certain. Trembling, he knelt and looked at the few grains of wheat. They glowed at his touch.

He groaned with relief. What if he had cut them down, never guessing? He blew out his breath and got up and took the scythe and stood back away from the wheat and stood for a long while looking down.

Molly thought it awfully strange when he came home early and kissed her on the cheek, for no reason at all.

XII

At dinner, Molly said, "You quit early today? Does—does the wheat still spoil when it falls?"

He nodded and took more meat.

She said, "You ought to write to the Agriculture people and have them come look at it."

"No," he said.

"I was just suggestin'," she said.

His eyes dilated. "I got to stay here all my life. Can't nobody else mess with that wheat; they wouldn't know where to cut and not to cut. They might cut the wrong parts."

"What wrong parts?"

"Nothin'," he said, chewing slowly. "Nothin' at all."

He slapped his fork down, hard. "Who knows *what* they might want to do! Those government men! They might even—might even want to plow the whole field under!"

Molly nodded. "That's just what it needs," she said. "And start all over again, with new seed."

He didn't finish eating. "I'm not writin' any gover'ment, and I'm not handin' this field over to no stranger to cut, and that's that!" he said, and the screen door banged behind him.

XIII

He detoured around that place where the lives of his children and his wife grew up in the sun, and used his scythe on the far end of the field where he knew he would make no mistakes.

But he no longer liked the work. At the end of an hour he knew he had brought death to three of his old, loved friends in Missouri. He read their names in the cut grain and couldn't go on.

He locked the scythe in the cellar and put the key away. He was done with the reaping, done for good and all.

XIV

He smoked his pipe in the evening, on the front porch, and told the kids stories to hear them laugh. But they didn't laugh much. They seemed withdrawn, tired and funny, like they weren't his children any more.

Molly complained of a headache, dragged around the house a little, went to bed early and fell into a deep sleep. That was funny, too. Molly always stayed up late and was full of vinegar.

The wheat field rippled with moonlight on it, making it into a sea.

It wanted cutting. Certain parts needed cutting *now*. Drew Erickson sat, swallowing quietly, trying not to look at it.

What'd happen to the world if he never went in the field again? What'd happen to people ripe for death, who waited the coming of the scythe?

He'd wait and see.

Molly was breathing softly when he blew out the oil lamp and got to bed. He couldn't sleep. He heard the wind in the wheat, felt the hunger to do the work in his arms and fingers.

In the middle of the night he found himself walking in the field, the scythe in his hands. Walking like a crazy man, walking and afraid, half-awake. He didn't remember unlocking the cellar door, getting the scythe, but here he was in the moonlight, walking in the grain.

Among these grains there were many who were old, weary, wanting so very much to sleep. The long, quiet, moonless sleep.

The scythe held him, grew into his palms, forced him to walk.

Somehow, struggling, he got free of it. He threw it down, ran off into the wheat, where he stopped and went down on his knees.

"I don't want to kill anymore," he said. "If I work with the scythe I'll have to kill Molly and the kids. Don't ask me to do that!"

The stars only sat in the sky, shining.

XV

Behind him, he heard a dull, thumping sound.

Something shot up over the hill into the sky. It was like a living thing, with arms of red color, licking at the stars. Sparks fell into his face. The thick, hot odor of fire came with it.

The house!

Crying out, he got sluggishly, hopelessly, to his feet, looking at the big fire.

The little white house with the live oaks was roaring up in one savage bloom of fire. Heat rolled over the hill and he swam in it and went down in it, stumbling, drowning over his head.

By the time he got down the hill there was not a shingle, bolt or threshhold of it that wasn't alive with flame. It made blistering, crackling, fumbling noises.

No one screamed inside. No one ran around or shouted.

He yelled in the yard. "Molly! Susie! Drew!"

He got no answer. He ran close in until his eyebrows withered and his skin crawled hot like paper burning, crisping, curling up in tight little curls.

"Molly! Susie!"

The fire settled contentedly down to feed. Drew ran around the house a dozen times, all alone, trying to find a way in. Then he sat down where the fire roasted his body and waited until all the walls had shrunken down with fluttering crashes, until the last ceilings bent, blanketing the floors with molten plaster and scorched lathing. Until the flames died and smoke coughed up, and the new day came slowly; and there was nothing but embering ashes and an acid smoldering.

Disregarding the heat fanning from the leveled frames, Drew walked into the ruin. It was still too dark to see much. Red light glowed on his sweating throat. He stood like a stranger in a new and different land. Here—the kitchen. Charred tables, chairs, the iron stove, the cupboards. Here—the hall. Here the parlor and then over here was the bedroom where—

Where Molly was still alive.

She slept among fallen timbers and angry-colored pieces of wire spring and metal.

She slept as if nothing had happened. Her small white hands lay at her sides, flaked with sparks. Her calm face slept with a flaming lath across one cheek.

Drew stopped and didn't believe it. In the ruin of her smoking bedroom she lay on a glittering bed of sparks, her skin intact, and her breast rising, falling, taking air.

"Molly!"

Alive and sleeping after the fire, after the walls had roared down, after ceilings had collapsed upon her and flame had lived all about her.

His shoes smoked as he pushed through piles of fuming litter. It could have seared his feet off at the ankles, he wouldn't have known.

"Molly . . ."

He bent over her. She didn't move or hear him, and she didn't speak. She wasn't dead. She wasn't alive. She just lay there with the fire surrounding her and not touching her, not harming her in any way. Her cotton nightgown was streaked with ashes, but not burnt. Her brown hair was pillowed on a tumble of red-hot coals.

He touched her cheek, and it was cold, cold in the middle of hell. Tiny breaths trembled her half-smiling lips.

The children were there, too. Behind a veil of smoke he made out two smaller figures huddled in the ashes sleeping.

He carried all three of them out to the edge of the wheat field.

"Molly. Molly, wake up! Kids! Kids, wake up!"

They breathed and didn't move and went on sleeping.

"Kids, wake up! Your mother is—"

Dead? No, not dead. But—

He shook the kids as if they were to blame. They paid no attention; they were busy with their dreams. He put them back down and stood over them, his face cut with lines.

He knew why they'd slept through the fire and continued to sleep now. He knew why Molly just lay there, never wanting to laugh again.

The power of the wheat and the scythe.

Their lives, supposed to end yesterday, May 30th, 1938, had been prolonged simply because he refused to cut the grain. They should have died in the fire. That's the way it was meant to *be*. But since he had not used the scythe, nothing could hurt them. A house had flamed and fallen and still they lived, caught halfway, not dead, not alive. Simply—waiting. And all over the world thousands more just like them, victims of accidents, fires, disease, suicide, waited, slept just like Molly and her children slept. Not able to die, not able to live. All because a man was afraid of harvesting the ripe grain. All because one man thought he could stop working with a scythe and never work with that scythe again.

He looked down upon the children. The job had to be done every day and every day with never a stopping but going on, with never a pause, but always the harvesting, forever and forever and forever.

XVI

All right, he thought. All right. I'll use the scythe.

He didn't say good-by to his family. He turned with a slow-feeding anger and found the scythe and walked rapidly, then he began to trot, then he ran with long jolting strides into the field, raving, feeling the hunger in his arms, as the wheat whipped and flailed his legs. He pounded through it, shouting. He stopped.

"Molly!" he cried, and raised the blade and swung it down.

"Susie!" he cried. "Drew!" And swung the blade down again.

Somebody screamed. He didn't turn to look at the fire-ruined house.

And then, sobbing wildly, he rose above the grain again and again and hewed to left and right and to left and to right and to left and to right. Over and over and over! Slicing out huge scars in green wheat and ripe wheat, with no selection and no care, cursing, over and over, swearing, laughing, the blade swinging up in the sun and falling in the sun with a singing whistle! Down!

Bombs shattered London, Moscow, Tokyo.

The blade swung insanely.

And the kilns of Belsen and Buchenwald took fire.

The blade sang, crimson wet.

And mushrooms vomited out blind suns at White Sands, Hiroshima, Bikini, and up, through, and in continental Siberian skies.

The grain wept in a green rain, falling.

Korea, Indo-China, Egypt, India trembled; Asia stirred, Africa woke in the night. . . .

And the blade went on rising, crashing, severing, with the fury and the rage of a man who has lost and lost so much that he no longer cares what he does to the world.

XVII

Just a few short miles off the main highway, down a rough dirt road that leads to nowhere, just a few short miles from a highway jammed with traffic bound for California.

Once in a while during the long years a jalopy gets off the main highway, pulls up steaming in front of the charred ruin of a little white house at the end of the dirt road, to ask instructions from the farmer they see just beyond, the one who works insanely, wildly, without ever stopping, night and day, in the endless fields of wheat.

But they get no help and no answer. The farmer in the field is too busy, even after all these years; too busy slashing and chopping the green wheat instead of the ripe.

And Drew Erickson moves on with his scythe, with the light of blind suns and a look of white fire in his never-sleeping eyes, on and on and on. . . .

Questions

1. Fantasy and allegory become believable only if the succession of events has an inner logic and if the details seem realistic. Discuss how Bradbury persuades us to accept the story through the opening scenes.

2. Drew's "conversation" with the old man in his grave is the first full statement of the allegory. Interpret the line in the following paragraph—"the same sky, the same wind, the same wheat."

3. What relation does the story have to the depression and World War II? Could Bradbury have set it in other times? Why, or why not?

4. The fire that destroys the house is a symbolic holocaust. Explore its relation to the larger allegory. What is the irony in Drew's determination to quit his job? In his acquiescence to go on with his job?

Don Carpenter

HOLLYWOOD HEART

Don Carpenter is an emerging young writer with a keen eye for the significant detail that instantly reveals a character, and a keen ear for vernacular speech. He was born in Berkeley, California, in 1931, and grew up in Portland, Oregon. He obtained degrees in English at Portland State University and in Creative Writing at San Francisco State College. While in college he began writing regularly for several hours a day to attain the sense of ease and the control over his material that mark his work. His first novel, Hard Rain Falling *(1966), was a tough, sensitive, but unsentimental book about poolroom hustlers and their lonely world. Set against the windy streets of Portland and in a cheerless prison in California, it was particularly successful in evoking the rootless lives of the unattached. His next novel,* Blade of Light *(1968), and a collection of short stories,* The Murder of the Frogs *(1969), from which "Hollywood Heart" is taken, increased Carpenter's reputation as a shrewd observer of some of the hidden aspects of modern American life—hope turned sour, success gone corrupt, the search for happiness ending in futility. These same themes were continued in another novel,* Getting Off *(1971.)*

"Hollywood Heart" is a particularly clear-eyed treatment of a common theme in literature—the rise of a poor boy to a position of power and influence, and is an examination of the means and the consequences of that rise. A notable feature of the story is the skill, well-concealed but clearly present, with which Carpenter uses the first-person point of view to allow the narrator both to characterize and to unconsciously reveal himself.

My son comes to me for advice. What can I tell him? What we did is not what they do now. Now it is all business, and the young ones don't even go to the movies or watch their own television shows. No heart. Forty years I fight to keep my studio going and to keep the wolves out, and now I sit in my wheel chair watching television, and you know what? The commercials are better than what my son does. Imagine. It all started when they took away my theaters. That was something. Those New Yorkers come to me and say sweet things, you are forty-five years old, it is time to get out of the business, and all the time behind my back they are saying Max is no good to us any more because they took away his theaters and if he doesn't own the theater who would book his pictures, but they are foolish if they thought I put thirty-three million dollars in some Swiss bank like actors I know about, or maybe they thought I spent most of it for taxes, but they didn't know about a certain amendment to a certain rule, that I get to keep my money. They found out quick enough. Now they are making all the pictures overseas to save money, and the town is going to die. The town will die before I do, and they will have nowhere to come home to. Let them. I could sell my stock tomorrow.

Orchids. It started as a joke. One of the very funny writers I bring in from New York City sends me a pot of orchids with a little sign on it, "Sweets to the Sweet," and naturally I thought he was saying "Orchids to you!"—a nice compliment, but all the writers are laughing and they are laughing at me. Traditionally the writers don't like me, and for a very simple reason. When I made a picture that picture had my name on it, the first thing you see, my name and the name of the studio. So it's my picture, I paid for it. The writers think it is their picture, and the directors think it is their picture, but they all know that it is mine. They hated me because I checked every word of every scene on this lot. I saw every daily and I closeted myself with the editors when I had to. So they hate me when I change their lines. They argue, if Max does not like the way we write, why does he hire us? And I argue back, if you do not like the way I change your lines, why do you keep taking my money? So this writer who I can't even remember his name is mad at me because he has some of his dialogue chopped up, and he sends me orchids. I have the pot on my desk and I look at it. How can such a dumb-looking plant have such a beautiful flower? I ask myself. It's so beautiful it looks fake. But I like it, and I decide that I don't want it to die. I hear that orchids are tropical plants from such places as Hawaii, and I wonder if my office is too cold for them, so I call a man in the research department to send me a brief on orchids, and then I understand the joke. Orchids, the word comes from the Greek word *orchis,* which means testicle, and nobody had to tell me what that meant. He was telling me, "Nuts to you!" and at the same time, "You are a nut!" A very funny joke from a man who went to Princeton or Harvard. So I get back at him the same way (in those days we had time for jokes) by sending him a vanilla milk shake with a note, "The same to you!" Let him tell everybody I am crazy, he doesn't know the brief on orchids tells me the vanilla plant is really an orchid, too, and I am saying back to him, "May your nuts be ground up for a milk shake!"

So now I have my home and my greenhouse and my television set, and my son has my studio. I am still the boss, but my son has the office. Everybody thinks I am crazy because I don't leave this house. They think I am locked up and there is no wheel chair. I tell you the truth, nobody comes here to see me because I don't want them to. I never had a friend in this business. This is not a business for friends. I am seventy-one years old. Kids I played with on the block are in old people's homes in Brooklyn and The Bronx. Am I so much better off? My son comes to me, thirty-seven years old and crying tears. Mister Nazi around the office and a baby at home, a boy who never had a mother but read a psychology book instead. To tell the truth, if he wasn't my own flesh and blood I wouldn't let him in the house.

When I was his age we worried about things, we worried about money and our personal lives. He worries about his *image*, that's all he's got to worry about. I think he should get married and I say so. "Everybody thinks you're a queer," I tell him, but I'm a Jew and I want grandchildren. I am also a realist and I know I won't have any unless I buy them from an orphanage. He cries because he is masterminding some rotten thing and he gets outsmarted. My son has no nerve. For five years he makes terrible pictures because he is afraid to make my kind of pictures and he is even more afraid to make the kind of pictures everybody at Yale told him were good. The Belknap picture is going to be good. Morgan Cleary is going to be a famous star after this picture comes out, and so my son tries to steal the picture from Belknap because it will improve his *image.* I could tell him. What image? You're my son, that's all the image you got. You could make *Gone With the Wind* and you would still be my son.

He comes in and I am watching a soap opera, my son's soap opera. Television is the only business in the world where my son could earn a dollar. Everything in it is stolen from radio or the comic strips. There is no size, no nerve. That picture fits my son like a glove. So he says to me, "What's that?" He doesn't even recognize the actors. Some producer.

He is not crying yet. The last time I cried I was eight years old and had the shoes stolen off my feet. The Lower East Side of New York City was no Bel Air to be raised in, but that was the last time I shed any tears. I have heard stories how Louis B. Mayer used to cry over stories, God rest his soul, but I never did. Who was it who came to his funeral to make sure he was dead? God forbid such a thing should happen to me, even though I made enough enemies in my time. Now they are all laughing. Max is crazy, locked up in his house eating orchid flowers. Notice: I am not locked in; you are locked out.

Cigarette commercial. A beautiful Western, good music, a handsome fellow on a horse. Then my son starts crying. He can't sleep. He can't eat. The pressure is killing him. We play our game. I tell him he didn't have to go into the business, and he tells me it is his profession. It is so simple. He is afraid. He shouts at me to turn off the television, and I push the wrong button and the sound goes up. He stamps his foot and leaves me. I am sorry but there is nothing I can do. I know he will spend the whole rest of the evening up in his room. He keeps it in all day and then lets it out in front of me, unloading it on me. This was not always the case. When he was a boy he never said hardly anything to me. Up until the day my legs go out from under me and I fall down the stairs and lay there on the fake marble steps, my legs up and my head down, black specks in front of my eyes, clearing up and me looking up at the green brass letters that spell out my name over the stone arch and hear the wind rushing around, only it is people's voices; that girl, she spent hours sitting waiting to get into the studio and comes out finally from the main entrance just in time to see me fall and comes to me, playing nurse with her knees showing and my head pillowed on her lap, the specks dancing and the needles not yet in my legs, feeling I got a scraped knuckle and wondering what is all the fuss, a man falls down some steps, but now instead of the letters of my name I am looking up into the upside-down face of a beautiful young girl with her mouth open in sympathy and her eyes calculating and frightened and hoping all at once, and I speak to her—this went out over the television news on two stations—"Haven't I seen you someplace before?" When I try to stand up and can't, she is right there, at my side, until the ambulance gets there, by right of accident she is my bodyguard, thinking, How can I tell him my name? and the time slipping by, her big break, the head of the studio falling in her lap, so to speak, and she hasn't got the hardness to take advantage. Some of the cunts in this business would have had a contract signed before the ambulance came, but not this one, so pretty and so young, hard in the face but not in the heart, where it counts, a girl with maybe two commercials to her credit and eating peanut butter until finally it is no use, she is finished and has to go. I was dizzy then. Everything felt bright. I could see all the faces and hear all the whispers. I could have helped her. I could have took her name and got her some work. Maybe I should have. No. I shouldn't have. In all this time no work for her. Instead, I tell her, "You and me, we're finished." I don't know how I knew, but it was like something pulled out of my guts, like a huge splinter, and the blood rushes out but I feel better.

The television shouts at me and I push the button, this time the right one, and it goes off. Blink! I always watch the tiny dot of light. I cross the entry hall under the picture of my wife, God rest her soul, and down the ramp into the greenhouse through the electric doors. It is warm and steamy, with the sun over the ocean low and coming in through the windows. I sit and look at the plants, thinking. The fans turn on and the place cools down. The sun is gone and the lights go on. Long tubes of light that make everything purple and yellow. I know I look like a corpse and so I leave, across the entry hall, back to the television. I have my supper in the library watching television, and I know the servants are in the back of the house having their supper and watching television, and my son is upstairs in his room eating from a tray on his desk, pretending to work. Work? He doesn't know the meaning of the word.

Who could sleep? My son is coming to the crisis of his life, and, to tell the truth, there is nothing I can do about it. The time for me to do is gone. I should have married. But suppose I did? Arlene dies in 1928, and like Hamlet in reverse the birthday cake served up cold becomes the funeral feast. I was forty-one at the time, Arlene was thirty-six. Give me a year or two to get over it, and I marry again at age forty-three. But I don't marry an old person, say a girl of twenty-two. So if she was twenty-two in 1930 she would have been about fifty or so when I fall down the steps, not ready to give up sex. But she could have been a mother to him. I don't know. Maybe now I would have a cracking-up son and a cracking-up wife on my hands. Not one breath of scandal in all that time. It wasn't worth it.

Like walking through a curtain, my mind. All those years fighting and keeping, my mind spread all over the place, from New York to here, keeping track, holding on. It was not money. It stopped being money so long ago I can't remember, still a kid shaking nickels and dimes, it wasn't even the money then. They call it power, some of them. At a dinner party in this very house one of them tells me, "We are men who have gone beyond money, into the deepest part of the water, power." What is power? Power is what you don't know you got until you find out you haven't got enough of it. That's what I told him. He looks at me funny. I don't bother to explain. Another story. My son reaches for it because he does not know it reaches for you. He does not know this because nobody taught him.

New York keeps banging on me, "Get young blood in the executive end, delegate, delegate!" That's easy to say in New York, where they don't understand anything but columns of figures. Come out here and try it. How many men turn out to be generals? I try to tell them, "You don't force it; when good men come along they take the reins themselves," only to be told confidentially that I am like a tyrant who has only kiss-asses around him. I tell this man, "Nonsense, no kiss-asses in my studio, I hate them. A kiss-ass will cut your throat while you're not looking!" But under the joke I am worried, because it might be true. And true or not, at that time they could have come in here and deposed me with their own bright young men all over the place spying and making trouble. It is hard to believe when you are forty-five years old that people are already thinking of replacing you. They couldn't cheat you or kill you, so they replace you. All your life you fight to make a thing with your own hand, and then they come and tell you, "This thing is permanent and you are not. Delegate!"

Isadore Rapfkin stole my shoes. I cried. A kid of eight. I learn the secret then, delegate. I work hard selling newspapers, steal a little money and buy some shoes. Isadore Rapfkin and his two brothers beat me up and take my shoes. They fit Izzy. I cry, but I think, Anybody bigger than me can take my money. All by myself I learn the secret of delegate and control. I go to Hesh. Hesh has a cap on pulled low to keep the cold wind off, but you can see his little eyes. Dumb Hesh. I offer him five cents to beat up Izzy and get back my shoes. I am scared he will steal the nickel but I have to hold it out, show it to him or he won't believe it. With a boy like Hesh you got to show the money. He doesn't steal the money, I never learn why. In all my life I never really learn why. Me, I would not steal the money because there might be more, but Hesh and those people don't think that way. I never learned how they think. A complicated chain of events, Izzy gets beat up pretty bad, I get my shoes back, Hesh gets beat up by Izzy's brothers, but for some reason nobody comes to me to get the shoes. For a couple of weeks I duck Hesh, but then I run into him on the roof and he grins, happy. He doesn't blame me Izzy's brothers beat him up. He thinks that's why I offered him the nickel. I meet Izzy and he has respect for me. He doesn't know about the nickel. Later he works for me.

They don't think it's work. Not like selling newspapers is work. I keep that job, but I sell in the poolrooms and see all that money go to the horses. I run errands, I do anything, I make money, and nobody tries to take the money away from me. They know if they do, Hesh will be on them, a dumb kid who don't know when to stop beating. I don't even pay Hesh salary. Piecework. By this time I am sharking, ten cents a day on the dollar, time limit seven days. No extensions. First to kids who are older, teen-agers they call them now, who need money, only kids who work, and then later around the poolrooms to grown men betting the horses or on the billiard games, but then I see the light what a sucker's game I have going for myself.

One day Hesh kills his father and the police come and take him away. I have to hide, because I know people will be after me. I hide in the back of the poolroom on Third Avenue, but a boy named Mordacai Felzer comes in and finds me, but he doesn't want to beat me up, only to ask if I need another muscle man. I hire him on the spot and tell him to forget the money he owes me. He grins and I know he thinks he has put one over on me. But he works for me. Then my grandfather, God rest his soul, finds out I charge interest to Jews and he reads me out of the family. By then I have enough money not to care, and I don't cry. Not then, not ever again. By the time I am twelve I have five employees, all older kids, and I personally shark money only to family men, mostly garment workers, and the rate of interest has dropped, because I know enough not to press people who are cornered like rats. I didn't know what the rest of the world was like; I thought everybody lived in this kind of misery and was afraid all their lives.

Isadore Rapfkin was the one who went a long way in the sharking, not me. While I was sharking garment workers, he still handled the fifty-cent and dollar gambler and kid trade for me, and nobody was supposed to know he worked for me. After some time, I find out he was buying up markers all over the Lower East Side that nobody else could collect, and collecting them. He really went strong-arm, and before he was twenty I think he had a couple of people killed. I never went that far. By then we are no longer associated and I am out of sharking entirely, but he went on and opened his own poolroom. He was a regular gangster, with cops working for him and everything. He got killed in the 1920's. Some woman got him.

Sex caught me when I was about fourteen and looked maybe twenty. She was a show girl who did an act with her brother, I thought, where he would throw her around to music. It was supposed to be a Spanish act, billed as José and Maria Catalan, but they were Jewish. Previously I had nothing to do with theaters or vaudeville except to go once in a while if I could get in free, and to tell the truth, the movies they had then didn't impress me very much. At that time they used movies to clear the house after the headliner. Niagara Falls, two people kissing, boxing matches. Feature films came later. People were always coming to me with propositions of how to make lots of money if only they had some to start with, and I got to admit that one out of a thousand really had good propositions, and a few good businesses got started on money I loaned out at six per cent. But the rest were something awful. One fellow I remember wanted me to loan him money to buy life insurance with so he could kill himself in an accident and the widow would pay me back. I never saw such a cold-blooded fellow. I had to turn him down.

There was a stuss parlor on Sixth Avenue where I used to sit from around ten in the morning until about two in the afternoon, and people would come to me there. Everybody except the owners thought I owned the place. Morton Chernig was a man of about thirty with a black suit, a derby and a long mustache, and little else except schemes. He had a father and two brothers working, and that was enough for him. I saw him out of the corner of my eye, hanging around, and as soon as I was alone, he came over and sat down without being asked.

"This is your lucky day," he told me. He reached over and took a cigar out of my pocket and started trimming it with a little gold-plated knife. "I am about to unveil a proposition which is both lucrative and entertaining, especially for a young fellow like yourself." To cut it short, he was offering me a partnership, as much as it broke his heart, because he knew I would not loan him a red cent, even though all he needed to make a cleanup was one hundred dollars for no more than one week. It took him half an hour to get down to what the proposition was about, what with people stopping by and him being nervous, but what it amounted to was he had a friend who just got back from Europe with "a very special reel of motion picture" which was nothing like what anybody had ever seen around here. He needed money to rent a store and some chairs and hire a fellow with a projector.

"What's the nature of this moving picture?" I asked, even though from the way he was carrying on, I had a good guess.

"Women, my boy," he said. "The subject is women. And let me tell you a secret, they ain't got any clothes on, either."

That afternoon he took me to a rooming house and introduced me to Sarah Greenglass, alias Maria Catalan, who was the friend with the movie. This made me a little shy, it being a woman, and they got the film out of its can and told me not to touch it with my fingertips, and pulled it off the spool, their fingers on the edges, and let me look, holding it up to the light. Sure enough, naked women, three of them. You could see the hair and everything, and so I knew they weren't wearing tights, which is what I had been afraid of. I avoided Sarah's eyes and said, "This looks interesting."

"I would be saving this," she said, "except we ain't been booked in six weeks. A triumphant tour of Europe and now we haven't got to eat. I ask you. This film cost Manny and me fifty dollars American in Paris."

I figured she had stolen it, and later she told me this was correct. But at the time she was trying to sell it outright to me for twenty-five dollars, while what Chernig wanted was for him and me to be partners. This didn't come out right away, not until Sarah told Chernig to go and wait for me at the stuss parlor. He didn't want to leave, seeing his dreams fluttering away, but she made him go, whispering something to him, and then closed the door and we were alone. I didn't know what to expect, being only fourteen although looking twenty.

"Such a handsome young man," she said in Yiddish, making eyes at me and coming up to put her hands on my cheeks. She had no trouble with me at all, and less than an hour later I left the place with the film in a package and memories of her muscles and the things she did to me in my mind. It was quite an experience, and the film only cost me twenty dollars after very little haggling. I went home to my boardinghouse and hid the film under my mattress. The next day I went back to the stuss parlor at my usual time, and Morton Chernig was there, his mustache up on one side and down on the other. His eyes had a worried look but his mouth looked mean. He sat down next to me.

"What happened?"

"The film is mine."

"You bought it from her? For how much?"

"None of your business."

"What's going on here? I thought we were partners."

"What do I need with a partner? Especially a broke one."

This is why he never got anywhere in life. He couldn't believe what I was saying. I purposely made it as tough on him as I could, because I had decided I could use him, not as a partner, but as the fellow who goes around telling the other fellows where the movie can be seen, what it is like, and how much. With such a picture, you don't put up signs.

"So I'm out in the cold," he said. He tipped his derby back and jammed his thumbs down into his vest pockets. "How do you like that?"

"You're entitled to something," I said. "After all, you did the arranging." I offered him a cigar.

The year before that the show people went on strike and a lot of theaters put in projectors and showed exclusively movies, so it was not difficult for me to pick up a used projector for seventy-two dollars and hire a fellow my own age to run it for fifty cents a night. I got the store from a man who owed me money and didn't bother with chairs. The only other expense was to take care of the police, and I let Morton Chernig handle that end of the business. I was not even slightly tempted to copper my bet by getting Chernig to sign a note; even then I had complete faith in the movies if only they were interesting to the public.

I had seen the movie before we opened for business. Three heavy-looking young tomatoes wearing nothing but ballet shoes and ribbons in their hair. They worked in front of a black curtain and kept disappearing and reappearing, which was trick photography. The film had been hand-tinted and must have been very expensive to make, even in France. I stayed completely away from the place after we opened, and it was not to be known that I owned it. A fellow who worked for me took the money, twenty cents per customer, paid the projectionist and Chernig and brought the rest to me.

In six months I had made a six-hundred-dollar profit and business was beginning to lag. I think every boy and man from the age of nine to twenty-five in the entire island of Manhattan had seen the picture twice by then, and it was time to either close up or find something else. Many people had come to me with propositions regarding the theater business in the meantime, since it was impossible for me to keep it secret that I owned the place. Consequently, at the age of fifteen I opened my second theater, just exactly like the first one, in a store in Brooklyn, and took the movie over there, but before that, I had my first experience as a maker of motion pictures.

I had been visiting Sarah Greenglass on and off for the whole six months, and, frankly, she and her husband were living off the money I gave her. I will confess to the fact that I loved her in a puppy-love way and that it came as a great shock and disappointment to learn that Manny was not her brother but her husband. And a very stupid man. He knew what was going on and he pretended to me that he didn't, and would come and see me at the stuss parlor, and ask me to back him in schemes. Always the heavy-handed hints about his *sister*, and how it would be too bad if they had to go out West to get any bookings. Sarah was much the smarter of the two, yet in retrospect I can say that she was a stupid woman, or she could have cleaned me out. In a sexual way she was quite an experience, and knew a number of tricks that even on the street I hadn't heard about, even though she was only three or four years older than me. Her big trouble was that she had the small-time schemer mind, and could not see past tomorrow. She would consider it an accomplishment to spend two or three days working on a scheme to steal five dollars. She even tried it on me, once. I think it was her idea, and not Manny's. I don't think Manny had enough brains for even such a stupid scheme.

I was in her room with my clothes off one night, about eight o'clock, and she was naked, too, lying on the bed. I was about to join her when Manny breaks into the room and starts shouting about me screwing his wife (I never had let them know I knew about their true relationship) and how he was going to call the law down on me for committing an act of adultery. Then she joins in and starts screaming at him, and he says he has had enough, he is going to call the cops, and she turns to me and says, "For God's sake pay him off, do something, or we'll be exposed!" Then it was supposed to be my turn. This was even then an old racket called "The Badger Game" and why they thought I would go for it is beyond me. I felt like laughing at them. I could have forced the issue by calling a cop myself and having Manny arrested, but already I had decided that it might be interesting to make use of them, and so instead I taught them a small lesson. I took all the money out of my pants pocket, counted it, and gave it to Manny, about thirty-five or forty dollars. You should have seen his eyes light up at the sight of the money. I guess Manny couldn't find a gun to use, because the way the racket is supposed to go, you wave a gun around and threaten to shoot everybody. But I gave the money and left, and then got in touch with an employee of mine and instructed him to get the money back, and be careful not to hurt Manny too much. He brought me the money in less than an hour.

A couple of days later I sent a kid to bring Manny to me at the stuss parlor. He showed up walking kind of stiff, but no marks on his face. He was a handsome fellow, with dark hair and eyes and skin, and just looking at him you would never know he was scared stiff. He just looked thoughtful, as if maybe he had to go to the dentist that afternoon.

"You and Sarah were going to leave town?" I asked him.

"Whatever you say."

"It figures. You needed getaway money, and you thought to take it from me. Why didn't you just ask me? Am I a friend of the *family* or not?"

"Aw, don't rub it in. We make a mistake, that's all."

"A terrible mistake. You should have come to me. As it happens, I have a method for you to earn a considerable amount of money, plenty enough to go as far away as San Francisco or Denver, which, by the way, might not be a bad idea. The South Pole would be even better, but I'll settle for the West."

"What's your proposition?"

"You know, it's a good thing you tried to crook me after all. Now we are all business, and none of this friendship stuff to get in the way. My proposition is simply this: I am going to make a moving picture myself. What I need is a couple actors to play the leading roles. The pay is fifty dollars apiece, and the job lasts one day tops. How does that strike you?"

He couldn't believe it. I think throughout the negotiations he was half sure I would have him beat up again after I paid him. But finally we got down to the crucial part of the conversation, in which I explained to him the nature of the movie I had in mind. "Fellows will pay good money to see some naked women running around," I said. "And you can imagine what they would also pay to see an act of sexual intercourse. Especially one full of tricks. You and Sarah are acrobats as well as Spanish dancers, it ought to be a very interesting movie."

I halfway expected him to look at me with hatred in his eyes, but he didn't. All he said was, "Fifty dollars?"

"Apiece," I stressed. "Your job will be to explain to Sarah."

"We have to get out of town," he said. "I can't stand it around here not working."

"I know just how you feel."

"We could get bookings in Kansas if we could get there," he said.

"Kansas would be fine," I said.

The cameraman was a young fellow no more than thirty who had inherited some money from his family and then spent it all on equipment and making a couple of movies, which he sold outright for less than it cost to make them. His name was Nargosian and he was very intense. He had his studio on a rooftop on Perry Street and that is where we made the movie. It took us half an hour to clear the junk out of his room and set up the black drapes all around, and while we did this Manny and Sarah sat out on the roof huddled together talking. We set it up so the camera was mostly hidden behind the drapes, giving them the appearance of being alone. Nargosian dragged in his own mattress from the next room, and covered it with a sheet and a shawl, and we called in the actors. I explained to them: "You just stand in there beside the mattress and take off your clothes and then lay down and start doing your tricks. Nargosian will be behind the drapes, and when he shouts at you, you do what he says, but don't look at the camera."

Nargosian said, "From time to time I'll ask you to stop, to change film or move the camera. Just stop cold and don't move. Just like the game of freeze, okay?"

"Boy, I don't feel like it," Manny said. He looked cold.

"What does it take to get you in the mood?" I said.

"I knew that would be a problem," Nargosian said.

"That can be part of the act," Sarah said. She didn't look at me at all. "Me getting him hot. How about that?"

They started to work and I went out on the roof. To tell the truth, I didn't feel any too good. I had not quite gotten her out of my system as yet and it made me a little sick to think of what was going on in there. I sat by the edge of the roof, looking five stories down to Perry Street, to all the little people. I could just hear the sound of the horses' hoofs on the pavement, and hear some kids yelling. Pigeons went up from a roof close by and I watched them go up and circle and fly away toward the Hudson River. There was a ledge around the edge of the roof, and I had my hands on top of it, holding on. I felt about a hundred years old. I tried to think about how much money I had in the bank, but I couldn't remember the exact amount. I took the money out of my pocket and counted it a couple of times, feeling pretty foolish. It was quite a sum of money, all I was going to pay for the making of the movie. A couple of hundred dollars, in the big bills like they don't make any more. I folded it double and put it back in my pants pocket. For some reason, I felt nauseous, and before I could stop myself, I puked over the edge of the building. I opened my eyes just in time to see it falling. It didn't land on anybody's head, but I saw some people start sideways, and the black dots showed a spot of white as they looked up toward me. I ducked and laughed, holding onto my knees. Then I went in and washed my face.

Some days later Nargosian sends for me to come up to his studio. He tries to act calm but his eyes are all lighted up. It is raining and I can hear the sound of it out on the roof while we stand in the dark room watching the final product. The movie lasted about six minutes and was very funny. Also, it was very carnal. I had never before watched people committing acts of sexual intercourse, and I have to admit that to a person my age it was like a tonic. Nargosian pulled back the curtains and let the gray light in.

"What do you think?" he asked me.

"Is that all?"

"Isn't it *enough*?"

"It took you three hours to make five minutes?"

He explained to me that he had to take lots more pictures than ended up in the movie. "A lot of it didn't work," he said.

"I paid for all of it, let me see it," I said, and we spent the rest of the afternoon looking over the stuff he had cut out. He had whole boxes full of it, not on reels, just laying there. Finally I said to him, "Put it together, any whichway, in five-minute reels. Then we have lots of shows."

"But it's just *junk*." He was upset. He ran his hands through his hair and begged me to not make him do it. I convinced him that since I paid for all of it, it was all mine. The upshot was that I had not one five- or six-minute film, but ten of them, some better than others, I'll admit, from an artistic standpoint, but at that time I was not much interested in artistry. I had another scheme. The good one I booked into my own theater, and the other ones I sent on the road with a fellow to sell other theater owners around the country, realizing a profit of something better than seven hundred dollars net just from that part. The good film showed at my place for three months, and then the old film, the one I sent over to Brooklyn, finally fell apart from too much splicing and burning, and I sent the good one over there, where it suffered the same fate in a few months. We were charging fifty cents to watch this particular movie, and so the audiences were somewhat smaller and older.

Through Nargosian I met a lot of fellows who were making movies. They would come to me naturally for money because even then it was a very expensive proposition to make a movie, although nothing like it is now. I did not think it was a safe proposition to go on making blue movies, and I also did not think there was going to be the money in it that there was in other forms of movies, but that was not really what got me out of the blue-movie business into the legitimate, not then. As a matter of fact, it was a thing we called later "Glamour," where a young fellow like myself could meet show-business people, especially girls. Once I got interested in girls I stayed interested for a long time, and it was always a search for the perfect girl of the moment, one who liked her sex and was beautiful and you could take her out in public. I knew that one way you could influence those girls to be co-operative was to give them gifts, but I was still a very careful person with a dollar, and I thought it would be more in keeping to attract the girls with something more substantial for both of us. I am not talking about putting them in the movies, that came much later on. I am talking about theaters wherein entertainers would perform. At that time, the good acts and the good theaters around the country were locked up by a handful of outfits centered in New York City, and I was young enough to think that with my pitiful amount of capital I could crack the combine. In the back of my mind it was always show girls, and maybe that was what clouded my thinking on this subject. So I wasted a lot of time midtown, which was not a complete waste because I got to know some people who turned out to be very useful to me. I wanted to back a play but I didn't have enough money, and I wanted to break into vaudeville on the ownership side of the fence but this was impossible. It was no wonder then, and I am not taking credit for being a genius, only a desperate young man, that I finally listened to Nargosian and his friends, some of whom being nice fellows were living off loans from me that frankly I never expected to see again.

The proposition was a simple one: we would make a short movie that was actually a play, with a plot and everything. There is a lot of talk in the history books about this idea, not just ours, but that movie about the train robbery and the one about the fire, which all came out at about the same time, but the talk is all about the cutting technique and the use of the close-up shot and other technical matters, which I left up to Nargosian and his friends, while I concentrated on the most important part. They wanted to make a movie like the kind of plays that were popular at that time, the plays of Dion What's-his-name, with the train about to run over the girl and the villain closing down the mortgage, but that was too difficult to do without words, so what we did was a nice short thing called *The Rescue*, where a girl falls off a ferryboat and nobody notices except a fellow on the shore. I must admit the cutting was interesting. They would show the girl and then the people on the boat not noticing and then the girl again, and then the fellow on shore, cutting back and forth until you are jumping out of your seat, and the fellow finally takes a rowboat and goes out and jumps in and saves her. Nargosian was so excited he couldn't stand it, because he didn't know what he had until he developed the pictures and edited them together, and then he went half crazy wondering if anybody else would see it the way he saw it, that is to say, suspenseful and exciting. I did. I was thrilled half to death.

It was expensive, but I had Nargosian make a number of prints, and then I went out on the road. I did not sell the prints, I rented them, and in the space of a year's time, I had made something like twenty-eight thousand dollars net. The picture cost me three hundred to make. There was no question in my mind that there was money in the movies. When I got back to New York Nargosian was gone, off to Europe someplace; I never heard of him again, but I still had many acquaintances in the picture-making business, and I bought outright a number of short feature films, some good, some awful, and went back out on the road. This time I did not rent or sell, I bought. I bought a theater in Portland, Maine, that is to say, I bought a store front, some chairs, equipment, a big sign, ads in the local papers, and opened a theater in direct competition to the existing theatrical enterprises, and mine made money because I had the good movies. Opening night was closed to the public, only the local civic leaders invited, free, and I gave a little speech before the show outlining how my place of business was going to help progress and art. I got a fellow in New York to write the speech for me, for two dollars. It was a good speech. After opening night the place did a fine business, and I hired a manager in the person of a young man recommended by the mayor of the town, and moved on. The same story, or practically, everywhere I went. In a couple of places I found something interesting: the person who owned the one local movie house would have his friends on the city council pass a law there could only be one movie house in town. In the first one, I opened my place in a sort of barn outside the city limits, did my advertising, invited the local nabobs and everything. On the second night the public came, a mean-looking bunch of men, and they tore my place apart. I got beat up, too, but it didn't bother me much, because I was too busy thinking about how to handle the situation. The best way, I decided, was to bypass the place and wait until I got back to New York. Before that I ran into another town with the one-movie-house ordinance, and I didn't even bother to try.

Back in New York I checked around to see where these people got their films. Neither of them had agents in the city. They would write to the film companies and rent their films in that manner. There were only a few companies, and I got a lawyer and signed contracts with them giving me one-year exclusive showing rights, in exchange for a higher percentage of the box-office receipts. These were very complicated agreements and I had to limit them to the two towns in question because the film companies weren't that crazy, but when I went back to these towns nobody objected to my opening my movie houses, because it was no longer a violation of the ordinance. The existing houses, by the time I got there, were showing stuff people had been tired of for years, and they were glad to sell to me. I booked my own pictures, and therefore did not have to lay out a cent on the contracts I had made with the New York companies, except for the fee I paid my lawyer.

I should say that before I went on the road in the first place I changed my name and got completely out of the sharking business. In New York I now lived midtown and never went below Sixteenth Street for anything whatsoever. I might add that with the passage of time, those people who ran the booking combine for vaudeville, who wouldn't let me in on it, or anybody else, for that matter, dried up and blew away. It was of great satisfaction to me.

There is one awful thing that happened in this particular period that made me feel sad. Sarah and Manny Greenglass were doing small towns in the Pacific Northwest when a very bad coincidence occurred. The blue movie they starred in was showed at a policeman and fireman smoker while they were doing their Spanish dancer act in this little town, and they were recognized and arrested. Manny got beat up pretty bad, and I would rather not know what happened to Sarah. The way I found out about it was that Sarah sent me a telegram to my New York office, using my new name, Max Meador, begging for money to get away from that town and buy Manny out of the jail, where he would die if he didn't get treatment. I sent her a thousand dollars care of Western Union San Francisco, and a hundred dollars care of Western Union in the town she was in. Don't ask me why. And for a long time I expected to hear from one or another of them with a blackmail demand or something of the sort, but I never did. I never heard of them again. I wonder where they are now? Probably dead.

Everything I did somebody else did, either before me or after me. The gold in the movies was easy to see. Some went into production, some went into distribution, and some like me went into exhibiting, with a little producing and distributing on the side. It was easy to see if you made your own pictures and distributed them to yourself and exhibited them yourself, the profits would be immense and the number of middlemen small. I did what I could. So did thousands of other young fellows. The competition was very fierce and there was many a time when I would be lying in a hotel bed without any sleep wishing I could get off the merry-go-round, especially times when I would come into a town where I had a theater and discover my manager had been cheating me and I would have to go to all kinds of trouble not to get ahead but just to stay even.

Here is what a lot of people would not understand, and it is the same thing that knocked off a lot of the competition early in the game. When you got everything you ever wanted, why don't you quit? A lot of fellows are after money, and so when they get together quite a pile of it, they retire from the business. With me I can say honestly that it was money only in the very beginning, and I sometimes wonder if it was money even then. Maybe it was fear even then. The glamour part wasn't what it was supposed to be. Once it was a big thrill to me to be around show-business people who had their names in the paper all the time and wore the beautiful clothes and so forth, but after you start dating show girls you wonder what you are going to do for some conversation, as all they talk about is themselves or show business. Also I know that somewhere down inside of me I wanted to build a family and be in the middle of it, but also I hated my own family and wanted no part of them, which is probably why I married late. It was a long time before I had occasion to meet nice family-type girls. And power. It didn't take me long to find out, for example, that a lot of girls would go to bed with me not because they thought they could get something out of me in the way of a job or cash money, but because they wanted some of my power. I can't find any other way to explain it. This power meant nothing to me, because so far in my life every time somebody pulled a shit trick on me, I pulled one right back on them but only if it was to my advantage to do so.

But underneath it all was the fear. I could not stop. There was something inside me telling me, "You stop now, you end up back on the Lower East Side cutting throats for nickels." I knew it wasn't true, but a person's feelings are not subject to the control of the mind. I used to wonder who I was. Everywhere I went outside New York City people would laugh behind their hands at the way I talked. For a while I tried to fix this up so I talked different, but that didn't work, and so after a while I talked like myself, only more so, and especially when I would be doing business with somebody who didn't like Jews and could not hide his feelings. It go to be a mask I could sit behind. I got to see other things, too, in little towns outside Chicago, St. Louis, and such places, where there were kids my own age playing baseball without a thought to the future, and green grass and trees on streets with houses on them, where people lived one family to a house. I used to think when I would get mad about this that I could buy and sell most of these people, but it was not a thought that could console me for long. I was hungry for that kind of life even though I knew I could not personally stand it.

So one day I am out in Los Angeles where I had a hand in a company producing pictures. They are shooting scenes on a beach near Malibu, and I am walking along the sand by myself, dressed in a business suit with a vest, feeling the sun and the wind come in off the ocean and wondering why the Pacific doesn't smell like the Atlantic, and I look around and I have gone over a hill of sand and can't see a single human being. I take off my coat and vest and sit down in the sand and watch the water come and go. It hisses in the sand, and I listen to that for a while. I feel at peace. Not a cloud in the sky. I pick up a seashell laying in the sand, and it is one that I recognize. A sand dollar. Even on the beach I am picking up dollars. I feel all black inside, like a man suddenly knows he is going to die. The blackness goes on for quite a while. I see my whole life, and it is ugly. My whole youth is gone scratching for dollars. I have no friends, no family. People laugh at me, but they are afraid. More blackness. I want to write a letter to my grandfather or my mother and beg them to forgive me. But in the blackness I can see that it would do no good. It would not mean anything to them and it would not mean anything to me. A cry in the dark, that's all. I think about God, and that don't do any good. I can't believe. I see kids kill each other for fifteen cents. More blackness. The face of God I can see in my mind turns away from me, not me from it. The inside of my mouth tastes all coppery, and I think not for the first time of killing myself and letting it all go. But I go past that. It would do no good.

Out of it all, I get a bad sunburn on the forehead and a resolve to get out of the exhibition business. The next day I cancel some meetings with production people and instead have a meeting with Karl M. Brannaman, a man who owns one hundred and sixty theaters. After two weeks of meetings and talks with lawyers we become partners, merging our theater operations under the name MBPC, with Brannaman as president. He handles the theaters, and I oversee the production of pictures. The year is 1915 and I am twenty-eight years old. I think the struggle is over, but of course it is just beginning. Ask my son.

Questions

1. Describe the narrator. In what ways does the reader's view of the narrator differ from his view of himself? Whose opinion is more valid?

2. Technique is an important factor in this story. For instance, point of view is skillfully used, for the narrator is made to reveal much more to the reader than he thinks he is revealing. Cite some instances where the reader's knowledge exceeds that of the speaker, Max Meador, himself. What ironies are revealed by this technique?

3. The story appears to be largely the chronicle of a life—a kind of expanded autobiographical sketch. What else is it? What judgments of its central character are made? What themes does it incorporate? In particular, what does it imply about the price of success and the compromises by which it is obtained?

4. Describe the conflict that emerges between father and son—more specifically, between their conflict of values. What is the basis of the father's complaint? What accounts for the differing aims of father and son? Is it only a matter of a generation gap?

Anton Chekhov

ANNA ON THE NECK

In both fiction and drama Chekhov is identified with a kind of artless simplicity, an apparent inclination to let the story tell itself. His output—half a dozen major plays and several short ones, and more than six hundred stories—has been great. However, his work is always found to exhibit total control of the artist over his material, and every detail is found to be necessary. This discipline is perhaps his most striking feature; "conciseness is the sister of talent," he once said, and his work is an object lesson in how to achieve the greatest effects with the minimum means. Chekhov was born in Russia in 1860, son of a grocer, and studied medicine at Moscow University. He began practicing medicine and writing at about the same time, and combined the two careers throughout the rest of his brief life, despite his failing health. In both careers he leavened the detachment of the medical scientist with strong humanitarian feelings. His stories came first, and then, at the end of his life, the plays that have become standard in the modern repertory: The Sea Gull *(1896),* Uncle Vanya *(1899),* The Three Sisters *(1901), and* The Cherry Orchard *(1904). He died in 1904 at a health resort in Germany where he had gone for a cure.*

The essence of Chekhov's style is his wistful-ironic view of life and his sympathy for well-intentioned but ineffectual persons. His characters are often aristocrats who have fallen on hard times, charming and well-mannered but no longer useful or productive. Their lives often consist of memories of the past or plans for the future rather than of present actions. "Anna on the Neck" (sometimes translated "An Anna Round Her Neck") relates Chekhov's sympathetic but unsentimental view of his characters.

After the ceremony not even light refreshments were served; the bride and groom each drank a glass of wine, changed their clothes, and drove to the station. Instead of having a gay ball and supper, instead of music and dancing, they traveled a hundred and fifty miles to perform their devotions at a shrine. Many people commended this, saying that Modest Alexeich had already reached a high rank in the service and was no longer young, and that a noisy wedding might not have seemed quite proper; and besides, music is likely to sound dreary when a fifty-two-year-old official marries a girl who has just turned eighteen. It was also said that Modest Alexeich, being a man of principle, had really arranged this visit to the monastery in order to make it clear to his young bride that in marriage, too, he gave the first place to religion and morality.

The couple were seen off by relatives and the groom's colleagues. The crowd stood, with the glasses in their hands, waiting to shout "hurrah" as soon as the train should start, and the bride's father, Pyotr Leontyich, in a top hat and the dress coat of a schoolmaster, already drunk and very pale, kept craning toward the window, glass in hand, and saying imploringly, "Anyuta! Anya, Anya! Just one word!"

Anya leaned out of the window toward him and he whispered something to her, enveloping her in a smell of alcohol and blowing into her ear—she could understand nothing—and made the sign of the cross over her face, her bosom, and her hands. His breathing came in gasps and tears shone in his eyes. And Anya's brothers, Petya and Andrusha, schoolboys, pulled at his coattails from behind, whispering embarrassedly: "Papa dear, enough . . . Papa dear, don't—"

When the train started, Anya saw her father run a little way after the coach, staggering and spilling his wine, and what a pitiful, kindly, guilty face he had! "Hurrah!" he shouted.

The couple were left alone. Modest Alexeich looked about the compartment, arranged their things on the shelves, and sat down opposite his young wife, smiling. He was an official of medium height, rather stout, who looked bloated and very well fed and wore Dundreary whiskers. His clean-shaven, round, sharply outlined chin looked like a heel. The most characteristic thing about his face was the absence of a mustache, this bare, freshly shaven spot which gradually passed into fat cheeks that quivered like jelly. His demeanor was dignified, his movements unhurried, his manners suave.

"At the moment I cannot help recalling one circumstance," he said smiling. "When, five years ago, Kosorotov received the order of St. Anna of the second class, and came to thank His Excellency for the honor, His Excellency expressed himself thus: 'So now you have three Annas: one in your buttonhole and two on your neck.' I must tell you that at that time Kosorotov's wife, a quarrelsome person of a giddy disposition, had just returned to him and that her name was Anna. I trust that when I receive the Anna of the second class, His Excellency will have no cause to say the same thing to me."

He smiled with his small eyes. And she, too, smiled, troubled by the thought that at any moment this man might kiss her with his full, moist lips and that she no longer had the right to prevent him from doing so. The soft movements of his bloated body frightened her; she felt both terrified and disgusted. He got up without haste, took the order off his neck, took off his dress coat and waistcoat and put on his dressing-gown. "That's better," he said, sitting down beside Anya.

She remembered what agony the marriage ceremony had been, when it had seemed to her that the priest, the guests, and everyone in the church had looked at her sadly: why was she, such a sweet, nice girl, marrying an elderly uninteresting man? Only that morning she had been in raptures over the fact that everything had been satisfactorily arranged, but during the ceremony and now in the railway carriage, she felt guilty, cheated, and ridiculous. Here she had married a rich man and yet she had no money. Her wedding dress had been bought on credit, and just now when her father and brothers had been saying good-by, she could see from their faces that they had not a kopeck to their name. Would they have any supper tonight? And tomorrow? And for some reason it seemed to her that her father and the boys without her were suffering from hunger and feeling as miserable as they did the day after their mother's funeral. "Oh, how unhappy I am," she thought. "Why am I so unhappy?"

With the awkwardness of a man of dignified habits who is unaccustomed to dealing with women, Modest Alexeich touched her on the waist and patted her on the shoulder while she thought of money, of her mother, and her mother's death. When her mother died, her father, a high school teacher of calligraphy and drawing, had taken to drink and they had begun to feel the pinch of poverty; the boys had no shoes or galoshes. Time and again her father was hauled before the justice of the peace, the process-server came and made an inventory of the furniture . . . What a disgrace! Anya had to look after her drunken father, darn her brothers' socks, do the marketing, and when she was complimented on her beauty, her youth, and her elegant manner, it seemed to her that the whole world was looking at her cheap hat and the holes in her shoes that were inked over. And at night there were tears and the disturbing persistent thought that soon, very soon, her father would be dismissed from the school for his failing and that he would not be able to endure it and would die like their mother. But then some ladies they knew had bestirred themselves and started looking about for a good match for Anya. This Modest Alexeich, who was neither young nor good-looking but had money, was soon found. He had 100,000 in the bank and a family estate which he rented to a tenant. He was a man of principle and was in favor with His Excellency; it would be very easy for him, Anya was told, to get a note from His Excellency to the high school principal or even to the trustee, and Pyotr Leontyich would not be dismissed . . .

While she was recalling these details, strains of music together with a sound of voices suddenly burst in at the window. The train had stopped at a small station. On the other side of the platform in the crowd an accordion and a cheap squeaky fiddle were being played briskly, and from beyond the tall birches and poplars and the small cottages that were flooded with moonlight came the sound of a military band: there must have been a dance in the place. Summer visitors and townspeople who came here by train in fine weather for a breath of fresh air were promenading on the platform. Among them was the owner of all the summer cottages, Artynov, a man of wealth. Tall, stout, black-haired, with prominent eyes, he looked like an Armenian. He wore a strange costume: an unbuttoned shirt that left his chest bare, high boots with spurs, and a black cloak which hung from his shoulders and trailed on the ground. Two borzois followed him with their sharp muzzles to the ground.

Tears were still glistening in Anya's eyes, but she was now no longer thinking of her mother or money or her marriage. She was shaking hands with high school boys and officers of her acquaintance, laughing gaily and saying quickly, "How do you do? How are you?"

She went out into the moonlight and stood so that they could all see her in her new splendid costume and hat.

"Why are we stopping here?" she asked.

"This is a siding. They are waiting for the mail train to pass."

Noticing that Artynov was looking at her, she screwed up her face coquettishly and began talking aloud in French; and because her voice sounded so well and because music was heard and the moon was reflected in the pond, and because Artynov, the notorious Don Juan and rake, was looking at her greedily and inquisitively, and because everyone was gay, she suddenly felt happy, and when the train started, and her friends the officers saluted her, she was humming a polka, the strains of which reached her from the military band which was blaring somewhere beyond the trees; and she returned to her compartment feeling as if she had been persuaded at the station that she would certainly be happy in spite of everything.

The couple spent two days at the monastery, then returned to town. They lived in an apartment supplied by the government. When Modest Alexeich left for the office, Anya would play the piano or cry out of sheer boredom or lie down on a couch and read novels or look through fashion journals. At dinner Modest Alexeich ate a great deal, talked about politics, new appointments, transfers and bonuses, and declared that one should work hard, that family life was not a pleasure but a duty, that if you took care of the kopecks, the rubles would take care of themselves, and that he put religion and morality above everything else in the world. And holding the knife in his fist like a sword, he would say:

"Everyone must have his duties!"

And Anya listened to him, was frightened, and could not eat, so that she usually rose from the table hungry. After dinner her husband took a nap and snored loudly while she went to see her own people. Her father and the boys looked at her in a peculiar way, as if just before she came they had been blaming her for having married for money a tedious, tiresome man whom she did not love. Her rustling skirts, her bracelets, and her general ladylike air made them uncomfortable, offended them. In her presence they felt a little embarrassed and did not know what to talk about; but they still loved her as before and were not used to having dinner without her. She sat down with them to cabbage soup, thick porridge, and potatoes fried in mutton fat that smelled of tallow candles. With a trembling hand Pyotr Leontyich filled his glass from a decanter and drank it off quickly, greedily, with disgust, then drank a second glass, then a third. Petya and Andrusha, thin, pale boys with big eyes, would take the decanter and say with embarrassment:

"You mustn't, Papa dear . . . Enough, Papa dear."

Anya, too, was troubled and would beg him to drink no more; and he would suddenly fly into a rage and strike the table with his fist. "I will not be dictated to!" he would shout. "Wretched boys! Wretched girl! I will turn you all out!"

But there was a note of weakness, of kindness in his voice, and no one was afraid of him. After dinner he usually spruced himself up. Pale, with cuts on his chin from shaving, he would stand for half an hour before the mirror, craning his thin neck, preening himself, combing his hair, twisting his black mustache, sprinkling himself with scent, tying his cravat in a bow; then he would put on his gloves and his top hat and would go off to give private lessons. If there was a holiday, he would stay at home and paint or play the harmonium, which hissed and growled; he would try to wrest melodious tones from it and would storm at the boys: "Scamps! Wretches! They have spoiled the instrument!"

Evenings Anya's husband played cards with his colleagues who lived under the same roof in the government quarters. During these parties the wives of the functionaries would also assemble—homely, tastelessly dressed women, as coarse as cooks, and gossip, as ugly and insipid as the women themselves, would start in the apartment. Sometimes Modest Alexeich would take Anya to the theater. During the intermissions he would not let her go a step from his side but walked about arm in arm with her through the corridors and the foyer. When he bowed to anyone, he immediately whispered to Anya: "A councilor of state . . . received by His Excellency," or "A man of means . . . has a house of his own." When they passed the buffet Anya had a great longing for sweets; she was fond of chocolate and apple tarts, but she had no money and she did not like to ask her husband. He would take a pear, feel it with his fingers, and ask uncertainly, "How much?"

"Twenty-five kopecks."

"I say!" he would exclaim and put the pear back, but as it was awkward to leave the buffet without buying anything, he would order a bottle of soda water and drink it all himself, and tears would come into his eyes. At such times Anya hated him.

Or suddenly turning quite red, he would say to her hurriedly: "Bow to that old lady!"

"But I am not acquainted with her–"

"No matter. That is the wife of the director of the local treasury office! Bow to her, I mean you," he said grumbling insistently. "Your head won't fall off."

Anya bowed and her head really didn't fall off, but it was very painful. She did everything her husband told her to do, and was very angry with herself that she had let herself be deceived like the silliest fool. She had married him only for his money, and yet she had less money now than before her marriage. Formerly her father would sometimes give her a twenty-kopeck piece, but now she never had a groat. To take money on the quiet or to ask for it, she couldn't; she was afraid of her husband. She trembled before him. It seemed to her as though she had been afraid of him for a long time. In her childhood the high school principal had always seemed to her the most imposing and terrible power in the world, moving along like a thundercloud or a steam locomotive ready to crush everything in its way. Another such power of which they often talked at home, and which for some reason they feared, was His Excellency. Then, there were a dozen other, less formidable powers, and among them were the high school teachers, strict and impeccable, with shaven upper lip. And now finally, it was Modest Alexeich, a man of principle, who resembled the head of the school in every particular, including his face. And in Anya's imagination, all these powers combined into one, and, in the shape of a terrible, huge white bear, bore down upon the weak and guilty, such as her father. And she was afraid to contradict her husband, and with a forced smile and a show of pleasure, submitted to his coarse caresses and defiling embraces which terrified her.

Only once did Pyotr Leontyich make bold to ask his son-in-law for a loan of fifty rubles in order to pay a very unpleasant debt, but what agony it was!

"Very well, I'll give you the money," said Modest Alexeich after a moment's thought, "but I warn you, I won't help you again until you stop drinking. Such a weakness is disgraceful in a man holding a government post! I cannot refrain from calling your attention to the well-known fact that many able people have been ruined by that passion, though temperance might perhaps have permitted them to attain a very high rank."

Followed long-winded sentences with such phrases as, "in proportion to," "whereas," "in view of the aforesaid," while poor Pyotr Leontyich was in an agony of humiliation and felt an intense craving for alcohol.

And when the boys came to visit Anya, generally in worn shoes and threadbare trousers, they too had to listen to lectures.

"Everyone must have his duties!" Modest Alexeich would say to them. But he would not give them money. To Anya, he would give rings, bracelets, brooches, saying that these things would come in handy on a rainy day. And he often unlocked her chest of drawers to see if they were all safe.

II

Meanwhile the cold season arrived. Before Christmas it was announced in the local newspaper that the usual winter ball would take place on December 29 in the Hall of the Nobility. Every evening after the card-playing, Modest Alexeich was excitedly conferring in whispers with his colleagues' wives and glancing anxiously at Anya, and afterwards he paced the room from corner to corner for a long time, thinking. At last, late one evening he stood before Anya and said, "You must have a ball dress made for yourself. Do you understand? Only, please consult Marya Grigoryevna and Natalya Kuzminishna."

And he gave her one hundred rubles. She took the money but didn't consult anyone when she ordered the gown. She spoke to no one but her father and tried to imagine how her mother would have dressed for the ball. Her mother had always dressed in the latest fashion and had always taken great pains with Anya, fitting her out elegantly like a doll, and had taught her to speak French and dance the mazurka magnificently (she had been a governess for five years prior to her marriage). Like her mother, Anya could make a new dress out of an old one, clean gloves with benzine, hire jewelry and, like her mother, she knew how to screw up her eyes, speak with a burr, strike pretty poses, fly into ecstasies when necessary and assume a sad and enigmatic air. And from her father she inherited dark hair and eyes, sensitive nerves, and the habit of always trying to look her best.

When, half an hour before they had to start for the ball, Modest Alexeich went into her room coatless to put his order round his neck in front of her mirror, he was so struck by her beauty and the splendor of her crisp gauzy attire, that he combed his side-whiskers complacently and said, "So that's how my wife can look . . . So that's how you can look!" And he went on, suddenly assuming a tone of solemnity, "Anyuta, I have made you happy, and tonight you can make me happy. I beg you to get yourself introduced to His Excellency's spouse. Do it for me, for God's sake! Through her I may get the post of senior reporting secretary."

They drove to the ball. There it was, the Hall of the Nobility, the lobby and the stately doorman. The vestibule was full of hangers, fur coats, footmen scurrying about and décolleté ladies putting up their fans to protect themselves from the draft; the place smelled of illuminating gas and soldiers.

When Anya, walking up the stairs on her husband's arm, heard the music and saw herself full-length in the huge pier glass glowing with numberless lights, her heart leapt with joy and with that presentiment of happiness which she had experienced in the moonlight at the station. She walked in proudly, confidently, for the first time feeling herself not a little girl but a lady, and unwittingly imitating her late mother's gait and manners. And for the first time in her life, she felt rich and free. Even her husband's presence did not embarrass her, for as she crossed the threshold of the hall she had guessed instinctively that the proximity of her elderly husband did not humiliate her in the least, but on the contrary, gave her that touch of piquant mystery that is so attractive to men.

In the ballroom the orchestra was already thundering, and dancing had already begun. After their apartment, Anya, overwhelmed by the lights, the bright colors, the music, the din, looked round the hall and thought: "Oh, how lovely!" and instantly spotted in the crowd all her acquaintances, everyone she had met before at parties or at picnics, all these officers, teachers, lawyers, officials, landowners. His Excellency, too, was there, and Artynov, and society ladies in low-neck dresses, the pretty ones and the ugly. These were already taking up positions in the booths and pavilions of the charity bazaar, ready to begin selling things for the benefit of the poor. A huge officer with shoulder-straps—she had been introduced to him when she was a schoolgirl and now could not remember his name—loomed up before her, as though he had sprung out of the ground and asked her for a waltz, and she flew away from her husband. She felt as though she were sailing in a boat during a violent storm, while her husband remained far away on the shore . . . She danced passionately, eagerly—waltzes, polkas, quadrilles—passing from one pair of arms to another, dizzy with the music and the hubbub, mixing Russian and French, speaking with a burr, laughing, and not giving a thought to her husband or anybody or anything. She scored a success with the men—that was clear and it couldn't have been otherwise. She was breathless with excitement, she squeezed her fan in her hand convulsively and felt thirsty. Her father in a crumpled coat that smelled of benzine came up to her offering her a saucer of pink ice cream.

"You are ravishing tonight," he said, looking at her enraptured, "and I have never so regretted that you were in such a hurry to get married . . . Why? I know you did it for our sake, but . . ." With a shaking hand, he drew out a roll of notes and said: "I got the money for lessons today, and can pay my debt to your husband."

She thrust the saucer back into his hand and, snatched by someone, was carried off far away. Over her partner's shoulder she caught a glimpse of her father gliding across the parquet putting his arm round a lady and whirling her down the hall.

"How charming he is when he is sober," she thought.

She danced the mazurka with the same huge officer. He moved gravely and heavily, like a lifeless carcass in uniform, twitching his shoulders and his chest, stamping his feet almost imperceptibly—he was loath to dance—while she fluttered round him, teasing him with her beauty, her bare neck. Her eyes glowed provokingly, her movements were passionate, while he grew more and more indifferent, and held out his hands to her graciously like a king.

"Bravo! Bravo!" people were exclaming in the crowd.

But little by little the huge officer, too, lost his composure; he came to life, grew excited, and yielding to her fascination, was carried away and danced lightly, youthfully, while she merely moved her shoulders and looked slyly at him as though she were now the queen and he were her slave. At that moment it seemed to her that the whole ballroom was looking at them, and that everyone was thrilled and envious of them.

The huge officer had hardly had time to thank her for the dance when the crowd suddenly parted and the men drew themselves up queerly and let their arms drop. It was His Excellency, with two stars on his dress coat, walking toward her. Yes, His Excellency was really walking toward her, for he was looking directly at her with a sugary smile and was chewing his lips as he always did when he saw pretty women.

"Delighted, delighted," he began, "I shall have your husband put under arrest for keeping such a treasure hidden from us till now. I have come to you with a commission from my wife," he went on, offering her his arm. "You must help us. M-m-yes . . . We ought to award you a prize for beauty as they do in America . . . M-m- yes . . . The Americans . . . My wife is waiting for you impatiently." He led her to a booth and presented her to an elderly lady, the lower part of whose face was disproportionately large, so that she looked as though she had a big stone in her mouth.

"You must help us," she said through her nose in a singsong voice. "All the pretty women are working for our charity bazaar, and for some reason, you alone are doing nothing. Why won't you help us?"

She went away and Anya took her place beside the silver samovar and the cups. She was soon doing a rushing business. Anya charged no less than a ruble for a cup of tea, and forced the huge officer to empty three cups. Artynov, the rich man with the bulging eyes, who suffered from asthma, came up too; he no longer wore the strange costume in which Anya had seen him in the summer at the station, but was in evening clothes like everyone else. Without taking his eyes off Anya, he drank a glass of champagne and paid one hundred rubles for it, then had a cup of tea and gave another hundred, all this without saying a word and wheezing with asthma. Anya solicited customers and got money out of them, firmly convinced by now that her smiles and glances could afford these people nothing but great pleasure. It had dawned upon her that she was made exclusively for this noisy, brilliant life, with laughter, music, dances, admirers, and her old dread of a power that was bearing down upon her and threatened to crush her now seemed ridiculous to her. She was afraid of no one and only regretted that her mother was not there to rejoice with her at her success. Her father, pale by this time, but still steady on his legs, came up to the booth and asked for a glass of cognac. Anya turned crimson, expecting him to say something inappropriate (she was already ashamed of having such a poor, ordinary father), but he emptied his glass, took a ten-ruble note from his roll, threw it down, and walked away with silent dignity. A little later she saw him dancing in the *grand rond* and by now he was staggering and kept calling out something, to his partner's great embarrassment. And Anya remembered how, at a ball three years before, he had staggered and called out in the same way, and it had ended by a police officer taking him home to bed, and the next day, the principal had threatened to dismiss him from his post. What an inappropriate recollection it was!

When the samovars in the booths were no longer alight and the weary charity workers had handed over their takings to the middle-aged lady with the stone in her mouth, Artynov led Anya on his arm to the hall where supper was being served for all who had helped at the bazaar.

There were some twenty people at supper, not more, but it was very noisy. His Excellency proposed this toast: "This luxurious dining room is the appropriate place in which to drink to the success of the soup kitchens for which the bazaar was held."

The Brigadier General proposed a toast "to the power to which even the artillery must bow," and all the men proceeded to clink glasses with the ladies. It was very, very jolly!

When Anya was escorted home, it was daylight and the cooks were going to market. Elated, intoxicated, full of new sensations, exhausted, she undressed, sank into bed and instantly fell asleep.

It was past one in the afternoon when the maid waked her and announced Mr. Artynov who had come to call on her. She dressed quickly and went into the drawing-room. Soon after Artynov left, His Excellency called to thank her for her part in the bazaar. Eyeing her with a sugary smile and chewing his lips, he kissed her hand, asked her permission to come again and took his leave, while she remained standing in the middle of the drawing room, amazed, entranced, unable to believe that a change in her life, a marvelous change, had occurred so quickly. And just then her husband walked in. He stood before her now with that ingratiating, sugary, cringingly respectful expression that she was accustomed to see on his face in the presence of the illustrious and the powerful, and with rapture, with indignation, with contempt, confident now that she could do it with impunity, she said, articulating each word distinctly:

"Get out, you blockhead!"

After that, Anya never had a single free day, as she was constantly taking part in picnics, excursions, private theatricals. Each day she returned home in the early hours of the morning and lay down on the floor in the drawing-room, and afterwards told everyone touchingly that she slept under flowers. She needed a great deal of money, but she was no longer afraid of Modest Alexeich, and spent his money as though it were her own; and she did not ask or demand it, but simply sent him the bills or brief notes like these: "Give the bearer 200 rubles," or "Pay 100 rubles at once."

At Easter Modest Alexeich received the order of St. Anna of the second class. When he went to offer his thanks, His Excellency put aside the newspaper he was reading and sank deeper into his armchair: "So now you have three Annas," he said, examining his white hands with their pink nails, "one in your buttonhole and two on your neck."

Modest Alexeich put two fingers to his lips as a precaution against laughing out loud and said: "Now I have only to look forward to the arrival of a little Vladimir. May I make bold to beg Your Excellency to stand godfather?"

He was alluding to the Vladimir of the fourth class and was already imagining how he would repeat everywhere this joke of his, so felicitous in its aptness and audacity, and he was making ready to say something equally good, but His Excellency was again absorbed in his newspaper and merely nodded to him.

And Anya went on driving about in troikas, hunting with Artynov, playing in one-acters, going out to supper parties, and she saw less and less of her own people. They dined alone now. Her father was drinking more heavily than ever; there was no money, and the harmonium had long since been sold for debt. The boys did not let him go out alone in the street now, but followed him for fear he might fall; and whenever they met Anya driving down Old Kiev Street in a smart carriage drawn by a team of two horses abreast and an outrunner, with Artynov on the box instead of a coachman, Pyotr Leontyich would take off his top hat, and would be about to shout something at her, but Petya and Andrusha would take him by the arms and say imploringly: "Don't, Papa dear . . . enough, Papa dear . . ."

Questions

1. "Anna on the Neck" is the simple story of a beautiful young girl who learns to use the power of her charms. Plot the steps Chekhov uses to make the change in Anya believable. Is this change considered acceptable?

2. With whom does Chekhov wish the reader to sympathize? How does he direct the reader's responses? Are there any wholly admirable characters?

3. How does Anya become an Anna? What is the hidden reference in the remark about the Vladimir? How do these puns add to the characterization of Modest Alexeich?

4. What is the relation of Alexeich's repeated remark about duties and Anya's action in the second part of the story? What other duties are suggested?

Julio Cortazar

BLOW-UP

The film version of "Blow-Up" made by the Italian director Michelangelo Antonioni in 1967 probably brought more attention to the work of Julio Cortazar than he had ever received before. It became a popular game, and the subject of much critical dispute, to figure out whether the photographer in the film had "really" witnessed a murder or only thought he had. Cortazar, however, had slowly been reaching an international audience, despite the perplexities and the dense texture of his work. Argentinian in descent, he was born in Brussels in 1914. He has lived and worked in Paris since 1952, but continues to write in Spanish. His most notable works in translation are two novels, The Winners *(1965) and* Hopscotch *(1966), and a collection,* End of the Game and Other Stories *(1967), from which "Blow-Up" is taken.*

Cortazar's work often baffles even his most ardent supporters, for it is difficult and often takes the form of inner monologues with little external action to relate to. The reader is, indeed, often uncertain whether the action is intended to be dream or reality, and whether its setting is an actual locale or a world of nightmarish fantasy. But if Cortazar perplexes, he also rewards. In "Blow-Up," he often forces the reader to question the appearances of actions he usually accepts readily and uncritically; to examine his own assumptions about things. He is particularly skillful at using a shifting or ambiguous point of view in keeping the reader alert.

It'll never be known how this has to be told, in the first person or in the second, using the third person plural or continually inventing modes that will serve for nothing. If one might say: I will see the moon rose, or: we hurt me at the back of my eyes, and especially: you the blond woman was the clouds that race before my your his our yours their faces. What the hell.

Seated ready to tell it, if one might go to drink a bock over there, and the typewriter continue by itself (because I use the machine), that would be perfection. And that's not just a manner of speaking. Perfection, yes, because here is the aperture which must be counted also as a machine (of another sort, a Contax 1.1.2) and it is possible that one machine may know more about another machine than I, you, she–the blond—and the clouds. But I have the dumb luck to know that if I go this Remington will sit turned to stone on top of the table with the air of being twice as quiet that mobile things have when they are not moving. So, I have to write. One of us all has to write, if this is going to get told. Better that it be me who am dead, for I'm less compromised than the rest; I who see only the clouds and can think without being distracted, write without being distracted (there goes another, with a grey edge) and remember without being distracted, I who am dead (and I'm alive, I'm not trying to fool anybody, you'll see when we get to the moment, because I have to begin some way and I've begun with this period, the last one back, the one at the beginning, which in the end is the best of the periods when you want to tell something).

All of a sudden I wonder why I have to tell this, but if one begins to wonder why he does all he does do, if one wonders why he accepts an invitation to lunch (now a pigeon's flying by and it seems to me a sparrow), or why when someone has told us a good joke immediately there starts up something like a tickling in the stomach and we are not at peace until we've gone into the office across the hall and told the joke over again; then it feels good immediately, one is fine, happy, and can get back to work. For I imagine that no one has explained this, that really the best thing is to put aside all decorum and tell it, because, after all's done, nobody is ashamed of breathing or of putting on his shoes; they're things that you do, and when something weird happens, when you find a spider in your shoe or if you take a breath and feel like a broken window, then you have to tell what's happening, tell it to the guys at the office or to the doctor. Oh, doctor, every time I take a breath . . . Always tell it, always get rid of that tickle in the stomach that bothers you.

And now that we're finally going to tell it, let's put things a little bit in order, we'd be walking down the staircase in this house as far as Sunday, November 7, just a month back. One goes down five floors and stands then in the Sunday in the sun one would not have suspected of Paris in November, with a large appetite to walk around, to see things, to take photos (because we were photographers, I'm a photographer). I know that the most difficult thing is going to be finding a way to tell it, and I'm not afraid of repeating myself. It's going to be difficult because nobody really knows who it is telling it, if I am I or what actually occurred or what I'm seeing (clouds, and once in a while a pigeon) or if, simply, I'm telling a truth which is only my truth, and then is the truth only for my stomach, for this impulse to go running out and to finish up in some manner with, this, whatever it is.

We're going to tell it slowly, what happens in the middle of what I'm writing is coming already. If they replace me, if, so soon, I don't know what to say, if the clouds stop coming and something else starts (because it's impossible that this keep coming, clouds passing continually and occasionally a pigeon), if something out of all this . . . And after the "if" what am I going to put if I'm going to close the sentence structure correctly? But if I begin to ask questions, I'll never tell anything, maybe to tell would be like an answer, at least for someone who's reading it.

Roberto Michel, French-Chilean, translator and in his spare time an amateur photographer, left number 11, rue Monsieur-le-Prince Sunday November 7 of the current year (now there're two small ones passing, with silver linings). He had spent three weeks working on the French version of a treatise on challenges and appeals by José Norberto Allende, professor at the University of Santiago. It's rare that there's wind in Paris, and even less seldom a wind like this that swirled around corners and rose up to whip at old wooden venetian blinds behind which astonished ladies commented variously on how unreliable the weather had been these last few years. But the sun was out also, riding the wind and friend of the cats, so there was nothing that would keep me from taking a walk along the docks of the Seine and taking photos of the Conservatoire and Sainte-Chapelle. It was hardly ten o'clock, and I figured that by eleven the light would be good, the best you can get in the fall; to kill some time I detoured around by the Isle Saint-Louis and started to walk along the quai d'Anjou, I stared for a bit at the hôtel de Lauzun, I recited bits from Apollinaire which always get into my head whenever I pass in front of the hôtel de Lauzun (and at that I ought to be remembering the other poet, but Michel is an obstinate beggar), and when the wind stopped all at once and the sun came out at least twice as hard (I mean warmer, but really it's the same thing), I sat down on the parapet and felt terribly happy in the Sunday morning.

One of the many ways of contesting level-zero, and one of the best, is to take photographs, an activity in which one should start becoming an adept very early in life, teach it to children since it requires discipline, aesthetic education, a good eye and steady fingers. I'm not talking about waylaying the lie like any old reporter, snapping the stupid silhouette of the VIP leaving number 10 Downing Street, but in all ways when one is walking about with a camera, one has almost a duty to be attentive, to not lose that abrupt and happy rebound of sun's rays off an old stone, or the pigtails-flying run of a small girl going home with a loaf of bread or a bottle of milk. Michel knew that the photographer always worked as a permutation of his personal way of seeing the world as other than the camera insidiously imposed upon it (now a large cloud is going by, almost black), but he lacked no confidence in himself, knowing that he had only to go out without the Contax to recover the keynote of distraction, the sight without a frame around it, light without the diaphragm aperture or 1/250 sec. Right now (what a word, *now*, what a dumb lie) I was able to sit quietly on the railing overlooking the river watching the red and black motorboats passing below without it occurring to me to think photographically of the scenes, nothing more than letting myself go in the letting go of objects, running immobile in the stream of time. And then the wind was not blowing.

After, I wandered down the quai de Bourbon until getting to the end of the isle where the intimate square was (intimate because it was small, not that it was hidden, it offered its whole breast to the river and the sky), I enjoyed it, a lot. Nothing there but a couple and, of course, pigeons; maybe even some of those which are flying past now so that I'm seeing them. A leap up and I settled on the wall, and let myself turn about and be caught and fixed by the sun, giving it my face and ears and hands (I kept my gloves in my pocket). I had no desire to shoot pictures, and lit a cigarette to be doing something; I think it was that moment when the match was about to touch the tobacco that I saw the young boy for the first time.

What I'd thought was a couple seemed much more now a boy with his mother, although at the same time I realized that it was not a kid and his mother, and that it was a couple in the sense that we always allegate to couples when we see them leaning up against the parapets or embracing on the benches in the squares. As I had nothing else to do, I had more than enough time to wonder why the boy was so nervous, like a young colt or a hare, sticking his hands into his pockets, taking them out immediately, one after the other, running his fingers through his hair, changing his stance, and especially why was he afraid, well, you could guess that from every gesture, a fear suffocated by his shyness, an impulse to step backwards which he telegraphed, his body standing as if it were on the edge of flight, holding itself back in a final, pitiful decorum.

All this was so clear, ten feet away—and we were alone against the parapet at the tip of the island—that at the beginning the boy's fright didn't let me see the blond very well. Now, thinking back on it, I see her much better at that first second when I read her face (she'd turned around suddenly, swinging like a metal weathercock, and the eyes, the eyes were there), when I vaguely understood what might have been occurring to the boy and figured it would be worth the trouble to stay and watch (the wind was blowing their words away and they were speaking in a low murmur). I think that I know how to look, if it's something I know, and also that every looking oozes with mendacity, because it's that which expels us furthest outside ourselves, without the least guarantee, whereas to smell, or (but Michel rambles on to himself easily enough, there's no need to let him harangue on this way). In any case, if the likely inaccuracy can be seen beforehand, it becomes possible again to look; perhaps it suffices to choose between looking and the reality looked at, to strip things of all their unnecessary clothing. And surely all that is difficult besides.

As for the boy I remember the image before his actual body (that will clear itself up later), while now I am sure that I remember the woman's body much better than the image. She was thin and willowy, two unfair words to describe what she was, and was wearing an almost-black fur coat, almost long, almost handsome. All the morning's wind (now it was hardly a breeze and it wasn't cold) had blown through her blond hair which pared away her white, bleak face—two unfair words—and put the world at her feet and horribly alone in front of her dark eyes, her eyes fell on things like two eagles, two leaps into nothingness, two puffs of green slime. I'm not describing anything, it's more a matter of trying to understand it. And I said two puffs of green slime.

Let's be fair, the boy was well enough dressed and was sporting yellow gloves which I would have sworn belonged to his older brother, a student of law or sociology; it was pleasant to see the fingers of the gloves sticking out of his jacket pocket. For a long time I didn't see his face, barely a profile, not stupid—a terrified bird, a Fra Filippo angel, rice pudding with milk—and the back of an adolescent who wants to take up judo and has had a scuffle or two in defense of an idea or his sister. Turning fourteen, perhaps fifteen, one would guess that he was dressed and fed by his parents but without a nickel in his pocket, having to debate with his buddies before making up his mind to buy a coffee, a cognac, a pack of cigarettes. He'd walk through the streets thinking of the girls in his class, about how good it would be to go to the movies and see the latest film, or to buy novels or neckties or bottles of liquor with green and white labels on them. At home (it would be a respectable home, lunch at noon and romantic landscapes on the walls, with a dark entryway and a mahogany umbrella stand inside the door) there'd be the slow rain of time, for studying, for being mama's hope, for looking like dad, for writing to his aunt in Avignon. So that there was a lot of walking the streets, the whole of the river for him (but without a nickel) and the mysterious city of fifteen-year-olds with its signs in doorways, its terrifying cats, a paper of fried potatoes for thirty francs, the pornographic magazine folded four ways, a solitude like the emptiness of his pockets, the eagerness for so much that was incomprehensible but illumined by a total love, by the availability analogous to the wind and the streets.

This biography was of the boy and of any boy whatsoever, but this particular one now, you could see he was insular, surrounded solely by the blond's presence as she continued talking with him. (I'm tired of insisting, but two long ragged ones just went by. That morning I don't think I looked at the sky once, because what was happening with the boy and the woman appeared so soon I could do nothing but look at them and wait, look at them and . . .) To cut it short, the boy was agitated and one could guess without too much trouble what had just occurred a few minutes before, at most half-an-hour. The boy had come onto the tip of the island, seen the woman and thought her marvelous. The woman was waiting for that because she was there waiting for that, or maybe the boy arrived before her and she saw him from one of the balconies or from a car and got out to meet him, starting the conversation with whatever, from the beginning she was sure that he was going to be afraid and want to run off, and that, naturally, he'd stay, stiff and sullen, pretending experience and the pleasure of the adventure. The rest was easy because it was happening ten feet away from me, and anyone could have gauged the stages of the game, the derisive, competitive fencing; its major attraction was not that it was happening but in foreseeing its denouement. The boy would try to end it by pretending a date, an obligation, whatever, and would go stumbling off disconcerted, wishing he were walking with some assurance, but naked under the mocking glance which would follow him until he was out of sight. Or rather, he would stay there, fascinated or simply incapable of taking the initiative, and the woman would begin to touch his face gently, muss his hair, still talking to him voicelessly, and soon would take him by the arm to lead him off, unless he, with an uneasiness beginning to tinge the edge of desire, even his stake in the adventure, would rouse himself to put his arm around her waist and to kiss her. Any of this could have happened, though it did not, and perversely Michel waited, sitting on the railing, making the settings almost without looking at the camera, ready to take a picturesque shot of a corner of the island with an uncommon couple talking and looking at one another.

Strange how the scene (almost nothing: two figures there mismatched in their youth) was taking on a disquieting aura. I thought it was I imposing it, and that my photo, if I shot it, would reconstitute things in their true stupidity. I would have liked to know what he was thinking, a man in a grey hat sitting at the wheel of a car parked on the dock which led up to the footbridge, and whether he was reading the paper or asleep. I had just discovered him because people inside a parked car have a tendency to disappear, they get lost in that wretched, private cage stripped of the beauty that motion and danger give it. And nevertheless, the car had been there the whole time, forming part (or deforming that part) of the isle. A car: like saying a lighted streetlamp, a park bench.

Never like saying wind, sunlight, those elements always new to the skin and the eyes, and also the boy and the woman, unique, put there to change the island, to show it to me in another way. Finally, it may have been that the man with the newspaper also became aware of what was happening and would, like me, feel that malicious sensation of waiting for everything to happen. Now the woman had swung around smoothly, putting the young boy between herself and the wall, I saw them almost in profile, and he was taller, though not much taller, and yet she dominated him, it seemed like she was hovering over him (her laugh, all at once, a whip of feathers), crushing him just by being there, smiling, one hand taking a stroll through the air. Why wait any longer? Aperture at sixteen, a sighting which would not include the horrible black car, but yes, that tree, necessary to break up too much grey space . . .

I raised the camera, pretended to study a focus which did not include them, and waited and watched closely, sure that I would finally catch the revealing expression, one that would sum it all up, life that is rhythmed by movement but which a stiff image destroys, taking time in cross section, if we do not choose the essential imperceptible fraction of it. I did not have to wait long. The woman was getting on with the job of handcuffing the boy smoothly, stripping from him what was left of his freedom a hair at a time, in an incredibly slow and delicious torture. I imagined the possible endings (now a small fluffy cloud appears, almost alone in the sky), I saw their arrival at the house (a basement apartment probably, which she would have filled with large cushions and cats) and conjectured the boy's terror and his desperate decision to play it cool and to be led off pretending there was nothing new in it for him. Closing my eyes, if I did in fact close my eyes, I set the scene: the teasing kisses, the woman mildly repelling the hands which were trying to undress her, like in novels, on a bed that would have a lilac-colored comforter, on the other hand she taking off his clothes, plainly mother and son under a milky yellow light, and everything would end up as usual, perhaps, but maybe everything would go otherwise, and the initiation of the adolescent would not happen, she would not let it happen, after a long prologue wherein the awkwardnesses, the exasperating caresses, the running of hands over bodies would be resolved in who knows what, in a separate and solitary pleasure, in a petulant denial mixed with the art of tiring and disconcerting so much poor innocence. It might go like that, it might very well go like that; that woman was not looking for the boy as a lover, and at the same time she was dominating him toward some end impossible to understand if you do not imagine it as a cruel game, the desire to desire without satisfaction, to excite herself for someone else, someone who in no way could be that kid.

Michel is guilty of making literature, of indulging in fabricated unrealities. Nothing pleases him more than to imagine exceptions to the rule, individuals outside the species, not-always-repugnant monsters. But that woman invited speculation, perhaps giving clues enough for the fantasy to hit the bullseye. Before she left, and now that she would fill my imaginings for several days, for I'm given to ruminating, I decided not to lose a moment more. I got it all into the view-finder (with the tree, the railing, the eleven-o'clock sun) and took the shot. In time to realize that they both had noticed and stood there looking at me, the boy surprised and as though questioning, but she was irritated, her face and body flat-footedly hostile, feeling robbed, ignominiously recorded on a small chemical image.

I might be able to tell it in much greater detail but it's not worth the trouble. The woman said that no one had the right to take a picture without permission, and demanded that I hand her over the film. All this in a dry, clear voice with a good Parisian accent, which rose in color and tone with every phrase. For my part, it hardly mattered whether she got the roll of film or not, but anyone who knows me will tell you, if you want anything from me, ask nicely. With the result that I restricted myself to formulating the opinion that not only was photography in public places not prohibited, but it was looked upon with decided favor, both private and official. And while that was getting said, I noticed on the sly how the boy was falling back, sort of actively backing up though without moving, and all at once (it seemed almost incredible) he turned and broke into a run, the poor kid, thinking that he was walking off and in fact in full flight, running past the side of the car, disappearing like a gossamer filament of angel-spit in the morning air.

But filaments of angel-spittle are also called devil-spit, and Michel had to endure rather particular curses, to hear himself called meddler and imbecile, taking great pains meanwhile to smile and to abate with simple movements of his head such a hard sell. As I was beginning to get tired, I heard the car door slam. The man in the grey hat was there, looking at us. It was only at that point that I realized he was playing a part in the comedy.

He began to walk toward us, carrying in his hand the paper he had been pretending to read. What I remember best is the grimace that twisted his mouth askew, it covered his face with wrinkles, changed somewhat both in location and shape because his lips trembled and the grimace went from one side of his mouth to the other as though it were on wheels, independent and involuntary. But the rest stayed fixed, a flour-powdered clown or bloodless man, dull dry skin, eyes deepset, the nostrils black and prominently visible, blacker than the eyebrows or hair or the black necktie. Walking cautiously as though the pavement hurt his feet; I saw patent-leather shoes with such thin soles that he must have felt every roughness in the pavement. I don't know why I got down off the railing, nor very well why I decided to not give them the photo, to refuse that demand in which I guessed at their fear and cowardice. The clown and the woman consulted one another in silence: we made a perfect and unbearable triangle, something I felt compelled to break with a crack of a whip. I laughed in their faces and began to walk off, a little more slowly, I imagine, than the boy. At the level of the first houses, beside the iron footbridge, I turned around to look at them. They were not moving, but the man had dropped his newspaper; it seemed to me that the woman, her back to the parapet, ran her hands over the stone with the classical and absurd gesture of someone pursued looking for a way out.

What happened after that happened here, almost just now, in a room on the fifth floor. Several days went by before Michel developed the photos he'd taken on Sunday; his shots of the Conservatoire and of Sainte-Chapelle were all they should be. Then he found two or three proof-shots he'd forgotten, a poor attempt to catch a cat perched astonishingly on the roof of a rambling public urinal, and also the shot of the blond and the kid. The negative was so good that he made an enlargement; the enlargement was so good that he made one very much larger, almost the size of a poster. It did not occur to him (now one wonders and wonders) that only the shots of the Conservatoire were worth so much work. Of the whole series, the snapshot of the tip of the island was the only one which interested him; he tacked up the enlargement on one wall of the room, and the first day he spent some time looking at it and remembering, that gloomy operation of comparing the memory with the gone reality; a frozen memory, like any photo, where nothing is missing, not even, and especially, nothingness, the true solidifier of the scene. There was the woman, there was the boy, the tree rigid above their heads, the sky as sharp as the stone of the parapet, clouds and stones melded into a single substance and inseparable (now one with sharp edges is going by, like a thunderhead). The first two days I accepted what I had done, from the photo itself to the enlargement on the wall, and didn't even question that every once in a while I would interrupt my translation of José Norberto Allende's treatise to encounter once more the woman's face, the dark splotches on the railing. I'm such a jerk; it had never occurred to me that when we look at a photo from the front, the eyes reproduce exactly the position and the vision of the lens; it's these things that are taken for granted and it never occurs to anyone to think about them. From my chair, with the typewriter directly in front of me, I looked at the photo ten feet away, and then it occurred to me that I had hung it exactly at the point of view of the lens. It looked very good that way; no doubt, it was the best way to appreciate a photo, though the angle from the diagonal doubtless has its pleasures and might even divulge different aspects. Every few minutes, for example when I was unable to find the way to say in good French what José Norberto Allende was saying in very good Spanish, I raised my eyes and looked at the photo; sometimes the woman would catch my eye, sometimes the boy, sometimes the pavement where a dry leaf had fallen admirably situated to heighten a lateral section. Then I rested a bit from my labors, and I enclosed myself again happily in that morning in which the photo was drenched, I recalled ironically the angry picture of the woman demanding I give her the photograph, the boy's pathetic and ridiculous flight, the entrance on the scene of the man with the white face. Basically, I was satisfied with myself; my part had not been too brilliant, and since the French have been given the gift of the sharp response, I did not see very well why I'd chosen to leave without a complete demonstration of the rights, privileges and prerogatives of citizens. The important thing, the really important thing was having helped the kid to escape in time (this in case my theorizing was correct, which was not sufficiently proven, but the running away itself seemed to show it so). Out of plain meddling, I have given him the opportunity finally to take advantage of his fright to do something useful; now he would be regretting it, feeling his honor impaired, his manhood diminished. That was better than the attentions of a woman capable of looking as she had looked at him on that island. Michel is something of a puritan at times, he believes that one should not seduce someone from a position of strength. In the last analysis, taking that photo had been a good act.

Well, it wasn't because of the good act that I looked at it between paragraphs while I was working. At that moment I didn't know the reason, the reason I had tacked the enlargement onto the wall; maybe all fatal acts happen that way, and that is the condition of their fulfillment. I don't think the almost-furtive trembling of the leaves on the tree alarmed me, I was working on a sentence and rounded it out successfully. Habits are like immense herbariums, in the end an enlargement of 32 x 28 looks like a movie screen, where, on the tip of the island, a woman is speaking with a boy and a tree is shaking its dry leaves over their heads.

But her hands were just too much. I had just translated: "In that case, the second key resides in the intrinsic nature of difficulties which societies . . ."—when I saw the woman's hand beginning to stir slowly, finger by finger. There was nothing left of me, a phrase in French which I would never have to finish, a typewriter on the floor, a chair that squeaked and shook, fog. The kid had ducked his head like boxers do when they've done all they can and are waiting for the final blow to fall; he had turned up the collar of his overcoat and seemed more a prisoner than ever, the perfect victim helping promote the catastrophe. Now the woman was talking into his ear, and her hand opened again to lay itself against his cheekbone, to caress and caress it, burning it, taking her time. The kid was less startled than he was suspicious, once or twice he poked his head over the woman's shoulder and she continued talking, saying something that made him look back every few minutes toward that area where Michel knew the car was parked and the man in the grey hat, carefully eliminated from the photo but present in the boy's eyes (how doubt that now) in the words of the woman, in the woman's hands, in the vicarious presence of the woman. When I saw the man come up, stop near them and look at them, his hands in his pockets and a stance somewhere between disgusted and demanding, the master who is about to whistle in his dog after a frolic in the square, I understood, if that was to understand, what had to happen now, what had to have happened then, what would have to happen at that moment, among these people, just where I had poked my nose in to upset an established order, interfering innocently in that which had not happened, but which was now going to happen, now was going to be fulfilled. And what I had imagined earlier was much less horrible than the reality, that woman, who was not there by herself, she was not caressing or propositioning or encouraging for her own pleasure, to lead the angel away with his tousled hair and play the tease with his terror and his eager grace. The real boss was waiting there, smiling petulantly, already certain of the business; he was not the first to send a woman in the vanguard, to bring him the prisoners manacled with flowers. The rest of it would be so simple, the car, some house or another, drinks, stimulating engravings, tardy tears, the awakening in hell. And there was nothing I could do, this time I could do absolutely nothing. My strength had been a photograph, that, there, where they were taking their revenge on me, demonstrating clearly what was going to happen. The photo had been taken, the time had run out, gone; we were so far from one another, the abusive act had certainly already taken place, the tears already shed, and the rest conjecture and sorrow. All at once the order was inverted, they were alive, moving, they were deciding and had decided, they were going to their future; and I on this side, prisoner of another time, in a room on the fifth floor, to not know who they were, that woman, that man, and that boy, to be only the lens of my camera, something fixed, rigid, incapable of intervention. It was horrible, their mocking me, deciding it before my impotent eye, mocking me, for the boy again was looking at the flour-faced clown and I had to accept the fact that he was going to say yes, that the proposition carried money with it or a gimmick, and I couldn't yell for him to run, or even open the road to him again with a new photo, a small and almost meek intervention which would ruin the framework of drool and perfume. Everything was going to resolve itself right there, at that moment; there was like an immense silence which had nothing to do with physical silence. It was stretching it out, setting itself up. I think I screamed, I screamed terribly, and that at that exact second I realized that I was beginning to move toward them, four inches, a step, another step, the tree swung its branches rhythmically in the foreground, a place where the railing was tarnished emerged from the frame, the woman's face turned toward me as though surprised, was enlarging, and then I turned a bit, I mean that the camera turned a little, and without losing sight of the woman, I began to close in on the man who was looking at me with the black holes he had in place of eyes, surprised and angered both, he looked, wanting to nail me onto the air, and at that instant I happened to see something like a large bird outside the focus that was flying in a single swoop in front of the picture, and I leaned up against the wall of my room and was happy because the boy had just managed to escape, I saw him running off, in focus again, sprinting with his hair flying in the wind, learning finally to fly across the island, to arrive at the footbridge, return to the city. For the second time he'd escaped them, for the second time I was helping him to escape, returning him to his precarious paradise. Out of breath, I stood in front of them; no need to step closer, the game was played out. Of the woman you could see just maybe a shoulder and a bit of the hair, brutally cut off by the frame of the picture; but the man was directly center, his mouth half open, you could see a shaking black tongue, and he lifted his hands slowly, bringing them into the foreground, an instant still in perfect focus, and then all of him a lump that blotted out the island, the tree, and I shut my eyes, I didn't want to see any more, and I covered my face and broke into tears like an idiot.

Now there's a big white cloud, as on all these days, all this untellable time. What remains to be said is always a cloud, two clouds, or long hours of a sky perfectly clear, a very clean, clear rectangle tacked up with pins on the wall of my room. That was what I saw when I opened my eyes and dried them with my fingers: the clear sky, and then a cloud that drifted in from the left, passed gracefully and slowly across and disappeared on the right. And then another, and for a change sometimes, everything gets grey, all one enormous cloud, and suddenly the splotches of rain cracking down, for a long spell you can see it raining over the picture, like a spell of weeping reversed, and little by little, the frame becomes clear, perhaps the sun comes out, and again the clouds begin to come, two at a time, three at a time. And the pigeons once in a while, and a sparrow or two.

Questions

1. Who is the narrator, and why is he telling the story? Why does he feel it necessary to dwell on the ambiguity of point of view, and the difficulty of telling the story?

2. How and why does the narrator's profession as a photographer lead him to question the nature of reality? How, when he wonders whether he is "telling a truth which is only my truth," does this reflect the concern of the story itself?

3. What does the narrator mean when he says, "If I begin to ask questions, I'll never tell anything"?

4. After speculating on the lives of the people he sees in the park, the photographer wonders if he is imposing too much of himself on what he sees. What larger question, implicit in the story itself, is he raising?

5. The narrator speculates on what he actually saw, and also, trying to be detached, on his own interpretation of what he saw. Can the two be separated? Does he try to separate them? Does the author of the story?

Roald Dahl

PIG

The Welsh-born writer Roald Dahl has specialized in the macabre horror tale, usually spiced with irresistible but grim humor. Born in 1916, he came to maturity under the threat of war, and served in World War II as an officer in the Royal Air Force. During the war he wrote The Gremlins *(1944), popularizing these mythical trouble-causing monsters. After the war he moved to the United States and began writing stories for the* New Yorker, *developing his distinctively flavored formula of making horror out of the ordinary. He twice won the Edgar Allan Poe award from the Mystery Writers of America, and is married to the American actress Patricia Neal. His collections of stories include* Some Time Never *(1948),* Someone Like You *(1953), and* Kiss Kiss *(1960). "Pig" is from the latter collection. Dahl's story examines whether a grotesque and even repellent subject can succeed in being entertaining.*

Once upon a time, in the City of New York, a beautiful baby boy was born into this world, and the joyful parents named him Lexington.

No sooner had the mother returned home from the hospital carrying Lexington in her arms than she said to her husband, "Darling, now you must take me out to a most marvellous restaurant for dinner so that we can celebrate the arrival of our son and heir."

Her husband embraced her tenderly and told her that any woman who could produce such a beautiful child as Lexington deserved to go absolutely any place she wanted. But was she strong enough yet, he enquired, to start running around the city late at night?

"No," she said, she wasn't. But what the hell.

So that evening they both dressed themselves up in fancy clothes, and leaving little Lexington in care of a trained infant's nurse who was costing them twenty dollars a day and was Scottish into the bargain, they went out to the finest and most expensive restaurant in town. There they each ate a giant lobster and drank a bottle of champagne between them, and after that, they went on to a nightclub, where they drank another bottle of champagne and then sat holding hands for several hours while they recalled and discussed and admired each individual physical feature of their lovely newborn son.

They arrived back at their house on the East Side of Manhattan at around two o'clock in the morning and the husband paid off the taxi-driver and then began feeling in his pockets for the key to the front door. After a while, he announced that he must have left it in the pocket of his other suit, and he suggested they ring the bell and get the nurse to come down and let them in. An infant's nurse at twenty dollars a day must expect to be hauled out of bed occasionally in the night, the husband said.

So he rang the bell. They waited. Nothing happened. He rang it again, long and loud. They waited another minute. Then they both stepped back onto the street and shouted the nurse's name (McPottle) up at the nursery windows on the third floor, but there was still no response. The house was dark and silent. The wife began to grow apprehensive. Her baby was imprisoned in this place, she told herself. Alone with McPottle. And who was McPottle? They had known her for two days, that was all, and she had a thin mouth, a small disapproving eye, and a starchy bosom, and quite clearly she was in the habit of sleeping much too soundly for safety. If she couldn't hear the front-door bell, then how on earth did she expect to hear a baby crying? Why, this very second the poor thing might be swallowing its tongue or suffocating on its pillow.

"He doesn't use a pillow," the husband said. "You are not to worry. But I'll get you in if that's what you want." He was feeling rather superb after all the champagne, and now he bent down and undid the laces of one of his black patent-leather shoes, and took it off. Then, holding it by the toe, he flung it hard and straight through the dining-room window on the ground floor.

"There you are," he said grinning. "We'll deduct it from McPottle's wages."

He stepped forward and very carefully put a hand through the hole in the glass and released the catch. Then he raised the window.

"I shall lift you in first, little mother," he said, and he took his wife around the waist and lifted her off the ground. This brought her big red mouth up level with his own, and very close, so he started kissing her. He knew from experience that women like very much to be kissed in this position, with their bodies held tight, and their legs dangling in the air, so he went on doing it for quite a long time, and she wiggled her feet, and made loud gulping noises down in her throat. Finally, the husband turned her round and began easing her gently through the open window into the dining-room. At this point, a police patrol car came nosing silently along the street toward them. It stopped about thirty yards away, and three cops of Irish extraction leaped out of the car and started running in the direction of the husband and wife, brandishing revolvers.

"Stick 'em up!" the cops shouted. "Stick 'em up!" But it was impossible for the husband to obey this order without letting go of his wife, and had he done this she would either have fallen to the ground or would have been left dangling half in and half out of the house, which is a terribly uncomfortable position for a woman; so he continued gallantly to push her upward and inward through the window. The cops, all of whom had received medals before for killing robbers, opened fire immediately, and although they were still running, and although the wife in particular was presenting them with a very small target indeed, they succeeded in scoring several direct hits on each body—sufficient anyway to prove fatal in both cases.

Thus, when he was no more than twelve days old, little Lexington became an orphan.

II

The news of this killing, for which the three policemen subsequently received citations, was eagerly conveyed to all relatives of the deceased couple by newspaper reporters, and the next morning, the closest of these relatives, as well as a couple of undertakers, three lawyers, and a priest, climbed into taxis and set out for the house with the broken window. They assembled in the living-room, men and women both, and they sat around in a circle on the sofas and armchairs, smoking cigarettes and sipping sherry and debating what on earth should be done now with the baby upstairs, the orphan Lexington.

It soon became apparent that none of the relatives was particularly keen to assume responsibility for the child, and the discussions and arguments continued all through the day. Everybody declared an enormous, almost an irresistible desire to look after him, and would have done so with the greatest of pleasure were it not for the fact that their apartment was too small, or that they already had one baby and couldn't possibly afford another, or that they wouldn't know what to do with the poor little thing when they went abroad in the summer, or that they were getting on in years, which surely would be most unfair to the boy when he grew up, and so on and so forth. They all knew, of course, that the father had been heavily in debt for a long time and that the house was mortgaged and that consequently there would be no money at all to go with the child.

They were still arguing like mad at six in the evening when suddenly, in the middle of it all, an old aunt of the deceased father (her name was Glosspan) swept in from Virginia, and without even removing her hat and coat, not even pausing to sit down, ignoring all offers of a martini, a whisky, a sherry, she announced firmly to the assembled relatives that she herself intended to take sole charge of the infant boy from then on. What was more, she said, she would assume full financial responsibility on all counts, including education, and everyone else could go on back home where they belonged and give their consciences a rest. So saying, she trotted upstairs to the nursery and snatched Lexington from his cradle and swept out of the house with the baby clutched tightly in her arms, while the relatives simply sat and stared and smiled and looked relieved, and McPottle the nurse stood stiff with disapproval at the head of the stairs, her lips compressed, her arms folded across her starchy bosom.

And thus it was that the infant Lexington, when he was thirteen days old, left the City of New York and travelled southward to live with his Great Aunt Glosspan in the State of Virginia.

III

Aunt Glosspan was nearly seventy when she became guardian to Lexington, but to look at her you would never have guessed it for one minute. She was as sprightly as a woman half her age, with a small, wrinkled, but still quite beautiful face and two lovely brown eyes that sparkled at you in the nicest way. She was also a spinster, though you would never have guessed that either, for there was nothing spinsterish about Aunt Glosspan. She was never bitter or gloomy or irritable; she didn't have a moustache; and she wasn't in the least bit jealous of other people, which in itself is something you can seldom say about either a spinster or a virgin lady, although of course it is not known for certain whether Aunt Glosspan qualified on both counts.

But she was an eccentric old woman, there was no doubt about that. For the past thirty years she had lived a strange isolated life all by herself in a tiny cottage high up on the slopes of the Blue Ridge Mountains, several miles from the nearest village. She had five acres of pasture, a plot for growing vegetables, a flower garden, three cows, a dozen hens, and a fine cockerel.

And now she had little Lexington as well.

She was a strict vegetarian and regarded the consumption of animal flesh as not only unhealthy and disgusting, but horribly cruel. She lived upon lovely clean foods like milk, butter, eggs, cheese, vegetables, nuts, herbs, and fruit, and she rejoiced in the conviction that no living creature would be slaughtered on her account, not even a shrimp. Once, when a brown hen of hers passed away in the prime of life from being egg-bound, Aunt Glosspan was so distressed that she nearly gave up egg-eating altogether.

She knew not the first thing about babies, but that didn't worry her in the least. At the railway station in New York, while waiting for the train that would take her and Lexington back to Virginia, she bought six feeding-bottles, two dozen diapers, a box of safety pins, a carton of milk for the journey, and a small paper-covered book called *The Care of Infants.* What more could anyone want? And when the train got going, she fed the baby some milk, changed its nappies after a fashion, and laid it down on the seat to sleep. Then she read *The Care of Infants* from cover to cover.

"There is no problem here," she said, throwing the book out the window. "No problem at all."

And curiously enough there wasn't. Back home in the cottage everything went just as smoothly as could be. Little Lexington drank his milk and belched and yelled and slept exactly as a good baby should, and Aunt Glosspan glowed with joy whenever she looked at him, and showered him with kisses all day long.

IV

By the time he was six years old, young Lexington had grown into a most beautiful boy with long golden hair and deep blue eyes the colour of cornflowers. He was bright and cheerful, and already he was learning to help his old aunt in all sorts of different ways around the property, collecting the eggs from the chicken house, turning the handle of the butter churn, digging up potatoes in the vegetable garden, and searching for wild herbs on the side of the mountain. Soon, Aunt Glosspan told herself, she would have to start thinking about his education.

But she couldn't bear the thought of sending him away to school. She loved him so much now that it would kill her to be parted from him for any length of time. There was, of course, that village school down in the valley, but it was a dreadful-looking place, and if she sent him there she knew they would start forcing him to eat meat the very first day he arrived.

"You know what, my darling?" she said to him one day when he was sitting on a stool in the kitchen watching her make cheese. "I don't really see why I shouldn't give you your lessons myself."

The boy looked up at her with his large blue eyes, and gave her a lovely trusting smile. "That would be nice," he said.

"And the very first thing I should do would be to teach you how to cook."

"I think I would like that, Aunt Glosspan."

"Whether you like it or not, you're going to have to learn some time," she said. "Vegetarians like us don't have nearly so many foods to choose from as ordinary people, and therefore they must learn to be doubly expert with what they have."

"Aunt Glosspan," the boy said, "what *do* ordinary people eat that we don't?"

"Animals," she answered, tossing her head in disgust.

"You mean *live* animals?"

"No," she said. "Dead ones."

The boy considered this for a moment.

"You mean when they die they *eat* them instead of *burying* them?"

"They don't wait for them to die, my pet. They kill them."

"How do they kill them, Aunt Glosspan?"

"They usually slit their throats with a knife."

"But what *kind* of animals?"

"Cows and pigs mostly, and sheep."

"Cows!" the boy cried. "You mean like Daisy and Snowdrop and Lily?"

"Exactly, my dear."

"But *how* do they eat them, Aunt Glosspan?"

"They cut them up into bits and they cook the bits. They like it best when its all red and bloody and sticking to the bones. They love to eat lumps of cow's flesh with the blood oozing out of it."

"Pigs too?"

"They adore pigs."

"Lumps of bloody pig's meat," the boy said. "Imagine that. What else do they eat, Aunt Glosspan?"

"Chickens."

"Chickens!"

"Millions of them."

"Feathers and all?"

"No dear, not the feathers. Now run along outside and get Aunt Glosspan a bunch of chives, will you, my darling?"

Shortly after that, the lessons began. They covered five subjects, reading, writing, geography, arithmetic, and cooking, but the latter was by far the most popular with both teacher and pupil. In fact, it very soon become apparent that young Lexington possessed a truly remarkable talent in this direction. He was a born cook. He was dextrous and quick. He could handle his pans like a juggler. He could slice a single potato into twenty paper-thin slivers in less time than it took his aunt to peel it. His palate was exquisitely sensitive, and he could taste a pot of strong onion soup and immediately detect the presence of a single tiny leaf of sage. In so young a boy, all this was a bit bewildering to Aunt Glosspan, and to tell the truth she didn't quite know what to make of it. But she was proud as proud could be, all the same, and predicted a brilliant future for the child.

"What a mercy it is," she said, "that I have such a wonderful little fellow to look after me in my dotage." And a couple of years later she retired from the kitchen for good, leaving Lexington in sole charge of all household cooking. The boy was now ten years old, and Aunt Glosspan was nearly eighty.

V

With the kitchen to himself, Lexington straight away began experimenting with dishes of his own invention. The old favourites no longer interested him. He had a violent urge to create. There were hundreds of fresh ideas in his head. "I will begin," he said, "by devising a chestnut soufflé." He made it and served it up for supper that very night. It was terrific. "You are a genius!" Aunt Glosspan cried, leaping up from her chair and kissing him on both cheeks. "You will make history!"

From then on, hardly a day went by without some new delectable creation being set up on the table. There was Brazil-nut soup, hominy cutlets, vegetable ragout, dandelion omelette, cream-cheese fritters, stuffed-cabbage surprise, stewed foggage, shallots *à la bonne femme,* beet-root mousse piquant, prunes Stroganoff, Dutch rarebit, turnips on horseback, flaming spruce-needle tarts, and many many other beautiful compositions. Never before in her life, Aunt Glosspan declared, had she tasted such food as this; and in the mornings, long before lunch was due she would go out onto the porch and sit there in her rocking-chair, speculating about the coming meal, licking her chops, sniffing the aromas that came wafting out through the kitchen window.

"What's that you're making in there today, boy?" she would call out.

"Try to guess, Aunt Glosspan."

"Smells like a bit of salsify fritters to me," she would say, sniffing vigorously.

Then out he would come, this ten-year-old child, a little grin of triumph on his face, and in his hands a big steaming pot of the most heavenly stew made entirely of parsnips and lovage.

"You know what you ought to do," his aunt said to him, gobbling the stew. "You ought to set yourself down this very minute with paper and pencil and write a cooking-book."

He looked across the table, chewing his parsnips slowly.

"Why not?" she cried. "I've taught you how to write and I've taught you how to cook and now all you've got to do is put the two things together. You write a cooking-book, my darling, and it'll make you famous the whole world over."

"All right," he said. "I will."

And that very day, Lexington began writing the first page of that monumental work which was to occupy him for the rest of his life. He called it *Eat Good and Healthy.*

VI

Seven years later, by the time he was seventeen, he had recorded over nine thousand different recipes, all of them original, all of them delicious.

But now, suddenly, his labors were interrupted by the tragic death of Aunt Glosspan. She was afflicted in the night by a violent seizure, and Lexington, who had rushed into her bedroom to see what all the noise was about, found her lying on her bed yelling and cussing and twisting herself up into all manner of complicated knots. Indeed, she was a terrible sight to behold, and the agitated youth danced around her in his pyjamas, wringing his hands, and wondering what on earth he should do. Finally, in an effort to cool her down, he fetched a bucket of water from the pond in the cow field and tipped it over her head, but this only intensified the paroxysms, and the old lady expired within the hour.

"This is really too bad," the poor boy said, pinching her several times to make sure that she was dead. "And how sudden! How quick and sudden! Why only a few hours ago she seemed in the very best of spirits. She even took three large helpings of my most recent creation, devilled mushroomburgers, and told me how succulent it was."

After weeping bitterly for several minutes, for he had loved his aunt very much, he pulled himself together and carried her outside and buried her behind the cowshed.

The next day, while tidying up her belongings, he came across an envelope that was addressed to him in Aunt Glosspan's handwriting.

He opened it and drew out two fifty-dollar bills and a letter. *Darling boy,* the letter said. *I know that you have never yet been down the mountain since you were thirteen days old, but as soon as I die you must put on a pair of shoes and a clean shirt and walk down to the village and find the doctor. Ask the doctor to give you a death certificate to prove that I am dead. Then take this certificate to my lawyer, a man called Mr. Samuel Zuckermann, who lives in New York City and who has a copy of my will. Mr. Zuckermann will arrange everything. The cash in this envelope is to pay the doctor for the certificate and to cover the cost of your journey to New York. Mr. Zuckermann will give you more money when you get there, and it is my earnest wish that you use it to further your researches into culinary and vegetarian matters, and that you continue to work upon the great book of yours until you are satisfied that it is complete in every way. Your loving aunt—Glosspan.*

Lexington, who had always done everything his aunt told him, pocketed the money, put on a pair of shoes and a clean shirt, and went down the mountain to the village where the doctor lived.

"Old Glosspan?" the doctor said. "My God, is *she* dead?"

"Certainly she's dead," the youth answered. "If you will come back home with me now I'll dig her up and you can see for yourself."

"How deep did you bury her?" the doctor asked.

"Six or seven feet down, I should think."

"And how long ago?"

"Oh, about eight hours."

"Then she's dead," the doctor announced. "Here's the certificate."

VII

Our hero now set out for the City of New York to find Mr. Samuel Zuckermann. He travelled on foot, and he slept under hedges, and he lived on berries and wild herbs, and it took him sixteen days to reach the metropolis.

"What a fabulous place this is!" he cried as he stood at the corner of Fifty-seventh Street and Fifth Avenue, staring around him. "There are no cows or chickens anywhere, and none of the women looks in the least like Aunt Glosspan."

As for Mr. Samuel Zuckermann, he looked like nothing that Lexington had ever seen before.

He was a small spongy man with livid jowls and a huge magenta nose, and when he smiled, bits of gold flashed at you marvellously from lots of different places inside his mouth. In his luxurious office, he shook Lexington warmly by the hand and congratulated him upon his aunt's death.

"I suppose you knew that your dearly beloved guardian was a woman of considerable wealth?" he said.

"You mean the cows and the chickens?"

"I mean half a million bucks," Mr. Zuckermann said.

"How much?"

"Half a million dollars, my boy. And she's left it all to you." Mr. Zuckermann leaned back in his chair and clasped his hands over his spongy paunch. At the same time, he began secretly working his right forefinger in through his waistcoat and under his shirt so as to scratch the skin around the circumference of his navel—a favourite exercise of his, and one that gave him a peculiar pleasure. "Of course, I shall have to deduct fifty per cent for my services," he said, "but that still leaves you with two hundred and fifty grand."

"I am rich!" Lexington cried. "This is wonderful! How soon can I have the money?"

"Well," Mr. Zuckermann said, "luckily for you, I happen to be on rather cordial terms with the tax authorities around here, and I am confident that I shall be able to persuade them to waive all death duties and back taxes."

"How kind you are," murmured Lexington.

"I should naturally have to give somebody a small honorarium."

"Whatever you say, Mr. Zuckermann."

"I think a hundred thousand would be sufficient."

"Good gracious, isn't that rather excessive?"

"Never undertip a tax-inspector or a policeman," Mr. Zuckermann said. "Remember that."

"But how much does it leave for me?" the youth asked meekly.

"One hundred and fifty thousand. But then you've got the funeral expenses to pay out of that."

"*Funeral* expenses?"

"You've got to pay the funeral parlour. Surely you know that?"

"But I buried her myself, Mr. Zuckermann, behind the cowshed."

"I don't doubt it," the lawyer said. "So what?"

"I never used a funeral parlour."

"Listen," Mr. Zuckermann said patiently. "You may not know it, but there is a law in this state which says that no beneficiary under a will may receive a single penny of his inheritance until the funeral parlour has been paid in full."

"You mean that's a *law?*"

"Certainly it's a law, and a very good one it is, too. The funeral parlour is one of our great national institutions. It must be protected at all cost."

Mr. Zuckermann himself, together with a group of public-spirited doctors, controlled a corporation that owned a chain of nine lavish funeral parlours in the city, not to mention a casket factory in Brooklyn and a postgraduate school for embalmers in Washington Heights. The celebration of death was therefore a deeply religious affair in Mr. Zuckermann's eyes. In fact, the whole business affected him profoundly, almost as profoundly, one might say, as the birth of Christ affected the shopkeeper.

"You had no right to go out and bury your aunt like that," he said. "None at all."

"I'm very sorry, Mr. Zuckermann."

"Why, it's downright subversive."

"I'll do whatever you say, Mr. Zuckermann. All I want to know is how much I'm going to get in the end, when everything's paid."

There was a pause. Mr. Zuckermann sighed and frowned and continued secretly to run the tip of his finger around the rim of his navel.

"Shall we say fifteen thousand?" he suggested, flashing a big gold smile. "That's a nice round figure."

"Can I take it with me this afternoon?"

"I don't see why not."

So Mr. Zuckermann summoned his chief cashier and told him to give Lexington fifteen thousand dollars out of the petty cash, and to obtain a receipt. The youth, who by this time was delighted to be getting anything at all, accepted the money gratefully and stowed it away in his knapsack. Then he shook Mr. Zuckermann warmly by the hand, thanked him for all his help, and went out of the office.

"The whole world is before me!" our hero cried as he emerged into the street. "I now have fifteen thousand dollars to see me through until my book is published. And after that, of course, I shall have a great deal more." He stood on the pavement, wondering which way to go. He turned left and began strolling down the street, staring at the sights of the city.

"What a revolting smell," he said, sniffing the air. "I can't stand this." His delicate olfactory nerves, tuned to receive only the most delicious kitchen aromas, were being tortured by the stench of the diesel-oil fumes pouring out of the backs of the buses.

"I must get out of this place before my nose is ruined altogether," he said. "But first, I've simply got to have something to eat. I'm starving." The poor boy had had nothing but berries and wild herbs for the past two weeks, and now his stomach was yearning for solid food. I'd like a nice hominy cutlet, he told himself. Or maybe a few juicy salsify fritters.

He crossed the street and entered a small restaurant. The place was hot inside, and dark and silent. There was a strong smell of cooking-fat and cabbage water. The only other customer was a man with a brown hat on his head, crouching intently over his food, who did not look up as Lexington came in.

Our hero seated himself at a corner table and hung his knapsack on the back of his chair. This, he told himself, is going to be most interesting. In all my seventeen years I have tasted only the cooking of two people, Aunt Glosspan and myself—unless one counts Nurse McPottle, who must have heated my bottle a few times when I was an infant. But I am now about to sample the art of a new chef altogether, and perhaps, if I am lucky, I may pick up a couple of useful ideas for my book.

A waiter approached out of the shadows at the back, and stood beside the table.

"How do you do," Lexington said. "I should like a large hominy cutlet please. Do it twenty-five seconds each side, in a very hot skillet with sour cream, and sprinkle a pinch of lovage on it before serving—unless of course your chef knows of a more original method, in which case I should be delighted to try it."

The waiter laid his head over to one side and looked carefully at his customer. "You want the roast pork and cabbage?" he asked. "That's all we got left."

"Roast what and cabbage?"

The waiter took a soiled handkerchief from his trouser pocket and shook it open with a violent flourish, as though he were cracking a whip. Then he blew his nose loud and wet.

"You want it or don't you?" he said, wiping his nostrils.

"I haven't the foggiest idea what it is," Lexington replied, "but I should love to try it. You see, I am writing a cooking-book and . . ."

"One pork and cabbage!" the waiter shouted, and somewhere in the back of the restaurant, far away in the darkness, a voice answered him.

The waiter disappeared. Lexington reached into his knapsack for his personal knife and fork. These were a present from Aunt Glosspan, given him when he was six years old, made of solid silver, and he had never eaten with any other instruments since. While waiting for the food to arrive, he polished them lovingly with a piece of soft muslin.

Soon the waiter returned carrying a plate on which there lay a thick greyish-white slab of something hot. Lexington leaned forward anxiously to smell it as it was put down before him. His nostrils were wide open now to receive the scent, quivering and sniffing.

"But this is absolute heaven!" he exclaimed. "What an aroma! It's tremendous!"

The waiter stepped back a pace, watching his customer carefully.

"Never in my life have I smelled anything as rich and wonderful as this!" our hero cried, seizing his knife and fork. "What on earth is it made of?"

The man in the brown hat looked around and stared, then returned to his eating. The waiter was backing away toward the kitchen.

Lexington cut off a small piece of the meat, impaled it on his silver fork, and carried it up to his nose so as to smell it again. Then he popped it into his mouth and began to chew it slowly, his eyes half closed, his body tense.

"This is fantastic!" he cried. "It is a brand-new flavour! Oh, Glosspan, my beloved Aunt, how I wish you were with me now so you could taste this remarkable dish! Waiter! Come here at once! I want you!"

The astonished waiter was now watching from the other end of the room, and he seemed reluctant to move any closer.

"If you will come and talk to me I will give you a present," Lexington said, waving a hundred-dollar bill. "Please come over here and talk to me."

The waiter sidled cautiously back to the table, snatched away the money, and held it up close to his face, peering at it from all angles. Then he slipped it quickly into his pocket.

"What can I do for you, my friend?" he asked.

"Look," Lexington said. "If you will tell me what this delicious dish is made of, and exactly how it is prepared, I will give you another hundred."

"I already told you," the man said. "It's pork."

"And what exactly is pork?"

"You never had roast pork before?" the waiter asked, staring.

"For heaven's sake, man, tell me what it is and stop keeping me in suspense like this."

"It's pig," the waiter said. "You just bung it in the oven."

"Pig!"

"All pork is pig. Didn't you know that?"

"You mean *this* is *pig's meat?"*

"I guarantee it."

"But . . . but . . . that's impossible," the youth stammered. "Aunt Glosspan, who knew more about food than anyone else in the world, said that meat of any kind was disgusting, revolting, horrible, foul, nauseating, and beastly. And yet this piece that I have here on my plate is without a doubt the most delicious thing that I have ever tasted. Now how on earth do you explain that? Aunt Glosspan certainly wouldn't have told me it was revolting if it wasn't."

"Maybe your aunt didn't know how to cook it," the waiter said.

"Is that possible?"

"You're damn right it is. Especially with pork. Pork has to be very well done or you can't eat it."

"Eureka!" Lexington cried. "I'll bet that's exactly what happened! She did it wrong!" He handed the man another hundred-dollar bill. "Lead me to the kitchen," he said. "Introduce me to the genius who prepared this meat."

Lexington was at once taken into the kitchen, and there he met the cook who was an elderly man with a rash on one side of his neck.

"This will cost you another hundred," the waiter said.

Lexington was only too glad to oblige, but this time he gave the money to the cook. "Now listen to me," he said, "I have to admit that I am really rather confused by what the waiter has just been telling me. Are you quite positive that the delectable dish which I have just been eating was prepared from pig's flesh?"

The cook raised his right hand and began scratching the rash on his neck.

"Well," he said, looking at the waiter and giving him a sly wink, "all I can tell you is that I *think* it was pig's meat."

"You mean you're not sure?"

"One can't ever be sure."

"Then what else could it have been?"

"Well," the cook said, speaking very slowly and still staring at the waiter. "There's just a chance, you see, that it might have been a piece of human stuff."

"You mean a man?"

"Yes."

"Good heavens."

"Or a woman. It could have been either. They both taste the same."

"Well—now you really do surprise me," the youth declared.

"One lives and learns."

"Indeed one does."

"As a matter of fact, we've been getting an awful lot of it just lately from the butcher's in place of pork," the cook declared.

"Have you really?"

"The trouble is, it's almost impossible to tell which is which. They're both very good."

"The piece I had just now was simply superb."

"I'm glad you liked it," the cook said. "But to be quite honest, I think that was a bit of pig. In fact, I'm almost sure it was."

"You are?"

"Yes, I am."

"In that case, we shall have to assume that you are right," Lexington said. "So now will you please tell me—and here is another hundred dollars for your trouble—will you please tell me precisely how you prepared it?"

The cook, after pocketing the money, launched out upon a colourful description of how to roast a loin of pork, while the youth, not wanting to miss a single word of so great a recipe, sat down at the kitchen table and recorded every detail in his notebook.

"Is that all?" he asked when the cook had finished.

"That's all."

"But there must be more to it than that, surely?"

"You got to get a good piece of meat to start off with," the cook said. "That's half the battle. It's got to be a good hog and it's got to be butchered right, otherwise it'll turn out lousy whichever way you cook it."

"Show me how," Lexington said. "Butcher me one now so I can learn."

"We don't butcher pigs in the kitchen," the cook said. "That lot you just ate came from a packing-house over in the Bronx."

"Then give me the address!"

The cook gave him the address, and our hero, after thanking them both many times for all their kindnesses, rushed outside and leapt into a taxi and headed for the Bronx.

VIII

The packing-house was a big four-storey brick building, and the air around it smelled sweet and heavy, like musk. At the main entrance gates, there was a large notice which said VISITORS WELCOME AT ANY TIME, and thus encouraged, Lexington walked through the gates and entered a cobbled yard which surrounded the building itself. He then followed a series of signposts (THIS WAY FOR THE GUIDED TOURS), and came eventually to a small corrugated-iron shed set well apart from the main building (VISITORS WAITING-ROOM). After knocking politely on the door, he went in.

There were six other people ahead of him in the waiting-room. There was a fat mother with her two little boys aged about nine and eleven.

There was a bright-eyed young couple who looked as though they might be on their honeymoon. And there was a pale woman with long white gloves, who sat very upright, looking straight ahead, with her hands folded on her lap. Nobody spoke. Lexington wondered whether they they were all writing cooking-books, like himself, but when he put this question to them aloud, he got no answer. The grown-ups merely smiled mysteriously to themselves and shook their heads, and the two children stared at him as though they were seeing a lunatic.

Soon, the door opened and a man with a merry pink face popped his head into the room and said, "Next, please." The mother and the two boys got up and went out.

About ten minutes later, the same man returned. "Next, please," he said again, and the honeymoon couple jumped up and followed him outside.

Two new visitors came in and sat down—a middle-aged husband and a middle-aged wife, the wife carrying a wicker shopping-basket containing groceries.

"Next, please," said the guide, and the woman with the long white gloves got up and left.

Several more people came in and took their places on the stiff-backed wooden chairs.

Soon the guide returned for the third time, and now it was Lexington's turn to go outside.

"Follow me, please," the guide said, leading the youth across the yard toward the main building.

"How exciting this is!" Lexington cried, hopping from one foot to the other."I only wish that my dear Aunt Glosspan could be with me now to see what I am going to see."

"I myself only do the preliminaries," the guide said. "Then I shall hand you over to someone else."

"Anything you say," cried the ecstatic youth.

First they visited a large penned-in area at the back of the building where several hundred pigs were wandering around. "Here's where they start," the guide said. "And over there's where they go in."

"Where?"

"Right there." The guide pointed to a long wooden shed that stood against the outside wall of the factory. "We call it the shackling-pen. This way, please."

Three men wearing long rubber boots were driving a dozen pigs into the shackling-pen just as Lexington and the guide approached, so they all went in together.

"Now," the guide said, "watch how they shackle them."

Inside, the shed was simply a bare wooden room with no roof, but there was a steel cable with hooks on it that kept moving slowly along the length of one wall, parallel with the ground, about three feet up. When it reached the end of the shed, this cable suddenly changed direction and climbed vertically upward through the open roof toward the top floor of the main building.

The twelve pigs were huddled together at the far end of the pen, standing quietly, looking apprehensive. One of the men in rubber boots pulled a length of metal chain down from the wall and advanced upon the nearest animal, approaching it from the rear. Then he bent down and quickly looped one end of the chain around one of the animal's hind legs. The other end he attached to a hook on the moving cable as it went by. The cable kept moving. The chain tightened. The pig's leg was pulled up and back, and then the pig itself began to be dragged backwards. But it didn't fall down. It was rather a nimble pig, and somehow it managed to keep its balance on three legs, hopping from foot to foot and struggling against the pull of the chain, but going back and back all the time until at the end of the pen where the cable changed direction and went vertically upward, the creature was suddenly jerked off its feet and borne aloft. Shrill protests filled the air.

"Truly a fascinating process," Lexington said. "But what was that funny cracking noise it made as it went up?"

"Probably the leg," the guide answered. "Either that or the pelvis."

"But doesn't that matter?"

"Why should it matter?" the guide asked. "You don't eat the bones."

The rubber-booted men were busy shackling the rest of the pigs, and one after another they were hooked to the moving cable and hoisted up through the roof, protesting loudly as they went.

"There's a good deal more in this recipe than just picking herbs," Lexington said. "Aunt Glosspan would never have made it."

At this point, while Lexington was gazing skyward at the last pig to go up, a man in rubber boots approached him quietly from behind and looped one end of a chain around the youth's own left ankle, hooking the other end to the moving belt. The next moment, before he had time to realize what was happening, our hero was jerked off his feet and dragged backwards along the concrete floor of the shackling-pen.

"Stop!" he cried. "Hold everything! My leg is caught!"

But nobody seemed to hear him, and five seconds later, the unhappy young man was jerked off the floor and hoisted vertically upward through the open roof of the pen, dangling upside down by one ankle, and wriggling like a fish.

"Help!" he shouted. "Help! There's been a frightful mistake! Stop the engines! Let me down!"

The guide removed a cigar from his mouth and looked up serenely at the rapidly ascending youth, but he said nothing. The men in rubber boots were already on their way out to collect the next batch of pigs.

"Oh save me!" our hero cried. "Let me down! Please let me down!" But he was now approaching the top floor of the building where the moving belt curled over like a snake and entered a large hole in the wall, a kind of doorway without a door; and there, on the threshold, waiting to greet him, clothed in a dark-stained yellow rubber apron, and looking for all the world like Saint Peter at the Gates of Heaven, the sticker stood.

Lexington saw him only from upside down, and very briefly at that, but even so he noticed at once the expression of absolute peace and benevolence on the man's face, the cheerful twinkle in the eyes, and little wistful smile, the dimples in his cheeks—and all this gave him hope.

"Hi there," the sticker said, smiling.

"Quick! Save me!" our hero cried.

"With pleasure," the sticker said, and taking Lexington gently by one ear with his left hand, he raised his right hand and deftly slit open the boy's jugular vein with a knife.

The belt moved on. Lexington went with it. Everything was still upside down and the blood was pouring out of his throat and getting into his eyes, but he could still see after a fashion, and he had a blurred impression of being in an enormously long room, and at the far end of the room there was a great smoking cauldron of water, and there were dark figures, half hidden in the steam, dancing around the edge of it, brandishing long poles. The conveyor-belt seemed to be travelling right over the top of the cauldron, and the pigs seemed to be dropping down one by one into the boiling water, and one of the pigs seemed to be wearing long white gloves on its front feet.

Suddenly our hero started to feel very sleepy, but it wasn't until his good strong heart had pumped the last drop of blood from his body that he passed on out of this, the best of all possible worlds, into the next.

Questions

1. A striking effect of this story is the change in tone that takes place. Describe and evaluate the appropriateness (in view of what is to come) of the rather ordinary, complacent tone at the beginning. Show where it starts to change.

2. After the reader recovers from the shock of the ending, he might examine whether it was prepared for or anticipated. Was it? Does a second reading increase or decrease one's respect for the skill of the author?

3. Is the story morbid? Comic? Ironic? Try to characterize its rather elusive nature.

4. Does the story have a point or theme, or is it largely an exercise in manipulating the sensibilities and the responses of the reader?

Edwin Granberry

A TRIP TO CZARDIS

Edwin Granberry has combined an academic career with his writing. Born in Meridian, Mississippi, in 1897, he was educated at the University of Florida and Columbia University, and then attended the famous 47 Workshop in drama at Harvard. He has taught romance languages and creative writing at various universities. Much of his own writing is set in the more remote regions of the South. He often uses back-woods characters who live close to the edge of bare existence. The short stories interpreting this life are his best-known works. He has also written several novels, among which are: The Ancient Hunger *(1927),* Strangers and Lovers *(1928), and* The Erl King *(1930).*

"A Trip to Czardis" (from Forum *magazine, April, 1932) is another "initiation" story—it deals with young characters who change and grow up because of a single experience that shatters their complacent world of childhood. Some readers have considered the story too melodramatic; others admire the skill with which Granberry leads the reader (along with his characters) toward the discovery of the horror of the situation by implication rather than by direct statement.*

It was still dark in the pine woods when the two brothers awoke. But it was plain that day had come, and in a little while there would be no more stars. Day itself would be in the sky and they would be going along the road. Jim waked first, coming quickly out of sleep and sitting up in the bed to take fresh hold of the things in his head, starting them up again out of the corners of his mind where sleep had tucked them. Then he waked Daniel and they sat up together in the bed. Jim put his arm around his young brother, for the night had been dewy and cool with the swamp wind. Daniel shivered a little and whimpered, it being dark in the room and his baby concerns still on him somewhat, making sleep heavy on his mind and slow to give understanding its way.

"Hit's the day, Dan'l. This day that's right here now, we are goen. You'll recollect it all in a minute."

"I recollect. We are goen in the wagon to see papa——"

"Then hush and don't whine."

"I were dreamen, Jim."

"What dreamen did you have?"

"I can't tell. But it were fearful what I dreamt."

"All the way we are goen this time. We won't stop at any places, but we will go all the way to Czardis to see papa. I never see such a place as Czardis."

"I recollect the water tower ——"

"Not in your own right, Dan'l. Hit's by my tellen it you see it in your mind."

"And lemonade with ice in it I saw ——"

"That too I seen and told to you."

"Then I never seen it at all?"

"Hit's me were there, Dan'l. I let you play like, but hit's me who went to Czardis. Yet I never till this day told half how much I see. There's sights I never told."

They stopped talking, listening for their mother's stir in the kitchen. But the night stillness was unlifted. Daniel began to shiver again.

"Hit's dark," he said.

"Hit's your eyes stuck," Jim said. "Would you want me to drip a little water on your eyes?"

"Oh!" cried the young one, pressing his face into his brother's side, "don't douse me, Jim, no more. The cold aches me."

The other soothed him, holding him around the body.

"You won't have e're chill or malarie ache to-day, Dan'l. Hit's a fair day ——"

"I won't be cold?"

"Hit's a bright day. I hear mournen doves starten a'ready. The sun will bake you warm. . . . Uncle Holly might buy us somethen new to eat in Czardis."

"What would it be?"

"Hit ain't decided yet. . . . He hasn't spoke. Hit might be somethen sweet. Maybe a candy ball fixed on to a rubber string."

"A candy ball!" Daniel showed a stir of happiness. "Oh, Jim!" But it was a deceit of the imagination, making his eyes shine wistfully; the grain of his flesh was against it. He settled into a stillness by himself.

"My stomach would retch it up, Jim. . . . I guess I couldn't eat it."

"You might could keep a little down."

"No . . . I would bring it home and keep it. . . ."

Their mother when they went to bed had laid a clean pair of pants and a waist for each on the chair. Jim crept out of bed and put on his clothes, then aided his brother on with his. They could not hear any noise in the kitchen, but hickory firewood burning in the kitchen stove worked a smell through the house, and in the forest guinea fowls were sailing down from the trees and poking their way along the half-dark ground toward the kitchen steps, making it known the door was open and that within someone was stirring about at the getting of food.

Jim led his brother by the hand down the dark way of yellow-pine stairs that went narrowly and without banisters to the rooms below. The young brother went huddling in his clothes, aguelike, knowing warmth was near, hungering for his place by the stove, to sit in peace on the bricks in the floor by the stove's side and watch the eating, it being his nature to have a sickness against food.

They came in silence to the kitchen, Jim leading and holding his brother by the hand. The floor was lately strewn with fresh bright sand that would sparkle when the daybreak got above the forest, though now it lay dull as hoarfrost and cold to the unshod feet of the brothers. The door to the firebox of the stove was open and in front of it their mother sat in a chair speaking low as they entered, uttering under her breath. The two boys went near and stood still, thinking she was blessing the food, there being mush dipped up and steaming in two bowls. And they stood cast down until she lifted her eyes to them and spoke.

"Your clothes on already," she said. "You look right neat." She did not rise, but kept her chair, looking cold and stiff, with the cloth of her black dress sagging between her knees. The sons stood in front of her and she laid her hand on first one head and then the other and spoke a little about the day, charging them to be sober and of few words, as she had raised them.

Jim sat on the bench by the table and began to eat, mixing dark molasses sugar through his bowl of mush. But a nausea began in Daniel's stomach at sight of the sweet and he lagged by the stove, gazing at the food as it passed into his brother's mouth.

Suddenly a shadow filled the back doorway and Holly, their uncle, stood there looking in. He was lean and big and dark from wind and weather, working in the timber as their father had done. He had no wife and children and would roam far off with the timber gangs in the Everglades. This latter year he did not go far, but stayed near them. Their mother stopped and looked at the man and he looked at her in silence. Then he looked at Jim and Daniel.

"You're goen to take them, after all?"

She waited a minute, seeming to get the words straight in her mind before bringing them out, making them say what was set there.

"He asked to see them. Nobody but God-Almighty ought to tell a soul hit can or can't have."

Having delivered her mind, she went out into the yard with the man and they spoke more words in an undertone, pausing in their speech.

In the silence of the kitchen, Daniel began to speak out and name what thing among his possessions he would take to Czardis to give his father. But the older boy belittled this and that and everything that was called up, saying one thing was of too little consequence for a man, and that another was of no account because it was food. But when the older boy had abolished the idea and silence had regained, he worked back to the thought, coming to it roundabout and making it new and as his own, letting it be decided that each of them would take their father a pomegranate from the tree in the yard.

They went to the kitchen door. The swamp fog had risen suddenly. They saw their mother standing in the lot while their uncle hitched the horse to the wagon. Leaving the steps, Jim climbed to the first crotch of the pomegranate tree. The reddest fruits were on the top branches. He worked his way up higher. The fog was now curling up out of the swamp, making gray mountains and rivers in the air and strange ghost shapes. Landmarks disappeared in the billows, or half-seen, they bewildered the sight and an eye could so little mark the known or strange that a befuddlement took hold of the mind, like the visitations sailors beheld in the fogs of Okeechobee. Jim could not find the ground. He seemed to have climbed into the mountains. The light was unnatural and dark and the pines were blue and dark over the mountains.

A voice cried out of the fog:

"Are worms gnawen you that you skin up a pomegranate tree at this hour? Don't I feed you enough?"

The boy worked his way down. At the foot of the tree he met his mother. She squatted and put her arm around him, her voice tight and quivering, and he felt tears on her face.

"We ain't come to the shame yet of you and Dan'l hunten your food off trees and grass. People seein' you gnawen on the road will say Jim Cameron's sons are starved, foragen like cattle of the field."

"I were getten the pomegranates for papa," said the boy, resigned to his mother's concern. She stood up when he said this, holding him in front of her skirts. In a while she said:

"I guess we won't take any, Jim. . . . But I'm proud it come to you to take your papa somethen."

And after a silence, the boy said:

"Hit were Dan'l it come to, Mamma."

Then she took his hand, not looking down, and in her throat, as if in her bosom, she repeated:

"Hit were a fine thought and I'm right proud . . . though to-day we won't take anything. . . ."

"I guess there's better pomegranates in Czardis where we are goen—"

"There's no better pomegranates in Czardis then right here over your head," she said grimly. "If pomegranates were needed, we would take him his own. . . . You are older'n Dan'l, Jim. When we get to the place we are goen, you won't know your papa after so long. He will be pale and he won't be as bright as you recollect. So don't labor him with questions . . . but speak when it behooves you and let him see you are upright."

When the horse was harnessed and all was ready for the departure, the sons were seated on a shallow bed of hay in the back of the wagon and the mother took the driver's seat alone. The uncle had argued for having the top up over the seat, but she refused the shelter, remarking that she had always driven under the sky and would do it still to-day. He gave in silently and got upon the seat of his own wagon, which took the road first, their wagon following. This was strange and the sons asked:

"Why don't we all ride in Uncle Holly's wagon?"

But their mother made no reply.

For several miles they traveled in silence through their own part of the woods, meeting no one. The boys whispered a little to themselves, but their mother and their uncle sat without speaking, nor did they turn their heads to look back. At last the narrow road they were following left the woods and came out to the highway and it was seen that other wagons besides their own were going to Czardis. And as they got farther along, they began to meet many other people going to the town, and the boys asked their mother what day it was. It was Wednesday. And then they asked her why so many wagons were going along the road if it wasn't Saturday and a market day. When she told them to be quiet, they settled down to watching the people go by. Some of them were faces that were strange and some were neighbors who lived in other parts of the woods. Some who passed them stared in silence and some went by looking straight to the front. But there were none of them who spoke, for their mother turned her eyes neither right nor left, but drove the horse on like a woman in her sleep. All was silent as the wagons passed, except the squeaking of the wheels and the thud of the horses' hoofs on the dry, packed sand.

At the edge of the town, the crowds increased and their wagon got lost in the press of people. All were moving in one direction.

Finally they were going along by a high brick wall on top of which ran a barbed-wire fence. Farther along the way in the middle of the wall was a tall, stone building with many people in front. There were trees along the outside of the wall and in the branches of one of the trees Daniel saw a man. He was looking over the brick wall down into the courtyard. All the wagons were stopping here and hitching through the grove in front of the building. But their Uncle Holly's wagon and their own drove on, making way slowly as through a crowd at a fair, for under the trees knots of men were gathered, talking in undertone. Daniel pulled at his mother's skirts and whispered:

"What made that man climb up that tree?"

Again she told him to be quiet.

"We're not to talk to-day," said Jim. "Papa is sick and we're not to make him worse." But his high, thin voice made his mother turn cold. She looked back and saw he had grown pale and still, staring at the iron-barred windows of the building. When he caught her gaze, his chin began to quiver and she turned back front to dodge the knowledge of his eyes.

For the two wagons had stopped now and the uncle gotten down and left them sitting alone while he went to the door of the building and talked with a man standing there. The crowd fell silent, staring at their mother.

"See, Jim, all the men up the trees!" Daniel whispered once more, leaning close in to his brother's side.

"Hush, Dan'l. Be still."

The young boy obeyed this time, falling into a bewildered stare at all the things about him he did not understand, for in all the trees along the brick wall men began to appear perched high in the branches, and on the roof of a building across the way stood other men, all gaping at something in the yard back of the wall.

Their uncle returned and hitched his horse to a ring in one of the trees. Then he hitched their mother's horse and all of them got out and stood on the ground in a huddle. The walls of the building rose before them. Strange faces at the barred windows laughed aloud and called down curses at the men below.

Now they were moving, with a wall of faces on either side of them, their uncle going first, followed by their mother who held to each of them by a hand. They went up the steps of the building. The door opened and their uncle stepped inside. He came back in a moment and all of them went in and followed a man down a corridor and into a bare room with two chairs and a wooden bench. A man in a black robe sat on one of the chairs, and in front of him on the bench, leaning forward looking down between his arms, sat their father. His face was lean and gray, which made him look very tall. But his hair was black, and his eyes were blue and mild and strange as he stood up and held the two sons against his body while he stooped his head to kiss their mother. The man in black left the room and walked up and down outside in the corridor. A second stranger stood in the doorway with his back to the room. The father picked up one of the sons and then the other in his arms and looked at them and leaned their faces on his own. Then he sat down on the bench and held them against him. Their mother sat down by them and they were all togther.

A few low words were spoken and then a silence fell over them all. And in a while the parents spoke a little more and touched one another. But the bare stone floor and the stone walls and the unaccustomed arms of their father hushed the sons with the new and strange. And when the time had passed, the father took his watch from his pocket:

"I'm goen to give you my watch, Jim. You are the oldest. I want you to keep it till you are a grown man. . . . And I want you to always do what mamma tells you. . . . I'm goen to give you the chain, Dan'l. . . ."

The young brother took the chain, slipped out of his father's arms, and went to his mother with it. He spread it out on her knee and began to talk to her in a whisper. She bent over him, and again all of them in the room grew silent.

A sudden sound of marching was heard in the corridor. The man rose up and took his sons in his arms, holding them abruptly. But their uncle, who had been standing with the man in the doorway, came suddenly and took them and went out and down through the big doorway by which they had entered the building. As the doors opened to let them pass, the crowd gathered around the steps pressed forward to look inside. The older boy cringed in his uncle's arms. His uncle turned and stood with his back to the crowd. Their mother came through the doors. The crowd fell back. Again through a passageway of gazing eyes, they reached the wagons. This time they sat on the seat beside their mother. Leaving their uncle and his wagon behind, they started off on the road that led out of town.

"Is papa coming home with Uncle Holly?" Jim asked in a still voice.

His mother nodded her head.

Reaching the woods once more and the silence he knew, Daniel whispered to his brother:

"We got a watch and chain instead, Jim."

But Jim neither answered nor turned his eyes.

Questions

1. What details early in the story create a certain tension? What details indicate that the day is of a special nature?
2. At what point in the story can the reader foresee the ending—

becoming aware of the reason for the trip to Czardis? At what point might the author *want* the reader to know the outcome? What is the effect of having the reader comprehend more than the characters do?

3. Many details of the father's situation are omitted—the nature of his crime, any question of his guilt or innocence, any facts about his trial. Why are they not given? In view of the theme of the story, what importance would they have?

4. On the way home, how much does each boy understand about what he has seen?

5. Why, at the end, does Jim neither answer nor turn his eyes? He is apparently lost in thought. What is he thinking? What new perception does he now have of the adult world?

Dashiell Hammett

THEY CAN ONLY HANG YOU ONCE

It is now possible to take Dashiell Hammett seriously as an important writer, though he was long regarded primarily as a pulp writer and an exponent of the hard-boiled school of detective fiction. Born in Maryland in 1894, he went to school only until he was fourteen, then held various laboring jobs until he became an operative for the Pinkerton Detective Agency. Service in World War I left his health impaired, and he turned to writing, drawing on his background with Pinkerton's. In the 1920s he wrote many crime stories for Black Mask *and other pulp magazines, where he developed his lean, economical prose style. This style at first seems impersonal and detached, but is a tightly controlled and highly appropriate vehicle for his stories whose subject matter is usually self- destructive greed, or violence which begets violence. After his apprenticeship in the pulps he quickly produced five novels—* Red Harvest *and* The Dain Curse *(both 1929),* The Maltese Falcon *(1930),* The Glass Key *(1931), and* The Thin Man *(1934)—and then very little more except film scripts in Hollywood. However, he changed the direction of the American detective story, making it hard, tough, and relentless, and he created the prototype of the private eye who moves through grim scenes of carnage and evil but strives to remain uncorrupted by them. In an editorial eulogy following his death in 1961, the* New York Times *described his stories as being "as consistent as mathematics and as intricate as psychology." After Hammett's death, his close friend Lillian Hellman edited a collection of his stories called* The Big Knockover *(1966), for which she provided a long and sympathetic introduction. She discussed his work and their friendship at greater length in her autobiographical memoir,* An Unfinished Woman *(1969).*

"They Can Only Hang You Once" was resurrected from the pulps and reprinted in Will Cuppy's anthology of detective stories, Murder Without Tears *(1946). It is typical of Hammett's plots in that it is*

tightly-knit and moves swiftly and relentlessly not only to expose criminal activities but to unmask deeper kinds of deceit.

Samuel Spade said, "My name is Ronald Ames. I want to see Mr. Binnett —Mr. Timothy Binnett."

"Mr. Binnett is resting now, sir," the butler replied hesitantly.

"Will you find out when I can see him? It's important." Spade cleared his throat. "I'm—uh—just back from Australia, and it's about some of his properties there."

The butler turned on his heel while saying, "I'll see, sir," and was going up the front stairs before he had finished speaking.

Spade made and lit a cigarette.

The butler came downstairs again.

"I'm sorry; he can't be disturbed now, but Mr. Wallace Binnett—Mr. Timothy's nephew—will see you."

Spade said, "Thanks," and followed the butler upstairs.

Wallace Binnett was a slender, handsome, dark man of about Spade's age—thirty-eight—who rose smiling from a brocaded chair, said, "How do you do, Mr. Ames?" waved his hand at another chair, and sat down again. "You're from Australia?"

"Got in this morning."

"You're a business associate of Uncle Tim's?"

Spade smiled and shook his head. "Hardly that, but I've some information I think he ought to have—quick."

Wallace Binnett looked thoughtfully at the floor, then up at Spade. "I'll do my best to persuade him to see you, Mr. Ames, but, frankly, I don't know."

Spade seemed mildly surprised. "Why?"

Binnett shrugged. "He's peculiar sometimes. Understand, his mind seems perfectly all right, but he has the testiness and eccentricity of an old man in ill health and—well—at times he can be difficult."

Spade asked slowly, "He's already refused to see me?"

"Yes."

Spade rose from his chair. His blond satan's face was expressionless.

Binnett raised a hand quickly.

"Wait, wait," he said. "I'll do what I can to make him change his mind. Perhaps if—" His dark eyes suddenly became wary. "You're not simply trying to sell him something, are you?"

"No."

The wary gleam went out of Binnett's eyes. "Well, then, I think I can—"

A young woman came in crying angrily, "Wally, that old fool has—" She broke off with a hand to her breast when she saw Spade.

Spade and Binnett had risen together.

Binnett said suavely, "Joyce, this is Mr. Ames. My sister-in-law, Joyce Court."

Spade bowed.

Joyce Court uttered a short, embarrassed laugh and said, "Please excuse my whirlwind entrance."

She was a tall, blue-eyed, dark woman of twenty-four or -five with good shoulders and a strong, slim body. Her features made up in warmth what they lacked in regularity. She wore wide-legged, blue satin pajamas.

Binnett smiled good-naturedly at her and asked:

"Now what's all the excitement?"

Anger darkened her eyes again and she started to speak. Then she looked at Spade and said:

"But we shouldn't bore Mr. Ames with our stupid domestic affairs. If—" She hesitated.

Spade bowed again. "Sure," he said, "certainly."

"I won't be a minute," Binnett promised, and left the room with her.

Spade went to the open doorway through which they had vanished and, standing just inside, listened. Their footsteps became inaudible. Nothing else could be heard.

Spade was standing there—his yellow-gray eyes dreamy—when he heard the scream. It was a woman's scream, high and shrill with terror. Spade was through the doorway when he heard the shot.

It was a pistol shot, magnified, reverberated by walls and ceilings.

Twenty feet from the doorway Spade found a staircase, and went up it three steps at a time. He turned to the left. Halfway down the hallway a woman lay on her back on the floor.

Wallace Binnett knelt beside her, fondling one of her hands desperately, crying in a low, beseeching voice, "Darling, Molly, darling!"

Joyce Court stood behind him and wrung her hands while tears streaked her cheeks.

The woman on the floor resembled Joyce Court but was older, and her face had a hardness the younger one's had not.

"She's dead, she's been killed," Wallace Binnett said incredulously, raising his white face toward Spade.

When Binnett moved his head Spade could see the round hole in the woman's tan dress over her heart and the dark stain which was rapidly spreading below it.

Spade touched Joyce Court's arm.

"Police, emergency hospital—phone," he said.

As she ran toward the stairs he addressed Wallace Binnett: "Who did—"

A voice groaned feebly behind Slade.

He turned swiftly. Through an open doorway he could see an old man in white pajamas lying sprawled across a rumpled bed. His head, a shoulder, an arm dangled over the edge of his bed. His other hand held his throat tightly. He groaned again and his eyelids twitched, but did not open.

Spade lifted the old man's head and shoulders and put them up on the pillows. The old man groaned again and took his hand from his throat. His throat was red with half a dozen bruises. He was a gaunt man with a seamed face that probably exaggerated his age.

A glass of water was on a table beside the bed. Spade put water on the old man's face and, when the old man's eyes twitched again, leaned down and growled softly:

"Who did it?"

The twitching eyelids went up far enough to show a narrow strip of bloodshot gray eyes. The old man spoke painfully, putting a hand to his throat again:

"A man—he—" He coughed.

Spade made an impatient grimace. His lips almost touched the old man's ear.

"Where'd he go?" His voice was urgent.

A gaunt hand moved weakly to indicate the rear of the house and fell back on the bed.

The butler and two frightened female servants had joined Wallace Binnett beside the dead woman in the hallway.

"Who did it?" Spade asked them.

They stared at him blankly.

"Somebody look after the old man," he growled, and went down the hallway.

At the end of the hallway was a rear staircase. He descended two flights and went through a pantry into the kitchen. He saw nobody. The kitchen door was shut but, when he tried it, not locked. He crossed a narrow back yard to a gate that was shut, not locked. He opened the gate. There was nobody in the narrow alley behind it.

He sighed, shut the gate, and returned to the house.

Spade sat comfortably slack in a deep leather chair in a room that ran across the front second story of Wallace Binnett's house. There were shelves of books and the lights were on. The window showed outer darkness weakly diluted by a distant street lamp.

Facing Spade, Detective Sergeant Polhaus—a big, carelessly shaven, florid man in dark clothes that needed pressing—was sprawled in another leather chair; Lieutenant Dundy—smaller, compactly built, square-faced—stood with legs apart, head thrust a little forward, in the center of the room.

Spade was saying:

"—and the doctor would only let me talk to the old man a couple of minutes. We can try it again when he's rested a little, but it doesn't look like he knows much. He was catching a nap and he woke up with somebody's hands on his throat dragging him around the bed. The best he got was a one-eyed look at the fellow choking him. A big fellow, he says, with a soft hat pulled down over his eyes, dark, needing a shave. Sounds like Tom." Spade nodded at Polhaus.

The detective sergeant chuckled, but Dundy said, "Go on," curtly.

Spade grinned and went on:

"He's pretty far gone when he hears Mrs. Binnett scream at the door. The hands go away from his throat and he hears the shot and just before passing out he gets a flash of the big fellow heading for the rear of the house and Mrs. Binnett tumbling down on the hall floor. He says he never saw the big fellow before."

"What size gun was it?" Dundy asked.

"Thirty-eight. Well, nobody in the house is much more help. Wallace and his sister-in-law, Joyce, were in her room, so they say, and didn't see anything but the dead woman when they ran out, though they think they heard something that could've been somebody running downstairs—the back stairs.

"The butler—his name's Jarboe—was in here when he heard the scream and shot, so he says. Irene Kelly, the maid, was down on the ground floor, so she says. The cook, Margaret Finn, was in her room—third floor back—and didn't even hear anything, so she says. She's deaf as a post, so everybody else says. The back door and gate were unlocked, but are supposed to be kept locked, so everybody says. Nobody says they were in or around the kitchen or yard at the time." Spade spread his hands in a gesture of finality. "That's the crop."

Dundy shook his head. "Not exactly," he said. "How come you were here?"

Spade's face brightened.

"Maybe my client killed her," he said. "He's Wallace's cousin, Ira Binnett. Know him?"

Dundy shook his head. His blue eyes were hard and suspicious.

"He's a San Francisco lawyer," Spade said, "respectable and all that. A couple of days ago he came to me with a story about his uncle Timothy, a miserly old skinflint, lousy with money and pretty well broken up by hard living. He was the black sheep of the family. None of them had heard of him for years. But six or eight months ago he showed up in pretty bad shape every way except financially—he seems to have taken a lot of money out of Australia—wanting to spend his last days with his only living relatives, his nephews Wallace and Ira.

"That was all right with them. 'Only living relatives' meant 'only heirs' in their language. But by and by the nephews began to think it was better to be an heir than to be one of a couple of heirs—twice as good, in fact—and started fiddling for the inside track with the old man. At least, that's what Ira told me about Wallace, and I wouldn't be surprised if Wallace would say the same thing about Ira, though Wallace seems to be the harder up of the two. Anyhow, the nephews fell out, and then Uncle Tim, who had been staying at Ira's, came over here. That was a couple of months ago, and Ira hasn't seen Uncle Tim since, and hasn't been able to get in touch with him by phone or mail.

"That's what he wanted a private detective about. He didn't think Uncle Tim would come to any harm here—oh, no, he went to a lot of trouble to make that clear—but he thought maybe undue pressure was being brought to bear on the old boy, or he was being hornswoggled somehow, and at least being told lies about his loving nephew Ira. He wanted to know what was what. I waited until today, when a boat from Australia docked, and came up here as a Mr. Ames with some important information for Uncle Tim about his properties down there. All I wanted was fifteen minutes alone with him."

Spade frowned thoughtfully. "Well, I didn't get them. Wallace told me the old man refused to see me. I don't know."

Suspicion had deepened in Dundy's cold blue eyes.

"And where is this Ira Binnett now?" he asked.

Spade's yellow-gray eyes were as guileless as his voice. "I wish I knew. I phoned his house and office and left word for him to come right over, but I'm afraid—"

Knuckles knocked sharply twice on the other side of the room's one door.

The three men in the room turned to face the door.

Dundy called, "Come in."

The door was opened by a sunburned blond policeman whose left hand held the right wrist of a plump man of forty or forty-five in well-fitting gray clothes. The policeman pushed the plump man into the room.

"Found him monkeying with the kitchen door," he said.

Spade looked up and said, "Ah!" His tone expressed satisfaction. "Mr. Ira Binnett, Lieutenant Dundy, Sergeant Polhaus."

Ira Binnett said rapidly, "Mr. Spade, will you tell this man that—"

Dundy addressed the policeman: "All right. Good work. You can leave him."

The policeman moved a hand vaguely toward his cap and went away.

Dundy glowered at Ira Binnett and demanded, "Well?"

Binnett looked from Dundy to Spade. "Has something—"

Spade said, "Better tell him why you were at the back door instead of the front."

Ira Binnett suddenly blushed. He cleared his throat in embarrassment. He said, "I—uh—I should explain. It wasn't my fault, of course, but when Jarboe—he's the butler—phoned me that Uncle Tim wanted to see me he told me he'd leave the kitchen door unlocked, so Wallace wouldn't have to know I'd—"

"What'd he want to see you about?" Dundy asked.

"I don't know. He didn't say. He said it was very important."

"Didn't you get my message?" Spade asked.

Ira Binnett's eyes widened. "No. What was it? Has anything happened? What is–"

Spade was moving toward the door.

"Go ahead," he said to Dundy. "I'll be right back."

He shut the door carefully behind him and went up to the third floor.

The butler Jarboe was on his knees at Timothy Binnett's door with an eye to the keyhole. On the floor beside him was a tray holding an egg in an egg-cup, toast, a pot of coffee, china, silver, and a napkin.

Spade said, "Your toast's going to get cold."

Jarboe, scrambling to his feet, almost upsetting the coffeepot in his haste, his face red and sheepish, stammered:

"I—er—beg your pardon, sir. I wanted to make sure Mr. Timothy was awake before I took this in." He picked up the tray. "I didn't want to disturb his rest if—"

Spade, who had reached the door, said, "Sure, sure," and bent over to put his eye to the keyhole. When he straightened up he said in a mildly complaining tone, "You can't see the bed—only a chair and part of the window."

The butler replied quickly, "Yes, sir, I found that out."

Spade laughed.

The butler coughed, seemed about to say something, but did not. He hesitated, then knocked lightly on the door.

A tired voice said, "Come in."

Spade asked quickly in a low voice, "Where's Miss Court?"

"In her room, I think, sir, the second door on the left," the butler said.

The tired voice inside the room said petulantly, "Well, come on in."

The butler opened the door and went in. Through the door, before the butler shut it, Spade caught a glimpse of Timothy Binnett propped up on pillows in his bed.

Spade went to the second door on the left and knocked. The door was opened almost immediately by Joyce Court. She stood in the doorway, not smiling, not speaking.

He said, "Miss Court, when you came into the room where I was with your brother-in-law you said, 'Wally, that old fool has—' Meaning Timothy?"

She stared at Spade for a moment. Then: "Yes."

"Mind telling me what the rest of the sentence would have been?"

She said slowly, "I don't know who you really are or why you ask, but I don't mind telling you. It would have been 'sent for Ira.' Jarboe had just told me."

"Thanks."

She shut the door before he had turned away.

He returned to Timothy Binnett's door and knocked on it.

"Who is it now?" the old man's voice demanded.

Spade opened the door. The old man was sitting up in bed. Spade said, "This Jarboe was peeping through your keyhole a few minutes ago," and returned to the library.

Ira Binnett, seated in the chair Spade had occupied, was saying to Dundy and Polhaus, "And Wallace got caught in the crash, like most of us, but he seems to have juggled accounts trying to save himself. He was expelled from the Stock Exchange."

Dundy waved a hand to indicate the room and its furnishings. "Pretty classy layout for a man that's busted."

"His wife has some money," Ira Binnett said, "and he always lived beyond his means."

Dundy scowled at Binnett. "And you really think he and his missus weren't on good terms?"

"I don't think it," Binnett replied evenly. "I know it."

Dundy nodded. "And you know he's got a yen for the sister-in-law, this Court?"

"I don't know that. But I've heard plenty of gossip to the same effect."

Dundy made a growling noise in his throat, then asked sharply, "How does the old man's will read?"

"I don't know. I don't know whether he's made one." He addressed Spade, now earnestly: "I've told everything I know, every single thing."

Dundy said, "It's not enough." He jerked a thumb at the door. "Show him where to wait, Tom, and let's have the widower in again."

Big Polhaus said, "Right," went out with Ira Binnett, and returned with Wallace Binnett, whose face was hard and pale.

Dundy asked, "Has your uncle made a will?"

"I don't know," Binnett replied.

Spade put the next question, softly: "Did your wife?"

Binnett's mouth tightened in a mirthless smile. He spoke deliberately: "I'm going to say some things I'd rather not have to say. My wife, properly, had no money. When I got into financial trouble some time ago I made some property over to her, to save it. She turned it into money without my knowing about it till afterward. She paid our bills—our living expenses—out of it, but she refused to return it to me and she assured me that in no event—whether she lived or died or we stayed together or were divorced—would I ever be able to get hold of a penny of it. I believed her, and still do."

"You wanted a divorce?" Dundy asked.

"Yes."

"Why?"

"It wasn't a happy marriage."

"Joyce Court?"

Binnett's face flushed. He said stiffly, "I admire Joyce Court tremendously, but I'd've wanted a divorce anyway."

Spade said, "And you're sure—still absolutely sure—you don't know anybody who fits your uncle's description of the man who choked him?"

"Absolutely sure."

The sound of the doorbell ringing came faintly into the room. Dundy said sourly, "That'll do."

Binnett went out.

Polhaus said, "That guy's as wrong as they make them. And–"

From below came the heavy report of a pistol fired indoors. The lights went out.

In the darkness the three detectives collided with one another going through the doorway into the dark hall.

Spade reached the stairs first. There was a clatter of footsteps below him, but nothing could be seen until he reached a bend in the stairs. Then enough light came from the street through the open front door to show the dark figure of a man standing with his back to the open door.

A flashlight clicked in Dundy's hand—he was at Spade's heels—and threw a glaring white beam of light on the man's face.

He was Ira Binnett. He blinked in the light and pointed at something on the floor in front of him.

Dundy turned the beam of his light down on the floor. Jarboe lay there on his face, bleeding from a bullet hole in the back of his head.

Spade grunted softly.

Tom Polhaus came blundering down the stairs, Wallace Binnett close behind him. Joyce Court's frightened voice came from farther up:

"Oh, what's happened? Wally, what's happened?"

"Where's the light switch?" Dundy barked.

"Inside the cellar door, under these stairs," Wallace Binnett said. "What is it?"

Polhaus pushed past Binnett toward the cellar door.

Spade made an inarticulate sound in his throat and, pushing Wallace

Binnett aside, sprang up the stairs. He brushed past Joyce Court and went on, heedless of her startled scream. He was halfway up the stairs to the third floor when the pistol went off up there.

He ran to Timothy Binnett's door. The door was open. He went in.

Something hard and angular struck him above his right ear, knocking him across the room, bringing him down on one knee. Something thumped and clattered on the floor just outside the door.

The lights came on.

On the floor, in the center of the room, Timothy Binnett lay on his back bleeding from a bullet wound in his left forearm. His pajama jacket was torn. His eyes were shut.

Spade stood up and put a hand to his head. He scowled at the old man on the floor, at the room, at the black automatic pistol lying on the hallway floor.

He said, "Come on, you old cutthroat. Get up and sit on a chair and I'll see if I can stop that bleeding till the doctor gets here."

The man on the floor did not move.

There were footsteps in the hallway and Dundy came in, followed by the two younger Binnetts. Dundy's face was dark and furious.

"Kitchen door wide open," he said in a choked voice. "They run in and out like—"

"Forget it," Spade said. "Uncle Tim is our meat." He paid no attention to Wallace Binnett's gasp, to the incredulous looks on Dundy's and Ira Binnett's faces. "Come on, get up," he said to the old man on the floor, "and tell us what it was the butler saw when he peeped through the keyhole."

The old man did not stir.

"He killed the butler because I told him the butler had peeped," Spade explained to Dundy. "I peeped, too, but didn't see anything except that chair and the window, though we'd made enough racket by then to scare him back to bed. Suppose you take the chair apart while I go over the window."

He went to the window and began to examine it carefully. He shook his head, put a hand out behind him, and said, "Give me the flashlight."

Dundy put the flashlight in his hand.

Spade raised the window and leaned out, turning the light on the outside of the building. Presently he grunted and put his other hand out, tugging at a brick a little below the sill. Presently the brick came loose. He put it on the window sill and stuck his hand into the hole its removal had made. Out of the opening, one at a time, he brought an empty black pistol holster, a partially filled box of cartridges, and an unsealed manila envelope.

Holding these things in his hands, he turned to face the others.

Joyce Court came in with a basin of water and a roll of gauze and knelt beside Timothy Binnett.

Spade put the holster and cartridges on a table and opened the manila envelope. Inside were two sheets of paper, covered on both sides with boldly penciled writing. Spade read a paragraph to himself, suddenly laughed, and began at the beginning again, reading aloud:

" 'I, Timothy Kieran Binnett, being sound of mind and body, do declare this to be my last will and testament. To my dear nephews, Ira Binnett and Wallace Bourke Binnett, in recognition of the loving kindness with which they have received me into their homes and attended my declining years, I give and bequeath, share and share alike, all my worldly possessions of whatever kind, to wit, my carcass and the clothes I stand in.

" 'I bequeath them, furthermore, the expense of my funeral and these memories: First, the memory of their credulity in believing that the fifteen years I spent in Sing Sing were spent in Australia; second, the memory of their optimism in supposing that those fifteen years had brought me great wealth, and that if I lived on them, borrowed from them, and never spent any of my own money, it was because I was a miser whose hoard they would inherit; and not because I had no money except what I shook them down for; third, for their hopefulness in thinking that I would leave either of them anything if I had it; and lastly, because their painful lack of any decent sense of humor will keep them from ever seeing how funny this has all been. Signed and sealed this—' "

Spade looked up to say, "There is no date, but it's signed Timothy Kieran Binnett with flourishes."

Ira Binnett was purple with anger.

Wallace's face was ghastly in its pallor and his whole body was trembling.

Joyce Court had stopped working on Timothy Binnett's arm.

The old man sat up and opened his eyes. He looked at his nephews and began to laugh. There was in his laughter neither hysteria nor madness: it was sane, hearty laughter, and subsided slowly.

Spade said, "All right, now you've had your fun. Let's talk about the killings."

"I know nothing more about the first one than I've told you," the old man said, "and this one's not a killing, since I'm only—"

Wallace Binnett, still trembling violently, said painfully through his teeth:

"That's a lie. You killed Molly. Joyce and I came out of her room when we heard Molly scream, and heard the shot and saw her fall out of your room, and nobody came out afterward."

The old man said calmly, "Well, I'll tell you: it was an accident. They told me there was a fellow from Australia here to see me about some of my properties there. I knew there was something funny about that somewhere"—he grinned—"not ever having been there. I didn't know whether one of my dear nephews was getting suspicious and putting up a game on me or what, but I knew that if Wally wasn't in on it he'd certainly try to pump the gentleman from Australia about me and maybe I'd lose one of my free boarding houses."

He chuckled.

"So I figured I'd get in touch with Ira so I could go back to his house if things worked out bad here, and I'd try to get rid of this Australian. Wally's always thought I'm half-cracked"— he leered at his nephew—"and's afraid they'll lug me off to a madhouse before I could make a will in his favor, or they'll break it if I do. You see, he's got a pretty bad reputation, what with that Stock Exchange trouble and all, and he knows no court would appoint him to handle my affairs if I went screwy—not as long as I've got another nephew"—he turned his leer on Ira—"who's a respectable lawyer. So now I know that rather than have me kick up a row that might wind me up in the madhouse, he'll chase this visitor, and I put on a show for Molly, who happened to be the nearest one to hand. She took it too seriously, though.

"I had a gun and I did a lot of raving about being spied on by my enemies in Australia and that I was going down and shoot this fellow. But she got too excited and tried to take the gun away from me, and the first thing I knew it had gone off, and I had to make these marks on my neck and think up that story about the big dark man."

He looked contemptuously at Wallace.

"I didn't know he was covering me up. Little as I thought of him, I never thought he'd be low enough to cover up his wife's murderer—even if he didn't like her—just for the sake of money."

Spade said, "Never mind that. Now about the butler?"

"I don't know anything about the butler," the old man replied, looking at Spade with steady eyes.

Spade said, "You had to kill him quick, before he had time to do or say anything. So you slip down the back stairs, open the kitchen door to fool people, go to the front door, ring the bell, shut the door, and hide in the shadow of the cellar door under the front steps. When Jarboe answered the doorbell you shot him—the hole was in the back of his head—pulled the light switch, just inside the cellar door, and ducked up the back stairs in the dark and shot yourself carefully in the arm. I got up there too soon for you; so you smacked me with the gun, chucked it through the door, and spread yourself on the floor while I was shaking pinwheels out of my noodle."

The old man sniffed again. "You're just—"

"Stop it," Spade said patiently. "Don't let's argue. The first killing was an accident—all right. The second couldn't be. And it ought to be easy to show that both bullets, and the one in your arm, were fired from the same gun. What difference does it make which killing we can prove first-degree murder on? They can only hang you once." He smiled pleasantly. "And they will."

Questions

1. The narrative style of this story seems to be totally objective, and there is virtually no description of the detective. Does the reader know anything of him beyond the few stated facts—that is, anything of his character, personality, or private beliefs? How does he find out such things?

2. The detective is presumably an impartial agent with no personal stake in the outcome of his investigation. Is this wholly true? Does he have any personal feelings toward the other characters? Does he influence the outcome of the plot—other than in a professional way?

3. This is largely a linear plot story, a narrative of events and little else. Does the story move too fast? Should the author have spent more time on characterization, setting, motivation? What would be gained, and what lost, by doing so?

4. To what extent is the ending a surprise? Has it been prepared for? Is it logical? Knowing the outcome of the story, could one reread it with any degree of interest? How would the second reading differ from the first? What does your answer suggest about this kind of story?

Nathaniel Hawthorne

ETHAN BRAND

Certainly one criterion by which a writer is evaluated is the importance or significance of his subject matter. On this point Nathaniel Hawthorne must be judged very highly, for, compared with earlier American writers, Hawthorne attempted the most difficult feats. He avoided the easy and sometimes sentimental subjects and conventional viewpoints of his time, and deliberately chose to deal in his work with some of the most difficult questions that perennially challenge men, such as: What constitutes sin? How is guilt atoned for? Why does evil exist? Can man surmount the fact of evil and grow from it, rather than be destroyed by it? Hawthorne, born in Salem, Mass., in 1804, came naturally to these questions, for one of his ancestors had been an early persecutor of the Quakers, and another, his son, had been a judge at the Salem witchcraft trials in 1692. His son, according to tradition, received a curse from one of the "witches" he sentenced to be hanged. After Hawthorne's graduation from Bowdoin College in 1825, he returned to the family home in Salem for a period of twelve years, where he apparently brooded over this burden of inherited guilt. It was during this time that he determined to confront the Puritan preoccupation with sin in order to make possible a satisfactory life in the present. Then began the outpouring of works on the subject—first the short stories collected in Twice-Told Tales *(1837) and* Mosses from an Old Manse *(1846), and then the four great novels,* The Scarlet Letter *(1850),* The House of the Seven Gables *(1851),* The Blithedale Romance *(1852), and finally* The Marble Faun *(1860). Hawthorne died in 1864.*

"Ethan Brand" is one of Hawthorne's dark, ambiguous stories on one of his recurrent themes, the "unpardonable sin." Perhaps the sin is pride; perhaps it is disdain for ordinary human contact; perhaps it is beyond specific identification. This story is from The Snow-Image and Other Tales *(1852).*

Bartram the lime-burner, a rough, heavy-looking man, begrimed with charcoal, sat watching his kiln, at nightfall, while his little son played at building houses with the scattered fragments of marble, when, on the hillside below them, they heard a roar of laughter, not mirthful, but slow, and even solemn, like a wind shaking the boughs of the forest.

"Father, what is that?" asked the little boy, leaving his play, and pressing betwixt his father's knees.

"Oh, some drunken man, I suppose," answered the lime-burner; "some merry fellow from the bar-room in the village, who dared not laugh loud enough within doors lest he should blow the roof of the house off. So here he is, shaking his jolly sides at the foot of Graylock."

"But, father," said the child, more sensitive than the obtuse, middle-aged clown, "he does not laugh like a man that is glad. So the noise frightens me!"

"Don't be a fool, child!" cried his father, gruffly. "You will never make a man, I do believe; there is too much of your mother in you. I have known the rustling of a leaf startle you. Hark! Here comes the merry fellow now. You shall see that there is no harm in him."

Bartram and his little son, while they were talking thus, sat watching the same lime-kiln that had been the scene of Ethan Brand's solitary and meditative life, before he began his search for the Unpardonable Sin. Many years, as we have seen, had now elapsed, since that portentous night when the IDEA was first developed. The kiln, however, on the mountain-side, stood unimpaired, and was in nothing changed since he had thrown his dark thoughts into the intense glow of its furnace, and melted them, as it were, into the one thought that took possession of his life. It was a rude, round, tower-like structure about twenty feet high, heavily built of rough stones, and with a hillock of earth heaped about the larger part of its circumference; so that the blocks and fragments of marble might be drawn by cart-loads, and thrown in at the top. There was an opening at the bottom of the tower, like an oven-mouth, but large enough to admit a man in a stooping posture, and provided with a massive iron door. With the smoke and jets of flame issuing from the chinks and crevices of this door, which seemed to give admittance into the hillside, it resembled nothing so much as the private entrance to the infernal regions, which the shepherds of the Delectable Mountains were accustomed to show to pilgrims.

There are many such lime-kilns in that tract of country, for the purpose of burning the white marble which composes a large part of the substance of the hills. Some of them, built years ago, and long deserted, with weeds growing in the vacant round of the interior, which is open to the sky, and grass and wild-flowers rooting themselves into the chinks of the stones, look already like relics of antiquity, and may yet be overspread with the lichens of centuries to come. Others, where the lime-burner still feeds his daily and night-long fire, afford points of interest to the wanderer among the hills, who seats himself on a log of wood or a fragment of marble, to hold a chat with the solitary man. It is a lonesome, and, when the character is inclined to thought, may be an intensely thoughtful occupation; as it proved in the case of Ethan Brand, who had mused to such strange purpose, in days gone by, while the fire in this very kiln was burning.

The man who now watched the fire was of a different order, and troubled himself with no thoughts save the very few that were requisite to his business. At frequent intervals, he flung back the clashing weight of the iron door, and, turning his face from the insufferable glare, thrust in huge logs of oak, or stirred the immense brands with a long pole. Within the furnace were seen the curling and riotous flames, and the burning marble, almost molten with the intensity of heat; while without, the reflection of the fire quivered on the dark intricacy of the surrounding forest, and showed in the foreground a bright and ruddy little picture of the hut, the spring beside its door, the athletic and coal-begrimed figure of the lime-burner, and the half-frightened child, shrinking into the protection of his father's shadow. And when again the iron door was closed, then reappeared the tender light of the half-full moon, which vainly strove to trace out the indistinct shapes of the neighboring mountains; and, in the upper sky, there was a flitting congregation of clouds, still faintly tinged with the rosy sunset, though thus far down into the valley the sunshine had vanished long and long ago.

The little boy now crept still closer to his father, as footsteps were heard ascending the hillside, and a human form thrust aside the bushes that clustered beneath the trees.

"Halloo! who is it?" cried the lime-burner, vexed at his son's timidity, yet half infected by it. "Come forward, and show yourself, like a man, or I'll fling this chunk of marble at your head!"

"You offer me a rough welcome," said a gloomy voice, as the unknown man drew nigh. "Yet I neither claim nor desire a kinder one, even at my own fireside."

To obtain a distincter view, Bartram threw open the iron door of the kiln, whence immediately issued a gush of fierce light, that smote full upon the stranger's face and figure. To a careless eye there appeared nothing very remarkable in his aspect, which was that of a man in a coarse, brown, country-made suit of clothes, tall and thin, with the staff and heavy shoes of a wayfarer. As he advanced, he fixed his eyes—which were very bright—intently upon the brightness of the furnace, as if he beheld, or expected to behold, some object worthy of note within it.

"Good evening, stranger," said the lime-burner; "whence come you, so late in the day?"

"I come from my search," answered the wayfarer; "for, at last, it is finished."

"Drunk!—or crazy!" muttered Bartram to himself. "I shall have trouble with the fellow. The sooner I drive him away, the better."

The little boy, all in a tremble, whispered to his father, and begged him to shut the door of the kiln, so that there might not be so much light; for that there was something in the man's face which he was afraid to look at, yet could not look away from. And, indeed, even the lime-burner's dull and torpid sense began to be impressed by an indescribable something in that thin, rugged, thoughtful visage, with the grizzled hair hanging wildly about it, and those deeply sunken eyes, which gleamed like fires within the entrance of a mysterious cavern. But, as he closed the door, the stranger turned towards him, and spoke in a quiet, familiar way, that made Bartram feel as if he were a sane and sensible man, after all.

"Your task draws to an end, I see," said he. "This marble has already been burning three days. A few hours more will convert the stone to lime."

"Why, who are you?" exclaimed the lime-burner. "You seem as well acquainted with my business as I am myself."

"And well I may be," said the stranger; "for I followed the same craft many a long year, and here, too, on this very spot. But you are a new-comer in these parts. Did you never hear of Ethan Brand?"

"The man that went in search of the Unpardonable Sin?" asked Bartram, with a laugh.

"The same," answered the stranger. "He has found what he sought, and therefore he comes back again."

"What! then you are Ethan Brand himself?" cried the lime-burner, in amazement. "I am a new-comer here, as you say, and they call it eighteen years since you left the foot of Graylock. But, I can tell you, the good folks still talk about Ethan Brand, in the village yonder, and what a strange errand took him away from his lime-kiln. Well, and so you have found the Unpardonable Sin?"

"Even so!" said the stranger, calmly.

"If the question is a fair one," proceeded Bartram, "where might it be?"

Ethan Brand laid his finger on his own heart.

"Here!" replied he.

And then, without mirth in his countenance, but as if moved by an involuntary recognition of the infinite absurdity of seeking throughout the world for what was the closest of all things to himself, and looking into every heart, save his own, for what was hidden in no other breast, he broke into a laugh of scorn. It was the same slow, heavy laugh, that had almost appalled the lime-burner when it heralded the wayfarer's approach.

The solitary mountain-side was made dismal by it. Laughter, when out of place, mistimed, or bursting forth from a disordered state of feeling, may be the most terrible modulation of the human voice. The laughter of one asleep, even if it be a little child,—the madman's laugh,—the wild, screaming laugh of a born idiot,—are sounds that we sometimes tremble to hear, and would always willingly forget. Poets have imagined no utterance of fiends or hobgoblins so fearfully appropriate as a laugh. And even the obtuse lime-burner felt his nerves shaken, as this strange man looked inward at his own heart, and burst into laughter that rolled away into the night, and was indistinctly reverberated among the hills.

"Joe," said he to his little son, "scamper down to the tavern in the village, and tell the jolly fellows there that Ethan Brand has come back, and that he has found the Unpardonable Sin!"

The boy darted away on his errand, to which Ethan Brand made no objection, nor seemed hardly to notice it. He sat on a log of wood, looking steadfastly at the iron door of the kiln. When the child was out of sight, and his swift and light footsteps ceased to be heard treading first on the fallen leaves and then on the rocky mountain-path, the lime-burner began to regret his departure. He felt that the little fellow's presence had been a barrier between his guest and himself, and that he must now deal, heart to heart, with a man who, on his own confession, had committed the one only crime for which Heaven could afford no mercy. That crime, in its indistinct blackness, seemed to overshadow him. The lime-burner's own sins rose up within him, and made his memory riotous with a throng of evil shapes that asserted their kindred with the Master Sin, whatever it might be, which it was within the scope of man's corrupted nature to conceive and cherish. They were all of one family; they went to and fro between his breast and Ethan Brand's, and carried dark greetings from one to the other.

Then Bartram remembered the stories which had grown traditionary in reference to this strange man, who had come upon him like a shadow of the night, and was making himself at home in his old place, after so long absence that the dead people, dead and buried for years, would have had more right to be at home, in any familiar spot, than he. Ethan Brand, it was said, had conversed with Satan himself in the lurid blaze of this very kiln. The legend had been matter of mirth heretofore, but looked grisly now. According to this tale, before Ethan Brand departed on his search, he had been accustomed to evoke a fiend from the hot furnace of the lime-kiln, night after night, in order to confer with him about the Unpardonable Sin; the man and the fiend each laboring to frame the image of some mode of guilt which could neither be atoned for nor forgiven. And, with the first gleam of light upon the mountain-top, the fiend crept in at the iron door, there to abide the intensest element of fire, until again summoned forth to share in the dreadful task of extending man's possible guilt beyond the scope of Heaven's else infinite mercy.

While the lime-burner was struggling with the horror of these thoughts, Ethan Brand rose from the log, and flung open the door of the kiln. The action was in such accordance with the idea in Bartram's mind, that he almost expected to see the Evil One issue forth, red-hot, from the raging furnace.

"Hold! hold!" cried he, with a tremulous attempt to laugh; for he was ashamed of his fears, although they overmastered him. "Don't, for mercy's sake, bring out your Devil now!"

"Man!" sternly replied Ethan Brand, "what need have I of the Devil? I have left him behind me, on my track. It is with such halfway sinners as you that he busies himself. Fear not, because I open the door. I do but act by old custom, and am going to trim your fire, like a lime-burner, as I was once."

He stirred the vast coals, thrust in more wood, and bent forward to gaze into the hollow prison-house of the fire, regardless of the fierce glow that reddened upon his face. The lime-burner sat watching him, and half suspected this strange guest of a purpose, if not to evoke a fiend, at least to plunge bodily into the flames, and thus vanish from the sight of man. Ethan Brand, however, drew quietly back, and closed the door of the kiln.

"I have looked," said he, "into many a human heart that was seven times hotter with sinful passions than yonder furnace is with fire. But I found not there what I sought. No, not the Unpardonable Sin!"

"What is the Unpardonable Sin?" asked the lime-burner; and then he shrank farther from his companion, trembling lest his question should be answered.

"It is a sin that grew within my own breast," replied Ethan Brand, standing erect, with a pride that distinguishes all enthusiasts of his stamp. "A sin that grew nowhere else! The sin of an intellect that triumphed over the sense of brotherhood with man and reverence for God, and sacrificed everything to its own mighty claims! The only sin that deserves a recompense of immortal agony! Freely, were it to do again, would I incur the guilt. Unshrinkingly I accept the retribution!"

"The man's head is turned," muttered the lime-burner to himself. "He may be a sinner like the rest of us,—nothing more likely,—but, I'll be sworn, he is a madman too."

Nevertheless, he felt uncomfortable at his situation, alone with Ethan Brand on the wild mountain-side, and was right glad to hear the rough murmur of tongues, and the footsteps of what seemed a pretty numerous party, stumbling over the stones and rustling through the underbrush. Soon appeared the whole lazy regiment that was wont to infest the village tavern, comprehending three or four individuals who had drunk flip beside the bar-room fire through all the winters, and smoked their pipes beneath the stoop through all the summers, since Ethan Brand's departure. Laughing boisterously, and mingling all their voices together in unceremonious talk, they now burst into the moonshine and narrow streaks of firelight that illuminated the open space before the lime-kiln. Bartram set the door ajar again, flooding the spot with light, that the whole company might get a fair view of Ethan Brand, and he of them.

There, among other old acquaintances, was a once ubiquitous man, now almost extinct, but whom we were formerly sure to encounter at the hotel of every thriving village throughout the country. It was the stage-agent. The present specimen of the genus was a wilted and smoke-dried man, wrinkled and red-nosed, in a smartly cut, brown, bob-tailed coat, with brass buttons, who, for a length of time unknown, had kept his desk and corner in the bar-room, and was still puffing what seemed to be the same cigar that he had lighted twenty years before. He had great fame as a dry joker, though, perhaps, less on account of any intrinsic humor than from a certain flavor of brandy-toddy and tobacco-smoke, which impregnated all his ideas and expressions, as well as his person. Another well-remembered, though strangely altered, face was that of Lawyer Giles, as people still called him in courtesy; an elderly ragamuffin, in his soiled shirt-sleeves and tow-cloth trousers. This poor fellow had been an attorney, in what he called his better days, a sharp practitioner, and in great vogue among the village litigants; but flip, and sling, and toddy, and cocktails, imbibed at all hours, morning, noon, and night, had caused him to slide from intellectual to various kinds and degrees of bodily labor, till at last, to adopt his own phrase, he slid into a soap-vat. In other words, Giles was now a soap-boiler, in a small way. He had come to be but the fragment of a human being, a part of one foot having been chopped off by an axe, and an entire hand torn away by the devilish grip of a steam engine. Yet, though the corporeal hand was gone, a spiritual member remained; for, stretching forth the stump, Giles steadfastly averred that he felt an invisible thumb and fingers with as vivid a sensation as before the real ones were amputated. A maimed and miserable wretch he was; but one, nevertheless, whom the world could not trample on, and had no right to scorn, either in this or any previous stage of his misfortunes, since he had still kept up the courage and spirit of a man, asked nothing in charity, and with his one hand—and that the left one—fought a stern battle against want and hostile circumstances.

Among the throng, too, came another personage, who, with certain points of similarity to Lawyer Giles, had many more of difference. It was the village doctor; a man of some fifty years, whom, at an earlier period of his life, we introduced as paying a professional visit to Ethan Brand during the latter's supposed insanity. He was now a purple-visaged, rude, and brutal, yet half-gentlemanly figure, with something wild, ruined, and desperate in his talk, and in all the details of his gesture and manners. Brandy possessed this man like an evil spirit, and made him as surly and savage as a wild beast, and as miserable as a lost soul; but there was supposed to be in him such wonderful skill, such native gifts of healing, beyond any which medical science could impart, that society caught hold of him, and would not let him sink out of its reach. So, swaying to and fro upon his horse, and grumbling thick accents at the bedside, he visited all the sick-chambers for miles about among the mountain towns, and sometimes raised a dying man, as it were, by miracle, or quite as often, no doubt, sent his patient to a grave that was dug many a year too soon. The doctor had an everlasting pipe in his mouth, and, as somebody said, in allusion to his habit of swearing, it was always alight with hell-fire.

These three worthies pressed forward, and greeted Ethan Brand each after his own fashion, earnestly inviting him to partake of the contents of a certain black bottle, in which, as they averred, he would find something far better worth seeking for than the Unpardonable Sin. No mind, which has wrought itself by intense and solitary meditation into a high state of enthusiasm, can endure the kind of contact with low and vulgar modes of thought and feeling to which Ethan Brand was now subjected. It made him doubt—and, strange to say, it was a painful doubt—whether he had indeed found the Unpardonable Sin, and found it within himself. The whole question on which he had exhausted life, and more than life, looked like a delusion.

"Leave me," he said bitterly, "ye brute beasts, that have made yourselves so, shrivelling up your souls with fiery liquors! I have done with you. Years and years ago, I groped into your hearts, and found nothing there for my purpose. Get ye gone!"

"Why, you uncivil scoundrel," cried the fierce doctor, "is that the way you respond to the kindness of your best friends? Then let me tell you the truth. You have no more found the Unpardonable Sin than yonder boy Joe has. You are but a crazy fellow,—I told you so twenty years ago, —neither better nor worse than a crazy fellow, and the fit companion of old Humphrey, here!"

He pointed to an old man, shabbily dressed, with long white hair, thin visage, and unsteady eyes. For some years past this aged person had been wandering about among the hills, inquiring of all travellers whom he met for his daughter. The girl, it seemed, had gone off with a company of circus-performers; and occasionally tidings of her came to the village, and fine stories were told of her glittering appearance as she rode on horseback in the ring, or performed marvellous feats on the tight-rope.

The white-haired father now approached Ethan Brand, and gazed unsteadily into his face.

"They tell me you have been all over the earth," said he, wringing his hands with earnestness. "You must have seen my daughter, for she makes a grand figure in the world, and everybody goes to see her. Did she send any word to her old father, or say when she was coming back?"

Ethan Brand's eye quailed beneath the old man's. That daughter, from whom he so earnestly desired a word of greeting, was the Esther of our tale, the very girl whom, with such cold and remorseless purpose, Ethan Brand had made the subject of a psychological experiment, and wasted, absorbed, and perhaps annihilated her soul, in the process.

"Yes," murmured he, turning away from the hoary wanderer; "it is no delusion. There is an Unpardonable Sin!"

While these things were passing, a merry scene was going forward in the area of cheerful light, beside the spring and before the door of the hut. A number of the youth of the village, young men and girls, had hurried up the hillside, impelled by curiosity to see Ethan Brand, the hero of so many a legend familiar to their childhood. Finding nothing, however, very remarkable in his aspect,— nothing but a sunburnt wayfarer, in plain garb and dusty shoes, who sat looking into the fire as if he fancied pictures among the coals,—these young people speedily grew tired of observing him. As it happened, there was other amusement at hand. An old German Jew, travelling with a diorama on his back, was passing down the mountain-road towards the village just as the party turned aside from it, and, in hopes of eking out the profits of the day, the showman had kept them company to the lime-kiln.

"Come, old Dutchman," cried one of the young men, "let us see your pictures, if you can swear they are worth looking at!"

"Oh, yes, Captain," answered the Jew,—whether as a matter of courtesy or craft, he styled everybody Captain,—"I shall show you, indeed, some very superb pictures!"

So, placing his box in a proper position, he invited the young men and girls to look through the glass orifices of the machine, and proceeded to exhibit a series of the most outrageous scratchings and daubings, as specimens of the fine arts, that ever an itinerant showman had the face to impose upon his circle of spectators. The pictures were worn out, moreover, tattered, full of cracks and wrinkles, dingy with tobacco-smoke, and otherwise in a most pitiable condition. Some purported to be cities, public edifices, and ruined castles in Europe; others represented Napoleon's battles and Nelson's sea-fights; and in the midst of these would be seen a gigantic, brown, hairy hand,—which might have been mistaken for the Hand of Destiny, though, in truth, it was only the showman's,—pointing its forefinger to various scenes of the conflict, while its owner gave historical illustrations. When, with much merriment at its abominable deficiency of merit, the exhibition was concluded, the German bade little Joe put his head into the box. Viewed through the magnifying-glasses, the boy's round, rosy visage assumed the strangest imaginable aspect of an immense Titanic child, the mouth grinning broadly, and the eyes and every other feature overflowing with fun at the joke. Suddenly, however, that merry face turned pale, and its expression changed to horror, for this easily impressed and excitable child had become sensible that the eye of Ethan Brand was fixed upon him through the glass.

"You make the little man to be afraid, Captain," said the German Jew, turning up the dark and strong outline of his visage, from his stooping posture. "But look again, and, by chance, I shall cause you to see somewhat that is very fine, upon my word!"

Ethan Brand gazed into the box for an instant, and then starting back, looked fixedly at the German. What had he seen? Nothing, apparently; for a curious youth, who had peeped in almost at the same moment, beheld only a vacant space of canvas.

"I remember you now," muttered Ethan Brand to the showman.

"Ah, Captain," whispered the Jew of Nuremberg, with a dark smile, "I find it to be a heavy matter in my show-box,—this Unpardonable Sin! By my faith, Captain, it has wearied my shoulders, this long day, to carry it over the mountain."

"Peace," answered Ethan Brand, sternly, "or get thee into the furnace yonder!"

The Jew's exhibition had scarcely concluded, when a great, elderly dog—who seemed to be his own master, as no person in the company laid claim to him—saw fit to render himself the object of public notice. Hitherto, he had shown himself a very quiet, well-disposed old dog, going round from one to another, and, by way of being sociable, offering his rough head to be patted by any kindly hand that would take so much trouble. But now, all of a sudden, this grave and venerable quadruped, of his own mere motion, and without the slightest suggestion from anybody else, began to run round after his tail, which, to heighten the absurdity of the proceeding, was a great deal shorter than it should have been. Never was seen such headlong eagerness in pursuit of an object that could not possibly be attained; never was heard such a tremendous outbreak of growling, snarling, barking, and snapping,—as if one end of the ridiculous brute's body were at deadly and most unforgivable enmity with the other. Faster and faster, round about went the cur; and faster and still faster fled the unapproachable brevity of his tail; and louder and fiercer grew his yells of rage and animosity; until, utterly exhausted, and as far from the goal as ever, the foolish old dog ceased his performance as suddenly as he had begun it. The next moment he was as mild, quiet, sensible, and respectable in his deportment, as when he first scraped acquaintance with the company.

As may be supposed, the exhibition was greeted with universal laughter, clapping of hands, and shouts of encore, to which the canine performer responded by wagging all that there was to wag of his tail, but appeared totally unable to repeat his very successful effort to amuse the spectators.

Meanwhile, Ethan Brand had resumed his seat upon the log, and moved, it might be, by a perception of some remote analogy between his own case and that of this self-pursuing cur, he broke into the awful laugh, which, more than any other token, expressed the condition of his inward being. From that moment, the merriment of the party was at an end; they stood aghast, dreading lest the inauspicious sound should be reverberated around the horizon, and that mountain would thunder it to mountain, and so the horror be prolonged upon their ears. Then, whispering one to another that it was late,—that the moon was almost down, —that the August night was growing chill,—they hurried homewards, leaving the lime-burner and little Joe to deal as they might with their unwelcome guest. Save for these three human beings, the open space on the hillside was a solitude, set in a vast gloom of forest. Beyond that darksome verge, the firelight glimmered on the stately trunks and almost black foliage of pines intermixed with the lighter verdure of sapling oaks, maples, and poplars, while here and there lay the gigantic corpses of dead trees, decaying on the leaf-strewn soil. And it seemed to little Joe —a timorous and imaginative child—that the silent forest was holding its breath until some fearful thing should happen.

Ethan Brand thrust more wood into the fire, and closed the door of the kiln; then looking over his shoulder at the lime-burner and his son, he bade, rather than advised, them to retire to rest.

"For myself, I cannot sleep," said he. "I have matters that it concerns me to meditate upon. I will watch the fire, as I used to do in the old time."

"And call the Devil out of the furnace to keep you company, I suppose," muttered Bartram, who had been making intimate acquaintance with the black bottle above mentioned. "But watch, if you like, and call as many devils as you like! For my part, I shall be all the better for a snooze. Come, Joe!"

As the boy followed his father into the hut, he looked back at the wayfarer, and the tears came into his eyes, for his tender spirit had an intuition of the bleak and terrible loneliness in which this man had enveloped himself.

When they had gone, Ethan Brand sat listening to the crackling of the kindled wood, and looking at the little spirits of fire that issued through the chinks of the door. These trifles, however, once so familiar, had but the slightest hold of his attention, while deep within his mind he was reviewing the gradual but marvellous change that had been wrought upon him by the search to which he had devoted himself. He remembered how the night dew had fallen upon him,— how the dark forest had whispered to him,—how the stars had gleamed upon him,—a simple and loving man, watching his fire in the years gone by, and ever musing as it burned. He remembered with what tenderness, with what love and sympathy for mankind, and what pity for human guilt and woe, he had first begun to contemplate those ideas which afterwards became the inspiration of his life; with what reverence he had then looked into the heart of man, viewing it as a temple originally divine, and, however desecrated, still to be held sacred by a brother; with what awful fear he had deprecated the success of his pursuit, and prayed that the Unpardonable Sin might never be revealed to him. Then ensued that vast intellectual development, which, in its progress, disturbed the counterpoise between his mind and heart. The Idea that possessed his life had operated as a means of education; it had gone on cultivating his powers to the highest point of which they were susceptible; it had raised him from the level of an unlettered laborer to stand on a starlit eminence, whither the philosophers of the earth, laden with the lore of universities, might vainly strive to clamber after him. So much for the intellect! But where was the heart? That, indeed, had withered,—had contracted,—had hardened,—had perished! It had ceased to partake of the universal throb. He had lost his hold of the magnetic chain of humanity. He was no longer a brother-man, opening the chambers or the dungeons of our common nature by the key of holy sympathy, which gave him a right to share in all its secrets; he was now a cold observer, looking on mankind as the subject of his experiment, and, at length, converting man and woman to be his puppets, and pulling the wires that moved them to such degrees of crime as were demanded for his study.

Thus Ethan Brand became a fiend. He began to be so from the moment that his moral nature had ceased to keep the pace of improvement with his intellect. And now, as his highest effort and inevitable development, —as the bright and gorgeous flower, and rich, delicious fruit of his life's labor,—he had produced the Unpardonable Sin!

"What more have I to seek? what more to achieve?" said Ethan Brand to himself. "My task is done, and well done!"

Starting from the log with a certain alacrity in his gait and ascending the hillock of earth that was raised against the stone circumference of the lime-kiln, he thus reached the top of the structure. It was a space of perhaps ten feet across, from edge to edge, presenting a view of the upper surface of the immense mass of broken marble with which the kiln was heaped. All these innumerable blocks and fragments of marble were red-hot and vividly on fire, sending up great spouts of blue flame, which quivered aloft and danced madly, as within a magic circle, and sank and rose again, with continual and multitudinous activity. As the lonely man bent forward over this terrible body of fire, the blasting heat smote up against his person with a breath that, it might be supposed, would have scorched and shrivelled him up in a moment.

Ethan Brand stood erect, and raised his arms on high. The blue flames played upon his face, and imparted the wild and ghastly light which alone could have suited its expression; it was that of a fiend on the verge of plunging into his gulf of intensest torment.

"O Mother Earth," cried he, "who art no more my Mother, and into whose bosom this frame shall never be resolved! O mankind, whose brotherhood I have cast off, and trampled thy great heart beneath my feet! O stars of heaven, that shone on me of old, as if to light me onward and upward!—farewell all, and forever. Come, deadly element of Fire,—henceforth my familiar frame! Embrace me, as I do thee!"

That night the sound of a fearful peal of laughter rolled heavily through the sleep of the lime-burner and his little son; dim shapes of horror and anguish haunted their dreams, and seemed still present in the rude hovel, when they opened their eyes to the daylight.

"Up, boy, up!" cried the lime-burner, staring about him. "Thank Heaven, the night is gone, at last; and rather than pass such another, I would watch my lime-kiln, wide awake, for a twelvemonth. This Ethan Brand, with his humbug of an Unpardonable Sin, has done me no such mighty favor, in taking my place!"

He issued from the hut, followed by little Joe, who kept fast hold of his father's hand. The early sunshine was already pouring its gold upon the mountain-tops, and though the valleys were still in shadow, they smiled cheerfully in the promise of the bright day that was hastening onward. The village, completely shut in by hills, which swelled away gently about it, looked as if it had rested peacefully in the hollow of the great hand of Providence. Every dwelling was distinctly visible; the little spires of the two churches pointed upwards, and caught a fore-glimmering of brightness from the sun-gilt skies upon their gilded weathercocks. The tavern was astir, and the figure of the old, smoke-dried stage-agent, cigar in mouth, was seen beneath the stoop. Old Graylock was glorified with a golden cloud upon his head. Scattered likewise over the breasts of the surrounding mountains, there were heaps of hoary mist, in fantastic shapes, some of them far down into the valley, others high up towards the summits, and still others, of the same family of mist or cloud, hovering in the gold radiance of the upper atmosphere.

Stepping from one to another of the clouds that rested on the hills, and thence to the loftier brotherhood that sailed in air, it seemed almost as if a mortal man might thus ascend into the heavenly regions. Earth was so mingled with sky that it was a day-dream to look at it.

To supply that charm of the familiar and homely, which Nature so readily adopts into a scene like this, the stage coach was rattling down the mountain-road, and the driver sounded his horn, while Echo caught up the notes, and intertwined them into a rich and varied and elaborate harmony, of which the original performer could lay claim to little share. The great hills played a concert among themselves, each contributing a strain of airy sweetness.

Little Joe's face brightened at once.

"Dear father," cried he, skipping cheerfully to and fro, "that strange man is gone, and the sky and the mountains all seem glad of it!"

"Yes," growled the lime-burner, with an oath, "but he has let the fire go down, and no thanks to him if five hundred bushels of lime are not spoiled. If I catch the fellow hereabouts again, I shall feel like tossing him into the furnace!"

With his long pole in his hand, he ascended to the top of the kiln. After a moment's pause, he called to his son.

"Come up here, Joe!" said he.

So little Joe ran up the hillock, and stood by his father's side. The marble was all burnt into perfect, snow-white lime. But on its surface, in the midst of the circle,— snow-white too, and thoroughly converted into lime,—lay a human skeleton, in the attitude of a person who, after long toil, lies down to long repose. Within the ribs—strange to say—was the shape of a human heart.

"Was the fellow's heart made of marble?" cried Bartram, in some perplexity at this phenomenon. "At any rate, it is burnt into what looks like special good lime; and, taking all the bones together, my kiln is half a bushel the richer for him."

So saying, the rude lime-burner lifted his pole, and, letting it fall upon the skeleton, the relics of Ethan Brand were crumbled into fragments.

Questions

1. How does Hawthorne prepare you in the opening of the story for the story's strange ending and its reference to the marble heart?

2. Is it important that Bartram's work is lime burning? Does it make the story remote and unbelievable today? What is the kiln and its fire a symbol of?

3. Is Ethan Brand "Everyman", or is his sin a special, unpardonable sin? If so, how would you describe the sin? How does Hawthorne convince you that it is special or universal?

4. How does Hawthorne involve the society around him in Brand's quest? What purpose is served by Brand's meeting with the Jew and the other "citizens"? What function does the incident with the dog serve?

Hermann Hesse

THE POET

The life and the work of Hermann Hesse can be conceived of as a pilgrimage. Much of his current popularity on college campuses is undoubtedly due to the emphasis he put on rejecting established or preordained values and on searching for those which satisfy one's own inner personal needs. Recognition and popularity came late to Hesse; he was little known in America until, in his old age, he was awarded the Nobel Prize in 1946. Some of his early novels and poetry are even now being translated and published for the first time. Hesse was born in Germany in 1877 and grew up under the combined influences of German romanticism—with its emphasis on poetic sensibility, aestheticism, and subjectivism—and of his father's missionary background—with its strains of passivity and Indian mysticism. His earliest novels were usually tales of sensitive, daydreaming schoolboys either falling in love for the first time or else seeking to escape from dull reality into the pure world of art. These include Peter Camenzind *(1904),* Beneath the Wheel *(1905), and* Gertrude *(1910). His best-known works are those of his middle period, in which his early romantic escape from the world is subjugated to the quest or search for new meaning and value that will permit him to come to a total acceptance of all that exists in that world. This reconciliation with life is shown in such works as* Demian *(1919),* Siddhartha *(1922), and* Steppenwolf *(1927). Perhaps his single greatest novel is the one translated variously as* Magister Ludi *and* The Glass Bead Game *(1943), a lengthy utopian allegory in which human existence is projected as a complicated game whose rules are mastered by very few. Disillusioned with German militarism at the time of World War I, Hesse moved to Switzerland and became a Swiss citizen in 1921. From this vantage point he carried on a vast correspondence with the world's intellectuals, among whom his influence was great. He died in Switzerland in 1962.*

Hesse did not write many short stories; "The Poet" is one of his few attempts. In "The Poet" he communicates something of his view of life as a quest for the ideal, more dependent on its artists than its materialists.

There is a story told that the Chinese poet, Han Fook, while yet a young man, had a strange and compelling wish to learn all there was to learn about the art of poetry, and to strive for perfection in the writing of it. In those days, he was still living in his home on the Yellow River, and with the help of his family who loved him dearly, he had just become engaged to a young lady of good family. The marriage was to be set for a day which promised good fortune. Han Fook was then twenty years old, a handsome youth, modest, well mannered, schooled in the sciences, and despite his youth, was already recognized among men of letters of his homeland for some excellent verse. Without being exactly rich, he had the prospect of an adequate fortune which would be augmented by the dowry of his bride. Since this bride was, moreover, very beautiful and virtuous, nothing seemed to be lacking for the young man's happiness. Nevertheless, he was not satisfied, for his heart was filled with the ambition to become a perfect poet.

One evening, as a festival of lanterns was being celebrated on the river, it so happened that Han Fook was wandering alone on the far bank of the river. He leaned against the trunk of a tree which grew over the water, and saw reflected in the river thousands of lights swimming and shimmering. He saw men and women and young girls greeting each other on the boats and floats, all glowing like beautiful flowers in their festive dress. He heard the soft murmur of the shining water, the songs of the girls, the humming of the zithers, the sweet tones of the flutes, and over the whole scene the blue night hovered like the vaulting of a temple. His heart beat faster as he gave in to the mood rising within him. He was the only witness to all this beauty! Even though he longed to cross the river and to enjoy the festival in the company of his bride and his friends, he wanted even more ardently to remain an observer, to drink in his own impressions of the scene, and then to transform them into a perfect poem. The poem would reflect the deep blue of the night, the play of light on the water, the joy of the festival guests, and also the yearning of the silent onlooker who leans on the trunk of the tree over the river. He sensed that if even he were to experience all the festivals and all the pleasures of the earth, they would not make him completely happy, for he knew that he would remain an onlooker, a stranger, as it were, isolated in the midst of life. He sensed the unique quality of his soul, which at once compelled him to feel deeply the beauty of the earth, and also to know the secret longings of an outsider. The thought made him sad, but as he pursued it further, he realized that true happiness and satisfaction could only be his if he could once succeed in creating with his poetry a perfect mirror image of the world. In this way he would possess the world itself, refined and immortalized in reflected images.

Han Fook scarcely knew whether he was still awake or had fallen asleep when he heard a slight sound and saw a stranger standing next to the tree trunk. It was an old man with a venerable air, clad in violet-colored robes. Han Fook rose and spoke to the stranger with the usual words of greeting for old men and eminent people. The stranger, however, smiled, and spoke a few lines of poetry. The young man's heart stood still in wonder, for in these lines was all the beauty and perfection which he had just experienced, expressed according to all the rules of the great poets. "Oh, who are you," he asked, bowing deeply, "you who can see into my soul and who speak more beautiful verses than I have ever heard from my teachers?"

The stranger smiled the smile of one who has attained perfection, and said, "If you wish to become a poet, then come with me. You will find my hut by the source of the great river in the northwest mountains. I am called the Master of the Perfect Word."

With that the old man stepped into the narrow shadow cast by the tree and disappeared immediately. Han Fook, after searching for him in vain and finding not even a trace, now firmly believed that everything had been a dream brought on by fatigue. He hurried over to the boats across the river and took part in the festival, but between conversations and the sound of the flutes, he continued to hear the voice of the stranger. Han Fook's very soul seemed to have gone away with the man, for he sat apart with dreaming eyes among the merrymakers who teased him for his lovesickness.

A few days later, Han Fook's father wanted to call his friends and relatives together in order to set the day of the wedding. But the bridegroom opposed his father, saying: "Forgive me if I seem to violate the obedience which a son owes his father. But you know how great is my longing to distinguish myself in the art of poetry. Even though a few of my friends praise my poems, I well know that I am still a beginner and still have a long way to go. Therefore I ask you to let me go for awhile into isolation in order to pursue my studies of poetry, because once I have a wife and a house to take care of, I will be held back from those things. Now, while I am still young and free from other duties, I would like to live for some time for my poetry alone—and my poetry will, I hope, bring me joy and fame."

The father was amazed at this speech, and he said, "You must love this art above everything else, since you even want to postpone your wedding because of it. Or, if something has come between you and your bride, then tell me so that I can help you bring about a reconciliation or provide you with another bride."

But the son swore that he loved his bride no less than before, and that not even the shadow of a disagreement had fallen between them. At the same time he told his father that a great master had revealed himself to him in a dream on the day of the lantern festival, and that it was his greatest wish in the world to become the pupil of this master.

"Well and good," said the father, "then I will give you a year. In this time you may pursue this dream of yours which may have been sent to you by a god."

"It may be two years," said Han Fook hesitantly, "who can tell?"

The father let him go and was grieved. The young man wrote a letter to his bride, took leave of his family, and went his way.

When he had traveled for a very long time, he reached the source of the river and found a bamboo hut standing by itself in the wilderness. On a braided mat in front of the hut sat the old man whom Han Fook had seen on the bank by the tree trunk. The old man sat and played his lute, and when he saw the guest approach respectfully, he did not get up, nor did he greet him. He only smiled and let his sensitive fingers play over the strings. A magic music flowed like a silver cloud through the valley, so that the young man stood in wondering astonishment and forgot everything else until the Master of the Perfect Word put aside his small lute and stepped into his hut. So Han Fook followed him with awe and remained with him as his servant and pupil.

A month passed, and Han Fook had learned to despise all poems which he had written before. He erased them from his memory. And after a few more months he erased even those poems from his memory which he had learned from his teachers at home. The Master spoke hardly a word with him. Silently, he taught Han Fook the art of lute playing until the very being of the pupil was filled with music. Once Han Fook composed a small poem, in which he described the flight of two birds across the autumnal sky, a poem which pleased him quite well. He didn't dare show it to the Master, but one evening he sang it near the hut. The Master heard it well but said not a word. He only played softly on his lute. Immediately the air became cool and the darkness increased; a sharp wind arose even though it was the middle of summer. Across the sky, which had now become gray, flew two lines of birds in their mighty yearning for new lands. All of this was so much more beautiful and more perfect than the verses of the pupil, that Han Fook became sad and silent, and felt himself worthless. The old man made this come to pass each time. When a year had gone by, Han Fook had learned lute playing almost to perfection, but the art of poetry appeared ever more difficult and more sublime.

When two years had gone by, the young man became overwhelmingly homesick for his family, for his homeland, and for his bride. So he asked the Master to let him travel.

The Master smiled and nodded. "You are free," he said, "and may go wherever you want. You may come again, you may stay away, just as you like."

So the pupil started on his journey and travelled without stopping until one morning in the dawn he stood on his native shore and looked over the vaulted bridge to his home town. He crept furtively into his father's garden, and heard through the bedroom window the breathing of his father who was still asleep. Stealing among the trees next to the house of his bride, he climbed to the top of a pear tree and saw his bride standing in her room, combing her hair. When he compared the sight before his eyes with the vision that he had painted of it in his homesick imaginings, it became clear to him that he was indeed destined to be a poet: that in the dreams of poets there is a beauty and grace which one searches for in vain in everyday reality. So he climbed down from the tree, fled from the garden, fled over the bridge out of his native town, and returned to the high valley in the mountains. There as before sat the Master in front of his hut on his simple mat, plucking the lute with his fingers. Instead of a greeting, he spoke two verses about the blessings of art. Upon hearing these deep and harmonious sounds, Han Fook's eyes became filled with tears.

Again Han Fook remained with the Master of the Perfect Word, who now gave him lessons on the zither since he had mastered the lute. The months vanished like snow in the west wind. Twice more it happened that homesickness overcame him. The first time he ran away secretly into the night, but before he had reached the last curve in the valley, the night wind blew over the zither which hung in the door of the hut and the sounds flowed after Han Fook and called him to return in such a way that he could not resist. The other time, however, he dreamed that he was planting a young tree in his garden and that his wife was standing by him and that his children were sprinkling the tree with wine and milk. When he awoke, the moon shone into his room. He got up, bewildered, and saw the Master lying asleep next to him, his gray beard trembling gently. Suddenly a feeling of bitter hatred towards this man came over him—this person who, it seemed to him, had destroyed his life and deceived him about his future. He wanted to fall upon him and murder him, when the old man opened his eyes and began immediately to smile with a fine, sad gentleness which disarmed the pupil. "Remember, Han Fook," said the old man quietly, "you are free to do whatever you wish. You may go into your home country and plant trees, you may hate me, or strike me dead,—it is of little importance."

"Oh, how could I hate you?" cried the poet deeply moved. "That would be like hating heaven itself."

So he remained, and learned to play the zither, and after that the flute. Later he began to write poems under the Master's direction. Slowly he learned the mysterious art of saying only that which is simple and straight-forward, but in such a way as to stir up the listener's soul as the wind stirs up the surface of the water. He described the coming of the sun as it hesitates on the edge of the mountains, and the soundless slipping away of fish when they flee like shadows under the water, and the gentle rocking of a young willow in the spring winds. To hear it was not just to hear about the sun, the play of the fish, or the murmuring of the willow; rather it seemed that heaven and earth harmonized each time for a moment of perfect music. Each listener thought with joy or sorrow on whatever he loved or hated: a boy's thoughts would turn to games, a young man's to his beloved, and the old man's to death.

Han Fook no longer knew how many years he spent with the Master at the source of the great river. Often it seemed to him that he had entered the valley only yesterday and been welcomed by the old man's string music. Often he felt as if all the ages of Man and Time itself had fallen away and become insubstantial.

One morning he awoke alone in the hut and though he looked and called everywhere, the Master had disappeared. Overnight fall seemed to have come. A raw wind shook the old hut and large flocks of migrating birds flew over the ridge of the mountain range, although it was not yet time for them to do so.

Then Han Fook took his little lute and descended into his native country. Wherever he encountered people, they greeted him with the sign of greeting which is due old men and eminent people. When he came to his native town, his father, his bride, and his relatives had died. Other people lived in their houses. That evening, a lantern festival was celebrated on the river. The poet Han Fook stood on the far side of the river, on the darker side of the river, leaning against the trunk of an old tree. When he began to play his little lute, then the women sighed and glanced, delighted and disturbed, into the night. The young men called to the lute player, but they could not find him. They called loudly, because not one of them had ever heard such sounds from a lute before. But Han Fook smiled. He looked into the river, where the reflected images of a thousand lanterns were swimming. Just as he no longer knew how to distinguish the reflected images from the real ones, so he found no difference in his soul between this festival and the first one, when he had stood here as a young man and heard the words of the strange Master.

Questions

1. Why does the young man, Han Fook, feel that he is only an onlooker, a stranger, and that he could not be happy even if he were to experience all life's pleasures?

2. As in many of Hesse's stories, the central character is one who searches for perfection. In this case he searches for the perfect world of art, by removing himself from ordinary society and denying himself usual human contact. What does he find as a result of his withdrawal?

3. What does poetry stand for in this story?

4. What does Han Fook finally learn from his teacher? Why does the teacher disappear?

5. It might be said that the subject of this story is the relationship between life and art, or the role of the artist in his society. What does the story "say" about this subject?

6. What is the story's conclusion? What does the story say about perfection?

Eugene Ionesco

THE STROLLER IN THE AIR

Perhaps the most imaginative and effervescent talent now at work in the theater is Eugene Ionesco, the Rumanian dramatist (born in 1912) who writes in French. From 1950, when his first play, The Bald Soprano, *was performed in Paris, it took him only a few years to become a figure known world-wide as one of the creators of the "theater of the absurd." The theater, Ionesco argued, is patently artificial; everyone knows that what he sees on a stage is not "really" happening there. Why then should it pretend to be a slice of life, an imitation of the actual? So, instead of pursuing an impossible realism, Ionesco determined to use every conceivable grotesque and exaggerated device. His plays are filled with "impossible" things: paintings that talk, corpses that grow, clocks that choose their own time and strike as often as they wish, and chairs, teacups, and other inanimate objects that insist on a life of their own. All these devices amuse audiences, but they also challenge them to examine their own enslavement to habit and their acceptance of meaningless conventions. Thus in* Amédée *(1953) a husband and wife who no longer love each other and who continue to live together only out of habit are forced out of their apartment by an enormous corpse that grows and grows until it finally knocks their wall down—a symbol of their dead love and the guilt feelings that pursue them. In* Rhinoceros *(1960) the inhabitants of a small provincial town are turned one by one into rhinoceroses; at first resisting, they gradually accept the change and even rush to be transformed into the ugly beasts—a powerful demonstration of the urge to conform. Ionesco's impact on the theater is the subject of a book by Martin Esslin,* The Theatre of the Absurd *(1961), and his own quixotic comments on his work can be found in* Notes and Counter Notes *(1964).*

Ionesco turned late to the writing of fiction, and so far has published only one collection, The Colonel's Photograph and Other Stories *(1970), from which "The Stroller in the Air" is taken. His fiction has as yet received little critical attention, but this ebullient story reveals many of the same qualities as his plays.*

"Now that you've given up the theatre, I take it that you'll give up the cinema too?"

I was finishing a book, that summer, in England. I had taken a little prefabricated house in Gloucestershire. It stood in the middle of a meadow in the green uplands above a valley. Down in that valley, between two wooded hills, there was a river, small but navigable. One day I had a letter from a young journalist whose questions I had promised to answer, and one of them was the question quoted above. I couldn't make head or tail of it.

"En abandonnant le théâtre, ne pensâtes-vous ne plus devoir écrire pour le cinéma?" Well, it was true that I had "given up the theatre" a year or two before. I had been tried beyond endurance by the ill-nature of certain critics and the persistent blindness of others. But I had gone on writing dialogue and screen-plays for the cinema.

I went over the question again. Why on earth should I give up the cinema, just because I had given up the theatre? What were these pseudo-problems, and why should I bother my conscience with them? Who stood to benefit by it? Did someone want to close my mouth, and prevent me expressing myself? I was enough of a worrier by nature without having new anxieties put in my way.

The question was not well put, in any case, and the phrasing seemed obscure. Was it really a piece of treachery to write for the cinema, in those conditions? That was what the little reporter seemed to be insinuating. It was too idiotic.

I was re-reading it for the twentieth or thirtieth time when suddenly I realized what had happened. My interrogator had left out one little three-letter word: *que*. What he had meant to say was: "En abandonnant le théâtre ne pensâtes-vous ne plus devoir écrire que pour le cinéma?" "Now that you've given up the theatre, I take it that you'll be writing *exclusively for* the cinema?" That would make perfect sense; for it was quite possible that once I took to writing for the cinema I should no longer be able to carry on with any other form of writing. The cinema takes all one's time and energy, as those who have worked for it well know. Besides, the cinema pays very well indeed. Why should one bust oneself writing novels and essays that nobody's going to buy?

This simple typing error—due, no doubt, to excessive haste—had caused me unnecessary disquiet. Luckily it was not more than a slip, for I very much dislike being accused of opportunism, self-satisfaction, cupidity, or bad faith. I like to live in comfort, but without extravagance, and without having to compromise for money's sake. I am quite capable of withdrawing from ventures that would bring in a great deal of money if I feel that my honour requires it: that was what had happened in the theatre. But had I set too much store by the critics? Possibly. . . .

I got up, as if to change the subject, and looked out of my window. My meadow-view had some white houses in the distance, and a steep descent to the right. Thinking how pleasant it would be to tread that green, green grass under the blue, blue sky of a June morning in England, I decided to go for a walk. But just as I reached the door a German bomber—the last survivor, no doubt, of the war of 1939–45—dropped a bomb that fell slap in the middle of my roof. The house went up in smoke. It was a miracle that I wasn't hurt.

Out in the meadow, my wife and daughter were waiting for me, surveying the landscape, the distant town, the croquet-playing children in their red-and-white Sunday suits, and the valley stretched out at their feet. They had come down from London, as they always did on Sundays, to see how I was getting on in my working-retreat.

"But it's enormous, your meadow!" said my wife. "And what marvellous weather you have here!"

"Didn't you see what just happened?" I said.

"You can't say I didn't warn you. You ought to have taken more care."

I was really rather irritated. "It's not my fault," I said. "What could I have done about it?"

"You could have taken a proper house, not that little cardboard thing that can't stand up even to the littlest bomb. It's so bad for your notebooks."

"Look how pretty Mama's hat is," said my daughter.

My wife had on a little pink hat that suited her very well, a sky-blue coat and skirt, more or less in the classic style, with a rose pinned to the lapel. She also had a black leather handbag that was out of key with the rest. I pointed this out.

"I can't buy everything all at once," she said. "I can't afford it. But I did see a beautiful bag in a shop-window in Piccadilly. It was light in colour—I can't describe just the shade—and it had flowers that moved. They opened and shut just like real ones. Perhaps they were real flowers? Or perhaps they worked like a fan?"

My daughter had on her Sunday dress, with white shoes. The light in her green-and-grey eyes had that invariable softness and sweetness, that childlike softness and sweetness that contrasted a little with the severity of her profile. I embraced them both, and took them by the hand, as we all went to sit on the bench that looked across the ravine.

"How much light there is here today!" I said. "How much light there is!" Down below, on the track that ran parallel to the little river, a train was passing, a tiny little train with its red locomotive and its shrill little cries that came to us from far, far down below. It was the kind of train I had longed to have for myself, as a child. Today's children, and tomorrow's, will have no use for it. Rockets are all that *they* want. Toys go out of fashion, too—more and more of them: academic toys, they've become, toys for the archives. Only the elderly scholar will find them amusing, and even he will need some misleading historical interpretation to get the point of them.

"You know I had a most disturbing dream last night." It was my wife speaking. "My father was alive. He'd come back to life, I mean. He'd only just died. . . . No, that's not how it was. He was thought to have died, but actually he hadn't. After the undertaker had been sent for my father was found to be still alive, and quite young, with all his hair and his big forehead. He was just a bit thin, because he'd come back from the war. His brother the doctor, my uncle, had come in a moment or two before to prepare us for the shock. For happiness can be killing, you know, if it's too intense and comes as too much of a surprise. The only tiresome thing was that we'd have to ring up the undertaker and cancel the funeral. They'd be very annoyed, of course. Such a thing had never happened before. They'd sue us for damages, and for interest on capital, beyond a doubt, and it would be in all the papers, quite probably: it was terribly annoying. What would people think of us? Could we avoid a court-case, at any rate? 'We must get a lawyer,' said my uncle, taking care not to look my father in the eye. 'There's no precedent in commercial law for a case of this sort. It'll have to go before a judge.' " My wife turned towards me: "What do you say to that, for a dream?"

"It's a dream, just a dream: nothing more. It simply means that you were very fond of your father, that you wish he was still alive, but that you realize that his return to life would lead to certain difficulties, all the same. Don't start worrying about dreams—just look at this beautiful grass, at those woods on the other side of the valley, and then turn round and look at the white walls of those houses on the outskirts of the town and see how they seem to dissolve in the light. Look up at the sky! Be content with the light!"

Just at that moment a man passed by. He was dressed in the old-fashioned style and had white side-whiskers. He almost bumped into us in order to get past, and he didn't even say "Sorry!": a rare omission, for an Englishman. My daughter was quite put out: "What manners!" she said. "Did you see that man?"

"What man?" said my wife. She hadn't seen him. And although my daughter and I assured her that he had really gone by, and had almost bumped into us, and that he was smoking a pipe, and that the smoke was going downwards instead of upwards, she said that it was a hallucination on our part.

"Yes and no," was what I said. "Yes and no," for the man had suddenly disappeared above the valley, as if he had melted into the air.

"He's fallen down," said my daughter.

"Not at all. 'Fallen' is a figure of speech. He's just gone on his way. We can no longer follow him. He is not one of us, although he's near to us. He is a member of the anti-world, who has passed through to the other side of the invisible and yet not transparent wall which divides that world from ours. I see him from time to time, in the morning. He must take his walk every day at the same hour, no doubt at some point where there's a break in the anti-world, a defect of some kind, a hole through which we can see him without his knowing it, a no-man's-land, a between-world. He certainly can't see us—that's why he didn't excuse himself for having nearly bumped into us. In any case, we can't really consider him as existing on the same plane as ourselves. His existence is relative, at most."

"What is the anti-world?" my daughter asked.

I tried to explain that there are an indeterminable number of universes. "Each of these overlaps and is interlocked with each of the others, and yet none of them interferes with the working of the others. They can lie one above the other, and they can even penetrate one another, without touching. They can even co-exist in an identical space. It's difficult to imagine but that's how it is. The glimpse that we had had of an inhabitant of one of these other worlds was a quite exceptional happening, and one that must be attributed to faulty shunting or signalling of some sort. It is on record that in Ireland, and in the islands of the Scottish coast, mirrors reflect, thanks to some as yet undefined property, silhouettes and countrysides which do not belong to the world as we know it. A certain quality in the air or the water is doubtless responsible; for if these same mirrors are taken to America, or Belgium, or merely on board a vessel flying the French flag, those images cease to appear. For a more exact account of all this, the student must address himself to a man of science. I've told you all I can," I said to my daughter. "And, anyway, the man who passed by just now is totally and inconceivably different from what we saw of him. What is he really like? And even if he did live in the universe which was most like our own, his hair would really be black, and not white, because what we could see of him corresponded to the negative of a photograph. If he seemed old to us, then very probably he's young. And what does 'really' mean, anyway? Let's stick to our own world," I said to my daughter. "You're not old enough to understand all that. Let's not ask too many questions. Sunday's not the day for philosophy."

But my daughter has a passion for learning. "Is that man what people call a ghost?"

"It's popularly believed," I said, "that when people die they pass into the anti-world. Certain facts appear to confirm this belief. When someone dies and is put into a coffin, his corpse disappears. That's why coffins weigh so little. What becomes of the body? There are no such things as ghosts. People who die get inlaid once and for all—of course that's again a figure of speech—into the anti-world. They have anti-heads, anti-limbs, anti-clothes, anti-feelings. It's pure chance if you happen to see them, as we saw the man or pseudo-man, who passed by just now. There are no ghosts, but there may be people who pass by, or pass back and forth, across a small part of our own universe. We ourselves may pass by in theirs. We are not conscious of it. And how do we look to them?"

"Those passers-by are simply phantoms, born of the winds' trickery," said my wife.

"Not at all! Not at all! There *is* a negative of our universe. Of that, there are proofs: or rather, indications, or verbal proofs. The word 'topsy-turvy' comes from that, though most people don't realize it. One might get some vague idea of topsy-turvydom through seeing the towers of a castle reflected in its moat, or a fly walking upside down on the ceiling, or handwriting that runs from right to left and from bottom to top of the page. Or an anagram, a juggler, an acrobat, or the sunlight as it is refracted, broken up, disintegrated into colour-dust as it passes through a prism of crystal only to reconstitute itself, a yard or two further on, on a wall, or on a screen, or on a face, once again bright and clear and transparent and unified . . . and upside down. Luckily the centre of our world never bumps into the centre of the anti-world. For if that were to happen there'd be mutual disintegration and annihilation. Some pessimists think that annihilation of all universes would result. Perhaps that's how it will end, and the whole thing will have to begin again from the beginning."

My wife looked at me, and reproached me, in the nicest way, for drinking too much. It stopped me from working—or so she said. "It did inspire me, at least," I replied, "to the sham literature of which I have just given you an example."

"Leave him alone," said my daughter. "Leave him alone. Surely he can do what he likes?"

"Instead of talking all round the point," said my wife, "why don't you come and walk in the grass with us? The grass will freshen your ideas."

I joined hands with the two dear beings who stood one on each side of me. My daughter is already taller than her mother. We often tease my wife about her tiny stature.

We must have made an amusing picture as we turned our backs on the white houses of the town and slowly ambled along the path beside the top of the steep descent.

To our right were some fragmentary ruins. Pink, they were, and flower-strewn, and gay: a column and some arcades, all shaky and tottery as if they were learning how to stand up again. Behind, my house had vanished. Even the debris was no longer there: sucked skywards, no doubt, by the pumps of Nothingness.

We all need, of course, to give our concepts a palpable image, and I had always imagined Nothingness as a sort of little ditch, or as the hollowed-out black section of a dice; but the capacity of that ditch, or that part of the dice, was vastly greater than that of the immeasurably larger boxes or spaces which exist in the world as we know it.

I went on with my thoughts: those bygone palaces to which the ruins bore witness were gone for ever—not a doubt of that. But just possibly they will be rebuilt and restored on the other side, after traversing Nothingness? Nothingness since it has no dimensions is smaller than Smallness itself. Yes, perhaps they have been rebuilt on the other side: upside-down, of course, since we are speaking of the other side. Their reconstruction may have already begun. The stones left behind here must feel it—that's why they have such a triumphant look, despite their provisional deterioration. The frontiers of Nothingness are imperceptible and it's easy to step over them without knowing it. The amazing thing is that there are people who imagine it as an enormous emptiness, a black, unfathomable void! For Nothingness is neither black nor white, and if it were "unfathomable" it would need a really unlimited amount of room.

"Where are you, my dear?" said my wife. "In Nothingness? Or in the Hereafter? I keep talking to you, and I never get an answer."

"How is it that you can guess even my most secret thoughts?"

"I was listening to you. I pay attention, even if you don't."

"And yet I wasn't thinking aloud. I didn't even move my lips."

"We only need to look at you to guess what you're thinking," said my daughter. "We only need to look at you—your face gives you away. You ought to have been a film actor, or a mime, or an impersonator."

I might have got irritated. But my daughter was holding a big bunch of daisies, fresh-picked and all a-quiver, in her arms, and when she put one in my buttonhole I was won over at once. I can never resist an affectionate impulse.

As we went on our way, a feeling of complete relaxation came over us. I felt within myself the beginnings of a felicity beyond description. It was bliss of the kind that one forgets about, and yet knows perfectly well; that one remembers exactly, when one is reminded of it; that comes back to one like something that belongs to one for all eternity; that is lost every day and yet never lost at all. Happiness of this kind is physical, concrete, localized. You can situate it exactly, between the solar plexus, where it begins, and the shoulders, where it climbs to after filling the lungs with an air more subtle than air itself. Its vapours rise into your mouth, pass through your nostrils, arrive at the brain. It's an intoxication born of the gods. You feel drunk with the sheer certainty of it.

"What certainty?" said my wife.

"Certainty," I replied. "Certainty. I don't know *what* certainty."

"Then it can't be certainty. It's an uncertain, an undefined certainty. The characteristic of certainty is precision."

"Well, as far as I'm concerned, certainty to which limits can be set is not certainty at all, because there are boundaries to it, and because it is menaced by what runs counter to it. And besides, nothing is more imprecise than precision. What does that mean?"

"You have a language all your own, and no one else can understand it. What else?"

"I understand it," said our daughter.

"Well, so much the worse for you," said my wife.

Suddenly I realized why I was so happy, and why, from that same happiness, I felt weightless and, without noticing it, had broken into a run. Going a little out of our way, I came upon the silver bridge: dazzling in the sun, it spanned the abyss, linking one side with the other, a great single-arched aerial structure that seemed to hang in the air high above the river, above the railway lines that ran beside the river, above the boats, above the houses, above the trees, above the sloping hills, above the terminus of the rack-railway and the funicular, riding easily among the summits of the upper air.

"Where are you going? Wait for us!" my wife cried.

And then when they too saw the bridge my two dear little women cried out in their turn, in amazement and incredulity and delight: "Goodness, how beautiful!"

They came beside me, and I took them by the shoulders, and we looked our fill. The silver arch reflected and multiplied the sun's rays and the glare of the sky.

There were some English families there too, in their Sunday best, and they too were looking in wonder at the bridge. They could see it every day, of course, but they only looked at it on Sundays. That's always the way. In France, no one would ever have looked at it, though the French have no equals when it comes to standing and staring. In America, too, they have enormous bridges; but the Americans go across them with their eyes shut. (That's why they have so many accidents.) In Australia they have them, too, and in Russia. But no one sees them, because they are not interested in the bridges, but merely in what they are used for. For this reason, there is no longer such a thing as a bridge. Only what is not a bridge still exists. Once you know what a thing is for, you destroy it.

"How d'you mean, destroy it?" said my wife, in irony, though she was touched by the beauty of the bridge. Her eyes remained sharp, even at moments of astonishment. We went over and joined the English families, just by the arch, where the little motor-cars were belting along as fast as they could, with the light bouncing off their side-windows and coming back at us in thousand upon thousand of multi-coloured fragments, like the sparkling facets of automobile diamonds.

"There you are," I said to my daughter. "As you're learning physics now you must recognize those—they are the celebrated luminous particles that scientists call photons."

"Really?"

"You'll make her more of a goose than she is already. She's taking you seriously."

"Oh, no, Mama! I know quite well that he's joking."

"And when isn't he joking?" Turning towards me, this time. "I prefer it when you're joking, actually. When you're not, it means that you're sad."

"Are you often sad? Why does it happen? What makes you sad?" asked my compassionate daughter. "It makes me sad that you should be sad," she went on, taking my hand and stroking it.

"I am sad when I think that the years go by like sacks that we mark 'Returned Empty,' sad when I think that we shall be separated from one another and from ourselves. But that sadness is just the bottom of the wave. Today I feel buoyed up by happiness, carried high by my joy. . . ."

And, in saying this, I began to hop and skip, working my arms wildly as if they had been wings.

"Steady on!" said my wife, as she took out a pocket-mirror to keep herself in countenance. "Steady on, now! People are looking."

Several groups of English people had, in effect, been studying my behaviour—not disapprovingly, but with a tranquil amazement, though they clearly thought that my exuberance smacked too much of the South for their latitudes.

I could not contain my wild gaiety. It overflowed, swept me away, lifted me right off the ground. I noticed that my feet had left the ground; the soles of my shoes skimmed the topmost tufts of grass.

The English hadn't realized this, as yet. As far as they were concerned I was simply walking fast—or, since I looked as if I was slithering along, I was imitating a skier or a skater. They might also have thought that I had put on an inch or two. But as I am of average height, and they are mostly rather tall, another or so on my part would not have added up to anything unusual.

But my daughter said: "That's funny—Papa's left the ground!"

"You must be mad," said my wife.

And then, as I went a little higher, she could see in her face-mirror the gap, now still wider, between my feet and the grass. She had to admit that my daughter was right.

"Now really, Herbert, what d'you think you're doing?" she said. "You simply can't behave like that in public!"

(She always gives me that name when she sees me doing things that she doesn't approve of.)

I was like a river in flood. I was drowning in my own happiness, and buoyed up by it at the same time. In actual fact I was walking on air; but I might equally well have been treading the sea-bed, for the air that morning had the density of water and the blue sky was deep as the ocean.

I had suddenly rediscovered how to fly. How could I ever have forgotten it? It was simple. Any child could do it. Flying is an act indispensable to mankind, a function as natural as breathing. The fact is that everyone can fly, must fly, knows how to fly. It's an innate faculty. Yet everyone forgets it. That's why we feel unhappy. It's worse than if we were deprived of food. Most of the time, not only do people no longer know how to fly, but they don't know that it's the fact of not flying that makes them unhappy. They feel their misfortune, but they can't identify it. Whence our wretchedness. What would people say if we forgot how to swim, or how to walk? Or how to stand up, quite simply? Or how to sit down? We must re-learn our take-off. Or rather: we must remember it. I myself, for most of the time, and like most of us, don't know how to leave the ground. But at least I know that it's vital for me to do it, and I know what it is that's wrong when I suffer for the lack of it. People may argue that we have invented the aeroplane, the rocket, and the satellite for that very reason: because humanity knows that flying is a part of its nature and has tried to reincorporate it. But does the paralytic walk in his wheel-chair? Not at all. He has to be pushed. That has nothing to do with walking. Does the motorist walk? No: he rolls along, shut up in his box. The aviator doesn't *fly*, any more than the paralytic flies in his wheel-chair or the motorist in his car. There are now in existence individual flying-kits that you wrap round yourself like life-belts, and with these you can jump, like a locust, over roads and gardens and rivers and coppices and bungalows. But as for taking off into the upper air—why, this apparatus is not even as much use as is the motorized bicycle to the man who wants to climb a mountain.

No. We must fly naturally, as we once did. It's nothing more than a habit we've got to get back into. Maybe it's simply from laziness that we've lost the habit of flying, and the feeling for it. If we have to have motors to help us fly, it's no longer natural. People call it "progress," but there's nothing progressive about walking with crutches. Soon we shall forget how to walk, too, if we don't look out. It's easy enough to see that things are already going that way. We're losing all our powers. What have we got on the roads? Nothing but motor-cars. Pedestrians are a rarity; the few that remain are objects of contempt. Before long they will have disappeared. But I want to go on being a man who walks on the road and a man who walks in the air. I want to walk on the grass, and I want to walk in the air as well: and for neither of them do I want any mechanical devices.

"How d'you do it? Do show me," said my daughter.

"He won't be able to go any higher," said my wife.

"Oh yes, I can," I said. "Nothing is easier. You just have to will yourself to do it. The will is power. You must have confidence. If you lose confidence, you fall backwards—you go down again, rather. For the remarkable thing is that you never fall down abruptly, like a stone. That's one more proof that it's natural to fly. When you're flying freely above the topmost trees, above the lake, above the high plateau, you never feel afraid. But in an aeroplane, or in a ski-lift, everyone is afraid from time to time. You can be astonished, certainly, to find yourself flying over mountain-tops, over cathedrals, over roofs. And if you're astonished beyond a certain point, if you begin to think that there's something abnormal about your being able to stay up without wings and a propeller, then your confidence is shaken, and you begin to lose height, and you drop down, but no faster than a lift. Sometimes, by an effort of the will, you can regain height, and climb again, as if you had thrown overboard some ballast. But not for long. Even the most trifling failure of will can bring on the downward movement again. How many times have I not rediscovered the secret within myself and said to myself as I took off "Now it's for ever that I know it! I shall never forget, I shall never forget it, any more than I shall forget how to hear and how to see."

But I was going down, all the same, like a child's balloon as it gradually lets out the air.

But now I no longer forget. This time I shall pay the closest attention to it all. I shall memorize every movement of heart and body, put them all down in my notebook, and reproduce them whenever I want to.

I was suddenly seized with an irresistible longing to go and take the air, or rather to let the air take me: to fly over the valley and see what there was to be seen in the other valleys that lay beyond the hills opposite. My feet touched ground again, but so far from losing my momentum I could hardly keep myself from taking off into the upper air. I was like a horse that paws the ground in its impatience. I tapped the ground with my foot, very lightly—just enough to hoist me a foot or two into the air.

"How d'you do it?" my daughter was asking.

"It's very easy. I'll teach you. You'll see. It's a game. You know how to ride a bicycle, don't you? Well, a bicycle is only a machine. But as we've got into the habit of using machines we might as well learn what we can from them, by analogy. They have taken the place of the human being and its functions—it's for us to retrieve our true functions by way of these mechanical imitations. Imagine that you're on your bicycle. Look: move your legs as if you were starting to ride, as if you had invisible wheels to keep moving. Hold yourself upright, as if you were on the saddle, and keep your hands in front of you, as if they were on your handlebars. After you've got the pedals turning seven or eight times you'll feel yourself getting under way—first about as high as the chimney-piece, and then higher and ever higher. You can ride a bicycle. Riding the air is the same thing—a matter of exactly the same balance. No difference at all. Just like this."

I did as I had told her to do. The English had formed a circle round me and were looking on.

"There's another procedure, a rather less mechanical one, for those who don't care for machines that climb, or roll on wheels, or fly, even if they are imaginary. It's a gymnastic procedure, and one nearer to nature. You jump in the air, as high as you can, and you raise your arms at the same time. Instead of allowing yourself to fall back, you hold on to an imaginary branch, rather as if you were climbing a tree. You pull yourself up by your wrists and grab hold of another, higher branch. And so you climb from one imaginary branch to the next. You can climb as high as you like, because your imaginary tree goes on until you've had enough of it, or can't go on any more. It's even infinite in its height, if you want to go on for ever and have the strength to do so. The first stages are very hard going, and you'll get awfully tired. But the more you climb, the easier it becomes. A mysterious strength that pushes you upwards. You don't feel your weight at all. You need a hand to get going, and then a finger, and then the mere wish to go higher is enough. It bears out the expression: 'Vouloir, c'est pouvoir.' "

But there's a danger in having too strong a will. You can end by destroying the natural resistance of the air to your ascent. Gravity capitulates: and you may disappear, carried away by the intoxication which characterizes extremes of height and depth.

In short, you must never take up arms against the forces of nature, and neither must you resist them.

"If you like," I said to my daughter, who was hesitating, and to my wife, who was terrified, "I can take you with me, each on one of my arms, if you don't want to fly by yourselves."

"Surely you won't take us by force!" said my wife. At that moment

I stamped a little too hard on the ground and took off without really meaning to. Probably I was drawn upwards by some movement of the atmosphere, for I found myself climbing very quickly. Then, once in the calm waters of the upper air, I slowed up and began to move sideways, parallel to the arch, though high above it. I no longer needed to make any complicated movements; the smallest gesture of one hand or the other was enough. In silence I headed for the hill opposite; I had only to look in that direction to keep on my course.

I was at a great height, midway between the two hills, when I stopped to look around, searching the four corners of the horizon below me.

And I saw it. I saw everything. And I grieved to see it. I was in despair. I thought to myself, "It can't be true. It can't." And then: "But *it is*, though." I turned in on myself, like a top that is running down, and over and over again I said: "It just can't be posible. But I'm not making a mistake. I'm not dreaming. Those atrocities that I have just seen are real. They and they only are real." I could have stayed on up there as long as I liked. But what was the point, if disaster and only disaster is in store for us?

Slowly, sadly, I came down, as a man comes down an invisible staircase. I brushed against the top of a tree and pulled at a single leaf, without thinking. It span round and round as it fell.

My wife, my daughter, and the others were waiting for me. I came down just over their heads, on to the grass, on to the firm ground.

"How did you manage it?"

"I flew."

"That's not true," said one of the Englishmen. "We saw what was happening. You were walking on an invisible arch. That was what kept you up. It was invisible because it's simply solidified air. Anyone could do what you did. You'd just have to show them where the arch starts from."

"There is no other arch. I was flying, I really was. That's all there was to it."

"Anyway there's nothing extraordinary about what you did. It's no more than a kite does. As for ourselves, we can cross the valley in a few seconds—by car, by aeroplane, by rocket—where it took you a good twenty minutes to get across. It's too long, your flying—it takes too much time. It's not a system we could put money into."

"What's the matter?" said my wife. "You ought to be proud of yourself. You look a bit down in the mouth—what did you see on the other side?"

"At the foot of the hill facing us, on the other side of the valley, there's a big gateway, and on it is written "PARADISE" in big letters, all lit up, like the ones at Battersea Fun Fair. Behind the gates, and open to the sky, is hell. Giant grasshoppers were nibbling at the severed skulls of those who had been imprudent enough to go in, and their headless trunks were being fitted with the heads of foxes, monkeys, and geese. Farther on, sows were in control. I climbed higher to see what was going on at other points of importance, and when I got near to the invisible rooftop where space and time meet—near enough to be able to touch it with my forehead—I looked to right and to left, in front of me and to the rear. Gigantic bombs were being pulled hither and thither, cutting deep as they went into flatlands long since ravaged and left empty. Where they came from, and who was in charge of them, I have no idea. And beyond there was nothing but ice, and fire beyond the ice, a desert of ice and a desert of fire, each fighting desperately to dominate the other as they moved steadily towards us."

"Tell that to these people, tell them what you saw."

"No one would believe me. And even if they did. . . ."

"Then what are you waiting for? Take us each under your arm, now that you've proved that you can fly."

"Where would we go?"

"Take us away, as far as you can, farther than the hell you spoke of."

"Alas, my darlings, I can't. Beyond that hell, there is nothing."

"What d'you mean—nothing?"

"Nothing. Just one bottomless abyss after another."

With heads bowed, and fear and desolation in our hearts, we walked on towards the town. The light was beginning to fade. We heard one or two loud explosions, and the sky glowed red for a moment. It was nothing, as yet—just a fête, a sort of English 14th of July.

Questions

1. Is it relevant that the narrator has been a writer for the theater? Or that he now writes for the cinema?

2. What relationships does the narrator have with his family? What differences are there between his wife and his daughter? What differing things are they interested in? Why do they even see (or fail to see) different things? Explain their varying reactions to the narrator's discovery of his ability to fly.

3. Summarize the narrator's argument for an indeterminable number of interlocking universes. Is this anything more than foolish fantasy?

4. Evaluate the narrator's argument that the ability to fly is simply a habit that man has lost but could rediscover if he wished. What is the implication of the view that flying is a natural act for man?

5. Account for the reactions of the spectators when the narrator comes down from his flight. Why do they first discredit him, saying he was only walking on an invisible arch, and then belittle his accomplishment, even if it is true?

6. Having proved he can fly, why does the narrator refuse to try to escape from the apocalyptic vision he has seen from the air?

Henry James

THE JOLLY CORNER

Henry James once remarked that a novelist must be a person "on whom nothing is lost." His large body of work illustrates his precept, for it is often concerned with the minute details and small perceptions that embody great significances. James came from a prominent American family; his grandfather was reputed to be one of the first millionaires in the country, and his father was a writer and lecturer on philosophy and religion. Henry, born in 1843, and his brother William, the psychologist, both received excellent educations, interspersed with trips to Europe and programs of independent reading. His own travels made him aware of the theme that, in numerous variations, was to preoccupy him throughout his life: the interaction between American and European cultures, particularly the impact of the sophisticated and worldly European on the naïve and innocent American. Europe for him, James said, represented "knowledge, pleasure, experience," while America was "innocence, health, honesty." He himself embodied this collision between cultures. In 1875 he decided to settle abroad. He lived first in Paris and then in England, where, except for occasional visits to America, he spent the rest of his life. He remained an American citizen and continued in an American outlook. But after war broke out in 1914 he did extensive work in England's behalf, and the next year he made the symbolic gesture of becoming a British citizen. He died soon after, in 1916. Among the most highly regarded of the many novels he produced are The American *(1877),* The Europeans *(1878),* The Portrait of a Lady *(1881),* The Princess Casamassima *(1886),* The Wings of the Dove *(1902),* The Ambassadors *(1903), and* The Golden Bowl *(1904).*

In his novels as well as in his numerous short stories, James was most interested in involving his characters in subtle moral dilemmas in which they must make fine distinctions and difficult choices based on their new perceptions. It would be easy to classify "The Jolly Corner" (written in 1908) as a ghost story and to read it largely for its super-

natural elements. However, its intentions go beyond this purpose, for here too James shows a character's increasing awareness of himself.

I

"Every one asks me what I 'think' of everything," said Spencer Brydon: "and I make answer as I can—begging or dodging the question, putting them off with any nonsense. It wouldn't matter to any of them really," he went on, "for, even were it possible to meet in that stand-and-deliver way so silly a demand on so big a subject, my 'thoughts' would still be almost altogether about something that concerns only myself." He was talking to Miss Staverton, with whom for a couple of months now he had availed himself of every possible occasion to talk; this disposition and this resource, this comfort and support, as the situation in fact presented itself, having promptly enough taken the first place in the considerable array of rather unattenuated surprises attending his so strangely belated return to America. Everything was somehow a surprise; and that might be natural when one had so long and so consistently neglected everything, taken pains to give surprises so much margin for play. He had given them more than thirty years—thirty-three, to be exact; and they now seemed to him to have organised their performance quite on the scale of that licence. He had been twenty-three on leaving New York—he was fifty-six to-day: unless indeed he were to reckon as he had sometimes, since his repatriation, found himself feeling; in which case he would have lived longer than is often allotted to a man. It would have taken a century, he repeatedly said to himself, and said also to Alice Staverton, it would have taken a longer absence and a more averted mind than those even of which he had been guilty, to pile up the differences, the newnesses, the queernesses, above all the bignesses, for the better or the worse, that at present assaulted his vision wherever he looked.

The great fact all the while however had been the incalculability; since he *had* supposed himself, from decade to decade, to be allowing, and in the most liberal and intelligent manner, for brilliancy of change. He actually saw that he had allowed for nothing; he missed what he would have been sure of finding, he found what he would never have imagined. Proportions and values were upside-down; the ugly things he had expected, the ugly things of his far-away youth, when he had too promptly waked up to a sense of the ugly—these uncanny phenomena placed him rather, as it happened, under the charm; whereas the "swagger" things, the modern, the monstrous, the famous things, those he had more particularly, like thousands of ingenuous enquirers every year, come over to see, were exactly his sources of dismay. They were as so many set traps for displeasure, above all for reaction, of which his restless tread was constantly pressing the spring. It was interesting, doubtless, the whole show, but it would have been too disconcerting hadn't a certain finer truth saved the situation. He had distinctly not, in this steadier light, come over *all* for the monstrosities; he had come, not only in the last analysis but quite on the face of the act, under an impulse with which they had nothing to do. He had come—putting the thing pompously—to look at his "property," which he had thus for a third of a century not been within four thousand miles of; or, expressing it less sordidly, he had yielded to the humour of seeing again his house on the jolly corner, as he usually, and quite fondly, described it—the one in which he had first seen the light, in which various members of his family had lived and had died, in which the holidays of his overschooled boyhood had been passed and the few social flowers of his chilled adolescence gathered, and which, alienated then for so long a period, had, through the successive deaths of his two brothers and the termination of old arrangements, come wholly into his hands. He was the owner of another, not quite so "good"—the jolly corner having been, from far back, superlatively extended and consecrated; and the value of the pair represented his main capital, with an income consisting, in these later years, of their respective rents which (thanks precisely to their original excellent type) had never been depressingly low. He could live in "Europe," as he had been in the habit of living, on the product of these flourishing New York leases, and all the better since, that of the second structure, the mere number in its long row, having within a twelvemonth fallen in, renovation at a high advance had proved beautifully possible.

These were items of property indeed, but he had found himself since his arrival distinguishing more than ever between them. The house within the street, two bristling blocks westward, was already in course of reconstruction as a tall mass of flats; he had acceded, some time before, to overtures for this conversion—in which, now that it was going forward, it has been not the least of his astonishments to find himself able, on the spot, and though without a previous ounce of such experience, to participate with a certain intelligence, almost with a certain authority. He had lived his life with his back so turned to such concerns and his face addressed to those of so different an order that he scarce knew what to make of this lively stir, in a compartment of his mind never yet penetrated, of a capacity for business and a sense for construction. These virtues, so common all round him now, had been dormant in his own organism—where it might be said of them perhaps that they had slept the sleep of the just. At present, in the splendid autumn weather—the autumn at least was a pure boon in the terrible place—he loafed about his "work" undeterred, secretly agitated; not in the least "minding" that the whole proposition, as they said, was vulgar and sordid, and ready to climb ladders, to walk the plank, to handle materials and look wise about them, to ask questions, in fine, and challenge explanations and really "go into" figures.

It amused, it verily quite charmed him; and, by the same stroke, it amused, and even more, Alice Staverton, though perhaps charming her perceptibly less. She wasn't however going to be better-off for it, as *he* was—and so astonishingly much: nothing was now likely, he knew, ever to make her better-off than she found herself, in the afternoon of life, as the delicately frugal possessor and tenant of the small house in Irving Place to which she had subtly managed to cling through her almost unbroken New York career. If he knew the way to it now better than to any other address among the dreadful multiplied numberings which seemed to him to reduce the whole place to some vast ledger-page overgrown, fantastic, of ruled and criss-crossed lines and figures—if he had formed, for his consolation, that habit, it was really not a little because of the charm of his having encountered and recognised, in the vast wilderness of the wholesale, breaking through the mere gross generalisation of wealth and force and success, a small still scene where items and shades, all delicate things, kept the sharpness of the notes of a high voice perfectly trained, and where economy hung about like the scent of a garden. His old friend lived with one maid and herself dusted her relics and trimmed her lamps and polished her silver; she stood off, in the awful modern crush, when she could, but she sallied forth and did battle when the challenge was really to "spirit," the spirit she after all confessed to, proudly and a little shyly, as to that of the better time, that of *their* common, their quite far-away and antediluvian social period and order. She made use of the street-cars when need be, the terrible things that people scrambled for as the panic-stricken at sea scramble for the boats; she affronted, inscrutably, under stress, all the public concussions and ordeals; and yet, with that slim mystifying grace of her appearance, which defied you to say if she were a fair young woman who looked older through trouble, or a fine smooth older one who looked young through successful indifference; with her precious reference, above all, to memories and histories into which he could enter, she was as exquisite for him as some pale pressed flower (a rarity to begin with), and, failing other sweetnesses, she was a sufficient reward of his effort. They had communities of knowledge, "their" knowledge (this discriminating possessive was always on her lips) of presences of the other age, presences all overlaid, in his case, by the experience of a man and the freedom of a wanderer, overlaid by pleasure, by infidelity, by passages of life that were strange and dim to her, just by "Europe" in short, but still unobscured, still exposed and cherished, under that pious visitation of the spirit from which she had never been diverted.

She had come with him one day to see how his "apartment house" was rising; he had helped her over gaps and explained to her plans, and while they were there had happened to have, before her, a brief but lively discussion with the man in charge, the representative of the building-firm that had undertaken his work. He had found himself quite "standing-up" to this personage over a failure on the latter's part to observe some detail of one of their noted conditions, and had lucidly argued his case that, besides ever so prettily flushing, at the time, for sympathy in his triumph, she had afterwards said to him (though to a slightly greater effect of irony) that he had clearly for too many years neglected a real gift. If he had but stayed at home he would have anticipated the inventor of the sky-scraper. If he had but stayed home he would have discovered his genius in time really to start some new variety of awful architectural hare and run it till it burrowed in a gold-mine. He was to remember these words, while the weeks elapsed, for the small silver ring they had sounded over the queerest and deepest of his own lately most disguised and most muffled vibrations.

It had begun to be present to him after the first fortnight, it had broken out with the oddest abruptness, this particular wanton wonderment: it met him there—and this was the image under which he himself judged the matter, or at least, not a little, thrilled and flushed with it—very much as he might have been met by some strange figure, some unexpected occupant, at a turn of one of the dim passages of an empty house. The quaint analogy quite hauntingly remained with him, when he didn't indeed rather improve it by a still intenser form: that of his opening a door behind which he would have made sure of finding nothing, a door into a room shuttered and void, and yet so coming, with a great suppressed start, on some quiet erect confronting presence, something planted in the middle of the place and facing him through the dusk. After that visit to the house in construction he walked with his companion to see the other and always so much the better one, which in the eastward direction formed one of the corners, the "jolly" one precisely, of the street now so generally dishonoured and disfigured in its westward reaches, and of the comparatively conservative Avenue. The Avenue still had pretensions, as Miss Staverton said, to decency; the old people had mostly gone, the old names were unknown, and here and there an old association seemed to stray, all vaguely, like some very aged person, out too late, whom you might meet and feel the impulse to watch or follow, in kindness, for safe restoration to shelter.

They went in together, our friends; he admitted himself with his key, as he kept no one there, he explained, preferring, for his reasons, to leave the place empty, under a simple arrangement with a good woman living in the neighbourhood and who came for a daily hour to open windows and dust and sweep. Spencer Brydon had his reasons and was growingly aware of them; they seemed to him better each time he was there, though he didn't name them all to his companion, any more than he told her as yet how often, how quite absurdly often, he himself came. He only let her see for the present, while they walked through the great blank rooms, that absolute vacancy reigned and that, from top to bottom, there was nothing but Mrs. Muldoon's broomstick, in a corner, to tempt the burglar. Mrs. Muldoon was then on the premises, and she loquaciously attended the visitors, preceding them from room to room and pushing back shutters and throwing up sashes—all to show them, as she remarked, how little there was to see. There was little indeed to see in the great gaunt shell where the main dispositions and the general apportionment of space, the style of an age of ampler allowances, had nevertheless for its master their honest pleading message, affecting him as some good old servant's, some lifelong retainer's appeal for a character, or even for a retiring-pension; yet it was also a remark of Mrs. Muldoon's that, glad as she was to oblige him by her noonday round, there was a request she greatly hoped he would never make of her. If he should wish her for any reason to come in after dark she would just tell him, if he "plased," that he must ask it of somebody else.

The fact that there was nothing to see didn't militate for the worthy woman against what one *might* see, and she put it frankly to Miss Staverton that no lady could be expected to like, could she? "craping up to thim top storeys in the ayvil hours." The gas and the electric light were off the house, and she fairly evoked a gruesome vision of her march through the great grey rooms—so many of them as there were too!—with her glimmering taper. Miss Staverton met her honest glare with a smile and the profession that she herself certainly would recoil from such an adventure. Spencer Brydon meanwhile held his peace—for the moment; the question of the "evil" hours in his old home had already become too grave for him. He had begun some time since to "crape," and he knew just why a packet of candles addressed to that pursuit had been stowed by his own hand, three weeks before, at the back of a drawer of the fine old sideboard that occupied, as a "fixture," the deep recess in the dining-room. Just now he laughed at his companions—quickly however changing the subject; for the reason that, in the first place, his laugh struck him even at that moment as starting the odd echo, the conscious human resonance (he scarce knew how to qualify it) that sounds made while he was there alone sent back to his ear or his fancy; and that, in the second, he imagined Alice Staverton for the instant on the point of asking him, with a divination, if he ever so prowled. There were divinations he was unprepared for, and he had at all events averted enquiry by the time Mrs. Muldoon had left them, passing on to other parts.

There was happily enough to say, on so consecrated a spot, that could be said freely and fairly; so that a whole train of declarations was precipitated by his friend's having herself broken out, after a yearning look around: "But I hope you don't mean they want you to pull *this* to pieces!" His answer came, promptly, with his re-awakened wrath: it was of course exactly what they wanted, and what they were "at" him for, daily, with the iteration of people who couldn't for their life understand a man's liability to decent feelings. He had found the place, just as it stood and beyond what he could express, an interest and a joy. There were values other than the beastly rent-values, and in short, in short—! But it was thus Miss Staverton took him up. "In short you're to make so good a thing of your sky-scraper that, living in luxury on *those* ill-gotten gains, you can afford for a while to be sentimental here!" Her smile had for him with the words, the particular mild irony with which he found half her talk suffused; an irony without bitterness and that came, exactly, from her having so much imagination—not, like the cheap sarcasms with which one heard most people, about the world of "society," bid for the reputation of cleverness, from nobody's really having any. It was agreeable to him at this very moment to be sure that when he had answered, after a brief demur, "Well yes: so, precisely, you may put it!" her imagination would still do him justice. He explained that even if never a dollar were to come to him from the other house he would nevertheless cherish this one; and he dwelt, further, while they lingered and wandered, on the fact of the stupefaction he was already exciting, the positive mystification he felt himself create.

He spoke of the value of all he read into it, into the mere sight of the walls, mere shapes of the rooms, mere sound of the floors, mere feel, in his hand, of the old silver-plated knobs of the several mahogany doors, which suggested the pressure of the palms of the dead; the seventy years of the past in fine that these things represented, the annals of nearly three generations, counting his grandfather's, the one that had ended there, and the impalpable ashes of his long-extinct youth, afloat in the very air like microscopic motes. She listened to everything; she was a woman who answered intimately but who utterly didn't chatter. She scattered abroad therefore no cloud of words; she could assent, she could agree, above all she could encourage, without doing that. Only at the last she went a little further than he had done himself. "And then how do you know? You may still, after all, want to live here." It rather indeed pulled him up, for it wasn't what he had been thinking, at least in her sense of the words. "You mean I may decide to stay on for the sake of it?"

"Well, *with* such a home—!" But, quite beautifully, she had too much tact to dot so monstrous an *i*, and it was precisely an illustration of the way she didn't rattle. How could any one—of any wit—insist on any one else's "wanting" to live in New York?

"Oh," he said "I *might* have lived here (since I had my opportunity early in life); I might have put in here all these years. Then everything would have been different enough—and, I dare say 'funny' enough. But that's another matter. And then the beauty of it—I mean of my perversity, of my refusal to agree to a 'deal'—is just in the total absence of a reason. Don't you see that if I had a reason about the matter at all it would *have* to be the other way, and would then be inevitably a reason of dollars? There are no reasons here *but* of dollars. Let us therefore have none whatever—not the ghost of one."

They were back in the hall then for departure, but from where they stood the vista was large, through an open door, into the great square main saloon, with its almost antique felicity of brave spaces between windows. Her eyes came back from that reach and met his own a moment. "Are you very sure the 'ghost' of one doesn't, much rather, serve—?"

He had a positive sense of turning pale. But it was as near as they were then to come. For he made answer, he believed, between a glare and a grin: "Oh ghosts—of course the place must swarm with them! I should be ashamed of it if it didn't. Poor Mrs. Muldoon's right, and it's why I haven't asked her to do more than look in."

Miss Staverton's gaze again lost itself, and things she didn't utter, it was clear, came and went in her mind. She might even for the moment, off there in the fine room, have imagined some element dimly gathering. Simplified like the death-mask of a handsome face, it perhaps produced for her just then an effect akin to the stir of an expression in the "set" commemorative plaster. Yet whatever her impression may have been she produced instead a vague platitude. "Well, if it were only furnished and lived in—!"

She appeared to imply that in case of its being still furnished he might have been a little less opposed to the idea of a return. But she passed straight into the vestibule, as if to leave her words behind her, and the next moment he had opened the house-door and was standing with her on the steps. He closed the door and, while he re-pocketed his key, looking up and down, they took in the comparatively harsh actuality of the Avenue, which reminded him of the assault of the outer light of the Desert on the traveller emerging from an Egyptian tomb. But he risked before they stepped into the street his gathered answer to her speech. "For me it *is* lived in. For me it *is* furnished." At which it was easy for her to sigh "Ah yes—!" all vaguely and discreetly; since his parents and his favourite sister, to say nothing of other kin, in numbers, had run their course and met their end there. That represented, within the walls, ineffaceable life.

It was a few days after this that, during an hour passed with her again, he had expressed his impatience of the too flattering curiosity—among the people he met—about his appreciation of New York. He had arrived at none at all that was socially producible, and as for that matter of his "thinking" (thinking the better or the worse of anything there) he was wholly taken up with one subject of thought. It was mere vain egoism, and it was moreover, if she liked, a morbid obsession. He found all things come back to the question of what he personally might have been, how he might have led his life and "turned out," if he had not so, at the outset, given it up. And confessing for the first time to the intensity within him of this absurd speculation—which but proved also, no doubt, the habit of too selfishly thinking—he affirmed the impotence there of any other source of interest, any other native appeal. "What would it have made of me, what would it have made of me? I keep for ever wondering, all idiotically; as if I could possibly know! I see what it has made of dozens of others, those I meet, and it positively aches within me, to the point of exasperation, that it would have made something of me as well. Only I can't make out *what*, and the worry of it, the small rage of curiosity never to be satisfied, brings back what I remember to have felt, once or twice, after judging best, for reasons, to burn some important letter unopened. I've been sorry, I've hated it—I've never known what was in the letter. You may of course say it's a trifle—!"

"I don't say it's a trifle," Miss Staverton gravely interrupted.

She was seated by her fire, and before her, on his feet and restless, he turned to and fro between this intensity of his idea and a fitful and unseeing inspection, through his single eye-glass, of the dear little old objects on her chimney-piece. Her interruption made him for an instant look at her harder. "I shouldn't care if you did!" he laughed, however; "and it's only a figure, at any rate, for the way I now feel. *Not* to have followed my perverse young course—and almost in the teeth of my father's curse, as I may say; not to have kept it up, so, 'over there,' from that day to this, without a doubt or a pang; not, above all, to have liked it, to have loved it, so much, loved it, no doubt, with such an abysmal conceit of my own preference: some variation from *that*, I say, must have produced some different effect for my life and for my form. I should have stuck here—if it had been possible; and I was too young, at twenty-three, to judge, *pour deux sous*, whether it *were* possible. If I had waited I might have seen it was, and then I might have been, by staying here, something nearer to one of these types who have been hammered so hard and made so keen by their conditions. It isn't that I admire them so much—the question of any charm in them, or of any charm, beyond that of the rank money-passion, exerted by their conditions *for* them, has nothing to do with the matter: it's only a question of what fantastic, yet perfectly possible, development of my own nature I mayn't have missed. It comes over me that I had then a strange *alter ego* deep down somewhere within me, as the full-blown flower is in the small tight bud, and that I just took the course, I just transferred him to the climate, that blighted him for once and for ever."

"And you wonder about the flower," Miss Staverton said. "So do I, if you want to know; and so I've been wondering these several weeks. I believe in the flower," she continued, "I feel it would have been quite splendid, quite huge and monstrous."

"Monstrous above all!" her visitor echoed; "and I imagine, by the same stroke, quite hideous and offensive."

"You don't believe that," she returned; "if you did you wouldn't wonder. You'd know, and that would be enough for you. What you feel —and what I feel *for* you—is that you'd have had power."

"You'd have liked me that way?" he asked.

She barely hung fire. "How should I not have liked you?"

"I see. You'd have liked me, have preferred me, a billionaire!"

"How should I not have liked you?" she simply again asked.

He stood before her still—her question kept him motionless. He took it in, so much there was of it; and indeed his not otherwise meeting it testified to that. "I know at least what I am," he simply went on; "the other side of the medal's clear enough. I've not been edifying—I believe I'm thought in a hundred quarters to have been barely decent. I've followed strange paths and worshipped strange gods; it must have come to you again and again—in fact you've admitted to me as much—that I was leading, at any time these thirty years, a selfish frivolous scandalous life. And you see what it has made of me."

She just waited, smiling at him. "You see what it has made of *me*."

"Oh you're a person whom nothing can have altered. You were born to be what you are, anywhere, anyway: you've the perfection nothing else could have blighted. And don't you see how, without my exile, I shouldn't have been waiting till now—?" But he pulled up for the strange pang.

"The great thing to see," she presently said, "seems to me to be that it has spoiled nothing. It hasn't spoiled your being here at last. It hasn't spoiled this. It hasn't spoiled your speaking—" She also however faltered.

He wondered at everything her controlled emotion might mean. "Do you believe then—too dreadfully!—that I *am* as good as I might ever have been?"

"Oh no! Far from it!" With which she got up from her chair and was nearer to him. "But I don't care," she smiled.

"You mean I'm good enough?"

She considered a little. "Will you believe it if I say so? I mean will you let that settle your question for you?" And then as if making out in his face that he drew back from this, that he had some idea which, however absurd, he couldn't yet bargain away: "Oh you don't care either—but very differently: you don't care for anything but yourself."

Spencer Brydon recognised it—it was in fact what he had absolutely professed. Yet he importantly qualified. "*He* isn't myself. He's the just so totally other person. But I do want to see him," he added. "And I can. And I shall."

Their eyes met for a minute while he guessed from something in hers that she divined his strange sense. But neither of them otherwise expressed it, and her apparent understanding, with no protesting shock, no easy derision, touched him more deeply than anything yet, constituting for his stifled perversity, on the spot, an element that was like breatheable air. What she said however was unexpected. "Well, *I've* seen him."

"You—?"

"I've seen him in a dream."

"Oh a 'dream'—!" It let him down.

"But twice over," she continued. "I saw him as I see you now."

"You've dreamed the same dream—?"

"Twice over," she repeated. "The very same."

This did somehow a little speak to him, as it also gratified him. "You dream about me at that rate?"

"Ah about *him!*" she smiled.

His eyes again sounded her. "Then you know all about him." And as she said nothing more: "What's the wretch like?"

She hesitated, and it was as if he were pressing her so hard that, resisting for reasons of her own, she had to turn away. "I'll tell you some other time!"

II

It was after this that there was most of a virtue for him, most of a cultivated charm, most of a preposterous secret thrill, in the particular form of surrender to his obsession and of address to what he more and more believed to be his privilege. It was what in these weeks he was living for—since he really felt life to begin but after Mrs. Muldoon had retired from the scene and, visiting the ample house from attic to cellar, making sure he was alone, he knew himself in safe possession and, as he tacitly expressed it, let himself go. He sometimes came twice in the twenty-four hours; the moments he liked best were those of gathering dusk, of the short autumn twilight; this was the time of which, again and again, he found himself hoping most. Then he could, as seemed to him, most intimately wander and wait, linger and listen, feel his fine attention, never in his life before so fine, on the pulse of the great vague place: he preferred the lampless hour and only wished he might have prolonged each day the deep crepuscular spell. Later—rarely much before midnight, but then for a considerable vigil—he watched with his glimmering light; moving slowly, holding it high, playing it far, rejoicing above all, as much as he might, in open vistas, reaches of communication between rooms and by passages; the long straight chance or show, as he would have called it, for the revelation he pretended to invite. It was a practice he found he could perfectly "work" without exciting remark; no one was in the least the wiser for it; even Alice Staverton, who was moreover a well of discretion, didn't quite fully imagine.

He let himself in and let himself out with the assurance of calm proprietorship; and accident so far favoured him that, if a fat Avenue "officer" had happened on occasion to see him entering at eleven-thirty, he had never yet, to the best of his belief, been noticed as emerging at two. He walked there on the crisp November nights, arrived regularly at the evening's end; it was as easy to do this after dining out as to take his way to a club or to his hotel. When he left his club, if he hadn't been dining out, it was ostensibly to go to his hotel; and when he left his hotel, if he had spent a part of the evening there, it was ostensibly to go to his club. Everything was easy in fine: everything conspired and promoted: there was truly even in the strain of his experience something that glossed over, something that salved and simplified, all the rest of consciousness. He circulated, talked, renewed, loosely and pleasantly, old relations—met indeed, so far as he could, new expectations and seemed to make out on the whole that in spite of the career, of such different contacts, which he had spoken of to Miss Staverton as ministering so little, for those who might have watched it, to edification, he was positively rather like than not. He was a dim secondary social success—and all with people who had truly not an idea of him. It was all mere surface sound, this murmur of their welcome, this popping of their corks—just as his gestures of response were the extravagant shadows, emphatic in proportion as they meant little, of some game of *ombres chinoises.* He projected himself all day, in thought, straight over the bristling line of hard unconscious heads and into the other, the real, the waiting life; the life that, as soon as he had heard behind him the click of his great house-door, began for him, on the jolly corner, as beguilingly as the slow opening bars of some rich music follows the tap of the conductor's wand.

He always caught the first effect of the steel point of his stick on the old marble of the hall pavement, large black-and-white squares that he remembered as the admiration of his childhood and that had then made in him, as he now saw, for the growth of an early conception of style. This effect was the dim reverberating tinkle as of some far-off bell hung who should say where?—in the depths of the house, of the past, of that mystical other world that might have flourished for him had he not, for weal or woe, abandoned it. On this impression he did ever the same thing; he put his stick noiselessly away in a corner—feeling the place once more in the likeness of some great glass bowl, all precious concave crystal, set delicately humming by the play of a moist finger round its edge. The concave crystal held, as it were, this mystical other world, and the indescribably fine murmur of its rim was the sigh there, the scarce audible pathetic wail to his strained ear, of all the old baffled forsworn possibilities. What he did therefore by this appeal of his hushed presence was to wake them into such measure of ghostly life as they might still enjoy. They were shy, all but unappeasably shy, but they weren't really sinister; at least they weren't as he had hitherto felt them—before they had taken the Form he so yearned to make them take, the Form he at moments saw himself in the light of fairly hunting on tiptoe, the points of his evening-shoes, from room to room and from storey to storey.

That was the essence of his vision—which was all rank folly, if one would, while he was out of the house and otherwise occupied, but which took on the last verisimilitude as soon as he was placed and posted. He knew what he meant and what he wanted; it was as clear as the figure on a cheque presented in demand for cash. His *alter ego* "walked"—that was the note of his image of him, while his image of his motive for his own odd pastime was the desire to waylay him and meet him. He roamed, slowly, warily, but all restlessly, he himself did—Mrs. Muldoon had been right, absolutely, with her figure of their "craping"; and the presence he watched for would roam restlessly too. But it would be as cautious and as shifty; the conviction of its probable, in fact its already quite sensible, quite audible evasion of pursuit grew for him from night to night, laying on him finally a rigour to which nothing in his life had been comparable. It had been the theory of many superficially-judging persons, he knew, that he was wasting that life in a surrender to sensations, but he had tasted of no pleasure so fine as his actual tension, had been introduced to no sport that demanded at once the patience and the nerve of this stalking of a creature more subtle, yet at bay perhaps more formidable, than any beast of the forest. The terms, the comparisons, the very practices of the chase positively came again into play; there were even moments when passages of his occasional experience as a sportsman, stirred memories, from his younger time, of moor and mountain and desert, revived for him—and to the increase of his keenness—by the tremendous force of analogy. He found himself at moments—once he had placed his single light on some mantel-shelf or in some recess—stepping back into shelter or shade, effacing himself behind a door or in an embrasure, as he had sought of old the vantage of rock and tree; he found himself holding his breath and living in the joy of the instant, the supreme suspense created by big game alone.

He wasn't afraid (though putting himself the question as he believed gentlemen on Bengal tiger-shoots or in close quarters with the great bear of the Rockies had been known to confess to having put it); and this indeed—since here at least he might be frank!—because of the impressions, so intimate and so strange, that he himself produced as yet a dread, produced certainly a strain, beyond the liveliest he was likely to feel. They fell for him into categories, they fairly became familiar, the signs, for his own perception, of the alarm his presence and his vigilance created; though leaving him always to remark, portentously, on his probably having formed a relation, his probably enjoying a consciousness, unique in the experience of man. People enough, first and last, had been in terror of apparitions, but who had ever before so turned the tables and become himself, in the apparitional world, an incalculable terror? He might have found this sublime had he quite dared to think of it; but he didn't too much insist, truly, on that side of his privilege. With habit and repetition he gained to an extraordinary degree the power to penetrate the dusk of distances and the darkness of corners, to resolve back into their innocence the treacheries of uncertain light, the evil-looking forms taken in the gloom by mere shadows, by accidents of the air, by shifting effects of perspective; putting down his dim luminary he could still wander on without it, pass into other rooms and, only knowing it was there behind him in case of need, see his way about, visually project for his purpose a comparative clearness. It made him feel, this acquired faculty, like some monstrous stealthy cat; he wondered if he would have glared at these moments with large shining yellow eyes, and what it mightn't verily be, for the poor hard-pressed *alter ego*, to be confronted with such a type.

He liked however the open shutters; he opened everywhere those Mrs. Muldoon had closed, closing them as carefully afterwards, so that she shouldn't notice: he liked—oh this he did like, and above all in the upper rooms!—the sense of the hard silver of the autumn stars through the window-panes, and scarcely less the flare of the street-lamps below, the white electric lustre which it would have taken curtains to keep out. This was human actual social; this was of the world he had lived in, and he was more at his ease certainly for the countenance, coldly general and impersonal, that all the while and in spite of his detachment it seemed to give him. He had support of course mostly in the rooms at the wide front and the prolonged side; it failed him considerably in the central shades and the parts at the back. But if he sometimes, on his rounds, was glad of his optical reach, so none the less often the rear of the house affected him as the very jungle of his prey. The place was there more subdivided; a large "extension" in particular, where small rooms for servants had been multiplied, abounded in nooks and corners, in closets and passages, in the ramifications especially of an ample back staircase over which he leaned, many a time, to look far down—not deterred from his gravity even while aware that he might, for a spectator, have figured some solemn simpleton playing at hide-and-seek. Outside in fact he might himself make that ironic *rapprochement;* but within the walls, and in spite of the clear windows, his consistency was proof against the cynical light of New York.

It had belonged to that idea of the exasperated consciousness of his victim to become a real test for him; since he had quite put it to himself from the first that, oh distinctly! he could "cultivate" his whole perception. He had felt it as above all open to cultivation—which indeed was but another name for his manner of spending his time. He was bringing it on, bringing it to perfection, by practice; in consequence of which it had grown so fine that he was now aware of impressions, attestations of his general postulate, that couldn't have broken upon him at once. This was the case more specifically with a phenomenon at last quite frequent for him in the upper rooms, the recognition—absolutely unmistakeable, and by a turn dating from a particular hour, his resumption of his campaign after a diplomatic drop, a calculated absence of three nights—of his being definitely followed, tracked at a distance carefully taken and to the express end that he should the less confidently, less arrogantly, appear to himself merely to pursue. It worried, it finally quite broke him up, for it proved, of all the conceivable impressions, the one least suited to his book. He was kept in sight while remaining himself—as regards the essence of his position—sightless, and his only recourse then was in abrupt turns, rapid recoveries of ground. He wheeled about, retracing his steps, as if he might so catch in his face at least the stirred air of some other quick revolution. It was indeed true that his fully dislocalised thought of these manoeuvres recalled to him Pantaloon, at the Christmas farce, buffeted and tricked from behind by ubiquitous Harlequin; but it left intact the influence of the conditions themselves each time he was re-exposed to them, so that in fact this association, had he suffered it to become constant, would on a certain side have but ministered to his intenser gravity. He had made, as I have said, to create on the premises the baseless sense of a reprieve, his three absences; and the result of the third was to confirm the after-effect of the second.

On his return, that night—the night succeeding his last intermission—he stood in the hall and looked up the staircase with a certainty more intimate than any he had yet known. "He's *there*, at the top, and waiting—not, as in general, falling back for disappearance. He's holding his ground, and it's the first time—which is a proof, isn't it? that something has happened for him." So Brydon argued with his hand on the banister and his foot on the lowest stair; in which position he felt as never before the air chilled by his logic. He himself turned cold in it, for he seemed of a sudden to know what now was involved. "Harder pressed?—yes, he takes it in, with its thus making clear to him that I've come, as they say, 'to stay.' He finally doesn't like and can't bear it, in the sense, I mean, that his wrath, his menaced interest, now balances with his dread. I've hunted him till he has 'turned': that, up there, is what has happened—he's the fanged or the antlered animal brought at last to bay." There came to him, as I say—but determined by an influence beyond my notation!—the acuteness of this certainty; under which however the next moment he had broken into a sweat that he would as little have consented to attribute to fear as he would have dared immediately to act upon it for enterprise. It marked none the less a prodigious thrill, a thrill that represented sudden dismay, no doubt, but also represented, and with the selfsame throb, the strangest, the most joyous, possibly the next minute almost the proudest, duplication of consciousness.

"He has been dodging, retreating, hiding, but now, worked up to anger, he'll fight!"—this intense impression made a single mouthful, as it were, of terror and applause. But what was wondrous was that the applause, for the felt fact, was so eager, since, if it was his other self he was running to earth, this ineffable identity was thus in the last resort not unworthy of him. It bristled there—somewhere near at hand, however unseen still—as the hunted thing, even as the trodden worm of the adage *must* at last bristle; and Brydon at this instant tasted probably of a sensation more complex than had ever before found itself consistent with sanity. It was as if it would have shamed him that a character so associated with his own should triumphantly succeed in just skulking, should to the end not risk the open; so that the drop of this danger was, on the spot, a great lift of the whole situation. Yet with another rare shift of the same subtlety he was already trying to measure by how much more he himself might now be in peril of fear; so rejoicing that he could, in another form, actively inspire that fear, and simultaneously quaking for the form in which he might passively know it.

The apprehension of knowing it must after a little have grown in him, and the strangest moment of his adventure perhaps, the most memorable or really most interesting, afterwards, of his crisis, was the lapse of certain instants of concentrated conscious *combat,* the sense of a need to hold on to something, even after the manner of a man slipping and slipping on some awful incline; the vivid impulse, above all, to move, to act, to charge, somehow and upon something—to show himself, in a word, that he wasn't afraid. The state of "holding-on" was thus the state to which he was momentarily reduced; if there had been anything, in the great vacancy, to seize, he would presently have been aware of having clutched it as he might under a shock at home have clutched the nearest chair-back. He had been surprised at any rate—of this he *was* aware—into something unprecedented since his original appropriation of the place; he had closed his eyes, held them tight, for a long minute, as with that instinct of dismay and that terror of vision. When he opened them the room, the other contiguous rooms, extraordinarily, seemed lighter—so light, almost, that at first he took the change for day. He stood firm, however that might be, just where he had paused; his resistance had helped him—it was as if there were something he had tided over. He knew after a little what this was—it had been in the imminent danger of flight. He had stiffened his will against going; without this he would have made for the stairs, and it seemed to him that, still with his eyes closed, he would have descended them, would have known how, straight and swiftly, to the bottom.

Well, as he had held out, here he was—still at the top, among the more intricate upper rooms and with the gauntlet of the others, of all the rest of the house, still to run when it should be his time to go. He would go at his time—only at his time: didn't he go every night very much at the same hour? He took out his watch—there was light for that: it was scarcely a quarter past one, and he had never withdrawn so soon. He reached his lodgings for the most part at two—with his walk of a quarter of an hour. He would wait for the last quarter—he wouldn't stir till then; and he kept his watch there with his eyes on it, reflecting while he held it that this deliberate wait, a wait with an effort, which he recognised, would serve perfectly for the attestation he desired to make. It would prove his courage—unless indeed the latter might most be proved by his budging at last from his place. What he mainly felt now was that, since he hadn't originally scuttled, he had his dignities—which had never in his life seemed so many—all to preserve and to carry aloft. This was before him in truth as a physical image, an image almost worthy of an age of greater romance. That remark indeed glimmered for him only to glow the next instant with a finer light; since what age of romance, after all, could have matched either the state of his mind or, "objectively," as they said, the wonder of his situation? The only difference would have been that, brandishing his dignities over his head as in a parchment scroll, he might then—that is in the heroic time—have proceeded downstairs with a drawn sword in his other grasp.

At present, really, the light he had set down on the mantel of the next room would have to figure his sword; which utensil, in the course of a minute, he had taken the requisite number of steps to possess himself of. The door between the rooms was open, and from the second another door opened to a third. These rooms, as he remembered, gave all three upon a common corridor as well, but there was a fourth, beyond them, without issue save through the preceding. To have moved, to have heard his step again, was appreciably a help; though even in recognising this he lingered once more a little by the chimney-piece on which his light had rested. When he next moved, just hesitating where to turn, he found himself considering a circumstance that, after his first and comparatively vague apprehension of it, produced in him the start that often attends some pang of recollection, the violent shock of having ceased happily to forget. He had come into sight of the door in which the brief chain of communication ended and which he now surveyed from the nearer threshold, the one not directly facing it. Placed at some distance to the left of this point, it would have admitted him to the last room of the four, the room without other approach or egress, had it not, to his intimate conviction, been closed *since* his former visitation, the matter probably of a quarter of an hour before. He stared with all his eyes at the wonder of the fact, arrested again where he stood and again holding his breath while he sounded its sense. Surely it had been *subsequently* closed—that is it had been on his previous passage indubitably open!

He took it full in the face that something had happened between—that he couldn't not have noticed before (by which he meant on his original tour of all the rooms that evening) that such a barrier had exceptionally presented itself. He had indeed since that moment undergone an agitation so extraordinary that it might have muddled for him any earlier view; and he tried to convince himself that he might perhaps then have gone into the room and, inadvertently, automatically, on coming out, have drawn the door after him. The difficulty was that this exactly was what he never did: it was against his whole policy, as he might have said, the essence of which was to keep vistas clear. He had them from the first, as he was well aware, quite on the brain: the strange apparition, at the far end of one of them, of his baffled "prey" (which had become by so sharp an irony so little the term now to apply!) was the form of success his imagination had most cherished, projecting into it always a refinement of beauty. He had known fifty times the start of perception that had afterwards dropped; had fifty times gasped to himself "There!" under some fond brief hallucination. The house, as the case stood, admirably lent itself; he might wonder at the taste, the native architecture of the particular time, which could rejoice so in the multiplication of doors—the opposite extreme to the modern, the actual almost complete proscription of them; but it had fairly contributed to provoke this obsession of the presence encountered telescopically, as he might say, focussed and studied in diminishing perspective and as by a rest for the elbow.

It was with these considerations that his present attention was charged—they perfectly availed to make what he saw portentous. He *couldn't*, by any lapse, have blocked that aperture; and if he hadn't, if it was unthinkable, why what else was clear but that there had been another agent? Another agent?—he had been catching, as he felt, a moment back, the very breath of him; but when had he been so close as in this simple, this logical, this completely personal act? It was so logical, that is, that one might have *taken* it for personal; yet for what did Brydon take it, he asked himself, while, softly panting, he felt his eyes almost leave their sockets. Ah this time at last they *were*, the two, the opposed projections of him, in presence; and this time, as much as one would, the question of danger loomed. With it rose, as not before, the question of courage—for what he knew the blank face of the door to say to him was "Show us how much you have!" It stared, it glared back at him with that challenge; it put to him the two alternatives: should he just push it open or not? Oh to have this consciousness was to *think*—and to think, Brydon knew, as he stood there, was, with lapsing moments, not to have acted! Not to have acted—that was the misery and the pang—was even still not to act; was in fact *all* to feel the thing in another, in a new and terrible way. How long did he pause and how long did he debate? There was presently nothing to measure it; for his vibration had already changed—as just by the effect of its intensity. Shut up there, at bay, defiant, and with the prodigy of the thing palpably proveably *done*, thus giving notice like some stark signboard—under that accession of accent the situation itself had turned; and Brydon at last remarkably made up his mind on what it had turned to.

It turned altogether to a different admonition; to a supreme hint, for him, of the value of Discretion! This slowly dawned, no doubt—for it could take its time; so perfectly, on his threshold, had he been stayed, so little as yet had he either advanced or retreated. It was the strangest of all things that now when, by his taking ten steps and applying his hand to a latch, or even his shoulder and his knee, if necessary, to a panel, all the hunger of his prime need might have been met, his high curiosity crowned, his unrest assuaged—it was amazing, but it was also exquisite and rare, that insistence should have, at a touch, quite dropped from him. Discretion—he jumped at that; and yet not, verily, at such a pitch, because it saved his nerves or his skin, but because, much more valuably, it saved the situation. When I say he "jumped" at it I feel the consonance of this term with the fact that—at the end indeed of I know not how long—he did move again, he crossed straight to the door. He wouldn't touch it—it seemed now that he might *if* he would: he would only just wait there a little, to show, to prove, that he wouldn't. He had thus another station, close to the thin partition by which revelation was denied him; but with his eyes bent and his hands held off in a mere intensity of stillness. He listened as if there had been something to hear, but this attitude, while it lasted, was his own communication. "If you won't then—good: I spare you and I give up. You affect me as by the appeal positively for pity: you convince me that for reasons rigid and sublime—what do I know?—we both of us should have suffered. I respect them then, and, though moved and privileged as, I believe, it has never been given to man, I retire, I renounce—never, on my honour, to try again. So rest for ever—and let *me!*"

That, for Brydon was the deep sense of this last demonstration—solemn, measured, directed, as he felt it to be. He brought it to a close, he turned away; and now verily he knew how deeply he had been stirred. He retraced his steps, taking up his candle, burnt, he observed, well-nigh to the socket, and marking again, lighten it as he would, the distinctness of his footfall; after which, in a moment, he knew himself at the other side of the house. He did here what he had not yet done at these hours—he opened half a casement, one of those in the front, and let in the air of the night; a thing he would have taken at any time previous for a sharp rupture of his spell. His spell was broken now, and it didn't matter—broken by his concession and his surrender, which made it idle henceforth that he should ever come back. The empty street—its other life so marked even by the great lamplit vacancy—was within call, within touch; he stayed there as to be in it again, high above it though he was still perched; he watched as for some comforting common fact, some vulgar human note, the passage of a scavenger or a thief, some night-bird however base. He would have blessed that sign of life; he would have welcomed positively the slow approach of his friend the policeman, whom he had hitherto only sought to avoid, and was not sure that if the patrol had come into sight he mightn't have felt the impulse to get into relation with it, to hail it, on some pretext, from his fourth floor.

The pretext that wouldn't have been too silly or too compromising, the explanation that would have saved his dignity and kept his name, in such a case, out of the papers, was not definite to him: he was so occupied with the thought of recording his Discretion—as an effect of the vow he had just uttered to his intimate adversary—that the importance of this loomed large and something had overtaken all ironically his sense of proportion. If there had been a ladder applied to the front of the house, even one of the vertiginous perpendiculars employed by painters and roofers and sometimes left standing overnight, he would have managed somehow, astride of the window-sill, to compass by outstretched leg and arm that mode of descent. If there had been some such uncanny thing as he had found in his room at hotels, a workable fire escape in the form of notched cable or a canvas shoot, he would have availed himself of it as a proof—well, of his present delicacy. He nursed that sentiment, as the question stood, a little in vain, and even—at the end of he scarce knew, once more, how long—found it, as by the action on his mind of the failure of response of the outer world, sinking back to vague anguish. It seemed to him he had waited an age for some stir of the great grim hush; the life of the town was itself under a spell—so unnaturally, up and down the whole prospect of known and rather ugly objects, the blankness and the silence lasted. Had they ever, he asked himself, the hard-faced houses, which had begun to look livid in the dim dawn, had they ever spoken so little to any need of his spirit? Great builded voids, great crowded stillnesses put on, often, in the heart of cities, for the small hours, a sort of sinister mask, and it was of this large collective negation that Brydon presently became conscious—all the more that the break of day was, almost incredibly, now at hand, proving to him what a night he had made of it.

He looked again at his watch, saw what had become of his time-values (he had taken hours for minutes—not, as in other tense situations, minutes for hours) and the strange air of the streets was but the weak, the sullen flush of a dawn in which everything was still locked up. His choked appeal from his own open window had been the sole note of life, and he could but break off at last as for a worse despair. Yet while so deeply demoralised he was capable again of an impulse denoting—at least by his present measure—extraordinary resolution; of retracing his steps to the spot where he had turned cold with the extinction of his last pulse of doubt as to there being in the place another presence than his own. This required an effort strong enough to sicken him; but he had his reason, which overmastered for the moment everything else. There was the whole of the rest of the house to traverse, and how should he screw himself to that if the door he had seen closed were at present open? He could hold to the idea that the closing had practically been for him an act of mercy, a chance offered him to descend, depart, get off the ground and never again profane it. This conception held together, it worked; but what it meant for him depended now clearly on the amount of forbearance his recent action, or rather his recent inaction, had engendered. The image of the "presence," whatever it was, waiting there for him to go—this image had not yet been so concrete for his nerves as when he stopped short of the point at which certainty would have come to him. For, with all his resolution, or more exactly with all his dread, he did stop short—he hung back from really seeing. The risk was too great and his fear too definite: it took at this moment an awful specific form.

He knew—yes, as he had never known anything—that, *should* he see the door open, it would all too abjectly be the end of him. It would mean that the agent of his shame—for his shame was the deep abjection —was once more at large and in general possession; and what glared him thus in the face was the act that this would determine for him. It would send him straight about to the window he had left open, and by that window, be long ladder and dangling rope as absent as they would, he saw himself uncontrollably insanely fatally take his way to the street. The hideous chance of this he at least could avert; but he could only avert it by recoiling in time from assurance. He had the whole house to deal with, this fact was still there; only he now knew that uncertainty alone could start him. He stole back from where he had checked himself—merely to do so was suddenly like safety—and, making blindly for the greater staircase, left gaping rooms and sounding passages behind. Here was the top of the stairs, with a fine large dim descent and three spacious landings to mark off. His instinct was all for mildness, but his feet were harsh on the floors, and, strangely, when he had in a couple of minutes become aware of this, it counted somehow for help. He couldn't have spoken, the tone of his voice would have scared him, and the common conceit or resource of "whistling in the dark" (whether literally or figuratively) have appeared basely vulgar; yet he liked none the less to hear himself go, and when he had reached his first landing—taking it all with no rush, but quite steadily—that stage of success drew from him a gasp of relief.

The house, withal, seemed immense, the scale of space again inordinate; the open rooms, to no one of which his eyes deflected, gloomed in their shuttered state like mouths of caverns; only the high skylight that formed the crown of the deep well created for him a medium in which he could advance, but which might have been, for queerness of colour, some watery under-world. He tried to think of something noble, as that his property was really grand, a splendid possession; but this nobleness took the form too of the clear delight with which he was finally to sacrifice it. They might come in now, the builders, the destroyers—they might come as soon as they would. At the end of two flights he had dropped to another zone, and from the middle of the third, with only one more left, he recognised the influence of the lower windows, of half-drawn blinds, of the occasional gleam of street lamps, of the glazed spaces of the vestibule. This was the bottom of the sea, which showed an illumination of its own and which he even saw paved—when at a given moment he drew up to sink a long look over the banisters—with the marble squares of his childhood. By that time indubitably he felt, as he might have said in a commoner cause, better; it had allowed him to stop and draw breath, and the ease increased with the sight of the old black-and-white slabs. But what he most felt was that now surely, with the element of impunity pulling him as by hard firm hands, the case was settled for what he might have seen above had he dared that last look. The closed door, blessedly remote now, was still closed—and he had only in short to reach that of the house.

He came down further, he crossed the passage forming the access to the last flight; and if here again he stopped an instant it was almost for the sharpness of the thrill of assured escape. It made him shut his eyes—which opened again to the straight slope of the remainder of the stairs. Here was impunity still, but impunity almost excessive; inasmuch as the sidelights and the high fan-tracery of the entrance were glimmering straight into the hall; an appearance produced, he the next instant saw, by the fact that the vestibule gaped wide, that the hinged halves of the inner door had been thrown far back. Out of that again the *question* sprang at him, making his eyes, as he felt, half-start from his head, as they had done, at the top of the house, before the sign of the other door. If he had left that one open, hadn't he left this one closed, and wasn't he now in *most* immediate presence of some inconceivable occult activity? It was as sharp, the question, as a knife in his side, but the answer hung fire still and seemed to lose itself in the vague darkness to which the thin admitted dawn, glimmering archwise over the whole outer door, made a semicircular margin, a cold silvery nimbus that seemed to play a little as he looked—to shift and expand and contract.

It was as if there had been something within it, protected by indistinctness and corresponding in extent with the opaque surface behind, the painted panels of the last barrier to his escape, of which the key was in his pocket. The indistinctness mocked him even while he stared, affected him as somehow shrouding or challenging certitude, so that after faltering an instant on his step he let himself go with the sense that here *was* at last something to meet, to touch, to take, to know—something all unnatural and dreadful, but to advance upon which was the condition for him either of liberation or of supreme defeat. The penumbra, dense and dark, was the virtual screen of a figure which stood in it as still as some image erect in a niche or as some black-vizored sentinel guarding a treasure. Brydon was to know afterwards, was to recall and make out, the particular thing he had believed during the rest of his descent. He saw, in its great grey glimmering margin, the central vagueness diminish, and he felt it to be taking the very form toward which, for so many days, the passion of his curiosity had yearned. It gloomed, it loomed, it was something, it was somebody, the prodigy of a personal presence.

Rigid and conscious, spectral yet human, a man of his own substance and stature waited there to measure himself with his power to dismay. This only could it be—this only till he recognised, with his advance, that what made the face dim was the pair of raised hands that covered it and in which, so far from being offered in defiance, it was buried as for dark deprecation. So Brydon, before him, took him in; with every fact of him now, in the higher light, hard and acute—his planted stillness, his vivid truth, his grizzled bent head and white masking hands, his queer actuality of evening-dress, of dangling double eye-glass, of gleaming silk lappet and white linen, of pearl button and gold watch-guard and polished shoe. No portrait by a great modern master could have presented him with more intensity, thrust him out of his frame with more art, as if there had been "treatment," of the consummate sort, in his every shade and salience. The revulsion, for our friend, had become, before he knew it, immense—this drop, in the act of apprehension, to the sense of his adversary's inscrutable manoeuvre. That meaning at least, while he gaped, it offered him; for he could but gape at his other self in this other anguish, gape as a proof that *he*, standing there for the achieved, the enjoyed, the triumphant life, couldn't be faced in his triumph. Wasn't the proof in the splendid covering hands, strong and completely spread?—so spread and so intentional that, in spite of a special verity that surpassed every other, the fact that one of these hands had lost two fingers, which were reduced to stumps, as if accidentally shot away, the face was effectually guarded and saved.

"Saved," though, *would* it be?—Brydon breathed his wonder till the very impunity of his attitude and the very insistence of his eyes produced, as he felt, a sudden stir which showed the next instant as a deeper portent, while the head raised itself, the betrayal of a braver purpose. The hands, as he looked, began to move, to open: then, as if deciding in a flash, dropped from the face and left it uncovered and presented. Horror, with the sight, had leaped into Brydon's throat, gasping there in a sound he couldn't utter; for the bared identity was too hideous as *his*, and his glare was the passion of his protest. The face, *that* face, Spencer Brydon's?—he searched it still, but looking away from it in dismay and denial, falling straight from his height of sublimity. It was unknown, inconceivable, awful, disconnected from any possibility—! He had been "sold," he inwardly moaned, stalking such game as this: the presence before him was a presence, the horror within him a horror, but the waste of his nights had been only grotesque and the success of his adventure an irony. Such an identity fitted his at *no* point, made its alternative monstrous. A thousand times yes, as it came upon him nearer now—the face was the face of a stranger. It came upon him nearer now, quite as one of those expanding fantastic images projected by the magic lantern of childhood; for the stranger, whoever he might be, evil, odious, blatant, vulgar, had advanced as for aggression, and he knew himself give ground. Then harder pressed still, sick with the force of his shock, and falling back as under the hot breath and the roused passion of a life larger than his own, a rage of personality before which his own collapsed, he felt the whole vision turn to darkness and his very feet give way. His head went round; he was going; he had gone.

III

What had next brought him back, clearly—though after how long? —was Mrs. Muldoon's voice, coming to him from quite near, from so near that he seemed presently to see her as kneeling on the ground before him while he lay looking up at her; himself not wholly on the ground, but half-raised and upheld—conscious, yes, of tenderness of support and, more particularly, of a head pillowed in extraordinary softness and faintly refreshing fragrance. He considered, he wondered, his wit but half at his service; then another face intervened, bending more directly over him, and he finally knew that Alice Staverton had made her lap an ample and perfect cushion to him, and that she had to this end seated herself on the lowest degree of the staircase, the rest of his long person remaining stretched on his old black-and-white slabs. They were cold, these marble squares of his youth; but *he* somehow was not, in this rich return of consciousness—the most wonderful hour, little by little, that he had ever known, leaving him, as it did, so gratefully, so abysmally passive, and yet as with a treasure of intelligence waiting all round him for quiet appropriation; dissolved, he might call it, in the air of the place and producing the golden glow of a late autumn afternoon. He had come back, yes—come back from further away than any man but himself had ever travelled; but it was strange how with this sense what he had come back *to* seemed really the great thing, and as if his prodigious journey had been all for the sake of it. Slowly but surely his consciousness grew, his vision of his state thus completing itself: he had been miraculously *carried* back—lifted and carefully borne as from where he had been picked up, the uttermost end of an interminable grey passage. Even with this he was suffered to rest, and what had now brought him to knowledge was the break in the long mild motion.

It had brought him to knowledge, to knowledge—yes, this was the beauty of his state; which came to resemble more and more that of a man who has gone to sleep on some news of a great inheritance, and then, after dreaming it away, after profaning it with matters strange to it, has waked up again to serenity of certitude and has only to lie and watch it grow. This was the drift of his patience—that he had only to let it shine on him. He must moreover, with intermissions, still have been lifted and borne; since why and how else should he have known himself, later on, with the afternoon glow intenser, no longer at the foot of his stairs—situated as these now seemed at that dark other end of his tunnel—but on a deep window-bench of his high saloon, over which had been spread, couch-fashion, a mantle of soft stuff lined with grey fur that was familiar to his eyes and that one of his hands kept fondly feeling as for its pledge of truth. Mrs. Muldoon's face had gone, but the other, the second he had recognised, hung over him in a way that showed how he was still propped and pillowed. He took it all in, and the more he took it the more it seemed to suffice: he was as much at peace as if he had had food and drink. It was the two women who had found him, on Mrs. Muldoon's having plied, at her usual hour, her latch-key—and on her having above all arrived while Miss Staverton still lingered near the house. She had been turning away, all anxiety, from worrying the vain bell-handle—her calculation having been of the hour of the good woman's visit; but the latter, blessedly, had come up while she was still there, and they had entered together. He had then lain, beyond the vestibule, very much as he was lying now—quite, that is, as he appeared to have fallen, but all so wondrously without bruise or gash; only in a depth of stupor. What he most took in, however, at present, with the steadier clearance, was that Alice Staverton had for a long unspeakable moment not doubted he was dead.

"It must have been that I *was*." He made it out as she held him. "Yes —I can only have died. You brought me literally to life. Only," he wondered, his eyes rising to her, "only, in the name of all the benedictions, how?"

It took her but an instant to bend her face and kiss him, and something in the manner of it, and in the way her hands clasped and locked his head while he felt the cool charity and virtue of her lips, something in all this beatitude somehow answered everything. "And now I keep you," she said.

"Oh keep me, keep me!" he pleaded while her face still hung over him: in response to which it dropped again and stayed close, clingingly close. It was the seal of their situation—of which he tasted the impress for a long blissful moment in silence. But he came back. "Yet how did you know—?"

"I was uneasy. You were to have come, you remember—and you had sent no word."

"Yes, I remember—I was to have gone to you at one to-day." It caught on to their "old" life and relation—which were so near and so far. "I was still out there in my strange darkness—where was it, what was it? I must have stayed there so long." He could but wonder at the depth and the duration of his swoon.

"Since last night?" she asked with a shade of fear for her possible indiscretion.

"Since this morning—it must have been: the cold dim dawn of to-day. Where have I been," he vaguely wailed, "where have I been?" He felt her hold him close, and it was as if this helped him now to make in all security his mild moan. "What a long dark day!"

All in her tenderness she had waited a moment. "In the cold dim dawn?" she quavered.

But he had already gone on piecing together the parts of the whole prodigy. "As I didn't turn up you came straight—?"

She barely cast about. "I went first to your hotel—where they told me of your absence. You had dined out last evening and hadn't been back since. But they appeared to know you had been at your club."

"So you had the idea of *this*—?"

"Of what?" she asked in a moment.

"Well—of what has happened."

"I believed at least you'd have been here. I've known, all along," she said, "that you've been coming."

" 'Known' it—?"

"Well, I've believed it. I said nothing to you after that talk we had a month ago—but I felt sure. I knew you *would*," she declared.

"That I'd persist, you mean?"

"That you'd see him."

"Ah but I didn't!" cried Brydon with his long wail. "There's somebody—an awful beast; whom I brought, too horribly, to bay. But it's not me."

At this she bent over him again, and her eyes were in his eyes. "No—it's not you." And it was as if, while her face hovered, he might have made out in it, hadn't it been so near, some particular meaning blurred by a smile." No, thank heaven," she repeated—"it's not you! Of course it wasn't to have been."

"Ah but it *was*," he gently insisted. And he stared before him now as he had been staring for so many weeks. "I was to have known myself."

"You couldn't!" she returned consolingly. And then reverting, and as if to account further for what she had herself done, "But it wasn't only *that,* that you hadn't been at home," she went on. "I waited till the hour at which we had found Mrs. Muldoon that day of my going with you; and she arrived, as I've told you, while, failing to bring any one to the door, I lingered in my despair on the steps. After a little, if she hadn't come, by such a mercy, I should have found means to hunt her up. But it wasn't," said Alice Staverton, as if once more with her fine intention—"it wasn't only that."

His eyes, as he lay, turned back to her. "What more then?"

She met it, the wonder she had stirred. "In the cold dim dawn, you say? Well, in the cold dim dawn of this morning I too saw you."

"Saw *me*—?"

"Saw *him,*" said Alice Staverton. "It must have been at the same moment."

He lay an instant taking it in—as if he wished to be quite reasonable. "At the same moment?"

"Yes—in my dream again, the same one I've named to you. He came back to me. Then I knew it for a sign. He had come to you."

At this Brydon raised himself; he had to see her better. She helped him when she understood his movement, and he sat up, steadying himself beside her there on the window-bench and with his right hand grasping her left. "*He* didn't come to me."

"You came to yourself," she beautifully smiled.

"Ah I've come to myself now—thanks to you, dearest. But this brute, with his awful face—this brute's a black stranger. He's none of *me,* even as I *might* have been," Brydon sturdily declared.

But she kept the clearness that was like the breath of infallibility. "Isn't the whole point that you'd have been different?"

He almost scowled for it. "As different as *that*—?"

Her look again was more beautiful to him than the things of this world. "Haven't you exactly wanted to know *how* different? So this morning," she said, "you appeared to me."

"Like *him*?"

"A black stranger!"

"Then how did you know it was I?"

"Because, as I told you weeks ago, my mind, my imagination, has worked so over what you might, what you mightn't have been—to show you, you see, how I've thought of you. In the midst of that you came to me—that my wonder might be answered. So I knew," she went on; "and believed that, since the question held you too so fast, as you told me that day, you too would see for yourself. And when this morning I again saw I knew it would be because you had—and also then, from the first moment, because you somehow wanted me. *He* seemed to tell me of that. So why," she strangely smiled, "shouldn't I like him?"

It brought Spencer Brydon to his feet. "You 'like' that horror—?"

"I could have liked him. And to me," she said, "he was no horror. I had accepted him."

" 'Accepted'—?" Brydon oddly sounded.

"Before, for the interest of his difference—yes. And as *I* didn't disown him, as *I* knew him—which you at last, confronted with him in his difference, so cruelly didn't, my dear—well, he must have been, you see, less dreadful to me. And it may have pleased him that I pitied him."

She was beside him on her feet, but still holding his hand—still with her arm supporting him. But though it all brought for him thus a dim light, "You 'pitied' him?" he grudgingly, resentfully asked.

"He has been unhappy, he has been ravaged," she said.

"And haven't I been unhappy? Am not I—you've only to look at me! —ravaged?"

"Ah I don't say I like him *better*," she granted after a thought. "But he's grim, he's worn—and things have happened to him. He doesn't make shift for sight, with your charming monocle."

"No"—it struck Brydon: "I couldn't have sported mine 'downtown.' They'd have guyed me there."

"His great convex pince-nez—I saw it, I recognised the kind—is for his poor ruined sight. And his poor right hand—!"

"Ah!" Brydon winced—whether for his proved identity or for his lost finger. Then, "He has a million a year," he lucidly added. "But he hasn't you."

"And he isn't—no, he isn't—*you!*" she murmured as he drew her to his breast.

Questions

1. Is "The Jolly Corner" primarily a ghost story, a love story, or a story of self-discovery? What would it be like without its ghost elements?

2. Alice Staverton says to Spencer Brydon near the end of Part 1, "You don't care for anything but yourself." Does her statement aptly characterize him at this point? Is she describing or accusing him?

3. What does his house come to represent to Spencer Brydon? How does it reflect him? Why does he feel compelled to return to it at odd hours?

4. Discuss: Did Spencer Brydon *see* a ghost, did he only *believe* he saw one, or did he think he was having hallucinations? Does Henry James specifically answer the question? Why, or why not?

5. How does Alice Staverton regard the ghost? Show evidence from the story which indicates whether she does or does not fully accept Brydon's account of his ghost experiences.

6. Why does Alice accept Spender Brydon as a husband? What is the relationship between the ghost story and the outcome of their love affair?

Franz Kafka

IN THE PENAL COLONY

The greatest work of the sensitive and tormented Franz Kafka was nearly lost to the world. He published a few short stories in his lifetime, but never completed any of the three novels he worked on sporadically. Before his death he asked his friend and literary executor Max Brod to destroy all his unfinished manuscripts. Brod refused, and saved for the world some of the most strikingly original fiction of the twentieth century. Kafka was born in Prague in 1883 to a Czech Jewish family. He took a law degree, but ill health throughout his life prevented him from practicing law or from marrying. His outward life was otherwise uneventful, and he seemed haunted by a sense of failure. He died at a sanatorium in Austria in 1924. His novels appeared a few years later in Europe, and finally were translated into English—first The Castle *(1930), then* The Trial *(1936), and finally* America *(1938), in the inverse order in which they had been written.*

The typical Kafka hero is an exile, seeking either something tangible like a homeland and a position, or else something intangible like justice or assurance. In vague, mysterious landscapes that seem clearly allegorical, he continues his quest in vain, usually meeting rebuff or defeat. The story "In the Penal Colony" is one of Kafka's most typical and most impressive works. It attempts to show man struggling to learn the rules of survival in an alien universe. This story occupies the central position in a collection, The Penal Colony, *published in 1948. Stylistically, it poses the difficult problem of using a point of view which is fundamentally opposed to the writer's own.*

"It's a remarkable piece of apparatus," said the officer to the explorer and surveyed with a certain air of admiration the apparatus which was after all quite familiar to him. The explorer seemed to have accepted merely out of politeness the Commandant's invitation to witness the execution of a soldier condemned to death for disobedience and insulting behaviour to a superior. Nor did the colony itself betray much interest in this execution. At least, in the small sandy valley, a deep hollow surrounded on all sides by naked crags, there was no one present save the officer, the explorer, the condemned man, who was a stupid-looking wide-mouthed creature with bewildered hair and face, and the soldier who held the heavy chain controlling the small chains locked on the prisoner's ankles, wrists and neck, chains which were themselves attached to each other by communicating links. In any case, the condemned man looked so like a submissive dog that one might have thought he could be left to run free on the surrounding hills and would only need to be whistled for when the execution was due to begin.

The explorer did not much care about the apparatus and walked up and down behind the prisoner with almost visible indifference while the officer made the last adjustments, now creeping beneath the structure, which was bedded deep in the earth, now climbing a ladder to inspect its upper parts. These were tasks that might well have been left to a mechanic, but the officer performed them with great zeal, whether because he was a devoted admirer of the apparatus or because of other reasons the work could be entrusted to no one else. "Ready now!" he called at last and climbed down from the ladder. He looked uncommonly limp, breathed with his mouth wide open and had tucked two fine ladies' handkerchiefs under the collar of his uniform. "These uniforms are too heavy for the tropics, surely," said the explorer, instead of making some inquiry about the apparatus, as the officer had expected. "Of course," said the officer, washing his oily and greasy hands in a bucket of water that stood ready, "but they mean home to us; we don't want to forget about home. Now just have a look at this machine," he added at once, simultaneously drying his hands on a towel and indicating the apparatus. "Up till now a few things still had to be set by hand, but from this moment it works all by itself." The explorer nodded and followed him. The officer, anxious to secure himself against all contingencies, said: "Things sometimes go wrong, of course; I hope that nothing goes wrong today, but we have to allow for the possibility. The machinery should go on working continuously for twelve hours. But if anything does go wrong it will only be some small matter that can be set right at once."

"Won't you take a seat?" he asked finally, drawing a cane chair out from among a heap of them and offering it to the explorer, who could not refuse it. He was now sitting at the edge of a pit, into which he glanced for a fleeting moment. It was not very deep. On one side of the pit the excavated soil had been piled up in a rampart, on the other side of it stood the apparatus. "I don't know," said the officer, "if the Commandant has already explained this apparatus to you." The explorer waved one hand vaguely; the officer asked for nothing better, since now he could explain the apparatus himself. "This apparatus," he said, taking hold of a crank handle and leaning against it, "was invented by our former Commandant. I assisted at the very earliest experiments and had a share in all the work until its completion. But the credit of inventing it belongs to him alone. Have you ever heard of our former Commandant? No? Well, it isn't saying too much if I tell you that the organization of the whole penal colony is his work. We who were his friends knew even before he died that the organization of the colony was so perfect that his successor, even with a thousand new schemes in his head, would find it impossible to alter anything, at least for many years to come. And our prophecy has come true; the new Commandant has had to acknowledge its truth. A pity you never met the old Commandant!—But," the officer interrupted himself, "I am rambling on, and here stands his apparatus before us. It consists, as you see, of three parts. In the course of time each of these parts has acquired a kind of popular nickname. The lower one is called the 'Bed,' the upper one the 'Designer,' and this one here in the middle that moves up and down is called the 'Harrow.' " "The Harrow?" asked the explorer. He had not been listening very attentively, the glare of the sun in the shadeless valley was altogether too strong, it was difficult to collect one's thoughts. All the more did he admire the officer, who in spite of his tight-fitting full-dress uniform coat, amply befrogged and weighed down by epaulettes, was pursuing his subject with such enthusiasm and, besides talking, was still tightening a screw here and there with a spanner. As for the soldier, he seemed to be in much the same condition as the explorer. He had wound the prisoner's chain round both his wrists, propped himself on his rifle, let his head hang and was paying no attention to anything. That did not surprise the explorer, for the officer was speaking French, and certainly neither the soldier nor the prisoner understood a word of French. It was all the more remarkable, therefore, that the prisoner was none the less making an effort to follow the officer's explanations. With a kind of drowsy persistence he directed his gaze wherever the officer pointed a finger, and at the interruption of the explorer's question he, too, as well as the officer, looked round.

"Yes, the Harrow," said the officer, "a good name for it. The needles are set in like the teeth of a harrow and the whole thing works something like a harrow, although its action is limited to one place and contrived with much more artistic skill. Anyhow, you'll soon understand it. On the Bed here the condemned man is laid—I'm going to describe the apparatus first before I set it in motion. Then you'll be able to follow the proceedings better. Besides, one of the cogwheels in the Designer is badly worn; it creaks a lot when it's working, you can hardly hear yourself speak; spare parts, unfortunately, are difficult to get here.—Well, here is the Bed, as I told you. It is completely covered with a layer of cotton wool; you'll find out why later. On this cotton wool the condemned man is laid, face down, quite naked, of course; here are straps for the hands, here for the feet, and here for the neck, to bind him fast. Here at the head of the bed, where the man, as I said, first lays down his face, is this little gag of felt, which can be easily regulated to go straight into his mouth. It is meant to keep him from screaming and biting his tongue. Of course the man is forced to take the felt into his mouth, for otherwise his neck would be broken by the strap." "Is that cotton wool?" asked the explorer, bending forward. "Yes, certainly," said the officer, with a smile. "Feel it for yourself." He took the explorer's hand and guided it over the bed. "It's specially prepared cotton wool; that's why it looks so different; I'll tell you presently what it's for." The explorer already felt a dawning interest in the apparatus; he sheltered his eyes from the sun with one hand and gazed up at the structure. It was a huge affair. The Bed and the Designer were of the same size and looked like two dark wooden chests. The Designer hung about two meters above the Bed; each of them was bound at the corners with four rods of brass that almost flashed out rays in the sunlight. Between the chests shuttled the Harrow on a ribbon of steel.

The officer had scarcely noticed the explorer's previous indifference, but he was now well aware of his dawning interest; so he stopped explaining in order to leave a space of time for quiet observation. The condemned man imitated the explorer; since he could not use a hand to shelter his eyes he gazed upwards without shade.

"Well, the man lies down," said the explorer, leaning back in his chair and crossing his legs.

"Yes," said the officer, pushing his cap back a little and passing one hand over his heated face, "now listen! Both the Bed and the Designer have an electric battery each; the Bed needs one for itself, the Designer for the Harrow. As soon as the man is strapped down, the Bed is set in motion. It quivers in minute, very rapid vibrations, both from side to side and up and down. You will have seen similar apparatus in hospitals; but in our Bed the movements are all precisely calculated; you see, they have to correspond very exactly to the movements of the Harrow. And the Harrow is the instrument for the actual execution of the sentence."

"And how does the sentence run?" asked the explorer.

"You don't know that either?" said the officer in amazement, and bit his lips. "Forgive me if my explanations seem rather incoherent. I do beg your pardon. You see, the Commandant always used to do the explaining; but the new Commandant shirks this duty; yet that such an important visitor"—the explorer tried to deprecate the honor with both hands; the officer, however, insisted—"that such an important visitor should not even be told about the kind of sentence we pass is a new development, which—" He was just on the point of using strong language but checked himself and said only: "I was not informed, it is not my fault. In any case, I am certainly the best person to explain our procedure, since I have here"—he patted his breast pocket—"the relevant drawings made by our former Commandant."

"The Commandant's own drawings?" asked the explorer. "Did he combine everything in himself, then? Was he soldier, judge, mechanic, chemist and draughtsman?"

"Indeed he was," said the officer, nodding assent, with a remote, glassy look. Then he inspected his hands critically; they did not seem clean enough to him for touching the drawings; so he went over to the bucket and washed them again. Then he drew out a small leather wallet and said: "Our sentence does not sound severe. Whatever commandment the prisoner has disobeyed is written upon his body by the Harrow. This prisoner, for instance"—the officer indicated the man—"will have written on his body: HONOR THY SUPERIORS!"

The explorer glanced at the man; he stood, as the officer pointed him out, with bent head, apparently listening with all his ears in an effort to catch what was being said. Yet the movement of his blubber lips, closely pressed together, showed clearly that he could not understand a word. Many questions were troubling the explorer, but at the sight of the prisoner he asked only:

"Does he know his sentence?" "No," said the officer, eager to go on with his exposition, but the explorer interrupted him: "He doesn't know the sentence that has been passed on him?" "No," said the officer again, pausing a moment as if to let the explorer elaborate his question, and then said: "There would be no point in telling him. He'll learn it on his body." The explorer intended to make no answer, but he felt the prisoner's gaze turned on him; it seemed to ask if he approved such goings on. So he bent forward again, having already leaned back in his chair, and put another question: "But surely he knows that he has been sentenced?" "Nor that either," said the officer, smiling at the explorer as if expecting him to make further surprising remarks. "No," said the explorer, wiping his forehead, "then he can't know either whether his defense was effective?" "He has had no chance of putting up a defense," said the officer, turning his eyes away as if speaking to himself and so sparing the explorer the shame of hearing self-evident matters explained. "But he must have had some chance of defending himself," said the explorer, and rose from his seat.

The officer realized that he was in danger of having his exposition of the apparatus held up for a long time; so he went up to the explorer, took him by the arm, waved a hand towards the condemned man, who was standing very straight now that he had so obviously become the center of attention—the soldier had also given the chain a jerk—and said: "This is how the matter stands. I have been appointed judge in this penal colony. Despite my youth. For I was the former Commandant's assistant in all penal matters and know more about the apparatus than anyone. My guiding principle is this: Guilt is never to be doubted. Other courts cannot follow that principle, for they consist of several opinions and have higher courts to scrutinize them. That is not the case here, or at least, it was not the case in the former Commandant's time. The new man has certainly shown some inclination to interfere with my judgments, but so far I have succeeded in fending him off and will go on succeeding. You wanted to have the case explained; it is quite simple, like all of them. A captain reported to me this morning that this man, who had been assigned to him as a servant and sleeps before his door, had been asleep on duty. It is his duty, you see, to get up every time the hour strikes and salute the captain's door. Not an exacting duty, and very necessary, since he has to be a sentry as well as a servant, and must be alert in both functions. Last night the captain wanted to see if the man was doing his duty. He opened the door as the clock struck two and there was his man curled up asleep. He took his riding whip and lashed him across the face. Instead of getting up and begging pardon, the man caught hold of his master's legs, shook him and cried: 'Throw that whip away or I'll eat you alive.'—That's the evidence. The captain came to me an hour ago, I wrote down his statement and appended the sentence to it. Then I had the man put in chains. That was all quite simple. If I had first called the man before me and interrogated him, things would have got into a confused tangle. He would have told lies, and had I exposed these lies he would have backed them up with more lies, and so on and so forth. As it is, I've got him and I won't let him go.—Is that quite clear now? But we're wasting time, the execution should be beginning and I haven't finished explaining the apparatus yet." He pressed the explorer back into his chair, went up again to the apparatus and began: "As you see, the shape of the Harrow corresponds to the human form; here is the harrow for the torso, here are the harrows for the legs. For the head there is only this one small spike. Is that quite clear?" He bent amiably forward towards the explorer, eager to provide the most comprehensive explanations.

The explorer considered the Harrow with a frown. The explanation of the judicial procedure had not satisfied him. He had to remind himself that this was in any case a penal colony where extraordinary measures were needed and that military discipline must be enforced to the last. He also felt that some hope might be set on the new Commandant, who was apparently of a mind to bring in, although gradually, a new kind of procedure which the officer's narrow mind was incapable of understanding. This train of thought prompted his next question: "Will the Commandant attend the execution?" "It is not certain," said the officer, wincing at the direct question, and his friendly expression darkened. "That is just why we have to lose no time. Much as I dislike it, I shall have to cut my explanations short. But of course tomorrow, when the apparatus has been cleaned—its one drawback is that it gets so messy—I can recapitulate all the details. For the present, then, only the essentials. —When the man lies down on the Bed and it begins to vibrate, the Harrow is lowered onto his body. It regulates itself automatically so that the needles barely touch his skin; once contact is made the steel ribbon stiffens immediately into a rigid band. And then the performance begins. An ignorant onlooker would see no difference between one punishment and another. The Harrow appears to do its work with uniform regularity. As it quivers, its points pierce the skin of the body which is itself quivering from the vibration of the Bed. So that the actual progress of the sentence can be watched, the Harrow is made of glass. Getting the needles fixed in the glass was a technical problem, but after many experiments we overcame the difficulty. No trouble was too great for us to take, you see. And now anyone can look through the glass and watch the inscription taking form on the body. Wouldn't you care to come a little nearer and have a look at the needles?"

The explorer got up slowly, walked across and bent over the Harrow. "You see," said the officer, "there are two kinds of needles arranged in multiple patterns. Each long needle has a short one beside it. The long needle does the writing, and the short needle sprays a jet of water to wash away the blood and keep the inscription clear. Blood and water together are then conducted here through small runnels into this main runnel and down a waste pipe into the pit." With his finger the officer traced the exact course taken by the blood and water. To make the picture as vivid as possible he held both hands below the outlet of the waste pipe as if to catch the outflow, and when he did this the explorer drew back his head and feeling behind him with one hand sought to return to his chair. To his horror he found that the condemned man too had obeyed the officer's invitation to examine the Harrow at close quarters and had followed him. He had pulled forward the sleepy soldier with the chain and was bending over the glass. One could see that his uncertain eyes were trying to perceive what the two gentlemen had been looking at, but since he had not understood the explanation he could not make head or tail of it. He was peering this way and that way. He kept running his eyes along the glass. The explorer wanted to drive him away, since what he was doing was probably culpable. But the officer firmly restrained the explorer with one hand and with the other took a clod of earth from the rampart and threw it at the soldier. He opened his eyes with a jerk, saw what the condemned man had dared to do, let his rifle fall, dug his heels into the ground, dragged his prisoner back so that he stumbled and fell immediately, and then stood looking down at him, watching him struggling and rattling in his chains. "Set him on his feet!" yelled the officer, for he noticed that the explorer's attention was being too much distracted by the prisoner. In fact he was even leaning right across the Harrow, without taking any notice of it, intent only on finding out what was happening to the prisoner. "Be careful with him!" cried the officer again. He ran round the apparatus, himself caught the condemned man under the shoulders and with the soldier's help got him up on his feet, which kept slithering from under him.

"Now I know all about it," said the explorer as the officer came back to him. "All except the most important thing," he answered, seizing the explorer's arm and pointing upwards: "In the Designer are all the cogwheels that control the movements of the Harrow, and this machinery is regulated according to the inscription demanded by the sentence. I am still using the guiding plans drawn by the former Commandant. Here they are"—he extracted some sheets from the leather wallet —"but I'm sorry I can't let you handle them; they are my most precious possessions. Just take a seat and I'll hold them in front of you like this, then you'll be able to see everything quite well." He spread out the first sheet of paper. The explorer would have liked to say something appreciative, but all he could see was a labyrinth of lines crossing and re-crossing each other, which covered the paper so thickly that it was difficult to discern the blank spaces between them. "Read it," said the officer. "I can't," said the explorer. "Yet it's clear enough," said the officer. "It's very ingenious," said the explorer evasively, "but I can't make it out." "Yes," said the officer with a laugh, putting the paper away again, "it's no calligraphy for school children. It needs to be studied closely. I'm quite sure that in the end you would understand it too. Of course the script can't be a simple one; it's not supposed to kill a man straight off, but only after an interval of, on an average, twelve hours; the turning point is reckoned to come at the sixth hour. So there have to be lots and lots of flourishes around the actual script; the script itself runs round the body only in a narrow girdle; the rest of the body is reserved for the embellishments. Can you appreciate now the work accomplished by the Harrow and the whole apparatus?—Just watch it!" He ran up the ladder, turned a wheel, called down: "Look out, keep to one side!" and everything started working. If the wheel had not creaked, it would have been marvelous. The officer, as if surprised by the noise of the wheel, shook his fist at it, then spread out his arms in excuse to the explorer and climbed down rapidly to peer at the working of the machine from below. Something perceptible to no one save himself was still not in order; he clambered up again, did something with both hands in the interior of the Designer, then slid down one of the rods, instead of using the ladder, so as to get down quicker, and with the full force of his lungs, to make himself heard at all in the noise, yelled in the explorer's ear: "Can you follow it? The Harrow is beginning to write; when it finishes the first draft of the inscription on the man's back, the layer of cotton wool begins to roll and slowly turns the body over, to give the Harrow fresh space for writing. Meanwhile the raw part that has been written on lies on the cotton wool, which is specially prepared to staunch the bleeding and so makes all ready for a new deepening of the script. Then these teeth at the edge of the Harrow, as the body turns further round, tear the cotton wool away from the wounds, throw it into the pit, and there is more work for the Harrow. So it keeps on writing deeper and deeper for the whole twelve hours. The first six hours the condemned man stays alive almost as before, he suffers only pain. After two hours the felt gag is taken away, for he has no longer strength to scream. Here, into this electrically heated basin at the head of the bed, some warm rice pap is poured, from which the man, if he feels like it, can take as much as his tongue can lap. Not one of them ever misses the chance. I can remember none, and my experience is extensive. Only about the sixth hour does the man lose all desire to eat. I usually kneel down here at that moment and observe what happens. The man rarely swallows his last mouthful, he only rolls it round his mouth and spits it out into the pit. I have to duck just then or he would spit it in my face. But how quiet he grows at just about the sixth hour! Enlightenment comes to the most dull-witted. It begins around the eyes. From there it radiates. A moment that might tempt one to get under the Harrow oneself. Nothing more happens than that the man begins to understand the inscription, he purses his mouth as if he were listening. You have seen how difficult it is to decipher the script with one's eyes; but our man deciphers it with his wounds. To be sure, that is a hard task; he needs six hours to accomplish it. By that time the Harrow has pierced him quite through and casts him into the pit, where he pitches down upon the blood and water and the cotton wool. Then the judgment has been fulfilled, and we, the soldier and I, bury him."

The explorer had inclined his ear to the officer and with his hands in his jacket pockets watched the machine at work. The condemned man watched it too, but uncomprehendingly. He bent forward a little and was intent on the moving needles when the soldier, at a sign from the officer, slashed through his shirt and trousers from behind with a knife, so that they fell off; he tried to catch at his falling clothes to cover his nakedness, but the soldier lifted him into the air and shook the last remnants from him. The officer stopped the machine, and in the sudden silence the condemned man was laid under the Harrow. The chains were loosened and the straps fastened on instead; in the first moment that seemed almost a relief to the prisoner. And now the Harrow was adjusted a little lower, since he was a thin man. When the needle points touched him a shudder ran over his skin; while the soldier was busy strapping his right hand, he flung out his left hand blindly; but it happened to be in the direction towards where the explorer was standing. The officer kept watching the explorer sideways, as if seeking to read from his face the impression made on him by the execution, which had been at least cursorily explained to him.

The wrist strap broke; probably the soldier had drawn it too tight. The officer had to intervene, the soldier held up the broken piece of strap to show him. So the officer went over to him and said, his face still turned towards the explorer: "This is a very complex machine, it can't be helped that things are breaking or giving way here and there; but one must not thereby allow oneself to be diverted in one's general judgment. In any case, this strap is easily made good; I shall simply use a chain; the delicacy of the vibrations for the right arm will of course be a little impaired." And while he fastened the chains, he added: "The resources for maintaining the machine are now very much reduced. Under the former Commandant I had free access to a sum of money set aside entirely for this purpose. There was a store, too, in which spare parts were kept for repairs of all kinds. I confess I have been almost prodigal with them, I mean in the past, not now as the new Commandant pretends, always looking for an excuse to attack our old way of doing things. Now he has taken charge of the machine money himself, and if I send for a new strap they ask for the broken old strap as evidence, and the new strap takes ten days to appear and then is of shoddy material and not much good. But how I am supposed to work the machine without a strap, that's something nobody bothers about."

The explorer thought to himself: It's always a ticklish matter to intervene decisively in other people's affairs. He was neither a member of the penal colony nor a citizen of the state to which it belonged. Were he to denounce this execution or actually try to stop it, they could say to him: You are a foreigner, mind your own business. He could make no answer to that, unless he were to add that he was amazed at himself in this connection, for he traveled only as an observer, with no intention at all of altering other people's methods of administering justice. Yet here he found himself strongly tempted. The injustice of the procedure and the inhumanity of the execution were undeniable. No one could suppose that he had any selfish interest in the matter, for the condemned man was a complete stranger, not a fellow countryman or even at all sympathetic to him. The explorer himself had recommendations from high quarters, had been received here with great courtesy, and the very fact that he had been invited to attend the execution seemed to suggest that his views would be welcome. And this was all the more likely since the Commandant, as he had heard only too plainly, was no upholder of the procedure and maintained an attitude almost of hostility to the officer.

At that moment the explorer heard the officer cry out in rage. He had just, with considerable difficulty, forced the felt gag into the condemned man's mouth when the man in an irresistible access of nausea shut his eyes and vomited. Hastily the officer snatched him away from the gag and tried to hold his head over the pit; but it was too late, the vomit was running all over the machine. "It's all the fault of that Commandant!" cried the officer, senselessly shaking the brass rods in front, "the machine is befouled like a pigsty." With trembling hands he indicated to the explorer what had happened. "Have I not tried for hours at a time to get the Commandant to understand that the prisoner must fast for a whole day before the execution? But our new, mild doctrine thinks otherwise. The Commandant's ladies stuff the man with sugar candy before he's led off. He has lived on stinking fish his whole life long and now he has to eat sugar candy! But it could still be possible, I should have nothing to say against it, but why won't they get me a new felt gag, which I have been begging for the last three months. How should a man not feel sick when he takes a felt gag into his mouth which more than a hundred men have already slobbered and gnawed in their dying moments?"

The condemned man had laid his head down and looked peaceful; the soldier was busy trying to clean the machine with the prisoner's shirt. The officer advanced towards the explorer, who in some vague presentiment fell back a pace, but the officer seized him by the hand, and drew him to one side. "I should like to exchange a few words with you in confidence," he said, "may I?" "Of course," said the explorer, and listened with downcast eyes.

"This procedure and method of execution, which you are now having the opportunity to admire, has at the moment no longer any open adherents in our colony. I am its sole advocate, and at the same time the sole advocate of the old Commandant's tradition. I can no longer reckon on any further extension of the method; it takes all my energy to maintain it as it is. During the old Commandant's lifetime the colony was full of his adherents; his strength of conviction I still have in some measure, but not an atom of his power; consequently the adherents have skulked out of sight, there are still many of them but none of them will admit it. If you were to go into the teahouse today, on execution day, and listen to what is being said, you would perhaps hear only ambiguous remarks. These would all be made by adherents, but under the present

Commandant and his present doctrines they are of no use to me. And now I ask you: because of this Commandant and the women who influence him, is such a piece of work, the work of a lifetime"—he pointed to the machine—"to perish? Ought one to let that happen? Even if one has only come as a stranger to our island for a few days? But there's no time to lose, an attack of some kind is impending on my function as judge; conferences are already being held in the Commandant's office from which I am excluded; even your coming here today seems to me a significant move; they are cowards and use you as a screen, you, a stranger.—How different an execution was in the old days! A whole day before the ceremony the valley was packed with people; they all came only to look on; early in the morning the Commandant appeared with his ladies; fanfares roused the whole camp; I reported that everything was in readiness; the assembled company—no high official dared to absent himself—arranged itself round the machine; this pile of cane chairs is a miserable survival from that epoch. The machine was freshly cleaned and glittering, I got new spare parts for almost every execution. Before hundreds of spectators—all of them standing on tip-toe as far as the heights there—the condemned man was laid under the Harrow by the Commandant himself. What is left today for a common soldier to do was then my task, the task of the presiding judge, and was an honor for me. And then the execution began! No discordant noise spoilt the working of the machine. Many did not care to watch it but lay with closed eyes in the sand; they all knew: Now Justice is being done. In the silence one heard nothing but the condemned man's sighs, half muffled by the felt gag. Nowadays the machine can no longer wring from anyone a sigh louder than the felt gag can stifle; but in those days the writing needles let drop an acid fluid, which we're no longer permitted to use. Well, and then came the sixth hour! It was impossible to grant all the requests to be allowed to watch it from near by. The Commandant in his wisdom ordained that the children should have the preference; I, of course, because of my office had the privilege of always being at hand; often enough I would be squatting there with a small child in either arm. How we all absorbed the look of transfiguration on the face of the sufferer, how we bathed our cheeks in the radiance of that justice, achieved at last and fading so quickly! What times these were, my comrade!" The officer had obviously forgotten whom he was addressing; he had embraced the explorer and laid his head on his shoulder. The explorer was deeply embarrassed, impatiently he stared over the officer's head. The soldier had finished his cleaning job and was now pouring rice pap from a pot into the basin. As soon as the condemned man, who seemed to have recovered entirely, noticed this action he began to reach for the rice with his tongue. The soldier kept pushing him away, since the rice pap was certainly meant for a later hour, yet it was just as unfitting that the soldier himself should thrust his dirty hands into the basin and eat out of it before the other's avid face.

The officer quickly pulled himself together. "I didn't want to upset you," he said. "I know it is impossible to make those days credible now. Anyhow, the machine is still working and it is still effective in itself. It is effective in itself even though it stands alone in this valley. And the corpse still falls at the last into the pit with an incomprehensibly gentle wafting motion, even although there are no hundreds of people swarming round like flies as formerly. In those days we had to put a strong fence round the pit; it has long since been torn down."

The explorer wanted to withdraw his face from the officer and looked round him at random. The officer thought he was surveying the valley's desolation; so he seized him by the hands, turned him round to meet his eyes, and asked: "Do you realise the shame of it?"

But the explorer said nothing. The officer left him alone for a little; with legs apart, hands on hips, he stood very still, gazing at the ground. Then he smiled encouragingly at the explorer and said: "I was quite near you yesterday when the Commandant gave you the invitation. I heard him giving it. I know the Commandant. I divined at once what he was after. Although he is powerful enough to take measures against me, he doesn't dare to do it yet, but he certainly means to use your verdict against me, the verdict of an illustrious foreigner. He has calculated it carefully: this is your second day on the island, you did not know the old Commandant and his ways, you are conditioned by European ways of thought, perhaps you object on principle to capital punishment in general and to such mechanical instruments of death in particular, besides you will see that the execution has no support from the public, a shabby ceremony—carried out with a machine already somewhat old and worn —now, taking all that into consideration, would it not be likely (so thinks the Commandant) that you might disapprove of my methods? And if you disapprove, you wouldn't conceal the fact (I'm still speaking from the Commandant's point of view), for you are a man to feel confidence in your own well-tried conclusions. True, you have seen and learned to appreciate the peculiarities of many peoples, and so you would not be likely to take a strong line against our proceedings, as you might do in your own country. But the Commandant has no need of that. A casual, even an unguarded remark will be enough. It doesn't even need to represent what you really think, so long as it can be used speciously to serve his purpose. He will try to prompt you with sly questions, of that I am certain. And his ladies will sit around you and prick up their ears; you might be saying something like this: 'In our country we have a different criminal procedure,' or 'In our country the prisoner is interrogated before he is sentenced,' or 'We haven't used torture since the Middle Ages.' All these statements are as true as they seem natural to you, harmless remarks that pass no judgment on my methods. But how would the Commandant react to them? I can see him, our good Commandant, pushing his chair away immediately and rushing onto the balcony, I can see his ladies streaming out after him. I can hear his voice—the ladies call it a voice of thunder—well, and this is what he says: 'A famous Western investigator, sent out to study criminal procedure in all the countries of the world, has just said that our old tradition of administering justice is inhumane. Such a verdict from such a personality makes it impossible for me to countenance these methods any longer. Therefore from this very day I ordain . . .' and so on. You many want to interpose that you never said any such thing, that you never called my methods inhumane; on the contrary your profound experience leads you to believe they are most humane and most in consonance with human dignity, and you admire the machine greatly—but it will be too late; you won't even get onto the balcony, crowded as it will be with ladies; you may try to draw attention to yourself; you may want to scream out; but a lady's hand will close your lips—and I and the work of the old Commandant will be done for."

The explorer had to suppress a smile; so easy, then, was the task he had felt to be so difficult. He said evasively: "You over-estimate my influence; the Commandant has read my letters of recommendation, he knows that I am no expert in criminal procedure. If I were to give an opinion, it would be as a private individual, an opinion no more influential than that of any ordinary person, and in any case much less influential than that of the Commandant, who, I am given to understand, has very extensive powers in this penal colony. If his attitude to your procedure is as definitely hostile as you believe, then I fear the end of your tradition is at hand, even without any humble assistance from me."

Had it dawned on the officer at last? No, he still did not understand. He shook his head emphatically, glanced briefly round at the condemned man and the soldier, who both flinched away from the rice, came close up to the explorer and without looking at his face but fixing his eye on some spot on his coat said in a lower voice than before: "You don't know the Commandant; you feel yourself—forgive the expression—a kind of outsider so far as all of us are concerned; yet, believe me, your influence cannot be rated too highly. I was simply delighted when I heard that you were to attend the execution all by yourself. The Commandant arranged it to aim a blow at me but I shall turn it to my advantage. Without being distracted by lying whispers and contemptuous glances—which could not have been avoided had a crowd of people attended the execution—you have heard my explanations, seen the machine and are now in course of watching the execution. You have doubtless already formed your own judgment; if you still have some small uncertainties the sight of the execution will resolve them. And now I make this request to you: help me against the Commandant!"

The explorer would not let him go on. "How could I do that?" he cried. "It's quite impossible. I can neither help nor hinder you."

"Yes, you can," the officer said. The explorer saw with a certain apprehension that the officer had clenched his fists. "Yes, you can," repeated the officer, still more insistently. "I have a plan that is bound to succeed. You believe your influence is insufficient. I know that it is sufficient. But even granted that you are right, is it not necessary, for the sake of preserving this tradition, to try even what might prove insufficient? Listen to my plan, then. The first thing necessary for you to carry it out is to be as reticent as possible today regarding your verdict on these proceedings. Unless you are asked a direct question you must say nothing at all; but what you do say must be brief and general; let it be remarked that you would prefer not to discuss the matter, that you are out of patience with it, that if you are to let yourself go you would use strong language. I don't ask you to tell any lies; by no means; you should only give curt answers, such as: 'Yes, I saw the execution,' or 'Yes, I had it explained to me.' Just that, nothing more. There are grounds enough for any impatience you betray, although not such as will occur to the Commandant. Of course, he will mistake your meaning and interpret it to please himself. That's what my plan depends on. Tomorrow in the Commandant's office there is to be a large conference of all the high administrative officials, the Commandant presiding. Of course the Commandant is the kind of man to have turned these conferences into public spectacles. He has had a gallery built that is always packed with spectators. I am compelled to take part in the conferences, but they make me sick with disgust. Now, whatever happens, you will certainly be invited to this conference; if you behave today as I suggest the invitation will become an urgent request. But if for some mysterious reason you're not invited, you'll have to ask for an invitation; there's no doubt of your getting it then. So tomorrow you're sitting in the Commandant's box with the ladies. He keeps looking up to make sure you're there. After various trivial and ridiculous matters, brought in merely to impress the audience—mostly harbor works, nothing but harbor works! —our judicial procedure comes up for discussion too. If the Commandant doesn't introduce it, or not soon enough, I'll see that it's mentioned. I'll stand up and report that today's execution has taken place. Quite briefly, only a statement. Such a statement is not usual, but I shall make it. The Commandant thanks me, as always, with an amiable smile, and then he can't restrain himself, he seizes the excellent opportunity. 'It has just been reported,' he will say, or words to that effect, 'that an execution has taken place. I should like merely to add that this execution was witnessed by the famous explorer who has, as you all know, honored our colony so greatly by his visit to us. His presence at today's session of our conference also contributes to the importance of this occasion. Should we not now ask the famous explorer to give us his verdict on our traditional mode of execution and the procedure that leads up to it?' Of course there is loud applause, general agreement, I am more insistent than anyone. The Commandant bows to you and says: 'Then in the name of the assembled company, I put the question to you.' And now you advance to the front of the box. Lay your hands where everyone can see them, or the ladies will catch them and press your fingers.—And then at last you can speak out. I don't know how I'm going to endure the tension of waiting for that moment. Don't put any restraint on yourself when you make your speech, publish the truth aloud, lean over the front of the box, shout, yes, indeed, shout your verdict, your unshakable conviction, at the Commandant. Yet perhaps you wouldn't care to do that, it's not in keeping with your character, in your country perhaps people do these things differently, well, that's all right too, that will be quite as effective, don't even stand up, just say a few words, even in a whisper, so that only the officials beneath you will hear them, that will be quite enough, you don't even need to mention the lack of public support for the execution, the creaking wheel, the broken strap, the filthy gag of felt, no, I'll take all that upon me, and, believe me, if my indictment doesn't drive him out of the conference hall, it will force him to his knees to make the acknowledgment: Old Commandant, I humble myself before you.—That is my plan; will you help me to carry it out? But of course you are willing, what is more, you must." And the officer seized the explorer by both arms and gazed, breathing heavily, into his face. He had shouted the last sentence so loudly that even the soldier and the condemned man were startled into attending; they had not understood a word but they stopped eating and looked over at the explorer, chewing their previous mouthfuls.

From the very beginning the explorer had no doubt about what answer he must give; in his lifetime he had experienced too much to have any uncertainty here; he was fundamentally honorable and unafraid. And yet now, facing the soldier and the condemned man, he did hesitate, for as long as it took to draw one breath. At last, however, he said, as he had to: "No." The officer blinked several times but did not turn his eyes away. "Would you like me to explain?" asked the explorer. The officer nodded wordlessly. "I do not approve of your procedure," said the explorer then, "even before you took me into your confidence—of course I shall never in any circumstances betray your confidence—I was already wondering whether it would be my duty to intervene and whether my intervention would have the slightest chance of success. I realized to whom I ought to turn: to the Commandant, of course. You have made that fact even clearer, but without having strengthened my resolution; on the contrary, your sincere conviction has touched me, even though it cannot influence my judgment."

The officer remained mute, turned to the machine, caught hold of a brass rod, and then, leaning back a little, gazed at the Designer as if to assure himself that all was in order. The soldier and the condemned man seemed to have come to some understanding; the condemned man was making signs to the soldier, difficult though his movements were because of the tight straps; the soldier was bending down to him; the condemned man whispered something and the soldier nodded.

The explorer followed the officer and said: "You don't know yet what I mean to do. I shall tell the Commandant what I think of the procedure, certainly, but not at a public conference, only in private; nor shall I stay here long enough to attend any conference; I am going away early tomorrow morning, or at least embarking on my ship."

It did not look as if the officer had been listening. "So you did not find the procedure convincing," he said to himself and smiled, as an old man smiles at childish nonsense and yet pursues his own meditations behind the smile.

"Then the time has come," he said at last, and suddenly looked at the explorer with bright eyes that held some challenge, some appeal for co-operation. "The time for what?" asked the explorer uneasily, but got no answer.

"You are free," said the officer to the condemned man in the native tongue. The man did not believe it at first. "Yes, you are set free," said the officer. For the first time the condemned man's face woke to real animation. Was it true? Was it only a caprice of the officer's that might change again? Had the foreign explorer begged him off? What was it? One could read these questions on his face. But not for long. Whatever it might be, he wanted to be really free if he might, and he began to struggle so far as the Harrow permitted him.

"You'll burst my straps," cried the officer. "Lie still! We'll soon loosen them." And signing the soldier to help him, he set about doing so. The condemned man laughed wordlessly to himself, now he turned his face left towards the officer, now right towards the soldier, nor did he forget the explorer.

"Draw him out," ordered the officer. Because of the Harrow this had to be done with some care. The condemned man had already torn himself a little in the back through his impatience.

From now on, however, the officer paid hardly any attention to him.

He went up to the explorer, pulled out the small leather wallet again, turned over the papers in it, found the one he wanted and showed it to the explorer. "Read it," he said. "I can't," said the explorer, "I told you before that I can't make out these scripts." "Try taking a close look at it," said the officer and came quite near to the explorer so that they might read it together. But when even that proved useless, he outlined the script with his little finger, holding it high above the paper as if the surface dared not be sullied by touch, in order to help the explorer to follow the script in that way. The explorer did make an effort, meaning to please the officer in this respect at least, but he was quite unable to follow. Now the officer began to spell it, letter by letter, and then read out the words. " 'BE JUST!' is what is written there," he said. "Surely you can read it now." The explorer bent so close to the paper that the officer feared he might touch it and drew it farther away; the explorer made no remark, yet it was clear that he still could not decipher it. " 'BE JUST!' is what is written there," said the officer once more. "Maybe," said the explorer, "I am prepared to believe you." "Well, then," said the officer, at least partly satisfied, and climbed up the ladder with the paper; very carefully he laid it inside the Designer and seemed to be changing the disposition of all the cogwheels; it was a troublesome piece of work and must have involved wheels that were extremely small, for sometimes the officer's head vanished altogether from sight inside the Designer, so precisely did he have to regulate the machinery.

The explorer, down below, watched the labor uninterruptedly, his neck grew stiff and his eyes smarted from the glare of sunshine over the sky. The soldier and the condemned man were now busy together. The man's shirt and trousers, which were already lying in the pit, were fished out by the point of the soldier's bayonet. The shirt was abominably dirty and its owner washed it in the bucket of water. When he put on the shirt and trousers both he and the soldier could not help guffawing, for the garments were of course slit up behind. Perhaps the condemned man felt it incumbent on him to amuse the soldier, he turned round and round in his slashed garments before the soldier, who squatted on the ground beating his knees with mirth. All the same, they presently controlled their mirth out of respect for the gentlemen.

When the officer had at length finished his task aloft, he surveyed the machinery in all its details once more, with a smile, but this time shut the lid of the Designer, which had stayed open till now, climbed down, looked into the pit and then at the condemned man, noting with satisfaction that the clothing had been taken out, then went over to wash his hands in the water bucket, perceived too late that it was disgustingly dirty, was unhappy because he could not wash his hands, in the end thrust them into the sand—this alternative did not please him, but he had to put up with it—then stood upright and began to unbutton his uniform jacket. As he did this, the two ladies' handkerchiefs he had tucked under his collar fell into his hands. "Here are your handkerchiefs," he said, and threw them to the condemned man. And to the explorer he said in explanation: "A gift from the ladies."

In spite of the obvious haste with which he was discarding first his uniform jacket and then all his clothing, he handled each garment with loving care, he even ran his fingers caressingly over the silver lace on the jacket and shook a tassel into place. This loving care was certainly out of keeping with the fact that as soon as he had a garment off he flung it at once with a kind of unwilling jerk into the pit. The last thing left to him was his short sword with the sword belt. He drew it out of the scabbard, broke it, then gathered all together, the bits of the sword, the scabbard and the belt, and flung them so violently down that they clattered into the pit.

Now he stood naked there. The explorer bit his lips and said nothing. He knew very well what was going to happen, but had no right to obstruct the officer in anything. If the judicial procedure which the officer cherished were really so near its end—possibly as a result of his own intervention, as to which he felt himself pledged—then the officer was doing the right thing; in his place the explorer would not have acted otherwise.

The soldier and the condemned man did not understand at first what was happening; at first they were not even looking on. The condemned man was gleeful at having got the handkerchiefs back, but he was not allowed to enjoy them for long, since the soldier snatched them with a sudden, unexpected grab. Now the condemned man in turn was trying to twitch them from under the belt where the soldier had tucked them, but the soldier was on his guard. So they were wrestling, half in jest. Only when the officer stood quite naked was their attention caught. The condemned man especially seemed struck with the notion that some great change was impending. What had happened to him was now going to happen to the officer. Perhaps even to the very end. Apparently the foreign explorer had given the order for it. So this was revenge. Although he himself had not suffered to the end, he was to be revenged to the end. A broad, silent grin now appeared on his face and stayed there all the rest of the time.

The officer, however, had turned to the machine. It had been clear enough previously that he understood the machine well, but now it was almost staggering to see how he managed it and how it obeyed him. His hand had only to approach the Harrow for it to rise and sink several times till it was adjusted to the right position for receiving him; he touched only the edge of the Bed and already it was vibrating; the felt gag came to meet his mouth, one could see that the officer was really reluctant to take it but he shrank from it only a moment, soon he submitted and received it. Everything was ready, only the straps hung down at the sides, yet they were obviously unnecessary, the officer did not need to be fastened down. Then the condemned man noticed the loose straps, in his opinion the execution was incomplete unless the straps were buckled, he gestured eagerly to the soldier and they ran together to strap the officer down. The latter had already stretched out one foot to push the lever that started the Designer; he saw the two men coming up; so he drew his foot back and let himself be buckled in. But now he could not reach the lever; neither the soldier nor the condemned man would be able to find it, and the explorer was determined not to lift a finger. It was not necessary; as soon as the straps were fastened the machine began to work; the Bed vibrated, the needles flickered above the skin, the Harrow rose and fell. The explorer had been staring at it quite a while before he remembered that a wheel in the Designer should have been creaking; but everything was quiet, not even the slightest hum could be heard.

Because it was working so silently the machine simply escaped one's attention. The explorer observed the soldier and the condemned man. The latter was the more animated of the two, everything in the machine interested him, now he was bending down and now stretching up on tiptoe, his forefinger was extended all the time pointing out details to the soldier. This annoyed the explorer. He was resolved to stay till the end, but he could not bear the sight of these two. "Go back home," he said. The soldier would have been willing enough, but the condemned man took the order as a punishment. With clasped hands he implored to be allowed to stay, and when the explorer shook his head and would not relent, he even went down on his knees. The explorer saw that it was no use merely giving orders; he was on the point of going over and driving them away. At that moment he heard a noise above him in the Designer. He looked up. Was that cogwheel going to make trouble after all? But it was something quite different. Slowly the lid of the Designer rose up and then clicked wide open. The teeth of a cogwheel showed themselves and rose higher, soon the whole wheel was visible; it was as if some enormous force were squeezing the Designer so that there was no longer room for the wheel; the wheel moved up till it came to the very edge of the Designer, fell down, rolled along the sand a little on its rim and then lay flat. But a second wheel was already rising after it. followed by many others, large and small and indistinguishably minute, the same thing happened to all of them, at every moment one imagined the Designer must now really be empty, but another complex of numerous wheels was already rising into sight, falling down, trundling along the sand and lying flat. This phenomenon made the condemned man completely forget the explorer's command, the cogwheels fascinated him, he was always trying to catch one and at the same time urging the soldier to help, but always drew back his hand in alarm, for another wheel always came hopping along which, at least on its first advance, scared him off.

The explorer, on the other hand, felt greatly troubled; the machine was obviously going to pieces; its silent working was a delusion; he had a feeling that he must now stand by the officer, since the officer was no longer able to look after himself. But while the tumbling cogwheels absorbed his whole attention he had forgotten to keep an eye on the rest of the machine; now that the last cogwheel had left the Designer, however, he bent over the Harrow and had a new and still more unpleasant surprise. The Harrow was not writing, it was only jabbing, and the bed was not turning the body over but only bringing it up quivering against the needles. The explorer wanted to do something, if possible, to bring the whole machine to a standstill, for this was no exquisite torture such as the officer desired, this was plain murder. He stretched out his hands. But at that moment the Harrow rose with the body spitted on it and moved to the side, as it usually did only when the twelfth hour had come. Blood was flowing in a hundred streams, not mingled with water, the water jets too had failed to function. And now the last action failed to fulfill itself, the body did not drop off the long needles, streaming with blood it went on hanging over the pit without falling into it. The Harrow tried to move back to its old position, but as if it had itself noticed that it had not yet got rid of its burden it stuck after all where it was, over the pit. "Come and help!" cried the explorer to the other two, and himself seized the officer's feet. He wanted to push against the feet while the others seized the head from the opposite side and so the officer might be slowly eased off the needles. But the other two could not make up their minds to come; the condemned man actually turned away; the explorer had to go over to them and force them into position at the officer's head. And here, almost against his will, he had to look at the face of the corpse. It was as it had been in life; no sign was visible of the promised redemption; what the others had found in the machine the officer had not found; the lips were firmly pressed together, the eyes were open, with the same expression as in life, the look was calm and convinced, through the forehead went the point of the great iron spike.

As the explorer, with the soldier and the condemned man behind him, reached the first houses of the colony, the soldier pointed to one of them and said: "There is the teahouse."

In the ground floor of the house was a deep, low, cavernous space, its walls and ceiling blackened with smoke. It was open to the road all along its length. Although this teahouse was very little different from the other houses of the colony, which were all very dilapidated, even up to the Commandant's palatial headquarters, it made on the explorer the impression of a historic tradition of some kind, and he felt the power of past days. He went near to it, followed by his companions, right up between the empty tables which stood in the street before it, and breathed the cool, heavy air that came from the interior. "The old man's buried here," said the soldier. "The priest wouldn't let him lie in the churchyard. Nobody knew where to bury him for a while, but in the end they buried him here. The officer never told you about that, for sure, because of course that's what he was most ashamed of. He even tried several times to dig the old man up by night, but he was always chased away." "Where is the grave?" asked the explorer, who found it impossible to believe the soldier. At once both of them, the soldier and the condemned man, ran before him pointing with outstretched hands in the direction where the grave should be. They led the explorer right up to the back wall, where guests were sitting at a few tables. They were apparently dock laborers, strong men with short, glistening, full black beards. None had a jacket, their shirts were torn, they were poor, humble creatures. As the explorer drew near, some of them got up, pressed close to the wall, and stared at him. "It's a foreigner," ran the whisper around him. "He wants to see the grave." They pushed one of the tables aside, and under it there was really a gravestone. It was a simple stone, low enough to be covered by a table. There was an inscription on it in very small letters, the explorer had to kneel down to read it. This was what it said: "Here rests the old Commandant. His adherents, who now must be nameless, have dug this grave and set up this stone. There is a prophecy that after a certain number of years the Commandant will rise again and lead his adherents from this house to recover the colony. Have faith and wait!" When the explorer had read this and risen to his feet he saw all the by-standers around him smiling, as if they too had read the inscription, had found it ridiculous and were expecting him to agree with them. The explorer ignored this, distributed a few coins among them, waiting till the table was pushed over the grave again, quitted the teahouse and made for the harbor.

The soldier and the condemned man had found some acquaintances in the teahouse, who detained them. But they must have soon shaken them off, for the explorer was only halfway down the long flight of steps leading to the boats when they came rushing after him. Probably they wanted to force him at the last minute to take them with him. While he was bargaining below with a ferryman to row him to the steamer, the two of them came headlong down the steps, in silence, for they did not dare to shout. But by the time they reached the foot of the steps the explorer was already in the boat, and the ferryman was just casting off from the shore. They could have jumped into the boat, but the explorer lifted a heavy knotted rope from the floor boards, threatened them with it and so kept them from attempting the leap.

—*Translated by* Willa and Edwin Muir.

Questions

1. Like most allegories of the human condition, "In the Penal Colony" may be read in social or political terms, in personal or psychoanalytic terms, or in religious or spiritual terms. Which context does each of the following relate to most obviously: the failure of the machine, the pail of water, the officer's uniform, and the prisoner's own reactions?

2. One critic identifies the explorer as the true modern scientist. Record what he observes and comment on his reactions, especially his attitude at the end of the story.

3. Explain why the machine writes a message on the back of the prisoner and what that message says. Is it intended for the reader also?

4. Kafka is said to have created this complex and often obscure allegory while using the most simple style. Characterize that style with special attention to his vocabulary and sentence structure. Consider also whether the plot and characters are equally simple.

Nigel Kneale

THE POND

After only one collection of his short stories had been published, Nigel Kneale became known as a distinctive stylist with a taste for quiet horror and a knack for the unexpected twist that produces a sudden chill on a sunny day. Born on the Isle of Man in 1922, he began writing in the 1940s, and had stories published in various British and American magazines. His stories were collected in book form in Tomato Cain and Other Stories *(1950). Most of these stories had ambiguous settings—either in what appeared to be Wales, Scotland, Brittany, or in the remote and primitive areas of America. What was more important than their physical setting was their psychological locale, a dark area where superstitions and ancient taboos reigned. Thus, the only identification in one story is "the far-off days before the preachers and the schoolmasters came," and in another, "one night in the gradual quietness that follows closing-time."*

In "The Pond" as well as some of Kneale's other stories, a seemingly calm and beneficent nature rouses itself and takes revenge in a peculiarly grotesque way. The shock of the ending shouldn't really come as a great surprise, though. The interested reader who survives this story may find another treatment of a similar theme in Arthur Machen's famous classic of the supernatural, The Terror, *published in 1917.*

It was deeply scooped from a corner of the field, a green stagnant hollow with thorn bushes on its banks.

From time to time something moved cautiously beneath the prickly branches that were laden with red autumn berries. It whistled and murmured coaxingly.

"Come, come, come, come," it whispered. An old man, squatting frog-like on the bank. His words were no louder than the rustling of the dry leaves above his head. "Come now. Sssst—ssst! Little dear—here's a bit of meat for thee." He tossed a tiny scrap of something into the pool. The weed rippled sluggishly.

The old man sighed and shifted his position. He was crouching on his haunches because the bank was damp.

He froze.

The green slime had parted on the far side of the pool. The disturbance travelled to the bank opposite, and a large frog drew itself half out of the water. It stayed quite still, watching; then with a swift crawl it was clear of the water. Its yellow throat throbbed.

"Oh!—little dear," breathed the old man. He did not move.

He waited, letting the frog grow accustomed to the air and slippery earth. When he judged the moment to be right, he made a low grating noise in his throat.

He saw the frog listen.

The sound was subtly like the call of its own kind. The old man paused, then made it again.

This time the frog answered. It sprang into the pool, sending the green weed slopping, and swam strongly. Only its eyes showed above the water. It crawled out a few feet distant from the old man and looked up the bank, as if eager to find the frog it had heard.

The old man waited patiently. The frog hopped twice, up the bank.

His hand was moving, so slowly that it did not seem to move, towards the handle of the light net at his side. He gripped it, watching the still frog.

Suddenly he struck.

A sweep of the net, and its wire frame whacked the ground about the frog. It leaped frantically, but was helpless in the green mesh.

"Dear! Oh, my dear!" said the old man delightedly.

He stood with much difficulty and pain, his foot on the thin rod. His joints had stiffened and it was some minutes before he could go to the net. The frog was still struggling desperately. He closed the net round its body and picked both up together.

"Ah, big beauty!" he said. "Pretty. Handsome fellow, you!"

He took a darning needle from his coat lapel and carefully killed the creature through the mouth, so that its skin would not be damaged, then put it in his pocket.

It was the last frog in the pond.

He lashed the water with the net rod, and the weed swirled and bobbed: there was no sign of life now but the little flies that flitted on the surface.

He went across the empty field with the net across his shoulder, shivering a little, feeling that the warmth had gone out of his body during the long wait. He climbed a stile, throwing the net over in front of him to leave his hands free. In the next field, by the road, was his cottage.

Hobbling through the grass with the sun striking a long shadow from him, he felt the weight of the dead frog in his pocket, and was glad.

"Big beauty!" he murmured again.

The cottage was small and dry, and ugly and very old. Its windows gave little light, and they had coloured panels, dark-blue and green, that gave the rooms the appearance of being under the sea.

The old man lit a lamp, for the sun had set; and the light became more cheerful. He put the frog on a plate, and poked the fire, and when he was warm again, took off his coat.

He settled down close beside the lamp and took a sharp knife from the drawer of the table. With great care and patience, he began to skin the frog.

From time to time he took off his spectacles and rubbed his eyes. The work was tiring; also the heat from the lamp made them sore. He would speak aloud to the dead creature, coaxing and cajoling it when he found his task difficult. But in time he had the skin neatly removed, a little heap of tumbled, slippery film. He dropped the stiff, stripped body into a pan of boiling water on the fire, and sat again, humming and fingering the limp skin.

"Pretty," he said. "You'll be so handsome."

There was a stump of black soap in the drawer and he took it out to rub the skin, with the slow, overcareful motion that showed the age in his hand. The little mottled thing began to stiffen under the curing action. He left it at last, and brewed himself a pot of tea, lifting the lid of the simmering pan occasionally to make sure that the tiny skull and bones were being boiled clean without damage.

Sipping his tea, he crossed the narrow living-room. Well away from the fire stood a high table, its top covered by a square of dark cloth supported on a frame. There was a faint smell of decay.

"How are you, little dears?" said the old man.

He lifted the covering with shaky scrupulousness. Beneath the wire support were dozens of stuffed frogs.

All had been posed in human attitudes; dressed in tiny coats and breeches to the fashion of an earlier time. There were ladies and gentlemen and bowing flunkeys. One, with lace at his yellow, waxen throat, held a wooden wine-cup. To the dried forepaw of its neighbour was stitched a tiny glassless monocle, raised to a black button eye. A third had a midget pipe pressed into its jaws, with a wisp of wool for smoke. The same coarse wool, cleaned and shaped, served the ladies for their miniature wigs; they wore long skirts and carried fans.

The old man looked proudly over the stiff little figures.

"You, my lord—what are you doing, with your mouth so glum?" His fingers prized open the jaws of a round-bellied frog dressed in satins; shrinkage must have closed them. "Now you can sing again, and drink up!"

His eyes searched the banqueting, motionless party.

"Where now—? Ah!"

In the middle of the table three of the creatures were fixed in the attitude of a dance.

The old man spoke to them. "Soon we'll have a partner for the lady there. He'll be the handsomest of the whole company, my dear, so don't forget to smile at him and look your prettiest!"

He hurried back to the fireplace and lifted the pan; poured off the steaming water into a bucket.

"Fine, shapely brain-box you have." He picked with his knife, cleaning the tiny skull. "Easy does it." He put it down on the table admiringly; it was like a transparent flake of ivory. One by one he found the delicate bones in the pan, knowing each for what it was.

"Now, little duke, we have all of them that we need," he said at last. "We can make you into a picture indeed. The beau of the ball. And such an object of jealousy for the lovely ladies!"

With wire and thread he fashioned a stiff little skeleton, binding in the bones to preserve the proportions. At the top went the skull.

The frog's skin had lost its earlier flaccidness. He threaded a needle, eyeing it close to the lamp. From the table drawer he now brought a loose wad of wool. Like a doctor reassuring his patient by describing his methods, he began to talk.

"This wool is coarse, I know, little friend. A poor substitute to fill that skin of yours, you may say: wool from the hedges, snatched by the thorns from a sheep's back." He was pulling the wad into tufts of the size he required. "But you'll find it gives you such a springiness that you'll thank me for it. Now, carefully does it—"

With perfect concentration he worked his needle through the skin, drawing it together round the wool with almost untraceable stitches.

"A piece of lace in your left hand, or shall it be a quizzing-glass?" With tiny scissors he trimmed away a fragment of skin. "But—wait, it's a dance and it is your right hand that we must see, guiding the lady."

He worked the skin precisely into place round the skull. He would attend to the empty eye-holes later.

Suddenly he lowered his needle.

He listened.

Puzzled, he put down the half-stuffed skin and went to the door and opened it.

It was dark now. He heard the sound more clearly. He knew it was coming from the pond. A far-off, harsh croaking, as of a great many frogs.

He frowned.

In the wall cupboard he found a lantern ready trimmed, and lit it with a flickering splinter. He put on an overcoat and hat: the evening was chilly. Lastly he took his net.

He went very cautiously. His eyes saw nothing at first, after working so close to the lamp. Then, as the croaking came to him more clearly and he became accustomed to the darkness, he hurried.

He climbed the stile as before, throwing the net ahead. This time, however, he had to search for it in the darkness, tantalized by the sounds from the pond. When it was in his hand again, he began to move stealthily.

About twenty yards from the pool he stopped and listened.

There was no wind and the noise astonished him. Hundreds of frogs must have travelled through the fields to this spot; perhaps from other water where danger had arisen, perhaps, or drought. He had heard of such instances.

Almost on tiptoe he crept towards the pond. He could see nothing yet. There was no moon, and the thorn bushes hid the surface of the water.

He was a few paces from the pond when, without warning, every sound ceased.

He froze again. There was absolute silence. Not even a watery plop or splashing told that one frog out of all those hundreds had dived for shelter into the weed. It was strange.

He stepped forward, and heard his boots brushing the grass.

He brought the net up across his chest, ready to strike if he saw anything move. He came to the thorn bushes, and still heard no sound. Yet, to judge by the noise they had made, they should be hopping in dozens from beneath his feet.

Peering, he made the throaty noise which had called the frog that afternoon. The hush continued.

He looked down at where the water must be. The surface of the pond, shadowed by the bushes, was too dark to be seen. He shivered, and waited.

Gradually, as he stood, he became aware of a smell.

It was wholly unpleasant. Seemingly it came from the weed, yet mixed with the vegetable odour was one of another kind of decay. A soft, oozy bubbling accompanied it. Gases must be rising from the mud at the bottom. It would not do to stay in this place and risk his health.

He stooped, still puzzled by the disappearance of the frogs, and stared once more at the dark surface. Pulling his net to a ready position, he tried the throaty call for the last time.

Instantly he threw himself backwards with a cry.

A vast, belching bubble of foul air shot from the pool. Another gushed up past his head; then another. Great patches of slimy weed were flung high among the thorn branches.

The whole pond seemed to boil.

He turned blindly to escape, and stepped into the thorns. He was in agony. A dreadful slobbering deafened his ears: the stench overcame his senses. He felt the net whipped from his hand. The icy weeds were wet on his face. Reeds lashed him.

Then he was in the midst of an immense, pulsating softness that yielded and received and held him. He knew he was shrieking. He knew there was no one to hear him.

An hour after the sun had risen, the rain slackened to a light drizzle.

A policeman cycled slowly on the road that ran by the cottage, shaking out his cape with one hand, and half-expecting the old man to appear and call out a comment on the weather. Then he caught sight of the lamp, still burning feebly in the kitchen, and dismounted. He found the door ajar, and wondered if something was wrong.

He called to the old man. He saw the uncommon handiwork lying on the table as if it had been suddenly dropped; and the unused bed.

For half an hour the policeman searched in the neighbourhood of the cottage, calling out the old man's name at intervals, before remembering the pond. He turned towards the stile.

Climbing over it, he frowned and began to hurry. He was disturbed by what he saw.

On the bank of the pond crouched a naked figure.

The policeman went closer. He saw it was the old man, on his haunches; his arms were straight; the hands resting between his feet. He did not move as the policeman approached.

"Hallo, there!" said the policeman. He ducked to avoid the thorn bushes catching his helmet. "This won't do, you know. You can get into trouble—"

He saw green slime in the old man's beard, and the staring eyes. His spine chilled. With an unprofessional distaste, he quickly put out a hand and took the old man by the upper arm. It was cold. He shivered, and moved the arm gently.

Then he groaned and ran from the pond.

For the arm had come away at the shoulder: reeds and green water-plants and slime tumbled from the broken joint.

As the old man fell backwards, tiny green stitches glistened across his belly.

Questions

1. What indications are there about setting, time or place in the story? Why is such information almost entirely absent?

2. What does the use to which the man puts the frogs he catches have to do with the reader's feelings about the revenge that overtakes him? How does it prepare for the ending?

3. How does the language used by the man in addressing the frogs —"Little friend," "little dears," "big beauty," etc.—further the point of the story?

4. Discuss the ultimate effect on the reader of the story's tone and language—the noncommital language, brief factual sentences, detached point of view, etc.

5. What is the force of the very last sentence of the story, and what is the reader's reaction to it?

D. H. Lawrence

THE HORSE-DEALER'S DAUGHTER

The troubled and disordered life of D. H. Lawrence would hardly seem conducive to his production of great literature; yet there never was any question, only astonishment, at the enormous quantity of work he did in his short lifetime. Now that the controversies that surrounded him have subsided, there is general recognition that he was one of the great, original forces in twentieth-century literature. Lawrence came out of unlikely circumstances. He was the sickly fourth child of a strong, hearty coal miner and a genteel schoolteacher, and was born in the grimy mining town of Eastwood, England, in 1885. Dominated by his mother, he was encouraged by her to go to school and become a teacher in order to escape the life of the mines. He taught, and almost simultaneously began to write. His first novel, The White Peacock, *was published in 1911. In quick succession came* The Trespasser *(1912),* Sons and Lovers *(1913),* The Rainbow *(1915), and* Women in Love *(1920). At the same time he wrote volumes of poems, plays, and collections of travel sketches, sometimes three or four titles in a single year. Lawrence also took up painting. All this work came against the background of his turbulent personal life. Lawrence's frank treatment of physical passion and sex produced many attacks and resulted in the censorship of some of his books. He eloped in 1912 with a married woman, Frieda von Richtofen Weekley, and received unjust charges of being pro-German during World War I, and censures as a sex maniac and a home wrecker. For the rest of their lives Lawrence and Frieda roamed the world, often in poverty. Taos, New Mexico, where the Lawrences arrived in 1922, probably provided as much peace and harmony as they were ever to know. Here, Lawrence felt a kind of mystical rapport with the primitivism and healthy sexual openness of Indian and Mexican cultures. One result of this was a novel celebrating their "blood consciousness,"* The Plumed Serpent *(1926). His most notorious novel,* Lady Chatterley's Lover, *for which he was much misunderstood, came two years later (1928). On a trip back to England*

and thence to Italy, Lawrence's health declined, and he died in Vence, France, in 1930.

Most of his short stories project the same sense of sexual urgency, hidden or suppressed, as his novels. "The Horse-Dealer's Daughter" deals with the theme of love's awakening as a kind of birth. "Follow the course of your blood," Lawrence urged; and in this story, especially through the symbolism of the dank pond and the escape from it, he dramatizes this belief of the superiority of instinct over reason and of sexual fulfillment over restraint.

"Well, Mabel, and what are you going to do with yourself?" asked Joe, with foolish flippancy. He felt quite safe himself. Without listening for an answer, he turned aside, worked a grain of tobacco to the tip of his tongue, and spat it out. He did not care about anything, since he felt safe himself.

The three brothers and the sister sat round the desolate breakfast table, attempting some sort of desultory consultation. The morning's post had given the final tap to the family fortunes, and all was over. The dreary dining-room itself, with its heavy mahogany furniture, looked as if it were waiting to be done away with.

But the consultation amounted to nothing. There was a strange air of ineffectuality about the three men, as they sprawled at table, smoking and reflecting vaguely on their own condition. The girl was alone, a rather short, sullen-looking young woman of twenty-seven. She did not share the same life as her brothers. She would have been good-looking, save for the impassive fixity of her face, "bull-dog," as her brothers called it.

There was a confused tramping of horses' feet outside. The three men all sprawled round in their chairs to watch. Beyond the dark holly-bushes that separated the strip of lawn from the highroad, they could see a cavalcade of shire horses swinging out of their own yard, being taken for exercise. This was the last time. These were the last horses that would go through their hands. The young men watched with critical, callous look. They were all frightened at the collapse of their lives, and the sense of disaster in which they were involved left them no inner freedom.

Yet they were three fine, well-set fellows enough. Joe, the eldest, was a man of thirty-three, broad and handsome in a hot, flushed way. His face was red, he twisted his black moustache over a thick finger, his eyes were shallow and restless. He had a sensual way of uncovering his teeth when he laughed, and his bearing was stupid. Now he watched the horses with a glazed look of helplessness in his eyes, a certain stupor of downfall.

The great draught-horses swung past. They were tied head to tail, four of them, and they heaved along to where a lane branched off from the highroad, planting their great hoofs floutingly in the fine black mud, swinging their great rounded haunches sumptuously, and trotting a few sudden steps as they were led into the lane, round the corner. Every movement showed a massive, slumbrous strength, and a stupidity which held them in subjection. The groom at the head looked back, jerking the leading rope. And the cavalcade moved out of sight up the lane, the tail of the last horse, bobbed up tight and stiff, held out taut from the swinging great haunches as they rocked behind the hedges in a motion-like sleep.

Joe watched with glazed hopeless eyes. The horses were almost like his own body to him. He felt he was done for now. Luckily he was engaged to a woman as old as himself, and therefore her father, who was steward of a neighbouring estate, would provide him with a job. He would marry and go into harness. His life was over, he would be a subject animal now.

He turned uneasily aside, the retreating steps of the horses echoing in his ears. Then, with foolish restlessness, he reached for the scraps of bacon-rind from the plates, and making a faint whistling sound, flung them to the terrier that lay against the fender. He watched the dog swallow them, and waited till the creature looked into his eyes. Then a faint grin came on his face, and in a high, foolish voice he said:

"You won't get much more bacon, shall you, you little b———?"

The dog faintly and dismally wagged its tail, then lowered its haunches, circled round, and lay down again.

There was another helpless silence at the table. Joe sprawled uneasily in his seat, not willing to go till the family conclave was dissolved. Fred Henry, the second brother, was erect, clean-limbed, alert. He had watched the passing of the horses with more *sang-froid.* If he was an animal, like Joe, he was an animal which controls, not one which is controlled. He was master of any horse, and he carried himself with a well-tempered air of mastery. But he was not master of the situations of life. He pushed his coarse brown moustache upwards, off his lip, and glanced irritably at his sister, who sat impassive and inscrutable.

"You'll go and stop with Lucy for a bit, shan't you?" he asked. The girl did not answer.

"I don't see what else you can do," persisted Fred Henry.

"Go as a skivvy," Joe interpolated laconically.

The girl did not move a muscle.

"If I was her, I should go in for training for a nurse," said Malcolm, the youngest of them all. He was the baby of the family, a young man of twenty-two, with a fresh, jaunty *museau.*

But Mabel did not take any notice of him. They had talked at her and round her for so many years, that she hardly heard them at all.

The marble clock on the mantel-piece softly chimed the half-hour, the dog rose uneasily from the hearthrug and looked at the party at the breakfast table. But still they sat on in ineffectual conclave.

"Oh, all right," said Joe suddenly, *à propos* of nothing. "I'll get a move on."

He pushed back his chair, straddled his knees with a downward jerk, to get them free, in horsey fashion, and went to the fire. Still he did not go out of the room; he was curious to know what the others would do or say. He began to charge his pipe, looking down at the dog and saying, in a high, affected voice:

"Going wi' me? Going wi' me are ter? Tha'rt goin' further than tha counts on just now, dost hear?"

The dog faintly wagged its tail, the man stuck out his jaw and covered his pipe with his hands, and puffed intently, losing himself in the tobacco, looking down all the while at the dog with an absent brown eye. The dog looked up at him in mournful distrust. Joe stood with his knees stuck out, in real horsey fashion.

"Have you had a letter from Lucy?" Fred Henry asked of his sister.

"Last week," came the neutral reply.

"And what does she say?"

There was no answer.

"Does she *ask* you to go and stop there?" persisted Fred Henry.

"She says I can if I like."

"Well, then, you'd better. Tell her you'll come on Monday."

This was received in silence.

"That's what you'll do then, is it?" said Fred Henry, in some exasperation.

But she made no answer. There was a silence of futility and irritation in the room. Malcolm grinned fatuously.

"You'll have to make up your mind between now and next Wednesday," said Joe loudly, "or else find yourself lodgings on the kerbstone."

The face of the young woman darkened, but she sat on immutable.

"Here's Jack Fergusson!" exclaimed Malcolm, who was looking aimlessly out of the window.

"Where?" exclaimed Joe, loudly.

"Just gone past."

"Coming in?"

Malcolm craned his neck to see the gate.

"Yes," he said.

There was a silence. Mabel sat on like one condemned, at the head of the table. Then a whistle was heard from the kitchen. The dog got up and barked sharply. Joe opened the door and shouted:

"Come on."

After a moment a young man entered. He was muffled up in overcoat and a purple woollen scarf, and his tweed cap, which he did not remove, was pulled down on his head. He was of medium height, his face was rather long and pale, his eyes looked tired.

"Hello, Jack! Well, Jack!" exclaimed Malcolm and Joe. Fred Henry merely said, "Jack."

"What's doing?" asked the newcomer, evidently addressing Fred Henry.

"Same. We've got to be out by Wednesday.—Got a cold?"

"I have—got it bad, too."

"Why don't you stop in?"

"*Me* stop in? When I can't stand on my legs, perhaps I shall have a chance." The young man spoke huskily. He had a slight Scotch accent.

"It's a knock-out, isn't it," said Joe, boisterously, "if a doctor goes round croaking with a cold. Looks bad for the patients, doesn't it?"

The young doctor looked at him slowly.

"Anything the matter with *you*, then?" he asked sarcastically.

"Not as I know of. Damn your eyes, I hope not. Why?"

"I thought you were very concerned about the patients, wondered if you might be one yourself."

"Damn it, no, I've never been patient to no flaming doctor, and hope I never shall be," returned Joe.

At this point Mabel rose from the table, and they all seemed to become aware of her existence. She began putting the dishes together. The young doctor looked at her, but did not address her. He had not greeted her. She went out of the room with the tray, her face impassive and unchanged.

"When are you off then, all of you?" asked the doctor.

"I'm catching the eleven-forty," replied Malcolm. "Are you goin' down wi' th' trap, Joe?"

"Yes, I've told you I'm going down wi' th' trap, haven't I?"

"We'd better be getting her in then.—So long, Jack, if I don't see you before I go," said Malcolm, shaking hands.

He went out, followed by Joe, who seemed to have his tail between his legs.

"Well, this is the devil's own," exclaimed the doctor, when he was left alone with Fred Henry. "Going before Wednesday, are you?"

"That's the orders," replied the other.

"Where, to Northampton?"

"That's it."

"The devil!" exclaimed Fergusson, with quiet chagrin.

And there was silence between the two.

"All settled up, are you?" asked Fergusson.

"About."

There was another pause.

"Well, I shall miss yer, Freddy, boy," said the young doctor.

"And I shall miss thee, Jack," returned the other.

"Miss you like hell," mused the doctor.

Fred Henry turned aside. There was nothing to say. Mabel came in again, to finish clearing the table.

"What are *you* going to do, then, Miss Pervin?" asked Fergusson. "Going to your sister's, are you?"

Mabel looked at him with her steady, dangerous eyes, that always made him uncomfortable, unsettling his superficial ease.

"No," she said.

"Well, what in the name of fortune *are* you going to do? Say what you mean to do," cried Fred Henry, with futile intensity.

But she only averted her head, and continued her work. She folded the white table-cloth, and put on the chenille cloth.

"The sulkiest bitch that ever trod!" muttered her brother.

But she finished her task with perfectly impassive face, the young doctor watching her interestedly all the while. Then she went out.

Fred Henry stared after her, clenching his lips, his blue eyes fixing in sharp antagonism, as he made a grimace of sour exasperation.

"You could bray her into bits, and that's all you'd get out of her," he said, in a small, narrowed tone.

The doctor smiled faintly.

"What's she *going* to do, then?" he asked.

"Strike me if *I* know!" returned the other.

There was a pause. Then the doctor stirred.

"I'll be seeing you to-night, shall I?" he said to his friend.

"Ay—where's it to be? Are we going over to Jessdale?"

"I don't know. I've got such a cold on me. I'll come round to the Moon and Stars, anyway."

"Let Lizzie and May miss their night for once, eh?"

"That's it—if I feel as I do now."

"All's one—"

The two young men went through the passage and down to the back door together. The house was large, but it was servantless now, and desolate. At the back was a small bricked house-yard, and beyond that a big square, gravelled fine and red, and having stables on two sides. Sloping, dank, winter-dark fields stretched away on the open sides.

But the stables were empty. Joseph Pervin, the father of the family, had been a man of no education, who had become a fairly large horse dealer. The stables had been full of horses, there was a great turmoil and come-and-go of horses and of dealers and grooms. Then the kitchen was full of servants. But of late things had declined. The old man had married a second time, to retrieve his fortunes. Now he was dead and everything was gone to the dogs, there was nothing but debt and threatening.

For months, Mabel had been servantless in the big house, keeping the home together in penury for her ineffectual brothers. She had kept house for ten years. But previously, it was with unstinted means. Then, however brutal and coarse everything was, the sense of money had kept her proud, confident. The men might be foul-mouthed, the women in the kitchen might have bad reputations, her brothers might have illegitimate children. But so long as there was money, the girl felt herself established, and brutally proud, reserved.

No company came to the house, save dealers and coarse men. Mabel had no associates of her own sex, after her sister went away. But she did not mind. She went regularly to church, she attended to her father. And she lived in the memory of her mother, who had died when she was fourteen, and whom she had loved. She had loved her father, too, in a different way, depending upon him, and feeling secure in him, until at the age of fifty-four he married again. And then she had set hard against him. Now he had died and left them all hopelessly in debt.

She had suffered badly during the period of poverty. Nothing, however, could shake the curious sullen, animal pride that dominated each member of the family. Now, for Mabel, the end had come. Still she would not cast about her. She would follow her own way just the same. She would always hold the keys of her own situation. Mindless and persistent, she endured from day to day. Why should she think? Why should she answer anybody? It was enough that this was the end, and there was no way out. She need not pass any more darkly along the main street of the small town, avoiding every eye. She need not demean herself any more, going into the shops and buying the cheapest food. This was at an end. She thought of nobody, not even of herself. Mindless and persistent, she seemed in a sort of ecstasy to be coming nearer to her fulfillment, her own glorification, approaching her dead mother, who was glorified.

In the afternoon she took a little bag, with shears and sponge and a small scrubbing brush, and went out. It was a grey, wintry day, with saddened, dark-green fields and an atmosphere blackened by the smoke of foundries not far off. She went quickly, darkly along the causeway, heeding nobody, through the town to the churchyard.

There she always felt secure, as if no one could see her, although as a matter of fact she was exposed to the stare of everyone who passed along under the churchyard wall. Nevertheless, once under the shadow of the great looming church, among the graves, she felt immune from the world, reserved within the thick churchyard wall as in another country.

Carefully she clipped the grass from the grave, and arranged the pinky-white, small chrysanthemums in the tin cross. When this was done, she took an empty jar from a neighbouring grave, brought water, and carefully, most scrupulously sponged the marble headstone and the coping-stone.

It gave her sincere satisfaction to do this. She felt an immediate contact with the world of her mother. She took minute pains, went through the park in a state bordering on pure happiness, as if in performing this task she came into a subtle, intimate connection with her mother. For the life she followed here in the world was far less real than the world of death she inherited from her mother.

The doctor's house was just by the church. Fergusson, being a mere hired assistant, was slave to the countryside. As he hurried now to attend to the outpatients in the surgery, glancing across the graveyard with his quick eye, he saw the girl at her task at the grave. She seemed so intent and remote, it was like looking into another world. Some mystical element was touched in him. He slowed down as he walked, watching her as if spellbound.

She lifted her eyes, feeling him looking. Their eyes met. And each looked again at once, each feeling, in some way, found out by the other. He lifted his cap and passed on down the road. There remained distinct in his consciousness, like a vision, the memory of her face, lifted from the tombstone in the churchyard, and looking at him with slow, large, portentous eyes. It *was* portentous, her face. It seemed to mesmerise him. There was a heavy power in her eyes which laid hold of his whole being, as if he had drunk some powerful drug. He had been feeling weak and done before. Now the life came back into him, he felt delivered from his own fretted, daily self.

He finished his duties at the surgery as quickly as might be, hastily filling up the bottles of the waiting people with cheap drugs. Then, in perpetual haste, he set off again to visit several cases in another part of his round, before teatime. At all times he preferred to walk, if he could, but particularly when he was not well. He fancied the motion restored him.

The afternoon was falling. It was grey, deadened, and wintry, with a slow, moist, heavy coldness sinking in and deadening all the faculties. But why should he think or notice? He hastily climbed the hill and turned across the dark-green fields, following the black cinder-track. In the distance, across a shallow dip in the country, the small town was clustered like smouldering ash, a tower, a spire, a heap of low, raw, extinct houses. And on the nearest fringe of the town, sloping into the dip, was Oldmeadow, the Pervins' house. He could see the stables and the outbuildings distinctly, as they lay towards him on the slope. Well, he would not go there many more times! Another resource would be lost to him, another place gone: the only company he cared for in the alien, ugly little town he was losing. Nothing but work, drudgery, constant hastening from dwelling to dwelling among the colliers and the iron-workers. It wore him out, but at the same time he had a craving for it. It was a stimulant to him to be in the homes of the working people, moving as it were through the innermost body of their life. His nerves were excited and gratified. He could come so near, into the very lives of the rough, inarticulate, powerfully emotional men and women. He grumbled, he said he hated the hellish hole. But as a matter of fact it excited him, the contact with the rough, strongly-feeling people was a stimulant applied direct to his nerves.

Below Oldmeadow, in the green, shallow, soddened hollow of fields, lay a square, deep pond. Roving across the landscape, the doctor's quick eye detected a figure in black passing through the gate of the field, down towards the pond. He looked again. It would be Mabel Pervin. His mind suddenly became alive and attentive.

Why was she going down there? He pulled up on the path on the slope above, and stood staring. He could just make sure of the small black figure moving in the hollow of the failing day. He seemed to see her in the midst of such obscurity, that he was like a clairvoyant, seeing rather with the mind's eye than with ordinary sight. Yet he could see her positively enough, whilst he kept his eye attentive. He felt, if he looked away from her, in the thick, ugly falling dusk, he would lose her altogether.

He followed her minutely as she moved, direct and intent, like something transmitted rather than stirring in voluntary activity, straight down the field towards the pond. There she stood on the bank for a moment. She never raised her head. Then she waded slowly into the water.

He stood motionless as the small black figure walked slowly and deliberately towards the centre of the pond, very slowly, gradually moving deeper into the motionless water, and still moving forward as the water got up to her breast. Then he could see her no more in the dusk of the dead afternoon.

"There!" he exclaimed. "Would you believe it?"

And he hastened straight down, running over the wet, soddened fields, pushing through the hedges, down into the depression of callous wintry obscurity. It took him several minutes to come to the pond. He stood on the bank, breathing heavily. He could see nothing. His eyes seemed to penetrate the dead water. Yes, perhaps that was the dark shadow of her black clothing beneath the surface of the water.

He slowly ventured into the pond. The bottom was deep, soft clay, he sank in, and the water clasped dead cold round his legs. As he stirred he could smell the cold, rotten clay that fouled up into the water. It was objectionable in his lungs. Still, repelled and yet not heeding, he moved deeper into the pond. The cold water rose over his thighs, over his loins, upon his abdomen. The lower part of his body was all sunk in the hideous cold element. And the bottom was so deeply soft and uncertain, he was afraid of pitching with his mouth underneath. He could not swim, and was afraid.

He crouched a little spreading his hands under the water and moving them round, trying to feel for her. The dead cold pond swayed upon his chest. He moved again, a little deeper, and again, with his hands underneath, he felt all around under the water. And he touched her clothing. But it evaded his fingers. He made a desperate effort to grasp it.

And so doing he lost his balance and went under, horribly, suffocating in the foul earthy water, struggling madly for a few moments. At last, after what seemed an eternity, he got his footing, rose again into the air and looked around. He gasped, and knew he was in the world. Then he looked at the water. She had risen near him. He grasped her clothing, and drawing her nearer, turned to take his way to land again.

He went very slowly, carefully, absorbed in the slow progress. He rose higher, climbing out of the pond. The water was now only about his legs; he was thankful, full of relief to be out of the clutches of the pond. He lifted her and staggered on to the bank, out of the horror of wet, grey clay.

He laid her down on the bank. She was quite unconscious and running with water. He made the water come from her mouth, he worked to restore her. He did not have to work very long before he could feel the breathing begin again in her; she was breathing naturally. He worked a little longer. He could feel her live beneath his hands; she was coming back. He wiped her face, wrapped her in his overcoat, looked round into the dim, dark-grey world, then lifted her and staggered down the bank and across the fields.

It seemed an unthinkably long way, and his burden so heavy he felt he would never get to the house. But at last he was in the stable-yard, and then in the house-yard. He opened the door and went into the house. In the kitchen he laid her down on the hearthrug, and called. The house was empty. But the fire was burning in the grate.

Then again he kneeled to attend to her. She was breathing regularly, her eyes were wide open and as if conscious, but there seemed something missing in her look. She was conscious in herself, but unconscious of her surroundings.

He ran upstairs, took blankets from a bed, and put them before the fire to warm. Then he removed her saturated, earthy-smelling clothing, rubbed her dry with a towel, and wrapped her naked in the blankets. Then he went into the dining room, to look for spirits. There was a little whiskey. He drank a gulp himself, and put some into her mouth.

The effect was instantaneous. She looked full into his face, as if she had been seeing him for some time, and yet had only just become conscious of him.

"Dr. Fergusson?" she said.

"What?" he answered.

He was divesting himself of his coat, intending to find some dry clothing upstairs. He could not bear the smell of the dead, clayey water, and he was mortally afraid for his own health.

"What did I do?" she asked.

"Walked into the pond," he replied. He had begun to shudder like one sick, and could hardly attend to her. Her eyes remained full on him, he seemed to be going dark in his mind, looking back at her helplessly. The shuddering became quieter in him, his life came back in him, dark and unknowing, but strong again.

"Was I out of my mind?" she asked, while her eyes were fixed on him all the time.

"Maybe, for the moment," he replied. He felt quiet, because his strength had come back. The strange fretful strain had left him.

"Am I out of my mind now?" she asked.

"Are you?" he reflected a moment. "No," he answered truthfully, "I don't see that you are." He turned his face aside. He was afraid now because he felt dazed, and felt dimly that her power was stronger than his, in this issue. And she continued to look at him fixedly all the time. "Can you tell me where I shall find some dry things to put on?" he asked.

"Did you dive into the pond for me?" she asked.

"No," he answered. "I walked in. But I went in overhead as well."

There was silence for a moment. He hesitated. He very much wanted to go upstairs to get into dry clothing. But there was another desire in him. And she seemed to hold him. His will seemed to have gone to sleep, and left him, standing there slack before her. But he felt warm inside himself. He did not shudder at all, though his clothes were sodden on him.

"Why did you?" she asked.

"Because I didn't want you to do such a foolish thing," he said.

"It wasn't foolish," she said, still gazing at him as she lay on the floor, with a sofa cushion under her head. "It was the right thing to do. I knew best, then."

"I'll go and shift these wet things," he said. But still he had not the power to move out of her presence, until she sent him. It was as if she had the life of his body in her hands, and he could not extricate himself. Or perhaps he did not want to.

Suddenly she sat up. Then she became aware of her own immediate condition. She felt the blankets about her, she knew her own limbs. For a moment it seemed as if her reason were going. She looked round, with wild eye, as if seeking something. He stood still with fear. She saw her clothing lying scattered.

"Who undressed me?" she asked, her eyes resting full and inevitable on his face.

"I did," he replied, "to bring you round."

For some moments she sat and gazed at him awfully, her lips parted.

"Do you love me then?" she asked.

He only stood and stared at her, fascinated. His soul seemed to melt.

She shuffled forward on her knees, and put her arms round him, round his legs, as he stood there, pressing her breasts against his knees and thighs, clutching him with strange, convulsive certainty, pressing his thighs against her, drawing him to her face, her throat, as she looked up at him with flaring, humble eyes of transfiguration, triumphant in first possession.

"You love me," she murmured, in strange transport, yearning and triumphant and confident. "You love me. I know you love me, I know."

And she was passionately kissing his knees, through the wet clothing, passionately and indiscriminately kissing his knees, his legs, as if unaware of everything.

He looked down at the tangled wet hair, the wild, bare, animal shoulders. He was amazed, bewildered, and afraid. He had never thought of loving her. He had never wanted to love her. When he rescued her and restored her, he was a doctor, and she was a patient. He had had no single personal thought of her. Nay, this introduction of the personal element was very distasteful to him, a violation of his professional honour. It was horrible to have her there embracing his knees. It was horrible. He revolted from it, violently. And yet—and yet—he had not the power to break away.

She looked at him again, with the same supplication of powerful love, and that same transcendent, frightening light of triumph. In view of the delicate flame which seemed to come from her face like a light, he was powerless. And yet he had never intended to love her. He had never intended. And something stubborn in him could not give way.

"You love me," she repeated, in a murmur of deep, rhapsodic assurance. "You love me."

Her hands were drawing him, drawing him down to her. He was afraid, even a little horrified. For he had, really, no intention of loving her. Yet her hands were drawing him towards her. He put out his hand quickly to steady himself, and grasped her bare shoulder. A flame seemed to burn the hand that grasped her soft shoulder. He had no intention of loving her: his whole will was against his yielding. It was horrible. And yet wonderful was the touch of her shoulders, beautiful the shining of her face. Was she perhaps mad? He had a horror of yielding to her. Yet something in him ached also.

He had been staring away at the door, away from her. But his hand remained on her shoulder. She had gone suddenly very still. He looked down at her. Her eyes were now wide with fear, with doubt, the light was dying from her face, a shadow of terrible greyness was returning. He could not bear the touch of her eyes' question upon him, and the look of death behind the question.

With an inward groan he gave way, and let his heart yield towards her. A sudden gentle smile came on his face. And her eyes, which never left his face, slowly, slowly filled with tears. He watched the strange water rise in her eyes, like some slow fountain coming up. And his heart seemed to burn and melt away in his breast.

He could not bear to look at her any more. He dropped on his knees and caught her head with his arms and pressed her face against his throat. She was very still. His heart, which seemed to have broken, was burning with a kind of agony in his breast. And he felt her slow, hot tears wetting his throat. But he could not move.

He felt the hot tears wet his neck and the hollows of his neck, and he remained motionless, suspended through one of man's eternities. Only now it had become indispensable to him to have her face pressed close to him; he could never let her go again. He could never let her head go away from the close clutch of his arm. He wanted to remain like that for ever, with his heart hurting him in a pain that was also life to him. Without knowing, he was looking down on her damp, soft brown hair.

Then, as it were suddenly, he smelt the horrid stagnant smell of that water. And at the same moment she drew away from him and looked at him. Her eyes were wistful and unfathomable. He was afraid of them, and he fell to kissing her, not knowing what he was doing. He wanted her eyes not to have that terrible, wistful, unfathomable look.

When she turned her face to him again, a faint delicate flush was glowing, and there was again dawning that terrible shining of joy in her eyes, which really terrified him, and yet which he now wanted to see, because he feared the look of doubt still more.

"You love me?" she said, rather faltering.

"Yes." The word cost him a painful effort. Not because it wasn't true. But because it was too newly true, the *saying* seemed to tear open again his newly-torn heart. And he hardly wanted it to be true, even now.

She lifted her face to him, and he bent forward and kissed her on the mouth, gently, with the one kiss that is an eternal pledge. And as he kissed her his heart strained again in his breast. He never intended to love her. But now it was over. He had crossed over the gulf to her, and all that he had left behind had shrivelled and become void.

After the kiss, her eyes again slowly filled with tears. She sat still, away from him, with her face drooped aside, and her hands folded in her lap. The tears fell very slowly. There was complete silence. He too sat there motionless and silent on the hearthrug. The strange pain of his heart that was broken seemed to consume him. That he should love her? That this was love! That he should be ripped open in this way!—Him, a doctor!—How they would all jeer if they knew!—It was agony to him to think they might know.

In the curious naked pain of the thought he looked again to her. She was sitting there drooped into a muse. He saw a tear fall, and his heart flared hot. He saw for the first time that one of her shoulders was quite uncovered, one arm bare, he could see one of her small breasts; dimly, because it had become almost dark in the room.

"Why are you crying?" he asked, in an altered voice.

She looked at him, and behind her tears the consciousness of her situation for the first time brought a dark look of shame to her eyes.

"I'm not crying, really," she said, watching him half frightened.

He reached his hand, and softly closed it on her bare arm.

"I love you! I love you!" he said in a soft, low vibrating voice, unlike himself.

She shrank, and dropped her head. The soft, penetrating grip of his hand on her arm distressed her. She looked up at him.

"I want to go," she said. "I want to go and get you some dry things."

"Why?" he said. "I'm all right."

"But I want to go," she said. "And I want you to change your things."

He released her arm, and she wrapped herself in the blanket, looking at him rather frightened. And still she did not rise.

"Kiss me," she said wistfully.

He kissed her, but briefly, half in anger.

Then, after a second, she rose nervously, all mixed up in the blanket. He watched her in her confusion, as she tried to extricate herself and wrap herself up so that she could walk. He watched her relentlessly, as she knew. And as she went, the blanket trailing, and as he saw a glimpse of her feet and her white leg, he tried to remember her as she was when he had wrapped her in the blanket. But then he didn't want to remember, because she had been nothing to him then, and his nature revolted from remembering her as she was when she was nothing to him.

A tumbling, muffled noise from within the dark house startled him. Then he heard her voice:—"There are clothes." He rose and went to the foot of the stairs, and gathered up the garments she had thrown down. Then he came back to the fire, to rub himself down and dress. He grinned at his own appearance when he had finished.

The fire was sinking, so he put on coal. The house was now quite dark, save for the light of a street-lamp that shone in faintly from beyond the holly trees. He lit the gas with matches he found on the mantelpiece. Then he emptied the pockets of his own clothes, and threw all his wet things in a heap into the scullery. After which he gathered up her sodden clothes, gently, and put them in a separate heap on the copper-top in the scullery.

It was six o'clock on the clock. His own watch had stopped. He ought to go back to the surgery. He waited, and still she did not come down. So he went to the foot of the stairs and called:

"I shall have to go."

Almost immediately he heard her coming down. She had on her best dress of black voile, and her hair was tidy, but still damp. She looked at him—and in spite of herself, smiled.

"I don't like you in those clothes," she said.

"Do I look a sight?" he answered.

They were shy of one another.

"I'll make you some tea," she said.

"No, I must go."

"Must you?" And she looked at him again with the wide, strained, doubtful eyes. And again, from the pain of his breast, he knew how he loved her. He went and bent to kiss her, gently, passionately, with his heart's painful kiss.

"And my hair smells so horrible," she murmured in distraction. "And I'm so awful, I'm so awful! Oh, no, I'm too awful." And she broke into bitter, heart-broken sobbing. "You can't want to love me, I'm horrible."

"Don't be silly, don't be silly," he said, trying to comfort her, kissing her, holding her in his arms. "I want you, I want to marry you, we're going to be married, quickly, quickly—to-morrow if I can."

But she only sobbed terribly, and cried:

"I feel awful. I feel awful. I feel I'm horrible to you."

"No, I want you, I want you," was all he answered, blindly, with that terrible intonation which frightened her almost more than her horror lest he should *not* want her.

Questions

1. The love relationship in this story is unusual. In fact, the two characters discover love as an aftermath of pain, and almost with surprise. In what other ways is the love between Mabel and Dr. Fergusson rather extraordinary, and even unconventional?

2. Can one say that, without knowing it, both characters were subconsciously prepared for love, and were only waiting for the right circumstances for discovering it? Cite evidence from the story which proves or disproves this view.

3. Characterize the relationship between Mabel and her three brothers, and explain how their attitude toward her helps to establish her character. How does their attitude relate to her suicide attempt?

4. Show how Mabel's suicide attempt is foreshadowed. In particular, show how the pond comes to be equated with death. In addition to actual descriptive details, what other elements of tone and atmosphere anticipate the suicide attempt?

5. After Mabel has been rescued from the pond, she undergoes a change; becoming less conscious of her surroundings, and more conscious of herself. What does this change portend? What discovery about herself is she making?

6. Dr. Fergusson changes too after he rescues Mabel. In what new way does he see Mabel? What does he really feel for her? Is the change in him plausible? What has motivated it?

7. Why are both characters more receptive to love after the suicide attempt than before?

Thomas Mann

MARIO AND THE MAGICIAN

Thomas Mann must be accounted one of the greatest writers of the twentieth century, and his masterpiece, The Magic Mountain, *is a title always present in debates about the greatest novel of the century. Yet Mann is not easily approachable. His stern sense of discipline, his detached and impersonal viewpoint, and his emphasis on form and order in his own work, all earn him respect if not affection. His avoidance of political activism and refusal to espouse causes often make him seem aloof and withdrawn. Mann was born in Lubeck, Germany, in 1875, son of a prosperous merchant and civic leader. He was prepared for a business career, but rejected it to study literature. His first novel,* Buddenbrooks *(1901), was a long family chronicle that introduced some of the conflicts he was repeatedly to deal with: that between bourgeois complacency and the uncertain but free life of the artist, or between the happy, accepting conformist on the one hand and the creative spirit, the rebel, the bohemian on the other; or between intellect and emotion, or between duty and desire. Mann concentrated on the artist in* Tonio Kroger *(1903) and on an amiable rogue in* Felix Krull *(1911), seeing many similarities; both young heroes discovered, as they grew up, the differences between what they had been told about life and what they found out for themselves. The great short novel* Death in Venice *came in 1913 and the long, allegorical* The Magic Mountain *in 1924, after Mann had been in a tuberculosis sanitorium. His Biblical tetralogy,* Joseph and His Brothers, *occupied him for a decade from 1933 to 1943. At the end of his life he returned to his one comic work and extended to novel length an early story,* Confessions of Felix Krull *(1954). He died in 1955.*

Mann generally believed that a writer should be apolitical and remain detached from controversial issues. Nevertheless, he was forced to make political decisions; his own books were burned by the Nazis, and he was deprived of German citizenship in 1936. Ultimately he moved to California and in 1944 became a United States citizen. His story

"Mario and the Magician"—the longest work in this book, actually a short novel—is a powerful political allegory about how a commanding figure manages to control the masses. Though written in 1930, before the rise of Hitler, it shows a profound awareness of the techniques of Fascism, of the way in which "good" people can be overpowered and destroyed.

The atmosphere of Torre di Venere remains unpleasant in the memory. From the first moment the air of the place made us uneasy, we felt irritable, on edge; then at the end came the shocking business of Cipolla, that dreadful being who seemed to incorporate, in so fateful and so humanly impressive a way, all the peculiar evilness of the situation as a whole. Looking back, we had the feeling that the horrible end of the affair had been preordained and lay in the nature of things; that the children had to be present at it was an added impropriety, due to the false colours in which the weird creature presented himself. Luckily for them, they did not know where the comedy left off and the tragedy began; and we let them remain in their happy belief that the whole thing had been a play up till the end.

Torre di Venere lies some fifteen kilometres from Portoclemente, one of the most popular summer resorts on the Tyrrhenian Sea. Portoclemente is urban and elegant and full to overflowing for months on end. Its gay and busy main street of shops and hotels runs down to a wide sandy beach covered with tents and pennanted sand-castles and sunburnt humanity, where at all times a lively social bustle reigns, and much noise. But this same spacious and inviting fine-sanded beach, this same border of pine grove and near, presiding mountains, continues all the way along the coast. No wonder then that some competition of a quiet kind should have sprung up further on. Torre di Venere—the tower that gave the town its name is gone long since, one looks for it in vain—is an offshoot of the larger resort, and for some years remained an idyll for the few, a refuge for more unworldly spirits. But the usual history of such places repeated itself: peace has had to retire further along the coast, to Marina Petriera and dear knows where else. We all know how the world at once seeks peace and puts her to flight—rushing upon her in the fond idea that they two will wed, and where she is, there it can be at home. It will even set up its Vanity Fair in a spot and be capable of thinking that peace is still by its side. Thus Torre—though its atmosphere so far is more modest and contemplative than that of Portoclemente—has been quite taken up, by both Italians and foreigners. It is no longer the thing to go to Portoclemente—though still so much the thing that it is as noisy and crowded as ever. One goes next door, so to speak: to Torre. So much more refined, even, and cheaper to boot. And the attractiveness of these qualities persists, though the qualities themselves long ago ceased to be evident. Torre has got a Grand Hotel. Numerous pensions have sprung up, some modest, some pretentious. The people who own or rent the villas and pinetas overlooking the sea no longer have it all their own way on the beach. In July and August it looks just like the beach at Portoclemente: it swarms with a screaming, squabbling, merrymaking crowd, and the sun, blazing down like mad, peels the skin off their necks. Garish little flat-bottomed boats rock on the glittering blue, manned by children, whose mothers hover afar and fill the air with anxious cries of Nino! and Sandro! and Bice! and Maria! Pedlars step across the legs of recumbent sun-bathers, selling flowers and corals, oysters, lemonade, and *cornetti al burro,* and crying their wares in the breathy, full-throated southern voice.

Such was the scene that greeted our arrival in Torre: pleasant enough, but after all, we thought, we had come too soon. It was the middle of August, the Italian season was still at its height, scarcely the moment for strangers to learn to love the special charms of the place. What an afternoon crowd in the cafés on the front! For instance, in the Esquisito, where we sometimes sat and were served by Mario, that very Mario of whom I shall have presently to tell. It is well-nigh impossible to find a table; and the various orchestras contend together in the midst of one's conversation with bewildering effect. Of course, it is in the afternoon that people come over from Portoclemente. The excursion is a favourite one for the restless denizens of that pleasure resort, and a Fiat motor-bus plies to and fro, coating inch-thick with dust the oleander and laurel hedges along the highroad—a notable if repulsive sight.

Yes, decidedly one should go to Torre in September, when the great public has left. Or else in May, before the water is warm enough to tempt the Southerner to bathe. Even in the before and after seasons Torre is not empty, but life is less national and more subdued. English, French, and German prevail under the tent-awnings and in the pension dining-rooms; whereas in August—in the Grand Hotel, at least, where, in default of private addresses, we had engaged rooms—the stranger finds the field so occupied by Florentine and Roman society that he feels quite isolated and even temporarily *déclassé.*

We had, rather to our annoyance, this experience on the evening we arrived, when we went in to dinner and were shown to our table by the waiter in charge. As a table, it had nothing against it, save that we had already fixed our eyes upon those on the veranda beyond, built out over the water, where little red-shaded lamps glowed—and there were still some tables empty, though it was as full as the dining-room within. The children went into raptures at the festive sight, and without more ado we announced our intention to take our meals by preference in the veranda. Our words, it appeared, were prompted by ignorance; for we were informed, with somewhat embarrassed politeness, that the cosy nook outside was reserved for the clients of the hotel: *ai nostri clienti.* Their clients? But we were their clients. We were not tourists or trippers, but boarders for a stay of some three or four weeks. However, we forbore to press for an explanation of the difference between the likes of us and that clientèle to whom it was vouchsafed to eat out there in the glow of the red lamps, and took our dinner by the prosaic common light of the dining-room chandelier—a thoroughly ordinary and monotonous hotel bill of fare, be it said. In Pensione Eleonora, a few steps landward, the table, as we were to discover, was much better.

And thither it was that we moved, three or four days later, before we had had time to settle in properly at the Grand Hotel. Not on account of the veranda and the lamps. The children, straightway on the best of terms with waiters and pages, absorbed in the joys of life on the beach, promptly forgot those colourful seductions. But now there arose, between ourselves and the veranda clientèle—or perhaps more correctly with the compliant management—one of those little unpleasantnesses which can quite spoil the pleasure of a holiday. Among the guests were some high Roman aristocracy, a Principe X and his family. These grand folk occupied rooms close to our own, and the Principessa, a great and a passionately maternal lady, was thrown into a panic by the vestiges of a whooping-cough which our little ones had lately got over, but which now and then still faintly troubled the unshatterable slumbers of our youngest-born. The nature of this illness is not clear, leaving some play for the imagination. So we took no offence at our elegant neighbour for clinging to the widely held view that whooping-cough is acoustically contagious and quite simply fearing lest her children yield to the bad example set by ours. In the fullness of her feminine self-confidence she protested to the management, which then, in the person of the proverbial frock-coated manager, hastened to represent to us, with many expressions of regret, that under the circumstances they were obliged to transfer us to the annexe. We did our best to assure him that the disease was in its very last stages, that it was actually over, and presented no danger of infection to anybody. All that we gained was permission to bring the case before the hotel physician—not one chosen by us—by whose verdict we must then abide. We agreed, convinced that thus we should at once pacify the Princess and escape the trouble of moving. The doctor appeared, and behaved like a faithful and honest servant of science. He examined the child and gave his opinion: the disease was quite over, no danger of contagion was present. We drew a long breath and considered the incident closed—until the manager announced that despite the doctor's verdict it would still be necessary for us to give up our rooms and retire to the *dépendance*. Byzantinism like this outraged us. It is not likely that the Principessa was responsible for the wilful breach of faith. Very likely the fawning management had not even dared to tell her what the physician said. Anyhow, we made it clear to his understanding that we preferred to leave the hotel altogether and at once—and packed our trunks. We could do so with a light heart, having already set up casual friendly relations with Casa Eleonora. We had noticed its pleasant exterior and formed the acquaintance of its proprietor, Signora Angiolieri, and her husband: she slender and black-haired, Tuscan in type, probably at the beginning of the thirties, with the dead ivory complexion of the southern woman, he quiet and bald and carefully dressed. They owned a larger establishment in Florence and presided only in summer and early autumn over the branch in Torre di Venere. But earlier, before her marriage, our new landlady had been companion, fellow-traveller, wardrobe mistress, yes, friend, of Eleonora Duse and manifestly regarded that period as the crown of her career. Even at our first visit she spoke of it with animation. Numerous photographs of the great actress, with affectionate inscriptions, were displayed about the drawing-room, and other souvenirs of their life together adorned the little tables and étagères. This cult of a so interesting past was calculated, of course, to heighten the advantages of the signora's present business. Nevertheless our pleasure and interest were quite genuine as we were conducted through the house by its owner and listened to her sonorous and staccato Tuscan voice relating anecdotes of that immortal mistress, depicting her suffering saintliness, her genius, her profound delicacy of feeling.

Thither, then, we moved our effects, to the dismay of the staff of the Grand Hotel, who, like all Italians, were very good to children. Our new quarters were retired and pleasant, we were within easy reach of the sea through the avenue of young plane trees that ran down to the esplanade. In the clean, cool dining-room Signora Angiolieri daily served the soup with her own hands, the service was attentive and good, the table capital. We even discovered some Viennese acquaintances, and enjoyed chatting with them after luncheon, in front of the house. They, in their turn, were the means of our finding others—in short, all seemed for the best, and we were heartily glad of the change we had made. Nothing was now wanting to a holiday of the most gratifying kind.

And yet no proper gratification ensued. Perhaps the stupid occasion of our change of quarters pursued us to the new ones we had found. Personally, I admit that I do not easily forget these collisions with ordinary humanity, the naïve misuse of power, the injustice, the sycophantic corruption. I dwelt upon the incident too much, it irritated me in retrospect—quite futilely, of course, since such phenomena are only all too natural and all too much the rule. And we had not broken off relations with the Grand Hotel. The children were as friendly as ever there, the porter mended their toys, and we sometimes took tea in the garden. We even saw the Principessa. She would come out, with her firm and delicate tread, her lips emphatically corallined, to look after her children, playing under the supervision of their English governess. She did not dream that we were anywhere near, for so soon as she appeared in the offing we sternly forbade our little one even to clear his throat.

The heat—if I may bring it in evidence—was extreme. It was African. The power of the sun, directly one left the border of the indigo-blue wave, was so frightful, so relentless, that the mere thought of the few steps between the beach and luncheon was a burden, clad though one might be only in pyjamas. Do you care for that sort of thing? Weeks on end? Yes, of course, it is proper to the south, it is classic weather, the sun of Homer, the climate wherein human culture came to flower—and all the rest of it. But after a while it is too much for me, I reach a point where I begin to find it dull. The burning void of the sky, day after day, weighs one down; the high coloration, the enormous naïveté of the unrefracted light—they do, I dare say, induce light-heartedness, a carefree mood born of immunity from downpours and other meteorological caprices. But slowly, slowly, there makes itself felt a lack: the deeper, more complex needs of the northern soul remain unsatisfied. You are left barren—even, it may be, in time, a little contemptuous. True, without that stupid business of the whooping-cough I might not have been feeling these things. I was annoyed, very likely I wanted to feel them and so half-unconsciously seized upon an idea lying ready to hand to induce, or if not to induce, at least to justify and strengthen, my attitude. Up to this point, then, if you like, let us grant some ill will on our part. But the sea; and the mornings spent extended upon the fine sand in face of its eternal splendours—no, the sea could not conceivably induce such feelings. Yet it was none the less true that, despite all previous experience, we were not at home on the beach, we were not happy.

It was too soon, too soon. The beach, as I have said, was still in the hands of the middle-class native. It is a pleasing breed to look at, and among the young we saw much shapeliness and charm. Still, we were necessarily surrounded by a great deal of very average humanity—a middle-class mob, which, you will admit, is not more charming under this sun than under one's own native sky. The voices these women have! It was sometimes hard to believe that we were in the land which is the western cradle of the art of song. *"Fuggièro!"* I can still hear that cry, as for twenty mornings long I heard it close behind me, breathy, full-throated, hideously stressed, with a harsh open *e*, uttered in accents of mechanical despair. *"Fuggièro! Rispondi almeno!"* Answer when I call you! The *sp* in *rispondi* was pronounced like *shp*, as Germans pronounce it; and this, on top of what I felt already, vexed my sensitive soul. The cry was addressed to a repulsive youngster whose sunburn had made disgusting raw sores on his shoulders. He outdid anything I have ever seen for ill-breeding, refractoriness, and temper and was a great coward to boot, putting the whole beach in an uproar, one day, because of his outrageous sensitiveness to the slightest pain. A sand-crab had pinched his toe in the water, and the minute injury made him set up a cry of heroic proportions—the shout of an antique hero in his agony—that pierced one to the marrow and called up visions of some frightful tragedy. Evidently he considered himself not only wounded, but poisoned as well; he crawled out on the sand and lay in apparently intolerable anguish, groaning *"Ohi!"* and *"Ohimè!"* and threshing about with arms and legs to ward off his mother's tragic appeals and the questions of the bystanders. An audience gathered round. A doctor was fetched—the same who had pronounced objective judgment on our whooping-cough—and here again acquitted himself like a man of science. Good-naturedly he reassured the boy, telling him that he was not hurt at all, he should simply go into the water again to relieve the smart. Instead of which, Fuggièro was borne off the beach, followed by a concourse of people. But he did not fail to appear next morning, nor did he leave off spoiling our children's sand-castles. Of course, always by accident. In short, a perfect terror.

And this twelve-year-old lad was prominent among the influences that, imperceptibly at first, combined to spoil our holiday and render it unwholesome. Somehow or other, there was a stiffness, a lack of innocent enjoyment. These people stood on their dignity—just why, and in what spirit, it was not easy at first to tell. They displayed much self-respectingness; towards each other and towards the foreigner their bearing was that of a person newly conscious of a sense of honour. And wherefore? Gradually we realized the political implications and understood that we were in the presence of a national ideal. The beach, in fact, was alive with patriotic children—a phenomenon as unnatural as it was depressing. Children are a human species and a society apart, a nation of their own, so to speak. On the basis of their common form of life, they find each other out with the greatest ease, no matter how different their small vocabularies. Ours soon played with natives and foreigners alike. Yet they were plainly both puzzled and disappointed at times. There were wounded sensibilities, displays of assertiveness—or rather hardly assertiveness, for it was too self-conscious and too didactic to deserve the name. There were quarrels over flags, disputes about authority and precedence. Grown-ups joined in, not so much to pacify as to render judgment and enunciate principles. Phrases were dropped about the greatness and dignity of Italy, solemn phrases that spoilt the fun. We saw our two little ones retreat, puzzled and hurt, and were put to it to explain the situation. These people, we told them, were just passing through a certain stage, something rather like an illness, perhaps; not very pleasant, but probably unavoidable.

We had only our own carelessness to thank that we came to blows in the end with this "stage"—which, after all, we had seen and sized up long before now. Yes, it came to another "cross-purposes," so evidently the earlier ones had not been sheer accident. In a word, we became an offence to the public morals. Our small daughter—eight years old, but in physical development a good year younger and thin as a chicken—had had a good long bathe and gone playing in the warm sun in her wet costume. We told her that she might take off her bathing-suit, which was stiff with sand, rinse it in the sea, and put it on again, after which she must take care to keep it cleaner. Off goes the costume and she runs down naked to the sea, rinses her little jersey, and comes back. Ought we to have foreseen the outburst of anger and resentment which her conduct, and thus our conduct, called forth? Without delivering a homily on the subject, I may say that in the last decade our attitude towards the nude body and our feeling regarding it have undergone, all over the world, a fundamental change. There are things we "never think about" any more, and among them is the freedom we had permitted to this by no means provocative little childish body. But in these parts it was taken as a challenge. The patriotic children hooted. Fuggièro whistled on his fingers. The sudden buzz of conversation among the grown people in our neighbourhood boded no good. A gentleman in city togs, with a not very apropos bowler hat on the back of his head, was assuring his outraged womenfolk that he proposed to take punitive measures; he stepped up to us, and a philippic descended on our unworthy heads, in which all the emotionalism of the sense-loving south spoke in the service of morality and discipline. The offence against decency of which we had been guilty was, he said, the more to be condemned because it was also a gross ingratitude and an insulting breach of his country's hospitality. We had criminally injured not only the letter and spirit of the public bathing regulations, but also the honour of Italy; he, the gentleman in the city togs, knew how to defend that honour and proposed to see to it that our offence against the national dignity should not go unpunished.

We did our best, bowing respectfully, to give ear to this eloquence. To contradict the man, overheated as he was, would probably be to fall from one error into another. On the tips of our tongues we had various answers: as, that the word "hospitality," in its strictest sense, was not quite the right one, taking all the circumstances into consideration. We were not literally the guests of Italy, but of Signora Angiolieri, who had assumed the rôle of dispenser of hospitality some years ago on laying down that of familiar friend of Eleonora Duse. We longed to say that surely this beautiful country had not sunk so low as to be reduced to a state of hypersensitive prudishness. But we confined ourselves to assuring the gentleman that any lack of respect, any provocation on our parts, had been the furthest from our thoughts. And as a mitigating circumstance we pointed out the tender age and physical slightness of the little culprit. In vain. Our protests were waved away, he did not believe in them; our defence would not hold water. We must be made an example of. The authorities were notified, by telephone, I believe, and their representative appeared on the beach. He said the case was "*molto grave.*" We had to go with him to the Municipio up in the Piazza, where a higher official confirmed the previous verdict of "*molto grave,*" launched into a stream of the usual didactic phrases—the selfsame tune and words as the man in the bowler hat—and levied a fine and ransom of fifty lire. We felt that the adventure must willy-nilly be worth to us this much of a contribution to the economy of the Italian government; paid, and left. Ought we not at this point to have left Torre as well?

If we only had! We should thus have escaped that fatal Cipolla. But circumstances combined to prevent us from making up our minds to a change. A certain poet says that it is indolence that makes us endure uncomfortable situations. The *aperçu* may serve as an explanation for our inaction. Anyhow, one dislikes voiding the field immediately upon such an event. Especially if sympathy from other quarters encourages one to defy it. And in the Villa Eleonora they pronounced as with one voice upon the injustice of our punishment. Some Italian after-dinner acquaintances found that the episode put their country in a very bad light, and proposed taking the man in the bowler hat to task, as one fellow-citizen to another. But the next day he and his party had vanished from the beach. Not on our account, of course. Though it might be that the consciousness of his impending departure had added energy to his rebuke; in any case his going was a relief. And, furthermore, we stayed because our stay had by now become remarkable in our own eyes, which is worth something in itself, quite apart from the comfort or discomfort involved. Shall we strike sail, avoid a certain experience so soon as it seems not expressly calculated to increase our enjoyment or our self-esteem? Shall we go away whenever life looks like turning in the slightest uncanny, or not quite normal, or even rather painful and mortifying? No, surely not. Rather stay and look matters in the face, brave them out; perhaps precisely in so doing lies a lesson for us to learn. We stayed on and reaped as the awful reward of our constancy the unholy and staggering experience with Cipolla.

I have not mentioned that the after season had begun, almost on the very day we were disciplined by the city authorities. The worshipful gentleman in the bowler hat, our denouncer, was not the only person to leave the resort. There was a regular exodus, on every hand you saw luggage-carts on their way to the station. The beach denationalized itself. Life in Torre, in the cafés and the pinetas, became more homelike and more European. Very likely we might even have eaten at a table in the glass veranda, but we refrained, being content at Signora Angiolieri's—as content, that is, as our evil star would let us be. But at the same time with this turn for the better came a change in the weather: almost to an hour it showed itself in harmony with the holiday calendar of the general public. The sky was overcast; not that it grew any cooler, but the unclouded heat of the entire eighteen days since our arrival, and probably long before that, gave place to a stifling sirocco air, while from time to time a little ineffectual rain sprinkled the velvety surface of the beach. Add to which, that two-thirds of our intended stay at Torre had passed. The colourless, lazy sea, with sluggish jellyfish floating in its shallows, was at least a change. And it would have been silly to feel retrospective longings after a sun that had caused us so many sighs when it burned down in all its arrogant power.

At this juncture, then, it was that Cipolla announced himself. Cavaliere Cipolla he was called on the posters that appeared one day stuck up everywhere, even in the dining-room of Pensione Eleonora. A travelling virtuoso, an entertainer, "*forzatore, illusionista, prestidigatore,*" as he called himself, who proposed to wait upon the highly respectable population of Torre di Venere with a display of extraordinary phenomena of a mysterious and staggering kind. A conjuror! The bare announcement was enough to turn our children's heads. They had never seen anything of the sort, and now our present holiday was to afford them this new excitement. From that moment on they besieged us with prayers to take tickets for the performance. We had doubts, from the first, on the score of the lateness of the hour, nine o'clock; but gave way, in the idea that we might see a little of what Cipolla had to offer, probably no great matter, and then go home. Besides, of course, the children could sleep late next day. We bought four tickets of Signora Angiolieri herself, she having taken a number of the stalls on commission to sell them to her guests. She could not vouch for the man's performance, and we had no great expectations. But we were conscious of a need for diversion, and the children's violent curiosity proved catching.

The Cavaliere's performance was to take place in a hall where during the season there had been a cinema with a weekly programme. We had never been there. You reached it by following the main street under the wall of the "palazzo," a ruin with a "For sale" sign, that suggested a castle and had obviously been built in lordlier days. In the same street were the chemist, the hairdresser, and all the better shops; it led, so to speak, from the feudal past the bourgeois into the proletarian, for it ended off between two rows of poor fishing-huts, where old women sat mending nets before the doors. And here, among the proletariat, was the hall, not much more, actually, than a wooden shed, though a large one, with a turreted entrance, plastered on either side with layers of gay placards. Some while after dinner, then, on the appointed evening, we wended our way thither in the dark, the children dressed in their best and blissful with the sense of so much irregularity. It was sultry, as it had been for days; there was heat lightning now and then, and a little rain; we proceeded under umbrellas. It took us a quarter of an hour.

Our tickets were collected at the entrance, our places we had to find ourselves. They were in the third row left, and as we sat down we saw that, late though the hour was for the performance, it was to be interpreted with even more laxity. Only very slowly did an audience—who seemed to be relied upon to come late—begin to fill the stalls. These comprised the whole auditorium; there were no boxes. This tardiness gave us some concern. The children's cheeks were already flushed as much with fatigue as with excitement. But even when we entered, the standing-room at the back and in the side aisles was already well occupied. There stood the manhood of Torre di Venere, all and sundry, fisherfolk, rough-and-ready youths with bare forearms crossed over their striped jerseys. We were well pleased with the presence of this native assemblage, which always adds colour and animation to occasions like the present; and the children were frankly delighted. For they had friends among these people—acquaintances picked up on afternoon strolls to the further ends of the beach. We would be turning homeward, at the hour when the sun dropped into the sea, spent with the huge effort it had made and gilding with reddish gold the oncoming surf; and we would come upon bare-legged fisherfolk standing in rows, bracing and hauling with long-drawn cries as they drew in the nets and harvested in dripping baskets their catch, often so scanty, of *frutta di mare*. The children looked on, helped to pull, brought out their little stock of Italian words, made friends. So now they exchanged nods with the "standing-room" clientèle; there was Guiscardo, there Antonio, they knew them by name and waved and called across in half-whispers, getting answering nods and smiles that displayed rows of healthy white teeth. Look, there is even Mario, Mario from the Esquisito, who brings us the chocolate. He wants to see the conjuror, too, and he must have come early, for he is almost in front; but he does not see us, he is not paying attention; that is a way he has, even though he is a waiter. So we wave instead to the man who lets out the little boats on the beach; he is there too, standing at the back.

It had got to a quarter past nine, it got to almost half past. It was natural that we should be nervous. When would the children get to bed? It had been a mistake to bring them, for now it would be very hard to suggest breaking off their enjoyment before it had got well under way. The stalls had filled in time; all Torre, apparently, was there: the guests of the Grand Hotel, the guests of Villa Eleonora, familiar faces from the beach. We heard English and German and the sort of French that Rumanians speak with Italians. Madame Angiolieri herself sat two rows behind us, with her quiet, bald-headed spouse, who kept stroking his moustache with the two middle fingers of his right hand. Everybody had come late, but nobody too late. Cipolla made us wait for him.

He made us wait. That is probably the way to put it. He heightened the suspense by his delay in appearing. And we could see the point of this, too—only not when it was carried to extremes. Towards half past nine the audience began to clap—an amiable way of expressing justifiable impatience, evincing as it does an eagerness to applaud. For the little ones, this was a joy in itself—all children love to clap. From the popular sphere came loud cries of *"Pronti!" "Cominciamo!"* And lo, it seemed now as easy to begin as before it had been hard. A gong sounded, greeted by the standing rows with a many-voiced "Ah-h!" and the curtains parted. They revealed a platform furnished more like a schoolroom than like the theatre of a conjuring performance—largely because of the blackboard in the left foreground. There was a common yellow hat-stand, a few ordinary straw-bottomed chairs, and further back a little round table holding a water carafe and glass, also a tray with a liqueur glass and a flask of pale yellow liquid. We had still a few seconds of time to let these things sink in. Then, with no darkening of the house, Cavaliere Cipolla made his entry.

He came forward with a rapid step that expressed his eagerness to appear before his public and gave rise to the illusion that he had already come a long way to put himself at their service—whereas, of course, he had only been standing in the wings. His costume supported the fiction. A man of an age hard to determine, but by no means young; with a sharp, ravaged face, piercing eyes, compressed lips, small black waxed moustache, and a so-called imperial in the curve between mouth and chin. He was dressed for the street with a sort of complicated evening elegance, in a wide black pelerine with velvet collar and satin lining; which, in the hampered state of his arms, he held together in front with his white-gloved hands. He had a white scarf round his neck; a top hat with a curving brim sat far back on his head. Perhaps more than anywhere else the eighteenth century is still alive in Italy, and with it the charlatan and mountebank type so characteristic of the period. Only there, at any rate, does one still encounter really well-preserved specimens. Cipolla had in his whole appearance much of the historic type; his very clothes helped to conjure up the traditional figure with its blatantly, fantastically foppish air. His pretentious costume sat upon him, or rather hung upon him, most curiously, being in one place drawn too tight, in another a mass of awkward folds. There was something not quite in order about his figure, both front and back—that was plain later on. But I must emphasize the fact that there was not a trace of personal jocularity or clownishness in his pose, manner, or behaviour. On the contrary, there was complete seriousness, an absence of any humorous appeal: occasionally even a cross-grained pride, along with that curious, self-satisfied air so characteristic of the deformed. None of all this, however, prevented his appearance from being greeted with laughter from more than one quarter of the hall.

All the eagerness had left his manner. The swift entry had been merely an expression of energy, not of zeal. Standing at the footlights he negligently drew off his gloves, to display long yellow hands, one of them adorned with a seal ring with a lapis-lazuli in a high setting. As he stood there, his small hard eyes, with flabby pouches beneath them, roved appraisingly about the hall, not quickly, rather in a considered examination, pausing here and there upon a face with his lips clipped together, not speaking a word. Then with a display of skill as surprising as it was casual, he rolled his gloves into a ball and tossed them across a considerable distance into the glass on the table. Next from an inner pocket he drew forth a packet of cigarettes; you could see by the wrapper that they were the cheapest sort the government sells. With his fingertips he pulled out a cigarette and lighted it, without looking, from a quick-firing benzine lighter. He drew the smoke deep into his lungs and let it out again, tapping his foot, with both lips drawn in an arrogant grimace and the grey smoke streaming out between broken and saw-edged teeth.

With a keenness equal to his own his audience eyed him. The youths at the rear scowled as they peered at this cocksure creature to search out his secret weaknesses. He betrayed none. In fetching out and putting back the cigarettes his clothes got in his way. He had to turn back his pelerine, and in so doing revealed a riding-whip with a silver claw-handle that hung by a leather thong from his left forearm and looked decidedly out of place. You could see that he had on not evening clothes but a frock-coat, and under this, as he lifted it to get at his pocket, could be seen a striped sash worn about the body. Somebody behind me whispered that this sash went with his title of Cavaliere. I give the information for what it may be worth—personally, I never heard that the title carried such insignia with it. Perhaps the sash was sheer pose, like the way he stood there, without a word, casually and arrogantly puffing smoke into his audience's face.

People laughed, as I said. The merriment had become almost general when somebody in the "standing seats," in a loud, dry voice, remarked: "*Buona sera.*"

Cipolla cocked his head. "Who was that?" asked he, as though he had been dared. "Who was that just spoke? Well? First so bold and now so modest? *Paura*, eh?" He spoke with a rather high, asthmatic voice, which yet had a metallic quality. He waited.

"That was me," a youth at the rear broke into the stillness, seeing himself thus challenged. He was not far from us, a handsome fellow in a woollen shirt, with his coat hanging over one shoulder. He wore his curly, wiry hair in a high, dishevelled mop, the style affected by the youth of the awakened Fatherland; it gave him an African appearance that rather spoiled his looks. "*Bè!* That was me. It was your business to say it first, but I was trying to be friendly."

More laughter. The chap had a tongue in his head. "*Ha sciolto la scilinguágnolo*," I heard near me. After all, the retort was deserved.

"Ah, bravo!" answered Cipolla. "I like you, *giovanotto*. Trust me, I've had my eye on you for some time. People like you are just in my line. I can use them. And you are the pick of the lot, that's plain to see. You do what you like. Or is it possible you have ever not done what you liked—or even, maybe, what you didn't like? What somebody else liked, in short? Hark ye, my friend, that might be a pleasant change for you, to divide up the willing and the doing and stop tackling both jobs at once. Division of labour, *sistema americano, sa'!* For instance, suppose you were to show your tongue to this select and honourable audience here—your whole tongue, right down to the roots?"

"No, I won't," said the youth, hostilely. "Sticking out your tongue shows a bad bringing-up."

"Nothing of the sort," retorted Cipolla. "You would only be *doing* it. With all due respect to your bringing-up, I suggest that before I count ten, you will perform a right turn and stick out your tongue at the company here further than you knew yourself that you could stick it out."

He gazed at the youth, and his piercing eyes seemed to sink deeper into their sockets. "*Uno!*" said he. He had let his riding-whip slide down his arm and made it whistle once through the air. The boy faced about and put out his tongue, so long, so extendedly, that you could see it was the very uttermost in tongue which he had to offer. Then turned back, stony-faced, to his former position.

"That was me," mocked Cipolla, with a jerk of his head towards the youth. "*Bè!* That was me." Leaving the audience to enjoy its sensations, he turned towards the little round table, lifted the bottle, poured out a small glass of what was obviously cognac, and tipped it up with a practised hand.

The children laughed with all their hearts. They had understood practically nothing of what had been said, but it pleased them hugely that something so funny should happen, straightaway, between that queer man up there and somebody out of the audience. They had no preconception of what an "evening" would be like and were quite ready to find this a priceless beginning. As for us, we exchanged a glance and I remember that involuntarily I made with my lips the sound that Cipolla's whip had made when it cut the air. For the rest, it was plain that people did not know what to make of a preposterous beginning like this to a sleight-of-hand performance. They could not see why the *giovanotto*, who after all in a way had been their spokesman, should suddenly have turned on them to vent his incivility. They felt that he had behaved like a silly ass and withdrew their countenances from him in favour of the artist, who now came back from his refreshment table and addressed them as follows:

"Ladies and gentlemen," said he, in his wheezing, metallic voice, "you saw just now that I was rather sensitive on the score of the rebuke this hopeful young linguist saw fit to give me"—"*questo linguista di belle speranze*" was what he said, and we all laughed at the pun. "I am a man who sets some store by himself, you may take it from me. And I see no point in being wished a good-evening unless it is done courteously and in all seriousness. For anything else there is no occasion. When a man wishes me a good-evening he wishes himself one, for the audience will have one only if I do. So this lady-killer of Torre di Venere" (another thrust) "did well to testify that I have one tonight and that I can dispense with any wishes of his in the matter. I can boast of having good evenings almost without exception. One not so good does come my way now and again, but very seldom. My calling is hard and my health not of the best. I have a little physical defect which prevented me from doing my bit in the war for the greater glory of the Fatherland. It is perforce with my mental and spiritual parts that I conquer life—which after all only means conquering oneself. And I flatter myself that my achievements have aroused interest and respect among the educated public. The leading newspapers have lauded me, the *Corriere della Sera* did me the courtesy of calling me a phenomenon, and in Rome the brother of the *Duce* honoured me by his presence at one of my evenings. I should not have thought that in a relatively less important place" (laughter here, at the expense of poor little Torre) "I should have to give up the small personal habits which brilliant and elevated audiences had been ready to overlook. Nor did I think I had to stand being heckled by a person who seems to have been rather spoilt by the favours of the fair sex." All this of course at the expense of the youth whom Cipolla never tired of presenting in the guise of *donnaiuolo* and rustic Don Juan. His persistent thin-skinnedness and animosity were in striking contrast to the self-confidence and the worldly success he boasted of. One might have assumed that the *giovanotto* was merely the chosen butt of Cipolla's customary professional sallies, had not the very pointed witticisms betrayed a genuine antagonism. No one looking at the physical parts of the two men need have been at a loss for the explanation, even if the deformed man had not constantly played on the other's supposed success with the fair sex. "Well," Cipolla went on, "before beginning our entertainment this evening, perhaps you will permit me to make myself comfortable."

And he went towards the hat-stand to take off his things.

"Parla benissimo," asserted somebody in our neighborhood. So far, the man had done nothing; but what he had said was accepted as an achievement, by means of that he had made an impression. Among southern peoples speech is a constituent part of the pleasure of living, it enjoys far livelier social esteem than in the north. That national cement, the mother tongue, is paid symbolic honours down here, and there is something blithely symbolical in the pleasure people take in their respect for its forms and phonetics. They enjoy speaking, they enjoy listening; and they listen with discrimination. For the way a man speaks serves as a measure of his personal rank; carelessness and clumsiness are greeted with scorn, elegance and mastery are rewarded with social èclat. Wherefore the small man too, where it is a question of getting his effect, chooses his phrase nicely and turns it with care. On this count, then, at least, Cipolla had won his audience; though he by no means belonged to the class of men which the Italian, in a singular mixture of moral and aesthetic judgments, labels *"simpatico."*

After removing his hat, scarf, and mantle he came to the front of the stage, settling his coat, pulling down his cuffs with their large cuff-buttons, adjusting his absurd sash. He had very ugly hair; the top of his head, that is, was almost bald, while a narrow, black-varnished frizz of curls ran from front to back as though stuck on; the side hair, likewise blackened, was brushed forward to the corners of the eyes—it was, in short, the hairdressing of an old-fashioned circus-director, fantastic, but entirely suited to his outmoded personal type and worn with so much assurance as to take the edge off the public's sense of humour. The little physical defect of which he had warned us was now all too visible, though the nature of it was even now not very clear: the chest was too high, as is usual in such cases; but the corresponding malformation of the back did not sit between the shoulders, it took the form of a sort of hips or buttocks hump, which did not indeed hinder his movements but gave him a grotesque and dipping stride at every step he took. However, by mentioning his deformity beforehand he had broken the shock of it, and a delicate propriety of feeling appeared to reign throughout the hall.

"At your service," said Cipolla. "With your kind permission, we will begin the evening with some arithmetical tests."

Arithmetic? That did not sound much like sleight-of-hand. We began to have our suspicions that the man was sailing under a false flag, only we did not yet know which was the right one. I felt sorry on the children's account; but for the moment they were content simply to be there.

The numerical test which Cipolla now introduced was as simple as it was baffling. He began by fastening a piece of paper to the upper right-hand corner of the blackboard; then lifting it up, he wrote something underneath. He talked all the while, relieving the dryness of his offering by a constant flow of words, and showed himself a practised speaker, never at a loss for conversational turns of phrase. It was in keeping with the nature of his performance, and at the same time vastly entertained the children, that he went on to eliminate the gap between stage and audience, which had already been bridged over by the curious skirmish with the fisher lad: he had representatives from the audience mount the stage, and himself descended the wooden steps to seek personal contact with his public. And again, with individuals, he fell into his former taunting tone. I do not know how far that was a deliberate feature of his system; he preserved a serious, even a peevish air, but his audience, at least the more popular section, seemed convinced that that was all part of the game. So then, after he had written something and covered the writing by the paper, he desired that two persons should come up on the platform and help to perform the calculations. They would not be difficult, even for people not clever at figures. As usual, nobody volunteered, and Cipolla took care not to molest the more select portion of his audience. He kept to the populace. Turning to two sturdy young louts standing behind us, he beckoned them to the front, encouraging and scolding by turns. They should not stand there gaping, he said, unwilling to oblige the company. Actually, he got them in motion; with clumsy tread they came down the middle aisle, climbed the steps, and stood in front of the blackboard, grinning sheepishly at their comrades' shouts and applause. Cipolla joked with them for a few minutes, praised their heroic firmness of limb and the size of their hands, so well calculated to do this service for the public. Then he handed one of them the chalk and told him to write down the numbers as they were called out. But now the creature declared that he could not write! "*Non so scrivere,*" said he in his gruff voice, and his companion added that neither did he.

God knows whether they told the truth or whether they wanted to make game of Cipolla. Anyhow, the latter was far from sharing the general merriment which their confession aroused. He was insulted and disgusted. He sat there on a straw-bottomed chair in the centre of the stage with his legs crossed, smoking a fresh cigarette out of his cheap packet; obviously it tasted the better for the cognac he had indulged in while the yokels were stumping up the steps. Again he inhaled the smoke and let it stream out between curling lips. Swinging his leg, with his gaze sternly averted from the two shamelessly chuckling creatures and from the audience as well, he stared into space as one who withdraws himself and his dignity from the contemplation of an utterly despicable phenomenon.

"Scandalous," said he, in a sort of icy snarl. "Go back to your places! In Italy everybody can write—in all her greatness there is no room for ignorance and unenlightenment. To accuse her of them, in the hearing of this international company, is a cheap joke, in which you yourselves cut a very poor figure and humiliate the government and the whole country as well. If it is true that Torre di Venere is indeed the last refuge of such ignorance, then I must blush to have visited the place—being, as I already was, aware of its inferiority to Rome in more than one respect—"

Here Cipolla was interrupted by the youth with the Nubian coiffure and his jacket across his shoulder. His fighting spirit, as we now saw, had only abdicated temporarily, and he now flung himself into the breach in defence of his native heath. "That will do," said he loudly. "That's enough jokes about Torre. We all come from the place and we won't stand strangers making fun of it. These two chaps are our friends. Maybe they are no scholars, but even so they may be straighter than some folks in the room who are so free with their boasts about Rome, though they did not build it either."

That was capital. The young man had certainly cut his eyeteeth. And this sort of spectacle was good fun, even though it still further delayed the regular performance. It is always fascinating to listen to an altercation. Some people it simply amuses, they take a sort of kill-joy pleasure in not being principals. Others feel upset and uneasy, and my sympathies are with these latter, although on the present occasion I was under the impression that all this was part of the show—the analphabetic yokels no less than the *giovanotto* with the jacket. The children listened well pleased. They understood not at all, but the sound of the voices made them hold their breath. So this was a "magic evening"—at least it was the kind they have in Italy. They expressly found it "lovely."

Cipolla had stood up and with two of his scooping strides was at the footlights.

"Well, well, see who's here!" said he with grim cordiality. "An old acquaintance! A young man with his heart at the end of his tongue" (he used the word *linguaccia,* which means a coated tongue, and gave rise to much hilarity). "That will do, my friends," he turned to the yokels. "I do not need you now, I have business with this deserving young man here, *con questo torregiano di Venere,* this tower of Venus, who no doubt expects the gratitude of the fair as a reward for his prowess—"

"*Ah, non scherziamo!* We're talking earnest," cried out the youth. His eyes flashed, and he actually made as though to pull off his jacket and proceed to direct methods of settlement.

Cipolla did not take him too seriously. We had exchanged apprehensive glances; but he was dealing with a fellow-countryman and had his native soil beneath his feet. He kept quite cool and showed complete mastery of the situation. He looked at his audience, smiled, and made a sideways motion of the head towards the young cockerel as though calling the public to witness how the man's bumptiousness only served to betray the simplicity of his mind. And then, for the second time, something strange happened, which set Cipolla's calm superiority in an uncanny light, and in some mysterious and irritating way turned all the explosiveness latent in the air into matter for laughter.

Cipolla drew still nearer to the fellow, looking him in the eye with a peculiar gaze. He even came half-way down the steps that led into the auditorium on our left, so that he stood directly in front of the troublemaker, on slightly higher ground. The riding-whip hung from his arm.

"My son, you do not feel much like joking," he said. "It is only too natural, for anyone can see that you are not feeling too well. Even your tongue, which leaves something to be desired on the score of cleanliness, indicates acute disorder of the gastric system. An evening entertainment is no place for people in your state; you yourself, I can tell, were of several minds whether you would not do better to put on a flannel bandage and go to bed. It was not good judgment to drink so much of that very sour white wine this afternoon. Now you have such a colic you would like to double up with the pain. Go ahead, don't be embarrassed. There is a distinct relief that comes from bending over, in cases of intestinal cramp."

He spoke thus, word for word, with quite impressiveness and a kind of stern sympathy, and his eyes, plunged the while deep in the young man's, seemed to grow very tired and at the same time burning above their enlarged tear-ducts—they were the strangest eyes, you could tell that not manly pride alone was preventing the young adversary from withdrawing his gaze. And presently, indeed, all trace of its former arrogance was gone from the bronzed young face. He looked open-mouthed at the Cavaliere and the open mouth was drawn in a rueful smile.

"Double over," repeated Cipolla. "What else can you do? With a colic like that you *must* bend. Surely you will not struggle against the performance of a perfectly natural action just because somebody suggests it to you?"

Slowly the youth lifted his forearms, folded and squeezed them across his body; it turned a little sideways, then bent, lower and lower, the feet shifted, the knees turned inward, until he had become a picture of writhing pain, until he all but grovelled upon the ground. Cipolla let him stand for some seconds thus, then made a short cut through the air with his whip and went with his scooping stride back to the little table, where he poured himself out a cognac.

"Il boit beaucoup," asserted a lady behind us. Was that the only thing that struck her? We could not tell how far the audience grasped the situation. The fellow was standing upright again, with a sheepish grin—he looked as though he scarcely knew how it had all happened. The scene had been followed with tense interest and applauded at the end; there were shouts of *"Bravo, Cipolla!"* and *"Bravo, giovanotto!"* Apparently the issue of the duel was not looked upon as a personal defeat for the young man. Rather the audience encouraged him as one does an actor who succeeds in an unsympathetic rôle. Certainly his way of screwing himself up with cramp had been highly picturesque, its appeal was directly calculated to impress the gallery—in short, a fine dramatic performance. But I am not sure how far the audience were moved by that natural tactfulness in which the south excels, or how far it penetrated into the nature of what was going on.

The Cavaliere, refreshed, had lighted another cigarette. The numerical tests might now proceed. A young man was easily found in the back row who was willing to write down on the blackboard the numbers as they were dictated to him. Him too we knew; the whole entertainment had taken on an intimate character through our acquaintance with so many of the actors. This was the man who worked at the greengrocer's in the main street; he had served us several times, with neatness and dispatch. He wielded the chalk with clerkly confidence, while Cipolla descended to our level and walked with his deformed gait through the audience, collecting numbers as they were given, in two, three, and four places, and calling them out to the grocer's assistant, who wrote them down in a column. In all this, everything on both sides was calculated to amuse, with its jokes and its oratorical asides. The artist could not fail to hit on foreigners, who were not ready with their figures, and with them he was elaborately patient and chivalrous, to the great amusement of the natives, whom he reduced to confusion in their turn, by making them translate numbers that were given in English or French. Some people gave dates concerned with great events in Italian history. Cipolla took them up at once and made patriotic comments. Somebody shouted "Number one!" The Cavaliere, incensed at this as at every attempt to make game of him, retorted over his shoulder that he could not take less than two-place figures. Whereupon another joker cried out "Number two!" and was greeted with the applause and laughter which every reference to natural functions is sure to win among southerners.

When fifteen numbers stood in a long straggling row on the board, Cipolla called for a general adding-match. Ready reckoners might add in their heads, but pencil and paper were not forbidden. Cipolla, while the work went on, sat on his chair near the blackboard, smoked and grimaced, with the complacent, pompous air cripples so often have. The five-place addition was soon done. Somebody announced the answer, somebody else confirmed it, a third had arrived at a slightly different result, but the fourth agreed with the first and second. Cipolla got up, tapped some ash from his coat, and lifted the paper at the upper right-hand corner of the board to display the writing. The correct answer, a sum close on a million, stood there; he had written it down beforehand.

Astonishment, and loud applause. The children were overwhelmed. How had he done that, they wanted to know. We told them it was a trick, not easily explainable offhand. In short, the man was a conjuror. This was what a sleight-of-hand evening was like, so now they knew. First the fisherman had cramp, and then the right answer was written down beforehand—it was all simply glorious, and we saw with dismay that despite the hot eyes and the hand of the clock at almost half past ten, it would be very hard to get them away. There would be tears. And yet it was plain that this magician did not "magick"—at least not in the accepted sense, of manual dexterity—and that the entertainment was not at all suitable for children. Again, I do not know, either, what the audience really thought. Obviously there was grave doubt whether its answers had been given of "free choice"; here and there an individual might have answered of his own motion, but on the whole Cipolla certainly selected his people and thus kept the whole procedure in his own hands and directed it towards the given result. Even so, one had to admire the quickness of his calculations, however much one felt disinclined to admire anything else about the performance. Then his patriotism, his irritable sense of dignity—the Cavaliere's own countrymen might feel in their element with all that and continue in a laughing mood; but the combination certainly gave us outsiders food for thought.

Cipolla himself saw to it—though without giving them a name—that the nature of his powers should be clear beyond a doubt to even the least-instructed person. He alluded to them, of course, in his talk—and he talked without stopping—but only in vague, boastful, self-advertising phrases. He went on awhile with experiments on the same lines as the first, merely making them more complicated by introducing operations in multiplying, subtracting, and dividing; then he simplified them to the last degree in order to bring out the method. He simply had numbers "guessed" which were previously written under the paper; and the guess was nearly always right. One guesser admitted that he had had in mind to give a certain number, when Cipolla's whip went whistling through the air, and a quite different one slipped out, which proved to be the "right" one. Cipolla's shoulders shook. He pretended admiration for the powers of the people he questioned. But in all his compliments there was something fleering and derogatory; the victims could scarcely have relished them much, although they smiled, and although they might easily have set down some part of the applause to their own credit. Moreover, I had not the impression that the artist was popular with his public. A certain ill will and reluctance were in the air, but courtesy kept such feelings in check, as did Cipolla's competency and his stern self-confidence. Even the riding-whip, I think, did much to keep rebellion from becoming overt.

From tricks with numbers he passed to tricks with cards. There were two packs, which he drew out of his pockets, and so much I still remember, that the basis of the tricks he played with them was as follows: from the first pack he drew three cards and thrust them without looking at them inside his coat. Another person then drew three out of the second pack, and these turned out to be the same as the first three—not invariably all the three, for it did happen that only two were the same. But in the majority of cases Cipolla triumphed, showing his three cards with a little bow in acknowledgment of the applause with which his audience conceded his possession of strange powers—strange whether for good or evil. A young man in the front row, to our right, an Italian, with proud, finely chiselled features, rose up and said that he intended to assert his own will in his choice and consciously to resist any influence, of whatever sort. Under these circumstances, what did Cipolla think would be the result? "You will," answered the Cavaliere, "make my task somewhat more difficult thereby. As for the result, your resistance will not alter it in the least. Freedom exists, and also the will exists; but freedom of the will does not exist, for a will that aims at its own freedom aims at the unknown. You are free to draw or not to draw. But if you draw, you will draw the right cards—the more certainly, the more wilfully obstinate your behaviour."

One must admit that he could not have chosen his words better, to trouble the waters and confuse the mind. The refractory youth hesitated before drawing. Then he pulled out a card and at once demanded to see if it was among the chosen three. "But why?" queried Cipolla. "Why do things by halves?" Then, as the other defiantly insisted, "*E servito,*" said the juggler, with a gesture of exaggerated servility; and held out the three cards fanwise, without looking at them himself. The left-hand card was the one drawn.

Amid general applause, the apostle of freedom sat down. How far Cipolla employed small tricks and manual dexterity to help out his natural talents, the deuce only knew. But even without them the result would have been the same: the curiosity of the entire audience was unbounded and universal, everybody both enjoyed the amazing character of the entertainment and unanimously conceded the professional skill of the performer. "*Lavora bene,*" we heard, here and there in our neighbourhood; it signified the triumph of objective judgment over antipathy and repressed resentment.

After his last, incomplete, yet so much the more telling success, Cipolla had at once fortified himself with another cognac. Truly he did "drink a lot," and the fact made a bad impression. But obviously he needed the liquor and the cigarettes for the replenishment of his energy, upon which, as he himself said, heavy demands were made in all directions. Certainly in the intervals he looked very ill, exhausted and hollow-eyed. Then the little glassful would redress the balance, and the flow of lively, self-confident chatter run on, while the smoke he inhaled gushed out grey from his lungs. I clearly recall that he passed from the card-tricks to parlour games—the kind based on certain powers which in human nature are higher or else lower than human reason: on intuition and "magnetic" transmission; in short, upon a low type of manifestation. What I do not remember is the precise order things came in. And I will not bore you with a description of these experiments; everybody knows them, everybody has at one time or another taken part in this finding of hidden articles, this blind carrying out of a series of acts, directed by a force that proceeds from organism to organism by unexplored paths. Everybody has had his little glimpse into the equivocal, impure, inexplicable nature of the occult, has been conscious of both curiosity and contempt, has shaken his head over the human tendency of those who deal in it to help themselves out with humbuggery, though, after all, the humbuggery is no disproof whatever of the genuineness of the other elements in the dubious amalgam. I can only say here that each single circumstance gains in weight and the whole greatly in impressiveness when it is a man like Cipolla who is the chief actor and guiding spirit in the sinister business. He sat smoking at the rear of the stage, his back to the audience while they conferred. The object passed from hand to hand which it was his task to find, with which he was to perform some action agreed upon beforehand. Then he would start to move zigzag through the hall, with his head thrown back and one hand outstretched, the other clasped in that of a guide who was in the secret but enjoined to keep himself perfectly passive, with his thoughts directed upon the agreed goal. Cipolla moved with the bearing typical in these experiments: now groping upon a false start, now with a quick forward thrust, now pausing as though to listen and by sudden inspiration correcting his course. The rôles seemed reversed, the stream of influence was moving in the contrary direction, as the artist himself pointed out, in his ceaseless flow of discourse. The suffering, receptive, performing part was now his, the will he had before imposed on others was shut out, he acted in obedience to a voiceless common will which was in the air. But he made it perfectly clear that it all came to the same thing. The capacity for self-surrender, he said, for becoming a tool, for the most unconditional and utter self-abnegation, was but the reverse side of that other power to will and to command. Commanding and obeying formed together one single principle, one indissoluble unity; he who knew how to obey knew also how to command, and conversely; the one idea was comprehended in the other, as people and leader were comprehended in one another. But that which was *done,* the highly exacting and exhausting performance, was in every case his, the leader's and mover's, in whom the will became obedience, the obedience will, whose person was the cradle and womb of both, and who thus suffered enormous hardship. Repeatedly he emphasized the fact that his lot was a hard one—presumably to account for his need of stimulant and his frequent recourse to the little glass.

Thus he groped his way forward, like a blind seer, led and sustained by the mysterious common will. He drew a pin set with a stone out of its hiding-place in an Englishwoman's shoe, carried it, halting and pressing on by turns, to another lady—Signora Angiolieri—and handed it to her on bended knee, with the words it had been agreed he was to utter. "I present you with this in token of my respect," was the sentence. Their sense was obvious, but the words themselves not easy to hit upon, for the reason that they had been agreed on in French; the language complication seemed to us a little malicious, implying as it did a conflict between the audience's natural interest in the success of the miracle, and their desire to witness the humiliation of this presumptuous man. It was a strange sight: Cipolla on his knees before the signora, wrestling, amid efforts at speech, after knowledge of the pre-ordained words. "I must say something," he said, "and I feel clearly what it is I must say. But I also feel that if it passed my lips it would be wrong. Be careful not to help me unintentionally!" he cried out, though very likely that was precisely what he was hoping for. *"Pensez très fort,"* he cried all at once, in bad French, and then burst out with the required words—in Italian, indeed, but with the final substantive pronounced in the sister tongue, in which he was probably far from fluent: he said *vénération* instead of *venerazione*, with an impossible nasal. And this partial success, after the complete success before it, the finding of the pin, the presentation of it on his knees to the right person—was almost more impressive than if he had got the sentence exactly right, and evoked bursts of admiring applause.

Cipolla got up from his knees and wiped the perspiration from his brow. You understand that this experiment with the pin was a single case, which I describe because it sticks in my memory. But he changed his method several times and improvised a number of variations suggested by his contact with his audience; a good deal of time thus went by. He seemed to get particular inspiration from the person of our landlady; she drew him on to the most extraordinary displays of clairvoyance. "It does not escape me, madame," he said to her, "that there is something unusual about you, some special and honourable distinction. He who has eyes to see descries about your lovely brow an aureola —if I mistake not, it once was stronger than now—a slowly paling radiance . . . hush, not a word! Don't help me. Beside you sits your husband—yes?" He turned towards the silent Signor Angiolieri. "You are the husband of this lady, and your happiness is complete. But in the midst of this happiness memories rise . . . the past, signora, so it seems to me, plays an important part in your present. You knew a king . . . has not a king crossed your path in bygone days?"

"No," breathed the dispenser of our midday soup, her golden-brown eyes gleaming in the noble pallor of her face.

"No? No, not a king; I meant that generally, I did not mean literally a king. Not a king, not a prince, and a prince after all, a king of a loftier realm; it was a great artist, at whose side you once—you would contradict me, and yet I am not wholly wrong. Well, then! It was a woman, a great, a world-renowned woman artist, whose friendship you enjoyed in your tender years, whose sacred memory overshadows and transfigures your whole existence. Her name? Need I utter it, whose fame has long been bound up with the Fatherland's, immortal as its own? Eleonora Duse," he finished, softly and with much solemnity.

The little woman bowed her head, overcome. The applause was like a patriotic demonstration. Nearly everyone there knew about Signora Angiolieri's wonderful past; they were all able to confirm the Cavaliere's intuition—not least the present guests of Casa Eleonora. But we wondered how much of the truth he had learned as the result of professional inquiries made on his arrival. Yet I see no reason at all to cast doubt, on rational grounds, upon powers which, before our very eyes, became fatal to their possessor.

At this point there was an intermission. Our lord and master withdrew. Now I confess that almost ever since the beginning of my tale I have looked forward with dread to this moment in it. The thoughts of men are mostly not hard to read; in this case they are very easy. You are sure to ask why we did not choose this moment to go away—and I must continue to owe you an answer. I do not know why. I cannot defend myself. By this time it was certainly eleven, probably later. The children were asleep. The last series of tests had been too long, nature had had her way. They were sleeping in our laps, the little one on mine, the boy on his mother's. That was, in a way, a consolation; but at the same time it was also ground for compassion and a clear leading to take them home to bed. And I give you my word that we wanted to obey this touching admonition, we seriously wanted to. We roused the poor things and told them it was now high time to go. But they were no sooner conscious than they began to resist and implore—you know how horrified children are at the thought of leaving before the end of a thing. No cajoling has any effect, you have to use force. It was so lovely, they wailed. How did we know what was coming next? Surely we could not leave until after the intermission; they liked a little nap now and again—only not go home, only not go to bed, while the beautiful evening was still going on!

We yielded, but only for the moment, of course—so far as we knew—only for a little while, just a few minutes longer. I cannot excuse our staying, scarcely can I even understand it. Did we think, having once said A, we had to say B—having once brought the children hither we had to let them stay? No, it is not good enough. Were we ourselves so highly entertained? Yes, and no. Our feelings for Cavaliere Cipolla were of a very mixed kind, but so were the feelings of the whole audience, if I mistake not, and nobody left. Were we under the sway of a fascination which emanated from this man who took so strange a way to earn his bread; a fascination which he gave out independently of the programme and even between the tricks and which paralysed our resolve? Again, sheer curiosity may account for something. One was curious to know how such an evening turned out; Cipolla in his remarks having all along hinted that he had tricks in his bag stranger than any he had yet produced.

But all that is not it—or at least it is not all of it. More correct it would be to answer the first question with another. Why had we not left Torre di Venere itself before now? To me the two questions are one and the same, and in order to get out of the impasse I might simply say that I had answered it already. For, as things had been in Torre in general: queer, uncomfortable, troublesome, tense, oppressive, so precisely they were here in this hall tonight. Yes, more than precisely. For it seemed to be the fountainhead of all the uncanniness and all the strained feelings which had oppressed the atmosphere of our holiday. This man whose return to the stage we were waiting was the personification of all that; and, as we had not gone away in general, so to speak, it would have been inconsistent to do it in the particular case. You may call this an explanation, you may call it inertia, as you see fit. Any argument more to the purpose I simply do not know how to adduce.

Well, there was an interval of ten minutes, which grew into nearly twenty. The children remained awake. They were enchanted by our compliance, and filled the break to their own satisfaction by renewing relations with the popular sphere, with Antonio, Guiscardo, and the canoe man. They put their hands to their mouths and called messages across, appealing to us for the Italian words. "Hope you have a good catch tomorrow, a whole netful!" They called to Mario, Esquisito Mario: *"Mario, una cioccolata e biscotti!"* And this time he heeded and answered with a smile: *"Subito, signorini!"* Later we had reason to recall this kindly, if rather absent and pensive smile.

Thus the interval passed, the gong sounded. The audience, which had scattered in conversation, took their places again, the children sat up straight in their chairs with their hands in their laps. The curtain had not been dropped. Cipolla came forward again, with his dipping stride, and began to introduce the second half of the programme with a lecture.

Let me state once for all that this self-confident cripple was the most powerful hypnotist I have ever seen in my life. It was pretty plain now that he threw dust in the public eye and advertised himself as a prestidigitator on account of police regulations which would have prevented him from making his living by the exercise of his powers. Perhaps this eye-wash is the usual thing in Italy; it may be permitted or even connived at by the authorities. Certainly the man had from the beginning made little concealment of the actual nature of his operations; and this second half of the programme was quite frankly and exclusively devoted to one sort of experiment. While he still practised some rhetorical circumlocutions, the tests themselves were one long series of attacks upon the will-power, the loss or compulsion of volition. Comic, exciting, amazing by turns, by midnight they were still in full swing; we ran the gamut of all the phenomena this natural-unnatural field has to show, from the unimpressive at one end of the scale to the monstrous at the other. The audience laughed and applauded as they followed the grotesque details; shook their heads, clapped their knees, fell very frankly under the spell of this stern, self-assured personality. At the same time I saw signs that they were not quite complacent, not quite unconscious of the peculiar ignominy which lay, for the individual and for the general, in Cipolla's triumphs.

Two main features were constant in all the experiments: the liquor glass and the claw-handled riding-whip. The first was always invoked to add fuel to his demoniac fires; without it, apparently, they might have burned out. On this score we might even have felt pity for the man; but the whistle of his scourge, the insulting symbol of his domination, before which we all cowered, drowned out every sensation save a dazed and outbraved submission to his power. Did he then lay claim to our sympathy to boot? I was struck by a remark he made—it suggested no less. At the climax of his experiments, by stroking and breathing upon a certain young man who had offered himself as a subject and already proved himself a particularly susceptible one, he had not only put him into the condition known as deep trance and extended his insensible body by neck and feet across the backs of two chairs, but had actually sat down on the rigid form as on a bench, without making it yield. The sight of this unholy figure in a frock-coat squatted on the stiff body was horrible and incredible; the audience, convinced that the victim of this scientific diversion must be suffering, expressed its sympathy: "*Ah, poveretto!*" Poor soul, poor soul! "*Poor soul!*" Cipolla mocked them, with some bitterness. "Ladies and gentlemen, you are barking up the wrong tree. *Sono io il poveretto.* I am the person who is suffering, I am the one to be pitied." We pocketed the information. Very good. Maybe the experiment was at his expense, maybe it was he who had suffered the cramp when the *giovanotto* over there had made the faces. But appearances were all against it; and one does not feel like saying *poveretto* to a man who is suffering to bring about the humiliation of others.

I have got ahead of my story and lost sight of the sequence of events. To this day my mind is full of the Cavaliere's feats of endurance; only I do not recall them in their order—which does not matter. So much I do know: that the longer and more circumstantial tests, which got the most applause, impressed me less than some of the small ones which passed quickly over. I remember the young man whose body Cipolla converted into a board, only because of the accompanying remarks which I have quoted. An elderly lady in a cane-seated chair was lulled by Cipolla in the delusion that she was on a voyage to India and gave a voluble account of her adventures by land and sea. But I found this phenomenon less impressive than one which followed immediately after the intermission. A tall, well-built, soldierly man was unable to lift his arm, after the hunchback had told him that he could not and given a cut through the air with his whip. I can still see the face of that stately, mustachioed colonel smiling and clenching his teeth as he struggled to regain his lost freedom of action. A staggering performance! He seemed to be exerting his will, and in vain; the trouble, however, was probably simply that he could not will. There was involved here that recoil of the will upon itself which paralyses choice—as our tyrant had previously explained to the Roman gentleman.

Still less can I forget the touching scene, at once comic and horrible, with Signora Angiolieri. The Cavaliere, probably in his first bold survey of the room, had spied out her ethereal lack of resistance to his power. For actually he bewitched her, literally drew her out of her seat, out of her row, and away with him whither he willed. And in order to enhance his effect, he bade Signor Angiolieri call upon his wife by her name, to throw, as it were, all the weight of his existence and his rights in her into the scale, to rouse by the voice of her husband everything in his spouse's soul which could shield her virtue against the evil assaults of magic. And how vain it all was! Cipolla was standing at some distance from the couple, when he made a single cut with his whip through the air. It caused our landlady to shudder violently and turn her face towards him. "Sofronia!" cried Signor Angiolieri—we had not known that Signora Angiolieri's name was Sofronia. And he did well to call, everybody saw that there was no time to lose. His wife kept her face turned in the direction of the diabolical Cavaliere, who with his ten long yellow fingers was making passes at his victim, moving backwards as he did so, step by step. Then Signora Angiolieri, her pale face gleaming, rose up from her seat, turned right round, and began to glide after him. Fatal and forbidding sight! Her face as though moonstruck, stiff-armed, her lovely hands lifted a little at the wrists, the feet as it were together, she seemed to float slowly out of her row and after the tempter. "Call her, sir, keep on calling," prompted the redoubtable man. And Signor Angiolieri, in a weak voice, called: "Sofronia!" Ah, again and again he called; as his wife went further off he even curved one hand round his lips and beckoned with the other as he called. But the poor voice of love and duty echoed unheard, in vain, behind the lost one's back; the signora swayed along, moonstruck, deaf, enslaved; she glided into the middle aisle and down it towards the fingering hunchback, towards the door. We were convinced, we were driven to the conviction, that she would have followed her master, had he so willed it, to the ends of the earth.

"*Accidente!*" cried out Signor Angiolieri, in genuine affright, springing up as the exit was reached. But at the same moment the Cavaliere put aside, as it were, the triumphal crown and broke off. "Enough, signora, I thank you," he said, and offered his arm to lead her back to her husband. "Signor," he greeted the latter, "here is your wife. Unharmed, with my compliments, I give her into your hands. Cherish with all the strength of your manhood a treasure which is so wholly yours, and let your zeal be quickened by knowing that there are powers stronger than reason or virtue, and not always so magnanimously ready to relinquish their prey!"

Poor Signor Angiolieri, so quiet, so bald! He did not look as though he would know how to defend his happiness, even against powers much less demoniac than these which were now adding mockery to frightfulness. Solemnly and pompously the Cavaliere retired to the stage, amid applause to which his eloquence gave double strength. It was this particular episode, I feel sure, that set the seal upon his ascendancy. For now he made them dance, yes, literally; and the dancing lent a dissolute, abandoned, topsy-turvy air to the scene, a drunken abdication of the critical spirit which had so long resisted the spell of this man. Yes, he had had to fight to get the upper hand—for instance against the animosity of the young Roman gentleman, whose rebellious spirit threatened to serve others as a rallying-point. But it was precisely upon the importance of example that the Cavaliere was so strong. He had the wit to make his attack at the weakest point and to choose as his first victim that feeble, ecstatic youth whom he had previously made into a board. The master had but to look at him, when this young man would fling himself back as though struck by lightning, place his hands rigidly at his sides, and fall into a state of military somnambulism, in which it was plain to any eye that he was open to the most absurd suggestion that might be made to him. He seemed quite content in his abject state, quite pleased to be relieved of the burden of voluntary choice. Again and again he offered himself as a subject and gloried in the model facility he had in losing consciousness. So now he mounted the platform, and a single cut of the whip was enough to make him dance to the Cavaliere's orders, in a kind of complacent ecstasy, eyes closed, head nodding, lank limbs flying in all directions.

It looked unmistakably like enjoyment, and other recruits were not long in coming forward: two other young men, one humbly and one well dressed, were soon jigging alongside the first. But now the gentleman from Rome bobbed up again, asking defiantly if the Cavaliere would engage to make him dance too, even against his will.

"Even against your will," answered Cipolla, in unforgettable accents. That frightful "*anche se non vuole*" still rings in my ears. The struggle began. After Cipolla had taken another little glass and lighted a fresh cigarette he stationed the Roman at a point in the middle aisle and himself took up a position some distance behind him, making his whip whistle through the air as he gave the order: "*Balla!*" His opponent did not stir. "*Balla!*" repeated the Cavaliere incisively, and snapped his whip. You saw the young man move his neck round in his collar; at the same time one hand lifted slightly at the wrist, one ankle turned outward. But that was all, for the time at least; merely a tendency to twitch, now sternly repressed, now seeming about to get the upper hand. It escaped nobody that here a heroic obstinacy, a fixed resolve to resist, must needs be conquered; we were beholding a gallant effort to strike out and save the honour of the human race. He twitched but danced not; and the struggle was so prolonged that the Cavaliere had to divide his attention between it and the stage, turning now and then to make his riding-whip whistle in the direction of the dancers, as it were to keep them in leash. At the same time he advised the audience that no fatigue was involved in such activities, however long they went on, since it was not the automatons up there who danced, but himself. Then once more his eye would bore itself into the back of the Roman's neck and lay siege to the strength of purpose which defied him.

One saw it waver, that strength of purpose, beneath the repeated summons and whip-crackings. Saw with an objective interest which yet was not quite free from traces of sympathetic emotion—from pity, even from a cruel kind of pleasure. If I understand what was going on, it was the negative character of the young man's fighting position which was his undoing. It is likely that *not* willing is not a practicable state of mind; *not* to want to do something may be in the long run a mental content impossible to subsist on. Between not willing a certain thing and not willing at all—in other words, yielding to another person's will—there may lie too small a space for the idea of freedom to squeeze into. Again, there were the Cavaliere's persuasive words, woven in among the whip-crackings and commands, as he mingled effects that were his own secret with others of a bewilderingly psychological kind. "*Balla!*" said he. "Who wants to torture himself like that? Is forcing yourself your idea of freedom? *Una ballatina!* Why, your arms and legs are aching for it. What a relief to give way to them—there, you are dancing already! That is no struggle any more, it is a pleasure!" And so it was. The jerking and twitching of the refractory youth's limbs had at last got the upper hand; he lifted his arms, then his knees, his joints quite suddenly relaxed, he flung his legs and danced, and amid bursts of applause the Cavaliere led him to join the row of puppets on the stage. Up there we could see his face as he "enjoyed" himself; it was clothed in a broad grin and the eyes were half-shut. In a way, it was consoling to see that he was having a better time than he had had in the hour of his pride.

His "fall" was, I may say, an epoch. The ice was completely broken, Cipolla's triumph had reached its height. The Circe's wand, that whistling leather whip with the claw handle, held absolute sway. At one time—it must have been well after midnight—not only were there eight or ten persons dancing on the little stage, but in the hall below a varied animation reigned, and a long-toothed Anglo-Saxoness in a pince-nez left her seat of her own motion to perform a tarantella in the centre aisle. Cipolla was lounging in a cane-seated chair at the left of the stage, gulping down the smoke of a cigarette and breathing it impudently out through his bad teeth. He tapped his foot and shrugged his shoulders, looking down upon the abandoned scene in the hall; now and then he snapped his whip backwards at a laggard upon the stage. The children were awake at the moment. With shame I speak of them. For it was not good to be here, least of all for them; that we had not taken them away can only be explained by saying that we had caught the general devil-may-careness of the hour. By that time it was all one. Anyhow, thank goodness, they lacked understanding for the disreputable side of the entertainment, and in their innocence were perpetually charmed by the unheard-of indulgence which permitted them to be present at such a thing as a magician's "evening." Whole quarter-hours at a time they drowsed on our laps, waking refreshed and rosy-cheeked, with sleep-drunken eyes, to laugh to bursting at the leaps and jumps the magician made those people up there make. They had not thought it would be so jolly; they joined with their clumsy little hands in every round of applause. And jumped for joy upon their chairs, as was their wont, when Cipolla beckoned to their friend Mario from the Esquisito, beckoned to him just like a picture in a book, holding his hand in front of his nose and bending and straightening the forefinger by turns.

Mario obeyed. I can see him now going up the stairs to Cipolla, who continued to beckon him, in that droll, picture-book sort of way. He hesitated for a moment at first; that, too, I recall quite clearly. During the whole evening he had lounged against a wooden pillar at the side entrance, with his arms folded, or else with his hands thrust into his jacket pockets. He was on our left, near the youth with the militant hair, and had followed the performance attentively, so far as we had seen, if with no particular animation and God knows how much comprehension. He could not much relish being summoned thus, at the end of the evening. But it was only too easy to see why he obeyed. After all, obedience was his calling in life; and then, how should a simple lad like him find it within his human capacity to refuse compliance to a man so throned and crowned as Cipolla at that hour? Willy-nilly he left his column and with a word of thanks to those making way for him he mounted the steps with a doubtful smile on his full lips.

Picture a thickset youth of twenty years, with clipt hair, a low forehead, and heavy-lidded eyes of an indefinite grey, shot with green and yellow. These things I knew from having spoken with him, as we often had. There was a saddle of freckles on the flat nose, the whole upper half of the face retreated behind the lower, and that again was dominated by thick lips that parted to show the salivated teeth. These thick lips and the veiled look of the eyes lent the whole face a primitive melancholy—it was that which had drawn us to him from the first. In it was not the faintest trace of brutality—indeed, his hands would have given the lie to such an idea, being unusually slender and delicate even for a southerner. They were hands by which one liked being served.

We knew him humanly without knowing him personally, if I may make that distinction. We saw him nearly every day, and felt a certain kindness for his dreamy ways, which might at times be actual inattentiveness, suddenly transformed into a redeeming zeal to serve. His mien was serious, only the children could bring a smile to his face. It was not sulky, but uningratiating, without intentional effort to please—or rather, it seemed to give up being pleasant in the conviction that it could not succeed. We should have remembered Mario in any case, as one of those homely recollections of travel which often stick in the mind better than more important ones. But of his circumstances we knew no more than that his father was a petty clerk in the Municipio and his mother took in washing.

His white waiter's-coat became him better than the faded striped suit he wore, with a gay coloured scarf instead of a collar, the ends tucked into his jacket. He neared Cipolla, who however did not leave off that motion of his finger before his nose, so that Mario had to come still closer, right up to the chair-seat and the master's legs. Whereupon the latter spread out his elbows and seized the lad, turning him so that we had a view of his face. Then gazed him briskly up and down, with a careless, commanding eye.

"Well, *ragazzo mio*, how comes it we make acquaintance so late in the day? But believe me, I made yours long ago. Yes, yes, I've had you in my eye this long while and known what good stuff you were made of. How could I go and forget you again? Well, I've had a good deal to think about. . . . Now tell me, what is your name? The first name, that's all I want."

"My name is Mario," the young man answered, in a low voice.

"Ah, Mario. Very good. Yes, yes, there is such a name, quite a common name, a classic name too, one of those which preserve the heroic traditions of the Fatherland. *Bravo! Salve!*" And he flung up his arm slantingly above his crooked shoulder, palm outward, in the Roman salute. He may have been slightly tipsy by now, and no wonder; but he spoke as before, clearly, fluently, and with emphasis. Though about this time there had crept into his voice a gross, autocratic note, and a kind of arrogance was in his sprawl.

"Well, now, Mario *mio*," he went on, "it's a good thing you came this evening, and that's a pretty scarf you've got on; it is becoming to your style of beauty. It must stand you in good stead with the girls, the pretty pretty girls of Torre—"

From the row of youths, close by the place where Mario had been standing, sounded a laugh. It came from the youth with the militant hair. He stood there, his jacket over his shoulder, and laughed outright, rudely and scornfully.

Mario gave a start. I think it was a shrug, but he may have started and then hastened to cover the movement by shrugging his shoulders, as much as to say that the neckerchief and the fair sex were matters of equal indifference to him.

The Cavaliere gave a downward glance.

"We needn't trouble about him," he said. "He is jealous, because your scarf is so popular with the girls, maybe partly because you and I are so friendly up here. Perhaps he'd like me to put him in mind of his colic—I could do it free of charge. Tell me, Mario. You've come here this evening for a bit of fun—and in the daytime you work in an ironmonger's shop?"

"In a café," corrected the youth.

"Oh, in a café. That's where Cipolla nearly came a cropper! What you are is a cup-bearer, a Ganymede—I like that, it is another classical allusion—*Salvietta!*" Again the Cavaliere saluted, to the huge gratification of his audience.

Mario smiled too. "But before that," he interpolated, in the interest of accuracy, "I worked for a while in a shop in Portoclemente." He seemed visited by a natural desire to assist the prophecy by dredging out its essential features.

"There, didn't I say so? In an ironmonger's shop?"

"They kept combs and brushes," Mario got round it.

"Didn't I say that you were not always a Ganymede? Not always at the sign of the serviette? Even when Cipolla makes a mistake, it is a kind that makes you believe in him. Now tell me: Do you believe in me?"

An indefinite gesture.

"A half-way answer," commented the Cavaliere. "Probably it is not easy to win your confidence. Even for me, I can see, it is not so easy. I see in your features a reserve, a sadness, *un tratto di malinconia* . . . tell me" (he seized Mario's hand persuasively) "have you troubles?"

"*Nossignore,*" answered Mario, promptly and decidedly.

"You *have* troubles," insisted the Cavaliere, bearing down the denial by the weight of his authority. "Can't I see? Trying to pull wool over Cipolla's eyes, are you? Of course, about the girls—it is a girl, isn't it? You have love troubles?"

Mario gave a vigorous head-shake. And again the *giovanotto's* brutal laugh rang out. The Cavaliere gave heed. His eyes were roving about somewhere in the air, but he cocked an ear to the sound, then swung his whip backwards, as he had once or twice before in his conversation with Mario, that none of his puppets might flag in their zeal. The gesture had nearly cost him his new prey: Mario gave a sudden start in the direction of the steps. But Cipolla had him in his clutch.

"Not so fast," said he. "That would be fine, wouldn't it? So you want to skip, do you, Granymede, right in the middle of the fun, or rather, when it is just beginning? Stay with me, I'll show you something nice. I'll convince you. You have no reason to worry, I promise you. This girl—you know her and others know her too—what's her name? Wait! I read the name in your eyes, it is on the tip of my tongue and yours too—"

"Silvestra!" shouted the *giovanotto* from below.

The Cavaliere's face did not change.

"Aren't there the forward people?" he asked, not looking down, more as in undisturbed converse with Mario. "Aren't there the young fighting-cocks that crow in season and out? Takes the word out of your mouth, the conceited fool, and seems to think he has some special right to it. Let him be. But Silvestra, your Silvestra—ah, what a girl that is! What a prize! Brings your heart into your mouth to see her walk or laugh or breathe, she is so lovely. And her round arms when she washes, and tosses her head back to get the hair out of her eyes! An angel from paradise!"

Mario stared at him, his head thrust forward. He seemed to have forgotten the audience, forgotten where he was. The red rings round his eyes had got larger, they looked as though they were painted on. His thick lips parted.

"And she makes you suffer, this angel," went on Cipolla, "or, rather, you make yourself suffer for her—there is a difference, my lad, a most important difference, let me tell you. There are misunderstandings in love, maybe nowhere else in the world are there so many. I know what you are thinking: what does this Cipolla, with his little physical defect, know about love? Wrong, all wrong, he knows a lot. He has a wide and powerful understanding of its workings, and it pays to listen to his advice. But let's leave Cipolla out, cut him out altogether and think only of Silvestra, your peerless Silvestra! What! Is she to give any young gamecock the preference, so that he can laugh while you cry? To prefer him to a chap like you, so full of feeling and so sympathetic? Not very likely, is it? It is impossible—we know better, Cipolla and she. If I were to put myself in her place and choose between the two of you, a tarry lout like that—a codfish, a sea-urchin—and a Mario, a knight of the serviette, who moves among gentlefolk and hands round refreshments with an air—my word, but my heart would speak in no uncertain tones—it knows to whom I gave it long ago. It is time that he should see and understand, my chosen one! It is time that you see me and recognize me, Mario, my beloved! Tell me, who am I?"

It was grisly, the way the betrayer made himself irresistible, wreathed and coquetted with his crooked shoulder, languished with the puffy eyes, and showed his splintered teeth in a sickly smile. And alas, at his beguiling words, what was come of our Mario? It is hard for me to tell, hard as it was for me to see; for here was nothing less than an utter abandonment of the inmost soul, a public exposure of timid and deluded passion and rapture. He put his hands across his mouth, his shoulders rose and fell with his pantings. He could not, it was plain, trust his eyes and ears for joy, and the one thing he forgot was precisely that he could not trust them. "Silvestra!" he breathed, from the very depths of his vanquished heart.

"Kiss me!" said the hunchback. "Trust me, I love thee. Kiss me here." And with the tip of his index finger, hand, arm, and little finger outspread, he pointed to his cheek, near the mouth. And Mario bent and kissed him.

It had grown very still in the room. That was a monstrous moment, grotesque and thrilling, the moment of Mario's bliss. In that evil span of time, crowded with a sense of the illusiveness of all joy, one sound became audible, and that not quite at once, but on the instant of the melancholy and ribald meeting between Mario's lips and the repulsive flesh which thrust itself forward for his caress. It was the sound of a laugh, from the *giovanotto* on our left. It broke into the dramatic suspense of the moment, coarse, mocking, and yet—or I must have been grossly mistaken—with an undertone of compassion for the poor bewildered, victimized creature. It had a faint ring of that "*Poveretto*" which Cipolla had declared was wasted on the wrong person, when he claimed the pity for his own.

The laugh still rang in the air when the recipient of the caress gave his whip a little swish, low down, close to his chair-leg, and Mario started up and flung himself back. He stood in that posture staring, his hands one over the other on those desecrated lips. Then he beat his temples with his clenched fists, over and over; turned and staggered down the steps, while the audience applauded, and Cipolla sat there with his hands in his lap, his shoulders shaking. Once below, and even while in full retreat, Mario hurled himself round with legs flung wide apart; one arm flew up, and two flat shattering detonations crashed through applause and laughter.

There was instant silence. Even the dancers came to a full stop and stared about, struck dumb. Cipolla bounded from his seat. He stood with his arms spread out, slanting as though to ward everybody off, as though next moment he would cry out: "Stop! Keep back! Silence! What was that?" Then, in that instant, he sank back in his seat, his head rolling on his chest; in the next he had fallen sideways to the floor, where he lay motionless, a huddled heap of clothing, with limbs awry.

The commotion was indescribable. Ladies hid their faces, shuddering, on the breasts of their escorts. There were shouts for a doctor, for the police. People flung themselves on Mario in a mob, to disarm him, to take away the weapon that hung from his fingers—that small, dull-metal, scarcely pistol-shaped tool with hardly any barrel—in how strange and unexpected a direction had fate levelled it!

And now—now finally, at last—we took the children and led them towards the exit, past the pair of *carabinieri* just entering. Was that the end, they wanted to know, that they might go in peace? Yes, we assured them, that was the end. An end of horror, a fatal end. And yet a liberation—for I could not, and I cannot, but find it so!

Questions

1. "Mario" is a two-part story held together by a common theme and narrative voice. Characterize the nameless, faceless society represented by the people who gather on the beach. What specific comments reveal the narrator's attitude toward them? How is this general characterization developed in the episodes dominated by Cipolla?

2. Cipolla is sometimes described as the great symbol of the evil political leader in twentieth century mass society. List all the symbolic elements you can find—from his name and deformity to his whip and his drinking—that Mann uses to specify the quality of that evil. Is Mann's position now out of date? Has the passing of fascist tyrannies made it inapplicable?

3. Though Cipolla and his activities dominate much of the surface of the story, the narrator often slips from describing the scene around him to commenting on his own feelings and his family. How are we supposed to account for the fact that they remain in the dreadful town, in the hall itself, through the whole performance? What leads does Mann give us?

4. The story closes with Mario's action described as "an act of liberation." Who was liberated from what? How does the ending take us back to the opening with its comment on children, comedy and tragedy?

Vladimir Nabokov

THE VANE SISTERS

An international man of letters with an imposing list of publications in several languages, Vladimir Nabokov did not achieve his now great reputation until rather late in his life, at least in America. Then it was on the basis of the sensational rather than the literary qualities of his novel, Lolita *(1958). Nabokov had already been publishing distinguished works for several decades, however. He was born in St. Petersburg, Russia, in 1899, and lived there until 1919, when he went to England to work for a degree at Cambridge University. After receiving his degree, he lived in Berlin for fifteen years, teaching English and writing novels in Russian. He came to the United States in 1940, and there combined the teaching of Russian literature and creative writing at various universities—Stanford, Wellesley, Cornell—with his own writing. After the success of* Lolita, *many of his earlier works were translated and published in English for the first time, and he continued to produce a stream of new novels, poems, and translations. Among his major works are a collection of poems (1959), the novels* Invitation to a Beheading *(1959),* Pale Fire *(1962), and* Ada *(1969), an extensively annotated translation of Pushkin's* Eugene Onegin *(1964), and an autobiography,* Speak, Memory *(1966).*

"The Vane Sisters" is from a collection of four stories, Nabokov's Quartet *(1966). It is a story that may appeal to a special taste, for it is one in which the language is as important as the content—in fact, its linguistic devices may be its real content. It is marked by the baroque ornamentation as well as the concealed word games—puns, acrostics, etc.—in which Nabokov delights. The sophisticated reader, while admiring this verbal trickery, may also detect the uses to which the name in the title itself is put.*

I might never have heard of Cynthia's death, had I not run, that night, into D., whom I had also lost track of for the last four years or so; and I might never have run into D., had I not got involved in a series of trivial investigations.

The day, a compunctious Sunday after a week of blizzards, had been part jewel, part mud. In the midst of my usual afternoon stroll through the small hilly town attached to the girls' college where I taught French literature, I had stopped to watch a family of brilliant icicles drip-dripping from the eaves of a frame house. So clear-cut were their pointed shadows on the white boards behind them that I was sure the shadows of the falling drops should be visible too. But they were not. The roof jutted too far out, perhaps, or the angle of vision was faulty, or, again, I did not chance to be watching the right icicle when the right drop fell. There was a rhythm, an alternation in the dripping that I found as teasing as a coin trick. It led me to inspect the corners of several house blocks, and this brought me to Kelly Road, and right to the house where D. used to live when he was instructor here. And as I looked up at the eaves of the adjacent garage with its full display of transparent stalactites backed by their blue silhouettes, I was rewarded at last, upon choosing one, by the sight of what might be described as the dot of an exclamation mark leaving its ordinary position to glide down very fast—a jot faster than the thaw-drop it raced. This twinned twinkle was delightful but not completely satisfying; or rather it only sharpened my appetite for other tidbits of light and shade, and I walked on in a state of raw awareness that seemed to transform the whole of my being into one big eyeball rolling in the world's socket.

Through peacocked lashes I saw the dazzling diamond reflection of the low sun on the round back of a parked automobile. To all kinds of things a vivid pictorial sense had been restored by the sponge of the thaw. Water in overlapping festoons flowed down one sloping street and turned into another. With ever so slight a note of meretricious appeal, narrow passages between buildings revealed treasures of brick and purple. I remarked for the first time the humble fluting—last echoes of grooves on the shafts of columns—ornamenting a garbage can, and I also saw the rippling upon its lid—circles diverging from a fantastically ancient center. Erect, dark-headed shapes of dead snow (left by the blades of a bulldozer last Friday) were lined up like rudimentary penguins along the curbs, above the brilliant vibration of live gutters.

I walked up, and I walked down, and I walked straight into a delicately dying sky, and finally the sequence of observed and observant things brought me, at my usual eating time, to a street so distant from my usual eating place that I decided to try a restaurant which stood on the fringe of the town. Night had fallen without sound or ceremony when I came out again. The lean ghost, the elongated umbra cast by a parking meter upon some damp snow, had a strange ruddy tinge; this I made out to be due to the tawny red light of the restaurant sign above the sidewalk; and it was then—as I loitered there, wondering rather wearily if in the course of my return tramp I might be lucky enough to find the same in neon blue—it was then that a car crunched to a standstill near me and D. got out of it with an exclamation of feigned pleasure.

He was passing, on his way from Albany to Boston, through the town he had dwelt in before, and more than once in my life have I felt that stab of vicarious emotion followed by a rush of personal irritation against travelers who seem to feel nothing at all upon revisiting spots that ought to harass them at every step with wailing and writhing memories. He ushered me back into the bar that I had just left, and after the usual exchange of buoyant platitudes came the inevitable vacuum which he filled with the random words: "Say, I never thought there was anything wrong with Cynthia Vane's heart. My lawyer tells me she died last week."

He was still young, still brash, still shifty, still married to the gentle, exquisitely pretty woman who had never learned or suspected anything about his disastrous affair with Cynthia's hysterical young sister, who in her turn had known nothing of the interview I had had with Cynthia when she suddenly summoned me to Boston to make me swear I would talk to D. and get him "kicked out" if he did not stop seeing Sybil at once—or did not divorce his wife (whom incidentally she visualized through the prism of Sybil's wild talk as a termagant and a fright). I had cornered him immediately. He had said there was nothing to worry about —had made up his mind, anyway, to give up his college job and move with his wife to Albany where he would work in his father's firm; and the whole matter, which had threatened to become one of those hopelessly entangled situations that drag on for years, with peripheral sets of well-meaning friends endlessly discussing it in universal secrecy—and even founding, among themselves, new intimacies upon its alien woes—came to an abrupt end.

I remember sitting next day at my raised desk in the large classroom where a midyear examination in French Lit was being held on the eve of Sybil's suicide. She came in on high heels, with a suitcase, dumped it in a corner where several other bags were stacked, with a single shrug slipped her fur coat off her thin shoulders, folded it on her bag, and with two or three other girls stopped before my desk to ask when would I mail them their grades. It would take me a week, beginning from tomorrow, I said, to read the stuff. I also remember wondering whether D. had already informed her of his decision—and I felt acutely unhappy about my dutiful little student as during one hundred and fifty minutes my gaze kept reverting to her, so childishly slight in closefitting gray, and kept observing that carefully waved dark hair, that small, small-flowered hat with a little hyaline veil as worn that season and under it her small face broken into a cubist pattern by scars due to a skin disease, pathetically masked by a sunlamp tan that hardened her features whose charm was further impaired by her having painted everything that could be painted, so that the pale gums of her teeth between cherry-red chapped lips and the diluted blue ink of her eyes under darkened lids were the only visible openings into her beauty.

Next day, having arranged the ugly copybooks alphabetically, I plunged into their chaos of scripts and came prematurely to Valevsky and Vane whose books I had somehow misplaced. The first was dressed up for the occasion in a semblance of legibility, but Sybil's work displayed her usual combination of several demon hands. She had begun in very pale, very hard pencil which had conspicuously embossed the blank verso, but had produced little of permanent value on the upperside of the page. Happily, the tip soon broke, and Sybil continued in another, darker, lead, gradually lapsing into the blurred thickness of what looked almost like charcoal, to which, by sucking the blunt point, she had contributed some traces of lipstick. Her work, although even poorer than I had expected, bore all the signs of a kind of desperate conscientiousness, with underscores, transposes, unnecessary footnotes, as if she were intent upon rounding up things in the most respectable manner possible. Then she had borrowed Mary Valevsky's fountain pen and added: "*Cette examain est finie ainsi que ma vie. Adieu, jeunes filles!* Please, *Monsieur le Professeur*, contact *ma soeur* and tell her that Death was not better than D minus, but definitely better than Life minus D."

I lost no time in ringing up Cynthia who told me it was all over—had been all over since eight in the morning—and asked me to bring her the note, and when I did, beamed through her tears with proud admiration for the whimsical use ("Just like her!") Sybil had made of an examination in French literature. In no time she "fixed" two highballs, while never parting with Sybil's notebook—by now splashed with soda water and tears—and went on studying the death message, whereupon I was impelled to point out to her the grammatical mistakes in it and to explain the way "girl" is translated in American colleges lest students innocently bandy around the French equivalent of "wench," or worse. These rather tasteless trivialities pleased Cynthia hugely as she rose, with gasps, above the heaving surface of her grief. And then, holding that limp notebook as if it were a kind of passport to a casual Elysium (where pencil points do not snap and a dreamy young beauty with an impeccable complexion winds a lock of her hair on a dreamy forefinger, as she meditates over some celestial test), Cynthia led me upstairs, to a chilly little bedroom just to show me, as if I were the police or a sympathetic Irish neighbor, two empty pill bottles and the tumbled bed from which a tender, inessential body, that D. must have known down to its last velvet detail, had been already removed.

It was four or five months after her sister's death that I began seeing Cynthia fairly often. By the time I had come to New York for some vacational research in the Public Library she had also moved to that city where for some odd reason (in vague connection, I presume, with artistic motives) she had taken what people, immune to gooseflesh, term a "cold water" flat, low down in the scale of the city's transverse streets. What attracted me were neither her ways, which I thought repulsively vivacious, nor her looks, which other men thought striking. She had wide-spaced eyes very much like her sister's, of a frank, frightened blue with dark points in a radial arrangement. The interval between her thick black eyebrows was always shiny, and shiny too were the fleshy volutes of her nostrils. The coarse texture of her epiderm looked almost masculine, and, in the stark lamplight of her studio, you could see the pores of her thirty-two-year-old face fairly gaping at you like something in an aquarium. She used cosmetics with as much zest as her little sister had, but with an additional slovenliness that would result in her big front teeth getting some of the rouge. She was handsomely dark, wore a not too tasteless mixture of fairly smart heterogeneous things, and had a so-called good figure; but all of her was curiously frowsy, after a way I obscurely associated with left-wing enthusiasms in politics and "advanced" banalities in art, although, actually, she cared for neither. Her coily hairdo, on a part-and-bun basis, might have looked feral and bizarre had it not been thoroughly domesticated by its own soft unkemptness at the vulnerable nape. Her fingernails were gaudily painted, but badly bitten and not clean. Her lovers were a silent young photographer with a sudden laugh and two older men, brothers, who owned a small printing establishment across the street. I wondered at their tastes whenever I glimpsed, with a secret shudder, the higgledy-piggledy striation of black hairs that showed all along her pale shins through the nylon of her stockings with the scientific distinctness of a preparation flattened under glass; or when I felt, at her every movement, the dullish, stalish, not particularly conspicuous but all-pervading and depressing emanation that her seldom-bathed flesh spread from under weary perfumes and creams.

Her father had gambled away the greater part of a comfortable fortune, and her mother's first husband had been of Slav origin, but otherwise Cynthia Vane belonged to a good, respectable family. For aught we know, it may have gone back to kings and soothsayers in the mists of ultimate islands. Transferred to a newer world, to a landscape of doomed, splendid deciduous trees, her ancestry presented, in one of its first phases, a white churchful of farmers against a black thunderhead, and then an imposing array of townsmen engaged in mercantile pursuits, as well as a number of learned men, such as Dr. Jonathan Vane, the gaunt bore (1780–1839), who perished in the conflagration of the steamer "Lexington" to become later an habitué of Cynthia's tilting table. I have always wished to stand genealogy on its head, and here I have an opportunity to do so, for it is the last scion, Cynthia, and Cynthia alone, who will remain of any importance in the Vane dynasty. I am alluding of course to her artistic gift, to her delightful, gay, but not very popular paintings which the friends of her friends bought at long intervals—and I dearly should like to know where they went after her death, those honest and poetical pictures that illuminated her living room—the wonderfully detailed images of metallic things, and my favorite "Seen Through a Windshield"—a windshield partly covered with rime, with a brilliant trickle (from an imaginary car roof) across its transparent part and, through it all, the sapphire flame of the sky and a green and white fir tree.

Cynthia had a feeling that her dead sister was not altogether pleased with her—had discovered by now that she and I had conspired to break her romance; and so, in order to disarm her shade, Cynthia reverted to a rather primitive type of sacrificial offering (tinged, however, with something of Sybil's humor), and began to send to D.'s business address, at deliberately unfixed dates, such trifles as snapshots of Sybil's tomb in a poor light; cuttings of her own hair which was indistinguishable from Sybil's; a New England sectional map with an inked-in cross, midway between two chaste towns, to mark the spot where D. and Sybil had stopped on October the twenty-third, in broad daylight, at a lenient motel, in a pink and brown forest; and, twice, a stuffed skunk.

Being as a conversationalist more voluble than explicit, she never could describe in full the theory of intervenient auras that she had somehow evolved. Fundamentally there was nothing particularly new about her private creed since it presupposed a fairly conventional hereafter, a silent solarium of immortal souls (spliced with mortal antecedents) whose main recreation consisted of periodical hoverings over the dear quick. The interesting point was a curious practical twist that Cynthia gave to her tame metaphysics. She was sure that her existence was influenced by all sorts of dead friends each of whom took turns in directing her fate much as if she were a stray kitten which a schoolgirl in passing gathers up, and presses to her cheek, and carefully puts down again, near some suburban hedge—to be stroked presently by another transient hand or carried off to a world of doors by some hospitable lady.

For a few hours, or for several days in a row, and sometimes recurrently, in an irregular series, for months or years, anything that happened to Cynthia, after a given person had died, would be, she said, in the manner and mood of that person. The event might be extraordinary, changing the course of one's life; or it might be a string of minute incidents just sufficiently clear to stand out in relief against one's usual day and then shading off into still vaguer trivia as the aura gradually faded. The influence might be good or bad; the main thing was that its source could be identified. It was like walking through a person's soul, she said. I tried to argue that she might not always be able to determine the exact source since not everybody has a recognizable soul; that there are anonymous letters and Christmas presents which anybody might send; that in fact, what Cynthia called "a usual day" might be itself a weak solution of mixed auras or simply the routine shift of a humdrum guardian angel. And what about God? Did or did not people who would resent any omnipotent dictator on earth look forward to one in heaven? And wars? What a dreadful idea—dead soldiers still fighting with living ones, or phantom armies trying to get at each other through the lives of crippled old men.

But Cynthia was above generalities as she was beyond logic. "Ah, that's Paul," she would say when the soup spitefully boiled over, or: "I guess good Betty Brown is dead"—when she won a beautiful and very welcome vacuum cleaner in a charity lottery. And, with Jamesian meanderings that exasperated my French mind, she would go back to a time when Betty and Paul had not yet departed, and tell me of the showers of well-meant, but odd and quite unacceptable bounties—beginning with an old purse that contained a check for three dollars which she picked up in the street and, of course, returned (to the aforesaid Betty Brown—this is where she first comes in—a decrepit colored woman hardly able to walk), and ending with an insulting proposal from an old beau of hers (this is where Paul comes in) to paint "straight" pictures of his house and family for a reasonable remuneration—all of which followed upon the demise of a certain Mrs. Page, a kindly but petty old party who had pestered her with bits of matter-of-fact advice since Cynthia had been a child.

Sybil's personality, she said, had a rainbow edge as if a little out of focus. She said that had I known Sybil better I would have at once understood how Sybil-like was the aura of minor events which, in spells, had suffused her, Cynthia's, existence after Sybil's suicide. Ever since they had lost their mother they had intended to give up their Boston home and move to New York, where Cynthia's paintings, they thought, would have a chance to be more widely admired; but the old home had clung to them with all its plush tentacles. Dead Sybil, however, had proceeded to separate the house from its view—a thing that affects fatally the sense of home. Right across the narrow street a building project had come into loud, ugly, scaffolded life. A pair of familiar poplars died that spring, turning to blond skeletons. Workmen came and broke up the warm-colored lovely old sidewalk that had a special violet sheen on wet April days and had echoed so memorably to the morning footsteps of Museum-bound Mr. Lever, who upon retiring from the business at sixty had devoted a full quarter of a century exclusively to the study of snails.

Speaking of old men, one should add that sometimes these posthumous auspices and interventions were in the nature of parody. Cynthia had been on friendly terms with an eccentric librarian called Porlock who in the last years of his dusty life had been engaged in examining old books for miraculous misprints such as the substitution of "l" for the second "h" in the word "hither." Contrary to Cynthia, he cared nothing for the thrill of obscure predictions; all he sought was the freak itself, the chance that mimics choice, the flaw that looks like a flower; and Cynthia, a much more perverse amateur of misshapen or illicitly connected words, puns, logogriphs and so on, had helped the poor crank to pursue a quest that in the light of the example she cited struck me as statistically insane. Anyway, she said, on the third day after his death she was reading a magazine and had just come across a quotation from an imperishable poem (that she, with other gullible readers, believed to have been really composed in a dream) when it dawned upon her that "Alph" was a prophetic sequence of the initial letters of Anna Livia Plurabelle (another sacred river running through, or rather around, yet another fake dream), while the additional "h" modestly stood, as a private signpost, for the word that had so hypnotized Mr. Porlock. And I wish I could recollect that novel or short story (by some contemporary writer, I believe) in which, unknown to its author, the first letters of the words in its last paragraphs formed, as deciphered by Cynthia, a message from his dead mother.

I am sorry to say that not content with these ingenious fancies Cynthia showed a ridiculous fondness for spiritualism. I refused to accompany her to sittings in which paid mediums took part: I knew too much about that from other sources. I did consent, however, to attend little farces rigged up by Cynthia and her two poker-faced gentlemen-friends of the printing shop. They were podgy, polite and rather eerie old fellows, but I satisfied myself that they possessed considerable wit and culture. We sat down at a light little table, and crackling tremors started almost as soon as we laid our fingertips upon it. I was treated to an assortment of ghosts who rapped out their reports most readily though refusing to elucidate anything that I did not quite catch. Oscar Wilde came and in rapid garbled French, with the usual anglicisms, obscurely accused Cynthia's dead parents of what appeared in my jottings as "*plagiatisme*." A brisk spirit contributed the unsolicited information that he, John Moore, and his brother Bill had been coal miners in Colorado and had perished in an avalanche at "Crested Beauty" in January 1883. Frederic Myers, an old hand at the game, hammered out a piece of verse (oddly resembling Cynthia's own fugitive productions) which in part reads in my notes:

What is this—a conjuror's rabbit,
Or a flawy but genuine gleam—
Which can check the perilous habit
And dispel the dolorous dream?

Finally, with a great crash and all kinds of shudderings and jig-like movements on the part of the table, Leo Tolstoy visited our little group and, when asked to identify himself by specific traits of terrene habitation, launched upon a complex description of what seemed to be some Russian type of architectural woodwork ("figures on boards—man, horse, cock, man, horse, cock"), all of which was difficult to take down, hard to understand and impossible to verify.

I attended two or three other sittings which were even sillier but I must confess that I preferred the childish entertainment they afforded and the cider we drank (Podgy and Pudgy were teetotalers) to Cynthia's awful house parties.

She gave them at the Wheeler's nice flat next door—the sort of arrangement dear to her centrifugal nature, but then, of course, her own living room always looked like a dirty old palette. Following a barbaric, unhygienic, and adulterous custom, the guests' coats, still warm on the inside, were carried by quiet baldish Bob Wheeler into the sanctity of a tidy bedroom and heaped on the conjugal bed. It was also he who poured out the drinks which were passed around by the young photographer while Cynthia and Mrs. Wheeler took care of the canapés.

A late arrival had the impression of lots of loud people unnecessarily grouped within a smoke-blue space between two mirrors gorged with reflections. Because, I suppose, Cynthia wished to be the youngest in the room, the women she used to invite, married or single, were, at the best, in their precarious forties; some of them would bring from their homes, in dark taxis, intact vestiges of good looks, which, however, they lost as the party progressed. It has always amazed me—the capacity sociable weekend revelers have of finding almost at once, by a purely empiric but very precise method, a common denominator of drunkenness, to which everybody loyally sticks before descending, all together, to the next level. The rich friendliness of the matrons was marked by tomboyish overtones, while the fixed inward look of amiably tight men was like a sacrilegious parody of pregnancy. Although some of the guests were connected in one way or another with the arts, there was no inspired talk, no wreathed, elbow-propped heads, and of course no flute girls. From some vantage point where she had been sitting in a stranded mermaid pose on the pale carpet with one or two younger fellows, Cynthia, her face varnished with a film of beaming sweat, would creep up on her knees, a proffered plate of nuts in one hand, and crisply tap with the other the athletic leg of Cochran of Corcoran, an art dealer, ensconced, on a pearl-gray sofa, between two flushed, happily disintegrating ladies.

At a further stage there would come spurts of more riotous gaiety. Corcoran or Coransky would grab Cynthia or some other wandering woman by the shoulder and lead her into a corner to comfort her with a grinning embroglio of private jokes and rumors, whereupon, with a laugh and a toss of her head, she would break away. And still later there would be flurries of intersexual chumminess, jocular reconciliations, a bare fleshy arm flung around another woman's husband (he standing very upright in the midst of a swaying room), or a sudden rush of flirtatious anger, of clumsy pursuit—and the quiet half smile of Bob Wheeler picking up glasses that grew like mushrooms in the shade of chairs.

After one last party of that sort, I wrote Cynthia a perfectly harmless and, on the whole, well-meant note, in which I poked a little Latin fun at some of her guests. I also apologized for not having touched her whiskey, saying that as a Frenchman I preferred the grape to the grain. A few days later I met her on the steps of the Public Library, in the broken sun, under a weak cloudburst, opening her amber umbrella, struggling with a couple of armpitted books (of which I relieved her for a moment). "Footfalls on the Boundary of Another World," by Robert Dale Owen, and something on "Spiritualism and Christianity"; when, suddenly, with no provocation on my part, she blazed out at me with vulgar vehemence, using poisonous words, saying—through pear-shaped drops of sparse rain—that I was a prig and a snob; that I only saw the gestures and disguises of people; that Corcoran had rescued from drowning, in two different oceans, two men—by an irrelevant coincidence both called Corcoran; that romping and screeching Joan Winter had a little girl doomed to grow completely blind in a few months; and that the woman in green with the freckled chest whom I had snubbed in some way or other had written a national best seller in 1932. Strange Cynthia! I had been told she could be thunderously rude to people whom she liked and respected; one had, however, to draw the line somewhere and since I had by then sufficiently studied her interesting auras and other odds and ids, I decided to stop seeing her altogether.

The night D. informed me of Cynthia's death I returned after eleven to the two-storied house I shared, in horizontal section, with an emeritus professor's widow. Upon reaching the porch I looked with the apprehension of solitude at the two kinds of darkness in the two rows of windows: the darkness of absence and the darkness of sleep.

I could do something about the first but could not duplicate the second. My bed gave me no sense of safety; its springs only made my nerves bounce. I plunged into Shakespeare's sonnets—and found myself idiotically checking the first letters of the lines to see what sacramental words they might form. I got FATE (LXX), ATOM (CXX) and, twice, TAFT (LXXXVIII, CXXXI). Every now and then I would glance around to see how the objects in my room were behaving. It was strange to think that if bombs began to fall I would feel little more than a gambler's excitement (and a great deal of earthy relief) whereas my heart would burst if a certain suspiciously tense-looking little bottle on yonder shelf moved a fraction of an inch to one side. The silence, too, was suspiciously compact as if deliberately forming a black backdrop for the nerve flash caused by any small sound of unknown origin. All traffic was dead. In vain did I pray for the groan of a truck up Perkins Street. The woman above who used to drive me crazy by the booming thuds occasioned by what seemed monstrous feet of stone (actually, in diurnal life, she was a small dumpy creature resembling a mummified guinea pig) would have earned my blessings had she now trudged to her bathroom. I put out my light and cleared my throat several times so as to be responsible for at least *that* sound. I thumbed a mental ride with a very remote automobile but it dropped me before I had a chance to doze off. Presently a crackle (due, I hoped, to a discarded and crushed sheet of paper opening like a mean, stubborn night flower)—started and stopped in the waste paper basket, and my bedtable responded with a click. It would have been just like Cynthia to put on right then a cheap poltergeist show.

I decided to fight Cynthia. I reviewed in thought the modern era of raps and apparitions, beginning with the knockings of 1848, at the hamlet of Hydesville, N.Y., and ending with grotesque phenomena at Cambridge, Mass.; I evoked the ankle-bones and other anatomical castanets of the Fox sisters (as described by the sages of the University of Buffalo); the mysteriously uniform type of delicate adolescent in bleak Epworth or Tedworth, radiating the same disturbances as in old Peru; solemn Victorian orgies with roses falling and accordions floating to the strains of sacred music; professional impostors regurgitating moist cheesecloth; Mr. Duncan, a lady medium's dignified husband, who, when asked if he would submit to a search, excused himself on the ground of soiled underwear; old Alfred Russel Wallace, the naive naturalist, refusing to believe that the white form with bare feet and unperforated earlobes before him, at a private pandemonium in Boston, could be prim Miss Cook whom he had just seen asleep, in her curtained corner, all dressed in black, wearing laced-up boots and earrings; two other investigators, small, puny, but reasonably intelligent and active men, closely clinging with arms and legs about Eusapia, a large plump elderly female reeking of garlic, who still managed to fool them; and Dingwall, the sceptical and embarrassed magician, instructed by charming young Margery's "control" not to get lost in the bathrobe's lining but to follow up the left stocking until he reached the bare thigh—upon the warm skin of which he felt a "teleplastic" mass that appeared to the touch uncommonly like cold uncooked liver.

I was appealing to flesh, and the corruption of flesh, to refute and defeat the possible persistence of discarnate life. Alas, these conjurations only enhanced my fear of Cynthia's phantom. Atavistic peace came with dawn, and when I slipped into sleep, the sun through the tawny window shades penetrated a dream that somehow was full of Cynthia.

This was disappointing. Secure in the fortress of daylight, I said to myself that I had expected more. She, a painter of glass-bright minutiae—and now so vague! I lay in bed, thinking my dream over and listening to the sparrows outside: who knows, if recorded and then run backward, those bird sounds might not become human speech, voiced words, just as the latter become a twitter when reversed? I set myself to reread my dream—backward, diagonally, up, down—trying hard to unravel something Cynthia-like in it, something strange and suggestive that must be there.

I could isolate, consciously, little. Everything seemed blurred, yellow-clouded, yielding nothing tangible. Her inept acrostics, maudlin evasions, theopathies–every recollection formed ripples of mysterious meaning. Everything seemed yellowly blurred, illusive, lost.

Questions

1. As in most Nabokov stories, the plot of "The Vane Sisters" is important though secondary to the speaking voice itself. Compare and contrast the opening and closing sections of the story in terms of what each part reveals about the narrator himself, and about the "real subject" of the story.

2. Nabokov gives us several very powerful portraits of the characters. Choose one—Sybil, Cynthia, D.—and describe him in your own terms. Refer back to the text and discuss how much of your impression comes from the physical details or reported actions and how much from Nabokov's tone—his attitude toward the characters and their lives.

3. Nabokov warns us to search for an acrostic that may, randomly, of course, provide some key to the story or life. Then he creates one in the last paragraph. Can you relate it to the story? Does it seem that the last paragraph is different in syntax, vocabulary, or style? Is it tacked on, like a happy ending to a melodrama, only for the acrostic?

4. Is "The Vane Sisters" a story about "real people" with real life problems or only the exercise of a word merchant—an intellectual fascinated by sounds which, like the sparrow sounds in the penultimate paragraph, may or may not have meaning when played backwards or forwards? Discuss where Nabokov finds "meaning"—in the events of the plot or in his speculations about them—using this story as evidence.

Joyce Carol Oates

UPON THE SWEEPING FLOOD

There can hardly be a more promising young writer in America than Joyce Carol Oates. Within a decade after she started writing, she won several O. Henry prizes for short stories, a Guggenheim fellowship, and a Rosenthal Foundation award for one novel, A Garden of Earthly Delights *(1967). This novel was also a candidate for the National Book Award, as was her next novel,* Expensive People *(1968). She finally received this award for* Them *(1969). Miss Oates was born at Lockport, New York, in 1938. She attended Syracuse University and then got a master's degree in English at the University of Wisconsin. She has since combined a productive writing career with teaching English at the University of Windsor in Ontario, Canada. Besides her novels, she has written numerous short stories and some poetry and critical essays.*

"Upon the Sweeping Flood" is the title story of a volume, Upon the Sweeping Flood *(1966). As in many of her other stories, Miss Oates displays particular skill in rendering with detachment but also with sympathy and understanding characters under stress. "I am concerned with only one thing," she once said, "the moral and social conditions of my generation." The attentive reader will discover this concern behind the sensual and sometimes violent surfaces of her stories.*

One day in Eden County, in the remote marsh and swamplands to the south, a man named Walter Stuart was stopped in the rain by a sheriff's deputy along a country road. Stuart was in a hurry to get home to his family—his wife and two daughters—after having endured a week at his father's old farm, arranging for his father's funeral, surrounded by aging relatives who had sucked at him for the strength of his youth. He was a stern, quiet man of thirty-nine, beginning now to lose some of the muscular hardness that had always baffled others, masking as it did Stuart's remoteness, his refinement, his faith in discipline and order that seem to have belonged, even in his youth, to a person already grown safely old. He was a district vice-president for one of the gypsum mining plants, a man to whom financial success and success in love had come naturally, without fuss. When only a child he had shifted his faith with little difficulty from the unreliable God of his family's tradition to the things and emotions of this world, which he admired in his thoughtful, rather conservative way, and this faith had given him access, as if by magic, to a communion with persons vastly different from himself—with someone like the sheriff's deputy, for example, who approached him that day in the hard, cold rain. "Is something wrong?" Stuart said. He rolled down the window and had nearly opened the door when the deputy, an old man with gray eyebrows and a slack, sunburned face, began shouting against the wind. "Just the weather, mister. You plan on going far? How far are you going?"

"Two hundred miles," Stuart said. "What about the weather? Is it a hurricane?"

"A hurricane—yes—a hurricane," the man said, bending to shout at Stuart's face. "You better go back to town and stay put. They're evacuating up there. We're not letting anyone through."

A long line of cars and pickup trucks, tarnished and gloomy in the rain, passed them on the other side of the road. "How bad is it?" said Stuart. "Do you need help?"

"Back at town, maybe, they need help," the man said. "They're putting up folks at the schoolhouse and the churches, and different families —The eye was spost to come by here, but last word we got it's veered further south. Just the same, though—"

"Yes, it's good to evacuate them," Stuart said. At the back window of an automobile passing them two children's faces peered out at the rain, white and blurred. "The last hurricane here—"

"Ah, God, leave off of that!" the old man said, so harshly that Stuart felt, inexplicably, hurt. "You better turn around now and get on back to town. You got money they can put you up somewheres good—not with these folks coming along here."

This was said without contempt, but Stuart flinched at its assumptions and, years afterward, he was to remember the old man's remark as the beginning of his adventure. The man's twisted face and unsteady, jumping eyes, his wind-snatched voice, would reappear to Stuart when he puzzled for reasons—but along with the deputy's face there would be the sad line of cars, the children's faces turned toward him, and, beyond them in his memory, the face of his dead father with skin wrinkled and precise as a withered apple.

"I'm going in to see if anybody needs help," Stuart said. He had the car going again before the deputy could even protest. "I know what I'm doing! I know what I'm doing!" Stuart said.

The car lunged forward into the rain, drowning out the deputy's outraged shouts. The slashing of rain against Stuart's face excited him. Faces staring out of oncoming cars were pale and startled, and Stuart felt rising in him a strange compulsion to grin, to laugh madly at their alarm. . . . He passed cars for some time. Houses looked deserted, yards bare. Things had the look of haste about them, even trees—in haste to rid themselves of their leaves, to be stripped bare. Grass was twisted and wild. A ditch by the road was overflowing and at spots the churning, muddy water stretched across the red clay road. Stuart drove, splashing, through it. After a while his enthusiasm slowed, his foot eased up on the gas pedal. He had not passed any cars or trucks for some time.

The sky had darkened and the storm had increased. Stuart thought of turning back when he saw, a short distance ahead, someone standing in the road. A car approached from the opposite direction. Stuart slowed, bearing to the right. He came upon a farm—a small, run-down one with just a few barns and a small pasture in which a horse stood drooping in the rain. Behind the roofs of the buildings a shifting edge of foliage from the trees beyond curled in the wind, now dark, now silver. In a neat harsh line against the bottom of the buildings the wind had driven up dust and red clay. Rain streamed off roofs, plunged into fat, tilted rain barrels, and exploded back out of them. As Stuart watched, another figure appeared, running out of the house. Both persons—they looked like children—jumped about in the road, waving their arms. A spray of leaves was driven against them and against the muddy windshield of the car that approached and passed them. They turned: a girl and a boy, waving their fists in rage, their faces white and distorted. As the car sped past Stuart, water and mud splashed up in a vicious wave.

When Stuart stopped and opened the door the girl was already there, shouting, "Going the wrong way! Wrong way!" Her face was coarse, pimply about her forehead and chin. The boy pounded up behind her, straining for air. "Where the hell are you going mister?" the girl cried. "The storm's coming from this way. Did you see that bastard, going right by us? Did you see him? If I see him when I get to town—" A wall of rain struck. The girl lunged forward and tried to push her way into the car; Stuart had to hold her back. "Where are your folks?" he shouted. "Let me in," cried the girl savagely. "We're getting out of here!" "Your folks," said Stuart. He had to cup his mouth to make her hear. "Your folks in there!" "There ain't nobody there—*Goddamn* you," she said, twisting about to slap her brother, who had been pushing at her from behind. She whirled upon Stuart again. "You letting us in, mister? You letting us in?" she screamed, raising her hands as if to claw him. But Stuart's size must have calmed her, for she shouted hoarsely and mechanically: "There ain't nobody in there. Our pa's been gone the last two days. *Last two days.* Gone into town *by himself*. Gone drunk somewhere. He ain't here. He left us here. LEFT US HERE!" Again she rushed at Stuart, and he leaned forward against the steering wheel to let her get in back. The boy was about to follow when something caught his eye back at the farm. "Get in," Stuart. "Get in. Please. Get in." "My horse there," the boy muttered. "You little bastard! You get in here!" his sister screamed.

But once the boy got in, once the door was closed, Stuart knew that it was too late. Rain struck the car in solid walls and the road, when he could see it, had turned to mud. "Let's go! Let's go!" cried the girl, pounding on the back of the seat. "Turn it around! Go up on our drive and turn it around!" The engine and the wind roared together. "Turn it! Get it going!" cried the girl. There was a scuffle and someone fell against Stuart. "It ain't no good," the boy said. "Let me out." He lunged for the door and Stuart grabbed him. "I'm going back to the house," the boy cried, appealing to Stuart with his frightened eyes, and his sister, giving up suddenly, pushed him violently forward. "It's no use," Stuart said. "Goddamn fool," the girl screamed, "goddamn fool!"

The water was ankle deep as they ran to the house. The girl splashed ahead of Stuart, running with her head up and her eyes wide open in spite of the flying scud. When Stuart shouted to the boy, his voice was slammed back to him as if he were being mocked. "Where are you going? Go to the house! Go to the house!" The boy had turned and was running toward the pasture. His sister took no notice but ran to the house. "Come back, kid!" Stuart cried. Wind tore at him, pushing him back. "What are you—"

The horse was undersized, skinny and brown. It ran to the boy as if it wanted to run him down but the boy, stooping through the fence, avoided the frightened hoofs and grabbed the rope that dangled from the horse's halter. "That's it! That's it!" Stuart shouted as if the boy could hear. At the gate the boy stopped and looked around wildly, up to the sky—he might have been looking for someone who had just called him; then he shook the gate madly. Stuart reached the gate and opened it, pushing it back against the boy, who now turned to gape at him. "What? What are you doing here?" he said.

The thought crossed Stuart's mind that the child was insane. "Bring the horse through!" he said. "We don't have much time."

"What are you doing here?" the boy shouted. The horse's eyes rolled, its mane lifted and haloed about its head. Suddenly it lunged through the gate and jerked the boy off the ground. The boy ran in the air, his legs kicking. "Hang on and bring him around!" Stuart shouted. "Let me take hold!" He grabbed the boy instead of the rope. They stumbled together against the horse. It had stopped now and was looking intently at something just to the right of Stuart's head. The boy pulled himself along the rope, hand over hand, and Stuart held onto him by the strap of his overalls. "He's scairt of you!" the boy said. "He's scairt of you!" Stuart reached over and took hold of the rope above the boy's fingers and tugged gently at it. His face was about a foot away from the horse's. "Watch out for him," said the boy. The horse reared and broke free, throwing Stuart back against the boy. "Hey, hey," screamed the boy, as if mad. The horse turned in mid-air as if whirled about by the wind, and Stuart looked up through his fingers to see its hoofs and a vicious flicking of its tail, and the face of the boy being yanked past him and away with incredible speed. The boy fell heavily on his side in the mud, arms outstretched above him, hands still gripping the rope with wooden fists. But he scrambled to his feet at once and ran alongside the horse. He flung one arm up around its neck as Stuart shouted, "Let him go! Forget about him!" Horse and boy pivoted together back toward the fence, slashing wildly at the earth, feet and hoofs together. The ground erupted beneath them. But the boy landed upright, still holding the rope, still with his arm about the horse's neck. "Let me help," Stuart said. "No," said the boy, "he's my horse, he knows me—" "Have you got him good?" Stuart shouted. "We got—we got each other here," the boy cried, his eyes shut tight.

Stuart went to the barn to open the door. While he struggled with it, the boy led the horse forward. When the door was open far enough, Stuart threw himself against it and slammed it around to the side of the barn. A cloud of hay and scud filled the air. Stuart stretched out his arms, as if pleading with the boy to hurry, and he murmured, "Come on. Please. Come on." The boy did not hear him or even glance at him: his own lips were moving as he caressed the horse's neck and head. The horse's muddy hoof had just begun to grope about the step before the door when something like an explosion came against the back of Stuart's head, slammed his back, and sent him sprawling out at the horse.

"Damn you! Damn you!" the boy screamed. Stuart saw nothing except rain. Then something struck him, his shoulder and hand, and his fingers were driven down into the mud. Something slammed beside him in the mud and he seized it—the horse's foreleg–and tried to pull himself up, insanely, lurching to his knees. The horse threw him backwards. It seemed to emerge out of the air before and above him, coming into sight as though out of a cloud. The boy he did not see at all—only the hoofs—and then the boy appeared, inexplicably, under the horse, peering intently at Stuart, his face struck completely blank. "Damn you!" Stuart heard, "he's my horse! My horse! I hope he kills you!" Stuart crawled back in the water, crab fashion, watching the horse form and dissolve, hearing its vicious tattoo against the barn. The door, swinging madly back and forth, parodied the horse's rage, seemed to challenge its frenzy; then the door was all Stuart heard, and he got to his feet, gasping, to see that the horse was out of sight.

The boy ran bent against the wind, out toward nowhere, and Stuart ran after him. "Come in the house, kid! Come on! Forget about it, kid!" He grabbed the boy's arm. The boy struck at him with his elbow. "He was my horse!" he cried.

In the kitchen of the house they pushed furniture against the door. Stuart had to stand between the boy and the girl to keep them from fighting. "Goddamn sniffling fool," said the girl. "So your goddamn horse run off for the night!" The boy crouched down on the floor, crying steadily. He was about thirteen: small for his age, with bony wrists and face. "We're all going to be blownt to hell, let alone your horse," the girl said. She sat with one big thigh and leg outstretched on the table, watching Stuart. He thought her perhaps eighteen. "Glad you come down to get us?" she said. "Where are you from, mister?" Stuart's revulsion surprised him; he had not supposed there was room in his stunned mind for emotion of this sort. If the girl noticed it she gave no sign, but only grinned at him. "I was—I was on my way home," he said. "My wife and daughters—" It occurred to him that he had forgotten about them entirely. He had not thought of them until now and, even now, no image came to his mind: no woman's face, no little girls' faces. Could he have imagined their lives, their love for him? For an instant he doubted everything. "Wife and daughters," said the girl, as if wondering whether to believe him. "Are they in this storm too?" "No—no," Stuart said. To get away from her he went to the window. He could no longer see the road. Something struck the house and he flinched away. "Them trees!" chortled the girl. "I knew it. Pa always said how he ought to cut them down, so close to the house like they are! I knew it! I knew it! And the old bastard off safe now where they can't get him!"

"Trees?" said Stuart slowly.

"Them trees! Old oak trees!" said the girl.

The boy, struck with fear, stopped crying suddenly. He crawled on the floor to a woodbox beside the big old iron stove and got in, patting the disorderly pile of wood as if he were blind. The girl ran to him and pushed him. "What are you doing?" Stuart cried in anguish. The girl took no notice of him. "What am I doing?" he said aloud. "What the hell am I doing here?" It seemed to him that the end would come in a minute or two, that the howling outside could get no louder, that the howling inside his mind could get no more intense, no more accusing. A goddamn fool! A goddamn fool! he thought. The deputy's face came to mind, and Stuart pictured himself groveling before the man, clutching at his knees, asking forgiveness and for time to be turned back. . . . Then he saw himself back at the old farm, the farm of his childhood, listening to tales of his father's agonizing sickness, the old peoples' heads craning around, seeing how he took it, their eyes charged with horror and delight. . . . "My wife and daughters," Stuart muttered.

The wind made a hollow, drumlike sound. It seemed to be tolling. The boy, crouching back in the woodbox, shouted: "I ain't scairt! I ain't scairt!" The girl gave a shriek. "Our chicken coop, I'll be gahdammed!" she cried. Try as he could, Stuart could see nothing out the window. "Come away from the window," Stuart said, pulling the girl's arm. She whirled upon him. "Watch yourself, mister," she said, "you want to go out to your gahdamn bastardly worthless car?" Her body was strong and big in her men's clothing; her shoulders looked muscular beneath the filthy shirt. Cords in her young neck stood out. Her hair had been cut short and was now wet, plastered about her blemished face. She grinned at Stuart as if she were about to poke him in the stomach, for fun. "I ain't scairt of what God can do!" the boy cried behind them.

When the water began to bubble up through the floor boards they decided to climb to the attic. "There's an ax!" Stuart exclaimed, but the boy got on his hands and knees and crawled to the corner where the ax was propped before Stuart could reach it. The boy cradled it in his arms. "What do you want with that?" Stuart said, and for an instant his heart was pierced with fear. "Let me take it. I'll take it." He grabbed it out of the boy's dazed fingers.

The attic was about half as large as the kitchen and the roof jutted down sharply on either side. Tree limbs rubbed and slammed against the roof on all sides. The three of them crouched on the middle beam, Stuart with the ax tight in his embrace, the boy pushing against him as if for warmth, and the girl kneeling, with her thighs straining her overalls. She watched the little paneless window at one end of the attic without much emotion or interest, like a large, wet turkey. The house trembled beneath them. "I'm going to the window," Stuart said, and was oddly relieved when the girl did not sneer at him. He crawled forward along the dirty beam, dragging the ax with him, and lay full length on the floor about a yard from the window. There was not much to see. At times the rain relaxed, and objects beneath in the water took shape: tree stumps, parts of buildings, junk whirling about in the water. The thumping on the roof was so loud at that end that he had to crawl backwards to the middle again. "I ain't scairt, nothing God can do!" the boy cried. "Listen to the sniveling baby," said the girl. "He thinks God pays him any mind! Hah!" Stuart crouched beside them, waiting for the boy to press against him again. "As if God gives a good damn about him," the girl said. Stuart looked at her. In the near dark her face did not seem so coarse; the set of her eyes was almost attractive. "You don't think

God cares about you?" Stuart said slowly. "No, not specially," the girl said, shrugging her shoulders. "The hell with it. You seen the last one of these?" She tugged at Stuart's arm. "Mister? It was something to see. Me an' Jackie was little then—him just a baby. We drove a far ways north to get out of it. When we come back the roads was so thick with sightseers from the cities! They took all the dead ones floating in the water and put them in one place, part of a swamp they cleared out. The families and things—they were mostly fruit pickers—had to come by on rafts and rowboats to look and see could they find the ones they knew. That was there for a day. The bodies would turn round and round in the wash from the boats. Then the faces all got alike and they wouldn't let anyone come any more and put oil on them and set them afire. We stood on top of the car and watched all that day. I wasn't but nine then."

When the house began to shake, some time later, Stuart cried aloud: "This is it!" He stumbled to his feet, waving the ax. He turned around and around as if he were in a daze. "You goin' to chop somethin' with that?" the boy said, pulling at him. "Hey, no, that ain't yours to—it ain't yours to chop—" They struggled for the ax. The boy sobbed, "It ain't yours! It ain't yours!" and Stuart's rage at his own helplessness, at the folly of his being here, for an instant almost made him strike the boy with the ax. But the girl slapped him furiously. "Get away from him! I swear I'll kill you!" she screamed.

Something exploded beneath them. "That's the windows," the girl muttered, clinging to Stuart, "and how am I to clean it again! The old bastard will want it clean, and mud over everything!" Stuart pushed her away so that he could swing the ax. Pieces of soft, rotted wood exploded back onto his face. The boy screamed insanely as the boards gave way to a deluge of wind and water, and even Stuart wondered if he had made a mistake. The three of them fell beneath the onslaught and Stuart lost the ax, felt the handle slam against his leg. "You! You!" Stuart cried, pulling at the girl—for an instant, blinded by pain, he could not think who he was, what he was doing, whether he had any life beyond this moment. The big-faced, husky girl made no effort to hide her fear and cried, "wait, wait!" But he dragged her to the hole and tried to force her out. "My brother—" she gasped. She seized his wrists and tried to get away. "Get out there! There isn't any time!" Stuart muttered. The house seemed about to collapse at any moment. He was pushing her through the hole, against the shattered wood, when she suddenly flinched back against him and he saw that her cheek was cut and she was choking. He snatched her hands away from her mouth as if he wanted to see something secret: blood welled out between her lips. She coughed and spat blood onto him. "You're all right," he said, oddly pleased. "Now get out there and I'll get the kid. I'll take care of him." This time she managed to crawl through the hole, with Stuart pushing her from behind; when he turned to seize the boy, the boy clung to his neck, sobbing something about God. "God loves you!" Stuart yelled. "Loves the least of you! The least of you!" The girl pulled her brother up in her great arms and Stuart was free to climb through himself.

It was actually quite a while—perhaps an hour—before the battering of the trees and the wind pushed the house in. The roof fell slowly, and the section to which they clung was washed free. "We're going somewheres!" shouted the girl. "Look at the house! That gahdamn old shanty seen the last storm!"

The boy lay with his legs pushed in under Stuart's and had not spoken for some time. When the girl cried, "Look at that!" he tried to burrow in farther. Stuart wiped his eyes to see the wall of darkness dissolve. The rain took on another look—a smooth, piercing, metallic glint, like nails driving against their faces and bodies. There was no horizon. They could see nothing except the rushing water and a thickening mist that must have been rain, miles and miles of rain, slammed by the wind into one great wall that moved remorselessly upon them. "Hang on," Stuart said, gripping the girl. "Hang on to me."

Waves washed over the roof, pushing objects at them with soft, muted thuds—pieces of fence, boards, branches heavy with foliage. Stuart tried to ward them off with his feet. Water swirled around them, sucking at them, sucking the roof until they were pushed against one of the farm buildings. Something crashed against the roof—another section of the house—and splintered, flying up against the girl. She was thrown backwards, away from Stuart, who lunged after her. They fell into the water while the boy screamed. The girl's arms threshed wildly against Stuart. The water was cold, and its aliveness, its sinister energy, surprised him more than the thought that he would drown—that he would never endure the night. Struggling with the girl, he forced her back to the roof, pushed her up. Bare, twisted nails raked his hands. "Gahdamn you, Jackie, you give a hand!" the girl said as Stuart crawled back up. He lay, exhausted, flat on his stomach and let the water and debris slosh over him.

His mind was calm beneath the surface buzzing. He liked to think that his mind was a clear, sane circle of quiet carefully preserved inside the chaos of the storm—that the three of them were safe within the sanctity of this circle; this was how man always conquered nature, how he subdued things greater than himself. But whenever he did speak to her it was in short grunts, in her own idiom: "This ain't so bad!" or "It'll let up pretty soon!" Now the girl held him in her arms as if he were a child, and he did not have the strength to pull away. Of his own free will he had given himself to this storm, or to the strange desire to save someone in it—but now he felt grateful for the girl, even for her brother, for they had saved him as much as he had saved them. Stuart thought of his wife at home, walking through the rooms, waiting for him; he thought of his daughters in their twin beds, two glasses of water on their bureau. . . . But these people knew nothing of him: in his experience now he did not belong to them. Perhaps he had misunderstood his role, his life? Perhaps he had blundered out of his way, drawn into the wrong life, surrendered to the wrong role. What had blinded him to the possibility of many lives, many masks, many arms that might so embrace him? A word not heard one day, a gesture misinterpreted, a leveling of someone's eyes in a certain unmistakable manner, which he had mistaken just the same! The consequences of such errors might trail insanely into the future, across miles of land, across worlds. He only now sensed the incompleteness of his former life. . . . "Look! Look!" the girl cried, jostling him out of his stupor. "Take a look at that, mister!"

He raised himself on one elbow. A streak of light broke out of the dark. Lanterns, he thought, a rescue party already. . . . But the rain dissolved the light; then it reappeared with a beauty that startled him. "What is it?" the boy screamed. "How come it's here?" They watched it filter through the rain, rays knifing through and showing, now, how buildings and trees crouched close about them. "It's the sun, the sun going down," the girl said. "The sun!" said Stuart, who had thought it was night. "The sun!" They stared at it until it disappeared.

The waves calmed sometime before dawn. By then the roof had lost its peak and water ran unchecked over it, in generous waves and then in thin waves, alternately, as the roof bobbed up and down. The three huddled together with their backs to the wind. Water came now in slow drifts. "It's just got to spread itself out far enough so's it will be even," said the girl, "then it'll go down." She spoke without sounding tired, only a little disgusted—as if things weren't working fast enough to suit her. "Soon as it goes down we'll start toward town and see if there ain't somebody coming out to get us in a boat," she said, chattily and comfortably, into Stuart's ear. Her manner astonished Stuart, who had been thinking all night of the humiliation and pain he had suffered. "Bet the old bastard will be glad to see us," she said, "even if he did go off like that. Well, he never knew a storm was coming. Me and him get along pretty well—he ain't so bad." She wiped her face; it was filthy with dirt and blood. "He'll buy you a drink, mister, for saving us how you did. That was something to have happen—a man just driving up to get us!" And she poked Stuart in the ribs.

The wind warmed as the sun rose. Rain turned to mist and back to rain again, still falling heavily, and now objects were clear about them. The roof had been shoved against the corner of the barn and a mound of dirt, and eddied there without much trouble. Right about them, in a kind of halo, a thick blanket of vegetation and filth bobbed. The fence had disappeared and the house had collapsed and been driven against a ridge of land. The barn itself had fallen in, but the stone support looked untouched, and it was against this they had been shoved. Stuart thought he could see his car—or something over there where the road used to be.

"I bet it ain't deep. Hell," said the girl sticking her foot into the water. The boy leaned over the edge and scooped up some of the filth in his hands. "Lookit all the spiders," he said. He wiped his face slowly. "Leave them gahdamn spiders alone," said the girl. "You want me to shove them down your throat?" She slid to the edge and lowered her legs. "Yah, I touched bottom. It ain't bad." But then she began coughing and drew herself back. Her coughing made Stuart cough: his chest and throat were ravaged, shaken. He lay exhausted when the fit left him and realized, suddenly, that they were all sick—that something had happened to them. They had to get off the roof. Now, with the sun up, things did not look so bad: there was a ridge of trees a short distance away on a long, red clay hill. "We'll go over there," Stuart said. "Do you think you can make it?"

The boy played in the filth, without looking up, but the girl gnawed at her lip to show she was thinking. "I spose so," she said. "But him—I don't know about him."

"Your brother? What's wrong?"

"Turn around. Hey, stupid. Turn around." She prodded the boy, who jerked around, terrified, to stare at Stuart. His thin bony face gave way to a drooping mouth. "Gone loony, it looks like," the girl said with a touch of regret. "Oh, he had times like this before. It might go away."

Stuart was transfixed by the boy's stare. The realization of what had happened struck him like a blow, sickening his stomach. "We'll get him over there," he said, making his words sound good. "We can wait there for someone to come. Someone in a boat. He'll be better there."

"I spose so," said the girl vaguely.

Stuart carried the boy while the girl splashed eagerly ahead. The water was sometimes up to his thighs. "Hold on another minute," he pleaded. The boy stared out at the water as if he thought he were taken somewhere to be drowned. "Put your arms around my neck. Hold on," Stuart said. He shut his eyes and every time he looked up the girl was still a few yards ahead and the hill looked no closer. The boy breathed hollowly, coughing into Stuart's face. His own face and neck were covered with small red bites. Ahead, the girl walked with her shoulders lunged forward as if to hurry her there, her great thighs straining against the water, more than a match for it. As Stuart watched her, something was on the side of his face—in his ear—and with a scream he slapped at it, nearly dropping the boy. The girl whirled around. Stuart slapped at his face and must have knocked it off—probably a spider. The boy, upset by Stuart's outcry, began sucking in air faster and faster as if he were dying. "I'm all right, I'm all right," Stuart whispered, "just hold on another minute. . . ."

When he finally got to the hill the girl helped pull him up. He set the boy down with a grunt, trying to put the boy's legs under him so he could stand. But the boy sank to the ground and turned over and vomited into the water; his body shook as if he were having convulsions. Again the thought that the night had poisoned them, their own breaths had sucked germs into their bodies, struck Stuart with an irresistible force. "Let him lay down and rest," the girl said, pulling tentatively at the back of her brother's belt, as if she were thinking of dragging him farther up the slope. "We sure do thank you, mister," she said.

Stuart climbed to the crest of the hill. His heart pounded madly, blood pounded in his ears. What was going to happen? Was anything going to happen? How disappointing it looked—ridges of land showing through the water and the healthy sunlight pushing back the mist. Who would believe him when he told of the night, of the times when death seemed certain . . . ? Anger welled up in him already as he imagined the tolerant faces of his friends, his children's faces ready to turn to other amusements, other oddities. His wife would believe him; she would shudder, holding him, burying her small face in his neck. But what could she understand of his experience, having had no part in it? . . . Stuart cried out; he had nearly stepped on a tangle of snakes. Were they alive? He backed away in terror. The snakes gleamed wetly in the morning light, heads together as if conspiring. Four . . . five of them—they too had swum for this land, they too had survived the night, they had as much reason to be proud of themselves as Stuart.

He gagged and turned away. Down by the water line the boy lay flat on his stomach and the girl squatted nearby, wringing out her denim jacket. The water behind them caught the sunlight and gleamed mightily, putting them into silhouette. The girl's arms moved slowly, hard with muscle. The boy lay coughing gently. Watching them, Stuart was beset by a strange desire: he wanted to run at them, demand their gratitude, their love. Why should they not love him, when he had saved their lives? When he had lost what he was just the day before, turned now into a different person, a stranger even to himself? Stuart stooped and picked up a rock. A broad hot hand seemed to press against his chest. He threw the rock out into the water and said, "Hey!"

The girl glanced around but the boy did not move. Stuart sat down on the soggy ground and waited. After a while the girl looked away; she spread the jacket out to dry. Great banked clouds rose into the sky, reflected in the water—jagged and bent in the waves. Stuart waited as the sun took over the sky. Mist at the horizon glowed, thinned, gave way to solid shapes. Light did not strike cleanly across the land, but was marred by ridges of trees and parts of buildings, and around a corner at any time Stuart expected to see a rescuing party—in a rowboat or something.

"Hey, mister." He woke; he must have been dozing. The girl had called him. "Hey. Whyn't you come down here? There's all them snakes up there."

Stuart scrambled to his feet. When he stumbled downhill, embarrassed and frightened, the girl said chattily, "The sons of bitches are crawling all over here. He chast some away." The boy was on his feet and looking around with an important air. His coming alive startled Stuart—indeed, the coming alive of the day, of the world, evoked alarm in him. All things came back to what they were. The girl's alert eyes, the firm set of her mouth, had not changed—the sunlight had not changed, or the land, really; only Stuart had been changed. He wondered at it . . . and the girl must have seen something in his face that he himself did not yet know about, for her eyes narrowed, her throat gulped a big swallow, her arms moved slowly up to show her raw elbows. "We'll get rid of them," Stuart said, breaking the silence. "Him and me. We'll do it."

The boy was delighted. "I got a stick," he said, waving a thin whip-like branch. "There's some over here."

"We'll get them," Stuart said. But when he started to walk, a rock slipped loose and he fell back into the mud. He laughed aloud. The girl, squatting a few feet away, watched him silently. Stuart got to his feet, still laughing. "You know much about it, kid?" he said, cupping his hand on the boy's head.

"About what?" said the boy.

"Killing snakes," said Stuart.

"I spose—I spose you just kill them."

The boy hurried alongside Stuart. "I need a stick," Stuart said; they got him one from the water, about the size of an ax. "Go by that bush," Stuart said, "there might be some there."

The boy attacked the bush in a frenzy. He nearly fell into it. His enthusiasm somehow pleased Stuart, but there were no snakes in the bush. "Go down that way," Stuart ordered. He glanced back at the girl: she watched them. Stuart and the boy went on with their sticks held in mid-air. "God put them here to keep us awake," the boy said brightly. "See we don't forget about Him." Mud sucked at their feet. "Last year we couldn't fire the woods on account of it so dry. This year can't either on account of the water. We got to get the snakes like this."

Stuart hurried as if he had somewhere to go. The boy, matching his steps, went faster and faster, panting, waving his stick angrily in the air. The boy complained about snakes and, listening to him, fascinated by him, in that instant Stuart saw everything. He saw the conventional dawn that had mocked the night, had mocked his desire to help people in trouble; he saw, beyond that, his father's home emptied now even of ghosts. He realized that the God of these people had indeed arranged things, had breathed the order of chaos into forms, had animated them, had animated even Stuart himself forty years ago. The knowledge of this fact struck him about the same way as the nest of snakes had struck him—an image leaping right to the eye, pouncing upon the mind, joining itself with the perceiver. "Hey, hey!" cried the boy, who had found a snake: the snake crawled noisily and not very quickly up the slope, a brown-speckled snake. The boy ran clumsily after it. Stuart was astonished at the boy's stupidity, at his inability to see, now that the snake had vanished. Still he ran along the slope, waving his stick, shouting, "I'll get you! I'll get you!" This must have been the sign Stuart was waiting for. When the boy turned, Stuart was right behind him. "It got away up there," the boy said. "We got to get it." When Stuart lifted his stick the boy fell back a step but went on in mechanical excitement, "It's up there, gotten hid in the weeds. It ain't me," he said, "it ain't me that—" Stuart's blow struck the boy on the side of the head, and the rotted limb shattered into soft wet pieces. The boy stumbled down toward the water. He was coughing when Stuart took hold of him and began shaking him madly, and he did nothing but cough, violently and with all his concentration, even when Stuart bent to grab a rock and brought it down on his head. Stuart let him fall into the water. He could hear him breathing and he could see, about the boy's lips, tiny flecks or bubbles of blood appearing and disappearing with his breath.

When the boy's eyes opened, Stuart fell upon him. They struggled savagely in the water. Again the boy went limp; Stuart stood, panting, and waited. Nothing happened for a minute or so. But then he saw something—the boy's fingers moving up through the water, soaring to the surface! "Will you quit it!" Stuart screamed. He was about to throw himself upon the boy again when the thought of the boy's life, bubbling out between his lips, moving his fingers, filled him with such outraged disgust that he backed away. He threw the rock out into the water and ran back, stumbling, to where the girl stood.

She had nothing to say: her jaw was hard, her mouth a narrow line, her thick nose oddly white against her dirty face. Only her eyes moved, and these were black, lustrous, at once demanding and terrified. She held a board in one hand. Stuart did not have time to think, but, as he lunged toward her, he could already see himself grappling with her in the mud, forcing her down, tearing her ugly clothing from her body—

"Lookit!" she cried, the way a person might speak to a horse, cautious and coaxing, and pointed behind him. Stuart turned to see a white boat moving toward them, a half mile or so away. Immediately his hands dropped, his mouth opened in awe. The girl still pointed, breathing carefully, and Stuart, his mind shattered by the broken sunshine upon the water, turned to the boat, raised his hands, cried out, "Save me! Save me!" He had waded out a short distance by the time the men arrived.

Questions

1. Is there anything in the story that prepares one for its ending? Does Stuart's attack on the boy come as a complete surprise? Is the attack motivated in any way? How can one explain it?

2. Look back and observe some of Stuart's needs and motives. Why does he proceed into the storm, even after being warned back? What does he want to do?

3. Stuart feels that his desire to help people in trouble has been mocked; this sense of rejection, somehow, is related to the trip he has just made to arrange for his father's funeral. What is the connection?

4. Is Stuart mad? Does he receive the reader's sympathy?

Flannery O'Connor

GREENLEAF

Another southern writer and creator of comic grotesques, Flannery O'Connor lived her brief life courageously in the presence of pain. A Georgia native, born in Savannah in 1925, she seldom traveled far, except to attend the State University of Iowa, where she received a master's degree in Creative Writing in 1947. Soon thereafter she was struck by a disease that kept her an invalid and eventually caused her death in 1964. She remained good humored and dedicated to her work, and was eased by the Catholic faith in which she had been raised.

Miss O'Connor wrote two novels, Wise Blood *(1952) and* The Violent Bear It Away *(1960), which treat southern religious fanaticism with some satire but never with condescension. She also wrote two collections of short stories,* A Good Man Is Hard to Find *(1955) and* Everything That Rises Must Converge *(1965). The latter is the source of "Greenleaf," a story that shows her humorous but sympathetic treatment of amiable southern eccentrics within an unexpected but devastatingly logical plot.*

Mrs. May's bedroom window was low and faced on the east and the bull, silvered in the moonlight, stood under it, his head raised as if he listened—like some patient god come down to woo her—for a stir inside the room. The window was dark and the sound of her breathing too light to be carried outside. Clouds crossing the moon blackened him and in the dark he began to tear at the hedge. Presently they passed and he appeared again in the same spot, chewing steadily, with a hedge-wreath that he had ripped loose for himself caught in the tips of his horns. When the moon drifted into retirement again, there was nothing to mark his place but the sound of steady chewing. Then abruptly a pink glow filled the window. Bars of light slid across him as the venetian blind was slit. He took a step backward and lowered his head as if to show the wreath across his horns.

For almost a minute there was no sound from inside, then as he raised his crowned head again, a woman's voice, guttural as if addressed to a dog, said, "Get away from here, Sir!" and in a second muttered, "Some nigger's scrub bull."

The animal pawed the ground and Mrs. May, standing bent forward behind the blind, closed it quickly lest the light make him charge into the shrubbery. For a second she waited, still bent forward, her nightgown hanging loosely from her narrow shoulders. Green rubber curlers sprouted neatly over her forehead and her face beneath them was smooth as concrete with an egg-white paste that drew the wrinkles out while she slept.

She had been conscious in her sleep of a steady rhythmic chewing as if something were eating one wall of the house. She had been aware that whatever it was had been eating as long as she had had the place and had eaten everything from the beginning of her fence line up to the house and now was eating the house and calmly with the same steady rhythm would continue through the house, eating her and the boys, and then on, eating everything but the Greenleafs, on and on, eating everything until nothing was left but the Greenleafs on a little island all their own in the middle of what had been her place. When the munching reached her elbow, she jumped up and found herself, fully awake, standing in the middle of her room. She identified the sound at once: a cow was tearing at the shrubbery under her window. Mr. Greenleaf had left the lane gate open and she didn't doubt that the entire herd was on her lawn. She turned on the dim pink table lamp and then went to the window and slit the blind. The bull, gaunt and long-legged, was standing about four feet from her, chewing calmly like an uncouth country suitor.

For fifteen years, she thought as she squinted at him fiercely, she had been having shiftless people's hogs root up her oats, their mules wallow on her lawn, their scrub bulls breed her cows. If this one was not put up now, he would be over the fence, ruining her herd before morning–and Mr. Greenleaf was soundly sleeping a half mile down the road in the tenant house. There was no way to get him unless she dressed and got in her car and rode down there and woke him up. He would come but his expression, his whole figure, his every pause, would say: "Hit looks to me like one or both of them boys would not make their maw ride out in the middle of the night thisaway. If hit was my boys, they would have got thet bull up theirself."

The bull lowered his head and shook it and the wreath slipped down to the base of his horns where it looked like a menacing prickly crown. She had closed the blind then; in a few seconds she heard him move off heavily.

Mr. Greenleaf would say, "If hit was my boys they would never have allowed their maw to go after hired help in the middle of the night. They would have did it theirself."

Weighing it, she decided not to bother Mr. Greenleaf. She returned to bed thinking that if the Greenleaf boys had risen in the world it was because she had given their father employment when no one else would have him. She had had Mr. Greenleaf fifteen years but no one else would have had him five minutes. Just the way he approached an object was enough to tell anybody with eyes what kind of a worker he was. He walked with a high-shouldered creep and he never appeared to come directly forward. He walked on the perimeter of some invisible circle and if you wanted to look him in the face, you had to move and get in front of him. She had not fired him because she had always doubted she could do better. He was too shiftless to go out and look for another job; he didn't have the initiative to steal, and after she had told him three or four times to do a thing, he did it; but he never told her about a sick cow until it was too late to call the veterinarian and if her barn had caught on fire, he would have called his wife to see the flames before he began to put them out. And of the wife, she didn't even like to think. Beside the wife, Mr. Greenleaf was an aristocrat.

"If it had been my boys," he would have said, "they would have cut off their right arm before they would have allowed their maw to . . ."

"If your boys had any pride, Mr. Greenleaf," she would like to say to him some day, "there are many things that they would not *allow* their mother to do."

The next morning as soon as Mr. Greenleaf came to the back door, she told him there was a stray bull on the place and that she wanted him penned up at once.

"Done already been here three days," he said, addressing his right foot which he held forward, turned slightly as if he were trying to look at the sole. He was standing at the bottom of the three back steps while she leaned out the kitchen door, a small woman with pale near-sighted eyes and grey hair that rose on top like the crest of some disturbed bird.

"Three days!" she said in the restrained screech that had become habitual with her.

Mr. Greenleaf, looking into the distance over the near pasture, removed a package of cigarets from his shirt pocket and let one fall into his hand. He put the package back and stood for a while looking at the cigaret. "I put him in the bull pen but he torn out of there," he said presently. "I didn't see him none after that." He bent over the cigaret and lit it and then turned his head briefly in her direction. The upper part of his face sloped gradually into the lower which was long and narrow, shaped like a rough chalice. He had deep-set fox-colored eyes shadowed under a grey felt hat that he wore slanted forward following the line of his nose. His build was insignificant.

"Mr. Greenleaf," she said, "get that bull up this morning before you do anything else. You know he'll ruin the breeding schedule. Get him up and keep him up and the next time there's a stray bull on this place, tell me at once. Do you understand?"

"Where do you want him put at?" Mr. Greenleaf asked.

"I don't care where you put him," she said. "You are supposed to have some sense. Put him where he can't get out. Whose bull is he?"

For a moment Mr. Greenleaf seemed to hesitate between silence and speech. He studied the air to the left of him. "He must be somebody's bull," he said after a while.

"Yes, he must!" she said and shut the door with a precise little slam.

She went into the dining room where the two boys were eating breakfast and sat down on the edge of her chair at the head of the table. She never ate breakfast but she sat with them to see that they had what they wanted. "Honestly!" she said, and began to tell about the bull, aping Mr. Greenleaf saying, "It must be *somebody's* bull."

Wesley continued to read the newspaper folded beside his plate but Scofield interrupted his eating from time to time to look at her and laugh. The two boys never had the same reaction to anything. They were as different, she said, as night and day. The only thing they did have in common was that neither of them cared what happened on the place. Scofield was a business type and Wesley was an intellectual.

Wesley, the younger child, had had rheumatic fever when he was seven and Mrs. May thought that this was what had caused him to be an intellectual. Scofield, who had never had a day's sickness in his life, was an insurance salesman. She would not have minded his selling insurance if he had sold a nicer kind but he sold the kind that only negroes buy. He was what negroes call a "policy man." He said there was more money in nigger-insurance than any other kind, and before company, he was very loud about it. He would shout, "Mamma don't like to hear me say it but I'm the best nigger-insurance salesman in this county!"

Scofield was thirty-six and he had a broad pleasant smiling face but he was not married. "Yes," Mrs. May would say, "and if you sold decent insurance, some *nice* girl would be willing to marry you. What nice girl wants to marry a nigger-insurance man? You'll wake up some day and it'll be too late."

And at this Scofield would yodel and say, "Why Mamma, I'm not going to marry until you're dead and gone and then I'm going to marry me some nice fat farm girl that can take over this place!" And once he had added, "—some nice lady like Mrs. Greenleaf." When he had said this, Mrs. May had risen from her chair, her back stiff as a rake handle, and had gone to her room. There she had sat down on the edge of her bed for some time with her small face drawn. Finally she had whispered, "I work and slave, I struggle and sweat to keep this place for them and as soon as I'm dead, they'll marry trash and bring it in here and ruin everything. They'll marry trash and ruin everything I've done," and she had made up her mind at that moment to change her will. The next day she had gone to her lawyer and had had the property entailed so that if they married, they could not leave it to their wives.

The idea that one of them might marry a woman even remotely like Mrs. Greenleaf was enough to make her ill. She had put up with Mr. Greenleaf for fifteen years, but the only way she had endured his wife had been by keeping entirely out of her sight. Mrs. Greenleaf was large and loose. The yard around her house looked like a dump and her five girls were always filthy; even the youngest one dipped snuff. Instead of making a garden or washing their clothes, her preoccupation was what she called "prayer healing."

Every day she cut all the morbid stories out of the newspaper—the accounts of women who had been raped and criminals who had escaped and children who had been burned and of train wrecks and plane crashes and the divorces of movie stars. She took these to the woods and dug a hole and buried them and then she fell on the ground over them and mumbled and groaned for an hour or so, moving her huge arms back and forth under her and out again and finally just lying down flat and, Mrs. May suspected, going to sleep in the dirt.

She had not found out about this until the Greenleafs had been with her a few months. One morning she had been out to inspect a field that she had wanted planted in rye but that had come up in clover because Mr. Greenleaf had used the wrong seeds in the grain drill. She was returning through a wooded path that separated two pastures, muttering to herself and hitting the ground methodically with a long stick she carried in case she saw a snake. "Mr. Greenleaf," she was saying in a low voice, "I cannot afford to pay for your mistakes. I am a poor woman and this place is all I have. I have two boys to educate. I cannot . . ."

Out of nowhere a guttural agonized voice groaned, "Jesus! Jesus!" In a second it came again with a terrible urgency. "Jesus! Jesus!"

Mrs. May stopped still, one hand lifted to her throat. The sound was so piercing that she felt as if some violent unleashed force had broken out of the ground and was charging toward her. Her second thought was more reasonable: somebody had been hurt on the place and would sue her for everything she had. She had no insurance. She rushed forward and turning a bend in the path, she saw Mrs. Greenleaf sprawled on her hands and knees off the side of the road, her head down.

"Mrs. Greenleaf!" she shrilled, "what's happened!"

Mrs. Greenleaf raised her head. Her face was a patchwork of dirt and tears and her small eyes, the color of two field peas, were red-rimmed and swollen, but her expression was as composed as a bulldog's. She swayed back and forth on her hands and knees and groaned, "Jesus, Jesus."

Mrs. May winced. She thought the word, Jesus, should be kept inside the church building like other words inside the bedroom. She was a good Christian woman with a large respect for religion, though she did not, of course, believe any of it was true. "What is the matter with you?" she asked sharply.

"You broken my healing," Mrs. Greenleaf said, waving her aside. "I can't talk to you until I finish."

Mrs. May stood, bent forward, her mouth open and her stick raised off the ground as if she were not sure what she wanted to strike with it.

"Oh Jesus, stab me in the heart!" Mrs. Greenleaf shrieked. "Jesus, stab me in the heart!" and she fell back flat in the dirt, a huge human mound, her legs and arms spread out as if she were trying to wrap them around the earth.

Mrs. May felt as furious and helpless as if she had been insulted by a child. "Jesus," she said, drawing herself back, "would be *ashamed* of you. He would tell you to get up from there this instant and go wash your children's clothes!" and she had turned and walked off as fast as she could.

Whenever she thought of how the Greenleaf boys had advanced in the world, she had only to think of Mrs. Greenleaf sprawled obscenely on the ground, and say to herself, "Well, no matter how far they *go*, they *came* from that."

She would like to have been able to put in her will that when she died, Wesley and Scofield were not to continue to employ Mr. Greenleaf. She was capable of handling Mr. Greenleaf; they were not. Mr. Greenleaf had pointed out to her once that her boys didn't know hay from silage. She had pointed out to him that they had other talents, that Scofield was a successful business man and Wesley a successful intellectual. Mr. Greenleaf did not comment, but he never lost an opportunity of letting her see, by his expression or some simple gesture, that he held the two of them in infinite contempt. As scrub-human as the Greenleafs were, he never hesitated to let her know that in any like circumstance in which his own boys might have been involved, they—O. T. and E. T. Greenleaf—would have acted to better advantage.

The Greenleaf boys were two or three years younger than the May boys. They were twins and you never knew when you spoke to one of them whether you were speaking to O. T. or E. T., and they never had the politeness to enlighten you. They were long-legged and raw-boned and red-skinned, with bright grasping fox-colored eyes like their father's. Mr. Greenleaf's pride in them began with the fact that they were twins. He acted, Mrs. May said, as if this were something smart they had thought of themselves. They were energetic and hard-working and she would admit to anyone that they had come a long way—and that the Second World War was responsible for it.

They had both joined the service and, disguised in their uniforms, they could not be told from other people's children. You could tell, of course, when they opened their mouths but they did that seldom. The smartest thing they had done was to get sent overseas and there to marry French wives. They hadn't married French trash either. They had married nice girls who naturally couldn't tell that they murdered the king's English or that the Greenleafs were who they were.

Wesley's heart condition had not permitted him to serve his country but Scofield had been in the army for two years. He had not cared for it and at the end of his military service, he was only a Private First Class. The Greenleaf boys were both some kind of sergeants, and Mr. Greenleaf, in those days, had never lost an opportunity of referring to them by their rank. They had both managed to get wounded and now they both had pensions. Further, as soon as they were released from the army, they took advantage of all the benefits and went to the school of agriculture at the university—the taxpayers meanwhile supporting their French wives. The two of them were living now about two miles down the highway on a piece of land that the government had helped them to buy and in a brick duplex bungalow that the government had helped to build and pay for. If the war had made anyone, Mrs. May said, it had made the Greenleaf boys. They each had three little children apiece, who spoke Greenleaf English and French, and who, on account of their mother's background, would be sent to the convent school and brought up with manners. "And in twenty years," Mrs. May asked Scofield and Wesley, "do you know what those people will be?"

"*Society*," she said blackly.

She had spent fifteen years coping with Mr. Greenleaf and, by now, handling him had become second nature with her. His disposition on any particular day was as much a factor in what she could and couldn't do as the weather was, and she had learned to read his face the way real country people read the sunrise and sunset.

She was a country woman only by persuasion. The late Mr. May, a business man, had bought the place when land was down, and when he died it was all he had to leave her. The boys had not been happy to move to the country to a broken-down farm, but there was nothing else for her to do. She had the timber on the place cut and with the proceeds had set herself up in the dairy business after Mr. Greenleaf had answered her ad. "i seen yor add and i will come have 2 boys," was all his letter said, but he arrived the next day in a pieced-together truck, his wife and five daughters sitting on the floor in the back, himself and the two boys in the cab.

Over the years they had been on her place, Mr. and Mrs. Greenleaf had aged hardly at all. They had no worries, no responsibilities. They lived like the lilies of the field, off the fat that she struggled to put into the land. When she was dead and gone from overwork and worry, the Greenleafs, healthy and thriving, would be just ready to begin draining Scofield and Wesley.

Wesley said the reason Mrs. Greenleaf had not aged was because she released all her emotions in prayer healing. "You ought to start praying, Sweetheart," he had said in the voice that, poor boy, he could not help making deliberately nasty.

Scofield only exasperated her beyond endurance but Wesley caused her real anxiety. He was thin and nervous and bald and being an intellectual was a terrible strain on his disposition. She doubted if he would marry until she died but she was certain that then the wrong woman would get him. Nice girls didn't like Scofield but Wesley didn't like nice girls. He didn't like anything. He drove twenty miles every day to the university where he taught and twenty miles back every night, but he said he hated the twenty-mile drive and he hated the second-rate university and he hated the morons who attended it. He hated the country and he hated the life he lived; he hated living with his mother and his idiot brother and he hated hearing about the damn dairy and the damn help and the damn broken machinery. But in spite of all he said, he never made any move to leave. He talked about Paris and Rome but he never went even to Atlanta.

"You'd go to those places and you'd get sick," Mrs. May would say. "Who in Paris is going to see that you get a salt-free diet? And do you think if you married one of those odd numbers you take out that *she* would cook a salt-free diet for you? No indeed, she would not!" When she took this line, Wesley would turn himself roughly around in his chair and ignore her. Once when she had kept it up too long, he had snarled, "Well, why don't you do something practical, Woman? Why don't you pray for me like Mrs. Greenleaf would?"

"I don't like to hear you boys make jokes about religion," she had said. "If you would go to church, you would meet some nice girls."

But it was impossible to tell them anything. When she looked at the two of them now, sitting on either side of the table, neither one caring the least if a stray bull ruined her herd—which was their herd, their future—when she looked at the two of them, one hunched over a paper and the other teetering back in his chair, grinning at her like an idiot, she wanted to jump up and beat her fist on the table and shout, "You'll find out one of these days, you'll find out what *Reality* is when it's too late!"

"Mamma," Scofield said, "don't you get excited now but I'll tell you whose bull that is." He was looking at her wickedly. He let his chair drop forward and he got up. Then with his shoulders bent and his hands held up to cover his head, he tiptoed to the door. He backed into the hall and pulled the door almost to so that it hid all of him but his face. "You want to know, Sugar-pie?" he asked.

Mrs. May sat looking at him coldly.

"That's O. T. and E. T.'s bull," he said. "I collected from their nigger yesterday and he told me they were missing it," and he showed her an exaggerated expanse of teeth and disappeared silently.

Wesley looked up and laughed.

Mrs. May turned her head forward again, her expression unaltered. "I am the only *adult* on this place," she said. She leaned across the table and pulled the paper from the side of his plate. "Do you see how it's going to be when I die and you boys have to handle him?" she began. "Do you see why he didn't know whose bull that was? Because it was theirs. Do you see what I have to put up with? Do you see that if I hadn't kept my foot on his neck all these years, you boys might be milking cows every morning at four o'clock?"

Wesley pulled the paper back toward his plate and staring at her full in the face, he murmured, "I wouldn't milk a cow to save your soul from hell."

"I know you wouldn't," she said in a brittle voice. She sat back and began rapidly turning her knife over at the side of her plate. "O. T. and E. T. are fine boys," she said. "They ought to have been my sons." The thought of this was so horrible that her vision of Wesley was blurred at once by a wall of tears. All she saw was his dark shape, rising quickly from the table. "And you two," she cried, "you two should have belonged to that woman!"

He was heading for the door.

"When I die," she said in a thin voice, "I don't know what's going to become of you."

"You're always yapping about when-you-die," he growled as he rushed out, "but you look pretty healthy to me."

For some time she sat where she was, looking straight ahead through the window across the room into a scene of indistinct greys and greens. She stretched her face and her neck muscles and drew in a long breath but the scene in front of her flowed together anyway into a watery grey mass. "They needn't think I'm going to die any time soon," she muttered, and some more defiant voice in her added: I'll die when I get good and ready.

She wiped her eyes with the table napkin and got up and went to the window and gazed at the scene in front of her. The cows were grazing in two pale green pastures across the road and behind them, fencing them in, was a black wall of trees with a sharp sawtooth edge that held off the indifferent sky. The pastures were enough to calm her. When she looked out any window in her house, she saw the reflection of her own character. Her city friends said she was the most remarkable woman they knew, to go, practically penniless and with no experience, out to a rundown farm and make a success of it. "Everything is against you," she would say, "the weather is against you and the dirt is against you and the help is against you. They're all in league against you. There's nothing for it but an iron hand!"

"Look at Mamma's iron hand!" Scofield would yell and grab her arm and hold it up so that her delicate blue-veined little hand would dangle from her wrist like the head of a broken lily. The company always laughed.

The sun, moving over the black and white grazing cows, was just a little brighter than the rest of the sky. Looking down, she saw a darker shape that might have been its shadow cast at an angle, moving among them. She uttered a sharp cry and turned and marched out of the house.

Mr. Greenleaf was in the trench silo, filling a wheelbarrow. She stood on the edge and looked down at him. "I told you to get up that bull. Now he's in with the milk herd."

"You can't do two thangs at oncet," Mr. Greenleaf remarked.

"I told you to do that first."

He wheeled the barrow out of the open end of the trench toward the barn and she followed close behind him. "And you needn't think, Mr. Greenleaf," she said, "that I don't know exactly whose bull that is or why you haven't been in any hurry to notify me he was here. I might as well feed O. T. and E. T.'s bull as long as I'm going to have him here ruining my herd."

Mr. Greenleaf paused with the wheelbarrow and looked behind him. "Is that them boys' bull?" he asked in an incredulous tone.

She did not say a word. She merely looked away with her mouth taut.

"They told me their bull was out but I never known that was him," he said.

"I want that bull put up now," she said, "and I'm going to drive over to O. T. and E. T.'s and tell them they'll have to come get him today. I ought to charge for the time he's been here—then it wouldn't happen again."

"They didn't pay but seventy-five dollars for him," Mr. Greenleaf offered.

"I wouldn't have had him as a gift," she said.

"They was just going to beef him," Mr. Greenleaf went on, "but he got loose and run his head into their pickup truck. He don't like cars and trucks. They had a time getting his horn out the fender and when they finally got him loose, he took off and they was too tired to run after him —but I never known that was him there."

"It wouldn't have paid you to know, Mr. Greenleaf," she said. "But you know now. Get a horse and get him."

In a half hour, from her front window she saw the bull, squirrel-colored, with jutting hips and long light horns, ambling down the dirt road that ran in front of the house. Mr. Greenleaf was behind him on the horse. "That's a Greenleaf bull if I ever saw one," she muttered. She went out on the porch and called, "Put him where he can't get out."

"He likes to bust loose," Mr. Greenleaf said, looking with approval at the bull's rump. "This gentleman is a sport."

"If those boys don't come for him, he's going to be a dead sport," she said. "I'm just warning you."

He heard her but he didn't answer.

"That the awfullest looking bull I ever saw," she called but he was too far down the road to hear.

It was mid-morning when she turned into O. T. and E. T.'s driveway. The house, a new red-brick, low-to-the-ground building that looked like a warehouse with windows, was on top of a treeless hill. The sun was beating down directly on the white roof of it. It was the kind of house that everybody built now and nothing marked it as belonging to Greenleafs except three dogs, part hound and part spitz, that rushed out from behind it as soon as she stopped her car. She reminded herself that you could always tell the class of people by the class of dog, and honked her horn. While she sat waiting for someone to come, she continued to study the house. All the windows were down and she wondered if the government could have air-conditioned the thing. No one came and she honked again. Presently a door opened and several children appeared in it and stood looking at her, making no move to come forward. She recognized this as a true Greenleaf trait—they could hang in a door, looking at you for hours.

"Can't one of you children come here?" she called.

After a minute they all began to move forward, slowly. They had on overalls and were barefooted but they were not as dirty as she might have expected. There were two or three that looked distinctly like Greenleafs; the others not so much so. The smallest child was a girl with untidy black hair. They stopped about six feet from the automobile and stood looking at her.

"You're mighty pretty," Mrs. May said, addressing herself to the smallest girl.

There was no answer. They appeared to share one dispassionate expression between them.

"Where's your Mamma?" she asked.

There was no answer to this for some time. Then one of them said something in French. Mrs. May did not speak French.

"Where's your daddy?" she asked.

After a while, one of the boys said, "He ain't hyar neither."

"Ahhhh," Mrs. May said as if something had been proven. "Where's the colored man?"

She waited and decided no one was going to answer. "The cat has six little tongues," she said. "How would you like to come home with me and let me teach you how to talk?" She laughed and her laugh died on the silent air. She felt as if she were on trial for her life, facing a jury of Greenleafs. "I'll go down and see if I can find the colored man," she said.

"You can go if you want to," one of the boys said.

"Well, thank you," she murmured and drove off.

The barn was down the lane from the house. She had not seen it before but Mr. Greenleaf had described it in detail for it had been built according to the latest specifications. It was a milking parlor arrangement where the cows are milked from below. The milk ran in pipes from the machines to the milk house and was never carried in no bucket, Mr. Greenleaf said, by no human hand. "When you gonter get you one?" he had asked.

"Mr. Greenleaf," she had said, "I have to do for myself. I am not assisted hand and foot by the government. It would cost me $20,000 to install a milking parlor. I barely make ends meet as it is."

"My boys done it," Mr. Greenleaf had murmured, and then—"but all boys ain't alike."

"No indeed!" she had said. "I thank God for that!"

"I thank Gawd for ever-thang," Mr. Greenleaf had drawled.

You might as well, she had thought in the fierce silence that followed; you've never done anything for yourself.

She stopped by the side of the barn and honked but no one appeared. For several minutes she sat in the car, observing the various machines parked around, wondering how many of them were paid for. They had a forage harvester and a rotary hay baler. She had those too. She decided that since no one was here, she would get out and have a look at the milking parlor and see if they kept it clean.

She opened the milking room door and stuck her head in and for the first second she felt as if she were going to lose her breath. The spotless white concrete room was filled with sunlight that came from a row of windows head-high along both walls. The metal stanchions gleamed ferociously and she had to squint to be able to look at all. She drew her head out the room quickly and closed the door and leaned against it, frowning. The light outside was not so bright but she was conscious that the sun was directly on top of her head, like a silver bullet ready to drop into her brain.

A negro carrying a yellow calf-feed bucket appeared from around the corner of the machine shed and came toward her. He was a light yellow boy dressed in the cast-off army clothes of the Greenleaf twins. He stopped at a respectable distance and set the bucket on the ground.

"Where's Mr. O. T. and Mr. E. T.?" she asked.

"Mist O. T. he in town, Mist E. T. he off yonder in the field," the negro said, pointing first to the left and then to the right as if he were naming the position of two planets.

"Can you remember a message?" she asked, looking as if she thought this doubtful.

"I'll remember it if I don't forget it," he said with a touch of sullenness.

"Well, I'll write it down then," she said. She got in her car and took a stub of pencil from her pocket book and began to write on the back of an empty envelope. The negro came and stood at the window. "I'm Mrs. May," she said as she wrote. "Their bull is on my place and I want him off *today*. You can tell them I'm furious about it."

"That bull lef here Sareday," the negro said, "and none of us ain't seen him since. We ain't knowed where he was."

"Well, you know now," she said, "and you can tell Mr. O. T. and Mr. E. T. that if they don't come get him today, I'm going to have their daddy shoot him the first thing in the morning. I can't have that bull ruining my herd." She handed him the note.

"If I knows Mist O. T. and Mist E. T.," he said, taking it, "they goin to say you go ahead and shoot him. He done busted up one of our trucks already and we be glad to see the last of him."

She pulled her head back and gave him a look from slightly blared eyes. "Do they expect me to take my time and my worker to shoot their bull?" she asked. "They don't want him so they just let him loose and expect somebody else to kill him? He's eating my oats and ruining my herd and I'm expected to shoot him too?"

"I speck you is," he said softly. "He done busted up . . ."

She gave him a very sharp look and said, "Well, I'm not surprised. That's just the way some people are," and after a second she asked, "Which is boss, Mr. O. T. or Mr. E. T.?" She had always suspected that they fought between themselves secretly.

"They never quarls," the boy said. "They like one man in two skins."

"Hmp. I expect you just never heard them quarrel."

"Nor nobody else heard them neither," he said, looking away as if this insolence were addressed to someone else.

"Well," she said, "I haven't put up with their father for fifteen years not to know a few things about Greenleafs."

The negro looked at her suddenly with a gleam of recognition. "Is you my policy man's mother?" he asked.

"I don't know who your policy man is," she said sharply. "You give them that note and tell them if they don't come for that bull today, they'll be making their father shoot it tomorrow," and she drove off.

She stayed at home all afternoon waiting for the Greenleaf twins to come for the bull. They did not come. I might as well be working for them, she thought furiously. They are simply going to use me to the limit. At the supper table, she went over it again for the boys' benefit because she wanted them to see exactly what O. T. and E. T. would do. "They don't want that bull," she said, "—pass the butter—so they simply turn him loose and let somebody else worry about getting rid of him for them. How do you like that? I'm the victim. I've always been the victim."

"Pass the butter to the victim," Wesley said. He was in a worse humor than usual because he had had a flat tire on the way home from the university.

Scofield handed her the butter and said, "Why Mamma, ain't you ashamed to shoot an old bull that ain't done nothing but give you a little scrub strain in your herd? I declare," he said, "with the Mamma I got it's a wonder I turned out to be such a nice boy!"

"You ain't her boy, Son," Wesley said.

She eased back in her chair, her fingertips on the edge of the table.

"All I know is," Scofield said, "I done mighty well to be as nice as I am seeing what I come from."

When they teased her they spoke Greenleaf English but Wesley made his own particular tone come through it like a knife edge. "Well lemme tell you one thang, Brother," he said, leaning over the table, "that if you had half a mind you would already know."

"What's that, Brother?" Scofield asked, his broad face grinning into the thin constricted one across from him.

"That is," Wesley said, "that neither you nor me is her boy . . . ," but he stopped abruptly as she gave a kind of hoarse wheeze like an old horse lashed unexpectedly. She reared up and ran from the room.

"Oh, for God's sake," Wesley growled, "what did you start her off for?"

"I never started her off," Scofield said. "You started her off."

"Hah."

"She's not as young as she used to be and she can't take it."

"She can only give it out," Wesley said. "I'm the one that takes it."

His brother's pleasant face had changed so that an ugly family resemblance showed between them. "Nobody feels sorry for a lousy bastard like you," he said and grabbed across the table for the other's shirtfront.

From her room she heard a crash of dishes and she rushed back through the kitchen into the dining room. The hall door was open and Scofield was going out of it. Wesley was lying like a large bug on his back with the edge of the over-turned table cutting him across the middle and broken dishes scattered on top of him. She pulled the table off him and caught his arm to help him rise but he scrambled up and pushed her off with a furious charge of energy and flung himself out the door after his brother.

She would have collapsed but a knock on the back door stiffened her and she swung around. Across the kitchen and back porch, she could see Mr. Greenleaf peering eagerly through the screenwire. All her resources returned in full strength as if she had only needed to be challenged by the devil himself to regain them. "I heard a thump," he called, "and I thought the plastering might have fell on you."

If he had been wanted someone would have had to go on a horse to find him. She crossed the kitchen and the porch and stood inside the screen and said, "No, nothing happened but the table turned over. One of the legs was weak," and without pausing, "the boys didn't come for the bull so tomorrow you'll have to shoot him."

The sky was crossed with thin red and purple bars and behind them the sun was moving down slowly as if it were descending a ladder. Mr. Greenleaf squatted down on the step, his back to her, the top of his hat on a level with her feet. "Tomorrow I'll drive him home for you," he said.

"Oh no, Mr. Greenleaf," she said in a mocking voice, "you drive him home tomorrow and next week he'll be back here. I know better than that." Then in a mournful tone, she said, "I'm surprised at O. T. and E. T. to treat me this way. I thought they'd have more gratitude. Those boys spent some mighty happy days on this place, didn't they, Mr. Greenleaf?"

Mr. Greenleaf didn't say anything.

"I think they did," she said. "I think they did. But they've forgotten all the nice little things I did for them now. If I recall, they wore my boys' old clothes and played with my boys' old toys and hunted with my boys' old guns. They swam in my pond and shot my birds and fished in my stream and I never forgot their birthday and Christmas seemed to roll around very often if I remember it right. And do they think of any of those things now?" she asked. "NOOOOO," she said.

For a few seconds she looked at the disappearing sun and Mr. Greenleaf examined the palms of his hands. Presently as if it had just occurred to her, she asked, "Do you know the real reason they didn't come for that bull?"

"Naw I don't," Mr. Greenleaf said in a surly voice.

"They didn't come because I'm a woman," she said. "You can get away with anything when you're dealing with a woman. If there were a man running this place . . ."

Quick as a snake striking Mr. Greenleaf said, "You got two boys. They know you got two men on the place."

The sun had disappeared behind the tree line. She looked down at the dark crafty face, upturned now, and at the wary eyes, bright under the shadow of the hatbrim. She waited long enough for him to see that she was hurt and then she said, "Some people learn gratitude too late, Mr. Greenleaf, and some never learn it at all," and she turned and left him sitting on the steps.

Half the night in her sleep she heard a sound as if some large stone were grinding a hole on the outside wall of her brain. She was walking on the inside, over a succession of beautiful rolling hills, planting her stick in front of each step. She became aware after a time that the noise was the sun trying to burn through the tree line and she stopped to watch, safe in the knowledge that it couldn't, that it had to sink the way it always did outside of her property. When she first stopped it was a swollen red ball, but as she stood watching it began to narrow and pale until it looked like a bullet. Then suddenly it burst through the tree line and raced down the hill toward her. She woke up with her hand over her mouth and the same noise, diminished but distinct, in her ear. It was the bull munching under her window. Mr. Greenleaf had let him out.

She got up and made her way to the window in the dark and looked out through the slit blind, but the bull had moved away from the hedge and at first she didn't see him. Then she saw a heavy form some distance away, paused as if observing her. This is the last night I am going to put up with this, she said, and watched until the iron shadow moved away in the darkness.

The next morning she waited until exactly eleven o'clock. Then she got in her car and drove to the barn. Mr. Greenleaf was cleaning milk cans. He had seven of them standing up outside the milk room to get the sun. She had been telling him to do this for two weeks. "All right, Mr. Greenleaf," she said, "go get your gun. We're going to shoot that bull."

"I thought you wanted theseyer cans . . ."

"Go get your gun, Mr. Greenleaf," she said. Her voice and face were expressionless.

"That gentleman torn out of there last night," he murmured in a tone of regret and bent again to the can he had his arm in.

"Go get your gun, Mr. Greenleaf," she said in the same triumphant toneless voice. "The bull is in the pasture with the dry cows. I saw him from my upstairs window. I'm going to drive you up to the field and you can run him into the empty pasture and shoot him there."

He detached himself from the can slowly. "Ain't nobody ever ast me to shoot my boys' own bull!" he said in a high rasping voice. He removed a rag from his back pocket and began to wipe his hands violently, then his nose.

She turned as if she had not heard this and said, "I'll wait for you in the car. Go get your gun."

She sat in the car and watched him stalk off toward the harness room where he kept a gun. After he had entered the room, there was a crash as if he had kicked something out of his way. Presently he emerged again with the gun, circled behind the car, opened the door violently and threw himself onto the seat beside her. He held the gun between his knees and looked straight ahead. He'd like to shoot me instead of the bull, she thought, and turned her face away so that he could not see her smile.

The morning was dry and clear. She drove through the woods for a quarter of a mile and then out into the open where there were fields on either side of the narrow road. The exhilaration of carrying her point had sharpened her senses. Birds were screaming everywhere, the grass was almost too bright to look at, the sky was an even piercing blue. "Spring is here!" she said gaily. Mr. Greenleaf lifted one muscle somewhere near his mouth as if he found this the most asinine remark ever made. When she stopped at the second pasture gate, he flung himself out of the car door and slammed it behind him. Then he opened the gate and she drove through. He closed it and flung himself back in, silently, and she drove around the rim of the pasture until she spotted the bull, almost in the center of it, grazing peacefully among the cows.

"The gentleman is waiting on you," she said and gave Mr. Greenleaf's furious profile a sly look. "Run him into that next pasture and when you get him in, I'll drive in behind you and shut the gate myself."

He flung himself out again, this time deliberately leaving the car door open so that she had to lean across the seat and close it. She sat smiling as she watched him make his way across the pasture toward the opposite gate. He seemed to throw himself forward at each step and then pull back as if he were calling on some power to witness that he was being forced. "Well," she said aloud as if he were still in the car, "it's your own boys who are making you do this, Mr. Greenleaf." O. T. and E. T. were probably splitting their sides laughing at him now. She could hear their identical nasal voices saying, "Made Daddy shoot our bull for us. Daddy don't know no better than to think that's a fine bull he's shooting. Gonna kill Daddy to shoot that bull!"

"If those boys cared a thing about you, Mr. Greenleaf," she said, "they would have come for that bull. I'm surprised at them."

He was circling around to open the gate first. The bull, dark among the spotted cows, had not moved. He kept his head down, eating constantly. Mr. Greenleaf opened the gate and then began circling back to approach him from the rear. When he was about ten feet behind him, he flapped his arms at his sides. The bull lifted his head indolently and then lowered it again and continued to eat. Mr. Greenleaf stopped again and picked up something and threw it at him with a vicious swing. She decided it was a sharp rock for the bull leapt and then began to gallop until he disappeared over the rim of the hill. Mr. Greenleaf followed at his leisure.

"You needn't think you're going to lose him!" she cried and started the car straight across the pasture. She had to drive slowly over the terraces and when she reached the gate, Mr. Greenleaf and the bull were nowhere in sight. This pasture was smaller than the last, a green arena, encircled almost entirely by woods. She got out and closed the gate and stood looking for some sign of Mr. Greenleaf but he had disappeared completely. She knew at once that his plan was to lose the bull in the woods. Eventually, she would see him emerge somewhere from the circle of trees and come limping toward her and when he finally reached her, he would say, "If you can find that gentleman in them woods, you're better than me."

She was going to say, "Mr. Greenleaf, if I have to walk into those woods with you and stay all afternoon, we are going to find that bull and shoot him. You are going to shoot him if I have to pull the trigger for you." When he saw she meant business, he would return and shoot the bull quickly himself.

She got back into the car and drove to the center of the pasture where he would not have so far to walk to reach her when he came out of the woods. At this moment she could picture him sitting on a stump, marking lines in the ground with a stick. She decided she would wait exactly ten minutes by her watch. Then she would begin to honk. She got out of the car and walked around a little and then sat down on the front bumper to wait and rest. She was very tired and she lay her head back against the hood and closed her eyes. She did not understand why she should be so tired when it was only mid-morning. Through her closed eyes, she could feel the sun, red-hot overhead. She opened her eyes slightly but the white light forced her to close them again.

For some time she lay back against the hood, wondering drowsily why she was so tired. With her eyes closed, she didn't think of time as divided into days and nights but into past and future. She decided she was tired because she had been working continuously for fifteen years.

She decided she had every right to be tired, and to rest for a few minutes before she began working again. Before any kind of judgment seat, she would be able to say: I've worked, I have not wallowed. At this very instant while she was recalling a lifetime of work, Mr. Greenleaf was loitering in the woods and Mrs. Greenleaf was probably flat on the ground, asleep over her holeful of clippings. The woman had got worse over the years and Mrs. May believed that now she was actually demented. "I'm afraid your wife has let religion warp her," she said once tactfully to Mr. Greenleaf. "Everything in moderation, you know."

"She cured a man oncet that half his gut was eat out with worms," Mr. Greenleaf said, and she had turned away, half-sickened. Poor souls, she thought now, so simple. For a few seconds she dozed.

When she sat up and looked at her watch, more than ten minutes had passed. She had not heard any shot. A new thought occurred to her; suppose Mr. Greenleaf had aroused the bull chunking stones at him and the animal had turned on him and run him up against a tree and gored him? The irony of it deepened: O. T. and E. T. would then get a shyster lawyer and sue her. It would be the fitting end to her fifteen years with the Greenleafs. She thought of it almost with pleasure as if she had hit on the perfect ending for a story she was telling her friends. Then she dropped it, for Mr. Greenleaf had a gun with him and she had insurance.

She decided to honk. She got up and reached inside the car window and gave three sustained honks and two or three shorter ones to let him know she was getting impatient. Then she went back and sat down on the bumper again.

In a few minutes something emerged from the tree line, a black heavy shadow that tossed its head several times and then bounded forward. After a second she saw it was the bull. He was crossing the pasture toward her at a slow gallop, a gay almost rocking gait as if he were overjoyed to find her again. She looked beyond him to see if Mr. Greenleaf was coming out of the woods too but he was not. "Here he is, Mr. Greenleaf!" she called and looked on the other side of the pasture to see if he could be coming out there but he was not in sight. She looked back and saw that the bull, his head lowered, was racing toward her. She remained perfectly still, not in fright, but in a freezing unbelief. She stared at the violent black streak bounding toward her as if she had no sense of distance, as if she could not decide at once what his intention was, and the bull had buried his head in her lap, like a wild tormented lover, before her expression changed. One of his horns sank until it pierced her heart and the other curved around her side and held her in an unbreakable grip. She continued to stare straight ahead but the entire scene in front of her had changed—the tree line was a dark wound in a world that was nothing but sky—and she had the look of a person whose sight has been suddenly restored but who finds the light unbearable.

Mr. Greenleaf was running toward her from the side with his gun raised and she saw him coming though she was not looking in his direction. She saw him approaching on the outside of some invisible circle, the tree line gaping behind him and nothing under his feet. He shot the bull four times through the eye. She did not hear the shots but she felt the quake in the huge body as it sank, pulling her forward on its head, so that she seemed, when Mr. Greenleaf reached her, to be bent over whispering some last discovery into the animal's ear.

Questions

1. Central to this story is the contrast between the May and Greenleaf families. One is portrayed as sterile and "on the way down," the other as thriving and "on the way up." Show the specific ways in which this contrast is developed.

2. In some primitive societies the bull has been worshiped as a symbol of the sun, as a male god, or as a life source. Consider the symbolic functions of the bull in this story, especially its identification with the Greenleafs. Why is it a particularly appropriate agent of revenge?

3. The attitude of the two families toward religion shows a good deal about them. What does religion mean to each one? How genuine is Mrs. May's belief? How genuine is Mrs. Greenleaf's? In a practical sense, which woman is best served by her religion?

4. The story is all seen from Mrs. May's standpoint though not told in the first person. What ironies does this technique make possible? To what extent are Mrs. May's observations of the other characters, as well as her image of herself, reliable? How do they differ from the reader's knowledge?

5. Account for the relationship between Mrs. May and Mrs. Greenleaf. Why have they put up with each other for so long?

6. One may think the ending of the story represents a kind of poetic justice. Why? Is it a good ending, or does it rely too much on pure chance? Is there any way in which Mrs. May has brought it on herself?

Gregoire Ouedrago

OUAGADOUGOU

Though the work of Gregoire Ouedrago is little known in America, he is one of an emerging group of African writers that is now beginning to interpret and reveal life on that vast continent to the rest of the world. He sets his work mainly in Ouagadougou, Upper Volta, which is his home. Ouedrago is an English teacher at l'Ecole Nationale d'Administration. He has spent a year in the United States, at San Jose State College, working in a government-sponsored program in the teaching of English as a second language. His story, "Ouagadougou," is hardly fiction in the ordinary sense, yet it distills the subjective essence of a city in much the same way in which a character's personality is usually revealed. The story is from the first volume of a collection of New African Literature and the Arts.

The sky is beginning to show some streaks of light over the East, behind Zoaghna. From the heart of the city the muezzin calls the Moslems to the central mosque for prayer. A bell rings sharply in the quietness, then from far away; this is the call for the main Catholic parish five o'clock mass. Once in a while dogs bark and roosters crow in the homes. Most women are already up, preparing breakfast. There is no traffic in the streets but a few early people here and there, some driving cars, others riding bicycles or motorcycles, or walking. In a moment, men will go to work and children to school. Another day in Ouagadougou has begun, just as usual.

Sixty years ago, Ouagadougou was the greatest of the kingdom capitals of the Mossi empire, the Mogho. Thus it was a farming town. There were neither churches nor schools or cars. But remote foreign tribes spoke of its greatness. Hamado's father was a young page of the Mogho-Naaba at that time. According to the old man, three roaring beats of drums, heard three miles around, announced both the sun and the Mogho-Naaba's waking every day. In the eyes of the Mossi, the Mogho-Naaba represented the sun on earth, and both rose together. When the sun was up, men walked to their fields outside the town, and children took care of the cows, sheep, and goats. Women usually had small fields around the compounds and worked there. In the dry season, when there was no field work, the men rubbed their walls with boalga and they looked beautiful. Those who could not find the good white boalga from a freshly dug well used red earth. They also spent this season making new mats, roofs and sheds, while the usual children's work was to feed the poultry. At noon, the sun burned hot. Most of the ten thousand inhabitants sat in their homes resting under their straw roofs, cooling their bodies with palmetto fans. Almost everywhere, children ran about under the karite trees, naked. Some people gathered under the big shady palaver-trees to chat about current matters. "Sometimes," tells Hamado's father, "I had some days off. Then I left the palace and went to live with relatives at Paspanga. There was a mat shed just across the Nongremassem pond. A woman sold good raam in the place. I used to meet your uncle there, boy, and we had some calabashes of the drink. Then years passed. The nine-century-old capital of the kingdom ruled by Ouedraogo, Zoungrana, Oubri" . . . he recited proudly a long list of emperors till the one he served . . . "met a queer stranger. He had no toes and spoke a savage language unknown to all Mossi. He had a skin disease that turned him all white. One white man had tried to come in Ouagadougou years before, but he was ordered by His Majesty not to step into his land. The second one who tried to come in was said to have shot off guns many miles from here, in a foreign land outside the Mogho. But he was kind and polite here. He sent messengers, accompanied by presents and good words to His Majesty. He was allowed in. Later, another white man came, but he was disloyal. Instead of acting like his brother who had come earlier, he surprised the Mogho-Naaba and his Tansoba. Before the Tansoba could gather his warriors, this man had already killed lots of people. This white man had come to stay for long. He sent words to his relatives to come and live with him. Some of them were, by tradition, forbidden to get married. The males were called fathers, though they had no children or wives. They said their sons were all of us because they liked us and wanted us to love their god called Zezu. Our elders laughed at their nonsense. Who ever got children without a wife? Tell me. Anyhow, how could whites have black offspring? These fathers asked the Owners-of-land for a place to built their huts and were given the devil forest. It was a place where even foolhardy ones feared to pass by at night. There, they could build a shrine for their Zezu and be the devil's fathers. Surprisingly, the devils did not do any harm to them. Our Sacrifice-Makers and the Moslem Imam later revealed that our devils had no common grounds with Whites; their own devils would harm them. The Mogho-Naaba continued to rule the kingdom and the people of Ouagadougou respected and revered him. At a cabinet meeting, the emperor said to the kingdom ministers and grandees that our people must read the Nassara's book, the Whites' book, to know his secrets and have two strengths: his and ours. Each minister and chief of district would send their children to the Whites. In the town, new houses called 'learning-houses' were built."

Hamado's father has passed away now, and Ouagadougou has changed. At the age of seven, Hamado and I went to school together. It was the main Catholic-parish Boys' school. Then Hamado was baptized a Catholic and became Marcellin. The old man was rather upset about his son's conversion. Before he died, he said that we young men will not feel at ease for a long time because we had become the strange result of two worlds that could not be separated. Ouagadougou, he added, was no longer the property of the Mossi. It belonged to everyone and no one in particular. With a submissive voice, he concluded that this was our time and not his.

When we were children, Marcellin and I knew everyone in our section of town. The entire city had only forty thousand inhabitants then. We had a pool at Saint Joseph—that Saint Leon claimed—where we went to swim and wash our clothes every Thursday. This pool has become part of a street. There was a barren area near our school, and we called it Boureima's Tobacco Field. None of us knew if anyone named Boureima had ever grown tobacco in the place, but no one claimed it, and there was always soft grass there. All our riotous play took place there. One day, I went home with a bloody nose. Marcellin, who had been waiting for me in our house, asked if I had gone to Boureima's Tobacco Field. Of course, I had. We laugh when we talk about these silly things today. There are buildings on Boureima's Tobacco Field now.

Ouagadougou today is a pleasant city, as it has always been. It is a place where scholars come to learn about the origins—sometimes buried in myths—and the long history of the most preserved and largest organized tribe in French-speaking West Africa. It is also the capital of a newly independent country. As you enter Ouagadougou, you see and feel this dual aspect of the city. For nine centuries, it has remained the capital of the Oubritenga, the most important kingdom of the Mossi empire. When Upper Volta was created in 1919, Ouagadougou was chosen capital of the territory. Side by side, modern buildings and traditional houses stand in the bright blue sky. In the classrooms, Negroes and Whites, Mossi and non-Mossi study together. In the grey brick-palace of His Majesty, Naaba Kougri, the thirty-sixth Mogho-Naaba sworn in in 1957, still confers with his ministers and the other kingdom grandees. About two miles from there, thousands of people from the whole country and the world had gathered in 1960 to hear the Declaration of Independence by President Maurice Yameogo. Ouagadouguians are proud of the dual aspect of their city. It is the symbol of two convergent ways of life. Naaba, his ministers, and district and village chiefs are no more than equal citizens with everyone else in the city and in the country. All together Ouagadouguians have honored the founders of their city, and the great men who made its history. Avenues, streets, squares and buildings have been dedicated to them. Right in the heart of the city, Avenue de la Princesse Yennenga welcomes visitors coming from the South or landing at the airport. Yennenga was the princess amazon from Gambaga in Ghana—who gave birth to Ouedraogo, the ancestor of all Mossi. As soon as they come out of the train station, visitors from the West are warmly welcomed by Place Naaba Koom II, a square dedicated to the thirty-fourth Mogho-Naaba who reigned from 1905 to 1942. Ouagadougou City Hospital bears the name of the late Yallegdo Ouedraogo, a great doctor who was president of the Constitutive Assembly of the country after Self Government was granted in 1956. French education has indeed changed Ouagadouguians into two worlds which cannot be separated, but they like it so. Every Tuesday night from nine to ten, they enjoy listening to Radio Upper Volta Folk Program, a program of Mossi folk tales and songs conducted by the Larhalle Naaba, a minister of the Mogho-Naaba. On such nights, many people who have no radio sets gather in front of small shops and bars to listen.

You may think that Ouagadougou, being so important, is just a nice place to visit but not to live in, as a great number of important cities are. It is not so. Ouagadougou is a pleasant and friendly city. There is no big hustle and bustle, and you would not feel lonesome in the middle of a keep-moving-to-nowhere crowd. There are only one hundred thousand inhabitants. The people are simple and like good jokes. Tease the merchant, who would think of bleeding you white, and take it easy. Say "laafi bala" to the unknown passer-by who greets you. Make a call on the Mogho-Naaba and ask to visit his palace and attend the Friday morning "false departure" ceremony. Go to the *Centre National de Recherches Scientifiques,* also called IFAN, if you are interested in reading about the people of the country. How about seeing the President's palace or the National Assembly? Buy a hat and a palmetto fan for almost nothing and cool yourself by a pool; then people would say: "He, look! This man likes it here." Don't get confused when you notice a winning smile at you for no reason. Sometimes you will meet a miserable beggar, half-naked at a corner. Give him a smile or something else good. A damnable robber may steal your wallet in the market. If you get him, tell him that if he is a "tampiri" (he will understand what it means and you do not need to in advance) he may keep the wallet. Then he may want to teach you some useful sentences in Morre, the Mossi language, and help you do your errands.

Ouagadougou is my native town. For years, earth-brick houses have given shelter to people of various walks of life; people have drunk good raam out of calabashes, and eaten good millet sagabo and hot sauce. The sky is bright and burns hot at noon. Ouagadougou is a nice town, and for me it is the nicest in the world. Why?—the sky is beginning to show some streaks of light over the East, behind Zoaghna. From the heart of the city, the muezzin calls the Moslems to the central mosque for prayer. A bell rings sharply in the quietness, then dies far away; this is the call for the main Catholic parish five o'clock mass. Once in a while dogs bark and roosters crow in the homes. Most women are already up, preparing breakfast. There is no traffic in the streets but a few early people here and there, some driving cars, others riding bicycles or motorcycles, or walking. In a moment, men will go to work and children to school. Another day in Ouagadougou has begun, just as usual.

Questions

1. One usually thinks of a short story as a narration of actions involving persons. "Ouagadougou" is almost entirely a description of a city. Does it still qualify as a "story"? Is it out of place in a collection of fiction?

2. How is the city "characterized" and made individual, similar to the characterization of human beings in most stories? Does this mean that places as well as persons have "personalities"?

3. This is one of the stories in this book—Jorge Luis Borges' "Funes the Memorious" and Virginia Woolf's "The Mark on the Wall" are others—that extend the usual boundaries of fiction. Can you formulate a definition of fiction that will include not only the conventional examples (stories by Hawthorne, James, Chekhov, Lawrence, Mann, etc.) but also fables, allegorical works like "The Bound Man" and "The Scythe," and stories like "Ouagadougou"?

Luigi Pirandello

THE JAR

Best-known as a dramatist, Luigi Pirandello also wrote several novels and some short stories. In most of his writing the same concerns are paramount: the ambiguous nature of truth, the shifting face of reality, and the superiority of illusion. Sometimes regarded as too cerebral—as an author of works designed to trick and puzzle his audiences rather than to enlighten them—Pirandello once suffered a decline in reputation. In recent years his affinity with many modern movements of thought—in psychology as well as in literature—has awakened new interest in him. Pirandello was born in Sicily in 1867, was educated at the University of Rome, and then took a doctorate in philosophy at the University of Bonn. Various events in his personal life—disillusionment with the revolutionary political causes he espoused, and the tragedy of his wife's insanity—led him to question the nature of reality and to ponder the subject of which is more "real," external appearances or the inner natures of things. This is the dilemma he confronts in most of his works. Among the major plays in which he treats shifting aspects of reality are Right You Are (If You Think You Are) *(1917),* Six Characters in Search of an Author *(1921),* Naked *(1922),* Henry IV *(1922),* Each in His Own Way *(1924), and* As You Desire Me *(1930). His novels include* The Late Mattia Pascal *(1904) and* Shoot *(1916). He died in 1936, two years after receiving the Nobel Prize.*

Though the short story received relatively little of Pirandello's attention, he still produced some distinguished works in this form—mostly at the very beginning and again at the end of his career. Preceding his later distrust of realism, his earliest works were folk tales of Italian life, using much realistic local color. "The Jar" (1909) is an example of this kind of work—a comic story on a very old theme, the tight-fisted trickster who meets his match, and it shows Pirandello's sympathetic but humorous treatment of the country people among whom he grew up.

There was a wonderful olive harvest as well that year. The mature trees, which had been groaning under the weight of olives the previous year, were all as heavily laden again, despite the mists which had attacked them at blossom-time.

Zirafa had a good acreage of them on his farm, Le Quote, at Primosole and, foreseeing that the five old glazed earthenware jars which he had in the cellar wouldn't be sufficient to contain the new harvest, he'd ordered (and in good time, too) a sixth from Santo Stefano di Camastra, where they made them. Tall as a man's chest it was, with a big fat belly, and most majestic-looking—admirably equipped to rank as a Mother Superior over the other five.

Needless to say, he'd had a row with the jar-maker over this jar. But then, who *didn't* Lollò Zirafa have rows with? Over every slightest trifle—even over a tiny slab of stone that had fallen off the boundary wall, even over a handful of straw! He'd yell at them to saddle his mule, so that he could rush into town and take out all sorts of summonses and things. And so, by sheer dint of using up vast quantities of legal documents (with heavy stamp-duty on the lot of them), meeting lawyers' fees, quoting this and quoting that, and always having in the end to pay everyone's costs, he'd just about half-ruined himself.

People said that his legal adviser had grown so tired of seeing him turning up in his office two or three times a week that, in order to get him from under his feet, he'd made him a present of a little book, which was just like a missal to look at. It was the *Civil Code.* So that he could drive *himself* round the bend rummaging through it on his own, to try and find out whether there was any judicial foundation for the lawsuits he was wanting to bring.

Whereas previously those with whom he had a difference of opinion would take the rise out of him by yelling after him 'Saddle my mule!' Now, instead, it was, 'Out with your *A.B.C.*, man!'

And Don Lollò would reply, 'I certainly *shall* get it out! And I'll blast you all off the face of the earth, you sons-of-bitches!'

That new jar, for which he'd paid four lovely, bouncing, chinking *onze,* had been lodged temporarily in the press-room—for convenience, while they were waiting for room to be found for it in the cellar. No one had ever seen such a jar. It really *hurt* you to see it there, lodged in that cavern stinking with must and that harsh crude smell which lurks in places that are deprived of light and air.

Two days earlier the knocking-down of the olives had begun, and Don Lollò was nearly going out of his mind with sheer rage because, what with the knockers-down to look after, and mule-drivers, who kept turning up with mules loaded with manure to deposit on the slope by the field where he was going to sow beans next year—well, he just didn't know how to split himself into enough selves to go round, and who to see to first. So he went about swearing like a trooper, threatening with direful extermination first this one, then that, if so much as one olive, *one single olive,* got overlooked; almost as if he'd counted them all beforehand, one by one, while they were still on the trees. Then off he'd go and threaten the others with all sorts of dreadful things if every heap of manure wasn't exactly the same size as the others. Wearing his battered old white hat, and in his shirt-sleeves, with his chest bare, his face ruddy to the point of apoplexy, and all dripping with sweat, he'd rush hither and thither, with his wolf-like eyes roaming all over the place, and angrily rubbing his cheeks—those cheeks on which his ferocious and indomitable beard virtually sprouted afresh as the razor cut away the old growth.

Now, at the end of the third day, three of the peasants who'd been knocking-down, on going into the press-room to put their ladders and poles, had been struck all of a heap by the sight of the new jar—cracked in two, just as if someone, with a neat cut, had taken the jar in all its fullness and removed the whole of the front bulge.

'Just look at that! Just look at that!'

'Who can possibly have done it?'

'Oh, God help us! Who's going to tell Don Lollò? Oh, what a pity! The new jar!'

The first of them, more terrified than the rest, proposed that they should shut the door immediately and go off ever so quietly, leaving their ladders and poles leaning up against the wall outside. The second, however, said, 'Are you mad? Try *that* one on *Don Lollò*? He's quite capable of believing that we broke it! No! We all stand fast here, every single one of us!'

He went out of the press-room and, making a megaphone with his hands, called, 'Don Lollò! Oh, Don Lollòòòò!'

There he was, at the bottom of the slope, with the men who were unloading the manure. As usual, he was gesticulating away furiously, and every so often banging his white hat on to his head with both hands. Sometimes he banged it on again so hard that he couldn't shift it, either at the nape of his neck or over his forehead. Already the last flames of sunset were being extinguished in the sky, and, cutting through the peace and quiet that was descending on the countryside–as the shadows of evening with its sweet coolness closed in—there came, *hurled* at you, those gestures on the part of that man who was always in a fury.

'Don Lollò! Oh, Don Lollòòòò!'

When he came on up and saw the damage, it looked just as if he was going to go out of his mind. He hurled himself first at the three men who'd made the discovery. One of them he grabbed by the throat and pinned against the wall, shouting, 'By the Blood of the Virgin Mary, you'll pay for it!'

When he in his turn had been grabbed by the other two, their earthy, bestial faces twisted with emotion, he turned all his mad rage against himself. He tore off his hat and flung it on the ground; he slapped himself hard on both cheeks, stamped his feet and bawled away like a man mourning the death of a relative. 'Oh, my new jar! Four *onze* worth of lovely jar! I hadn't even christened it!'

He wanted to know who'd broken it! Was it conceivable that it had got broken all by itself? Somebody *must* have broken it, either out of envy or out of sheer human wickedness! But when? And how? There wasn't any sign of violence! Had it by any chance been broken when it had arrived from the jar-maker's? Of course it hadn't! It had rung like a bell when it'd come!

As soon as the peasants saw that his immediate anger was abating, they started urging him to calm down. The jar could be mended. After all, it wasn't very *badly* damaged. Only one piece had got broken off. A good jar-mender would be able to put it together again so that it came up just like new. There was Zi' Dima Licasi, for instance. Just the man for the job! He'd discovered a miraculous cement, the secret of which he guarded most jealously. A cement you couldn't even bash apart with a hammer, once it had set. Look! If Don Lollò would like him to, Zi' Dima Licasi could come along tomorrow morning—at the crack of dawn—and before you could say two twos are four the jar would be mended and better than ever.

Don Lollò said 'No' to all their exhortations. It was quite useless. There wasn't any way he could see of making good the damage. In the end, however, he let them talk him round. So next morning, punctually at the crack of dawn, Zi' Dima Licasi presented himself at Primosole, with his tool kit slung over his shoulder.

He was a misshapen old man, with swollen, knotty joints, just like an ancient Saracen olive log. Every word had to be dragged out of him. His deformed body positively bristled with stand-offishness. Or was it really *sadness*? Or was it disappointment that no one was able to appreciate at their proper value—or even to *comprehend*—his merits as an inventor? Zi' Dima Licasi hadn't yet patented his discovery because he wanted deeds to speak louder than words on a bit of paper. So he had to keep a sharp look-out, fore and aft, as it were, to make sure that no one stole his secret from him.

'Show me this cement of yours,' were Don Lollò's first words to him after he'd looked him mistrustfully up and down for several minutes.

Zi' Dima, the acme of dignity, shook his head.

'You'll see how good it is when the job's done.'

'Will it end up all right?'

Zi' Dima put his tool-kit on the ground. He fished out a rolled up and very well-worn cotton kerchief. Very slowly he started to unroll it, while they all stood around him, consumed with curiosity, their whole attention riveted upon him. When, finally, a pair of spectacles appeared, with the bridge and sides broken and tied up with string, *he* gave a sigh and all the rest of them burst into hearty laughter. Zi' Dima took no notice. He wiped his fingers before handling the spectacles and then fitted them carefully on to his nose and over his ears. Then very, very solemnly he began his examination of the jar—which by now had been brought out into the threshing-yard. Finally he said, 'It'll be all right.'

Zirafa started laying down his conditions. 'I don't trust it with cement alone. I want rivets as well.'

'I'm off,' replied Zi' Dima, and, without even pausing to argue the point, he got up and slung his tool-kit over his shoulder again.

Don Lollò grabbed him by one arm. 'Where are you off to? Is this the way you treat people, you high-and-mighty old swine? Huh! Look at him! As full of airs and graces as if he was Lord Tomnoddy himself! Ger, you old hunk of cat's meat! You stupid old donkey! I've got to use that jar for putting oil in! It'll ooze through! You don't mean to say you think you can mend a crack a mile long—*look at it!*—just with cement! I want rivets as well. Cement and rivets. Those are my orders!'

Zi' Dima closed his eyes, pursed his lips and shook his head. They were all the same! He was always being deprived of the opportunity of doing a good clean job, conscientiously carried out according to the rules of his craft. He was always being deprived, too, of an opportunity of demonstrating the virtues of his cement.

'If that jar,' he said, 'doesn't ring like a bell again——'

'I'm not listening to a word you say,' interrupted Don Lollò. '*Rivets!* I'm paying you to use cement and rivets. How much do I have to give you?'

'If, with my cement alone——'

'Oh, God rot me! What a stubborn brute the man is!' exclaimed Don Lollò. 'Am I talking sense or *aren't* I? I tell you, *I want rivets*. We'll settle things when the job's done. I haven't got any more time to waste on you!'

And off he went to look after his workmen.

Zi' Dima started on his job, simply bristling with anger and contempt. And his anger and contempt grew with every hole that he drilled in the main body of the jar and in the broken-off bit—this was to make it possible for the steel wire used in the riveting to be threaded through. He accompanied the *frou-frou* of the bit with a running commentary of grunts, which gradually got louder and louder. And his face took on an ever more bilious hue and his eyes became ever sharper and more flaming with annoyance. The first stage of the operation completed, he flung the drill angrily back into the tool-bag. He stuck the broken-off piece back into position in the jar, to see if the holes were the right distance apart and to see if they corresponded with one another, then, with his wire-cutters, he cut off as many pieces of steel wire as he'd need to insert rivets, and called over one of the peasants who were knocking-down to help him.

'Cheer up, Zi' Dima!' said this fellow, seeing his face twisted with anger.

Zi' Dima raised his hand in an angry gesture. He opened the old tin which contained his cement, and, holding it up to heaven, brandished it in the air, as if offering it up to God—seeing that men had no desire to recognize its virtues. Then with his finger he began to spread it along the edge of the broken-off piece and the edge of the jar where it had come away. He took the wire-cutters and the pieces of wire he'd prepared in advance and tucked himself away inside the open belly of the jar, instructing the peasant to stick the broken-off piece in position, just as he himself had done only a few moments earlier. Before he started putting in the rivets, he said to the farm-hand, from inside the jar, 'Go on, tug away! Tug away with all your might! *See*? You can't get them apart, can you? So to hell with anyone who doesn't believe me! Bang away! Bang away! Does it, or does it not, ring like a bell? Even with me inside it! Run along! Run along and tell your boss all about it!'

And Zi' Dima began to pass the pieces of wire through the pairs of holes that lay next to one another, one this side, the other that side of the mend. Then with his wire-cutters he twisted the ends together. It took him an hour to do the lot of them. The sweat was pouring off him, there inside the jar. As he worked, he lamented his wretched fate. And the peasant on the outside spent *his* time comforting him.

'Now help me to get out!' said Zi' Dima at the end of it all.

But, no matter how large in the belly it was, that jar was very tight in the neck. Zi' Dima had been so angry that he hadn't checked up on *that* detail. Now, try as he would, he couldn't find any way of getting out again. And the peasant, instead of helping him—look at him, the idle lout, doubled up with laughter!—there was Zi' Dima, *imprisoned*! Imprisoned in the jar which he himself had mended, and which now—there was no possibility of half-measures—would have to be broken all over again! And broken for good this time!

Hearing all the laughter and shouting, Don Lollò came up. Zi' Dima, inside the jar, was like a demented tomcat.

'Let me out!' he was howling. 'God Almighty, I want to get out! At once! Help!'

At first Don Lollò just stood there like a man dazed. He simply couldn't believe his eyes. 'But, how on——? In there? Has he riveted himself up in there?'

He went up to the jar and yelled at the old man, '*Help?* What sort of help can *I* give you, you obstinate old dodder? It was your job to take your own measurements before you got in, wasn't it? Now, come on. Try getting an arm out first—that's the way. Now your head—come on! Come on! No, gently—— What the——! Down with it! Now, wait a minute! Like *that*! No! Down with it! Down with it! How the devil did you manage to——? Hey, what about the jar now? Now, keep calm! Keep calm! Keep calm!' he started advising all and sundry around him—just as if *they* and not he were likely to begin getting all worked up. 'Oh, my brains are boiling! Now, keep calm! This is a completely new case. Where's my mule?'

He rapped on the jar with his knuckles. It really *did* ring like a bell.

'Lovely! Come up like new! Hang on a minute!' he said to the prisoner. '*You*, go and saddle me my mule!' he said to the farm-hand. Then, rubbing his head vigorously with both hands, he went on muttering away to himself. 'Just look at the sort of thing that happens to me!' This isn't a jar—it's the devil incarnate! Keep still! *You in there*, keep still!'

And he rushed over to steady the jar, in which an infuriated Zi' Dima was bashing about like an animal in a trap.

'It's a completely new case, my dear fellow! I must get my lawyer to sort it out for me. I don't trust my own judgment. Where's my mule? Get me my mule! I'm going now! I'll be back immediately! Just be patient! It's in your own interest. . . . Meanwhile, *keep quiet*! Keep calm! I must look after my own interests. And first of all, just so as to preserve my rights, I'll do my duty. Here you are! I'm paying you for your work. I'm paying you a day's wages. Five lire? That do you?'

'I don't want anything!' yelled Zi' Dima. 'I want to get out of here!'

'You'll get out all right! But meanwhile, I'm paying you. Here you are—five lire!'

He took the money out of his waistcoat pocket and threw it into the jar. Then he asked, solicitously, 'Have you had your breakfast? Bread and something to go with it, eh? Right away! You don't want it? Throw it to the dogs, then! It's enough for me to know that I've given it to you!'

He ordered them to give him the food, leapt into the saddle, and he went to town at a gallop. Everyone who saw him as he galloped along gesticulating, thought he must be off to shut himself up in the lunatic asylum, so extraordinarily was he behaving.

As luck would have it, he didn't have to wait long before the lawyer was free to see him. But, when he'd laid the case before him, he *did* have to wait a long time before the lawyer had finished laughing. Thoroughly annoyed by the lawyer's laughter, he said, 'Forgive the question, but what's there to laugh at? It's not your lordship's backside that's getting burnt! The jar's *mine*!'

But the other man just went on laughing. He insisted on his telling him the story all over again. On his telling him exactly what had happened. So that he could have another good laugh. Inside it, eh? He'd riveted himself up inside it, had he? And what was it Don Lollò thought he was entitled to? Did he think he was entitled to—k-k-keep him in there? Ha! Ha! Ha! Ho! Ho! Ho! Keep him in there, so as not to lose the jar?

'Oh, so I'm supposed just to write it off, am I?' asked Don Lollò, clenching his fists. 'What about all the harm he's done me? What about all the derision I'm going to have to put up with?'

'But do you know what they call this?' the lawyer finally managed to ask him. 'They call this sort of thing kidnapping!'

'Kidnapping? Who's kidnapping him?' exclaimed Don Lollò. 'He kidnapped *himself*! Off his own bat! What fault is it of mine?'

The lawyer then explained to him that there were two sides to the case. On the one hand he—Don Lollò—had immediately to set the prisoner free, in order not to be answerable to a charge of kidnapping. On the other hand, the jar-mender was answerable for the harm he'd caused with his stupidity and uppitiness.

'Ah!' Don Lollò breathed again. 'By paying me for the jar?'

'Gently!' observed the lawyer. 'Not as if it were new, mind!'

'Why not?'

'Oh, good grief, man, because it was broken!'

'Broken? Oh, no! It's mended now. It's *better* than mended! He says so himself! And now, if I break it again, I shan't be able to get it mended again. One jar lost, Mr. Lawyer!'

The lawyer assured him that that would be taken into account, by making him pay whatever the jar was worth in the state in which it now was.

'So!' he advised him, 'I should get him to give you an estimate of its worth before you go any further.'

'I kiss your hand!' said Don Lollò and off he went at a hell of a lick.

When he got back, towards evening, he found the peasants having a high old time round the inhabited jar. Even the watchdog was taking part in the fun and games, jumping about all over the place and barking. Zi' Dima had not only calmed down, but had also come round to enjoying his bizarre adventure, and he was laughing away with that sick gaiety that characterizes the unfortunate of this world.

Zirafa shoved them all to one side and stuck his neck over the top and peered into the jar.

'Hey! All right in there?'

'Absolutely all right! Beautifully cool,' replied Zi' Dima. 'I'm better off here than in my own home.'

'Glad to hear it. Meanwhile, allow me to inform you that that jar cost me four *onze* new. How much do you think it would cost now?'

'With me inside?' asked Zi'Dima.

The farm-hands laughed.

'Shut up!' shouted Zirafa. 'Two propositions–take your choice. Either your cement's good for nothing or it's good for something. If it's good for nothing, then you're a downright twister. If it's good for something, then the jar, just as it is now, must have some sort of value. What value? *You* say! Give me an estimate!'

Zi' Dima paused for a moment, reflecting. Then he said, 'Here's my answer. If you'd let me mend it with cement alone, as I wanted to, first of all I shouldn't be stuck inside here, and the jar would have more or less the same value as it had originally. All mucked-up as it is now, with these filthy rivets stuck in it, which I had necessarily to do from the inside, what value could it possibly have? A third of what it was worth in the first place—more or less.'

'A third?' asked Zirafa. 'One *onza*, thirty three?'

'Maybe less. Certainly not more.'

'Well, then,' said Don Lollò, 'I'll take your word for it. Hand over the *onza* and thirty three.'

'What?' said Zi' Dima, as if he didn't understand what he'd said.

'I'll break the jar and let you out,' replied Don Lollò, 'and you, so my lawyer says, must pay me whatever you value it at. One *onza* and thirty three.'

'Me *pay*?' sniggered Zi' Dima. 'Your lordship will have his little joke! I'd sooner stay in here till I make food for the worms!'

And, pulling his tar-encrusted pipe out of his pocket with some difficulty, he lit it and started smoking, puffing the smoke out through the neck of the jar.

Don Lollò was utterly taken aback. This other possibility, that Zi' Dima would no longer wish to quit the jar, neither he nor the lawyer had foreseen. How was this new difficulty to be resolved? He was on the verge of again ordering them instantly to saddle his mule, when it occurred to him that it was already evening.

'Oh, indeed?' he said. 'So you wish to take up permanent residence in my jar? You lot—you're all my witnesses! He doesn't want to come out again, so as not to have to pay for it. I'm ready to break the jar! Meanwhile, since he wishes to remain in there, tomorrow I'll sue him for trespassing on my property, and for wilfully preventing me from using the jar!'

Zi' Dima puffed another mouthful of smoke out of the jar, then he placidly replied. 'No, sir. I'm not trying to stop you from doing anything. Not me. Do you think I'm in here for my own amusement? You get me out of here, and I'll be off willingly. As for paying you anything—— Not on your sweet life, your lordship!'

In an excess of rage, Don Lollò lifted his foot to launch a kick at the jar. He refrained, however. He seized hold of it instead with both hands and shook it vigorously, trembling all over.

'See? Wonderful stuff, my cement!' said Zi' Dima to him.

'Jailbird!' roared Zirafa. 'Who's done the harm, you or me? And have I got to pay for it? You can starve to death in there! We'll see who wins this little battle!'

And off he went, quite forgetting the five lire which that morning he'd thrown into the jar. To start off with, Zi' Dima thought it would be a good idea to have a party with the farm-hands who, having been kept late because of that strange accident, were going to spend the night in the country, out in the open, on the threshing-yard. One of them went off to the pub nearby to lay in stocks. Most appropriately, there was a moon—so bright that it seemed as if day had come again.

Don Lollò went to bed, but in the middle of the night he was awakened by an infernal din. He went out on to the balcony of the farmhouse, and, by the light of the moon, he saw out in the threshing-yard hordes and hordes of devils. They were the drunk farm-hands who'd linked hands and who were dancing round the jar, inside which Zi' Dima was singing away at the top of his voice.

This time Don Lollò couldn't restrain himself. He hurled himself at the jar like a mad bull, and before they had time to stop him he'd given it a huge shove and sent it rolling down the slope. The jar rolled on and on, accompanied by the laughter of the drunks, and ended up by splitting open against an olive-tree.

Zi' Dima had won.

Questions

1. Part of the comic effect of this story depends on the establishment of the tight-fisted character of Don Lollò Zirafa. Point out how this trait is established by the author.

2. In Pirandello's story the ultimate effect is comic, but literature is full of treatments of the same theme—a greedy person punished by his greed—that are tragic in tone. How is this treatment different? Does a "comic" treatment of the theme make the subject any less serious?

3. In one sense "The Jar" pits the person of power and intelligence (Don Lollò) against the relatively ignorant but inherently shrewd peasant (Zi' Dima Licasi). Why is the reader's sympathy almost invariably on the side of the weaker? Does Pirandello himself seem to take sides in the contest? Does he direct the reader's sympathies?

4. Is there, or could there be, a legal solution to the problem of getting Zi' Dima out of the jar? Is the resolution in the story satisfactory?

Katherine Anne Porter

THE GRAVE

Few writers have established so high a reputation on such a small body of work as Kathrine Anne Porter. Her stories appeared infrequently, and she spent many years refining and polishing her only novel before it was published. Yet, everything she has written has received high critical acclaim, and the precision and control she brings to her work mark her as one of the most conscientious and deliberately literary craftsmen of the century. Her background is rural and traditional—she was born in Indian Creek, Texas, in 1894, and educated in convents in the South. Her extensive travels and wide reading made her one of the world's sophisticates, at home in world capitals such as Paris, Mexico City, New York, and Washington. She experienced the Mexican revolution, and used it as the setting for many of her first stories, collected in book form in Flowering Judas *(1930). Other collections of her stories are* Noon Wine *(1937),* Pale Horse, Pale Rider *(1939), and* The Leaning Tower and Other Stories *(1944), from which "The Grave" is taken. Her novel,* Ship of Fools, *long awaited and eagerly expected, finally appeared in 1962. A collected edition of her stories and short novels, containing some new material, appeared in 1965, and a collection of literary essays and autobiographical sketches was published in 1970.*

In many of her short stories, such as "The Grave," she returns to the scenes of her early childhood, the small towns and the dusty plains of the southwest. She treats many of the same themes as William Faulkner—the inherited burden of guilt from the past, the stern sense of retribution, and the coming to terms with the present. She often sees these happenings through the eyes of a character named Miranda, the daughter of a genteel Southern family who in "The Grave" and other stories seems to represent Miss Porter's own viewpoint. Although she does not have Faulkner's somewhat romantic view of the past, she is more concerned with the difficult process of human adjustment to the present.

The grandfather, dead for more than thirty years, had been twice disturbed in his long repose by the constancy and possessiveness of his widow. She removed his bones first to Louisiana and then to Texas as if she had set out to find her own burial place, knowing well she would never return to the places she had left. In Texas she set up a small cemetery in a corner of her first farm, and as the family connection grew, and oddments of relations came over from Kentucky to settle, it contained at last about twenty graves. After the grandmother's death, part of her land was to be sold for the benefit of certain of her children, and the cemetery happened to lie in the part set aside for sale. It was necessary to take up the bodies and bury them again in the family plot in the big new public cemetery, where the grandmother had been buried. At last her husband was to lie beside her for eternity, as she had planned.

The family cemetery had been a pleasant small neglected garden of tangled rose bushes and ragged cedar trees and cypress, the simple flat stones rising out of uncropped sweet-smelling wild grass. The graves were lying open and empty one burning day when Miranda and her brother Paul, who often went together to hunt rabbits and doves, propped their twenty-two Winchester rifles carefully against the rail fence, climbed over and explored among the graves. She was nine years old and he was twelve.

They peered into the pits all shaped alike with such purposeful accuracy, and looking at each other with pleased adventurous eyes, they said in solemn tones: "These were graves!" trying by words to shape a special, suitable emotion in their minds, but they felt nothing except an agreeable thrill of wonder: they were seeing a new sight, doing something they had not done before. In them both there was also a small disappointment at the entire commonplaceness of the actual spectacle. Even if it had once contained a coffin for years upon years, when the coffin was gone a grave was just a hole in the ground. Miranda leaped into the pit that had held her grandfather's bones. Scratching around aimlessly and pleasurably as any young animal, she scooped up a lump of earth and weighed it in her palm. It had a pleasantly sweet, corrupt smell, being mixed with cedar needles and small leaves, and as the crumbs fell apart, she saw a silver dove no larger than a hazel nut, with spread wings and a neat fan-shaped tail. The breast had a deep round hollow in it. Turning it up to the fierce sunlight, she saw that the inside of the hollow was cut in little whorls. She scrambled out, over the pile of loose earth that had fallen back into one end of the grave, calling to Paul that she had found something, he must guess what. . . . His head appeared smiling over the rim of another grave. He waved a closed hand at her. "I've got something too!" They ran to compare treasures, making a game of it, so many guesses each, all wrong, and a final show-down with opened palms. Paul had found a thin wide gold ring curved with intricate flowers and leaves. Miranda was smitten at sight of the ring and wished to have it. Paul seemed more impressed by the dove. They made a trade, with some little bickering. After he had got the dove in his hand, Paul said, "Don't you know what this is? This is a screw head for a *coffin*! . . . I'll bet nobody else in the world has one like this!"

Miranda glanced at it without covetousness. She had the gold ring on her thumb; it fitted perfectly. "Maybe we ought to go now," she said, "maybe one of the niggers 'll see us and tell somebody." They knew the land had been sold, the cemetery was no longer theirs, and they felt like trespassers. They climbed back over the fence, slung their rifles loosely under their arms—they had been shooting at targets with various kinds of firearms since they were seven years old—and set out to look for the rabbits and doves or whatever small game might happen along. On these expeditions Miranda always followed at Paul's heels along the path, obeying instructions about handling her gun when going through fences; learning how to stand it up properly so it would not slip and fire unexpectedly; how to wait her time for a shot and not just bang away in the air without looking, spoiling shots for Paul, who really could hit things if given a chance. Now and then, in her excitement at seeing birds whizz up suddenly before her face, or a rabbit leap across her very toes, she lost her head, and almost without sighting she flung her rifle up and pulled the trigger. She hardly ever hit any sort of mark. She had no proper sense of hunting at all. Her brother would be often completely disgusted with her. "You don't care whether you get your bird or not," he said. "That's no way to hunt." Miranda could not understand his indignation. She had seen him smash his hat and yell with fury when he had missed his aim. "What I like about shooting," said Miranda, with exasperating inconsequence, "is pulling the trigger and hearing the noise."

"Then, by golly," said Paul, "whyn't you go back to the range and shoot at bullseyes?"

"I'd just as soon," said Miranda, "only like this, we walk around more."

"Well, you just stay behind and stop spoiling my shots," said Paul, who, when he made a kill, wanted to be certain he had made it. Miranda, who alone brought down a bird once in twenty rounds, always claimed as her own any game they got when they fired at the same moment. It was tiresome and unfair and her brother was sick of it.

"Now, the first dove we see, or the first rabbit, is mine," he told her. "And the next will be yours. Remember that and don't get smarty."

"What about snakes?" asked Miranda idly. "Can I have the first snake?"

Waving her thumb gently and watching her gold ring glitter, Miranda lost interest in shooting. She was wearing her summer roughing outfit: dark blue overalls, a light blue shirt, a hired-man's straw hat, and thick brown sandals. Her brother had the same outfit except his was a sober hickory-nut color. Ordinarily Miranda preferred her overalls to any other dress, though it was making rather a scandal in the countryside, for the year was 1903, and in the back country the law of female decorum had teeth in it. Her father had been criticized for letting his girls dress like boys and go careering around astride barebacked horses. Big sister Maria, the really independent and fearless one, in spite of her rather affected ways, rode at a dead run with only a rope knotted around her horse's nose. It was said the motherless family was running down, with the Grandmother no longer there to hold it together. It was known that she had discriminated against her son Harry in her will, and that he was in straits about money. Some of his old neighbors reflected with vicious satisfaction that now he would probably not be so stiffnecked, nor have any more high-stepping horses either. Miranda knew this, though she could not say how. She had met along the road old women of the kind who smoked corn-cob pipes, who had treated her grandmother with most sincere respect. They slanted their gummy old eyes side-ways at the granddaughter and said, "Ain't you ashamed of yoself, Missy? It's against the Scriptures to dress like that. Whut yo Pappy thinkin' about?" Miranda, with her powerful social sense, which was like a fine set of antennae radiating from every pore of her skin, would feel ashamed because she knew well it was rude and ill-bred to shock anybody, even bad-tempered old crones, though she had faith in her father's judgment and was perfectly comfortable in the clothes. Her father had said, "They're just what you need, and they'll save your dresses for school. . . ." This sounded quite simple and natural to her. She had been brought up in rigorous economy. Wastefulness was vulgar. It was also a sin. These were truths; she had heard them repeated many times and never once disputed.

Now the ring, shining with the serene purity of fine gold on her rather grubby thumb, turned her feelings against her overalls and sockless feet, toes sticking through the thick brown leather straps. She wanted to go back to the farmhouse, take a good cold bath, dust herself with plenty of Maria's violent talcum powder—provided Maria was not present to object, of course—put on the thinnest, most becoming dress she owned, with a big sash, and sit in a wicker chair under the trees. . . . These things were not all she wanted, of course; she had vague stirrings of desire for luxury and a grand way of living which could not take precise form in her imagination but were founded on family legend of past wealth and leisure. These immediate comforts were what she could have, and she wanted them at once. She lagged rather far behind Paul, and once she thought of just turning back without a word and going home. She stopped, thinking that Paul would never do that to her, and so she would have to tell him. When a rabbit leaped, she let Paul have it without dispute. He killed it with one shot.

When she came up with him, he was already kneeling, examining the wound, the rabbit trailing from his hands. "Right through the head," he said complacently, as if he had aimed for it. He took out his sharp competent bowie knife and started to skin the body. He did it very cleanly and quickly. Uncle Jimbilly knew how to prepare the skins so that Miranda always had fur coats for her dolls, for though she never cared much for her dolls she liked seeing them in fur coats. The children knelt facing each other over the dead animal. Miranda watched admiringly while her brother stripped the skin away as if he were taking off a glove. The flayed flesh emerged dark scarlet, sleek, firm; Miranda with thumb and finger felt the long fine muscles with the silvery flat strips binding them to the joints. Brother lifted the oddly bloated belly. "Look," he said, in a low amazed voice. "It was going to have young ones."

Very carefully he slit the thin flesh from the centre ribs to the flanks, and a scarlet bag appeared. He slit again and pulled the bag open, and there lay a bundle of tiny rabbits, each wrapped in a thin scarlet veil. The brother pulled these off and there they were, dark gray, their sleek wet down lying in minute even ripples, like a baby's head just washed, their unbelievably small delicate ears folded close, their little blind faces almost featureless.

Miranda said, "Oh, I want to *see*," under her breath. She looked and looked—excited but not frightened, for she was accustomed to the sight of animals killed in hunting—filled with pity and astonishment and a kind of shocked delight in the wonderful little creatures for their own sakes, they were so pretty. She touched one of them ever so carefully, "Ah, there's blood running over them," she said and began to tremble without knowing why. Yet she wanted most deeply to see and to know. Having seen, she felt at once as if she had known all along. The very memory of her former ignorance faded, she had always known just this. No one had ever told her anything outright, she had been rather unobservant of the animal life around her because she was so accustomed to animals. They seemed simply disorderly and unaccountably rude in their habits, but altogether natural and not very interesting. Her brother had spoken as if he had known about everything all along. He may have seen all this before. He had never said a word to her, but she knew now a part at least of what he knew. She understood a little of the secret, formless intuitions in her own mind and body, which had been clearing up, taking form, so gradually and so steadily she had not realized that she was learning what she had to know. Paul said cautiously, as if he were talking about something forbidden: "They were just about ready to be born." His voice dropped on the last word. "I know," said Miranda, "like kittens. I know, like babies." She was quietly and terribly agitated, standing again with her rifle under her arm, looking down at the bloody heap. "I don't want the skin," she said, "I won't have it." Paul buried the young rabbits again in their mother's body, wrapped the skin around her, carried her to a clump of sage bushes, and hid her away. He came out again at once and said to Miranda, with an eager friendliness, a confidential tone quite unusual in him, as if he were taking her into an important secret on equal terms: "Listen now. Now you listen to me, and don't ever forget. Don't you ever tell a living soul that you saw this. Don't tell a soul. Don't tell Dad because I'll get into trouble. He'll say I'm leading you into things you ought not to do. He's always saying that. So now don't you go and forget and blab out sometime the way you're always doing. . . . Now, that's a secret. Don't you tell."

Miranda never told, she did not even wish to tell anybody. She thought about the whole worrisome affair with confused unhappiness for a few days. Then it sank quietly into her mind and was heaped over by accumulated thousands of impressions, for nearly twenty years. One day she was picking her path among the puddles and crushed refuse of a market street in a strange city of a strange country, when without warning, plain and clear in its true colors as if she looked through a frame upon a scene that had not stirred nor changed since the moment it happened, the episode of that far-off day leaped from its burial place before her mind's eye. She was so reasonlessly horrified she halted suddenly staring, the scene before her eyes dimmed by the vision back of them. An Indian vendor had held up before her a tray of dyed sugar sweets, in the shapes of all kinds of small creatures: birds, baby chicks, baby rabbits, lambs, baby pigs. They were in gay colors and smelled of vanilla, maybe. . . . It was a very hot day and the smell in the market, with its piles of raw flesh and wilting flowers, was like the mingled sweetness and corruption she had smelled that other day in the empty cemetery at home: the day she had remembered always until now vaguely as the time she and her brother had found treasure in the opened graves. Instantly upon this thought the dreadful vision faded, and she saw clearly her brother, whose childhood face she had forgotten, standing again in the blazing sunshine, again twelve years old, a pleased sober smile in his eyes, turning the silver dove over and over in his hands.

Questions

1. What are the objects that Paul and Miranda find in the grave—a gold ring and a silver dove—symbols of?

2. Why is Miranda excited, then troubled, by the sight of the dead rabbit and her babies?

3. Why do the children feel they must keep the killing and dissection of the rabbit a secret? If they have not been guilty of any actual act of disobedience, what do they feel they have done wrong?

4. When at the end of the story Miranda sees the "piles of raw flesh and wilting flowers" in an Indian market, why does she unexpectedly recall the episode, years earlier, in the cemetery?

5. Why does the recollection seem to her at first a "dreadful vision," and why is it replaced by the memory of Paul smiling?

B. Traven

WHEN THE PRIEST IS NOT AT HOME

The world's most mysterious literary figure is the writer known as B. Traven, whose real name may (or may not) be Berick (or Bruno) Traven Torsvan. He may have been born in Chicago about 1890, and very likely spent some years in Germany during and after World War I. He was first an actor and then an editor of a radical anti-war, anti-capitalist newspaper. He then fled to Mexico, where he lived in anonymity until his death in 1969. Even his publishers insisted they did not know the real identity of the man who wrote as Traven, affirming that they could approach him only through an agent—who may have been Traven himself. A remarkable piece of literary detective work, attempting to solve the mystery of Traven's identity and the reasons for his anonymity, was done by Judy Stone in Ramparts *magazine for September and October, 1967. One theory offered in these articles was that he was the illegitimate son of Kaiser Wilhelm II, and that his lack of acceptance turned him into an embittered wanderer. What is known for sure, though, is that he did produce a stream of notable novels and stories, most of them with Mexican settings, in which he exhibited intense sympathy for the economic underdogs, the exploited, the victims of overgrown governments with their maze of bureaus and offices. Some of these works were first published in Mexico and Europe, where Traven's reputation is higher than in the United States.* The Death Ship *(first published in Germany, 1926; in the U.S., 1934) in particular was an international success, perhaps because its picture of a homeless, legally dead sailor captured convincingly the world of the European war victim and refugee, the stateless person entrapped in a bureaucratic world of passports, visas, and identity cards. "The fact that you are sitting in front of me," one consul tells the sailor, in closing his case, "is no proof of your birth." This sympathy was extended to American drifters and Mexican laborers in such works as* The Treasure of the Sierra Madre *(1935), his best-known novel, largely because of the brilliant film version made by John Huston in 1948,* The Bridge in the Jungle *(1938), and* The Rebellion of the Hanged *(1952). Many of his other works yet remain to be translated and published.*

"When the Priest Is Not at Home," from The Night Visitors and Other Stories *(1966), is less bitter than many of Traven's works, but it still conveys much of his distrust of any established authority, political or religious. It shows that things often arrange themselves better when common people, who have nothing personal to gain, take over. The point of view from which the events are seen very skillfully increases the irony.*

The good padre of a village populated entirely by Indian peasants had to leave for the capital of the state to attend a conference called by the bishop. There were no trains and no buses and so our good padre had to travel by mule. Because he did not want to overexert himself he only rode by day, from one hacienda where he had spent the night to the next, where he would remain until the following day. Everywhere he was of course well received and treated with the best of food and drink.

No wonder he considered this trip a well-earned vacation after three years of doing his duty as village priest to peasants whose homes were scattered over a vast region. The round trip would take from four to six weeks. Consequently, before leaving, he blessed the community, warning the faithful against the slings of Satan and of the ever and ever expected return of the ancient Indian gods, more feared by him than Satan himself.

He called in Cipriano, his sacristan, and officially turned the care of the church over to him. Cipriano was by profession a woodchopper and charcoal-burner, and as a human being he was neither better nor worse than any other man in the village.

Extremely proud of his duties as sacristan, he took his job very seriously. In his opinion, there existed only two persons of real importance in the region: el padre and el sacristan, and he realized well enough that without the help of a sacristan a padre isn't much to speak of.

Frequently he had let his friends know confidentially that a sacristan was perhaps even more important than a padre, but this of course he would never say out very loud for surely that might be considered sinful. Truth was, if the padre was respected in the community, it was the sacristan who was feared. The padre was a Mestizo whereas Cipriano was a full-blooded Indian. For that reason his position was more or less like that of a medicine man, or *brujo,* among his people. And that was easy to understand. Cipriano was as close to the saints as was the padre. He, Cipriano, knew all the secrets of religion just as well as the padre. He had access to the most Holy. He could chant and conduct the ceremonies of the Mass out of memory better than the padre, who sometimes would forget certain lines and had to consult the book.

He had been sacristan for thirty years and during that long time had served under four different priests. Not only did he know every line of the liturgy by heart, but he also knew every single glass pearl on every one of the many holy images which crowded the church; he knew every holy day and every saint's day without ever making a mistake. In fact, the members of the community, especially the children and adolescents, thought that Cipriano was more important in carrying out the many intricate ceremonies than the padre himself.

Just as all Indians first appeal to the saints when they want something from God, so the members of the parroquia first appealed to Cipriano when they wanted something from the padre. Whether it was a marriage, a baptism or a funeral, they first came to Cipriano for advice. Even when the girls and boys went to confession they inquired first of Cipriano whether this or that was a deadly sin if one did not confess it, or how to indicate this or that without expressing it directly. Cipriano counselled everyone and he had help for all. He was the confidant of every single member of the community to a much greater extent by far than the best priest could ever be.

For all these reasons Cipriano was comparatively well-off. He got a chicken here and a rooster there, here a bottle of tequila and there one of rum. And on his saint's day he got so many good things that he could live on them for a whole month.

When the señor padre was ready to depart for his trip, he said to Cipriano: "You know very well what to do around here. I don't have to tell you anything about that. You will open the church early in the morning, see to it that the bells are rung rightly and at night you will lock up the holy place as always. Sunday mornings and Wednesday and Saturday evenings you will sing the service and say the prayers. You know them all well enough. And don't forget to fill the fonts with the blessed water when you see them empty. That you also know. And then there is something of great importance. Clean all the saints, dust them and remove the droppings of the birds. It's a shame to see how they look. You know the señor bishop might perhaps pay us an unexpected visit any day. I would be embarrassed to have all the images so dirty and the church so full of sh— Well, Cipriano, you know yourself how dirty the whole place has gone during the years, what with those terrible dust storms we've had."

"Si, Padre, the place is in a horrible state and 'specially the poor santitos."

"Now that's exactly what I'm telling you. You clean them well, all of them. Where the paint has come off, put on some new. But don't paint the Mother of God over the altar. Just wash off the dirt and then cover Her with colorless varnish. I'll show you how to use it."

"I'm sure I can do it fine, Padre."

"So am I, Cipriano. Now, tomorrow morning I'll buy all the material you need. And from there I'll be on my way to the conference."

The various paints and the varnish had been bought and the use of it explained by the merchant.

Then, before taking his leave, the padre took his money belt and shelled out eight pesos in silver.

"There, Cipriano, take this money so that you won't have to work in the bush but can take full charge of cleaning up the holy place instead, so that when I come back I can be proud of our church. May the good Lord and the Holy Virgin bless you and help you in your pious task. And now, Cipriano, let's have a drink together and wish me good luck on my trip."

The drinks—it wasn't just one—consumed, the padre went on his way, his simple suitcase tied on behind the saddle.

Cipriano rode home on his burro content with the world and in particular with religion. He arrived just in time for the vespers service.

Next morning he started cleaning up the church and beautifying the saints, washing them with tender care as he would babies. Though he was no expert in using paint, instinctively, with the inborn love for colors of the Indian, he felt sure he would do a satisfactory job.

The paint he had at his disposal was rather limited because it was expensive and the padre was a poor man who could not afford to spend more on anything even for his personal wants than was absolutely essential.

In consequence of that, Cipriano handled Judas Iscariot first, who anyway in his opinion was really only a half saint because his true relationship to Christ had never been made clear. Some say he betrayed the Lord and for that he is roasting in hell for two thousand years already.

Others maintain that God ordered Judas Iscariot to betray the Lord. For if he had not betrayed Him, Christ would not have been taken prisoner and Christ could not have been crucified and so He would not have died laden with all the sins of the world to redeem humanity. But since Judas Iscariot was absolutely necessary to fulfill the miracle of redemption, the Indian looks upon him as a half saint who now and then can perhaps put in a good word for him in heaven.

One should not blame an Indian peasant for such a strange attitude, because among the ancient Aztecs the evil gods who could do much harm to men were worshiped as devotedly as were the good gods. By all means it is considered wise to stand on a good footing with all and every personage mentioned in the Bible. You can never know for sure whether a certain patriarch was not perhaps God's tool even if he behaved himself badly on earth.

Now as to Judas Iscariot, he always stood in a dark corner of the church like a schoolboy who has put a frog into the teacher's handbag. There he will stand, Judas will, all during the whole year until Holy Week when he is taken out, dusted off and cleaned, and set at the table of the Last Supper put up in the church. At this table Judas Iscariot must not be missed even though other saints as for instance San Augustin or San Jerónimo may be substituted for some of those originally present at the Last Supper.

Like anybody else Cipriano had to learn by practicing. And Judas to practice on was as good as anyone on whom to try out how much and how well one might wash without harming the original paint still good and how much new paint to use. He, Cipriano, could to his heart's content paint and lacquer on Judas to find out how the paint took and how it came out without overdoing it. If he spoiled something on Judas it was but of little importance. Judas would be put into his dark corner again until Easter Week and by that time enough dust would have accumulated to hide Cipriano's miscalculated artistic efforts. The principal idea was to keep the beard and the money bag intact so as to recognize the image as Judas Iscariot, for it had happened, and might happen again any odd day, that he was taken for St. Joe and given presents such as candles or trinkets of silver.

Cipriano painted Judas Iscariot with real zest, almost with devotion, and when he had finished he could hardly tear himself away. He hated to put him into his dark corner again where rats and mice would molest him. At this moment Cipriano felt a profound pity for Judas that he had allowed himself to be bribed and that he had betrayed the Lord. Had he, Judas, only not done it so openly Cipriano might have been able to put him in front so that everybody could see him shine. But that could not be done because all the faithful, especially the women, knew the story of that infamous betrayal and they would object violently.

Cipriano even had a blasphemic intention to change the beard of Judas, take away from him his money bag and make a St. Marcus out of him. But this change of course would have been detected very soon, as the features of Judas Iscariot were better known to all members of the community than those of any other image.

The thought of making such a change had occurred to Cipriano because on Judas he tried out all the colors and saw their effects. As for the other images he had to keep to the original basic colors so that they would be recognized by the worshipers whereas it did not matter much where Judas was concerned.

The next few days Cipriano put all his work and effort into cleaning and repainting the images but constantly his thoughts would return to the beautiful artistic expressions he had bestowed upon Judas. No doubt since he was no longer under the padre's protection he must have worked under Satan's influence to perform such a remarkable job, and of all images, on that of the greatest sinner that ever walked on earth. In no other way could it be explained why, in the course of time, all that occurred thereafter might well be traced back to the fact that Cipriano had wasted his talents so lavishly on that arch-villain Judas. What now happened showed plainly and unmistakably how smartly Satan works, that even such a good man as was Cipriano fell into the abyss.

On purpose he had kept the Virgin waiting to be the very last of the images to be handled so that in the meantime he would become a great expert in cleaning and repairing the holy effigies.

At last Cipriano arrived at the task of cleaning and varnishing the adored statue of the Holy Virgin enthroned over the altar. He realized that this was the holiest of all his tasks which could have been conferred upon him. The different likenesses of the Lord he had handled easily and with no more particular respect than he gave the saints. But the Holy Virgin was the holiest of the holy, to him, the simple-minded Indian peasant, more important than God the Father Himself. To him, the way he had been taught, the Virgin was the very essence, yes, the fundamental base of the only true religion.

Before taking Her likeness down from the little stage on which it stood he kneeled down and said two dozen Ave Marias besides various other prayers by which She usually was addressed. He crossed himself several times and finally he brought down the image and set it on the floor. He took off Her mantle to dust and wash it. Then he washed Her face while he mumbled prayers incessantly. Now he rubbed and polished the figure with soft cotton rags. Then he carefully applied the varnish. The body was made out in such a manner that the inner garments appeared to be carved woodwork. The Virgin's garments he laid out in the yard to dry.

On the brick floor of the church Cipriano had kept a small fire burning for warming the water a little and also to keep the glue liquid with which he repaired broken parts of the images. On this same fire he now boiled some coffee and heated his frijoles and tortillas because he did not want to lose time going home to eat.

His meal finished he left to sit in the sun for a short rest. While he smoked a self-rolled cigarette his thoughts again turned to Judas Iscariot, how he might perhaps paint him better still since he discovered that he had some little paint left over. He hoped that perhaps even the padre would be pleased with his great work of art and give Judas a better place to live than the darkest corner of the church where he was condemned to contemplate his unforgivable sin. He thought that after all a big injustice had been done to Judas, making him atone for two thousand years because of a lousy thirty pieces of silver which he surely must have needed to pay his back rent or buy his daughter a much needed dress or maybe even medicine for his sick wife. With the heavy strain of these thoughts over such complicated problems and questions concerning religion, and at the same time thinking that the relations of the señor padre with doña Elodia and doña Agapita, both good-looking widows, might fairly well be interpreted in more than one way, Cipriano fell asleep. That was only natural because at the moment he had nothing else to do but wait for the sun to dry the Virgin's mantle. He was just dreaming that Judas Iscariot had come to life complaining to him that the thirty pesos he had received for his job had turned out all counterfeit and caused him lots of trouble when the ferocious barking of several dogs, fighting inside the church over some tortillas Cipriano had left, brutally awoke him. He hurried into the church and drove the dogs out by the back door.

When his eyes got used to the darkness inside the church and he approached the image of the Holy Virgin, cold shivers ran up and down his spine. He had to look several times before he could convince himself that what he saw was real and not a dream.

The dogs in their fighting for the tortillas had pushed the Most Holy Mother of God into the fire, where She lay helplessly and with the same natural consequences as any other piece of wood when tossed into any fire. Cipriano, without being told so, knew at once that Satan had sent the dogs to keep him out of heaven.

With a resolute grip he rescued the Godmother from the fire. Her left hand was held pressed to Her heart hanging outside the center of her body from where rays of gold, red and bronze radiated in all directions. Her right hand was raised to the level of Her chin with the palm down in a gesture as if to bless someone, or cover the head of an invisible child. This hand the fire had completely charred. The right side of the image was blackened in a most ugly way.

Cipriano extinguished the still burning parts of the figure with the last few drops of his coffee. When this did not altogether help he used his spit. Not for one moment did he consider this spitting on the Virgin an act of disrespect. In spite of all his education as a faithful Christian he, without realizing it, turned heathen again when confronted by reality.

Now he had to think of what to do. He completely forgot that he held in his hands the Mother of God who was worshiped and prayed to as if she really was the Mother of God alive and in person and not just a wooden figure.

Automatically he closed the church so that nobody should come in to witness the damage that had been done. He was aware of the fact that there was no excuse for his negligence. He would lose his position and, what was a hundred times worse, he might even be excommunicated. Not that his job brought in much money, ten centavos for a baptism, twenty-five centavos for a good wedding, fifteen centavos for a funeral. But what bothered him more than the possible loss of his job as sacristan was to lose the respectful position he now held. If the disaster for which he alone was to blame should become known he no longer could be the one closest to the padre, no longer would he be allowed to attend to all that was holy, no longer would he substitute for the padre during his occasional absences, nor would he have the envied privilege to light the candles in the presence of the whole community, nor would he have the unbelievably great honor to hand the wash basin and towel or the chasuble to the padre. Nobody would ask or heed his advice, there would not be any more chicken or rooster on his saint's day, no tequila here or pumpkin cooked in wild honey there. In other words, life would not be worth living anymore. In his thirty years of service he had become so involved with the church that nobody could even imagine the church without him. The present generation had been raised in the belief that his person was irreplaceable. Perhaps, so he thought, he might pray very ardently and a great miracle would happen, and the hand of the Mother of God would grow again. But Cipriano's belief did not reach out that far. He was too much Indian to know that charred wood does not grow under any circumstances, no matter how much you pray for that to happen.

After hours of thinking and speculating he contemplated the idea of sawing off the charred hand, carving a new one and gluing it onto the stump. He then would apply a thick coat of paint, and once the image was again set up over the altar nobody would notice the difference. The carving of the hand would take a day. During this time the Virgin would have to be in Her place or the worshipers who come to pray would surely miss her immediately. Without the image before him, an Indian cannot concentrate on his prayers but thinks of his corn, his goats, his sheep and his wife instead.

Cipriano clothed the Virgin again in her dark-blue velvet mantle and put Her back on Her little stage over the altar once more. He arranged the candles in such a way that in the twilight of the church one would not easily notice the charred hand. He draped some folds of the cloak over the hand in such a smart way that no one could easily distinguish the charred hand from the dark cloth. Before the padre returned, a new hand perfectly well painted would have been glued onto the arm.

Meanwhile it became late, Cipriano opened the main door and a few elderly women entered to pray. When it was time to close he locked the church and went home reassured that during the night nothing would happen to make the calamity known. He looked for a piece of wood and started to carve the hand as best he could. The finer points he would do in full daylight during the next forenoon. He worked fast and figured that he would have his job finished by noon the following day.

While he was busy carving a terrific storm broke loose. Thunder rattled from all sides, lightning flashed over the skies and tore the black night into flaming shreds. A more pious person than Cipriano would have connected the storm with the Virgin in disgrace. And surely the padre would have said: "There you are, Cipriano, see what you did, the wrath of God Almighty is over you. Repent, Cipriano, repent!"

Cipriano was pious but not pious enough to believe for one moment that the storm happened in consequence of his carelessness in regard to the Virgin's image. As an Indian he was well acquainted with nature and he had already seen in the early afternoon how heavy storm clouds gathered far out on the horizon. In fact he had told his neighbors Mateo and Eusebio when they came visiting for a while in the churchyard: "Watch out, you cuates, we'll have a severe storm such as we haven't had for a long time. Who knows whether or not a few jacalitos might not burn down." And that happened at least one hour before the hand of the Virgin was lost. So what had the thunderstorm to do with that lamentable mishap?

The padre though would have said: "The Virgin knew all this long before and therefore arranged the thunderstorm beforehand." And Cipriano would have answered: "Si, Padre, that's so." For he had been taught as a little boy that one commits sin arguing with a priest. What a priest says is the truth of God. But to himself Cipriano would have said: "If the Virgin had known all this beforehand, She would also have known that a few hungry village dogs would throw Her into the fire. Would She really have allowed those dogs to do that to Her for no other reason but to cause me trouble? I can't believe that, so help me the Lord."

Cipriano rolled himself a cigarette and waited, for he knew that, in his situation, praying would not help anyway. The tempest would wear itself out. He remembered doña Lucina, the wife of Pancho Lazcano, who was killed by lightning while fingering the rosary. So it was better to roll a cigarette and stand in the open door to watch the splendor of the storm.

While he so watched the sky, a tremendous burst of thunder exploded right above his head which shook him so that he had to hold fast to the doorpost of his choza to avoid dropping to the ground. At the same fraction of a second he saw a flash hitting the roof of the church. Roof tiles crackled all over and he expected the church to go up in flames at any moment. But nothing happened. The dark outline of the church stood out quietly against the night. Slowly the thunders began to retreat, the flashes quivered away and a heavy rain started pouring down. After half an hour the rain stopped, the storm had abated, and only in the far distance could one see an occasional flash.

While Cipriano was still standing in his door, a few men came running, shouting: "Don Cipriano, did you see that last flash which hit the church? Quickly, bring your keys and open up. We must see if something is burning inside. Still time to put out any fire that may have caught on somewhere."

When they arrived at the church many people were waiting already and many more were coming fast, men, women and children. Everyone had seen the flash strike the church straight over the altar and they now wanted to see what damage had been done.

Cipriano opened the door, the men went in and looked around but could see no fire anywhere. Until midnight they searched around. When finally they had made sure that not even a glimmer had been overlooked they all went home satisfied.

Very early next morning Cipriano opened the church and women entered to pray.

Having lighted the candles as usual, he stood near the door filling the font when suddenly two women right in front of the altar let out a shriek, crossing themselves violently at the same time.

Cipriano turned around, terribly frightened. He knew that everything had been discovered and that he only had to wait for the padre's return to be dishonorably discharged from duty. Other women in the church also were running now toward the altar to see what had caused that horrifying shriek. Hardly had they come close when they stopped, screaming and crossing themselves.

Cipriano heard a word here and a scream there but finally he could make out what they were shouting: "A miracle has happened! A great miracle! Blessed be the Mother of God. Glory to the Holy Virgin! A great miracle!" The women hurried toward Cipriano, dragging him to the altar.

He had become entirely indifferent. He would have liked best to go home, lie down in bed and say that he was deadly sick. But they pulled him along, shouting at the same time: "Look, Don Cipriano! Have you no eyes for the great miracle that has happened? A lightning struck the church. Up there the tiles have fallen out from the roof. A great miracle has happened to our church. The hand of the Holy Virgin caught the flash! La Madre Santísima sacrificed Her adored hand to protect the holy flesh of Christ our Lord. She saved our church! Be She blessed for ever and ever, She kept the fire away that would have destroyed our church. A miracle! A great, great miracle has happened. Glory be to God!"

In less than three days the church was surrounded by Indians and

Mestizos alike, thousands of people. Cipriano could not do anything anymore. He had become convinced that there surely must be a higher power which determines fate on earth, in particular his own.

In no time the church became an important source of income in solid cash and it has stayed so to this very day because faithful pilgrims adore that Virgin, praying for her protection against injuries lightning might cause.

It was only human that Cipriano never said anything. How would he dare tell the princes of the church, archbishops and bishops who came to celebrate Masses here, that a little error had occurred? These dignitaries would have laughed out loud and told him that he was getting too old and a little weak in the head.

A true Indian, he was endowed with an inborn worldly wisdom and knew when and how to hold his tongue. After all, he did not believe it his duty to reform religions. Less so as they were good enough for him the way they existed. Everything concerned, he thought it most beneficial for him to leave the matters as they stood, because soon he learned that a sacristan of a rich church can live much better than one of a poor Indian community. No longer did he have to go out, cutting wood and burning coal in the bush under a tropical sun. And for this convenience he remained forever grateful to his half saint, Judas Iscariot.

Questions

1. What does the setting, a rather backward, remote region in Mexico, contribute to the story? Could the story appropriately be set in a more sophisticated place?

2. Cipriano, for all his lack of formal learning, has an inherent shrewdness; in a more worldly setting, he would be known as a "smooth operator." In view of the ironic tone of the story as well as of its theme, why is it fitting that he is the only person who knows the inside story of the miracle?

3. For what professed reasons, and for what "real" ones, does Cipriano remain silent at the end?

4. This is a story in which the reader knows a good deal more about what has really happened than do any of the characters (except, of course, Cipriano). How does the reader's knowledge alter his view of the events? What irony does it make possible? How does it contribute to the theme of the story?

John Updike

THE CHRISTIAN ROOMMATES

John Updike is a talented young writer whose precise diction and controlled style sometimes seem of more concern to him than his subject matter. He was born in Shillington, Pennsylvania, in 1932, graduated from Harvard, and then studied art before joining the staff of the New Yorker. *He wrote both stories and poems that exhibited a lively but subdued comic sense at the little oddities and pretenses of ordinary human life for this magazine. His first book was a collection of poems,* The Carpentered Hen *(1958); and the next year he published both a novel,* The Poorhouse Fair, *and a collection of stories,* The Same Door. *Another novel,* Rabbit, Run *(1960) was about the monotonous lives of trapped Americans; another,* The Centaur *(1963), imposed a pattern from classical mythology on a contemporary family. His greatest commercial success was* Couples *(1968), a long novel about bored suburbanites and their shifting sexual patterns. Probably his major critical success to date has been* Bech: A Book *(1970)—a satirical account of a writer.*

Updike's stories usually have a surface of detached amusement, and he has been accused of having no depth of feeling. "The Christian Roommates," from the collection, The Music School *(1966), may challenge this judgment, for certainly it reveals genuine concern for the values by which a life is lived. The character in the story who puzzles over what he has missed is a figure of both irony and pity.*

Orson Ziegler came straight to Harvard from the small South Dakota town where his father was the doctor. Orson, at eighteen, was half an inch under six feet tall, with a weight of 164 and an I.Q. of 152. His eczematous cheeks and vaguely irritated squint—as if his face had been for too long transected by the sight of a level horizon—masked a definite self-confidence. As the doctor's son, he had always mattered in the town. In his high school he had been class president, valedictorian, and captain of the football and baseball teams. (The captain of the basketball team had been Lester Spotted Elk, a full-blooded Chippewa with dirty fingernails and brilliant teeth, a smoker, a drinker, a discipline problem, and the only boy Orson ever had met who was better than he at anything that mattered.) Orson was the first native of his town to go to Harvard, and would probably be the last, at least until his son was of age. His future was firm in his mind: the pre-med course here, medical school either at Harvard, Penn, or Yale, and then back to South Dakota, where he had his wife already selected and claimed and primed to wait. Two nights before he left for Harvard, he had taken her virginity. She had cried, and he had felt foolish, having, somehow, failed. It had been his virginity, too. Orson was sane, sane enough to know that he had lots to learn, and to be, within limits, willing. Harvard processes thousands of such boys and restores them to the world with little apparent damage. Presumably because he was from west of the Mississippi and a Protestant Christian (Methodist), the authorities had given him as a freshman roommate a self-converted Episcopalian from Oregon.

When Orson arrived at Harvard on the morning of Registration Day, bleary and stiff from the series of airplane rides that had begun fourteen hours before, his roommate was already installed. "H. Palamountain" was floridly inscribed in the upper of the two name slots on the door of Room 14. The bed by the window had been slept in, and the desk by the window was neatly loaded with books. Standing sleepless inside the door, inertly clinging to his two heavy suitcases, Orson was conscious of another presence in the room without being able to locate it; optically and mentally, he focused with a slight slowness.

The roommate was sitting on the floor, barefoot, before a small spinning wheel. He jumped up nimbly. Orson's first impression was of the wiry quickness that almost magically brought close to his face the thick-lipped, pop-eyed face of the other boy. He was a head shorter than Orson, and wore, above his bare feet, pegged sky-blue slacks, a lumberjack shirt whose throat was dashingly stuffed with a silk foulard, and a white cap such as Orson had seen before only in photographs of Pandit Nehru. Dropping a suitcase, Orson offered his hand. Instead of taking it, the roommate touched his palms together, bowed his head, and murmured something Orson didn't catch. Then he gracefully swept off the white cap, revealing a narrow crest of curly blond hair that stood up like a rooster's comb. "I am Henry Palamountain." His voice, clear and colorless in the way of West Coast voices, suggested a radio announcer. His handshake was metallically firm and seemed to have a pinch of malice in it. Like Orson, he wore glasses. The thick lenses emphasized the hyperthyroid bulge of his eyes and their fishy, searching expression.

"Orson Ziegler," Orson said.

"I know."

Orson felt a need to add something adequately solemn, standing as they were on the verge of a kind of marriage. "Well, Henry"—he lamely lowered the other suitcase to the floor—"I guess we'll be seeing a lot of each other."

"You may call me Hub," the roommate said. "Most people do. However, call me Henry if you insist. I don't wish to diminish your dreadful freedom. You may not wish to call me anything at all. Already I've made three hopeless enemies in the dormitory."

Every sentence in this smoothly enunciated speech bothered Orson, beginning with the first. He himself had never been given a nickname; it was the one honor his classmates had withheld from him. In his adolescence he had coined nicknames for himself—Orrie, Ziggy—and tried to insinuate them into popular usage, without success. And what was meant by "dreadful freedom"? It sounded sarcastic. And why might he not wish to call him anything at all? And how had the roommate had the time to make enemies? Orson asked irritably, "How long have you *been* here?"

"Eight days." Henry concluded every statement with a strange little pucker of his lips, a kind of satisfied silent click, as if to say, "And what do you think of *that?*"

Orson felt that he had been sized up as someone easy to startle. But he slid helplessly into the straight-man role that, like the second-best bed, had been reserved for him. "That *long?*"

"Yes. I was totally alone until the day before yesterday. You see, I hitch-hiked."

"From Oregon?"

"Yes. And I wished to allow time enough for any contingency. In case I was robbed, I had sewed a fifty-dollar bill inside my shirt. As it turned out, I made smooth connections all the way. I had painted a large cardboard sign saying 'Harvard.' You should try it sometime. One meets some very interesting Harvard graduates."

"Didn't your parents worry?"

"Of course. My parents are divorced. My father was furious. He wanted me to fly. I told him to give the plane fare to the Indian Relief Fund. He never gives a penny to charity. And, of course, I'm old. I'm twenty."

"You've been in the Army?"

Henry lifted his hands and staggered back as if from a blow. He put the back of his hand to his brow, whimpered "Never," shuddered, straightened up smartly, and saluted. "In fact, the Portland draft board is after me right now." With a preening tug of his two agile hands—which did look, Orson realized, old: bony and veined and red-tipped, like a woman's—he broadened his foulard. "They refuse to recognize any conscientious objectors except Quakers and Mennonites. My bishop agrees with them. They offered me an out if I'd say I was willing to work in a hospital, but I explained that this released a man for combat duty and if it came to that I'd just as soon carry a gun. I'm an excellent shot. I mind killing only on principle."

The Korean War had begun that summer, and Orson, who had been nagged by a suspicion that his duty was to enlist, bristled at such blithe pacifism. He squinted and asked, "What *have* you been doing for two years, then?"

'Working in a plywood mill. As a gluer. The actual gluing is done by machines, but they become swamped in their own glue now and then. It's a kind of excessive introspection—you've read *Hamlet?*"

"Just *Macbeth* and *The Merchant of Venice.*"

"Yes. Anyway. They have to be cleaned with solvent. One wears long rubber gloves up to one's elbows. It's very soothing work. The inside of a gluer is an excellent place for revolving Greek quotations in your head. I memorized nearly the whole of the *Phaedo* that way." He gestured toward his desk, and Orson saw that many of the books were green Loeb editions of Plato and Aristotle, in Greek. Their spines were worn; they looked read and reread. For the first time, the thought of being at Harvard frightened him. Orson had been standing between his suitcases and now he moved to unpack. "Have you left me a bureau?"

"Of course. The better one." Henry jumped on the bed that had not been slept in and bounced up and down as if it were a trampoline. "And I've given you the bed with the better mattress," he said, still bouncing, "and the desk that doesn't have the glare from the window."

"Thanks," Orson said.

Henry was quick to notice his tone. "Would you rather have my bed? My desk?" He jumped from the bed and dashed to his desk and scooped a stack of books from it.

Orson had to touch him to stop him, and was startled by the tense muscularity of the arm he touched. "Don't be silly," he said. "They're exactly alike."

Henry replaced his books. "I don't want any bitterness," he said, "or immature squabbling. As the older man, it's my responsibility to yield. Here. I'll give you the shirt off my back." And he began to peel off his lumberjack shirt, leaving the foulard dramatically knotted around his naked throat. He wore no undershirt.

Having won from Orson a facial expression that Orson himself could not see, Henry smiled and rebuttoned the shirt. "Do you mind my name being in the upper slot on the door? I'll remove it. I apologize. I did it without realizing how sensitive you would be."

Perhaps it was all a kind of humor. Orson tried to make a joke. He pointed and asked, "Do I get a spinning wheel, too?"

"Oh, *that*." Henry hopped backward on one bare foot and became rather shy. "That's an experiment. I ordered it from Calcutta. I spin for a half hour a day, after Yoga."

"You do Yoga, too?"

"Just some of the elementary positions. My ankles can't take more than five minutes of the Lotus yet."

"And you say you have a bishop."

The roommate glanced up with a glint of fresh interest. "Say. You listen, don't you? Yes. I consider myself an Anglican Christian Platonist strongly influenced by Gandhi." He touched his palms before his chest, bowed, straightened, and giggled. "My bishop hates me," he said. "The one in Oregon, who wants me to be a soldier. I've introduced myself to the bishop here and I don't think he likes me, either. For that matter, I've antagonized my adviser. I told him I had no intention of fulfilling the science requirement."

"For God's sake, why *not*?"

"You don't really want to know."

Orson felt this rebuff as a small test of strength. "Not really," he agreed.

"I consider science a demonic illusion of human *hubris*. Its phantasmal nature is proved by its constant revision. I asked him, 'Why should I waste an entire fourth of my study time, time that could be spent with Plato, mastering a mass of hypotheses that will be obsolete by the time I graduate?' "

"My Lord, Henry," Orson exclaimed, indignantly defending the millions of lives saved by medical science, "you can't be serious!"

"Please. Hub. I may be difficult for you, and I think it would help if you were to call me by my name. Now let's talk about you. Your father is a doctor, you received all A's in high school—I received rather mediocre grades myself—and you've come to Harvard because you believe it affords a cosmopolitan Eastern environment that will be valuable to you after spending your entire life in a small provincial town."

"Who the hell told you this?" The recital of his application statement made Orson blush. He already felt much older than the boy who had written it.

"University Hall," Henry said. "I went over and asked to see your folder. They didn't want to let me at first, but I explained that if they were going to give me a roommate, after I had specifically requested to live alone, I had a right to information about you, so I could minimize possible friction."

"And they *let* you?"

"Of course. People without convictions have no powers of resistance." His mouth made its little satisfied click, and Orson was goaded to ask, "Why did *you* come to Harvard?"

"Two reasons." He ticked them off on two fingers. "Raphael Demos and Werner Jaeger."

Orson did not know these names, but he suspected that "Friends of yours?" was a stupid question, once it was out of his mouth.

But Henry nodded. "I've introduced myself to Demos. A charming old scholar, with a beautiful young wife."

"You mean you just went to his house and pushed yourself *in?*" Orson heard his own voice grow shrill; his voice, rather high and unstable, was one of the things about himself that he liked least.

Henry blinked, and looked unexpectedly vulnerable, so slender and bravely dressed, his ugly, yellowish, flat-nailed feet naked on the floor, which was uncarpeted and painted black. "That isn't how I would describe it. I went as a pilgrim. He seemed pleased to talk to me." He spoke carefully, and his mouth abstained from clicking.

That he could hurt his roommate's feelings—that this jaunty apparition had feelings—disconcerted Orson more deeply than any of the surprises he had been deliberately offered. As quickly as he had popped up, Henry dropped to the floor, as if through a trapdoor in the plane of conversation. He resumed spinning. The method apparently called for one thread to be wound around the big toe of a foot and to be kept taut by a kind of absent-minded pedal motion. While engaged in this, he seemed hermetically sealed inside one of the gluing machines that had incubated his garbled philosophy. Unpacking, Orson was slowed and snagged by a complicated mood of discomfort. He tried to remember how his mother had arranged his bureau drawers at home—socks and underwear in one, shirts and handkerchiefs in another. Home seemed infinitely far from him, and he was dizzily conscious of a great depth of space beneath his feet, as if the blackness of the floor were the color of an abyss. The spinning wheel steadily chuckled. Orson's buzz of unease circled and settled on his roommate, who, it was clear, had thought earnestly about profound matters, matters that Orson, busy as he had been with the practical business of being a good student, had hardly considered. It was also clear that Henry had thought unintelligently. This unintelligence ("I received rather mediocre grades myself") was more of a menace than a comfort. Bent above the bureau drawers, Orson felt cramped in his mind, able neither to stand erect in wholehearted contempt nor to lie down in honest admiration. His mood was complicated by the repugnance his roommate's physical presence aroused in him. An almost morbidly clean boy, Orson was haunted by glue, and a tacky ambience resisted every motion of his unpacking.

The silence between the roommates continued until a great bell rang ponderously. The sound was near and yet far, like a heartbeat within the bosom of time, and it seemed to bring with it into the room the muffling foliation of the trees in the Yard, which to Orson's prairie-honed eyes had looked tropically tall and lush; the walls of the room vibrated with leaf shadows, and many minute presences—dust motes, traffic sounds, or angels of whom several could dance on the head of a pin—thronged the air and made it difficult to breathe. The stairways of the dormitory rumbled. Boys dressed in jackets and neckties crowded the doorway and entered the room, laughing and calling "Hub. Hey, Hub."

"Get up off the floor, dad."

"Jesus, Hub, put your shoes on."

"Pee-*yew*."

"And take off that seductive sarong around your neck."

"Consider the lilies, Hub. They toil not, neither do they spin, and yet I say unto you that Solomon in all his glory was not arrayed like one of these."

"Amen, brothers!"

"Fitch, you should be a preacher."

They were all strangers to Orson. Hub stood and smoothly performed introductions.

In a few days, Orson had sorted them out. That jostling conglomerate, so apparently secure and homogeneous, broke down, under habitual exposure, into double individuals: roommates. There were Silverstein and Koshland, Dawson and Kern, Young and Carter, Petersen and Fitch.

Silverstein and Koshland, who lived in the room overhead, were Jews from New York City. All Orson knew about non-biblical Jews was that they were a sad race, full of music, shrewdness, and woe. But Silverstein and Koshland were always clowning, always wisecracking. They played bridge and poker and chess and Go and went to the movies in Boston and drank coffee in the luncheonettes around the Square. They came from the "gifted" high schools of the Bronx and Brooklyn respectively, and treated Cambridge as if it were another borough. Most of what the freshman year sought to teach them they seemed to know already. As winter approached, Koshland went out for basketball, and he and his teammates made the floor above bounce to the thump and rattle of scrimmages with a tennis ball and a wastebasket. One afternoon, a section of ceiling collapsed on Orson's bed.

Next door, in Room 12, Dawson and Kern wanted to be writers. Dawson was from Ohio and Kern from Pennsylvania. Dawson had a sulky, slouching bearing, a certain puppyish facial eagerness, and a terrible temper. He was a disciple of Anderson and Hemingway and himself wrote as austerely as a newspaper. He had been raised as an atheist, and no one in the dormitory incited his temper more often than Hub. Orson, feeling that he and Dawson came from opposite edges of that great psychological realm called the Midwest, liked him. He felt less at ease with Kern, who seemed Eastern and subtly vicious. A farm boy driven by an unnatural sophistication, riddled with nervous ailments ranging from conjunctivitis to hemorrhoids, Kern smoked and talked incessantly. He and Dawson maintained between them a battery of running jokes. At night Orson could hear them on the other side of the wall keeping each other awake with improvised parodies and musical comedies based on their teachers, their courses, or their fellow-freshmen. One midnight, Orson distinctly heard Dawson sing, "My name is Orson Ziegler, I come from South Dakota." There was a pause, then Kern sang back, "I tend to be a niggler, and masturbate by quota."

Across the hall, in 15, lived Young and Carter, Negroes. Carter was from Detroit and very black, very clipped in speech, very well dressed, and apt to collapse, at the jab of a rightly angled joke, into a spastic giggling fit that left his cheeks gleaming with tears; Kern was expert at breaking Carter up. Young was a lean, malt-pale colored boy from North Carolina, here on a national scholarship, out of his depth, homesick, and cold. Kern called him Br'er Possum. He slept all day and at night sat on his bed playing the mouthpiece of a trumpet to himself. At first, he had played the full horn in the afternoon, flooding the dormitory and its green envelope of trees with golden, tremulous versions of languorous tunes like "Sentimental Journey" and "The Tennessee Waltz." It had been nice. But Young's sombre sense of tact—a slavish drive toward self-effacement that the shock of Harvard had awakened in him—soon cancelled these harmless performances. He took to hiding from the sun, and at night the furtive spitting sound from across the hall seemed to Orson, as he struggled into sleep, music drowning in shame. Carter always referred to his roommate as "Jonathan," mouthing the syllables fastidiously, as if he were pronouncing the name of a remote being he had just learned about, like Rochefoucald or Demosthenes.

Cattycorner up the hall, in unlucky 13, Petersen and Fitch kept a strange household. Both were tall, narrow-shouldered, and broad-bottomed; physiques aside, it was hard to see what they had in common, or why Harvard had put them together. Fitch, with dark staring eyes and the flat full cranium of Frankenstein's monster, was a child prodigy from Maine, choked with philosophy, wild with ideas, and pregnant with the seeds of the nervous breakdown he was to have, eventually, in April. Petersen was an amiable Swede with a transparent skin that revealed blue veins in his nose. For several summers he had worked as a reporter for the Duluth *Herald*. He had all the newsman's tricks: the side-of-the-mouth quip, the nip of whiskey, the hat on the back of the head, the habit of throwing still-burning cigarettes onto the floor. He did not seem quite to know why he was at Harvard, and in fact did not return at the end of the freshman year. But, while these two drifted toward their respective failures, they made a strangely well-suited couple. Each was strong where the other was helpless. Fitch was so uncoördinated and unorganized he could not even type; he would lie on his bed in pajamas, writhing and grimacing, and dictate a tangled humanities paper, twice the requested length and mostly about books that had not been assigned, while Petersen, typing with a hectic two-finger system, would obligingly turn this chaotic monologue into "copy." His patience verged on the maternal. When Fitch appeared for a meal wearing a coat and tie, the joke ran in the dormitory that Petersen had dressed him. In return, Fitch gave Petersen ideas out of the superabundance painfully cramming his big flat head. Petersen had absolutely no ideas; he could neither compare, contrast, nor criticize St. Augustine and Marcus Aurelius. Perhaps having seen, so young, so many corpses and fires and policemen and prostitutes had prematurely blighted his mind. At any rate, mothering Fitch gave him something practical to do, and Orson envied them.

He envied all the roommates, whatever the bond between them—geography, race, ambition, physical size—for between himself and Hub Palamountain he could see no link except forced cohabitation. Not that living with Hub was superficially unpleasant. Hub was tidy, industrious, and ostentatiously considerate. He rose at seven, prayed, did Yoga, spun, and was off to breakfast, often not to be seen again until the end of the day. He went to sleep, generally, at eleven sharp. If there was noise in the room, he would insert rubber plugs in his ears, put a black mask over his eyes, and go to sleep anyway. During the day, he kept a rigorous round of appointments: he audited two courses in addition to taking four, he wrestled three times a week for his physical-training requirement, he wangled tea invitations from Demos and Jaeger and the Bishop of Massachusetts, he attended free evening lectures and readings, he associated himself with Phillips Brooks House and spent two afternoons a week supervising slum boys in a Roxbury redevelopment house. In addition, he had begun to take piano lessons in Brookline. Many days, Orson saw him only at meals in the Union, where the dormitory neighbors, in those first fall months when their acquaintance was crisp and young and differing interests had not yet scattered them, tended to regroup around a long table. In these months there was often a debate about the subject posed under their eyes: Hub's vegetarianism. There he would sit, his tray heaped high with a steaming double helping of squash and lima beans, while Fitch would try to locate the exact point at which vegetarianism became inconsistent. "You eat eggs," he said.

"Yes," Hub said.

"You realize that every egg, from the chicken's point of reference, is a newborn baby?"

"But in fact it is not unless it has been fertilized by a rooster."

"But suppose," Fitch pursued, "as sometimes happens—which I happen to know, from working in my uncle's henhouse in Maine—an egg that *should* be sterile has in fact been fertilized and contains an embryo?"

"If I see it, I naturally don't eat that particular egg," Hub said, his lips making that satisfied concluding snap.

Fitch pounced triumphantly, spilling a fork to the floor with a lurch of his hand. "But *why?* The hen feels the same pain on being parted from an egg whether sterile or fertile. The embryo is unconscious—a vegetable. As a vegetarian, you should eat it with special relish." He tipped back in his chair so hard he had to grab the table edge to keep from toppling over.

"It seems to me," Dawson said, frowning darkly—these discussions, clogging some twist of his ego, often spilled him into a vile temper—"that psychoanalysis of hens is hardly relevant."

"On the contrary," Kern said lightly, clearing his throat and narrowing his pink, infected eyes, "it seems to me that there, in the tiny, dim mind of the hen—the minimal mind, as it were—is where the tragedy of the universe achieves a pinpoint focus. Picture the emotional life of a hen. What does she know of companionship? A flock of pecking, harsh-voiced gossips. Of shelter? A few dung-bespattered slats. Of food? Some flecks of mash and grit insolently tossed on the ground. Of love? The casual assault of a polygamous cock—cock in the Biblical sense. Then, into this heartless world, there suddenly arrives, as if by magic, an egg. An egg of her own. An egg, it must seem to her, that she and God have made. How she must cherish it, its beautiful baldness, its gentle lustre its firm yet somehow fragile, softly swaying weight."

Carter had broken up. He bent above his tray, his eyes tight shut, his dark face contorted joyfully. "Puhleese," he gasped at last. "You're making my stomach hurt."

"Ah, Carter," Kern said loftily, "if that were only the worst of it. For then, one day, while the innocent hen sits cradling this strange, faceless, oval child, its little weight swaying softly in her wings"—he glanced hopefully at Carter, but the colored boy bit his lower lips and withstood the jab—"an enormous man, smelling of beer and manure, comes and tears the egg from her grasp. And why? Because *he*"—Kern pointed, arm fully extended, across the table, so that his index finger, orange with nicotine, almost touched Hub's nose—"*he*, Saint Henry Palamountain, wants more eggs to eat. 'More eggs!' he cries voraciously, so that brutal steers and faithless pigs can continue to menace the children of American mothers!"

Dawson slammed his silver down, got up from the table, and slouched out of the dining room. Kern blushed. In the silence, Petersen put a folded slice of roast beef in his mouth and said, chewing, "Jesus, Hub, if somebody else kills the animals you might as well eat 'em. They don't give a damn any more."

"You understand nothing," Hub said simply.

"Hey, Hub," Silverstein called down from the far end of the table. "What's the word on milk? Don't calves drink milk? Maybe you're taking milk out of some calf's mouth."

Orson felt impelled to speak. "*No*," he said, and his voice seemed to have burst, its pitch was so unsteady and excited. "As anybody except somebody from New York would know, milch cows have weaned their calves. What I wonder about, Hub, is your shoes. You wear leather shoes."

"I do." The gaiety left Hub's defense of himself. His lips became prim.

"Leather is the skin of a steer."

"But the animal has already been slaughtered."

"You sound like Petersen. Your purchase of leather goods—what about your wallet and belt, for that matter?—encourages the slaughter. You're as much of a murderer as the rest of us. More of one—because you think about it."

Hub folded his hands carefully in front of him, propping them, almost in prayer, on the table edge. His voice became like that of a radio announcer, but an announcer rapidly, softly describing the home stretch of a race. "My belt, I believe, is a form of plastic. My wallet was given to me by my mother years ago, before I became a vegetarian. Please remember that I ate meat for eighteen years and I still have an appetite for it. If there were any other concentrated source of protein, I would not eat eggs. Some vegetarians do not. On the other hand, some vegetarians eat fish and take liver extract. I would not do this. Shoes are a problem. There is a firm in Chicago that makes non-leather shoes for extreme vegetarians, but they're very expensive and not comfortable. I once ordered a pair. They killed my feet. Leather, you see, 'breathes' in a way no synthetic substitute does. My feet are tender; I have compromised. I apologize. For that matter, when I play the piano I encourage the slaughter of elephants, and in brushing my teeth, which I must do faithfully because a vegetable diet is so heavy in carbohydrates, I use a brush of pig bristles. I am covered with blood, and pray daily for forgiveness." He took up his fork and resumed eating the mound of squash.

Orson was amazed; he had been impelled to speak by a kind of sympathy, and Hub had answered as if he alone were an enemy. He tried to defend himself. "There are perfectly wearable shoes," he said, "made out of canvas, with crêpe-rubber soles."

"I'll look into them," Hub said. "They sound a little sporty to me."

Laughter swept the table and ended the subject. After lunch Orson walked to the library with the beginnings of indigestion; a backwash of emotion was upsetting his stomach. There was a growing confusion inside him he could not resolve. He resented being associated with Hub, and yet felt attacked when Hub was attacked. It seemed to him that Hub deserved credit for putting his beliefs into practice, and that people like Fitch and Kern, in mocking, merely belittled themselves. Yet Hub smiled at their criticism, took it as a game, and fought back in earnest only at Orson, forcing him into a false position. Why? Was it because in being also a Christian he alone qualified for serious rebuke? But Carter went to church, wearing a blue pin-striped suit with a monogrammed handkerchief peaked in the breast pocket, every Sunday; Petersen was a nominal Presbyterian; Orson had once seen Kern sneaking out of Mem Chapel; and even Koshland observed his holidays, by cutting classes and skipping lunch. Why, therefore, Orson asked himself, should Hub pick on him? And why should he care? He had no real respect for Hub. Hub's handwriting was childishly large and careful and his first set of hour exams, even in the course on Plato and Aristotle, had yielded a batch of C's. Orson resented being condescended to by an intellectual inferior. The knowledge that at the table he had come off second best galled him like an unfair grade. His situation with Hub became in his head a diagram in which all his intentions curved off at right angles and his strengths inversely tapered into nothing. Behind the diagram hung the tuck of complacence in Hub's lips, the fishy impudence of his eyes, and the keenly irksome shape and tint of his hands and feet. These images—Hub disembodied—Orson carried with him into the library, back and forth to classes, and along the congested streets around the Square; now and then the glaze of an eye or the flat yellowish nail of a big toe welled up distinctly through the pages of a book and, greatly magnified, slid with Orson into the unconsciousness of sleep. Nevertheless, he surprised himself, sitting one February afternoon in Room 12 with Dawson and Kern, by blurting, "I hate him." He considered what he had said, liked the taste of it, and repeated, "I hate the bastard. I've never hated anybody before in my life." His voice cracked and his eyes warmed with abortive tears.

They had all returned from Christmas vacation to plunge into the weird limbo of reading period and the novel ordeal of midyear exams. This was a dormitory, by and large, of public-school graduates, who feel the strain of Harvard most in their freshman year. The private-school boys, launched by little Harvards like Exeter and Groton, tend to glide through this year and to run aground later on strange reefs, foundering in alcohol, or sinking into dandified apathy. But the institution demands of each man, before it releases him, a wrenching sacrifice of ballast. At Christmas, Orson's mother thought he looked haggard, and set about fattening him up. On the other hand, he was struck by how much his father had aged and shrunk. Orson spent his first days home listening to the mindless music on the radio, hours of it, and driving through farmland on narrow straight roads already banked bright with plowed snow. The South Dakota sky had never looked so open, so clean; he had never realized before that the high dry sun that made even sub-zero days feel warm at noon was a local phenomenon. He made love to his girl again, and again she cried. He said to her he blamed himself, for ineptitude; but in his heart he blamed her. She was not helping him. Back in Cambridge, it was raining, raining in January, and the entryway of the Coop was full of gray footprints and wet bicycles and Radcliffe girls in slickers and sneakers. Hub had stayed here, alone in their room, and had celebrated Christmas with a fast.

In the monotonous, almost hallucinatory month of rereading, outlining, and memorizing, Orson perceived how little he knew, how stupid he was, how unnatural all learning is, and how futile. Harvard rewarded him with three A's and a B. Hub pulled out two B's and two C's. Kern, Dawson, and Silverstein did well; Petersen, Koshland, and Carter got mediocre grades; Fitch flunked one subject, and Young flunked three. The pale Negro slunk in and out of the dorm as if he were diseased and marked for destruction; he became, while still among them, a rumor. The suppressed whistling of the trumpet mouthpiece was no longer heard. Silverstein and Koshland and the basketball crowd adopted Carter and took him to movies in Boston three or four times a week.

After exams, in the heart of the Cambridge winter, there is a grateful pause. New courses are selected, and even the full-year courses, heading into their second half, sometimes put on, like a new hat, a fresh professor. The days quietly lengthen; there is a snowstorm or two; the swimming and squash teams lend the sports pages of the *Crimson* an unaccustomed note of victory. A kind of foreshadow of spring falls bluely on the snow. The elms are seen to be shaped like fountains. The discs of snow pressed by boots into the sidewalk by Albiani's seem large precious coins; the brick buildings, the arched gates, the archaic lecterns, and the barny mansions along Brattle Street dawn upon the freshman as a heritage he temporarily possesses. The thumb-worn spines of his now familiar textbooks seem proof of a certain knowingness, and the strap of the green book bag tugs at his wrist like a living falcon. The letters from home dwindle in importance. The hours open up. There is more time. Experiments are made. Courtships begin. Conversations go on and on; and an almost rapacious desire for mutual discovery possesses acquaintances. It was in this atmosphere, then, that Orson made his confession.

Dawson turned his head away as if the words had menaced him personally. Kern blinked, lit a cigarette, and asked, "What don't you like about him?"

"Well"—Orson shifted his weight uncomfortably in the black but graceful, shapely but hard Harvard chair—"it's little things. Whenever he gets a notice from the Portland draft board, he tears it up without opening it and scatters it out the window."

"And you're afraid that this incriminates you as an accessory and they'll put you in jail?"

"No—I don't know. It seems exaggerated. He exaggerates everything. You should see how he prays."

"How do you know he prays?"

"He shows me. Every morning, he gets down on his knees and *throws* himself across the bed, his face in the blanket, his arms way out." He showed them.

"God," Dawson said. "That's marvellous. It's medieval. It's more than medieval. It's Counter-Reformation."

"I mean," Orson said, grimacing in realization of how deeply he had betrayed Hub, "I pray, too, but I don't make a show of myself."

A frown clotted Dawson's expression, and passed.

"He's a saint," Kern said.

"He's *not*," Orson said. "He's not intelligent. I'm taking Chem 1 with him, and he's worse than a child with the math. And those Greek books he keeps on his desk, they look worn because he bought them second-hand."

"Saints don't have to be intelligent," Kern said. "What saints have to have is energy. Hub has it."

"Look how he wrestles," Dawson said.

"I doubt if he wrestles very *well*," Orson said. "He didn't make the freshman team. I'm sure if we heard him play the piano, it'd be awful."

"You seem to miss the point," Kern said, eyes closed, "of what Hub's all about."

"I know goddam well what he thinks he's all about," Orson said, "but it's fake. It doesn't go. All this vegetarianism and love of the starving Indian—he's really a terribly cold bastard. I think he's about the coldest person I've ever met in my life."

"I don't think Orson thinks that, do you?" Kern asked Dawson.

"No," Dawson said, and his puppyish smile cleared his cloudy face. "That's not what Orson the Parson thinks."

Kern squirmed. "Is it Orson the Parson, or Orson the Person?"

"I think Hub is the nub," Dawson said.

"Or the rub," Kern added, and both burst into grinding laughter. Orson felt he was being sacrificed to the precarious peace the two roommates kept between themselves, and left, superficially insulted but secretly flattered to have been given, at last, a nickname of sorts: Orson the Parson.

Several nights later they went to hear Carl Sandburg read in New Lecture Hall—the four adjacent roommates, plus Fitch. To avoid sitting next to Hub, who aggressively led them into a row of seats, Orson delayed, and so sat the farthest away from the girl Hub sat directly behind. Orson noticed her immediately; she had a lavish mane of coppery red hair which hung down loose over the back of her seat. The color of it, and the abundance, reminded him, all at once, of horses, earth, sun, wheat, and home. From Orson's angle she was nearly in profile; her face was small, with a tilted shadowy cheekbone and a pale prominent ear. Toward the pallor of her profile he felt an orgasmic surge; she seemed suspended in the crowd and was floating, a crest of whiteness, toward him. She turned away. Hub had leaned forward and was saying something into her other ear. Fitch overheard it, and gleefully relayed it to Dawson, who whispered to Kern and Orson, *"Hub said to the girl, 'You have beautiful hair.'"*

Several times during the reading, Hub leaned forward to add something more into her ear, each time springing spurts of choked laughter from Fitch, Dawson, and Kern. Meanwhile, Sandburg, his white bangs as straight and shiny as a doll's wig of artificial fibre, incanted above the lectern and quaintly strummed a guitar. Afterward, Hub walked with the girl into the outdoors. From a distance Orson saw her white face turn and crumple into a laugh. Hub returned to his friends with the complacent nick in the corner of his mouth deepened, in the darkness, to a gash.

It was not the next day, or the next week, but within the month that Hub brought back to the room a heap of red hair. Orson found it lying like a disastrous corpse on a newspaper spread on his bed. "Hub, what the hell is this?"

Hub was on the floor playing with his spinning wheel. "Hair."

"*Human* hair?"

"Of course."

"Whose?"

"A girl's."

"What happened?" The question sounded strange; Orson meant to ask, "What girl's?"

Hub answered as if he had asked that question. "It's a girl I met at the Sandburg reading; you don't know her."

"This is *her* hair?"

"Yes. I asked her for it. She said she was planning to cut it all off this spring anyway."

Orson stood stunned above the bed, gripped by an urge to bury his face and hands in the hair. "You've been *seeing* her?" This effeminate stridence in his voice: he despised it and only Hub brought it out.

"A little. My schedule doesn't allow for much social life, but my adviser has recommended that I relax now and then."

"You take her to movies?"

"Once in a while. She pays her admission, of course."

"Of *course*."

Hub took him up on his tone. "Please remember I'm here on my savings alone. I have refused all financial assistance from my father."

"Hub"—the very syllable seemed an expression of pain—"what are you going to do with her hair?"

"Spin it into a rope."

"A *rope*?"

"Yes. It'll be very difficult; her hair is terribly fine."

"And what will you do with the rope?"

"Make a knot of it."

"A *knot*?"

"I think that's the term. I'll coil it and secure it so it can't come undone and give it to her. So she'll always have her hair the way it was when she was nineteen."

"How the hell did you talk this poor girl into it?"

"I didn't talk her into it. I merely offered, and she thought it was a lovely idea. Really, Orson, I don't see why this should offend your bourgeois scruples. Women cut their hair all the time."

"She must think you're insane. She was humoring you."

"As you like. It was a perfectly rational suggestion, and my sanity has never been raised as an issue between us."

"Well, *I* think you're insane. Hub, you're a *nut*."

Orson left the room and slammed the door, and didn't return until eleven, when Hub was asleep in his eye mask. The heap of hair had been transferred to the floor beside the spinning wheel, and already some strands were entangled with the machine. In time a rope was produced, a braided cord as thick as a woman's little finger, about a foot long, weightless and waxen. The earthy, horsy fire in the hair's color had been quenched in the process. Hub carefully coiled it and with black thread and long pins secured and stiffened the spiral into a disc the size of a small saucer. This he presented to the girl one Friday night. The presentation appeared to satisfy him, for, as far as Orson knew, Hub had no further dates with her. Once in a while Orson passed her in the Yard, and without her hair she scarcely seemed female, her small pale face fringed in curt tufts, her ears looking enormous. He wanted to speak to her; some obscure force of pity, or hope of rescue, impelled him to greet this wan androgyne, but the opening word stuck in his throat. She did not look as if she pitied herself, or knew what had been done to her.

Something magical protected Hub; things deflected from him. The doubt Orson had cast upon his sanity bounced back onto himself. As spring slowly broke, he lost the ability to sleep. Figures and facts churned sluggishly in an insomnious mire. His courses became four parallel puzzles. In mathematics, the crucial transposition upon which the solution pivoted consistently eluded him, vanishing into the chinks between the numbers. The quantities in chemistry became impishly unstable; the unbalanced scales clicked down sharply and the system of interlocked elements that fanned from the lab to the far stars collapsed. In the history survey course, they had reached the Enlightenment, and Orson found himself disturbingly impressed by Voltaire's indictment of God, though the lecturer handled it calmly, as one more dead item of intellectual history, neither true nor false. And in German, which Orson had taken to satisfy his language requirement, the words piled on remorselessly, and the existence of languages other than English, the existence of so many, each so vast, intricate, and opaque, seemed to prove cosmic dementia. He felt his mind, which was always more steady than quick, grow slower and slower. His chair threatened to adhere to him, and he would leap up in panic. Sleepless, stuffed with information he could neither forget nor manipulate, he became prey to obsessive delusions; he became convinced that his girl in South Dakota had taken up with another boy and was making love to him happily, Orson having shouldered the awkwardness and blame of taking her virginity. In the very loops that Emily's ballpoint pen described in her bland letters to him he read the pleased rotundity, the inner fatness of a well-loved woman. He even knew the man. It was Spotted Elk, the black-nailed Chippewa, whose impassive nimbleness had so often mocked Orson on the basketball court, whose terrible ease and speed of reaction had seemed so unjust, and whose defense—he recalled now—Emily had often undertaken. His wife had become a whore, a squaw; the scraggly mute reservation children his father had doctored in the charity clinic became, amid the sliding transparencies of Orson's mind, his own children. In his dreams—or in those limp elisions of imagery which in the absence of sleep passed for dreams—he seemed to be rooming with Spotted Elk, and his roommate, who sometimes wore a mask, invariably had won, by underhanded means, the affection and admiration that were rightfully his. There was a conspiracy. Whenever Orson heard Kern and Dawson laughing on the other side of the wall, he knew it was about him, and about his most secret habits. This ultimate privacy was outrageously invaded; in bed, half-relaxed, he would suddenly see himself bodily involved with Hub's lips, Hub's legs, with Hub's veined, vaguely womanish hands. At first he resisted these visions, tried to erase them; it was like trying to erase ripples on water. He learned to submit to them, to let the attack—for it was an attack, with teeth and sharp acrobatic movements—wash over him, leaving him limp enough to sleep. These dives became the only route to sleep. In the morning he would awake and see Hub sprawled flamboyantly across his bed in prayer, or sitting hunched at his spinning wheel, or, gaudily dressed, tiptoeing to the door and with ostentatious care closing it softly behind him; and he would hate him—hate his appearance, his form, his manner, his pretensions with an avidity of detail he had never known in love. The tiny details of his roommate's physical existence—the wrinkles flickering beside his mouth, the slightly withered look about his hands, the complacently polished creases of his leather shoes—seemed a poisonous food Orson could not stop eating. His eczema worsened alarmingly.

By April, Orson was on the verge of going to the student clinic, which had a department called Mental Health. But at this point Fitch relieved him by having, it seemed, his nervous breakdown for him. For weeks, Fitch had been taking several showers a day. Toward the end he stopped going to classes and was almost constantly naked, except for a towel tucked around his waist. He was trying to complete a humanities paper that was already a month overdue and twenty pages too long. He left the dormitory only to eat and to take more books from the library. One night around nine, Petersen was called to the phone on the second-floor landing. The Watertown police had picked Fitch up as he was struggling through the underbrush on the banks of the Charles four miles away. He claimed he was walking to the West, where he had been told there was enough space to contain God, and proceeded to talk with wild animation to the police chief about the differences and affinities between Kierkegaard and Nietzsche. Hub, ever alert for an opportunity to intrude in the guise of doing good, went to the hall proctor—a spindly and murmurous graduate student of astronomy engaged, under Harlow Shapley, in an endless galaxy count—and volunteered himself as an expert on the case, and even conferred with the infirmary psychologist. Hub's interpretation was that Fitch had been punished for *hubris*. The psychologist felt the problem was fundamentally Oedipal. Fitch was sent back to Maine. Hub suggested to Orson that now Petersen would need a roommate next year. "I think you and he would hit it off splendidly. You're both materialists."

"I'm *not* a materialist."

Hub lifted his dreadful hands in half-blessing. "Have it your way. I'm determined to minimize friction."

"Dammit, Hub, all the friction between us comes from *you*."

"How? What do I do? Tell me, and I'll change. I'll give you the shirt off my back." He began to unbutton, and stopped, seeing that the laugh wasn't going to come.

Orson felt weak and empty, and in spite of himself he cringed inwardly, with a helpless affection for his unreal, unreachable friend. "I don't know, Hub," he admitted. "I don't know what it is you're doing to me."

A paste of silence dried in the air between them.

Orson with an effort unstuck himself. "I think you're right, we shouldn't room together next year."

Hub seemed a bit bewildered, but nodded, saying, "I told them in the beginning that I ought to live alone." And his hurt eyes bulging behind their lenses settled into an invulnerable Byzantine stare.

One afternoon in middle May, Orson was sitting stumped at his desk, trying to study. He had taken two exams and had two to go. They stood between him and release like two towering walls of muddy paper. His position seemed extremely precarious: he was unable to retreat and able to advance only along a very thin thread, a high wire of sanity on which he balanced above an abyss of statistics and formulae, his brain a firmament of winking cells. A push would kill him. There was then a hurried pounding up the stairs, and Hub pushed into the room carrying cradled in his arm a metal object the color of a gun and the size of a cat. It had a red tongue. Hub slammed the door behind him, snapped the lock, and dumped the object on Orson's bed. It was the head of a parking meter, sheared from its post. A keen quick pain cut through Orson's groin. "For God's sake," he cried in his contemptible high voice, "what's *that*?"

"It's a parking meter."

"I *know*, I can *see* that. Where the hell did you *get* it?"

"I won't talk to you until you stop being hysterical," Hub said, and crossed to his desk, where Orson had put his mail. He took the top letter, a special delivery from the Portland draft board, and tore it in half. This time, the pain went through Orson's chest. He put his head in his arms on the desk and whirled and groped in the black-red darkness there. His body was frightening him; his nerves listened for a third psychosomatic slash.

There was a rap on the door; from the force of the knock, it could only be the police. Hub nimbly dashed to the bed and hid the meter under Orson's pillow. Then he pranced to the door and opened it.

It was Dawson and Kern. "What's up?" Dawson asked, frowning as if the disturbance had been created to annoy him.

"It sounded like Ziegler was being tortured," Kern said.

Orson pointed at Hub and explained, "He's castrated a parking meter!"

"I did not," Hub said. "A car went out of control on Mass. Avenue and hit a parked car, which knocked a meter down. A crowd gathered. The head of the meter was lying in the gutter, so I picked it up and carried it away. I was afraid someone might be tempted to steal it."

"Nobody tried to stop you?" Kern asked.

"Of course not. They were all gathered around the driver of the car."

"Was he hurt?"

"I doubt it. I didn't look."

"You didn't *look!*" Orson cried. "You're a great Samaritan."

"I am not prey," Hub said, "to morbid curiosity."

"Where were the police?" Kern asked.

"They hadn't arrived yet."

Dawson asked, "Well, why didn't you wait till a cop arrived and give the meter to him?"

"Why should I give it to an agent of the State? It's no more his than mine."

"But it *is,*" Orson said.

"It was a plain act of Providence that placed it in my hands," Hub said, the corners of his lips dented securely. "I haven't decided yet which charity should receive the money it contains."

Dawson asked, "But isn't that stealing?"

"No more stealing than the State is stealing in making people pay money for space in which to park their own cars."

"Huh," Orson said, getting to his feet. "You give it back or we'll both go to jail." He saw himself ruined, the scarcely commenced career of his life destroyed.

Hub turned serenely. "I'm not afraid. Going to jail under a totalitarian regime is a mark of honor. If you had a conscience, you'd understand."

Petersen and Carter and Silverstein came into the room. Some boys from the lower floors followed them. The story was hilariously retold. The meter was produced from under the pillow and passed around and shaken to demonstrate the weight of pennies it contained. Hub always carried, as a vestige of the lumberjack country he came from, an intricate all-purpose pocket knife. He began to pry open the little money door. Orson came up behind him and got him around the neck with one arm. Hub's body stiffened. He passed the head of the meter and the open knife to Carter, and then Orson experienced sensations of being lifted, of flying, and of lying on the floor, looking up at Hub's face, which was upside down in his vision. He scrambled to his feet and went for him again, rigid with anger and yet, in his heart, happily relaxed; Hub's body was tough and quick and satisfying to grip, though, being a wrestler, he somehow deflected Orson's hands and again lifted and dropped him to the black floor. This time, Orson felt a blow as his coccyx hit the wood; yet even through the pain he perceived, gazing into the heart of this marriage, that Hub was being as gentle with him as he could be. And that he could try in earnest to kill Hub and be in no danger of succeeding was also a comfort. He renewed the attack and again enjoyed the tense defensive skill that made Hub's body a kind of warp in space through which his own body, after an ecstatic instant of contention, was converted to the supine position. He got to his feet and would have gone for Hub the fourth time, but his fellow-freshmen grabbed his arms and held him. He shook them off and without a word returned to his desk and concentrated down into his book, turning the page. The type looked extremely distinct, though it was trembling too hard to be deciphered.

The head of the parking meter stayed in the room for one night. The next day, Hub allowed himself to be persuaded (by the others; Orson had stopped speaking to him) to take it to the Cambridge police headquarters in Central Square. Dawson and Kern tied a ribbon around it, and attached a note: "Please take good care of my baby." None of them, however, had the nerve to go with Hub to the headquarters, though when he came back he said the chief was delighted to get the meter, and had thanked him, and had agreed to donate the pennies to the local orphans' home. In another week, the last exams were over. The freshmen all went home. When they returned in the fall, they were different: sophomores. Petersen and Young did not come back at all. Fitch returned, made up the lost credits, and eventually graduated *magna cum* in History and Lit. He now teaches in a Quaker prep school. Silverstein is a bio-chemist, Koshland a lawyer. Dawson writes conservative editorials in Cleveland, Kern is in advertising in New York. Carter, as if obliged to join Young in oblivion, disappeared between his junior and senior years. The dormitory neighbors tended to lose sight of each other, though Hub, who had had his case shifted to the Massachusetts jurisdiction, was now and then pictured in the *Crimson,* and once gave an evening lecture, "Why I Am an Episcopalian Pacifist." As the litigation progressed, the Bishop of Massachusetts rather grudgingly vouched for him, and by the time of his final hearing the Korean War was over, and the judge who heard the case ruled that Hub's convictions were sincere, as witnessed by his willingness to go to jail. Hub was rather disappointed at the verdict, since he had prepared a three-year reading list to occupy him in his cell and was intending to memorize all four Gospels in the original Greek. After graduation, he went to Union Theological Seminary, spent several years as the assistant rector of an urban parish in Baltimore, and learned to play the piano well enough to be the background music in a Charles Street cocktail lounge. He insisted on wearing his clerical collar, and as a consequence gave the bar a small celebrity. After a year of overriding people of less strong convictions, he was allowed to go to South Africa, where he worked and preached among the Bantus until the government requested that he leave the country. From there he went to Nigeria, and when last heard from—on a Christmas card, with French salutations and Negro Magi, which arrived, soiled and wrinkled, in South Dakota in February—Hub was in Madagascar, as a "combination missionary, political agitator, and soccer coach." The description struck Orson as probably facetious, and Hub's childish and confident handwriting, with every letter formed individually, afflicted him with some of the old exasperation. Having vowed to answer the card, he mislaid it, uncharacteristically.

Orson didn't speak to Hub for two days after the parking-meter incident. By then, it seemed rather silly, and they finished out the year sitting side by side at their desks as amiably as two cramped passengers who have endured a long bus trip together. When they parted, they shook hands, and Hub would have walked Orson to the subway kiosk except that he had an appointment in the opposite direction. Orson received two A's and two B's on his final exams; for the remaining three years at Harvard, he roomed uneventfully with two other colorless pre-med students, named Wallace and Neuhauser. After graduation, he married Emily, attended the Yale School of Medicine, and interned in St. Louis. He is now the father of four children and, since the death of his own father, the only doctor in the town. His life has gone much the way he planned it, and he is much the kind of man he intended to be when he was eighteen. He delivers babies, assists the dying, attends the necessary meetings, plays golf, and does good. He is honorable and irritable. If not as much loved as his father, he is perhaps even more respected. In one particular only—a kind of scar he carries without pain and without any clear memory of the amputation—does the man he is differ from the man he assumed he would become. He never prays.

Questions

1. A conflict between the two roommates, Orson Ziegler and Henry Palamountain, arises over what "matters" to each one. For Orson, many things "matter," and for Henry almost nothing does. Explain how this conflict reveals what things are important to each one.

2. Specifically, the two roommates have very different reasons for coming to Harvard. What are those reasons? What does each one want, and expect, from college? How much does each one understand of his own and of each other's reasons? In particular, Henry names his two reasons: "Raphael Demos and Werner Jaeger." What does his answer suggest about what is important to him in college? Why does Orson fail to understand?

3. What preconceptions about other people has Orson brought with him? Why is he less ready than Henry to be friendly with the new boys they meet in the dormitory?

4. Why is Orson irritated by Henry's constant round of activities? What are his real feelings toward him?

5. The story ends with a succinct summary of the lives of its characters after their first year of college. Why? Is the story over at this point? What has it shown? What is its theme?

6. We are told that, after college, Orson's life "has gone much the way he planned it." Is this what he wished? Discuss the irony of the statement. Had college changed him in any way? Is he ever aware of anything he has missed?

Eudora Welty

DEATH OF A TRAVELLING SALESMAN

Eudora Welty has gone her own individualistic way, quite apart from literary centers and influences, creating a body of distinguished work based wholly on her own perceptions of small-town southern life. Miss Welty was born in Jackson, Mississippi, in 1909, and was educated there and at the University of Wisconsin. She also studied advertising at Columbia University. Her outside experiences, however, had little effect on the content of her work, for she has written almost exclusively about her native Mississippi. More proficient in the short story form with its brief controlled glimpses into one or two characters' lives than in the sustained narrative of the novel, Miss Welty first made her reputation with A Curtain of Green *(1941), a group of stories introduced and praised by Katherine Anne Porter. Other collections of stories are* The Wide Net *(1943) and* The Golden Apples *(1949). Her novels include* Delta Wedding *(1946),* The Ponder Heart *(1954), and her most ambitious work,* Losing Battles *(1970), a long novel about a family gathering in Mississippi which is almost entirely dialogue.*

In her stories Miss Welty finds comic and even grotesque elements beneath the surface of the ordinary lives of her characters. She has an accurate ear for colloquial and regional speech, which she renders with comic relish and often uses in place of exposition to achieve characterization. Her typical characters are often unschooled in a formal way, but possess a natural, tough shrewdness. "Death of a Travelling Salesman," from A Curtain of Green, *is more serious in tone and intent than many of her stories. It shows her deep sympathy for a man at the end of his life who is forced to recognize all his insecure foundations.*

R. J. Bowman, who for fourteen years had travelled for a shoe company through Mississippi, drove his Ford along a rutted dirt path. It was a long day! The time did not seem to clear the noon hurdle and settle into soft afternoon. The sun, keeping its strength here even in winter, stayed at the top of the sky, and every time Bowman stuck his head out of the dusty car to stare up the road, it seemed to reach a long arm down and push against the top of his head, right through his hat—like the practical joke of an old drummer, long on the road. It made him feel all the more angry and helpless. He was feverish, and he was not quite sure of the way.

This was his first day back on the road after a long siege of influenza. He had had very high fever, and dreams, and had become weakened and pale, enough to tell the difference in the mirror, and he could not think clearly. . . . All afternoon, in the midst of his anger, and for no reason, he had thought of his dead grandmother. She had been a comfortable soul. Once more Bowman wished he could fall into the big feather bed that had been in her room. . . . Then he forgot her again.

This desolate hill country! And he seemed to be going the wrong way—it was as if he were going back, far back. There was not a house in sight. . . . There was no use wishing he were back in bed, though. By paying the hotel doctor his bill he had proved his recovery. He had not even been sorry when the pretty trained nurse said good-bye. He did not like illness, he distrusted it, as he distrusted the road without signposts. It angered him. He had given the nurse a really expensive bracelet, just because she was packing up her bag and leaving.

But now—what if in fourteen years on the road he had never been ill before and never had an accident? His record was broken, and he had even begun almost to question it. . . . He had gradually put up at better hotels, in the bigger towns, but weren't they all, eternally, stuffy in summer and draughty in winter? Women? He could only remember little rooms within little rooms, like a nest of Chinese paper boxes, and if he thought of one woman he saw the worn loneliness that the furniture of that room seemed built of. And he himself—he was a man who always wore rather wide-brimmed black hats, and in the wavy hotel mirrors had looked something like a bull-fighter, as he paused for that inevitable instant on the landing, walking downstairs to supper. . . . He leaned out of the car again, and once more the sun pushed at his head.

Bowman had wanted to reach Beulah by dark, to go to bed and sleep off his fatigue. As he remembered, Beulah was fifty miles away from the last town, on a gravelled road. This was only a cow trail. How had he ever come to such a place? One hand wiped the sweat from his face, and he drove on.

He had made the Beulah trip before. But he had never seen this hill or this petering-out path before—or that cloud, he thought shyly, looking up and then down quickly—any more than he had seen this day before. Why did he not admit he was simply lost and had been for miles? . . .

He was not in the habit of asking the way of strangers, and these people never knew where the very roads they lived on went to; but then he had not even been close enough to anyone to call out. People standing in the fields now and then, or on top of the haystacks, had been too far away, looking like leaning sticks or weeds, turning a little at the solitary rattle of his car across their countryside, watching the pale sobered winter dust where it chunked out behind like big squashes down the road. The stares of these distant people had followed him solidly like a wall, impenetrable, behind which they turned back after he had passed.

The cloud floated there to one side like the bolster on his grandmother's bed. It went over a cabin on the edge of a hill, where two bare chinaberry trees clutched at the sky. He drove through a heap of dead oak leaves, his wheels stirring their weightless sides to make a silvery melancholy whistle as the car passed through their bed. No car had been along this way ahead of him. Then he saw that he was on the edge of a ravine that fell away, a red erosion, and that this was indeed the road's end.

He pulled the brake. But it did not hold, though he put all his strength into it. The car, tipped toward the edge, rolled a little. Without doubt, it was going over the bank.

He got out quietly, as though some mischief had been done him and he had his dignity to remember. He lifted his bag and sample case out, set them down, and stood back and watched the car roll over the edge. He heard something–not the crash he was listening for, but a slow unuproarious crackle. Rather distastefully he went to look over, and he saw that his car had fallen into a tangle of immense grape vines as thick as his arm, which caught it and held it, rocked it like a grotesque child in a dark cradle, and then, as he watched, concerned somehow that he was not still inside it, released it gently to the ground.

He sighed.

Where am I? he wondered with a shock. Why didn't I do something? All his anger seemed to have drifted away from him. There was the house, back on the hill. He took a bag in each hand and with almost childlike willingness went toward it. But his breathing came with difficulty, and he had to stop to rest.

It was a shotgun house, two rooms and an open passage between, perched on the hill. The whole cabin slanted a little under the heavy heaped-up vine that covered the roof, light and green, as though forgotten from summer. A woman stood in the passage.

He stopped still. Then all of a sudden his heart began to behave strangely. Like a rocket set off, it began to expand into uneven patterns of beats which showered into his brain, and he could not think. But in scattering and falling it made no noise. It shot up with great power, almost elation, and fell gently, like acrobats into nets. It began to pound profoundly, then waited irresponsibly, hitting in some sort of inward mockery first at his ribs, then against his eyes, then under his shoulder blades, and against the roof of his mouth when he tried to say, "Good afternoon, madam." But he could not hear his heart—it was as quiet as ashes falling: This was rather comforting; still, it was shocking to Bowman to feel his heart beating at all.

Stockstill in his confusion, he dropped his bags, which seemed to drift in slow bulks gracefully through the air and to cushion themselves on the grey prostrate grass near the doorstep.

As for the woman standing there, he saw at once that she was old. Since she could not possibly hear his heart, he ignored the pounding and now looked at her carefully, and yet in his distraction dreamily, with his mouth open.

She had been cleaning the lamp, and held it, half blackened, half clear, in front of her. He saw her with the dark passage behind her. She was a big woman with a weather-beaten but unwrinkled face; her lips were held tightly together, and her eyes looked with a curious dulled brightness into his. He looked at her shoes, which were like bundles. If it were summer she would be barefoot. . . . Bowman, who automatically judged a woman's age on sight, set her age at fifty. She wore a formless garment of some grey coarse material, rough-dried from a washing, from which her arms appeared pink and unexpectedly round. When she never said a word, and sustained her quiet pose of holding the lamp, he was convinced of the strength in her body.

"Good afternoon, madam," he said.

She stared on, whether at him or at the air around him he could not tell, but after a moment she lowered her eyes to show that she would listen to whatever he had to say.

"I wonder if you would be interested—" He tried once more. "An accident—my car . . ."

Her voice emerged low and remote, like a sound across a lake. "Sonny he ain't here."

"Sonny?"

"Sonny ain't here now."

Her son—a fellow able to bring my car up, he decided in blurred relief. He pointed down the hill. "My car's in the bottom of the ditch. I'll need help."

"Sonny ain't here, but he'll be here."

She was becoming clearer to him and her voice stronger, and Bowman saw that she was stupid.

He was hardly surprised at the deepening postponement and tedium of his journey. He took a breath, and heard his voice speaking over the silent blows of his heart. "I was sick. I am not strong yet. . . . May I come in?"

He stooped and laid his big black hat over the handle on his bag. It was a humble motion, almost a bow, that instantly struck him as absurd and betraying of all his weakness. He looked up at the woman, the wind blowing his hair. He might have continued for a long time in this unfamiliar attitude; he had never been a patient man, but when he was sick he had learned to sink submissively into the pillows, to wait for his medicine. He waited on the woman.

Then she, looking at him with blue eyes, turned and held open the door, and after a moment Bowman, as if convinced in his action, stood erect and followed her in.

Inside, the darkness of the house touched him like a professional hand, the doctor's. The woman set the half-cleaned lamp on a table in the centre of the room and pointed, also like a professional person, a guide, to a chair with a yellow cowhide seat. She herself crouched on the hearth, drawing her knees up under the shapeless dress.

At first he felt hopefully secure. His heart was quieter. The room was enclosed in the gloom of yellow pine boards. He could see the other room, with the foot of an iron bed showing, across the passage. The bed had been made up with a red-and-yellow pieced quilt that looked like a map or a picture, a little like his grandmother's girlhood painting of Rome burning.

He had ached for coolness, but in this room it was cold. He stared at the hearth with dead coals lying on it and iron pots in the corners. The hearth and smoked chimney were of the stone he had seen ribbing the hills, mostly slate. Why is there no fire? he wondered.

And it was so still. The silence of the fields seemed to enter and move familiarly through the house. The wind used the open hall. He felt that he was in a mysterious, quiet, cool danger. It was necessary to do what? . . . To talk.

"I have a nice line of women's low-priced shoes . . ." he said.

But the woman answered, "Sonny'll be here. He's strong. Sonny'll move your car."

"Where is he now?"

"Farms for Mr. Redmond."

Mr. Redmond. Mr. Redmond. That was someone he would never have to encounter, and he was glad. Somehow the name did not appeal to him. . . . In a flare of touchiness and anxiety, Bowman wished to avoid even mention of unknown men and their unknown farms.

"Do you two live here alone?" He was surprised to hear his old voice, chatty, confidential, inflected for selling shoes, asking a question like that—a thing he did not even want to know.

"Yes. We are alone."

He was surprised at the way she answered. She had taken a long time to say that. She had nodded her head in a deep way too. Had she wished to affect him with some sort of premonition? he wondered unhappily. Or was it only that she would not help him, after all, by talking with him? For he was not strong enough to receive the impact of unfamiliar things without a little talk to break their fall. He had lived a month in which nothing had happened except in his head and his body—an almost inaudible life of heartbeats and dreams that came back, a life of fever and privacy, a delicate life which had left him weak to the point of—what? Of begging. The pulse in his palm leapt like a trout in a brook.

He wondered over and over why the woman did not go ahead with cleaning the lamp. What prompted her to stay there across the room, silently bestowing her presence upon him? He saw that with her it was not a time for doing little tasks. Her face was grave; she was feeling how right she was. Perhaps it was only politeness. In docility he held his eyes stiffly wide; they fixed themselves on the woman's clasped hands as though she held the cord they were strung on.

Then, "Sonny's coming," she said.

He himself had not heard anything, but there came a man passing the window and then plunging in at the door, with two hounds beside him. Sonny was a big enough man, with his belt slung low about his hips. He looked at least thirty. He had a hot, red face that was yet full of silence. He wore muddy blue pants and an old military coat stained and patched. World War? Bowman wondered. Great God, it was a Confederate coat. On the back of his light hair he had a wide filthy black hat which seemed to insult Bowman's own. He pushed down the dogs from his chest. He was strong with dignity and heaviness in his way of moving. . . . There was the resemblance to his mother.

They stood side by side. . . . He must account again for his presence here.

"Sonny, this man, he had his car to run off over the prec'pice an' wants to know if you will git it out for him," the woman said after a few minutes.

Bowman could not even state his case.

Sonny's eyes lay upon him.

He knew he should offer explanations and show money–at least appear either penitent or authoritative. But all he could do was to shrug slightly.

Sonny brushed by him going to the window, followed by the eager dogs, and looked out. There was effort even in the way he was looking, as if he could throw his sight out like a rope. Without turning Bowman felt that his own eyes could have seen nothing: it was too far.

"Got me a mule out there an' got me a block an' tackle," said Sonny meaningfully. "I *could* catch me my mule an' git me my ropes, an' before long I'd git your car out the ravine."

He looked completely round the room, as if in meditation, his eyes roving in their own distance. Then he pressed his lips firmly and yet shyly together, and with the dogs ahead of him this time, he lowered his head and strode out. The hard earth sounded, cupping to his powerful way of walking—almost a stagger.

Mischievously, at the suggestion of those sounds, Bowman's heart leapt again. It seemed to walk about inside him.

"Sonny's goin' to do it," the woman said. She said it again, singing it almost, like a song. She was sitting in her place by the hearth.

Without looking out, he heard some shouts and the dogs barking and the pounding of hoofs in short runs on the hill. In a few minutes Sonny passed under the window with a rope, and there was a brown mule with quivering, shining, purple-looking ears. The mule actually looked in the window. Under its eyelashes it turned target-like eyes into his. Bowman averted his head and saw the woman looking serenely back at the mule, with only satisfaction in her face.

She sang a little more, under her breath. It occurred to him, and it seemed quite marvellous, that she was not really talking to him, but rather following the thing that came about with words that were unconscious and part of her looking.

So he said nothing, and this time when he did not reply he felt a curious and strong emotion, not fear, rise up in him.

This time, when his heart leapt, something—his soul—seemed to leap too, like a little colt invited out of a pen. He stared at the woman while the frantic nimbleness of his feeling made his head sway. He could not move; there was nothing he could do, unless perhaps he might embrace this woman who sat there growing old and shapeless before him.

But he wanted to leap up, to say to her, I have been sick and I found out then, only then, how lonely I am. Is it too late? My heart puts up a struggle inside me, and you may have heard it, protesting against emptiness. . . . It should be full, he would rush on to tell her, thinking of his heart now as a deep lake, it should be holding love like other hearts. It should be flooded with love. There would be a warm spring day . . . Come and stand in my heart, whoever you are, and a whole river would cover your feet and rise higher and take your knees in whirlpools, and draw you down to itself, your whole body, your heart too.

But he moved a trembling hand across his eyes, and looked at the placid crouching woman across the room. She was still as a statue. He felt ashamed and exhausted by the thought that he might, in one more moment, have tried by simple words and embraces to communicate some strange thing—something which seemed always to have just escaped him . . .

Sunlight touched the farthest pot on the hearth. It was late afternoon. This time to-morrow he would be somewhere on a good gravelled road, driving his car past things that happened to people, quicker than their happening. Seeing ahead to the next day, he was glad, and knew that this was no time to embrace an old woman. He could feel in his pounding temples the readying of his blood for motion and for hurrying away.

"Sonny's hitched up your car by now," said the woman. "He'll git it out the ravine right shortly."

"Fine!" he cried with his customary enthusiasm.

Yet it seemed a long time that they waited. It began to get dark. Bowman was cramped in his chair. Any man should know enough to get up and walk around while he waited. There was something like guilt in such stillness and silence.

But instead of getting up, he listened. . . His breathing restrained, his eyes powerless in the growing dark, he listened uneasily for a warning sound, forgetting in wariness what it would be. Before long he heard something—soft, continuous, insinuating.

"What's the noise?" he asked, his voice jumping into the dark. Then wildly he was afraid it would be his heart beating so plainly in the quiet room, and she would tell him so.

"You might hear the stream," she said grudgingly.

Her voice was closer. She was standing by the table. He wondered why she did not light the lamp. She stood there in the dark and did not light it.

Bowman would never speak to her now, for the time was past. I'll sleep in the dark, he thought, in his bewilderment pitying himself.

Heavily she moved on to the window. Her arm, vaguely white, rose straight from her full side and she pointed out into the darkness.

"That white speck's Sonny," she said, talking to herself.

He turned unwillingly and peered over her shoulder; he hesitated to rise and stand beside her. His eyes searched the dusky air. The white speck floated smoothly toward her finger, like a leaf on a river, growing whiter in the dark. It was as if she had shown him something secret, part of her life, but had offered no explanation. He looked away. He was moved almost to tears, feeling for no reason that she had made a silent declaration equivalent to his own. His hand waited upon his chest.

Then a step shook the house, and Sonny was in the room. Bowman felt how the woman left him there and went to the other man's side.

"I done got your car out, mister," said Sonny's voice in the dark. "She's settin' a-waitin' in the road, turned to go back where she come from."

"Fine!" said Bowman, projecting his own voice to loudness. "I'm surely much obliged—I could never have done it myself—I was sick. . . ."

"I could do it easy," said Sonny.

Bowman could feel them both waiting in the dark, and he could hear the dogs panting out in the yard, waiting to bark when he should go. He felt strangely helpless and resentful. Now that he could go, he longed to stay. From what was he being deprived? His chest was rudely shaken by the violence of his heart. These people cherished something here that he could not see, they withheld some ancient promise of food and warmth and light. Between them they had a conspiracy. He thought of the way she had moved away from him and gone to Sonny, she had flowed toward him. He was shaking with cold, he was tired, and it was not fair. Humbly and yet angrily he stuck his hand into his pocket.

"Of course I'm going to pay you for everything–"

"We don't take money for such," said Sonny's voice belligerently.

"I want to pay. But do something more . . . Let me stay—tonight. . . ." He took another step toward them. If only they could see him, they would know his sincerity, his real need! His voice went on, "I'm not very strong yet, I'm not able to walk far, even back to my car, maybe, I don't know—I don't know exactly where I am—"

He stopped. He felt as if he might burst into tears. What would they think of him!

Sonny came over and put his hands on him. Bowman felt them pass (they were professional too) across his chest, over his hips. He could feel Sonny's eyes upon him in the dark.

"You ain't no revenuer come sneakin' here, mister, ain't got no gun?"

To this end of nowhere! And yet *he* had come. He made a grave answer. "No."

"You can stay."

"Sonny," said the woman, "you'll have to borry some fire."

"I'll go git it from Redmond's," said Sonny.

"What?" Bowman strained to hear their words to each other.

"Our fire, it's out, and Sonny's got to borry some, because it's dark an' cold," she said.

"But matches—I have matches—"

"We don't have no need for 'em," she said proudly. "Sonny's goin' after his own fire."

"I'm goin' to Redmond's," said Sonny with an air of importance, and he went out.

After they had waited a while, Bowman looked out the window and saw a light moving over the hill. It spread itself out like a little fan. It zigzagged along the field, darting and swift, not like Sonny at all. . . . Soon enough, Sonny staggered in, holding a burning stick behind him in tongs, fire flowing in his wake, blazing light into the corners of the room.

"We'll make a fire now," the woman said, taking the brand.

When that was done she lit the lamp. It showed its dark and light. The whole room turned golden-yellow like some sort of flower, and the walls smelled of it and seemed to tremble with the quiet rushing of the fire and the waving of the burning lampwick in its funnel of light.

The woman moved among the iron pots. With the tongs she dropped hot coals on top of the iron lids. They made a set of soft vibrations, like the sound of a bell far away.

She looked up and over at Bowman, but he could not answer. He was trembling. . . .

"Have a drink, mister?" Sonny asked. He had brought in a chair from the other room and sat astride it with his folded arms across the back. Now we are all visible, to one another, Bowman thought, and cried, "Yes sir, you bet, thanks!"

"Come after me and do just what I do," said Sonny.

It was another excursion into the dark. They went through the hall, out to the back of the house, past a shed and a hooded well. They came to a wilderness of thicket.

"Down on your knees," said Sonny.

"What?" Sweat broke out on his forehead.

He understood when Sonny began to crawl through a sort of tunnel that the bushes made over the ground. He followed, startled in spite of himself when a twig or a thorn touched him gently without making a sound, clinging to him and finally letting him go.

Sonny stopped crawling and, crouched on his knees, began to dig with both hands into the dirt. Bowman shyly struck matches and made a light. In a few minutes Sonny pulled up a jug. He poured out some of the whisky into a bottle from his coat pocket, and buried the jug again. "You never know who's liable to knock at your door," he said, and laughed. "Start back," he said, almost formally. "Ain't no need for us to drink outdoors, like hogs."

At the table by the fire, sitting opposite each other in their chairs, Sonny and Bowman took drinks out of the bottle, passing it across. The dogs slept; one of them was having a dream.

"This is good," said Bowman. "That is what I needed." It was just as though he were drinking the fire off the hearth.

"He makes it," said the woman with quiet pride.

She was pushing the coals off the pots, and the smells of corn bread and coffee circled the room. She set everything on the table before the men, with a bone-handled knife stuck into one of the potatoes, splitting out its golden fibre. Then she stood for a minute looking at them, tall and full above them where they sat. She leaned a little toward them.

"You-all can eat now," she said, and suddenly smiled.

Bowman had just happened to be looking at her. He set his cup back on the table in unbelieving protest. A pain pressed at his eyes. He saw that she was not an old woman. She was young, still young. He could think of no number of years for her. She was the same age as Sonny, and she belonged to him. She stood with the deep dark corner of the room behind her, the shifting yellow light scattering over her head and her grey formless dress, trembling over her tall body when it bent over them in its sudden communication. She was young. Her teeth were shining and her eyes glowed. She turned and walked slowly and heavily out of the room, and he heard her sit down on the cot and then lie down. The pattern on the quilt moved.

"She goin' to have a baby," said Sonny, popping a bite into his mouth.

Bowman could not speak. He was shocked with knowing what was really in this house. A marriage, a fruitful marriage. That simple thing. Anyone could have had that.

Somehow he felt unable to be indignant or protest, although some sort of joke had certainly had been played upon him. There was nothing remote or mysterious here—only something private. The only secret was the ancient communication between two people. But the memory of the woman's waiting silently by the cold hearth, of the man's stubborn journey a mile away to get fire, and how they finally brought out their food and drink and filled the room proudly with all they had to show, was suddenly too clear and too enormous within him for response. . . .

"You ain't as hungry as you look," said Sonny.

The woman came out of the bedroom as soon as the men had finished, and ate her supper while her husband stared peacefully into the fire.

Then they put the dogs out, with the food that was left.

"I think I'd better sleep here by the fire, on the floor," said Bowman.

He felt that he had been cheated, and that he could afford now to be generous. Ill though he was, he was not going to ask them for their bed. He was through with asking favours in this house, now that he understood what was there.

"Sure, mister."

But he had not known yet how slowly he understood. They had not meant to give him their bed. After a little interval they both rose and looking at him gravely went into the other room.

He lay stretched by the fire until it grew low and dying. He watched every tongue of blaze lick out and vanish. "There will be special reduced prices on all footwear during the month of January," he found himself repeating quietly, and then he lay with his lips tight shut.

How many noises the night had! He heard the stream running, the fire dying, and he was sure now that he heard his heart beating, too, the sound it made under his ribs. He heard breathing, round and deep, of the man and his wife in the room across the passage. And that was all. But emotion swelled patiently within him, and he wished that the child were his.

He must get back to where he had been before. He stood weakly before the red coals, and put on his overcoat. It felt too heavy on his shoulders. As he started out he looked and saw that the woman had never got through with cleaning the lamp. On some impulse he put all the money from his billfold under its fluted glass base, almost ostentatiously.

Ashamed, shrugging a little, and then shivering, he took his bags and went out. The cold of the air seemed to lift him bodily. The moon was in the sky.

On the slope he began to run, he could not help it. Just as he reached the road, where his car seemed to sit in the moonlight like a boat, his heart began to give off tremendous explosions like a rifle, bang bang bang.

He sank in fright onto the road, his bags falling about him. He felt as if all this had happened before. He covered his heart with both hands to keep anyone from hearing the noise it made.

But nobody heard it.

Questions

1. Show how the reader becomes aware of Bowman's deepening realization of his own emotional insecurity. We learn of his plight largely from his own reactions; point out some of them.

2. What does the woman represent to Bowman? While seeming rather patronizing toward her, he also envies some of the things she has. How does his attitude toward her change?

3. The house itself is a kind of symbolic haven. How does Bowman see it? What kind of security does he find there?

4. The story develops several contrasts between Bowman and his hosts. Identify some of them and show how they advance the theme of the story (such as the contrast between the woman's fertility and Bowman's sterility).

5. What does one come to know of Bowman's past, and of his whole life? Show what clues lead to this awareness. Does the story make any judgment of this life?

6. Death references and death symbols increase as the story progresses. Point out some of these symbols and show how they further the theme of the story.

E. B. White

THE HOUR OF LETDOWN

The gentle tone and urbane manner of E. B. White's prose should not divert attention from his serious purpose and his broad humanitarian sympathies. Though his reputation is as a satirist and humorist, his comedy is tinged with melancholy as he measures man's oddities and little failures against his potentialities. Eastern and urban in background—born in Mt. Vernon, New York, in 1899, and educated at Cornell—he went west and did newspaper work in Seattle before returning to New York and becoming one of the guiding spirits of the New Yorker *magazine. He wrote many of the items in the "Talk of the Town" section of that magazine, as well as reviews, short stories, and even cartoon captions. He developed a knack for poking holes in the windy rhetoric of politicians and for exposing pretension wherever he found it. At the same time he celebrated the triumph of sheer common sense. As one of his admiring critics said of him, "When he writes of small things they are never unimportant." Most of his published books are collections of short pieces that originally appeared in* The New Yorker. *They include* One Man's Meat *(1942),* The Wild Flag *(1946),* The Second Tree from the Corner *(1953), and* The Points of My Compass *(1962). Not least among his achievements are three books ostensibly for children that have been quickly elevated to the status of classics, perhaps because adults read them with even more pleasure than their children:* Stuart Little (1945), Charlotte's Web (1952), *and* The Trumpet of the Swan (1970).

"The Hour of Letdown" is from The Second Tree from the Corner. *However brief, it is more than an anecdote.*

When the man came in, carrying the machine, most of us looked up from our drinks, because we had never seen anything like it before. The man set the thing down on top of the bar near the beerpulls. It took up an ungodly amount of room and you could see the bartender didn't like it any too well, having this big, ugly-looking gadget parked right there.

"Two rye-and-water," the man said.

The bartender went on puddling an Old-Fashioned that he was working on, but he was obviously turning over the request in his mind.

"You want a double?" he asked, after a bit.

"No," said the man. "Two rye-and-water, please." He stared straight at the bartender, not exactly unfriendly but on the other hand not affirmatively friendly.

Many years of catering to the kind of people that come into saloons had provided the bartender with an adjustable mind. Nevertheless, he did not adjust readily to this fellow, and he did not like the machine—that was sure. He picked up a live cigarette that was idling on the edge of the cash register, took a drag out of it, and returned it thoughtfully. Then he poured two shots of rye whiskey, drew two glasses of water, and shoved the drinks in front of the man. People were watching. When something a little out of the ordinary takes place at a bar, the sense of it spreads quickly all along the line and pulls the customers together.

The man gave no sign of being the center of attention. He laid a five-dollar bill down on the bar. Then he drank one of the ryes and chased it with water. He picked up the other rye, opened a small vent in the machine (it was like an oil cup) and poured the whiskey in, and then poured the water in.

The bartender watched grimly. "Not funny," he said in an even voice. "And furthermore, your companion takes up too much room. Why'n you put it over on that bench by the door, make more room here."

"There's plenty of room for everyone here," replied the man.

"I ain't amused," said the bartender. "Put the goddam thing over near the door like I say. Nobody will touch it."

The man smiled. "You should have seen it this afternoon," he said. "It was magnificent. Today was the third day of the tournament. Imagine it—three days of continuous brainwork! And against the top players in the country, too. Early in the game it gained an advantage; then for two hours it exploited the advantage brilliantly, ending with the opponent's king backed in a corner. The sudden capture of a knight, the neutralization of a bishop, and it was all over. You know how much money it won, all told, in three days of playing chess?"

"How much?" asked the bartender.

"Five thousand dollars," said the man. "Now it wants to let down, wants to get a little drunk."

The bartender ran his towel vaguely over some wet spots. "Take it somewheres else and get it drunk there!" he said firmly. "I got enough troubles."

The man shook his head and smiled. "No, we like it here." He pointed at the empty glasses. "Do this again, will you, please?"

The bartender slowly shook his head. He seemed dazed but dogged. "You stow the thing away," he ordered. "I'm not ladling out whiskey for jokestersmiths."

" 'Jokesmiths,' " said the machine. "The word is 'jokesmiths.' "

A few feet down the bar, a customer who was on his third highball seemed ready to participate in this conversation to which we had all been listening so attentively. He was a middle-aged man. His necktie was pulled down away from his collar, and he had eased the collar by unbuttoning it. He had pretty nearly finished his third drink, and the alcohol tended to make him throw his support in with the underprivileged and the thirsty.

"If the machine wants another drink, give it another drink," he said to the bartender. "Let's not have haggling."

The fellow with the machine turned to his new-found friend and gravely raised his hand to his temple, giving him a salute of gratitude and fellowship. He addressed his next remark to him, as though deliberately snubbing the bartender.

"You know how it is when you're all fagged out mentally, how you want a drink?"

"Certainly do," replied the friend. "Most natural thing in the world."

There was a stir all along the bar, some seeming to side with the bartender, others with the machine group. A tall, gloomy man standing next to me spoke up.

"Another whiskey sour, Bill," he said. "And go easy on the lemon juice."

"Picric acid," said the machine, sullenly. "They don't use lemon juice in these places."

"That does it!" said the bartender, smacking his hand on the bar. "Will you put that thing away or else beat it out of here. I ain't in the mood, I tell you. I got this saloon to run and I don't want lip from a mechanical brain or whatever the hell you've got there."

The man ignored this ultimatum. He addressed his friend, whose glass was now empty.

"It's not just that it's all tuckered out after three days of chess," he said amiably. "You know another reason it wants a drink?"

"No," said the friend. "Why?"

"It cheated," said the man.

At this remark, the machine chuckled. One of its arms dipped slightly, and a light glowed in a dial.

The friend frowned. He looked as though his dignity had been hurt, as though his trust had been misplaced. "Nobody can cheat at chess," he said. "Simpossible. In chess, everything is open and above the board. The nature of the game of chess is such that cheating is impossible."

"That's what I used to think, too," said the man. "But there *is* a way."

"Well, it doesn't surprise me any," put in the bartender. "The first time I laid my eyes on that crummy thing I spotted it for a crook."

"Two rye-and-water," said the man.

"You can't have the whiskey," said the bartender. He glared at the mechanical brain. "How do I know it ain't drunk already?"

"That's simple. Ask it something," said the man.

The customers shifted and stared into the mirror. We were all in this thing now, up to our necks. We waited. It was the bartender's move.

"Ask it what? Such as?" said the bartender.

"Makes no difference. Pick a couple big figures, ask it to multiply them together. You couldn't multiply big figures together if you were drunk, could you?"

The machine shook slightly, as though making internal preparations.

"Ten thousand eight hundred and sixty-two, multiply it by ninety-nine," said the bartender, viciously. We could tell that he was throwing in the two nines to make it hard.

The machine flickered. One of its tubes spat, and a hand changed position, jerkily.

"One million seventy-five thousand three hundred and thirty-eight," said the machine.

Not a glass was raised all along the bar. People just stared gloomily into the mirror; some of us studied our own faces, others took carom shots at the man and the machine.

Finally, a youngish, mathematically minded customer got out a piece of paper and a pencil and went into retirement. "It works out," he reported, after some minutes of calculating. "You can't say the machine is drunk!"

Everyone now glared at the bartender. Reluctantly he poured two shots of rye, drew two glasses of water. The man drank his drink. Then he fed the machine its drink. The machine's light grew fainter. One of its cranky little arms wilted.

For a while the saloon simmered along like a ship at sea in calm weather. Every one of us seemed to be trying to digest the situation, with the help of liquor. Quite a few glasses were refilled. Most of us sought help in the mirror—the court of last appeal.

The fellow with the unbuttoned collar settled his score. He walked stiffly over and stood between the man and the machine. He put one arm around the man, the other arm around the machine. "Let's get out of here and go to a good place," he said.

The machine glowed slightly. It seemed to be a little drunk now.

"All right," said the man. "That suits me fine. I've got my car outside."

He settled for the drinks and put down a tip. Quietly and a trifle uncertainly he tucked the machine under his arm, and he and his companion of the night walked to the door and out into the street.

The bartender stared fixedly, then resumed his light housekeeping. "So he's got his car outside," he said, with heavy sarcasm. "Now isn't that nice!"

A customer at the end of the bar near the door left his drink, stepped to the window, parted the curtains, and looked out. He watched for a moment, then returned to his place and addressed the bartender. "It's even nicer than you think," he said. "It's a Cadillac. And which one of the three of them d'ya think is doing the driving?"

Questions

1. Fantasy with comic overtones makes possible gentle comments on human behavior. Trace the steps of White's characterization of the bartender as he responds to this passing incident.

2. What function does setting play in this story? Could the story happen anywhere else?

3. Would the story be more believable if the human characteristics attributed to the machine were embodied in a person? Would there be a story to tell under those conditions?

4. Explain the title of the story. Why not call it "The Happy Hour"? or "The Mirror"?

5. Is the ending prepared for? Does it make the story less real? Less believable?

Thomas Wolfe

THE LOST BOY

*A continuing literary debate centers around the question of where a writer gets his material—his subject matter, his characters, his vision of life. Does he invent them, or does he discover them within his own experience? There is no doubt about Thomas Wolfe's sources, for the autobiographical content of his work is clear. He wrote four long novels—*Look Homeward, Angel *(1929),* Of Time and the River *(1935),* The Web and the Rock *(1939), and* You Can't Go Home Again *(1940)—which told the continuing story of his own process of growing up, discovering life, going through the cycle of rebellion and acceptance. Wolfe was born in Asheville, North Carolina, in 1900, and went to the University of North Carolina, then to Harvard for a master's degree. He taught English at New York University until the great success of his first novel left him free to write and travel. Then, in the brief time left him—he died in 1938, after a writing career of only about ten years–he worked feverishly to produce the enormous novels which recorded, in voluminous detail, his own experience. His heroes—Eugene Gant in the first two novels, George Webber in the latter two—are thin disguises for Wolfe himself. Both of them, like their creator, are sensitive, searching young men who rebel against the provincialism and the restraints of their Southern backgrounds, and who see their lives as pilgrimages devoted to the discovery and assimilation of every possible human experience. Reactions to Wolfe's work have always been divided; some readers find him self-centered and totally lacking in artistic control. Others are willing to forgive him any sin for the sake of his exuberance and vigor. One sure thing is that no one can be neutral about his work.*

"The Lost Boy" first appeared in a magazine in 1937, then in book form in The Hills Beyond *(1943). It is a fuller treatment of an incident in* Look Homeward, Angel, *the death of the hero Eugene Gant's brother. It reveals Wolfe's compulsion to return again and again to those events that moved him most, viewing them from every*

angle. The shifting point of view he uses in the story illustrates that, contrary to the claims of some of his critics, he could sometimes escape from the confines of his own ego and see his subject from a larger perspective.

I

Light came and went and came again, the booming strokes of three o'clock beat out across the town in thronging bronze from the courthouse bell, light winds of April blew the fountain out in rainbow sheets, until the plume returned and pulsed, as Grover turned into the Square. He was a child, dark-eyed and grave, birthmarked upon his neck—a berry of warm brown—and with a gentle face, too quiet and too listening for his years. The scuffed boy's shoes, the thick-ribbed stockings gartered at the knees, the short knee pants cut straight with three small useless buttons at the side, the sailor blouse, the old cap battered out of shape, perched sideways up on top of the raven head, the old soiled canvas bag slung from the shoulder, empty now, but waiting for the crisp sheets of the afternoon—these friendly, shabby garments, shaped by Grover, uttered him. He turned and passed along the north side of the Square and in that moment saw the union of Forever and of Now.

Light came and went and came again, the great plume of the fountain pulsed and winds of April sheeted it across the Square in a rainbow gossamer of spray. The fire department horses drummed on the floors with wooden stomp, most casually, and with dry whiskings of their clean, coarse tails. The street cars ground into the Square from every position of the compass and halted briefly like wound toys in their familiar quarter-hourly formula. A dray, hauled by a boneyard nag, rattled across the cobbles on the other side before his father's shop. The courthouse bell boomed out its solemn warning of immediate three, and everything was just the same as it had always been.

He saw that haggis of vexed shapes with quiet eyes—that hodgepodge of ill-sorted architectures that made up the Square, and he did not feel lost. For "Here," thought Grover, "here is the Square as it has always been—and papa's shop, the fire department and the City Hall, the fountain pulsing with its plume, the street cars coming in and halting at the quarter hour, the hardware store on the corner there, the row of old brick buildings on this side of the street, the people passing and the light that comes and changes and that always will come back again, and everything that comes and goes and changes in the Square, and yet will be the same again. And here," the boy thought, "is Grover with his paper bag. Here is old Grover, almost twelve years old. Here is the month of April, 1904. Here is the courthouse bell and three o'clock. Here is Grover on the Square that never changes. Here is Grover, caught upon this point of time."

It seemed to him that the Square, itself the accidental masonry of many years, the chance agglomeration of time and of disrupted strivings, was the center of the universe. It was for him, in his soul's picture, the earth's pivot, the granite core of changelessness, the eternal place where all things came and passed, and yet abode forever and would never change.

He passed the old shack on the corner—the wooden fire-trap where S. Goldberg ran his wiener stand. Then he passed the Singer place next door, with its gleaming display of new machines. He saw them and admired them, but he felt no joy. They brought back to him the busy hum of housework and of women sewing, the intricacy of stitch and weave, the mystery of style and pattern, the memory of women bending over flashing needles, the pedaled tread, the busy whir. It was women's work: it filled him with unknown associations of dullness and of vague depression. And always, also, with a moment's twinge of horror, for his dark eye would always travel toward that needle stitching up and down so fast the eye could never follow it. And then he would remember how his mother once had told him she had driven the needle through her finger, and always, when he passed this place, he would remember it and for a moment crane his neck and turn his head away.

He passed on then, but had to stop again next door before the music store. He always had to stop by places that had shining perfect things in them. He loved hardware stores and windows full of accurate geometric tools. He loved windows full of hammers, saws, and planing boards. He liked windows full of strong new rakes and hoes, with unworn handles, of white perfect wood, stamped hard and vivid with the maker's seal. He loved to see such things as these in the windows of hardware stores. And he would fairly gloat upon them and think that some day he would own a set himself.

Also, he always stopped before the music and piano store. It was a splendid store. And in the window was a small white dog upon his haunches, with head cocked gravely to one side, a small white dog that never moved, that never barked, that listened attentively at the flaring funnel of a horn to hear "His Master's Voice"—a horn forever silent, and a voice that never spoke. And within were many rich and shining shapes of great pianos, an air of splendor and of wealth.

And now, indeed, he *was* caught, held suspended. A waft of air, warm, chocolate-laden, filled his nostrils. He tried to pass the white front of the little eight-foot shop; he paused, struggling with conscience; he could not go on. It was the little candy shop run by old Crocker and his wife. And Grover could not pass.

"Old stingy Crockers!" he thought scornfully. "I'll not go there any more. But—" as the maddening fragrance of rich cooking chocolate touched him once again—"I'll just look in the window and see what they've got." He paused a moment, looking with his dark and quiet eyes into the window of the little candy shop. The window, spotlessly clean, was filled with trays of fresh-made candy. His eyes rested on a tray of chocolate drops. Unconsciously he licked his lips. Put one of them upon your tongue and it just melted there, like honeydew. And then the trays full of rich home-made fudge. He gazed longingly at the deep body of the chocolate fudge, reflectively at maple walnut, more critically, yet with longing, of the mints, the nougatines, and all the other dainties.

"Old stingy Crockers!" Grover muttered once again, and turned to go. "I wouldn't go in *there* again."

And yet he did not go away. "Old stingy Crockers" they might be; still, they did make the best candy in town, the best, in fact, that he had ever tasted.

He looked through the window back into the little shop and saw Mrs. Crocker there. A customer had gone in and had made a purchase, and as Grover looked he saw Mrs. Crocker, with her little wrenny face, her pinched features, lean over and peer primly at the scales. She had a piece of fudge in her clean, bony, little fingers, and as Grover looked, she broke it, primly, in her little bony hands. She dropped a morsel down into the scales. They weighted down alarmingly, and her thin lips tightened. She snatched the piece of fudge out of the scales and broke it carefully once again. This time the scales wavered, went down very slowly, and came back again. Mrs. Crocker carefully put the reclaimed piece of fudge back in the tray, dumped the remainder in a paper bag, folded it and gave it to the customer, counted the money carefully and doled it out into the till, the pennies in one place, the nickels in another.

Grover stood there, looking scornfully. "Old stingy Crocker—afraid that she might give a crumb away!"

He grunted scornfully and again he turned to go. But now Mr. Crocker came out from the little partitioned place where they made all their candy, bearing a tray of fresh-made fudge in his skinny hands. Old Man Crocker rocked along the counter to the front and put it down. He really rocked along. He was a cripple. And like his wife, he was a wrenny, wizened little creature, with bony hands, thin lips, a pinched and meager face. One leg was inches shorter than the other, and on this leg there was an enormous thick-soled boot, with a kind of wooden, rocker-like arrangement, six inches high at least, to make up for the deficiency. On this wooden cradle Mr. Crocker rocked along, with a prim and apprehensive little smile, as if he were afraid he was going to lose something.

"Old stingy Crocker!" muttered Grover. "Humph! He wouldn't give you anything!"

And yet—he did not go away. He hung there curiously, peering through the window, with his dark and gentle face now focused and intent, alert and curious, flattening his nose against the glass. Unconsciously he scratched the thick-ribbed fabric of one stockinged leg with the scuffed and worn toe of his old shoe. The fresh, warm odor of the new-made fudge was delicious. It was a little maddening. Half consciously he began to fumble in one trouser pocket, and pulled out his purse, a shabby worn old black one with a twisted clasp. He opened it and prowled about inside.

What he found was not inspiring—a nickel and two pennies and—he had forgotten them—the stamps. He took the stamps out and unfolded them. There were five twos, eight ones, all that remained of the dollar-sixty-cents' worth which Reed, the pharmacist, had given him for running errands a week or two before.

"Old Crocker," Grover thought, and looked somberly at the grotesque little form as it rocked back into the shop again, around the counter, and up the other side. "Well—" again he looked indefinitely at the stamps in his hand—"he's had all the rest of them. He might as well take these."

So, soothing conscience with this sop of scorn, he went into the shop and stood looking at the trays in the glass case and finally decided. Pointing with a slightly grimy finger at the fresh-made tray of chocolate fudge, he said, "I'll take fifteen cents' worth of this, Mr. Crocker." He paused a moment, fighting with embarrassment, then he lifted his dark face and said quietly, "And please, I'll have to give you stamps again."

Mr. Crocker made no answer. He did not look at Grover. He pressed his lips together primly. He went rocking away and got the candy scoop, came back, slid open the door of the glass case, put fudge into the scoop, and, rocking to the scales, began to weigh the candy out. Grover watched him as he peered and squinted, he watched him purse and press his lips together, he saw him take a piece of fudge and break it in two parts. And then old Crocker broke two parts in two again. He weighed, he squinted, and he hovered, until it seemed to Grover that by calling *Mrs.* Crocker stingy he had been guilty of a rank injustice. But finally, to his vast relief, the job was over, the scales hung there, quivering apprehensively, upon the very hair-line of nervous balance, as if even the scales were afraid that one more move from Old Man Crocker and they would be undone.

Mr. Crocker took the candy then and dumped it in a paper bag and, rocking back along the counter toward the boy, he dryly said: "Where are the stamps?" Grover gave them to him. Mr. Crocker relinquished his claw-like hold upon the bag and set it down upon the counter. Grover took the bag and dropped it in his canvas sack, and then remembered. "Mr. Crocker—" again he felt the old embarrassment that was almost like strong pain—"I gave you too much," Grover said. "There were eighteen cents in stamps. You—you can just give me three ones back."

Mr. Crocker did not answer. He was busy with his bony little hands, unfolding the stamps and flattening them out on top of the glass counter. When he had done so, he peered at them sharply for a moment, thrusting his scrawny neck forward and running his eye up and down, like a bookkeeper who totes up rows of figures.

When he had finished, he said tartly: "I don't like this kind of business. If you want candy, you should have the money for it. I'm not a post office. The next time you come in here and want anything, you'll have to pay me money for it."

Hot anger rose in Grover's throat. His olive face suffused with angry color. His tarry eyes got black and bright. He was on the verge of saying: "Then why did you take my other stamps? Why do you tell me now, when you have taken all the stamps I had, that you don't want them?"

But he was a boy, a boy of eleven years, a quiet, gentle, gravely thoughtful boy, and he had been taught how to respect his elders. So he just stood there looking with his tar-black eyes. Old Man Crocker, pursing at the mouth a little, without meeting Grover's gaze, took the stamps up in his thin, parched fingers and, turning, rocked away with them down to the till.

He took the twos and folded them and laid them in one rounded scallop, then took the ones and folded them and put them in the one next to it. Then he closed the till and started to rock off, down toward the other end. Grover, his face now quiet and grave, kept looking at him, but Mr. Crocker did not look at Grover. Instead he began to take some stamped cardboard shapes and fold them into boxes.

In a moment Grover said, "Mr. Crocker, will you give me the three ones, please?"

Mr. Crocker did not answer. He kept folding boxes, and he compressed his thin lips quickly as he did so. But Mrs. Crocker, back turned to her spouse, also folding boxes with her birdlike hands, muttered: "Hm! *I'd* give him nothing!"

Mr. Crocker looked up, looked at Grover, said, "What are you waiting for?"

"Will you give me the three ones, please?" Grover said.

"I'll give you nothing," Mr. Crocker said.

He left his work and came rocking forward along the counter. "Now you get out of here! Don't you come in here with any more of those stamps," said Mr. Crocker.

"I should like to know where he gets them—that's what *I* should like to know," said Mrs. Crocker.

She did not look up as she said these words. She inclined her head a little to the side, in Mr. Crocker's direction, and continued to fold the boxes with her bony fingers.

"You get out of here!" said Mr. Crocker. "And don't you come back here with any stamps. . . . Where did you get those stamps?" he said.

"That's just what *I've* been thinking," Mrs. Crocker said. "*I've* been thinking all along."

"You've been coming in here for the last two weeks with those stamps," said Mr. Crocker. "I don't like the look of it. Where did you get those stamps?" he said.

"That's what *I've* been thinking," said Mrs. Crocker, for a second time.

Grover had got white underneath his olive skin. His eyes had lost their luster. They looked like dull, stunned balls of tar. "From Mr. Reed," he said. "I got the stamps from Mr. Reed." Then he burst out desperately. "Mr. Crocker—Mr. Reed will tell you how I got the stamps. I did some work for Mr. Reed, he gave me those stamps two weeks ago."

"Mr. Reed," said Mrs. Crocker acidly. She did not turn her head. "I call it mighty funny."

"Mr. Crocker," Grover said, "if you'll just let me have three ones—"

"You get out of here!" cried Mr. Crocker, and he began rocking forward toward Grover. "Now don't you come in here again, boy! There's something funny about this whole business! I don't like the look of it," said Mr. Crocker. "If you can't pay as other people do, then I don't want your trade."

"Mr. Crocker," Grover said again, and underneath the olive skin his face was gray, "if you'll just let me have those three—"

"You get out of here!" Mr. Crocker cried, rocking down toward the counter's end. "If you don't get out, boy—"

"*I'd* call a policeman, that's what I'd do," Mrs. Crocker said.

Mr. Crocker rocked around the lower end of the counter. He came rocking up to Grover. "You get out," he said.

He took the boy and pushed him with his bony little hands, and Grover was sick and gray down to the hollow pit of his stomach.

"You've got to give me those three ones," he said.

"You get out of here!" shrilled Mr. Crocker. He seized the screen door, pulled it open, and pushed Grover out. "Don't you come back in here," he said, pausing for a moment, and working thinly at the lips. He turned and rocked back in the shop again. The screen door slammed behind him. Grover stood there on the pavement. And light came and went and came again into the Square.

The boy stood there, and a wagon rattled past. There were some people passing by, but Grover did not notice them. He stood there blindly, in the watches of the sun, feeling this was Time, this was the center of the universe, the granite core of changelessness, and feeling, this is Grover, this the Square, this is Now.

But something had gone out of day. He felt the overwhelming, soul-sickening guilt that all the children, all the good men of the earth, have felt since Time began. And even anger had died down, had been drowned out, in this swelling tide of guilt, and "This is the Square"—thought Grover as before—"This is Now. There is my father's shop. And all of it is as it has always been—save I."

And the Square reeled drunkenly around him, light went in blind gray motes before his eyes, the fountain sheeted out to rainbow iridescence and returned to its proud, pulsing plume again. But all the brightness had gone out of day, and "Here is the Square, and here is permanence, and here is Time—and all of it is the same as it has always been, save I."

The scuffed boots of the lost boy moved and stumbled blindly. The numb feet crossed the pavement—reached the cobbled street, reached the plotted central square—the grass plots, and the flower beds, so soon to be packed with red geraniums.

"I want to be alone," thought Grover, "where I cannot go near him. . . . Oh God, I hope he never hears, that no one ever tells him—"

The plume blew out, the iridescent sheet of spray blew over him. He passed through, found the other side and crossed the street, and—"Oh God, if papa ever hears!" thought Grover, as his numb feet started up the steps into his father's shop.

He found and felt the steps—the width and thickness of old lumber twenty feet in length. He saw it all—the iron columns on his father's porch, painted with the dull anomalous black-green that all such columns in this land and weather come to; two angels, fly-specked, and the waiting stones. Beyond and all around, in the stonecutter's shop, cold shapes of white and marble, rounded stone, the languid angel with strong marble hands of love.

He went on down the aisle, the white shapes stood around him. He went on to the back of the workroom. This he knew—the little cast-iron stove in left-hand corner, caked, brown, heat-blistered, and the elbow of the long stack running out across the shop; the high and dirty window looking down across the Market Square toward Niggertown; the rude old shelves, plank-boarded, thick, the wood not smooth but pulpy, like the strong hair of an animal; upon the shelves the chisels of all sizes and a layer of stone dust; an emery wheel with pump tread; and a door that let out on the alleyway, yet the alleyway twelve feet below. Here in the room, two trestles of this coarse spiked wood upon which rested gravestones, and at one, his father at work.

The boy looked, saw the name was Creasman: saw the carved analysis of John, the symmetry of the s, the fine sentiment that was being polished off beneath the name and date: "John Creasman, November 7, 1903."

Gant looked up. He was a man of fifty-three, gaunt-visaged, mustache cropped, immensely long and tall and gaunt. He wore good dark clothes —heavy, massive—save he had no coat. He worked in shirtsleeves with his vest on, a strong watch chain stretching across his vest, wing collar and black tie, Adam's apple, bony forehead, bony nose, light eyes, gray-green, undeep and cold, and, somehow, lonely-looking, a striped apron going up around his shoulders and starched cuffs. And in one hand a tremendous rounded wooden mallet like a butcher's bole; and in his other hand, a strong cold chisel.

"How are you, son?"

He did not look up as he spoke. He spoke quietly, absently. He worked upon the chisel and the wooden mallet, as a jeweler might work on a watch, except that in the man and in the wooden mallet there was power too.

"What is it, son?" he said.

He moved around the table from the head, started up on "J" once again.

"Papa, I never stole the stamps," said Grover.

Gant put down the mallet, laid the chisel down. He came around the trestle.

"What?" he said.

As Grover winked his tar-black eyes, they brightened, the hot tears shot out. "I never stole the stamps," he said.

"Hey? What is this?" his father said. "What stamps?"

"That Mr. Reed gave me, when the other boy was sick and I worked there for three days. . . . And Old Man Crocker," Grover said, "he took all the stamps. And I told him Mr. Reed had given them to me. And now he owes me three ones—and Old Man Crocker says he don't believe that they were mine. He says—he says—that I must have taken them somewhere," Grover blurted out.

"The stamps that Reed gave you—hey?" the stonecutter said. "The stamps you had—" He wet his thumb upon his lips, threw back his head and slowly swung his gaze around the ceiling, then turned and strode quickly from his workshop out into the storeroom.

Almost at once he came back again, and as he passed the old gray painted-board partition of his office he cleared his throat and wet his thumb and said, "Now I tell you—"

Then he turned and strode up toward the front again and cleared his throat and said, "I tell you now—" He wheeled about and started back, and as he came along the aisle between the marshaled rows of gravestones he said beneath his breath, "By God, now—"

He took Grover by the hand and they went out flying. Down the aisle they went by all the gravestones, past the fly-specked angels waiting there, and down the wooden steps and across the Square. The fountain pulsed, the plume blew out in sheeted iridescence, and it swept across them; an old gray horse, with a peaceful look about his torn lips, sucked up the cool mountain water from the trough as Grover and his father went across the Square, but they did not notice it.

They crossed swiftly to the other side in a direct line to the candy shop. Gant was still dressed in his long striped apron, and he was still holding Grover by the hand. He opened the screen door and stepped inside.

"Give him the stamps," Gant said.

Mr. Crocker came rocking forward behind the counter, with the prim and careful look that now was somewhat like a smile. "It was just—" he said.

"Give him the stamps," Gant said, and threw some coins down on the counter.

Mr. Crocker rocked away and got the stamps. He came rocking back. "I just didn't know—" he said.

The stonecutter took the stamps and gave them to the boy. And Mr. Crocker took the coins.

"It was just that—" Mr. Crocker began again, and smiled.

Gant cleared his throat: "You never were a father," he said. "You never knew the feelings of a father, or understood the feelings of a child; and that is why you acted as you did. But a judgment is upon you. God has cursed you. He has afflicted you. He has made you lame and childless as you are—and lame and childless, miserable as you are, you will go to your grave and be forgotten!"

And Crocker's wife kept kneading her bony little hands and said, imploringly, "Oh, no—oh don't say that, please don't say that."

The stonecutter, the breath still hoarse in him, left the store, still holding the boy tightly by the hand. Light came again into the day.

"Well, son," he said, and laid his hand on the boy's back. "Well, son," he said, "now don't you mind."

They walked across the Square, the sheeted spray of iridescent light swept out on them, the horse swizzled at the water-trough, and "Well, son," the stonecutter said.

And the old horse sloped down, ringing with his hoofs upon the cobblestones.

"Well, son," said the stonecutter once again, "be a good boy."

And he trod his own steps then with his great stride and went back again into his shop.

The lost boy stood upon the Square, hard by the porch of his father's shop.

"This is Time," thought Grover. "Here is the Square, here is my father's shop, and here am I."

And light came and went and came again—but now not quite the same as it had done before. The boy saw the pattern of familiar shapes and knew that they were just the same as they had always been. But something had gone out of day, and something had come in again. Out of the vision of those quiet eyes some brightness had gone, and into their vision had come some deeper color. He could not say, he did not know through what transforming shadows life had passed within that quarter hour. He only knew that something had been lost—something forever gained.

Just then a buggy curved out through the Square, and fastened to the rear end was a poster, and it said "St. Louis" and "Excursion" and "The Fair."

II The Mother

As we went down through Indiana—you were too young, child, to remember it—but I always think of all of you the way you looked that morning, when we went down through Indiana, going to the Fair. All of the apple trees were coming out, and it was April; it was the beginning of spring in southern Indiana and everything was getting green. Of course we don't have farms at home like those in Indiana. The children had never seen such farms as those, and I reckon, kidlike, they had to take it in.

So all of them kept running up and down the aisle—well, no, except for you and Grover. *You* were too young, Eugene. You were just three, I kept you with me. As for Grover—well, I'm going to tell you about that.

But the rest of them kept running up and down the aisle and from one window to another. They kept calling out and hollering to each other every time they saw something new. They kept trying to look out on all sides, in every way at once, as if they wished they had eyes at the back of their heads. It was the first time any of them had ever been in Indiana, and I reckon that it all seemed strange and new.

And so it seemed they couldn't get enough. It seemed they never could be still. They kept running up and down and back and forth, hollering and shouting to each other, until—"I'll vow! You children! I never saw the beat of you!" I said. "The way that you keep running up and down and back and forth and never can be quiet for a minute beats all I ever saw," I said.

You see, they were excited about going to St. Louis, and so curious over everything they saw. They couldn't help it, and they wanted to see everything. But—"I'll vow!" I said. "If you children don't sit down and rest you'll be worn to a frazzle before we ever get to see St. Louis and the Fair!"

Except for Grover! He—no, sir! not him. Now, boy, I want to tell you—I've raised the lot of you—and if I do say so, there wasn't a numbskull in the lot. But *Grover!* Well, you've all grown up now, all of you have gone away, and none of you are children any more. . . . And of course, I hope that, as the fellow says, you have reached the dignity of man's estate. I suppose you have the judgment of grown men. . . . But *Grover! Grover* had it even then!

Oh, even as a child, you know—at a time when I was almost afraid to trust the rest of you out of my sight—I could depend on Grover. He could go anywhere, I could send him anywhere, and I'd always know he'd get back safe, and do exactly what I told him to!

Why, I didn't even have to tell him. You could send that child to market and tell him what you wanted, and he'd come home with *twice* as much as you could get yourself for the same money!

Now you know, I've always been considered a good trader. But *Grover!*—why, it got so finally that I wouldn't even tell him. Your papa said to me: "You'd be better off if you'd just tell him what you want and leave the rest to him. For," your papa says, "damned if I don't believe he's a better trader than you are. He gets more for the money than anyone I ever saw."

Well, I had to admit it, you know. I had to own up then. Grover, even as a child, was a far better trader than I was. . . . Why, yes, they told it on him all over town, you know. They said all of the market men, all of the farmers, knew him. They'd begin to laugh when they saw him coming—they'd say: "Look out! Here's Grover! Here's one trader you're not going to fool!"

And they were right! *That* child! I'd say, "Grover, suppose you run uptown and see if they've got anything good to *eat* today"—and I'd just wink at him, you know, but he'd know what I meant. I wouldn't let on that I *wanted* anything exactly, but I'd say, "Now it just occurs to me that some good fresh stuff may be coming in from the country, so suppose you take this dollar and just see what you can do with it."

Well, sir, that was all that was needed. The minute you told that child that you depended on his judgment, he'd have gone to the ends of the earth for you—and, let me tell you something, he wouldn't *miss*, either!

His eyes would get as black as coals—oh! the way that child would look at you, the intelligence and sense in his expression. He'd say: "Yes, *ma'am!* Now don't you worry, mama. You leave it all to me—and I'll do *good!*" said Grover.

And he'd be off like a streak of lightning and—oh Lord! As your father said to me, "I've been living in this town for almost thirty years," he said—"I've seen it grow up from a crossroads village, and I thought I knew everything there was to know about it—but that child—" your papa says—"he knows places that I never heard of!" . . . Oh, he'd go right down there to that place below your papa's shop where the draymen and the country people used to park their wagons—or he'd go down there to those old lots on Concord Street where the farmers used to keep their wagons. And, child that he was, he'd go right in among them, sir—*Grover* would!—go right in and barter with them like a grown man!

And he'd come home with things he'd bought that would make your eyes stick out. . . . Here he comes one time with another boy, dragging a great bushel basket full of ripe termaters between them. "Why, Grover!" I says. "How on earth are we ever going to use them? Why they'll go bad on us before we're half way through with them." "Well, mama," he says, "I know—" oh, just as solemn as a judge—"but they were the last the man had," he says, "and he wanted to go home, and so I got them for ten cents," he says. "They were so cheap," said Grover, "I thought it was a shame to let 'em go; and I figgered that what we couldn't eat—why," says Grover, "you could *put up!*" Well, the way he said it —so earnest and so serious—I had to laugh. "But I'll vow!" I said. "If you don't beat all!" . . . But that was *Grover!*—the way he was in *those* days! As everyone said, boy that he was, he had the sense and judgment of a grown man. . . . Child, child, I've seen you all grow up, and all of you were bright enough. There were no half-wits in *my* family. But for all-round intelligence, judgment, and general ability, Grover surpassed the whole crowd. I've never seen his equal, and everyone who knew him as a child will say the same.

So that's what I tell them now when they ask me about all of you. I have to tell the truth. I always said that *you* were smart enough, Eugene—but when they come around and brag to me about you, and about how you have got on and have a kind of name—I don't let on, you know. I just sit there and let them talk. I don't brag on you—if *they* want to brag on you, that's *their* business. I never bragged on one of my own children in my life. When father raised us up, we were all brought up to believe that it was not good breeding to brag about your kin. "If the others want to do it," father said, "well, let *them* do it. Don't ever let on by a word or sign that you know what they are talking about. Just let *them* do the talking, and say nothing."

So when they come around and tell me about the things *you've* done —I don't let on to them, I never say a word. Why yes!—why, here, you know—oh, along about a month or so ago, this feller comes—a well-dressed man, you know—he looked intelligent, a good substantial sort of person. He said he came from New Jersey, or somewhere up in that part of the country, and he began to ask me all sorts of questions—what you were like when you were a boy, and all such stuff as that.

I just pretended to study it all over and then I said, "Well, yes"—real serious-like, you know—"well, yes—I reckon I ought to know a little something about him. Eugene was my child, just the same as all the others were. I brought him up just the way I brought up all the others. And," I says—oh, just as solemn as you please—"he wasn't a *bad* sort of a boy. Why," I says, "up to the time that he was twelve years old he was just about the same as any other boy—a good, average, normal sort of fellow."

"Oh," he says, "But didn't you notice something? Wasn't there something kind of strange?" he says—"something different from what you noticed in the other children?"

I didn't let on, you know—I just took it all in and looked as solemn as an owl—I just pretended to study it all over, just as serious as you please.

"Why no," I says, real slow-like, after I'd studied it all over. "As I remember it, he was a good, ordinary, normal sort of boy, just like all the others."

"Yes," he says—oh, all excited-like, you know–"But didn't you notice how brilliant he was? Eugene must have been more brilliant than the rest!"

"Well, now," I says, and pretended to study that all over too. "Now let me see. . . . Yes," I says—I just looked him in the eye, as solemn as you please—"he did pretty well. . . . Well, yes," I says, "I guess he was a fairly bright sort of a boy. I never had no complaints to make of him on that score. He was bright enough," I says. "The only trouble with him was that he was lazy."

"Lazy!" he says—oh, you should have seen the look upon his face, you know—he jumped like someone had stuck a pin in him. "Lazy!" he says. "Why, you don't mean to tell me—"

"Yes," I says—oh, I never cracked a smile–"I was telling him the same thing myself the last time that I saw him. I told him it was a mighty lucky thing for him that he had the gift of gab. Of course, he went off to college and read a lot of books, and I reckon that's where he got this flow of language they say he has. But as I said to him the last time that I saw him: 'Now look a-here,' I said. 'If you can earn your living doing a light, easy class of work like this you do,' I says, 'you're mighty lucky, because none of the rest of your people,' I says, 'had any such luck as that. They had to work for a living.' "

Oh, I told him, you know. I came right out with it. I made no bones about it. And I tell you what—I wish you could have seen his face. It was a study.

"Well," he says, at last, "you've got to admit this, haven't you—he was the brightest boy you had, now wasn't he?"

I just looked at him a moment. I had to tell the truth. I couldn't fool him any longer. "No," I says. "He was a good, bright boy—I got no complaint to make about him on that score—but the brightest boy I had, the one that surpassed all the rest of them in sense, and understanding, and in judgment—the best boy I had—the smartest boy I ever saw—was—well, it wasn't Eugene," I said. "It was another one."

He looked at me a moment, then he said, "Which boy was that?"

Well, I just looked a him, and smiled. I shook my head, you know. I wouldn't tell him. "I never brag about my own," I said. "You'll have to find out for yourself."

But—I'll have to tell *you*—and you know yourself, I brought the whole crowd up, I knew you all. And you can take my word for it—the best one of the lot was—*Grover!*

And when I think of Grover as he was along about that time, I always see him sitting there, so grave and earnest-like, with his nose pressed to the window, as we went down through Indiana in the morning, to the Fair.

All through that morning we were going down along beside the Wabash River—the Wabash River flows through Indiana, it is the river that they wrote the song about—so all that morning we were going down along the river. And I sat with all you children gathered about me as we went down through Indiana, going to St. Louis, to the Fair.

And Grover sat there, so still and earnest-like, looking out the window, and he didn't move. He sat there like a man. He was just eleven and a half years old, but he had more sense, more judgment and more understanding that any child I ever saw.

So here he sat beside this gentleman and looked out the window. I never knew the man—I never asked his name—but I tell you what! He was certainly a fine-looking, well-dressed, good, substantial sort of man, and I could see that he had taken a great liking to Grover. And Grover sat there looking out, and then turned to this gentleman, as grave and earnest as a grown-up man, and says, "What kind of crops grow here, sir?" Well, this gentleman threw his head back and just hah-hahed. "Well, I'll see if I can tell you," says this gentleman, and then, you know, he talked to him, they talked together, and Grover took it all in, as solemn as you please, and asked this gentleman every sort of question—what the trees were, what was growing there, how big the farms were—all sorts of questions, which this gentleman would answer, until I said: "Why, I'll vow, Grover! You shouldn't ask so many questions. You'll bother the very life out of this gentleman."

The gentleman threw his head back and laughed right out. "Now you leave that boy alone. He's all right," he said. "He doesn't bother me a bit, and if I know the answers to his questions I will answer him. And if I don't know, why, then, I'll tell him so. But he's *all right*," he said, and put his arm around Grover's shoulders. "You leave him alone. He doesn't bother me a bit."

And I can still remember how he looked that morning, with his black eyes, his black hair, and with the birthmark on his neck—so grave, so serious, so earnest-like—as he sat by the train window and watched the apple trees, the farms, the barns, the houses, and the orchards, taking it all in, I reckon, because it was strange and new to him.

It was so long ago, but when I think of it, it all comes back, as if it happened yesterday. Now all of you have either died or grown up and gone away, and nothing is the same as it was then. But all of you were there with me that morning and I guess I should remember how the others looked, but somehow I don't. Yet I can still see Grover just the way he was, the way he looked that morning when we went down through Indiana, by the river, to the Fair.

III The Sister

Can you remember, Eugene, how Grover used to look? I mean the birthmark, the black eyes, the olive skin. The birthmark always showed because of those open sailor blouses kids used to wear. But I guess you must have been too young when Grover died. . . . I was looking at that old photograph the other day. You know the one I mean—that picture showing mama and papa and all of us children before the house on Woodson Street. *You* weren't there, Eugene. *You* didn't get in. *You* hadn't arrived when that was taken. . . . You remember how mad you used to get when we'd tell you that you were only a dishrag hanging out in Heaven when something happened?

You were the baby. That's what you get for being the baby. You don't get in the picture, do you? . . . I was looking at that old picture just the other day. There we were. And, my God, what is it all about? I mean, when you see the way we were—Daisy and Ben and Grover, Steve and all of us—and then how everyone either dies or grows up and goes away—and then—look at us now! Do you ever get to feeling funny? You know what I mean—do you ever get to feeling *queer*—when you try to figure these things out? You've been to college and you ought to know the answer—and I wish you'd tell me if you know.

My Lord, when I think sometimes of the way I used to be—the dreams I used to have. Playing the piano, practicing seven hours a day, thinking that some day I would be a great pianist. Taking singing lessons from Aunt Nell because I felt that some day I was going to have a great career in opera. . . . Can you beat it now? Can you imagine it? *Me!* In grand opera! . . . Now I want to ask you. I'd like to know.

My Lord! When I go uptown and walk down the street and see all these funny-looking little boys and girls hanging around the drug store—do you suppose any of them have ambitions the way we did? Do you suppose any of these funny-looking little girls are thinking about a big career in opera? . . . Didn't you ever see that picture of us? I was looking at it just the other day. It was made before the old house down on Woodson Street, with papa standing there in his swallow-tail, and mama there beside him—and Grover, and Ben, and Steve, and Daisy, and myself, with our feet upon our bicycles. Luke, poor kid, was only four or five. *He* didn't have a bicycle like us. But there he was. And there were all of us together.

Well, there I was, and my poor old skinny legs and long white dress, and two pigtails hanging down my back. And all the funny-looking clothes we wore, with the doo-lolley business on them. . . . But I guess you can't remember. You weren't born.

But, well, we were a right nice-looking set of people, if I do say so. And there was "86" the way it used to be, with the front porch, the grape vines, and the flower beds before the house—and "Miss Eliza" standing there by papa, with a watch charm pinned upon her waist. . . . I shouldn't laugh, but "Miss Eliza"—well, mama was a pretty woman then. Do you know what I mean? "Miss Eliza" was a right good-looking woman, and papa in his swallow-tail was a good-looking man. Do you remember how he used to get dressed up on Sunday? And how grand we thought he was? And how he let me take his money out and count it? And how rich we all thought he was? And how wonderful that dinkey little shop on the Square looked to us? . . . Can you beat it, now? Why we thought that papa was the biggest man in town and—oh, you can't tell me! You can't tell me! He had his faults, but papa was a wonderful man. You know he was!

And there was Steve and Ben and Grover, Daisy, Luke, and me lined up there before the house with one foot on our bicycles. And I got to thinking back about it all. It all came back.

Do you remember anything about St. Louis? You were only three or four years old then, but you must remember something. . . . Do you remember how you used to bawl when I would scrub you? How you'd bawl for Grover? Poor kid, you used to yell for Grover every time I'd get you in the tub. . . . He was a sweet kid and he was crazy about you—he almost brought you up.

That year Grover was working at the Inside Inn out on the Fair Grounds. Do you remember the old Inside Inn? That big old wooden thing inside the Fair? And how I used to take you there to wait for Grover when he got through working? And old fat Billy Pelham at the newsstand—how he always used to give you a stick of chewing gum?

They were all crazy about Grover. Everybody liked him. . . . And how proud Grover was of you! Don't you remember how he used to show you off? How he used to take you around and make you talk to Billy Pelham? And Mr. Curtis at the desk? And how Grover would try to make you talk and get you to say "Grover?" And you couldn't say it—you couldn't pronounce the "r." You'd say "Gova." Have you forgotten that? You shouldn't forget *that,* because—you were a *cute* kid, then—Ho-ho-ho-ho-ho—I don't know where it's gone to, but you were a big hit in those days. . . . I tell you, boy, you were Somebody back in those days.

And I was thinking of it all the other day when I was looking at that photograph. How we used to go and meet Grover there, and how he'd take us to the Midway. Do you remember the Midway? The Snake-Eater and the Living Skeleton, the Fat Woman and the Chute-the-chute, the Scenic Railway and the Ferris Wheel? How you bawled the night we took you up on the Ferris Wheel? You yelled your head off—I tried to laugh it off, but I tell you, I was scared myself. Back in those days, that was Something. And how Grover laughed at us and told us there was no danger. . . . My Lord! poor little Grover. He wasn't quite twelve years old at the time, but he seemed so grown up to us. I was two years older, but I thought he knew it all.

It was always that way with him. Looking back now, it sometimes seems that it was Grover who brought us up. He was always looking after us, telling us what to do, bringing us something—some ice cream or some candy, something he had bought out of the poor little money he'd gotten at the Inn.

Then I got to thinking of the afternoon we sneaked away from home. Mama had gone out somewhere. And Grover and I got on the street car and went downtown. And my Lord, we thought that we were going

Somewhere. In those days, that was what we called a *trip*. A ride in the street car was something to write home about in those days. . . . I hear that it's all built up around there now.

So we got on the car and rode the whole way down into the business section of St. Louis. We got out on Washington Street and walked up and down. And I tell you, boy, we thought that that was Something. Grover took me into a drug store and set me up to soda water. Then we came out and walked around some more, down to the Union Station and clear over to the river. And both of us half scared to death at what we'd done and wondering what mama would say if she found out.

We stayed down there till it was getting dark, and we passed by a lunchroom—an old one-armed joint with one-armed chairs and people sitting on stools and eating at the counter. We read all the signs to see what they had to eat and how much it cost, and I guess nothing on the menu was more than fifteen cents, but it couldn't have looked grander to us if it had been Delmonico's. So we stood there with our noses pressed against the window, looking in. Two skinny little kids, both of us scared half to death, getting the thrill of a lifetime out of it. You know what I mean? And smelling everything with all our might and thinking how good it all smelled. . . . Then Grover turned to me and whispered: "Come on, Helen. Let's go in. It says fifteen cents for pork and beans. And I've got the money," Grover said. "I've got sixty cents."

I was so scared I couldn't speak. I'd never been in a place like that before. But I kept thinking, "Oh Lord, if mama should find out!" I felt as if we were committing some big crime. . . . Don't you know how it is when you're a kid? It was the thrill of a lifetime. . . . I couldn't resist. So we both went in and sat down on those high stools before the counter and ordered pork and beans and a cup of coffee. I suppose we were too frightened at what we'd done really to enjoy anything. We just gobbled it all up in a hurry, and gulped our coffee down. And I don't know whether it was the excitement—I guess the poor kid was already sick when we came in there and didn't know it. But I turned and looked at him, and he was white as death. . . . And when I asked him what was the matter, he wouldn't tell me. He was too proud. He said he was all right, but I could see that he was sick as a dog. . . . So he paid the bill. It came to forty cents—I'll never forget *that* as long as I live. . . . And sure enough, we no more than got out the door—he hardly had time to reach the curb—before it all came up.

And the poor kid was so scared and so ashamed. And what scared him so was not that he had gotten sick, but that he had spent all that money and it had come to nothing. And mama would find out. . . . Poor kid, he just stood there looking at me and he whispered: "Oh Helen, don't tell mama. She'll be mad if she finds out." Then we hurried home, and he was still white as a sheet when we got there.

Mama was waiting for us. She looked at us—you know how "Miss Eliza" looks at you when she thinks you've been doing something that you shouldn't. Mama said, "Why, where on earth have you two children been?" I guess she was all set to lay us out. Then she took one look at Grover's face. That was enough for her. She said, "Why, child, what in the world!" She was white as a sheet herself. . . . And all that Grover said was—"Mama, I feel sick."

He was sick as a dog. He fell over on the bed, and we undressed him and mama put her hand upon his forehead and came out in the hall—she was so white you could have made a black mark on her face with chalk—and whispered to me, "Go get the doctor quick, he's burning up."

And I went chasing up the street, my pigtails flying, to Dr. Packer's house. I brought him back with me. When he came out of Grover's room he told mama what to do but I don't know if she even heard him.

Her face was white as a sheet. She looked at me and looked right through me. She never saw me. And oh, my Lord, I'll never forget the way she looked, the way my heart stopped and came up in my throat. I was only a skinny little kid of fourteen. But she looked as if she was dying right before my eyes. And I knew that if anything happened to him, she'd never get over it if she lived to be a hundred.

Poor old mama. You know, he always was her eyeballs—you know that, don't you?—not the rest of us!—no, sir! I know what I'm talking about. It always has been Grover—she always thought more of him than she did of any of the others. And—poor kid!—he was a sweet kid. I can still see him lying there, and remember how sick he was, and how scared I was! I don't know why I was so scared. All we'd done had been to sneak away from home and go into a lunchroom—but I felt guilty about the whole thing, as if it was my fault.

It all came back to me the other day when I was looking at that picture, and I thought, my God, we were two kids together, and I was only two years older than Grover was, and now I'm forty-six. . . . Can you believe it? Can you figure it out—the way we grow up and change and go away? . . . And my Lord, Grover seemed so grown-up to me. He was such a quiet kid—I guess that's why he seemed older than the rest of us.

I wonder what Grover would say now if he could see that picture. All my hopes and dreams and big ambitions have come to nothing, and it's all so long ago, as if it happened in another world. Then it comes back, as if it happened yesterday. . . . Sometimes I lie awake at night and think of all the people who have come and gone, and how everything is different from the way we thought that it would be. Then I go out on the street the next day and see the faces of the people that I pass.

. . . Don't they look strange to you? Don't you see something funny in people's eyes, as if all of them were puzzled about something? As if they were wondering what had happened to them since they were kids? Wondering what it is that they have lost? . . . Now am I crazy, or do you know what I mean? You've been to college, Gene, and I want you to tell me if you know the answer. Now do they look that way to you? I never noticed that look in people's eyes when I was a kid—did you?

My God, I wish I knew the answer to these things. I'd like to find out what is wrong—what has changed since then—and if we have the same queer look in our eyes, too. Does it happen to us all, to everyone? . . . Grover and Ben, Steve, Daisy, Luke, and me—all standing there before that house on Woodson Street in Altamont—there we are, and you see the way we were—and how it all gets lost. What is it, anyway, that people lose?

How is it that nothing turns out the way we thought it would be? It all gets lost until it seems that it has never happened—that it is something we dreamed somewhere. . . . You see what I mean? . . . It seems that it must be something we heard somewhere—that it happened to someone else. And then it all comes back again.

And suddenly you remember just how it was, and see again those two funny, frightened, skinny little kids with their noses pressed against the dirty window of that lunchroom thirty years ago. You remember the way it felt, the way it smelled, even the strange smell in the old pantry in that house we lived in then. And the steps before the house, the way the rooms looked. And those two little boys in sailor suits who used to ride up and down before the house on tricycles. . . . And the birthmark on Grover's neck. . . . The Inside Inn. . . . St. Louis and the Fair.

It all comes back as if it happened yesterday. And then it goes away again, and seems farther off and stranger than if it happened in a dream.

IV The Brother

"*This* is King's Highway," the man said.

And then Eugene looked and saw that it was just a street. There were some big new buildings, a large hotel, some restaurants and "bar-grill" places of the modern kind, the livid monotone of neon lights, the ceaseless traffic of motor cars—all this was new, but it was just a street. And he knew that it had always been just a street and nothing more—but somehow—well, he stood there looking at it, wondering what else he had expected to find.

The man kept looking at him with inquiry in his eyes, and Eugene asked him if the Fair had not been out this way.

"Sure, the Fair was out beyond here," the man said. "Out where the park is now. But this street you're looking for—don't you remember the name of it or nothing?" the man said.

Eugene said he thought the name of the street was Edgemont, but that he wasn't sure. Anyhow it was something like that. And he said the house was on the corner of that street and of another street.

Then the man said: "What was that other street?"

Eugene said he did not know, but that King's Highway was a block or so away, and that an interurban line ran past about half a block from where he once had lived.

"What line was this?" the man said, and stared at him.

"The interurban line," Eugene said.

Then the man stared at him again, and finally, "I don't know no interurban line," he said.

Eugene said it was a line that ran behind some houses, and that there were board fences there and grass beside the tracks. But somehow he could not say that it was summer in those days and that you could smell the ties, a wooden, tarry smell, and feel a kind of absence in the afternoon after the car had gone. He only said the interurban line was back behind somewhere between the backyards of some houses and some old board fences, and that King's Highway was a block or two away.

He did not say that King's Highway had not been a street in those days but a kind of road that wound from magic out of some dim and haunted land, and that along the way it had got mixed in with Tom the Piper's son, with hot cross buns, with all the light that came and went, and with coming down through Indiana in the morning, and the smell of engine smoke, the Union Station, and most of all with voices lost and far and long ago that said "King's Highway."

He did not say these things about King's Highway because he looked about him and he saw what King's Highway was. All he could say was that the street was near King's Highway, and was on the corner, and that the interurban trolley line was close to there. He said it was a stone house, and that there were stone steps before it, and a strip of grass. He said he thought the house had had a turret at one corner, he could not be sure.

The man looked at him again, and said, "This is King's Highway, but I never heard of any street like that."

Eugene left him then, and went on till he found the place. And so at last he turned into the street, finding the place where the two corners met, the huddled block, the turret, and the steps, and paused a moment, looking back, as if the street were Time.

For a moment he stood there, waiting—for a word, and for a door to open, for the child to come. He waited but no words were spoken; no one came.

Yet all of it was just as it had always been, except that the steps were lower, the porch less high, the strip of grass less wide, than he had thought. All the rest of it was as he had known it would be. A gray-stone front, three-storied, with a slant slate roof, the side red brick and windowed, still with the old arched entrance in the center for the doctor's use.

There was a tree in front, and a lamp post; and behind and to the side, more trees than he had known there would be. And all the slatey turret gables, all the slatey window gables, going into points, and the two arched windows, in strong stone, in the front room.

It was all so strong, so solid, and so ugly—and all so enduring and so good, the way he had remembered it, except he did not smell the tar, the hot and caulky dryness of the old cracked ties, the boards of back-yard fences and the coarse and sultry grass, and absence in the afternoon when the street car had gone, and the twins, sharp-visaged in their sailor suits, pumping with furious shrillness on tricycles up and down before the house, and the feel of the hot afternoon, and the sense that everyone was absent at the Fair.

Except for this, it all was just the same; except for this and for King's Highway, which was now a street; except for this, and for the child that did not come.

It was a hot day. Darkness had come. The heat rose up and hung and sweltered like a sodden blanket in St. Louis. It was wet heat, and one knew that there would be no relief or coolness in the night. And when one tried to think of the time when the heat would go away, one said: "It cannot last. It's bound to go away," as we always say it in America. But one did not believe it when he said it. The heat soaked down and men sweltered in it; the faces of people were pale and greasy with the heat. And in their faces was a patient wretchedness, and one felt the kind of desolation that one feels at the end of a hot day in a great city in America—when one's home is far away, across the continent, and he thinks of all that distance, all that heat, and feels, "Oh God! but it's a big country!"

And he feels nothing but absence, absence, and the desolation of America, the loneliness and sadness of the high, hot skies, and evening coming on across the Middle West, across the sweltering and heat-sunken land, across all the lonely little towns, the farms, the fields, the oven swelter of Ohio, Kansas, Iowa, and Indiana at the close of day, and voices, casual in the heat, voices at the little stations, quiet, casual, somehow faded into that enormous vacancy and weariness of heat, of space, and of the immense, the sorrowful, the most high and awful skies.

Then he hears the engine and the wheel again, the wailing whistle and the bell, the sound of shifting in the sweltering yard, and walks the street, and walks the street, beneath the clusters of hard lights, and by the people with sagged faces, and is drowned in desolation and in no belief.

He feels the way one feels when one comes back, and knows that he should not have come, and when he sees that, after all, King's Highway is—a street; and St. Louis—the enchanted name—a big, hot, common town upon the river, sweltering in wet, dreary heat, and not quite South, and nothing else enough to make it better.

It had not been like this before. He could remember how it would get hot, and how good the heat was, and how he would lie out in the backyard on an airing mattress, and how the mattress would get hot and dry and smell like a hot mattress full of sun, and how the sun would make him want to sleep, and how, sometimes, he would go down into the basement to feel coolness, and how the cellar smelled as cellars always smell—a cool, stale smell, the smell of cobwebs and of grimy bottles. And he could remember, when you opened the door upstairs, the smell of the cellar would come up to you—cool, musty, stale and dank and dark—and how the thought of the dark cellar always filled him with a kind of numb excitement, a kind of visceral expectancy.

He could remember how it got hot in the afternoons, and how he would feel a sense of absence and vague sadness in the afternoons, when everyone had gone away. The house would seem so lonely, and sometimes he would sit inside, on the second step of the hall stairs, and listen to the sound of silence and of absence in the afternoon. He could smell the oil upon the floor and on the stairs, and see the sliding doors with their brown varnish and the beady chains across the door, and thrust his hands among the beady chains, and gather them together in his arms, and let them clash, and swish with light beady swishings all around him. He could feel darkness, absence, varnished darkness, and stained light within the house, through the stained glass of the window on the stairs, through the small stained glasses by the door, stained light and absence, silence and the smell of floor oil and vague sadness in the house on a hot mid-afternoon. And all these things themselves would have a kind of life: would seem to wait attentively, to be most living and most still.

He would sit there and listen. He could hear the girl next door practice her piano lessons in the afternoon, and hear the street car coming by between the backyard fences, half a block away, and smell the dry and sultry smell of backyard fences, the smell of coarse hot grasses by the car tracks in the afternoon, the smell of tar, of dry caulked ties, the smell of bright worn flanges, and feel the loneliness of backyards in the afternoon and the sense of absence when the car was gone.

Then he would long for evening and return, the slant of light, and feet along the street, the sharp-faced twins in sailor suits upon their tricycles, the smell of supper and the sound of voices in the house again, and Grover coming from the Fair.

That is how it was when he came into the street, and found the place where the two corners met, and turned at last to see if Time was there. He passed the house: some lights were burning, the door was open, and a woman sat upon the porch. And presently he turned, came back, and stopped before the house again. The corner light fell blank upon the house. He stood looking at it, and put his foot upon the step.

Then he said to the woman who was sitting on the porch: "This house —excuse me—but could you tell me, please, who lives here in this house?"

He knew his words were strange and hollow, and he had not said what he wished to say. She stared at him a moment, puzzled.

Then she said: "I live here. Who are you looking for?"

He said, "Why, I am looking for—"

And then he stopped, because he knew he could not tell her what it was that he was looking for.

"There used to be a house—" he said.

The woman was now staring at him hard.

He said, "I think I used to live here."

She said nothing.

In a moment he continued, "I used to live here in this house," he said, "when I was a little boy."

She was silent, looking at him, then she said: "Oh. Are you sure this was the house? Do you remember the address?"

"I have forgotten the address," he said, "but it was Edgemont Street, and it was on the corner. And I know this is the house."

"This isn't Edgemont Street," the woman said. "The name is Bates."

"Well, then, they changed the name of the street," he said, "but this is the same house. It hasn't changed."

She was silent a moment, then she nodded: "Yes. They did change the name of the street. I remember when I was a child they called it something else," she said. "But that was a long time ago. When was it that you lived here?"

"In 1904."

Again she was silent, looking at him. Then presently: "Oh. That was the year of the Fair. You were here then?"

"Yes." He now spoke rapidly, with more confidence. "My mother had the house, and we were here for seven months. And the house belonged to Dr. Packer," he went on. "We rented it from him."

"Yes," the woman said, and nodded, "this was Dr. Packer's house. He's dead now, he's been dead for many years. But this was the Packer house, all right."

"That entrance on the side," he said, "where the steps go up, that was for Dr. Packer's patients. That was the entrance to his office."

"Oh," the woman said. "I didn't know that. I've often wondered what it was. I didn't know what it was for."

"And this big room in front here," he continued, "that was the office. And there were sliding doors, and next to it, a kind of alcove for his patients—"

"Yes, the alcove is still there, only all of it has been made into one room now—and I never knew just what the alcove was for."

"And there were sliding doors on this side, too, that opened on the hall—and a stairway going up upon this side. And halfway up the stairway, at the landing, a little window of colored glass—and across the sliding doors here in the hall, a kind of curtain made of strings of beads."

She nodded, smiling. "Yes, it's just the same—we still have the sliding doors and the stained glass window on the stairs. There's no bead curtain any more," she said, "but I remember when people had them. I know what you mean."

"When we were here," he said, "we used the doctor's office for a parlor—except later on—the last month or two—and then we used it for—a bedroom."

"It is a bedroom now," she said. "I run the house—I rent rooms—all of the rooms upstairs are rented—but I have two brothers and they sleep in this front room."

Both of them were silent for a moment, then Eugene said, "My brother stayed there too."

"In the front room?" the woman said.

He answered, "Yes."

She paused, then said: "Won't you come in? I don't believe it's changed much. Would you like to see?"

He thanked her and said he would, and he went up the steps. She opened the screen door to let him in.

Inside it was just the same—the stairs, the hallway, the sliding doors, the window of stained glass upon the stairs. And all of it was just the same, except for absence, the stained light of absence in the afternoon, and the child who once had sat there, waiting on the stairs.

It was all the same except that as a child he had sat there feeling things were *Somewhere*—and now he *knew*. He had sat there feeling that a vast and sultry river was somewhere—and now he knew! He had sat there wondering what King's Highway was, where it began, and where it ended—now he knew! He had sat there haunted by the magic word "downtown"—now he knew!—and by the street car, after it had gone—and by all things that came and went and came again, like the cloud shadows passing in a wood, that never could be captured.

And he felt that if he could only sit there on the stairs once more, in solitude and absence in the afternoon, he would be able to get it back again. Then would he be able to remember all that he had seen and been —the brief sum of himself, the universe of his four years, with all the light of Time upon it—that universe which was so short to measure, and yet so far, so endless, to remember. Then would he be able to see his own small face again, pooled in the dark mirror of the hall, and peer once more into the grave eyes of the child that he had been, and discover there in his quiet three-years' self the lone integrity of "I," knowing: "Here is the House, and here House listening; here is Absence, Absence in the afternoon; and here in this House, this Absence, is my core, my kernel—here am I!"

But as he thought it, he knew that even if he could sit here alone and get it back again, it would be gone as soon as seized, just as it had been then—first coming like the vast and drowsy rumors of the distant and enchanted Fair, then fading like cloud shadows on a hill, going like faces in a dream—coming, going, coming, possessed and held but never captured, like lost voices in the mountains long ago—and like the dark eyes and quiet face of the dark, lost boy, his brother, who, in the mysterious rhythms of his life and work, used to come into this house, then go, and return again.

The woman took Eugene back into the house and through the hall. He told her of the pantry, told her where it was and pointed to the place, but now it was no longer there. And he told her of the backyard, and of the old board fence around the yard. But the old board fence was gone. And he told her of the carriage house, and told her it was painted red. But now there was a small garage. And the backyard was still there, but smaller than he thought, and now there was a tree.

"I did not know there was a tree," he said. "I do not remember any tree."

"Perhaps it was not there," she said. "A tree could grow in thirty years." And then they came back through the house again and paused at the sliding doors.

"And could I see this room?" he said.

She slid the doors back. They slid open smoothly, with a rolling heaviness, as they used to do. And then he saw the room again. It was the same. There was a window at the side, the two arched windows at the front, the alcove and the sliding doors, the fireplace with the tiles of mottled green, the mantel of dark mission wood, the mantel posts, a dresser and a bed, just where the dresser and the bed had been so long ago.

"Is this the room?" the woman said. "It hasn't changed?"

He told her that it was the same.

"And your brother slept here where my brothers sleep?"

"This is his room," he said.

They were silent. He turned to go, and said, "Well, thank you. I appreciate your showing me."

She said that she was glad and that it was no trouble. "And when you see your family, you can tell them that you saw the house," she said. "My name is Mrs. Bell. You can tell your mother that a Mrs. Bell has the house now. And when you see your brother, you can tell him that you saw the room he slept in, and that you found it just the same."

He told her then that his brother was dead.

The woman was silent for a moment. Then she looked at him and said: "He died here, didn't he? In this room?"

He told her that it was so.

"Well, then," she said, "I knew it. I don't know how. But when you told me he was here, I knew it."

He said nothing. In a moment the woman said, "What did he die of?"

"Typhoid."

She looked shocked and troubled, and said involuntarily, "My two brothers—"

"That was a long time ago," he said. "I don't think you need to worry now."

"Oh, I wasn't thinking about that," she said. "It was just hearing that a little boy—your brother—was—was in this room that my two brothers sleep in now—"

"Well, maybe I shouldn't have told you then. But he was a good boy —and if you'd known him you wouldn't mind."

She said nothing, and he added quickly: "Besides, he didn't stay here long. This wasn't really his room—but the night he came back with my sister he was so sick—they didn't move him."

"Oh," the woman said, "I see." And then: "Are you going to tell your mother you were here?"

"I don't think so."

"I—I wonder how she feels about this room."

"I don't know. She never speaks of it."

"Oh. . . . How old was he?"

"He was twelve."

"You must have been pretty young yourself."

"I was not quite four."

"And—you just wanted to see the room, didn't you? That's why you came back."

"Yes."

"Well—" indefinitely—"I guess you've seen it now."

"Yes, thank you."

"I guess you don't remember much about him, do you? I shouldn't think you would."

"No, not much."

The years dropped off like fallen leaves: the face came back again—the soft dark oval, the dark eyes, the soft brown berry on the neck, the raven hair, all bending down, approaching—the whole appearing to him ghostwise, intent and instant.

"Now say it—*Grover!*"

"Gova."

"No—not Gova.—*Grover!* . . . Say it!"

"Gova."

"Ah-h—you didn't say it. You said Gova. *Grover*—now say it!"

"Gova."

"Look, I tell you what I'll do if you say it right. Would you like to go down to King's Highway? Would you like Grover to set you up? All right, then. If you say Grover and say it right, I'll take you to King's Highway and set you up to ice cream. Now say it right—*Grover!*"

"Gova."

"Ah-h, you-u. You're the craziest little old boy I ever did see. Can't you even say Grover?"

"Gova."

"Ah-h, you-u. Old Tongue-Tie, that's what you are. . . . Well, come on, then, I'll set you up anyway."

It all came back, and faded, and was lost again. Eugene turned to go, and thanked the woman and said good-by.

"Well, then, good-by," the woman said, and they shook hands. "I'm glad if I could show you. I'm glad if—" She did not finish, and at length she said: "Well, then, that was a long time ago. You'll find everything changed now, I guess. It's all built up around here now—and way out beyond here, out beyond where the Fair Grounds used to be. I guess you'll find it changed."

They had nothing more to say. They just stood there for a moment on the steps, and then shook hands once more.

"Well, good-by."

And again he was in the street, and found the place where the corners met, and for the last time turned to see where Time had gone.

And he knew that he would never come again, and that lost magic would not come again. Lost now was all of it—the street, the heat, King's Highway, and Tom the Piper's son, all mixed in with the vast and drowsy murmur of the Fair, and with the sense of absence in the afternoon, and the house that waited, and the child that dreamed. And out of the enchanted wood, that thicket of man's memory, Eugene knew that the dark eye and the quiet face of his friend and brother—poor child, life's stranger, and life's exile, lost like all of us, a cipher in blind mazes, long ago—the lost boy was gone forever, and would not return.

Questions

1. A key clue to the author's intention in this story lies in the fact that it is not told by an omniscient author, or even from the point of view of any one character, but rather from a shifting point of view, showing the central action through the eyes of different characters. Evaluate some of the possible advantages and disadvantages of this method.

2. All the sections of the story are preceded by an identification of a character—The Mother, The Sister, The Brother—except Part I. Explain the omission here, and show how the author lets the reader discover through whose eyes he is seeing this part of the story.

3. In Part I, Grover thinks the "pattern of familiar shapes" of his life will always remain the same. In Parts 2, 3, and 4 we see how wrong his idea is. Show what these sections reveal about the relentless march of time. What is relevant about the fact that they all represent the viewpoint of older people?

4. The story is mainly about time. Exactly what is the time chronology of the story? What is the relation of Part I, in time, to the other parts of the story?

5. Explain the very last line: "The lost boy was gone forever, and would not return." What has been lost, and will never return?

6. Of what does Grover become the symbol? What does the memory of his loss mean to Eugene? What, finally, has Eugene "learned" at the end of the story?

Virginia Woolf

THE MARK ON THE WALL

Associated with the "stream of consciousness" school in modern fiction, Virginia Woolf was one of the writers, along with Dorothy Richardson and James Joyce, who abandoned the traditional linear plot novel, like those of Arnold Bennett and John Galsworthy, and chose to explore the inner life of their characters, often at the subconscious level. Thus the movement in her work is often that of deepening awareness rather than progression in time. Mrs. Woolf was born in London in 1882 to a distinguished family; her father was Sir Leslie Stephen, editor and biographer. As she grew up she moved in circles that included artists, writers, critics, theater people—those who later came to be known as the Bloomsbury Group, from their residence in that area of London. She married Leonard Woolf, and together they founded the Hogarth Press, which published not only their own works but also early work by Katherine Mansfield, E. M. Forster, T. S. Eliot, and others. Virginia Woolf's own first work was fairly conventional, consisting of two novels, The Voyage Out *(1915) and* Night and Day *(1919). However, she soon began the distinctive experiments with interior monologues and other innovative techniques that marked her best work:* Jacob's Room *(1922),* Mrs. Dalloway *(1925),* To the Lighthouse *(1927),* The Waves *(1931), and* The Years *(1937). In 1941, depressed by the death of friends and the onset of war, and fearful of oncoming mental illness, she committed suicide by drowning. Her posthumously published* A Writer's Diary *(1953) gives sensitive insight not only into Virginia Woolf herself but into the relationship between a writer and her works.*

"The Mark on the Wall" is a story in which quite literally nothing happens except the exploration of consciousness. From the collection, A Haunted House *(1944), it suggests an attempt to clutch a reality that shimmers just beyond one's grasp. At the end of one of Mrs. Woolf's novels,* The Years, *the heroine says she "wanted to enclose the moment; to make it stay; to fill it fuller and fuller with the past, the*

present, and the future, until it shone whole, bright, deep with understanding." Something of this attempt is shown also in "The Mark on the Wall."

Perhaps it was the middle of January in the present year that I first looked up and saw the mark on the wall. In order to fix a date it is necessary to remember what one saw. So now I think of the fire; the steady film of yellow light upon the page of my book; the three chrysanthemums in the round glass bowl on the mantelpiece. Yes, it must have been the winter time, and we had just finished our tea, for I remember that I was smoking a cigarette when I looked up and saw the mark on the wall for the first time. I looked up through the smoke of my cigarette and my eye lodged for a moment upon the burning coals, and that old fancy of the crimson flag flapping from the castle tower came into my mind, and I thought of the cavalcade of red knights riding up the side of the black rock. Rather to my relief the sight of the mark interrupted the fancy, for it is an old fancy, an automatic fancy, made as a child perhaps. The mark was a small round mark, black upon the white wall, about six or seven inches above the mantelpiece.

How readily our thoughts swarm upon a new object, lifting it a little way, as ants carry a blade of straw so feverishly, and then leave it. . . . If that mark was made by a nail, it can't have been for a picture, it must have been for a miniature—the miniature of a lady with white powdered curls, powder-dusted cheeks, and lips like red carnations. A fraud of course, for the people who had this house before us would have chosen pictures in that way—an old picture for an old room. That is the sort of people they were—very interesting people, and I think of them so often, in such queer places, because one will never see them again, never know what happened next. They wanted to leave this house because they wanted to change their style of furniture, so he said, and he was in process of saying that in his opinion art should have ideas behind it when we were torn asunder, as one is torn from the old lady about to pour out tea and the young man about to hit the tennis ball in the back garden of the suburban villa as one rushes past in the train.

But for that mark, I'm not sure about it; I don't believe it was made by a nail after all; it's too big, too round, for that. I might get up, but if I got up and looked at it, ten to one I shouldn't be able to say for certain; because once a thing's done, no one ever knows how it happened. Oh! dear me, the mystery of life; the inaccuracy of thought! The ignorance of humanity! To show how very little control of our possessions we have—what an accidental affair this living is after all our civilization—let me just count over a few of the things lost in one lifetime, beginning, for that seems always the most mysterious of losses—what cat would gnaw, what rat would nibble—three pale blue canisters of bookbinding tools? Then there were the bird cages, the iron hoops, the steel skates, the Queen Anne coal-scuttle, the bagatelle board, the hand organ—all gone, and jewels, too. Opals and emeralds, they lie about the roots of turnips. What a scraping paring affair it is to be sure! The wonder is that I've any clothes on my back, that I sit surrounded by solid furniture at this moment. Why, if one wants to compare life to anything, one must liken it to being blown through the Tube at fifty miles an hour—landing at the other end without a single hairpin in one's hair! Shot out at the feet of God entirely naked! Tumbling head over heels in the asphodel meadows like brown paper parcels pitched down a shoot in the post office! With one's hair flying back like the tail of a race-horse. Yes, that seems to express the rapidity of life, the perpetual waste and repair; all so casual, all so haphazard. . . .

But after life. The slow pulling down of thick green stalks so that the cup of the flower, as it turns over, deluges one with purple and red light. Why, after all, should one not be born there as one is born here, helpless, speechless, unable to focus one's eyesight, groping at the roots of the grass, at the toes of the Giants? As for saying which are trees, and which are men and women, or whether there are such things, that one won't be in a condition to do for fifty years or so. There will be nothing but spaces of light and dark, intersected by thick stalks, and rather higher up perhaps, rose-shaped blots of an indistinct colour—dim pinks and blues—which will, as time goes on, become more definite, become—I don't know what. . . .

And yet that mark on the wall is not a hole at all. It may even be caused by some round black substance, such as a small rose leaf, left over from the summer, and I, not being a very vigilant housekeeper—look at the dust on the mantelpiece, for example, the dust which, so they say, buried Troy three times over, only fragments of pots utterly refusing annihilation, as one can believe.

The tree outside the window taps very gently on the pane. . . . I want to think quietly, calmly, spaciously, never to be interrupted, never to have to rise from my chair, to slip easily from one thing to another, without any sense of hostility, or obstacle. I want to sink deeper and deeper, away from the surface, with its hard separate facts. To steady myself, let me catch hold of the first idea that passes. . . . Shakespeare. . . . Well, he will do as well as another. A man who sat himself solidly in an arm-chair, and looked into the fire, so—A shower of ideas fell perpetually from some very high Heaven down through his mind. He leant his forehead on his hand, and people, looking in through the open door—for this scene is supposed to take place on a summer's evening—But how dull this is, this historical fiction! It doesn't interest me at all. I wish

I could hit upon a pleasant track of thought, a track indirectly reflecting credit upon myself, for those are the pleasantest thoughts, and very frequent even in the minds of modest mouse-coloured people, who believe genuinely that they dislike to hear their own praises. They are not thoughts directly praising oneself; that is the beauty of them; they are thoughts like this:

"And then I came into the room. They were discussing botany. I said how I'd seen a flower growing on a dust heap on the site of an old house in Kingsway. The seed, I said, must have been sown in the reign of Charles the First. What flowers grew in the reign of Charles the First?" I asked—(but I don't remember the answer). Tall flowers with purple tassels to them perhaps. And so it goes on. All the time I'm dressing up the figure of myself in my own mind, lovingly, stealthily, not openly adoring it, for if I did that, I should catch myself out, and stretch my hand at once for a book in self-protection. Indeed, it is curious how instinctively one protects the image of oneself from idolatry or any other handling that could make it ridiculous, or too unlike the original to be believed in any longer. Or is it not so very curious after all? It is a matter of great importance. Supposing the looking-glass smashes, the image disappears, and the romantic figure with the green of forest depths all about it is there no longer, but only that shell of a person which is seen by other people—what an airless, shallow, bald, prominent world it becomes! A world not to be lived in. As we face each other in omnibuses and underground railways we are looking into the mirror; that accounts for the vagueness, the gleam of glassiness, in our eyes. And the novelists in future will realize more and more the importance of these reflections, for of course there is not one reflection but an almost infinite number; those are the depths they will explore, those the phantoms they will pursue, leaving the description of reality more and more out of their stories, taking a knowledge of it for granted, as the Greeks did and Shakespeare perhaps—but these generalizations are very worthless. The military sound of the word is enough. It recalls leading articles, cabinet ministers—a whole class of things indeed which, as a child, one thought the thing itself, the standard thing, the real thing, from which one could not depart save at the risk of nameless damnation. Generalizations bring back somehow Sunday in London, Sunday afternoon walks, Sunday luncheons, and also ways of speaking of the dead, clothes, and habits—like the habit of sitting all together in one room until a certain hour, although nobody liked it. There was a rule for everything. The rule for tablecloths at that particular period was that they should be made of tapestry with little yellow compartments marked upon them, such as you may see in photographs of the carpets in the corridors of the royal palaces. Tablecloths of a different kind were not real tablecloths. How shocking, and yet how wonderful it was to discover that these real things, Sunday luncheons, Sunday walks, country houses, and tablecloths were not entirely real, were indeed half phantoms, and the damnation which visited the disbeliever in them was only a sense of illegitimate freedom. What now takes the place of those things I wonder, those real standard things? Men perhaps, should you be a woman; the masculine point of view which governs our lives, which sets the standard, which established Whitaker's Table of Precedency, which has become, I suppose, since the war, half a phantom to many men and women, which soon, one may hope, will be laughed into the dustbin where the phantoms go, the mahogany sideboards and the Landseer prints, Gods and Devils, Hell and so forth, leaving us all with an intoxicating sense of illegitimate freedom—if freedom exists. . . .

In certain lights that mark on the wall seems actually to project from the wall. Nor is it entirely circular. I cannot be sure, but it seems to cast a perceptible shadow, suggesting that if I ran my finger down that strip of the wall it would, at a certain point, mount and descend a small tumulus, a smooth tumulus like those barrows on the South Downs which are, they say, either tombs or camps. Of the two I should prefer them to be tombs, desiring melancholy like most English people, and finding it natural at the end of a walk to think of the bones stretched beneath the turf. . . . There must be some book about it. Some antiquary must have dug up those bones and given them a name. . . . What sort of a man is an antiquary, I wonder? Retired Colonels for the most part, I daresay, leading parties of aged labourers to the top here, examining clods of earth and stone, and getting into correspondence with the neighbouring clergy, which, being opened at breakfast time, gives them a feeling of importance, and the comparison of arrow-heads necessitates cross-country journeys to the county towns, an agreeable necessity both to them and to their elderly wives, who wish to make plum jam or to clean out the study, and have every reason for keeping that great question of the camp or the tomb in perpetual suspension, while the Colonel himself feels agreeably philosophic in accumulating evidence on both sides of the question. It is true that he does finally incline to believe in the camp; and, being opposed, indites a pamphlet which he is about to read at the quarterly meeting of the local society when a stroke lays him low, and his last conscious thoughts are not of wife or child, but of the camp and that arrow-head there, which is now in the case at the local museum, together with the foot of a Chinese murderess, a handful of Elizabethan nails, a great many Tudor clay pipes, a piece of Roman pottery, and the wineglass that Nelson drank out of—proving I really don't know what.

No, no, nothing is proved, nothing is known. And if I were to get up at this very moment and ascertain that the mark on the wall is really—

what shall we say?—the head of a gigantic old nail, driven in two hundred years ago, which has now, owing to the patient attrition of many generations of housemaids, revealed its head above the coat of paint, and is taking its first view of modern life in the sight of a white-walled fire-lit room, what should I gain?—Knowledge? Matter for further speculation? I can think sitting still as well as standing up. And what is knowledge? What are our learned men save the descendants of witches and hermits who crouched in caves and in woods brewing herbs, interrogating shrew-mice and writing down the language of the stars? And the less we honour them as our superstitions dwindle and our respect for beauty and health of mind increases. . . . Yes, one could imagine a very pleasant world. A quiet, spacious world, with the flowers so red and blue in the open fields. A world without professors or specialists or house-keepers with the profiles of policemen, a world which one could slice with one's thought as a fish slices the water with his fin, grazing the stems of the water-lilies, hanging suspended over nests of white sea eggs. . . . How peaceful it is down here, rooted in the centre of the world and gazing up through the grey waters, with their sudden gleams of light, and their reflections—if it were not for Whitaker's Almanack—if it were not for the Table of Precedency!

I must jump up and see for myself what that mark on the wall really is—a nail, a rose-leaf, a crack in the wood?

Here is nature once more at her old game of self-preservation. This train of thought, she perceives, is threatening mere waste of energy, even some collision with reality, for who will ever be able to lift a finger against Whitaker's Table of Precedency? The Archbishop of Canterbury is followed by the Lord High Chancellor; the Lord High Chancellor is followed by the Archbishop of York. Everybody follows somebody, such is the philosophy of Whitaker; and the great thing is to know who follows whom. Whitaker knows, and let that, so Nature counsels, comfort you, instead of enraging you; and if you can't be comforted, if you must shatter this hour of peace, think of the mark on the wall.

I understand Nature's game—her prompting to take action as a way of ending any thought that threatens to excite or to pain. Hence, I suppose, comes our slight contempt for men of action—men, we assume, who don't think. Still, there's no harm in putting a full stop to one's disagreeable thoughts by looking at a mark on the wall.

Indeed, now that I have fixed my eyes upon it, I feel that I have grasped a plank in the sea; I feel a satisfying sense of reality which at once turns the two Archbishops and the Lord High Chancellor to the shadows of shades. Here is something definite, something real. Thus, waking from a midnight dream of horror, one hastily turns on the light and lies quiescent, worshipping the chest of drawers, worshipping solidity, worshipping reality, worshipping the impersonal world which is a proof of some existence other than ours. That is what one wants to be sure of. . . . Wood is a pleasant thing to think about. It comes from a tree; and trees grow, and we don't know how they grow. For years and years they grow, without paying any attention to us, in meadows, in forests, and by the side of rivers—all things one likes to think about. The cows swish their tails beneath them on hot afternoons; they paint rivers so green that when a moorhen dives one expects to see its feathers all green when it comes up again. I like to think of the fish balanced against the stream like flags blown out; and of water-beetles slowly raising domes of mud upon the bed of the river. I like to think of the tree itself: first the close dry sensation of being wood; then the grinding of the storm; then the slow, delicious ooze of sap. I like to think of it, too, on winter's nights standing in the empty field with all leaves close-furled, nothing tender exposed to the iron bullets of the moon, a naked mast upon an earth that goes tumbling, tumbling, all night long. The song of birds must sound very loud and strange in June; and how cold the feet of insects must feel upon it, as they make laborious progresses up the creases of the bark, or sun themselves upon the thin green awning of the leaves, and look straight in front of them with diamond-cut red eyes. . . . One by one the fibres snap beneath the immense cold pressure of the earth, then the last storm comes and, falling, the highest branches drive deep into the ground again. Even so, life isn't done with; there are a million patient, watchful lives still for a tree, all over the world, in bedrooms, in ships, on the pavement, lining rooms, where men and women sit after tea, smoking cigarettes. It is full of peaceful thoughts, happy thoughts, this tree. I should like to take each one separately—but something is getting in the way. . . . Where was I? What has it all been about? A tree? A river? The Downs? Whitaker's Almanack? The fields of asphodel? I can't remember a thing. Everything's moving, falling, slipping, vanishing. . . . There is a vast upheaval of matter. Someone is standing over me and saying:

"I'm going out to buy a newspaper."

"Yes?"

"Though it's no good buying newspapers. . . . Nothing ever happens. Curse this war; God damn this war! . . . All the same, I don't see why we should have a snail on our wall."

Ah, the mark on the wall! It was a snail.

Questions

1. The subject of this story is not so much an event or occurrence as a series of reflections caused by something unexpected—in this case the appearance of a strange mark on a wall. Explain how the observation of this simple phenomenon brings about the narrator's meditations on larger subjects such as "the mystery of life" and "the inaccuracy of thought."

2. Does the narrator really want to know what the mark on the wall is? Why, or why not?

3. What is the purpose in the story of the narrator's recollection of possessions she has lost?

4. The narrator recalls facts from the past, relics dug up in tombs and barrows, "proving I really don't know what." How does her rather disdainful attitude toward this kind of knowledge relate to her present situation?

5. The narrator says she distrusts "hard separate facts." Why? Is the mark on the wall such a "fact"?

6. What effect does the revelation at the end of the story—the identity of the mark—have on the validity of the narrator's earlier reflections? For the purposes of the story, would it have been better for the mark to have remained unidentified? Why, or why not?